CW00552797

THE MIDNIGHT TRILOGY

L.M. HATCHELL

The Midnight Trilogy

First published by ALX Publishing 2023

Cover Design by CBC Designs

Editing by Three Point Author Services
& Sian Phillips

For the readers that made this possible

MIDNIGHT COMES

PHOENIX'S PREQUEL

CHAPTER ONE

120 years ago

A sense of dread gripped Aria as she watched Marcus stand before his Sire, head held high and shoulders tensed, waiting for the final decision. Aria was under no illusion as to what that decision would be; her family hadn't accepted their relationship and neither would his clan.

The room around them was completely silent and filled with an unnatural stillness that only vampires could accomplish. Out of the twenty people present to witness them plead their case, Aria was the only one breathing, and she was acutely aware that her heartbeat was like a drumroll to the vampire ears.

Marcus stood directly ahead of her, facing Lucian alone. Every cell in her body screamed to be by his side and lend him her strength, but Aria knew the rules. Her support would be seen as a sign of weakness and provide them with further proof that their relationship was wrong.

But it wasn't wrong. Her heart didn't lie.

They should be grateful, she supposed. The fact they managed to walk out of Faerie alive in order to stand here was a miracle in itself.

The Council's edict was clear: interspecies relationships were not tolerated. It was one of the few rules all members of the Lore abided by, and death was the penalty for defiance.

As a member of the royal lineage, her indiscretion could bring ruin to the fae and would have easily justified such retribution. When she'd stood before her parents with Marcus by her side, she'd actually wondered if they'd do it. If they'd condemn their daughter to death. The look on her mother's face had been so cold that even the touch of the sun couldn't warm Aria's skin. But worse than that had been the tears in her father's eyes. Tears that now mirrored her own.

As Lucian finally spoke the words she'd known would come, a single one of those tears freed itself of her hold and slid down her cheek.

"I'm sorry, my son, but if this truly is your choice then you have left me with none. You will no longer be recognised as part of this clan, or of our bloodline.

"From this moment on, you are banished."

CHAPTER TWO

120 years later

Aria gently touched the brittle leaves of the blueberry bush. Frost had settled overnight and the garden was coated with a glistening shimmer that, although pretty to look at, wreaked havoc on her plants. The bone-deep chill pervaded everything and she had to pull on the sun's energy more than normal that winter to keep the plants alive.

"They don't look like they're doing too well."

She turned with a smile at the sound of her daughter's voice. Phoenix's vibrant green eyes were somewhat dulled by concern, but they were no less striking for it. Her blood-red hair formed a fiery contrast to the frosty colours of the winter landscape, reminding Aria that she needed to check on her roses too.

From a young age, Phoenix had loved helping her in the garden. She'd been fascinated by the array of colours and the cycle of rebirth that nature brought. At fifteen year's old, she was more interested now in the martial arts lessons Marcus encouraged since they were so much cooler. But occasionally, on rare mornings, she'd find her way back to Aria's side.

"Winter's not been kind to them this year." Aria turned back to the blueberries with a frown. She could feel Phoenix's eyes on her as she closed her own and pushed back the niggling concern that settled in the centre of her chest.

As natural as breathing, the heat came. The sun, though hidden in the white blanket of the sky, reached out to her. Like calling to like. It wrapped around her and sank through the layers of skin to coalesce with the DNA that resided in her cells. Aria knelt and placed her hands on the hard, cracked earth. For a moment there was resistance, but then the frost began to melt beneath her fingertips. The soil became soft and welcoming, and when she opened her eyes, she was met with vibrant greens and deep, succulent purples.

A hand reached over her shoulder and she looked back to see Phoenix pluck a blueberry from the bush, awe mixing with delight on her young face as she took a bite.

"Can I try?"

Aria swallowed her surprise, careful to keep her face neutral. Although Phoenix had always shown an affinity to the sun, she'd displayed no obvious signs of fae powers to date. Her hybrid nature was so unique that they had no way of knowing what to expect, and she was hesitant to put pressure on her daughter.

"I need to check on the roses, how about you join me?" she said carefully as she stood up.

Phoenix plucked another blueberry from the bush and nodded.

The grass crunched beneath their feet as they trudged back up the hill to the bungalow they called home. Hidden in the Wicklow Mountains, the small house afforded them stunning views of sprawling emerald hills. And privacy. Most importantly, privacy.

Phoenix hesitated as they reached the roses.

The row of colourful blooms that ran perpendicular to the house appeared lacklustre and drooped in defeat. Only the harsh thorns stood strong against the punishing onslaught of the Irish winter, and once more Aria was struck by how much harder she'd had to work to keep them blooming.

"I don't know if I ..." Phoenix came to a stop and bit her lip as she assessed the task before her.

6

Aria could see her daughter's shoulders inch forwards, even as her feet remained rooted to the ground, afraid to take that final step. As a mother, her automatic instinct was to comfort her – she could easily tend the roses herself – but she held back and waited.

Finally, Phoenix took a deep breath and tentatively reached a hand towards the wilting petals. Serious green eyes turned to Aria. "How do I do it?"

And that was the million-dollar question. How did she teach her daughter something that was so innate within herself?

Aria moved to stand behind Phoenix and placed both hands on her shoulders. "Close your eyes."

She forced her breathing to slow, feeling Phoenix's breathing fall into sync with hers. Step by step she guided her daughter, trying hard to put the intangible sensations into words.

Then she closed her eyes and waited.

———

Only when Aria felt the sun drift low on the horizon did she realise how much time had passed. With each hour, the furrow in Phoenix's forehead had grown deeper, and with each failed attempt, her daughter's frustration had become more heart-breaking to watch.

"Dammit, why can't I do it?" Phoenix balled her hands into fists as she glared at the roses.

Half of the row was now a vibrant rainbow of colours – Aria having decided that a practical demonstration might be of more use – but the other half remained dejected and wilting. It wasn't working.

Aria wanted desperately to pull her daughter close for a hug, but sensed the invisible barrier that had been erected to numb the pain of disappointment. She was about to suggest they try again another day when she felt Marcus's presence. His nearness brought a comfort that helped to lift the heaviness from her chest and she smiled as she turned to seek him out.

"I was wondering where my girls had gotten to."

Marcus held the front door of the bungalow ajar as he leaned

7

against the doorframe. Even from a distance, Aria could see the happiness glinting in his dark eyes as he watched them.

When Phoenix failed to acknowledge him, Marcus raised a questioning eyebrow in Aria's direction. A sigh and a shrug were all she could offer by way of answer.

"Hey, Phoenix," Marcus tried again, "if you're not busy, I could use your help with something?"

That finally got her attention.

"Are we going to train?" Phoenix's voice was hopeful as she tilted her head in her father's direction.

Aria bit back a groan. She knew the martial arts lessons were important, but she hated the fact they were necessary. In the Lore, all species learned to fight from a young age. But they weren't part of the Lore anymore, and she'd grown attached to the idea of giving her daughter a "normal" life.

"Maybe later. If you do a good job."

That was all it took for Phoenix to abandon her task and slip past Marcus into the house. Aria would've laughed at her eagerness if not for the twinge of sadness it elicited. With one more look at the rose bushes, she followed her daughter's path to the house.

Marcus waited in the doorway, blocking her path.

"Nope." He shook his head. "Not you. Why don't you take a walk and clear your head?" With a sexy grin and a soft kiss, he turned on his heel and closed the door on her.

For a moment, Aria stared dumbfounded at the chipped wood of their front door. She didn't know whether to be curious or worried about what he was up to, but she eventually decided ignorance was bliss. Her energy needed a recharge after tending the plants, and a walk in the woods sounded like just the ticket.

With the sun setting low on the horizon, she made her way down the hill and through a break in the tree line. Instantly the world around her changed. The afternoon light was already fading and the canopy of twisted branches forced the final rays to compete for a place within their hidden sanctuary. Leaves crunched under her feet and Aria breathed deeply, savouring the woody aromas that filled her nose.

8

Soft rustling echoed around her as the trees whispered their secrets, and animals assessed the newcomer in their midst. She closed her eyes and let her senses guide her travel. Time became irrelevant as her cells rejuvenated with the cycle of life and rebirth all around her.

The gurgling sound of water was the first thing that brought her back to her surroundings. The soft "caw" of a crow was the second. Aria froze, her whole body still as she slowly opened her eyes.

A small stream ran in a jagged line across the path ahead of her. Clear water bubbled over the rocks that littered the ground and a fallen branch lay across the stream. A large crow was perched on the crumbling bark of the log, red eyes watching her.

For a moment Aria was mesmerised by the kaleidoscope of colours reflected on the bird's feathers: blues, purples, turquoise. It had been a long time since she'd seen the beauty of that particular rainbow.

Then realisation hit her, quickly followed by fear.

"How did you find me?" The words came out in a gasp of breath, and her body tensed to run.

It'd be no use.

The crow merely watched her, its strange eyes seeming almost sad.

"Will you tell them we're here?" Her thoughts instantly turned to the family that awaited her beyond the woods, and everything she stood to lose.

A single "caw" was her only reply before the crow turned its head to the trees and took flight. Muffled voices and the snap of twigs came from the same direction. A second later, two people stumbled from the treeline and splashed into the stream cursing.

The man and woman were so busy arguing that it took them a moment to notice her. Wrapped in warm coats and woolly hats that had obviously never seen the outdoors, they looked completely bewildered with their surroundings. The man held a crumpled map and the woman looked beyond pissed off.

Ignoring her partner's protests, the woman turned to Aria, hands on her hips. "Can you help us? We seem to be lost?" She threw a pointed look towards the man in the stream.

CHAPTER THREE

Aria stood at the front door of the bungalow and scrunched her eyes closed. She could hear the distant sound of her daughter's laughter, and a deep ache filled her chest. How would she tell Marcus?

They'd worked so hard to build a life for themselves here, had given up everything they'd ever known to be together as a family. If the Council came for them now, it would all be destroyed.

Shoring up her resolve, she pushed open the front door only to find herself face-to-face with Marcus's warm smile.

"I was wondering if you were going to stay out there all night."

Aria opened her mouth, ready to tell him everything, but the words froze in her throat. The lights were dimmed in the hallway, but through the open door that led to their dining room, she could see flickering candlelight and hear the soft strands of music. She looked into Marcus's brown eyes and the love she saw there made her heart stutter.

"Do you know what day it is?" He took her hand in his and raised it to his lips for a soft kiss.

Aria tried to make sense of the question, her mind a jumble of confused thoughts as it tried to deal with the sudden shift in focus.

"Marcus, I –"

He kissed her on the lips, stopping all words and thoughts for that split second.

"C'mon," he said with a grin, and pulled her down the hallway.

As they reached the dining room, Phoenix slipped out the door, a shy smile on her face.

"Happy anniversary, Mam," she said, giving Aria a quick kiss on the cheek before running down the hall to her bedroom.

Aria looked in askance at Marcus as she tried in vain to remember what day it was.

"Today is the day I first saw you," he clarified. "The day I fell in love."

The burn in her throat was instantaneous and tears pricked her eyes as she thought of the crow in the woods.

Eager to reveal his surprise, Marcus pulled her the rest of the way into the dining room. Candles lined each wall of the large open-plan room and their oak dining table was set with the most exquisite feast of her favourite foods: fruits from their garden, warm doughy bread, and cheese platters to make her mouth water.

The melodic harmonies of her favourite song filled the room and Marcus held out a hand to her. "Dance with me?"

He pulled her close, and as she rested her head against his chest, she allowed herself that moment. Tomorrow, everything would change. But tonight ... she would cherish.

"What do you think she wanted?" A frown marred Marcus's features as he paced the length of their small sitting room.

From her curled-up position on the sofa, Aria shrugged help-lessly and dropped her head into her hands. She didn't know whether it was a blessing or curse that the hikers had interrupted them; maybe she could've found out more information and wouldn't be in such a blind panic now.

Marcus, as usual, was trying to remain calm and think through the situation logically, but Aria could see the stiffness in his shoulders and the slight creasing at his temples as he concentrated.

"Darius will warn us of any murmurings in the Council."

He spoke of their only remaining Lore contact with a surety born of many years' loyalty. Darius had been their closest friend and staunchest ally for more than a century, standing by them when all others turned their back. His position as Witness to the Council provided them advance warning of the Council's plans and would hopefully prove invaluable if the time came to run.

"But he has no connection to the fae." Aria pushed away the dull emptiness that formed in her chest when she thought of her people.

Marcus stopped his pacing and sat down beside her. His brown eyes were filled with sympathetic understanding as he pulled her close. "We'll figure it out," he whispered, pressing his lips to her forehead.

Phoenix chose that moment to come barrelling into the sitting room. Her eyes were alight with excitement and her mobile phone was held tightly in her hand. She came to a sliding stop when she saw them and rolled her eyes. "Do you two ever stop?"

Aria could feel Marcus's rumbling chuckle through her body and couldn't help but smile. "What is it, sweetheart?"

"Well ... you know how we talked about me having a bit more independence now that I'm fifteen?"

Aria opened her mouth to point out that the discussion had been the fairly one-sided opinion of teenage delusion, but Phoenix continued on in a hurry.

"Some girls from school have invited me to go into the city with them on Saturday. They're going to the cinema and maybe a bit of shopping. I'm not too arsed on the shopping part, but the film sounds ..."

Phoenix trailed off and her face dropped as she took in their less than enthusiastic expressions. She wrapped her arms around her midsection and her face became a blank mask.

"I'm sorry, sweetheart, now's just really not a good time." Marcus gave Aria a quick, reassuring squeeze as he addressed their daughter gently. "Maybe you can go the next time –"

"Liar," Phoenix spat, arms dropping to her sides as she balled her hands into fists. "You always say no. The other girls are allowed to go and I'm always the one left out. Why can't I be the same as them for once?" Her voice cracked as she threw the question at them, demanding an answer to an issue she hadn't even begun to truly fathom yet.

Tears glistened in Phoenix's eyes, and Aria's heart broke. They wanted so much to give her a normal childhood, a normal life, but it felt like they were forever failing.

"Phoenix," Marcus stood from the sofa, hands held out placatingly, "I promise we're only trying to do what's best for you."

He moved towards her, but Phoenix stepped back.

"When will I be old enough to decide what's best for me?"

A tingle of energy ran over Aria's skin, causing panic to shoot through her. She looked at Phoenix's face only to be met with luminous green eyes full of anger and frustration. The air in the room grew heavy, as if charged with electricity. She could feel the growing heat of the sun's energy.

Aria stood slowly, afraid to make any sudden movements. "Sweetheart, why don't you take a walk with me? We can talk about it. Maybe we can come to a compromise."

Phoenix just shook her head, tears threatening to spill over. The mobile phone was still held tightly in one fist and Aria noticed with trepidation the small line of smoke that drifted from it.

Completely unaware of the danger that stood before him, Marcus took another step towards his daughter, concern furrowing his forehead. Aria opened her mouth to yell, but it was too late. He extended a hand to grasp Phoenix by the shoulder and this time she didn't pull away. Instead, she let the smoking phone drop to the floor and lifted her hand to knock his away.

Time stood still for a second before a flash of scalding white light filled the room.

Marcus was thrown back into the wall at such force that the wall erupted in a spiderweb of cracks and he slid unmoving to the ground. His left arm was a mess of blackened skin from hand to shoulder, and the room smelled of burnt flesh.

Phoenix stood staring at her father's crumpled form, eyes wide with shock and skin deathly pale. Her whole body trembled as a pained sob wrenched itself from her throat and she dropped to the floor, keening like a wounded animal.

CHAPTER FOUR

Aria opened the door to her daughter's room to find Phoenix huddled in a small ball on her bed, her favourite purple blanket wrapped tightly around her. The curtains were closed, cloaking the room in darkness that seemed to magnify the soft sounds of crying. Even with concern for Marcus filling her thoughts, the sight made Aria's heart ache with an instinctual need to make it better. Quietly she closed the door behind her and sat down on the edge of the bed.

"Is he –" Phoenix's words cut off in sob that was muffled by her pillow.

Tears burned Aria's eyes. She had to swallow hard before answering. "It's okay. Your father will be okay." She made soothing noises as she rubbed her daughter's back.

Phoenix finally raised her head from the pillow, her gaze filled with trepidation and just a tinge of hope. "I didn't hurt him?"

Aria wanted to lie so badly, to take the pain and fear from those innocent eyes. But even if she wasn't prevented from doing so by virtue of her fae nature, she couldn't do it. Phoenix needed to understand the power she held, and exactly how dangerous it could be.

"You didn't hurt him intentionally." A sharp pain shot through her chest as she watched Phoenix's face crumble once more. "But yes, he is hurt."

At her words, Phoenix sat up in the bed and pulled her knees against her chest, gripping them so tightly her knuckles turned white. "He'll heal, won't he? He's a vampire, so he'll heal quickly?"

Memories of burnt skin and raw flesh filled Aria's mind as she thought of Marcus lying asleep in their bed. She'd had just enough herbs from the garden to coat the wounds and help him sleep, but it wouldn't be enough.

"I've given him some blood ..."

Phoenix's eyes widened but she stayed quiet.

"... and a remedy to help him sleep. The injuries are limited to the arm you made contact with, thankfully. They'll heal, but not without help."

Confusion warred with guilt on Phoenix's face. "Why isn't he healing?" Her tone grew more frantic as she read between the lines of what Aria was saying. "He's never needed help before if he's been injured. Why does he need help now?"

"Shh, it's okay." Aria brushed the flame-red hair back from Phoenix's face and gave her a sad smile. "The power you used today was a fae power. When you got upset you called on the sun. Your father is extremely strong, but even he can't withstand the sun in its purest form."

Understanding turned Phoenix's face to a mask of shock before the tears started again. "I didn't mean to do it, I swear." She dropped her head to her knees and her body shook.

Aria wrapped her arms around her daughter, no longer able to hold back. She gently rocked her and whispered soothing words that were little consolation to either of them. For so long she'd yearned to see traits of her fae heritage in her daughter. Other than Phoenix's immunity to sunlight, it had seemed the vampire side of her genetics dominated: speed, strength, a fondness for extra rare steak. Aria had gotten her wish, but at what cost?

The argument had started because Phoenix craved a normal life, and now it seemed as if that possibility was moving further and further from their reach.

Aria closed her eyes and took a deep breath, trying to tune out the crowds and noise of the city. Grafton Street was particularly busy that Saturday. She normally loved the random music acts and entertainers scattered about, but she found no joy in their passion now. Each act was just another obstacle to delay her, and the crowds they attracted were another frustrating barrier to her goal.

Marcus had slept through the night, the healing process numbing even his natural waking instincts. Once she calmed down, Phoenix had waited diligently by his side, and with each hour that passed without him waking, Aria watched her grow more uneasy. She'd tried to explain that it was his body's way of helping, but this seemed to do little to console Phoenix, and it was with a heavy heart that Aria left them to stock up on vital supplies.

A low rumble of thunder sounded overhead as thick, grey clouds darkened the sky. Aria pulled the hood of her jacket tight around her face and veered down one of the smaller side-streets.

The difference was instantaneous.

The melodic strains of an Irish ballad followed her, but the crowds disappeared. Clean, well-finished shopfronts were replaced by graffitied walls and cardboard box remnants from the homeless that had taken shelter that night.

She took turn after turn until she eventually ended up outside the small apothecary.

The brown wooden door was as nondescript as they came, and the windows showed little of the dimly lit shop beyond. Passers-by would be forgiven for assuming it had been long abandoned and few spared it a second glance as they rushed to their next destination before the heavens opened.

Aria pushed open the door and was greeted by a jingling bell. The mild wave of electricity that ran over her skin was expected, but it still made her shiver. The ward flagged her as a Supe and announced her presence to the shop's owner; although the witch could've easily identified her as a fae without the magical assistance.

Inside, the shop appeared perfectly innocuous. Wooden shelves lined the walls, and herbal remedies filled the various pots and jars.

The soothing scent of lavender drifted from an oil burner by the till, and baskets of glittering crystals offered creativity, good health, and true love. Everything a human might expect to see if they happened to venture in off the street.

A young woman with long, straw-coloured hair stepped from a doorway at the back of the shop. Sapphire blue eyes assessed Aria carefully.

"I'm afraid I do not allow glamours in my shop." The woman's voice was not unfriendly, but held an edge of expectation. She was not going to be refused on her property.

Aria gave the room a quick scan before inclining her head and letting the hood of her jacket fall back. The glamour had been a part of her life for so long, it was almost as natural as breathing. Whereas most would've had to concentrate to hold one, she now had to concentrate to remove it.

The change was subtle as the soft rounding of her ears returned to their natural points. Aria pushed the golden strands of her hair back so the witch could see clearly and received an acknowledging smile in return.

"Thank you. Now, how can I help you?"

Aria pulled the list of ingredients from her pocket and handed it to the witch.

A raised eyebrow and slight stilling of the body were the only physical signs of surprise before the witch looked at her and nodded. "I'll need a few minutes."

With that, she disappeared through the doorway at the back of the shop once more. Time slowed to a crawl as Aria paced anxiously. Each minute she spent interacting with the Lore increased the risk to her family. But Marcus needed this remedy, and even her extensive garden couldn't provide ingredients this rare.

Finally, the witch returned, holding a small package wrapped in brown paper and tied with rope. She looked at the package in her hands and back to Aria, a frown marring the smooth skin of her forehead.

"This isn't cheap."

Aria nodded silently and an unexpected lump formed in her

throat as she reached into her pocket for the gold. She could feel the embossed edges of the sun emblem as she gripped the coins in her hand. Her eyes closed for a moment as the memories flooded back.

Her father's face had been tight with anguish when he pressed the coins into her hand and urged her to use the money wisely. Behind him, her mother had sat with a steely gaze, showing no emotion at having just banished her youngest daughter from Faerie.

The coins were one of the few symbols she held of her people, and though valuable and tainted with grief, she'd held onto them for more than a hundred years. Until now.

With a deep breath, Aria handed over the coins and took the offered package. She didn't give the witch a chance to say anything further, just turned and left the small shop with her eyes downcast, glamour firmly back in place.

The ominous rumble of thunder met her as she stepped back onto the street and a flash of lightning split the sky. Fat, heavy raindrops began to splatter the pavement and within seconds, the rain was teeming down, mercilessly drenching anyone who dared cross its path.

Aria pulled her hood tightly around her head, but as soon as she moved from the shelter of the building, rain pelted her in the face. She wiped the water from her eyes, but it was a futile exercise. As eager as she was to get home, she just didn't have the energy to battle the elements, so she followed the surge of pedestrians diving for cover under the metal archways of George's Street Shopping Arcade, a couple of shops down from the apothecary.

Men, women, and children huddled at the entrance looking like drowned rats. The rain formed an almost solid wall in front of the arcade opening, and nobody seemed inclined to venture back out.

Aria huddled back into the crowd and a strange feeling washed over her as she watched the Irish weather in its furious glory. There was an energy to the air that spoke to a primal part of her, the part so intricately linked to the elements. Something like trepidation settled heavily in her gut.

Feeling stupid for being so edgy, she turned away from the opening and delved further into the arcade. Various smells assaulted her nose: the calming scent of incense, the invigorating aroma of freshly ground coffee. The eclectic mix of boutiques that spanned the small shopping arcade offered a tantalising feast for the senses.

Aria wove aimlessly between shoppers, keeping her head down. She was so lost in her thoughts that she didn't see the woman in front of her until they collided, sending the brown paper package flying from her hands.

Panic rushed through her, but before she could dive for the package, the woman grabbed her wrist. She looked up, prepared to fight, only to find herself staring into eyes so pale they were almost white.

The woman holding her had short black hair, and aside from the unusual eyes and powerful supernatural aura, she was about as nondescript as they came.

There was nothing threatening in her expression. In fact, there was nothing in her expression at all, just a blank stare into the distance and the slightest vibration around her eyes that would only be noticed from up close.

Aria gasped, recognising the telltale signs of a Seer – a gift so rare she'd only ever read about it.

The woman began to speak in mumbled tongues, her words low and incoherent, but growing more frantic by the second. Aria struggled to free her wrist, terrified the woman might see something that would put her family in danger. The grip was unwavering, however, and passers-by started to cast concerned glances in their direction.

Suddenly the frantic mumbling stopped and the woman stilled, eyes rolling upwards so that only the whites were visible.

"It has begun," the Seer said, words coming on a gasp of breath. "The bloodlines have mixed."

A wave of nausea rolled over Aria and the fear she'd felt before paled in comparison to the feeling that enveloped her now. No longer concerned about drawing attention from the humans, she reached deep inside her, preparing to draw on the power of the sun.

There was nothing.

The spot deep within her solar plexus that normally pulsed with heat was silent. She could still feel the connection to her element, but it was like a door had been closed, cutting off her access.

"They are coming," the Seer continued, oblivious to Aria's distress. "With her immortality, the fabric weakens. Death. Destruction. Devastation. They bring the end."

The woman's eyes flickered once more and her grip tightened further as she turned sightless eyes towards Aria. "She must not stand alone."

With a gasp, the Seer released her hold. Her eyes returned to her normal pale blue as she looked around in confusion before her gaze came to rest on Aria.

"Oh, I'm sorry." The woman gave an apologetic smile. "I really should look where I'm going."

And with that, she continued past Aria and out into the pouring rain, leaving Aria frozen to the spot with fear as heat pulsed in her chest once more.

CHAPTER FIVE

Phoenix bolted upright with a start. She'd no idea what had woken her, or when she'd fallen asleep for that matter. The last she remembered she'd been sitting by her father's side diligently watching for any sign of movement from his still form.

She was still in the stiff-backed wooden chair, arse aching from the hours spent on bed-watch. But the bedroom was dark, and the bed she'd been resting her head on was now empty.

Dad? Shit!

Adrenaline shot through her veins and her heart somersaulted. Phoenix jumped to her feet and looked around wildly, not quite sure what she was expecting to see. Was her father lying hurt on the bedroom floor?

It took a moment for the voices to filter through her groggy consciousness. And another minute before she realised what had woken her from sleep.

Her mother's voice was low enough that it should have been inaudible in her exhaustion-induced slumber, but there was something in the tone that spoke to a primal instinct deep within Phoenix. Fear.

"What if the woman tells someone, Marcus? What if she already has?"

Phoenix froze, trying to listen past the pounding of her heart. She could hear the soft shushing of her father as he comforted her mother, and for a moment, the relief at hearing his voice overshadowed the tense conversation on the other side of the door. Her knees grew weak.

"We need to talk to him. He'll know more," Marcus said calmly.

"You're not well enough –"

"This is too important to wait."

Movement sounded in the hallway beyond the bedroom and any response from her mother was muffled as Phoenix scurried back to her seat by the bed. When the door to the bedroom opened, she forced her face to remain completely blank.

Aria stood in the doorway, still wearing the jacket she'd had on earlier that day. There was a tightness around her green eyes that was almost imperceptible on her smooth skin and the smile she gave didn't quite ring true.

"Phoenix, sweetheart, we need to go out for a little while. Something important has come up."

The earlier relief Phoenix felt at hearing her father's voice disappeared in a flash and suddenly every worst-case scenario was running through her head in giant technicolour.

"Is Dad –" She choked off, not able to finish her question.

The door to the bedroom opened wider to reveal Marcus standing at Aria's shoulder, a wan smile on his sickly pale face. There were dark circles under his eyes, and with his shirt open, Phoenix could clearly see the edges of bandages running across his chest and up the left side of his neck. But he was awake, and he was standing, so she took what little comfort she could from the image.

"Dad, I'm so sorry." She heard her voice crack despite her best efforts and stared intently at her hands, gripped firmly together in her lap.

Marcus moved past Aria and came to kneel in front of Phoenix, lifting her chin so that she'd meet his gentle gaze. "It was an accident, sweetheart. Just an accident."

He waited until she nodded a reluctant acceptance of his words before continuing. "Your mother and I need to go out. We won't be long, but I need you to stay here, okay?"

Phoenix opened her mouth to ask what was going on, but he just shook his head.

"It's nothing for you to worry about, but I need you to stay inside and keep the doors locked." He gave her a quick kiss on the forehead, and before she could say anything further, he stood and left the room.

Her mother paused for a moment longer in the doorway, a haunted look in her eyes. That look burned itself into Phoenix's memory and stayed with her long after her mother had turned and left.

Phoenix paced the length of the kitchen, eyes flicking to the clock on the wall every few seconds.

Where are they?

It had been four hours since her parents left and she'd spent the whole time replaying their hushed words in her head. None of what she'd heard made sense. What could be serious enough that it trumped her father's injuries?

All attempts to distract herself had failed miserably. Homework had provided a measly five minutes of entertainment before she got fed up. Martial arts practice had fared a little better at thirty minutes, but her heart hadn't been in it.

Every once in a while, she'd reach for her phone, only to curse herself as she remembered the battery was fried from her little hormonal outburst. It was no use; she needed to do something useful.

Her stomach took that opportune moment to start grumbling and she smiled. Food. That's what she could do to help. She was pretty sure neither of her parents had had time to eat before they left, so the least she could do was have something ready when they came back.

Eight hours later and Phoenix stared at the now cold dinner laid out on the table, eyes burning with unshed tears. The early morning sunlight streamed in through the kitchen window, casting streaks of red light across the table and coating the uneaten food in an odd, blood-like hue. Through the hours of darkness, hundreds of scenarios had flashed across her mind, and not a single one of them had been comforting. Now, as the daylight spread, lighting the kitchen in its glaring reality, she couldn't shake the feeling that something was wrong.

She'd promised her dad that she'd stay in the house, but the longer they were gone, the harder it was to sit idly by and wait. If she just slipped into the village, she could find somewhere to buy a new phone and call them, then she would know they were okay. Surely he couldn't be angry with her for that?

Eventually, fear of the unknown outweighed her guilt at breaking a promise and Phoenix made the five-mile round trip to the village. Her pocket money stash was severely depleted – as in non-existent – but at least her sim card was now sitting in a functioning phone.

Every fifteen minutes she made the same call with the same result: no answer.

By the time dusk fell, the ringtone had become a soundtrack to echo the terror that was settling in the deep, uncomfortable pit of her stomach. But she couldn't help herself; she just kept pressing the call button. Even though she'd given up on an answer hours ago.

Darkness brought with it a new fear – fear of herself. Each time the clock in the kitchen passed the hour mark, her anxiety would ratchet up another level, and with it came the heat.

It started in the palms of her hands. A strange burning sensation that didn't quite hurt. Then, as her consciousness registered the sensation, her whole body began to tremble and sweat trailed down the back of her neck. She knew this feeling. She'd felt it once before ...

Every time the heat flared within her, images of her father's injuries would follow. So, she learned to push it back. Slow, controlled breathing helped her to calm her racing heart until eventually the flare-ups reduced and all that was left was the ticking of the clock. Taunting her.

Morning came, and still her parents hadn't returned. At some point during the night a cold numbness had settled in, cushioning her from the reality of the empty house. Practical thoughts replaced horror-filled scenarios. A bag now sat at her feet, packed with clothes and uncertainty.

Phoenix looked at her phone resting on the kitchen table. Silent. She knew what she was supposed to do if something happened to her parents; she'd had it drilled into her from as young as she could remember. Call Darius. Go with him to safety.

But still she held off making the call.

If she took that step, it would mean admitting that something was seriously wrong, and her parents weren't going to walk back through the door any minute. It would also mean entering his world, however temporarily. She loved Darius, and she knew he'd do anything to protect her, but she wasn't ready to step into the vampire's lair just yet.

One more day. She'd wait one more day and then she'd make the call.

With the decision made, Phoenix looked at the bag resting on the floor. There was something missing. She pushed up from the table and made her way down the hall to her parents' bedroom. The door was slightly ajar, and even in the darkness beyond, she could see the abandoned signs of her bedside vigil. The sight made her breath catch in her throat and for a brief moment the world seemed to spin. When her gaze steadied, she realised her hand was clutching the doorframe and the area surrounding her hand was black and charred.

She pulled her hand away as if she, and not the doorframe, had been burned. With a deep breath, she moved into the room, blocking out everything except her goal.

The medallion was resting on the bedside locker where she last saw it. Even in the dim light, the embossed image of the sun was clearly visible – her mother's family emblem. As she ran the platinum chain through her fingers, she suddenly realised she'd never seen her mother without the medallion. Why had she taken it off now?

Phoenix bowed her head and slipped the chain around her neck, tucking it under her top. The metal felt warm where it rested against her breast bone, and for a brief moment, she felt comforted.

Next stop was the wardrobe.

She had to stretch on her tiptoes to reach the highest shelf, but with a bit of nudging, the long mahogany box came into view. The side of it was carved with beautiful intricate swirls and the Celtic symbols called to her in a way she couldn't explain.

Gently, she manoeuvred the box to the edge of the shelf until she could slide it down into her hands. Phoenix didn't need to open the lid to picture the sword inside. She'd spent many hours sat by her father's feet as he cleaned the precious metal and had memorised every little detail of the weapon. Her motivation through many training sessions had been to master her art so that he'd teach her how to wield it. Would he ever get the chance now?

As she rose to leave, one more thing occurred to her. Ignoring the burning in her throat, she reached for another, smaller wooden box that sat at the bottom of the wardrobe. This, too, bore the sun emblem of her mother's people, and the scent of herbs was strong despite the lid being firmly closed. She prayed to a god she didn't believe in that she'd never have to use the contents, and left the room to wait.

Minutes passed, followed by hours; each accentuated by the incessant ticking of the clock. And with the fading light, something inside of Phoenix died.

Unable to wait any longer, she made the call.

"Uncle D, I need your help."

CHAPTER SIX

6 years later

Phoenix didn't look back. Not even for a second. She could feel the large, white building looming at her back, its dark windows watching her silently. Many of the occupants were settling down for their daily slumber, satiated from a rich feast of blood. Most of them wouldn't realise she'd gone. Most of them didn't even know she'd been there.

Darius, however, would be watching her closely, waiting for her to change her stubborn mind – his words – and return.

Instead, she focused her gaze on the tendrils of red seeping into the sky as the sun breached the horizon. The merest hint of light sent tingles across her skin, causing her fingers to twitch. Even in the cold depths of winter, she felt her fae side awaken from its long slumber.

Phoenix inhaled deeply, relishing the crisp morning air. As she took her first tentative step towards her new life, her hand gripped the money in her pocket. Uncertainty made her stomach churn.

The keys Darius had given her to the new apartment rested stubbornly on the bedside table where she'd left them. The money had been harder to leave behind. She promised herself she'd pay him back.

At the end of the winding driveway, large, wrought-iron gates acted as an imposing deterrent to passers-by. Not many people truly knew what lay under the Ambassador's residence, but some instincts lingered even in the most human of humans; anyone with sense knew to stay away.

Phoenix didn't wait to see if the gates would open in acceptance of her decision. With a short sprint, she rebounded off one of the concrete pillars and used her momentum to grab the top of the gate. She swung herself over the barrier and landed with a jarring thud on the other side.

For a moment everything was silent. Then the subtle creak of metal broke through the stillness as the gates began to open behind her.

A weight lifted from her shoulders and for the first time that morning, she smiled, giving a small wave to the security cameras behind her. The smile didn't last though. As she looked at the open fields surrounding her, she suddenly felt lost. Where the hell was she going?

A loud squawk from a nearby oak tree startled her. She looked up at the tree to find a large crow watching her from a gnarled branch. The bird's dark feathers formed a kaleidoscope of colours in the morning light and there was something unusual about its beady eyes.

The bird tilted its head, appearing to assess her for a moment longer before taking flight towards the distant sound of traffic. And with no better plan, Phoenix followed the crow.

3 MINUTES TO MIDNIGHT

CHAPTER ONE

Abi is going to kill me!

Phoenix pushed through the throng of arms and legs that flooded towards her in a never-ending sea of bodies. Visibility was almost non-existent thanks to the relentless downpour of rain and her vibrant red hair plastered to her face. More than once she had to duck to avoid the kamikaze pigeons dive-bombing their way through the crowds while giant seagulls circled ominously overhead.

The bitter wind stabbed at her as she navigated her way through the city streets back to Connolly Train Station. Darkness fell around her and she longed for the warm comforts of home: the cosy pub that was her sanctuary as she worked, the easy chatter and friendly banter with customers. Being dry.

She sighed.

What the hell had she been thinking coming into Dublin, on New Year's Eve of all days? Sure, Abi's incessant party planning was getting on her already frazzled nerves, but she'd just swapped one form of torture for another.

The crowds grew even thicker as she neared the grey stone building. Rowdy cheers and enthusiastic conversations announced the revellers ready to see in the New Year. Weather be damned.

As she pushed through the doors of the station, Phoenix held her breath against the stench of sweat and stale smoke, grateful her sense of smell was only slightly heightened, unlike some species of the Lore.

Occasionally the telltale signature of another Supe tingled across her skin, making her gut clench. Some she recognised – vampire or the occasional fae – others were less familiar. None seemed to pay attention to her, but still her senses remained on high alert, waiting for a strange look or a finger pointed in her direction.

The green digital clock glared at her from the notice board, as if she needed a reminder of just how late she was. *This would be a great time to have teleportation powers,* she thought as she jumped in line for the ticket turnstile.

Not that she'd use them if she did.

A sudden insistent buzzing against her hip made her stomach drop. *Shit, please don't be Abi.*

Inching along with the queue, Phoenix reached into the tight pocket of her leather trousers and pulled out her phone, preparing to apologise profusely. Relief flooded her when she looked at the screen to find Darius's name flashing back.

"Uncle D." She covered her free ear in the slim hope of being able to hear the voice at the end of the phone.

"Did I catch you at a bad time? I wanted to wish you a happy birthday."

Darius's rich tone was warming in its familiarity, and Phoenix smiled. "No, you're fine. I'm just trying to get home before Abi hands me my arse on a plate for being late to my own party."

"It's nice that she wants to celebrate your birthday."

She gave a non-committal grunt. "Are we still good for dinner on Thursday?"

"Of course. I've gotten us a reservation at the new Italian restaurant I mentioned. The table's booked for nine."

Phoenix whistled low to herself. From what she'd heard, it was almost impossible to get a reservation at Bella's. Even with Darius's vast connections, it was impressive he'd managed.

"Nine is good for me," she said.

"Perfect, I'll send a car for you at –"

"No, no, there's no need. I'll meet you there."

"Now, Phoenix, don't be silly."

"Honestly, Uncle D. It'll be easier if I meet you there. Look, I gotta go –"

"Phoenix." His softer tone stopped her in her tracks surer than any argument could. "How are you feeling? Really?"

She paused for a second and debated lying, but this was Darius. He knew her too well. "I don't really know … I don't even know what I'm expecting to feel. Maybe nothing will even happen."

"I know this is hard for you, but you can't bury your head in the sand."

Funny because that's exactly what she planned on doing.

As if reading her mind, Darius's voice turned harder, the familiar impatience evident in his tone. "Your mother settled into her immortality at twenty-five. It stands to reason you will too."

"We don't know that."

"No, we don't. With your unique nature we don't know anything for sure, but ignoring it won't make it go away either."

Her hand clenched around her phone and she closed her eyes against the pounding headache that was beginning to form.

The crackling static of the intercom announced the arrival of her train.

Her words were barely a whisper when she finally spoke. "My train's here, Uncle D. I'll see you on Thursday." She hung up before he had a chance to respond.

Lost in her thoughts, Phoenix hardly noticed the man-mountain barrelling towards her from the waiting train. He ploughed into her with a force so unexpected that in a blink she was on her arse on the cold ground, watching in shock as his back faded into the distance.

Stunned, it took her a moment to notice the rough hand reaching out to her. She looked up into the rich, brown eyes of another man. His gaze was fixed intently on her, even as his body language was poised for pursuit.

The supernatural energy that thrummed through him was enough to send sparks of electricity skittering across her skin. She backed away from the offered assistance and stumbled, not so gracefully, to her feet. The man regarded her with an odd expression and ran a hand through his dark, tousled hair.

A sudden yell drew his attention in the direction the man-mountain had fled. And with a cheeky grin he was gone, leaving Phoenix staring at the empty space he'd been, heart racing.

The pounding in her head grew stronger and for a moment, her vision blurred. She shook her head, trying to clear the strange mugginess, but her hands started to tremble and heat built in her right palm.

Fear washed over her and she clenched her hand in a fist.

Please don't let me lose control. Not here.

Her fae powers had become increasingly unpredictable of late; any form of stress acted as a potential trigger. With no control over her power and no one to ask, she clung to the only thing she knew how to do. With slow, controlled breaths, she pushed the energy deep down inside and locked it firmly away.

Eventually the heat receded, and her heart slowed its frantic pace. The pounding headache, however, grew worse as she turned to see the train pull away from the platform, and a large crow with strange red eyes watching her from the electricity mast.

CHAPTER TWO

The party was in full swing by the time Phoenix arrived at the pub, drenched to the bone and far past fashionably late. Music was blasting out of the old-style jukebox, thumping in time to her headache, while the band set up in the corner. The lights were low and the drinks were flowing freely. A comforting sense of home welcomed her as the door closed with a thud, shutting out the miserable night.

A scan of the pub found Abi at her usual spot behind the bar. Phoenix made a beeline in her direction, more than prepared to grovel if necessary.

"Abi, I'm so sorry. I honestly didn't mean to be so late. I missed the train and ..."

Abi glared at her, hands on her hips, lips pursed.

Phoenix's heart dropped, and she said the only thing she could, "I'm sorry for being an ungrateful bitch."

Abi glared for a moment longer before her face finally softened. Her blue eyes sparkled with a hint of laughter as she took in Phoenix's dishevelled appearance. "I'll get you a drink."

Just like that, she was forgiven, and for the first time all day, she felt a bit lighter. Giving Abi a small smile, she slipped behind the bar and upstairs to the apartment they shared.

The headache was just stress, she assured herself. Turning twenty-five wasn't a big deal; Darius was overreacting. There was every chance she'd keep ageing as normal. She needed to get cleaned up and celebrate with her friend.

Anyway, even if she did follow in her mother's footsteps, it didn't mean anything had to change ... did it?

"... Five, four, three, two, one!"

Just as the clock struck midnight and the crowd around her cheered at the top of their lungs, the room began to swim and Phoenix's vision blurred. A violent shudder ran down her spine and her hands gripped the edge of the bar, knuckles turning white.

A mere second and the moment passed. Everything came back into sharp focus and Abi's voice reverberated loudly in her ear.

"Happy birthday!"

Phoenix shook her head, trying to get her bearings. She returned Abi's embrace and let her friend's ever-contagious enthusiasm wash over her as she pushed back the sense of unease. It was just the drink, that's all.

One arm still locked around her waist, Abi swayed along with the crowd of people, singing a very out of tune "Auld Lang Syne". Phoenix dutifully followed suit, but the niggle of unease refused to leave her.

When the crowd broke into a rowdy rendition of "The Fields of Athenry", Phoenix extricated herself from her friend's grip and slipped away in search of a strong drink. She grabbed an empty glass and made her way to the bar to fetch a fresh bottle.

You can't have a celebration without rum. And that's what this is, isn't it? A celebration.

Pouring a generous measure, she took a breath and knocked it back straight. She waited a moment, expecting the room to spin, or some sign the drink was going to her head.

Nothing happened.

Her vision didn't blur, and the room didn't spin. She tried another large gulp straight from the bottle.

Nothing.

With a sigh, she poured more rum into her glass and topped it with a wedge of lime. Who was she kidding? Her metabolism was far too accelerated for the alcohol to affect her. Maybe she was coming down with the flu. Sure, human diseases didn't normally affect her, but it was possible. All these crazy super bugs going around, who knew?

Clutching the glass, her free hand played with the platinum medallion hanging from her neck. The hard, embossed edges of the sun pressed into the palm of her hand. Her mother's emblem. One of the only things she had left of her.

She never thought of asking her mother what it would feel like when her immortality kicked in. She'd always assumed her parents would be with her when the time came.

Her father had been in his thirties when he was turned. Sure, he had to die for it to happen, but who says her fae side would be more dominant anyway? Just because the fae reached their immortality at twenty-five, didn't mean she would. Maybe she'd need to die before it happened, like her father. Hell, maybe a hybrid wouldn't even become immortal at all …

Looking around, she was filled with an over-whelming sense of gratitude for the life she'd built. Abi had saved her by giving her this job, a place to stay, and a way to escape the Lore. She couldn't ever imagine leaving it behind. But how many years would she have before people noticed she wasn't aging? How long would it take before Abi asked questions she couldn't answer? How long before she would have to say goodbye?

No sooner had the thought formed in her head than a shudder ran through her and her vision turned black. The glass slipped from her grasp and smashed to pieces on the tiled floor.

CHAPTER THREE

"You don't scream for me anymore."

Il Maestro pondered this, tilting his head as he looked at the frail figures curled up on the hard, stone floor. A chain made with thick iron links swung lazily in his left hand as he licked the blood from the fingers of his right.

The smaller of the two forms tensed, no doubt waiting on the inevitable blow. The larger form remained still, unmoving, as it had for a long time now.

"It's started already, you know," Il Maestro continued, pacing slowly around the small, dank cell, in no hurry to make use of the heavy chain. "I felt it as soon as the clock struck midnight. The shift.

"All those years waiting patiently. It will be worth it when the prophecy is fulfilled and I take my rightful place at their side. We will hide in the shadows no more."

He stopped pacing and stared at the torches that lined the wall, their flames flickering hungrily in the dark.

"At least she'll know her life meant something in the end. That must make you proud."

Lifting his arm high, he let the chain fly and felt the satisfying crunch of bone beneath the iron.

Again, his arm raised.

"Let's see if we can make you scream, shall we?"

The tightness in his shoulders had eased significantly by the time he left the chamber. Blood splatter covered the front of his black Armani suit and he made a mental note to get it dry cleaned as he settled behind the large mahogany desk in his office and wiped his hands with the embroidered handkerchief.

"You called for me, Il Maestro?"

Il Maestro looked up at the vampire before him. Even compared to his own impressive height, Raphael was tall. The broad expanse of muscle only served to heighten his intimidating aura; a useful quality to have as head of security.

"I want a full debriefing on the status of all outstanding projects at midnight tonight."

"Yes, Il Maestro." Raphael stood straight with his hands clasped behind his back, a not-so-subtle military air to his posture.

"How are the new recruits coming along?"

"The wolves are reacting well to the new formula. Their aggression has increased significantly but with fewer obedience issues."

Il Maestro nodded, pleased with this development. The mangy dogs had been the most difficult to control. As much as he enjoyed their viciousness – it took very little for them to tear each other's throats out – discipline was paramount.

"Good, it's time we start escalating our preparations. We need to be ready."

He reached for the crystal decanter on his desk and poured a generous measure of the rich, golden liquid into a glass. "Arrange a meeting with the witches and get the newest batch of wolves ready for a field test."

With a swift nod, Raphael turned on his heel and left the office.

The tingling anticipation was starting to build now that preparations were fully underway, but it was important he didn't lose focus.

The clock had finally begun its countdown.

CHAPTER FOUR

Wiping the bar counter absently, Phoenix considered the previous few days. There had been no more blackouts since New Year's Eve, but a sense of dread still lingered insidiously with every waking thought. More than one customer had commented on her distraction, and Abi was regularly throwing concerned glances her way.

Not being able to confide in her friend made it even harder. But what could she say? *Oh hey, did I forget to mention I'm a vampire-fae hybrid? Don't worry I don't suck your blood while you sleep or anything, but I think I might be immortal now and I could really use a shoulder to cry on about all of it.*

Probably wouldn't go down too well.

Abi's shout from above pulled her out of her imaginary conversation with a start. "Hey, Fifi, get your butt up here or I'm going to eat all the popcorn by myself."

Phoenix grimaced at the nickname she detested. Looking down, she was surprised to realise the cloth in her hand had turned to tatters; her aggressive cleaning of a single spot causing the threads to wear through. With a sigh she threw the cloth in the bin and rushed upstairs to where Abi was waiting, surrounded by a sea of puffy cushions in the sitting room of their apartment.

The apartment that occupied the upper floor of the pub wasn't the largest, but Abi's unique flair had given it a homely feel not many could have replicated. Quirky pictures hung on the wall, and each room was a strange mish-mash of colours, but it worked somehow. It was the antithesis of the vampire lair where she'd spent so much of her teenage years and Phoenix had loved it from the moment Abi took her in as a lodger.

"So, what did we settle on?" Phoenix asked, dropping into the oversized sofa and grabbing a handful of popcorn from the bowl in Abi's lap.

"Well, Mary – you know the one with the black hair? Well, she was telling me about this TV series called True Blood. It's like Twilight, but for grown-ups, if you know what I mean." Abi's blue eyes twinkled as she wiggled her eyebrows suggestively.

Phoenix choked, a popcorn kernel lodging in her throat at the wrong moment. "I didn't think vampires were your thing," she spluttered, when she could finally speak again.

Abi shrugged. "The main guy is kind of cute. Figured it's worth a look." She grabbed the remote control and pressed play before adding, "Afterwards we can decide what your New Year's resolutions are going to be."

Covering her face with a cushion, Phoenix groaned. Going back to the vampire lair suddenly didn't seem like such a bad idea.

Watching the crowds around him, Ethan shook his head. Even midweek, Temple Bar was heaving with tourists. Lairy stags and cackling hens stumbled from pub to pub, seemingly oblivious to the almost freezing temperatures and cutting wind. The rain-slick cobblestones were proving too much of a challenge for many a high heel, and more than once he winced in sympathy for the ankles that paid the price.

He'd been patrolling the city since the last attack on New Year's Eve, and so far, things had been quiet. But it wouldn't last. It never lasted.

As if to prove his point, a high-pitched scream pulled Ethan

43

roughly from his thoughts. He took off at a run, heading for the shadowed alley the sound had come from. The sense of déjà vu that washed over him was becoming frustratingly common.

What will it be this time?

The putrid smell of rubbish, mixed with the fresh scent of human excrement, assaulted his senses before he even reached the mouth of the alley. It made him wish, not for the first time, that his senses weren't quite so heightened.

Sticking to the shadows cast by the graffitied brick walls, he could hear the muffled sounds of terror punctuated by low growls in the darkness. But it was the sharp scent of fear that sent Ethan's pulse racing.

He worked hard to control the wolf inside him. He knew his eyes would be glowing yellow from the adrenaline, and the last thing he needed was to scare the woman even more.

A number of industrial bins lined the wall ahead, partially blocking his view. Quietly, he leapt on top of the closest one and took in the scene before him. Rage flared through him at what he saw.

Five large wolves had a woman surrounded. Though they weren't in full wolf form, their beasts were clearly in control; madness visible in their yellow eyes, razor-sharp fangs and fully extended claws.

Well, that explained the fear anyway.

The largest of the pack had the woman pinned to the wall, one huge hand holding her by the throat as he slowly sniffed the length of her neck. Tears flowed freely down her cheeks as she held herself rigid. The scent of her fear was only driving them wilder and Ethan knew he didn't have long before they would tire of their teasing and attack.

The numbers were against him, and even though none had signatures strong enough to be an Alpha, five-to-one odds were not good. But walking away wasn't an option either. So, he extended his claws and allowed his wolf to come to the fore just enough to give him a fighting chance.

Moving so fast he appeared as little more than a blur, Ethan grabbed the closest wolf from behind and raked his claws clean across his throat. The element of surprise gave him enough time to turn towards the second wolf before anyone could react. Grabbing him by the throat, he lifted the large frame two foot in the air and slammed his body into the hard concrete, stunning him.

And that was where his luck ran out.

By this time, the remaining three wolves had turned their full attention to him, and the woman, finally coming to her senses, fled to the safety of the street beyond. The snarling wolves surrounded him, their obvious show of logic and organisation posing a strange contrast to their crazed looks and bloodthirsty behaviour.

Ethan braced for the attack.

With his body in a half-crouched position, he was able to quickly shift to the left as one of the wolves lunged at him. The first strike missed him, but it was followed immediately by a second. A sharp claw raked across his bicep, sending a burning sensation down his arm and seriously pissing him off.

Using the offending wolf's momentum against him, Ethan turned and aimed a kick at his ribs, sending the wolf stumbling with a grunt into the large bins.

The next wolf came for him and he dropped low, sweeping the wolf's leg. But as he began to rise, Ethan was caught from behind in a strangling chokehold. His airway was quickly cut off and pressure began to build behind his eyes.

Using all his weight, he shoved back against the wolf and slammed him into the wall behind. Despite the crushing sound of skull hitting brick, the pressure around his throat refused to let up. He pushed back again, weaker this time, as the blood flow to his head slowed and he started getting woozy.

Through his now blurring vision, Ethan could see the largest wolf stalking towards him. Foam dripped from the corner of its mouth and the whites of his crazed eyes were mottled a strange red colour.

Something is seriously not right with these wolves, Ethan thought numbly as he tried in vain to loosen the ironclad grip around his neck.

Suddenly, the wolf stopped his advance. A look of surprise widened the wolf's eyes, and without warning, he slumped forward onto the ground. A large knife protruded from his back.

The wolf holding him growled in confusion, and as he tried to peer around his captive, his grip loosened just enough for Ethan to suck in some air. Taking advantage of the brief reprieve, Ethan launched an elbow into the wolf's gut and twisted out of his grasp. Barely a second later, he heard a guttural yelp and a second knife lodged in the wolf's throat.

"C'mon, big guy. They won't be out for long."

Ethan turned to see Nate's wide grin and the laughter evident in his amber eyes.

Dammit. That was the second time Nate had saved his ass from his own kind. The kid was going to be even more insufferable now.

"What is it with you wolves and all that aggression? Did mammy and daddy not cuddle you enough as pups?"

Ethan took a long sup from his pint, savouring the cool freshness as he ignored Nate's playful ribbing. Now that they were away from the crowds of Temple Bar, he could think a bit clearer, his wolf finally content to take a back seat once the danger had passed. Cocooned in the cosy darkness of the small pub they'd found, he analysed the scene in his head and tried to pinpoint exactly what it was about the encounter that bothered him so much – aside from the fact he needed saving, of course.

"That wasn't normal wolf behaviour." He sighed, rolling his head from side to side until his neck gave a resounding crack.

Hell, he didn't even know what normal was any more. Ever since he started tracking the vamp that killed Sean, it seemed things were just getting weirder and weirder.

Nate looked at him sceptically, one eyebrow raised. He said nothing, merely took a mouthful of his own pint.

Ethan grimaced. The aches were starting to set in as his body healed itself and he wasn't feeling better for it. "The last time was different –"

"Ye mean the last time I saved your hairy ass?" Nate interjected, and a wide grin conveyed just how pleased he was with himself.

Gritting his teeth, Ethan ignored the taunt. "That was about territory. This was just mindless violence."

"They were controlled though. Organised."

Ethan nodded. "And none of the wolves were Alphas. They shouldn't have been that strong."

As he played with the pint glass in front of him, he didn't miss the flash of concern that passed in Nate's eyes; he was pretty sure it mirrored his own. And not for the first time, he wondered what the hell they'd gotten caught up in.

The two sat in companionable silence for a while, each lost in their own thoughts. All Ethan had wanted was a break from the pack. Some time to be free of everyone's expectations and the constant weight of responsibility. But Sean had to go and follow him. Had to go and get killed.

Ever since, it seemed like things had completely gone to shit.

Tracking the vamp responsible for Sean's death had been a lesson in dead ends. Yet somehow, he kept finding himself in strange situations like the one tonight; it couldn't be a coincidence. More and more innocent people were getting caught in the crossfire of the Lore, and it only appeared to be escalating.

The Lore may not have been known for peace, love, and bunny rabbits, but it was one of their most solemn edicts that humans were to be kept ignorant of their existence. The mistakes of the past had been hard-learned and the Council decreed death to anyone stupid enough to defy them.

"So what, aside from luck, brought you down here tonight?" Ethan eventually asked. He looked sideways at the kid next to him, because that's all he was really, little more than a kid.

Guilt gnawed at Ethan. At barely twenty-one, Nate hadn't even settled into his immortality yet – something that normally happened later for shifters – he shouldn't have been caught up in this mess.

Nate shook his floppy brown hair out of his eyes and perked up. "I came to find you 'cause it looks like we might've finally gotten a lead."

Ethan's hand froze, pint midway to his mouth. "And you're only telling me now?"

"Well, you seemed a bit preoccupied back there –" Nate ducked just in time to avoid the clip across the ear. "Okay, okay. Lily's gotten some info from a witch friend of hers. Someone with connections to the Dublin coven."

Ethan smiled to himself at the way Nate's voice changed when he mentioned Lily's name, but refrained from interrupting.

"Apparently word on the grapevine is that there's some kind of prophecy at play, and it's causing all this bad juju."

"A prophecy?"

Ethan heard the scepticism in his own tone. The witches were often more clued in than the rest of the Lore. Without the strength and speed benefits of other species, their resilience relied on knowledge. But blaming everything on some random act of fate just seemed too convenient to him.

"Yeah, something about a hybrid and the end of humanity," Nate said, knocking back the remainder of his pint. "All sounds like something from a bad movie if you ask me."

It took a few seconds for the words to register with Ethan, and another few seconds for the shock to follow. "A hybrid? How in the Lore would a hybrid have been created?"

"Well you know when two people love each other ..." Nate gave a cheeky grin as he highlighted his not so subtle point with even less subtle hand gestures.

Ethan's head was spinning.

Nate was right. If a hybrid existed, there had to have been an inter-species relationship. One that produced an offspring. Not only was that breaking Council edict, another crime punishable by death, but it was also unheard of. Hell, their very nature made it near impossible for members of the same species to procreate – an unfortunate trade-off for being difficult to kill, or nature's culling mechanism, who knew. He couldn't even imagine how challenging it would be for two members of different species.

Something niggled at the back of Ethan's consciousness, a fleeting memory that wouldn't quite solidify. Pulling himself from his own thoughts, he forced himself to focus on one thing at a time.

"So, if the witches know what's causing this, why aren't they doing anything about it?"

Nate shrugged. "That's the million-dollar question, I guess. It all seems pretty sketchy to me, and Lily's friend was pretty nervous talking about it."

"Did the witch give any more details about the prophecy?"

"She was pretty vague according to Lily. But she did say that a hybrid would bring about an 'eternal night and the end of humanity'."

Ethan drummed his fingers on the table, trying to piece it all together. "Is this why we've been seeing so much crazy shit with the Lore lately?"

Nate shrugged again. "Maybe. Either way I'm guessing we're in for a bumpy ride."

CHAPTER FIVE

Phoenix puffed out a cold gust of air and rubbed her hands together briskly as she stepped into the warm cocoon of the restaurant. A low murmur of conversation surrounded her, almost as if the soft candle-light encouraged the patrons to speak in hushed, intimate tones. The occasional clink of glasses added harmony to the almost musical flow of voices.

For the second time in less than a week, she'd left the warm comfort of home to trek into the city. And just like a few days ago, the possibility of her immortality was weighing heavy on her mind. She could only hope Darius would have useful advice for her.

Looking around the lavish space, she tugged self-consciously at her black dress as she searched the room for Darius. Bella's was the newest in a range of high-end restaurants that had been popping up along the quays. She'd heard it was so in demand that few, other than the stupidly rich and famous, could even hope to get a reservation. Phoenix was neither, and as she stood awkwardly in the doorway, she wished Darius had chosen somewhere a little less impressive for her annual birthday dinner.

A maître d' wearing the obligatory black and white suit came to greet her, pausing for a second to assess her windswept appearance before plastering a welcoming smile on his face.

"Welcome to Bella's. Do you have a reservation?"

It was at that moment she heard Darius's rich, seductive voice, followed closely by a girlish giggle. Seeking the sound with her eyes, she spotted him by a large window that looked out at the picturesque lights of the city.

"I'm here to meet my uncle." Phoenix returned the fake smile and pointed in Darius's direction.

"Oh, of course. You're most welcome, Ms. Crawford." The maître d' flushed as he took her coat.

Not waiting to be shown the way, Phoenix made a beeline for the table where Darius sat. All this yes Ma'am, no Ma'am, can I take your coat Ma'am, just made her feel awkward and out of place. Give her a nice dingy pub any day.

Darius appeared extra suave in his charcoal, tailored suit, most likely made by some designer she'd never heard of. The look perfectly accentuated his thick, black hair and pale, flawless skin. He was clean shaven like always and the epitome of class as he graced the waitress with one of his most charming smiles – fangs retracted, of course.

Phoenix cringed as the woman again dissolved into a fit of girlish giggles, just short of fanning herself with the white cloth she held. She'd love to see the waitress's reaction if she found out she was talking to one of the most powerful vampires in Ireland. Hell, probably in all of Europe. Then again, with the way movies had been romanticising vampires and werewolves lately, it would probably only make the woman worse.

Rolling her eyes, she took the last few steps and moved into Darius's line of sight. He quickly stood from the table, shifting his charming smile to her. His dark eyes were the only thing that showed his amusement as he kissed her on both cheeks in welcome.

The blustering waitress had the grace to look embarrassed as she quickly pulled out Phoenix's chair and offered her a glass of wine. Declining the expensive vinegar, she ordered a rum and coke and shook her head as the woman left the table with a mere fragment of her composure intact.

"You didn't give her a chance at all, did you?" Phoenix attempted to give Darius a disapproving look, but she couldn't stop her lips from quirking up in amused fondness for the man before her.

He really hadn't changed much in all the years she'd known him. Being as old as dust tended to make people set in their ways. The charming sophistication never faltered, and even his expensive fashion tastes had a timeless quality. He didn't have the softest disposition, but he'd stood by her parents when everyone else turned their back. That made him family.

"Oh, Phoenix, darling, I really wasn't trying in the slightest. Merely passing the time." He raised one perfectly manicured eyebrow as if to say, "What can I do if they find me irresistible?"

With a resigned laugh, Phoenix focused her attention on the menu. The reprieve from her troubled thoughts had been brief, and as her amusement faded, she found herself once more distracted by the concerns of recent days. What if Darius couldn't answer her questions? She had no one else to ask. But the memory of their conversation on New Year's Eve was fresh in her mind, and she suddenly found herself reluctant to broach the subject. Instead, she forced herself to focus on the insanely expensive food options.

Once the waitress had taken their order – two steaks, extra rare – they settled into their usual routine. Darius asked about the pub and her friends, and she diverted his prying by asking about his many business ventures. Before long, she was finding it hard to concentrate and he quickly noticed.

"What's wrong, Phoenix?" Darius looked disapprovingly at the half-eaten steak she was pushing around her plate.

"Do all fae become immortal at twenty-five?"

There was a long moment of silence, and Phoenix forced herself to meet his gaze. He regarded her closely, a stillness to him that only vampires could achieve.

"As far as I know, yes." His tone remained neutral, but the intensity of his gaze never wavered.

"Do you know what it feels like? When it happens?"

A furrow creased his brow as he considered her question. "I was turned, Phoenix. As your father was. For us, immortality was a side effect rather than a birthright."

What little she'd eaten of her dinner felt heavy in her stomach. He wasn't telling her anything new, yet she'd hoped he could give her more information. Anything to put her mind at ease.

"Is there something you need to tell me, Phoenix?"

The temptation to lie, to brush it off, was strong. Once she said the words out loud, she couldn't ignore them anymore. If she remained silent, she could stay ignorant and get on with her normal, happy life.

Until she couldn't any longer.

"I've just been feeling a bit strange since my birthday. It could be nothing. Maybe I have the flu."

Darius scoffed. "The flu? What, like a human? Don't be ridiculous."

She frowned, his tone taking her by surprise. Yes, she knew there was very little chance of her getting sick, but Darius actually seemed disgusted by the suggestion.

"It doesn't matter. Like I said, it was probably nothing." She pushed her plate aside, appetite completely gone.

"Maybe, but why don't you tell me what happened?" His face softened as he reached for her hand.

Taking a deep breath, she told him everything: the strange dizziness, the moment of blackness, the edgy feeling she'd had ever since. For a while, he mulled over the information and rolled his wine glass back and forth between his fingers. Eventually, he sat back and looked at her.

"We never did know what to expect with you. Given the two elements that make up your dual nature, it would make sense for your fae side to be dominant. In this respect, at least."

The heavy weight in her stomach dropped, and it was only then that she acknowledged the truth. She'd been hoping he would give her a reason to dismiss her fears.

As far as they knew, she was the first of her kind. The first hybrid. It brought with it a lot of unknowns, and with no one they could ask, each potential milestone was filled with trepidation and an increasing fear of what the change might mean.

"I know you don't want to face this, but I think we really need to assume you're settling into your immortality," he continued.

A faint buzz started in her head. She rested her forehead in her hands, trying to think past the pressure that was building behind her eyes.

"Is there any way to find out for sure?"

He stared at her.

Sure, she could die and see what happens.

Darius grew grave once more. "Phoenix, if you have reached your immortality, then I think it's time you come home."

"Home?" Confusion distracted her momentarily from the growing headache.

"Back to the lair."

Phoenix froze.

Taking a sip of her drink, she chose her words carefully, though the racing of her heart was no doubt advertising her feelings on the suggestion.

"Why would I need to come back to the lair?"

"Where else will you go once you cut ties with the humans?"

She choked on the sweet, burning liquid that ran down her throat, her eyes watering.

"You know you won't be able to stay with them," Darius said as he pulled a silk handkerchief from his pocket and handed it to her. "And it's not like other members of the Lore will welcome you with open arms. It's better if you come back to the lair where I can keep you safe."

Her heart stuttered at the very thought.

Go back to the way things were before? To being alone? She'd been a shell of herself, merely surviving. She knew now that wasn't how she wanted to live.

"I can't go back to the dark, Uncle D," she said quietly.

Before he could argue any further, she shook herself off and plastered a smile on her face. "Let's not worry about it for now. We're here to celebrate."

CHAPTER SIX

"Okay, so what's the plan?" Ethan turned from the panoramic view of the city and looked at the odd assortment of people gathered in his apartment. A vamp, a shifter, and two witches. It almost sounded like the start of a bad joke.

"We're going to do a spell, apparently."

Ethan threw an irritated look at the vampire slouched in the over-sized leather sofa next to Nate. Shade's ice blue eyes stared back with the insolent look he seemed to have perfected. A black hoody and baggy jeans only added to the angsty teenage vibe he was projecting, something Ethan strongly felt he should have outgrown at nineteen years of age.

"We're going to search for the hybrid's signature," Annabelle said, swatting Shade with a magazine before she moved to stand by Ethan at the window.

He couldn't help but smile as he pulled the young girl close for a hug. Her small, freckled nose scrunched up as she squeezed him tight and he could almost feel her humming with excitement.

Annabelle's sister, Lily, stood with her back to them in the kitchen, lost in thought as she mixed a variety of strange-smelling concoctions. The sisters looked very similar with their long blonde hair and green eyes, but there was a seriousness to Lily that made her seem older than her eighteen years. Where Annabelle had held tightly to her youthful optimism in the face of their parent's death, Lily had taken on the burden of responsibility and wore it like a visible weight. It hurt his heart to see on someone so young.

"I got that part, but how can we search for it if we don't know what the signature is?" Ethan knew the girls were talented witches, but they were still young and still learning to use their power. This seemed like a big ask, even for an advanced witch.

"Process of elimination," Lily said, finally focusing her attention on the group around her. "We know how a human signature reads. And most of the common supernatural signatures. So, we look for something ... other."

Ethan watched as she moved to the dining room table, unfolded a large map, and placed three small bowls beside it. Annabelle left his side to join her sister and a curious silence fell over the room. Nate and Shade both sat forward on the sofa. It was as if the room held its breath.

"You ready?" Lily's voice was quiet as she looked at her sister.

Annabelle exhaled slowly and nodded. With her shoulders relaxed, the excited energy of minutes ago seemed to slip away from her. She calmly took Lily's hands, and the girls began chanting, eyes closed.

The words were unintelligible to Ethan, but a strange sensation tingled over his skin in time with their cadence. It wasn't an unpleasant feeling; nothing like the sickening weight that came with dark magic. This was pure, natural energy, channelled and moulded to their will.

Ethan closed his eyes and let the power flow over him, focusing his thoughts on their intention: find the hybrid. Unbidden, the vague snippets of a memory flashed through his mind. Green eyes. More vivid than any he had ever seen before. But as he tried to grasp it, remember where he had seen them before, the memory faded in a haze.

When he dragged his attention back to the room, he had no idea how much time had passed. The girls and Nate all stood over the map, talking quietly. Shade watched him from the sofa with an odd expression on his face.

Shaking his head, Ethan pushed away from the window and went to join the others at the table.

"She's somewhere near Dublin, somewhere in the outskirts," Nate said, glancing up as he approached.

"She?"

Lily nodded. "The signature feels ... feminine."

Ethan was surprised. He shouldn't have been – hell, plenty of the women in his pack back home were scarier than the men – but he was.

"Can we narrow down her location?"

"We picked up a few hotspots." Lily pointed to marks on the map. "We can't narrow it down further without having something that belongs to her, but I'm sure she's in one of these locations."

"We think if you can get close enough, you'll be able to identify her from her signature," Nate said, making a note of the marked locations on his phone.

Again, the remnants of a thought flitted at the edge of Ethan's subconscious, just out of reach.

"Have we managed to find out what combination the hybrid is?" he asked, directing the question at Nate since he was their go-to for research, but also sparing a glance at Lily in case she'd picked up anything from the signature. Both of them shook their heads.

The question made him curious and anxious at the same time. He'd no idea what kind of traits a hybrid might have – or why she'd be looking to end humanity for that matter – but if she'd gotten the best of two strong species, and coupled it with some psychotic tendencies, they could be in serious trouble.

The increased speed of a vamp.

The strength of a wolf.

Some neat magic tricks courtesy of a witch or fae.

Near impossible to kill.

Shit.

Of course, there was no guarantee she had any of those traits. But who, other than an especially powerful Supe, could have wolves all over the country going feral? Vamps succumbing to bloodlust? An unprecedented uptake in dark magic practices? Because that was what he'd been encountering on a weekly basis ever since he'd left Donegal.

"You have to kill her." Shade's words cut through the silence that had fallen around them, turning everyone's attention to him.

"Shade –"

"No." He shook his head and stood. "I know what you're going to say Ethan. But it's the only way to make sure this stops."

"She could be innocent in all this too," Annabelle said, a look of horror on her face.

"It's one life, Annie," Lily's voice was soft as she stared at the table in front of her. "What about all the innocent people that are getting hurt? What about our parents?"

Annabelle's eyes brightened with tears, but the look on her face remained defiant as she shook her head. "It's not right."

Lily refused to look at her, choosing instead to level her gaze on Ethan. "You said you'd help us find out what happened to them. You'd help us make it right. If she's the cause, you need to fix this."

Ethan's chest constricted at the pain shadowing her young eyes and the truth of her statement. He'd promised to help them, and he was failing. They were all innocent victims in this, each caught up somehow in the events that were unfolding. And they'd placed their trust in him. A trust that wasn't deserved.

Around him, everyone was talking over one another, arguing the morals of murder and the value of one life compared to millions. He couldn't think straight.

"Enough," Ethan growled, not able to listen any longer. "Enough."

He pushed away from the table. They made it sound so simple. Murder the hybrid and everything goes back to normal; they all get on with their lives. Well, life didn't work that way. All actions had consequences. And how many people would be affected by his actions now? Hundreds? Thousands? More? Hell, he'd left his pack to avoid shit like this. Sighing, he grabbed his jacket and headed for the door.

"What are you going to do, man?" Nate called after him, the others watching quietly.

Damned if he knew.

CHAPTER SEVEN

Phoenix hummed softly along to the music as she wiped down the bar and restocked the shelves. Aside from a random group of tourists that looked to have set up camp for the night, it had been quiet for a Sunday. Normally she'd have enjoyed the lull, but tonight it gave her too much time to think.

The conversation with Darius earlier that week had been replaying itself on a loop in her head. His assertion that she would need to come back to the lair and leave this life behind was somewhat understandable. Still, the thought alone made her break out in a cold sweat.

He couldn't know how it affected her, spending so much time in the darkness. As a vampire, she craved that very thing. But she wasn't just a vampire, she was also half fae – a sun elemental – and that half of her died a slow death every day she spent away from the sun. Six years had been a very slow death.

That didn't even factor in the consequences for Darius if the Council found out he'd been hiding her. They'd crucify him. Aiding and abetting an inter-species relationship. Harbouring the results of such a relationship. She didn't know much about the Council, but she was pretty sure they'd be pissed.

Darius had taken her in without question when her parents

disappeared and she'd be forever grateful to him, but she was older now. It was time to stand on her own two feet.

Lost in her thoughts, she jumped a mile when she turned to find a man standing patiently at the bar behind her with an amused smile on his face. He was vaguely familiar and she was pretty sure he'd come in with the group of tourists. He'd made a few attempts to talk to her earlier in the night, but her head had been too far up her arse to appreciate the attention.

"Sorry, was miles away." Phoenix forced a friendly smile onto her face as her eyes scanned the pub floor for Abi. Her friend stood by the stage with a grin on her face, giving a not-so-subtle two thumbs up.

Phoenix groaned inwardly, "What can I get you?"

"A pint of the black stuff, please."

His Scottish accent seemed to have gotten thicker from earlier in the night and he had a cute dimple when he smiled. He really wasn't bad looking, Phoenix acknowledged, as she grabbed a pint glass and held it under the Guinness tap.

"Any chance I can buy you a drink?" His eyes watched her with unmasked interest as she waited for the pint to settle before topping it up.

"Thanks, but I'm working." Phoenix waved at the half-empty bar around her, giving him a small smile.

The poor guy really had no idea what a loaded question that was. She hadn't let herself feed from anyone in weeks, and the idea of a "drink" sounded pretty appealing. Generally, her fae side was dominant enough to gain sustenance from the sun without the need to take blood regularly. It was one of the few mercies of her hybrid nature, and one of the ways she could maintain the illusion of being normal. But with the stress of the past week, not to mention the serious lack of sun, the urge was making itself known.

"Maybe later." He smiled and looked at her for a moment longer before taking his drink back to his friends.

Maybe ...

Phoenix turned back to her morose thoughts while stocking the shelves. She had no idea how much time had passed when a cold breeze brushed the back of her neck and she heard the creaking of the door. A strange sense of awareness sent a shiver down her spine.

She froze. Arm paused mid-air clutching the bottle of Jack Daniels, she swivelled her head to locate the source of her unease. But all she found was empty space. The door swung closed, bringing with it the icy draught of the winter night beyond.

It was official, she was losing her marbles.

Ever since her birthday, she'd been on edge, feeling eyes on her everywhere she went. She was starting to think becoming immortal wasn't her problem at all. Going crazy was.

"Oh my God, Phoenix, you've *got* to check out this guy that just walked in. Hot is not even the word!" Abi came up behind her, squealing with excitement as she reached around to grab a glass from the back wall.

Phoenix laughed, her earlier irritation forgotten as she turned to watch Abi fill the glass with a pint of Blue Moon. It wasn't unusual for Abi to get excited about a cute guy, but she didn't often reach the girly, high-pitched level she was currently at.

"Now, don't make it too obvious, but he's over in the corner booth beside the stage." Abi placed the pint on the bar and ran her fingers through her long, wavy hair.

"I think you're probably over-exaggerating a bit, there's no way he's that ..."

The words trailed off as Phoenix turned to look in the direction Abi indicated, only to find the man staring intensely back at her. The guy from New Year's Eve.

Even across the open space of the bar his dark eyes burned into her; the awareness she'd felt only moments before wrapping around her like a blanket.

"Uh huh, told ye so ..."

Abi continued on in the background, but Phoenix was no longer listening. Her head was spinning. What the hell was he doing here? Abi had been right about his looks. Even beneath the black V-neck jumper he wore, Phoenix could see the muscles rippling as he settled back in the seat and ran a hand through his dark tousled hair. His eyes were piercing and a light stubble covered his jaw, just enough to offset the strong lines of his face.

Everything about him screamed male.

And everything about him screamed predator.

Having been sheltered from the Lore most of her life, Phoenix wasn't very good at reading the different signatures of Supes. From this distance, she could tell his energy was strong, much stronger than any human, but nothing like her parents' energy. So, that ruled out vampire or fae. The feral quality of his looks made her guess werewolf, or shifter of some sort, and that meant heightened senses.

Phoenix squirmed and tore her eyes away from him. It was just a coincidence that he'd come into the bar, wasn't it? Sure, Whitethorn wasn't exactly Lore territory, one of the main reasons she'd come here, but it was possible.

It wasn't a big deal anyway. Very few people knew about her true nature. Most Supes would simply mistake her for a vamp, as long as they didn't pay too close attention.

He was paying very close attention ...

Ethan watched her from the dark corner where he sat. The small, innocuous pub was the third place he'd tried on the list, and he'd known immediately he was in the right place.

The girl from the train station. The green eyes.

His wolf stirred to attention as soon as it caught a hint of her scent, rich and warm, bringing to mind thoughts of vivid sunsets. Her vibrant red hair only heightened the image. The energy emanating from her was unlike anything he'd ever felt before; familiar enough to mark her as supernatural, but so very unique in its undertones.

He saw recognition flash across her face as her eyes met his. The connection sent a jolt through him, and he couldn't look away. For what seemed like an eternity, her gaze held his. Eventually she turned away and went back to her work. Tension was evident in the stiff set of her shoulders as she busied herself behind the bar.

Ethan found himself fascinated by the sinuous flow of her movements and wondered again what mix of hybrid she was. At a quick glance, he would have dismissed her as a vamp, but her signature was too rich and too full of life.

The more he watched her, the more confused he became. What was she doing working in such a quaint pub in a small suburb? It didn't exactly reek of world-domination ambitions. He hadn't even come across another Supe the whole time he'd been in the area. It was almost like a Lore blackout zone.

The sudden blaring of music from the jukebox broke Ethan out of his reverie. A moment later he found his view of the bar obscured as the group of tourists enthusiastically took to the small dancefloor. Downing his pint, he stood quickly from the table. That was his cue to get back to business. With one last glance in her direction, he slipped out the door and back into the cold January night to wait.

Phoenix put all of her focus into emptying the bins behind the bar. She was more shaken than she'd like to admit by the pull she felt from Mr. Tall, Dark, and Inconvenient. Her pulse thrummed in her ears. An uncomfortable nervousness flitted in her stomach, making her fidgety.

Why the hell is he here?

She'd left the vampire lair behind four years ago, and with it, the Lore and all its bullshit. In that time, she'd largely managed to avoid the hundreds of Supes that called Dublin home. She'd mostly lived a nice, normal life. So why was one landing on her doorstep now? And why was he looking so interested in her?

"Hey –"

Phoenix jumped a mile. The cute tourist from earlier was standing to the side of the bar, hands up in surrender. It took a second for her to realise she'd stepped back into a fighting stance on reflex. Heat crept up her cheeks as she forced herself to relax back into a normal posture.

"Sorry, I didn't mean to startle you ... again." He flashed his dimple as he lowered his hands and gestured towards the bags at her feet. "I thought you might like a hand?"

Looking at the four bulging black bags, she was about to dismiss his offer as unnecessary. After all, she could probably lift him and the bags without breaking a sweat. But then the soft thud of his heartbeat echoed in her ears.

Her breath caught sharply. She found herself taking a step back, her mouth watering at the mere thought of the rich, coppery liquid. She stopped that thought in its tracks. There was still the problem of the other Supe. No way could she feed with him around.

A sideways glance towards the stage found her an empty table, complete with an empty pint glass. Surprised, she turned to scan the pub. No sign.

Is he gone?

His signature still tingled over her skin, but faint, like a scent that lingered after a person had left the room. A sigh of relief escaped her lips, and for the first time since he'd come in, Phoenix's heart rate began to calm.

A loud clearing of the throat drew her attention back to the cute tourist that was now starting to fidget awkwardly. "I'll just leave you to it, will I?"

Phoenix glanced around the pub once more. The Supe definitely seemed to be gone. Abi had the floor covered, and it was pretty quiet; she wouldn't notice if Phoenix snuck out for a quick break. Maybe just a little sip to soothe her nerves ...

"I'd love some help." She gave him the first genuine smile of the night as she handed him two bags and followed him out the side exit.

His eyes rolled back when Phoenix slid her fangs gently out of his neck. A look of ecstasy relaxed the lines of his face as he leaned against the wall, dazed and weak from blood loss. He'd have one hell of a hangover tomorrow, but at least she wouldn't have to worry about him remembering anything. The alcohol and blood loss combination nicely made up for her inability to wipe memories.

Pressing against the solid angles of his chest, she licked slowly over the two small puncture wounds. The natural healing property of her saliva was already beginning to remove all trace of the feeding. The masculine groan and obvious feel of his arousal against her hip made her smile.

Glad you had fun too.

She nudged him back through the emergency exit and closed the door so she could have a minute to tidy herself up. It was only then that she noticed the unusual quiet of the night and the rush of air as something moved unnaturally fast behind her.

Before she could react, a large, solid form hit her from behind and pinned her to the wall. A surprised yelp slipped from her lips, and for a moment, all of the self-defence training her father had taught her left her mind completely.

A large hand covered her mouth as a deep voice growled low in her ear, "Don't scream."

Don't scream? Fuck that!

Phoenix began struggling in earnest. She should have been strong enough – she was half vamp, dammit – but she wasn't. No matter how hard she tried, she remained wedged between a solid wall of muscle and the rough brick wall. Anger and frustration threatened to over-whelm her at the sense of weakness, but she fought to push it back down.

The grip holding her lessened for the briefest moment as her attacker removed his hand from her mouth and turned her to face him. She had only a second to recognise the Supe from the bar before a glint of metal drew her attention to a large hunting knife tucked into his belt.

Fear spiked through her as the dim light of the moon flashed off the razor-sharp blade. Her vision blurred and everything went black. When it cleared, she found the Supe from the bar sprawled on the ground looking stunned, and the knife lying far out of reach.

Before she could figure out what had happened, or what to do next, she heard a sound that caused her blood to freeze in her veins.

"Fifi, what in God's name are you doing out here making all that racket?"

CHAPTER EIGHT

Ethan watched from his horizontal position on the ground as the human bartender stuck her head out the emergency exit. The shadows hid him from sight, but he remained completely still so as not to attract her attention.

His head was reeling from the blinding flash of light that the hybrid – *Fifi? Really?* – had emitted. The force had thrown him well clear of her and blobs of light now floated in front of his eyes as if he'd looked directly at the sun.

At least that clarified the other half of her nature.

The thought of her recent feeding rose unbidden to Ethan's mind, causing blood to rush to places that made his current position even more uncomfortable. He should've been disgusted watching her, but all he could remember was the look of ecstasy on the guy's face. The memory caused a low growl from his wolf and he forced the image from his mind.

Cleary she was half vamp, but as for the rest, there was only one power he knew of like the one she'd used, and only one species with that power. Fae.

But it was night, and it took the strongest of the elemental fae to call on the sun at night. She'd looked as shocked by the power as he was. None of this made sense.

"Oh, I uh tripped over a stupid cat and stubbed my toe. Go inside. I got this."

Her nervous babbling drew his attention back to the scene before him. The hybrid stood with her back to him – *brave move* – blocking him further from sight. Her shoulders were stiff and the tension was pronounced enough that he could see the lines of taut muscle through her tight, black top. The scent of fear oozed from her, stronger now than it had been a moment ago.

"Are you sure you don't need help?" the human asked, her eyebrows raised.

"No, no, I'm good. Go inside before you get cold."

The hybrid urged the other girl through the door and quickly closed it behind her. She slumped against the metal, her chest rising and falling in deep hypnotic movements as she turned to eye him warily.

Ethan knew that he'd gone the wrong way about this if he was hoping for her cooperation, but he still needed answers. He'd just have to make the most of the situation.

"You seem awfully worried about the human for someone who's trying to kill them all." He kept his tone casual and watched her reaction closely for the slightest tick or flinch. Just two old pals talking about getting rid of that pesky human race.

The look of wariness on her face turned to confusion, swiftly followed by anger. "What the hell are you talking about?"

Ethan shifted himself to a seated position, moving his back to the wall. Her confusion appeared genuine; the indignation most definitely was.

"You're not really going to tell me you know nothing about the prophecy are you?"

She looked at him blankly.

"You know," he prompted, "the one where you bring about the end of humanity."

"Are you insane?" Anger gave way to a look of utter disbelief as she gaped at him. "Who the hell are you?"

"You *are* the hybrid, aren't you?"

The quick change of direction caused a shift in her demeanour so slight he would've missed it if he'd blinked.

"It's okay, you don't have to answer that. I already know you are."

"What do you want from me?"

"Well I was hoping we could have a chat, but I'll settle for your name to start. Tell me it's not really Fifi?"

Lucky for him, shooting the sun from your eyes wasn't a real power, because with the glare now fixed on him, he was pretty sure he'd be burned to a crisp.

"No, it's not Fifi," she said through gritted teeth.

He waited, but no other name was forthcoming.

Fifi it is.

"So, Fifi, about this prophecy –"

"How many times do I need to tell you? I don't know anything about a goddamn prophecy! All I want is to be left alone."

"That makes two of us." His laugh held no trace of humour. "But somehow it seems to have become my problem. And from what I hear, you're the one I need to talk to."

"Well, I've no intention of hurting anyone, so your information is obviously wrong." She pushed away from the door, standing straight and defiant.

Ethan looked at her, then down at himself and raised one eyebrow.

"Well you deserved it. You attacked me first." She huffed and crossed her arms over her chest.

Ethan felt his lips quirk at the gesture. This girl fascinated him.

Nothing about her reactions felt forced or faked, and all of his instincts were telling him she was being truthful. At least in her mind. If she was to be responsible for ending humanity, he didn't believe it would be intentional. But that didn't rule out unintentional, so where did that leave them?

"Okay, let's say you really don't know anything about this prophecy." Ethan leaned forward and rested his forearms loosely on bent knees. "Do you know of any other hybrids like you?"

For a moment he thought she would refuse to answer, but she sighed and shook her head mutely.

69

"I don't either." He nodded in acknowledgement of her honesty. "So, let's – for argument's sake – assume you're the hybrid in the prophecy. How might you be involved in bringing about the end of humanity?"

Her jaw dropped and she stared at him dumbfounded for a minute before speaking. "Are you seriously asking me that? What the hell does this so-called prophecy say anyway?"

"Well, the details are a bit vague at the moment –"

"Are you fucking kidding me?"

Her voice reached glass-shattering pitches as she picked up one of the bags of rubbish that had been discarded in favour of feeding and flung it at him.

"You came here to kill me because of some vague, bullshit prophecy you don't even know the details of?"

Ethan held his hands up, palms forward, as he struggled to stand. He was way too much of a sitting duck for flying projectiles if he stayed on the ground.

"Whoa, whoa, whoa! I didn't come here to kill you."

Her hand froze as it reached for the next bag of rubbish and she gaped at him. Opening and closing her mouth repeatedly as if she couldn't form the words, she jabbed her finger towards the ground to the left of him.

He glanced quickly to where she pointed and realisation dawned on him when he caught sight of his hunting knife glinting in the moonlight.

"Oh, that." He grinned sheepishly. "Yeah, I kind of forgot that was there. I always carry it on me."

"What, like a safety blanket?" She snorted her disbelief.

"Things are bad out there." Ethan grew serious. For some inexplicable reason, he needed her to understand.

"What do you expect me to do about it?"

He blew out a breath. How the hell could he get through to her?

"I know you don't want to hear this, and I know I've gone about this the wrong way, but when I say things are bad, I mean they're really bad."

He ran his fingers through his hair, forcing it out of his eyes. "Innocent people are dying, and I can't stop it. I don't know how you fit into all this, but you do. Help me figure it out ... please."

She shook her head and took a step back until she was wedged more firmly against the door. "No way. I'm not getting dragged into this. You people wanted nothing to do with me, so I want nothing to do with you people."

With that she grabbed the handle of the door, her forearm tensed to tug it open.

"But it's not us that will suffer, is it? It's the humans. It's people like your friend inside."

She hesitated, and for a minute, Ethan felt hopeful, but then she pulled the door open and rushed inside, leaving him with a resounding thud as the door closed behind her.

Ethan blew out the breath he didn't realise he was holding and bent to pick up his knife.

That really went to plan, didn't it?

Phoenix was still shaking as the door slammed behind her.

How dare he!

Coming to her job, attacking her, accusing her of trying to hurt people, and then having the nerve to ask for her help. Where the hell did he get off?

"I hope you gave that cat a piece of your mind."

Phoenix jumped as Abi walked towards her, throwing a towel in her direction, her blue eyes twinkling. She looked at the towel she was now holding and smiled weakly at her friend.

"Hey, you okay?" Abi's smile quickly faded as concern caused her forehead to crease.

"I'm fine, just a bit of a headache."

"Well look, the bar is quiet, why don't you head upstairs and I can finish down here?" Abi began gathering the empty glasses from tables around her, obviously satisfied the matter was settled.

71

It was only then that Phoenix noticed the lack of music, the jukebox sitting silently in the corner. Most of the customers had gone home for the night and the last few stragglers, the tourists, were preparing themselves to head out into the cold night beyond. The cute guy smiled sleepily and waved as he followed his friends out the door.

She looked back in Abi's direction and her throat constricted. If anything had happened to Abi tonight, Phoenix wasn't sure what she'd have done.

But if what the Supe said was true, then something could happen to her. And it would be all her fault.

And what about everyone else? The people she saw every day? The regulars who would sit at the bar laughing and joking with them while she and Abi worked through the night? Dear old Betty who always had a tale to tell when she came in to help them clean? The other bar staff who helped out when they were busy?

Innocent people are dying. His words repeated in her head. She wanted to cover her ears so she wouldn't continue to hear them.

What could she do? She didn't know anything about a so-called prophecy, never mind how to stop it. How could she be involved in something she knew nothing about? Sure, maybe he was just some unhinged lunatic, and it was pure coincidence that he happened to land on her doorstep. But could she really take that chance? Could she hope everything he said was rubbish and nothing came of it? Hope the people she cared about weren't hurt?

"Abi?" Phoenix heard her voice crack slightly as she called out. "How about you choose the movie tonight?"

Abi smiled at her and made a shooing motion with her hands.

Still clutching the towel, Phoenix headed to the back of the bar and made her way upstairs. Maybe Darius could do some digging if she asked him. After all, he was the head of the most powerful vampire clan in Ireland, and a Witness on the Council. Surely if something was going on, he'd know about it.

Plus, she'd been avoiding his calls since their dinner on Thursday. If she didn't make contact soon, he'd land on her doorstep too.

Resolving to call him tomorrow, she threw on an oversized hoody and headed into the sitting room. She grabbed the soft, blue throw off the back of the sofa and wrapped it tightly around herself, attempting in vain to stop the shivers while she waited for Abi.

CHAPTER NINE

"Where the hell have you been?"

Ethan shifted his gaze from his city view to the icy blue eyes glaring at him from the doorway and grinned. "What's wrong, Shade? You miss me?"

"Dammit, man. We didn't know what the hell happened to you." Shade's glare softened only fractionally.

"Yeah, Ethan. Considering how much you've needed saving lately, you could've been getting your ass whooped somewhere." Nate grinned as he pushed past Shade into the large open-plan apartment, Lily and Annabelle hot on his heels.

Dragging himself up from the nice comfortable groove he'd made in the sofa, Ethan sighed and made a mental note to start locking his door. He walked to the large fridge and pulled out a beer, two cans of coke, and a cool bag of O negative fresh from the blood bank, then set the items onto the marble island where the others were now sitting.

After grabbing himself a beer, he twisted the cap off and walked to the large window that ran the length of the open plan room. He looked out over the dimming lights of the docklands and allowed himself to get lost in the hypnotic flow of the water for a few moments.

Nate was closer to the truth than he'd like to admit. He'd fucked up royally with the hybrid and gotten his ass burned in the process. Now, not only did he have to figure out a way to get her onside, but he also had to convince the others it was the right thing to do.

"I found her." The noise from the apartment stopped abruptly at his words. "I didn't kill her if that's what you were expecting."

It was Annabelle that spoke first, her soft voice curious but holding no judgement. "What happened?"

Ethan turned his back to the window and met the stares of the four faces in front of him. "She didn't know anything about the prophecy."

Shade raised a pierced eyebrow in his direction before turning his attention dismissively to the old penknife he was playing with.

When no one commented, Ethan continued, "She was more worried about a human than her own safety. Hell, I don't even think she realised I was there until the last minute."

Taking a swig of his beer, almost to himself he said, "I really can't see her masterminding a doomsday prophecy."

"So, she was hot then." Nate's face remained innocent as he spoke, but laughter danced behind his amber eyes.

"Nate!" Lily swatted at him, glaring.

Ethan complemented her glare with one of his own and his wolf growled softly. "What she looks like is irrelevant. The only question now is how we get her to help us."

"What?" Shade's head snapped up. "Help us? The other day we were talking about killing her. Now we're going to be best buds?"

"No Shade, *you* were talking about killing her. What would you have me do? Murder an innocent woman just because it's the easy option?" The muscles at the side of his cheek jumped as his jaw clenched. "If she's not driving this, then she's as much a victim as the rest of us."

"How do you know you can trust her?" Shade countered, his eyes blazing.

It was a valid question. One Ethan had been asking himself all day. And he still couldn't come up with a good answer. But any time he considered the alternative, his wolf reared its head, ready and willing to defend her. Every instinct he had told him they needed her.

Lily stood suddenly from her stool and slapped her palms down on the counter. "Okay, enough of the testosterone, both of you." Turning to Ethan, she said, "If killing her isn't an option, where does it leave us? What's plan B?"

Taking a deep breath, Ethan walked back to the sofa and dropped into the still warm spot he'd vacated. "Whether intentionally or not, she's involved in this. I'd rather keep her close until when we figure out how."

He gave Shade a warning look, daring him to protest. "I'll keep working on the girl. Convince her to help –" damned if he knew how. "But in the meantime, we need more information. We need to know what we're facing with this prophecy."

"Shouldn't we maybe think about contacting the Council? Let them sort it?" Lily said.

Nate jerked his head up from the laptop in front of him. "Fuck, no. We don't need to attract their attention on top of everything else."

"Nate's right." Ethan nodded. "Lily, can you try your contact again? See if she can give you anything more specific that might help us put a stop to all this."

"I have a friend in the Dublin coven," Annabelle chimed in. "I can get her to do some digging –"

"No way, it's too dangerous, Annie!" Lily softened somewhat as she saw the look of hurt of her younger sister's face. "You can help by searching the wiccan archives. Surely if the covens know about it there must be some other references to the prophecy."

Annabelle nodded a reluctant agreement, her eyes no longer meeting those in the room.

Not having the energy to salve hurt feelings, Ethan turned to the others. "Shade, you and me are on patrol tonight. Nate, see if you can hack into the Gardaí database and find out what spin the humans have been putting on these attacks. They might have spotted a pattern we're missing."

With a wide grin, Nate saluted him, grabbing his laptop as he pushed his chair back from the kitchen island. Shade grunted and followed him out the door without another word.

Ethan rubbed the stubble on his chin and reminded himself

again that they were just kids. Hell, hadn't he been as much of a pain in the arse at their age? He grabbed his keys and followed them, ushering Lily and Annabelle out the door ahead of him.

He looked up as he locked the door and was surprised to find Annabelle watching him curiously. Tousling her hair, he asked, "What's up, kid?"

"What was she like? The hybrid?"

Ethan thought for a moment but could only come up with a single answer.

"Unique."

Phoenix had gone to her room with the intention of calling Darius. Instead, she found herself buried among the soft pillows of her bed and staring at the blank screen of her phone.

Doubts started creeping in with the cold light of day, and though she knew he'd be up long before sunset, she held off, reluctant to make the call. He'd use it against her. Use it as proof that his argument was correct; she should return to the lair.

The sudden ringing of her phone jarred her from her thoughts. Her heart pounded when she saw Darius's name flash on the screen. Feeling unnecessarily guilty, she fumbled to answer.

"Uncle D."

"Phoenix, darling. I'm glad I caught you. I was beginning to get worried when I hadn't heard from you in a while."

"Sorry, things have been a bit mad at the bar lately. I've been meaning to call."

She wound the platinum chain of her mother's medallion around her fingers and wondered how she could broach the subject of the Supe without worrying him too much.

"I'm glad to hear business is thriving. I would still very much like to come visit this establishment. Perhaps I could offer some investment options for expansion if it's doing that well?"

Phoenix felt her throat go dry. "I don't think Abi is looking to expand, but the offer is appreciated."

"I suppose she'll have enough on her hands, managing the pub when you leave," Darius said.

"I'm not coming back, Uncle D. I told you that."

She forced her voice to be firm, her decision very clear on the matter. Going back wasn't an option, no matter what else happened. She would stay, or she would find another alternative, anything but that one.

"We talked about this. You can't continue living with the human."

"That human is my friend."

"Phoenix –"

"Have you told anyone about me?" The question left her mouth before she could think it through.

Darius stopped in his tracks, silent for a moment on the other end of the phone.

"What's going on, Phoenix?"

"Have you told anyone I'm a hybrid –" She faltered. "I mean, aside from the few vamps that already know?"

"Of course not. Do you think I'd risk your safety like that?"

Shame heated her cheeks. What had she been thinking? Darius had worked tirelessly with her parents to keep her identity secret. Why would that suddenly change now?

"You're right. I'm sorry, Uncle D. It's just, there was a guy in the bar last night. A Supe. He knew what I was. It kind of threw me."

"Do you know who he was?"

There was an edge to Darius's voice that made Phoenix pause. Had she made a mistake mentioning it? Maybe she shouldn't be making such a big deal of it.

"No. I think he may have been a werewolf, but I'm not sure."

More silence.

"Has anything strange been happening lately?" She paused, wondering how much to say. "You know, like, in the Lore?"

Darius released a harsh laugh. "There are always strange things happening in the Lore. Why do you ask?"

"He said there'd been attacks, and that people were being killed. He seemed to think I was involved somehow."

"That's ludicrous."

"I know that, and you know that, but why would he think I was involved?" The question had plagued her all night. She still couldn't think of a reasonable explanation.

"Unless …"

Phoenix sat up straighter, letting the chain fall from her fingers. "Unless what, Uncle D?"

"Unless the Council has heard rumours of your existence. It's possible they might fabricate stories, to act as a … deterrent to others."

"But why would they –" She broke off with a bitter laugh. "Oh, I get it. Make me out to be the Lore equivalent of the bogeyman, so others will be too afraid to follow the same path my parents did."

"It's just a thought, Phoenix. I could be wrong."

A heavy lump settled in her stomach at the harsh reminder of where she fit within the Lore. She was the ultimate symbol of defiance. One of their most sacred edicts broken and unpunished. There was no way they would take her existence lightly if they found out.

"Is there any chance he could have been telling the truth? About the people being killed?" She didn't say what she was really thinking; she didn't dare ask about the humans.

"I would be fairly confident the wolf is not to be trusted, but let me talk to some of my contacts in the Council and see if they've heard anything of concern."

"Thanks, Uncle D."

"Oh, and Phoenix. If this wolf bothers you again, I want you to let me know immediately."

She smiled at his stern tone and hung up the phone.

At least she had one person in the Lore on her side. Funny how it didn't stop the lump in her stomach from getting a little bit heavier.

CHAPTER TEN

With the door to the frigid morning open in front of her, Phoenix stared at the heavy grey sky.

Figures.

She sighed and stepped into the miserable, hazy rain before turning left, away from the pub. A steady jog quickly loosened her limbs, and the rhythmic pounding of feet on the pavement became a meditative mantra, clearing her mind of the worries that had plagued her all night.

It wasn't long before the gentle incline carried her to the gate of Whitethorn Park. Instantly, her spirits lifted. She took a deep breath, savouring the freshness of the air and the energy that hummed around her. The park was blissfully quiet with only the occasional jogger or bird braving the elements. Gravel crunched under her feet as water splashed her from above and below, the bare tree branches offering little shelter from the elements.

Consumed by the physicality of her movement, she almost missed him – the Supe from the bar. He sat sprawled on a wooden park bench, his arm resting casually across the back as he watched her. A dusting of dark hair and thick sinuous muscle peeked out from the sleeve of the black V-neck jumper that was starting to soak through.

Geez, doesn't this guy feel the cold at all?

A slow, sexy smile spread across his face as she slowed her pace, and Phoenix felt an almost irresistible urge to slap that smirk right off.

"Are you following me?" She came to a stop with her hands on her hips and discreetly surveyed the park for any nearby humans. She was counting her safety on him not wanting to attract attention.

His grin didn't falter at her cold tone. "I thought maybe we got off on the wrong foot."

"I guess you could call trying to kill me the wrong foot."

An indignant pout replaced the grin as he sat up straight. "I told you that was a misunderstanding. I just wanted to talk."

Having the grace to look sheepish, he relaxed back into the bench. "I may have gone slightly the wrong way about it."

"You think?" Phoenix almost choked in disbelief. *The absolute gall of him!*

She turned, ready to continue her run and leave this madman to his games, when he stood and reached for her wrist.

"Get your hands off me, wolf," she growled, sounding almost wolf-like herself.

To her surprise, he let go, and a brief flash of annoyance crossed his face at her chosen nickname.

"I just want to talk to you, nothing more. I promise."

"We have nothing to talk about," she said, and turned to continue her jog. She noted vaguely that he hadn't corrected her wolf assumption, which ruled out running away. There was no outrunning a wolf's hunting instincts.

He kept pace with her easily. "Are you not even slightly curious about the prophecy?"

"You assume I believe there is a prophecy."

"Don't you?"

Darius's words replayed in her mind, causing her to bite her lip. In a way she would rather believe there was a prophecy. The alternative, that the Council might know of her existence, was terrifying.

"I only have your word to take for it. And considering I don't even know you, why would I believe you?"

"Well, what if I start by introducing myself?" He stopped in front of her, rich brown eyes watching her closely as he held out his hand. "I'm Ethan."

She ignored the offered hand, trying, with difficulty, not to step back from the intensity of his gaze. "I'd love to say it was a pleasure meeting you, Ethan, but I was brought up not to lie."

He chuckled, a deep rumbling sound. "I guess that's just one more thing that's unique about you."

A thunderous bang from the sky overhead pulled her attention to the heavy black clouds that hung like a thick blanket above them. The previously light haze of rain turned to heavy droplets that splashed against her like miniature puddles and drew her attention to the fact she was getting cold and wet.

"Look, I'm done with this conversation. I'd like to get back to my run now if you don't mind."

For a moment, she thought he was going to keep badgering her, but instead he held out his hand and presented a small, folded piece of paper.

"Just do me a favour and take my number. You never know when you might need it."

A strange sense of unease washed over Phoenix at his words, effectively quelling her urge to tell him where to shove it. Silently, she took the paper and turned towards the park entrance, wanting nothing more than to go home.

CHAPTER ELEVEN

The silver coin burned as Il Maestro flipped it over each finger, but he ignored it; pain was just a state of mind. Leaning back in the large leather chair, he poured himself a generous measure of whiskey from the crystal decanter on the desk in front of him.

After a few moments, he turned his gaze to the vampire standing to attention by the large mahogany desk. "What's the status?"

"All of the wolves are recovering after the attack, but they were severely injured." Raphael paused and eyed him warily. "It will take time for them to heal."

He gripped the glass tightly. "We don't have time."

"How would you like me to proceed, Il Maestro?"

"Kill them. Get me more test subjects and implement the same formula."

Raphael nodded before turning abruptly on his heel.

"Oh, Raphael."

The vampire stopped with his hand hovering near the door handle. "Yes, Il Maestro?"

"Make sure I don't have to kill this group."

Raphael nodded again and walked out of the office.

Throwing back the glass of whiskey, Il Maestro savoured the burn that slid down his throat as he mused on the condition the wolves had returned in. It would have taken a lot of strength and skill to overpower a group of wolves under normal circumstances, but these wolves were formulated for strength and aggression.

It also wasn't the first time someone had derailed his plans in recent months, and it was starting to become inconvenient. Maybe it was time to escalate matters further.

The air was cool as Il Maestro stepped into the large stone chamber, buried deep beneath the earth. The head of the Dublin witch's coven was already present, standing tall with her arms resting at her sides. Not quite meeting his gaze.

Curious.

"Belinda, so good of you to meet me here on such short notice."

He took one of her hands in his as he bowed to place a light kiss on the back of the smooth hand, noting the ever so subtle stiffening of her body.

"You said it was urgent. I felt it best not to keep you waiting," she said, the aging husky voice belying her youthful complexion.

"Indeed." He turned his back and walked further into the darkness of the chamber. "We are at the precipice of a vital change. It is more important now than ever that our intentions are clear to those we support."

"What would you have of me?"

He raised an eyebrow at her choice of wording. "I think a blood sacrifice might be appropriate, don't you?"

If she was affected by his suggestion, she didn't show it. Then again, he was sure she'd resorted to much worse purely for the sake of vanity alone.

"There's a full moon in three nights," Belinda said, a simple practicality to her tone. "The sacrifice will be more potent then."

"Good." He watched her as he trailed his fingers along the large stone altar that stood in the centre of the room. "It is vital that we keep the favour of the Horsemen. We haven't yet reached the end game and already there have been … interferences."

The change in her posture was so subtle it could easily have been missed, but there was no hiding the ratcheting of her heartbeat. Not from him.

She nodded and moved quickly towards the chamber entrance. "I'll see to the arrangements immediately."

"Belinda."

The softly spoken word stopped her in her tracks.

"Is there something you'd like to tell me?"

She turned, and her eyes defiantly met his for the first time since she'd arrived. "It's nothing you need to worry about."

"Humour me." He waited calmly.

Her right hand slipped into her coat pocket where she no doubt carried a protection charm of some form. Nonetheless, she answered him.

"It appears rumours may have been leaked about the prophecy. The leak did not come from my coven and the details were minimal," she hastened to clarify. "But I have seen to it that the source has been dealt with accordingly."

The smile dropped from his face, and with it, fell any air of friendliness. "There is more."

A brief hesitation, then a nod. "I believe a member of my coven may have also betrayed us recently."

"And what do you intend to do about it?"

A chilling calm settled over the witch's features. "As I said, I have a sacrifice to prepare." With that, she turned and left the chamber.

Il Maestro watched her go while digesting the new information.

The witches were becoming unreliable. Their thirst for power was overly complicated by a tendency towards inconvenient human emotions. It was possible, of course, that this had no relevance to the attack on his wolves, or earlier complications, but he didn't believe in coincidences.

Anger simmered in his veins at the thought of everything being ruined by such simple incompetency. Everything he had worked for.

Everything he had waited for. Belinda would rectify the situation or she would find herself the next to be sacrificed.

Needing a release for his anger, he turned to the door that sat, almost invisible, in the stone wall and took the key from his pocket. The heavy metal lock opened and he stepped into the utter blackness of the cell. He smiled serenely as he lifted the blood-stained chain from its hook on the wall and closed the door tightly behind him.

CHAPTER TWELVE

As usual, Phoenix felt his presence before he even sat down. The wolf – Ethan – had become such a permanent fixture in the pub over the last few days that she hardly had the energy to get angry anymore. He'd kept things relatively light-hearted in his attempts to speak to her, but she'd be damned if she let him trick her into dropping her guard.

With Abi unloading stock in the back, and the other bar staff not due in until later that evening, she had no choice but to serve him. *Although the less contact he has with Abi the better*, she thought as she remembered Abi's shameless flirting the night before.

"What do you want, wolf?"

"Now is that any way to speak to a paying customer?" He gave her his trademark cheeky grin and rested his forearms on the bar. "I'll have a bottle of Blue Moon please."

Shaking her head at his usual choice of poison, she twisted the top off an ice-cold bottle and plopped it unceremoniously in front of him.

"What, no glass?"

Her hand tightened around a pint glass, and for a moment she considered throwing it at his head. Instead, she placed it calmly on the bar and gave him her sweetest smile.

He put his hand on hers before she could pull it away and watched her with open curiosity. "How have you managed to stay off the radar for so long?"

Phoenix tensed and pulled her hand back. She didn't sense any form of malice or threat behind the words, but his eyes were probing, and his curiosity made her uncomfortable in ways she couldn't explain.

"You know you were less annoying when you were trying to kill me," she said before hurrying to the far end of the bar, and the safety of waiting customers.

Her snarky comment elicited a rich laugh that followed in her wake and sent shivers along her bare arms.

For a while, she worked in peace, chatting and laughing with some of the regular Friday-nighters. She told herself repeatedly that the big lump of testosterone sitting a few seats away was merely a figment of her very annoying imagination. And that worked fine until the big lump of testosterone once again began working his charms on her very human, very breakable friend.

From the other end of the bar she could hear Abi's laughter. Phoenix sighed, and accepting her fate, she trudged back to the corner where Abi stood animatedly chatting to Ethan.

At her approach, Abi turned and grinned. "Hey, Fifi. I was just telling this lovely gentleman about that time I managed to get you really drunk, and we –"

"Abi! I don't think our customers need to hear about how well their bartenders hold their drink." Phoenix glared, all thoughts of safeguarding Abi's wellbeing suddenly replaced with thoughts of throttling her.

"Oh, I think your customers would love to hear all about it." Ethan threw Abi a cheeky wink.

"Why don't you go for your break now, Abi?" Phoenix shifted her glare to Ethan as she gave Abi a not-so-subtle nudge.

"Okay, okay, I can take a hint." With a grin and a wave, Abi sauntered off to the kitchen, the sway of her shapely hips most definitely exaggerated.

88

"So, *Fifi*, did you want to talk to me about something?" Ethan asked, once he was finished watching the show.

"Nobody except Abi gets to call me that without losing vital body parts." Phoenix reached for a large, serrated kitchen knife and began slicing lemons. The implicit threat earned her little more than a chuckle.

Ethan held up his hands in surrender. "Okay, why don't you tell me your actual name then?"

"And why would I do that?"

"Well, I could always call your cute friend back and ask her." He took a casual swig of his beer.

The thought made her shudder. She really didn't want to witness any more of Abi's blatant drooling. Anyway, why was she even fighting it? He already knew enough to cause her trouble if he wanted to.

"Fine, it's Phoenix."

"Hmm, Phoenix." He rotated the bottle of beer idly in his hands as he seemed to test the sound of her name on his tongue. "I like it."

Oh goody, my life is now complete.

When he didn't elaborate any further regarding his opinion of her name, Phoenix grabbed a cloth and moved to wipe up the pools of condensation along the bar top. Surely she could get back to ignoring him now that she'd been polite for a few minutes?

"You haven't asked me anything more about the prophecy," Ethan said after a brief silence.

Nope, obviously she couldn't ignore him.

Flashing back on the follow-up call she'd had with Darius the day before, she sighed in frustration. As expected, his enquiries with the Council had been fruitless. There were no murmurings of a hybrid, and as he couldn't ask outright without drawing attention, it made questioning difficult. Of course, Darius was a master of wordplay so it didn't stop him digging, but his conclusion was the same as before: either Ethan was lying or the Council had intentionally started the rumour.

The more time that passed, the less option one made sense to her. Why would some random guy seek her out just to tell her lies? Actually, how would some random guy even know she existed to seek her out in the first place?

Which left option two ...

Phoenix finally stopped what she was doing and looked at Ethan. "Okay, I'll play ball. Who told you there was a prophecy?"

"We have some connections with the witches."

We?

"And how did you find out about me?"

"The same way."

Shit, now the witches knew about her too?

"That day at the train station, did you know what I was?"

"No. I could sense there was something ... unusual about you, but I didn't know."

"So, how did you find me?"

Ethan gave a small smile. "To be honest, I'm not even sure myself."

Ignoring his ambiguity, she hugged her arms around her stomach and asked the question that worried her the most. "How do you know it's true? How do you know this isn't just a rumour the Council started?"

He eyed her quizzically. "Why would they do that?"

She said nothing, but clutched her midsection tighter.

"Look, Phoenix." Ethan leaned forward and lowered his voice. "In the past week alone we've had to prevent six attacks on humans. I'm not talking about your normal day-to-day violence. I'm talking serious shit that would give you nightmares. There's something really wrong out there."

"And how do you think I'd be able to help?"

He raised his eyebrows and a cheeky glint stirred in his eyes before he grew serious once more. "Truth be told, I don't know. But the prophecy refers to a hybrid, so whether you like it or not, someone decided you're involved."

Taking a final swig of his beer, he stood. "You have my number when you're ready to call me. Just don't wait too long." With that, he left the bar, a strange sense of emptiness remaining in his place.

He was right, she did have his number. So why hadn't she given it to Darius?

The cracked leather was rough under her knuckles, the heavy punching bag offering little resistance to her onslaught. Sounds echoed from the stone walls and linoleum floors around her, and sweat and adrenaline permeated the air. Phoenix loved the starkness of the gym; all niceties had been stripped back until the only thing left was determination and drive. Focus. Just what she needed.

She'd been coming to this gym ever since she found herself in Whitethorn, continuing the training her father had started with her before he disappeared. Recently though, she'd been slacking, and something told her it was time to get her act together.

"Not bad for a woman," Ethan's deep, familiar voice teased her from behind.

Without hesitating and driven by sheer frustration, she turned mid-strike and sent a back-fist straight towards his head. He parried at the last second. His look of surprise was quickly replaced with a grin as he moved just out of reach.

"I thought you were going to wait for me to call?" Phoenix dug her fists into her hips to avoid the temptation of a second swing.

Less than two days of peace, that's all she'd gotten – two bloody days!

"I am. I just had some energy to burn and fancied a spot of training."

She stared in disbelief at the impressive v-taper of his back as he strolled towards the large boxing ring in the centre of the gym. Should he even be allowed out on a full moon? Surely there were rules about that kind of thing.

Looking back over his shoulder, he called, "You coming or what?"

What is it with this guy?

Although ... maybe it would be fun to take some of her frustrations out on him. They still had a few hours yet before the moon would be up. Looking around, she took stock of the other people training nearby. There were enough humans that he couldn't really try anything too shady, and she could do with the practice.

With her mind made up, she strolled casually towards him. She folded her arms across her chest and eyed him up and down. "What do I get out of it?"

He appeared to think for a moment, but something about the glint in his eye told her he already had the answer prepared.

"You win, I leave you alone for good. I win … and I don't."

Her steps faltered.

Tempting offer. But it hinged on one key factor. Could she beat him? Sure, he had the height advantage and was packing significantly more muscle than her. Hell, he was a werewolf; he'd probably chew her up and spit her out without blinking. But she had speed on her side, and with humans present, they'd have to dampen down their Supe abilities anyway.

Was it worth it for the chance to be left alone? Chewing on her lip, she decided the answer was simple – she just needed to make sure she won.

"Deal," she said as she closed the distance between them. Ignoring the hand he held out, Phoenix stepped lithely onto the high platform of the ring and jumped over the ropes.

He followed, slipping off his t-shirt as he went.

When she looked up, she was met with a solid, finely sculpted chest, dusted in hairs the colour of rich chocolate that she imagined would match his wolf's coat when he turned.

He was obviously trying to distract her.

Giving herself a mental shake, Phoenix shifted on the balls of her feet and pushed all distractions from her mind.

"First to pin the other wins." The words were barely out of his mouth before she launched her first attack.

The low roundhouse to the side of the knee knocked him off balance momentarily, but he recovered quickly, blocking her follow up strikes with a speed that belied his size, even when it was obviously being restrained.

They moved in a blur of strikes, parries, twists, turns, and locks. Phoenix struggled to dredge up a very rusty repertoire of moves, but her body quickly settled into a comfortable rhythm; her muscles remembering what her mind had forgotten.

She caught him with a kick to the gut and pressed her advantage as she turned swiftly into a spinning back kick. Her foot met only with air.

An unexpected low sweep from the side caused her to stumble backwards, and she suddenly found herself pressed up against the corner of the ring. Before she could move, Ethan's imposing form was in front of her, taking advantage of her momentary lapse to pin her in tight.

Her breath caught in her throat and her heart pounded like thunder in her ears as she realised she couldn't move. A memory flashed unbidden into her mind. Fear. Helplessness. A blinding light she couldn't control. Her chest grew tight and she began to struggle in earnest.

But there was nothing holding her.

She blinked in confusion and tried to focus past the pounding bass of her heartbeat. The sounds of the gym slowly filtered back into her consciousness: weights thudding to the floor, fists hitting canvas.

Ethan was standing at arms-length, watching her with concern. He was close enough that she could smell the musky scent of his sweat, but he stood to the side, clearly allowing her a path to move from the corner.

When she didn't move or speak, he turned and walked to the far side of the ring, grabbing his towel to wipe the sweat off his forehead.

"Let's just call that a win for me," he said as he threw her a cheeky grin and jumped over the ropes.

Still shaken, Phoenix pushed herself out of the corner and moved to follow him. "Ethan?"

He stopped and looked at her expectantly.

"Why do you care?"

"Because I can't just sit back while innocent people are hurt."

His words were quiet, but she heard them crystal clear. And she watched quietly while he turned and walked out of the gym, more confused than ever before.

CHAPTER THIRTEEN

Ethan could feel the pull of the moon as he left the gym. It would be completely dark soon, and if he was back home in Donegal, he'd have been preparing to hunt. But this close to the city, he couldn't chance it. Besides, it didn't feel right without his pack. Each month he was away from them, he fought the change – something only the strongest of wolves could do.

It helped that his head was so full of questions about the woman he'd just left. She was fascinating in ways that could only mean trouble for him. There was no point pushing her though, he knew that now. Phoenix had her walls up so high that she didn't even realise they were there. It would take a miracle to get her to trust him. He just hoped they had enough time for that miracle.

The musical tones of "Wild Thing" dragged Ethan's attention back to the present and he made a mental note to kick Nate's arse. The kid was forever changing his ringtone, thinking he was hilarious when he wasn't.

He pulled his phone from his pocket and was surprised to see Annabelle's name flash on the screen. "Hey, kid, what's up?"

Annabelle's voice was unusually low at the other end of the phone. Her fear was almost palpable, as if reaching through the phone to claw at him.

"Ethan, I think I'm in trouble. I don't know what to do."

"Okay, tell me where you are." He forced his voice to stay calm, but his heart ricocheted in his chest.

"I'm in an old warehouse near Celbridge. The witches are doing dark magic. Ethan, I'm trapped."

"Dammit, Annabelle, what the hell were you thinking?"

The words were out before he could stop them, fear for her safety getting the better of him. She wasn't far away, less than five minutes if he floored it, but he needed to be with her *now*.

"I know. I'm sorry. But they have my friend, Ethan." Her voice broke in a whispered sob that gripped his heart. "They're going to sacrifice her."

"Shh, kid. It's okay, it's okay. Just give me the exact address."

She quickly relayed the location to him, and with a promise to stay hidden until he arrived, she hung up the phone. Moving with renewed purpose, Ethan jumped on the oil-slick black Harley he'd taken to the gym. He quickly dialled Nate's number, tapping his hand impatiently against his leg.

No answer.

Dammit, he needed to go. There was no way they'd make it in time anyway. He could only hope he would.

A silence that was almost unnatural hung in the air as Ethan arrived at the address Annabelle had given him. The abandoned warehouses looked like jagged teeth against the dark night sky, and a sense of emptiness pervaded everything in the area.

He'd have known the warehouse he was looking for even without the address. A weight fell over him as soon as he pulled close to the dilapidated structure. The weight of dark magic.

The sensation was almost tangible, like trying to move through a wall of sludge. A cold chill washed over his skin and Ethan felt like he would never be clean again. He kept his mind firmly focused on his goal and pushed through the oppressive feeling. Once he was close enough for an easy escape, he switched off the engine and rolled the bike into the shadows.

Inching along the side of the building, he found a piece of corrugated iron, bottom edge bent upwards. The scent of blood rose up to meet him and his gut clenched – Annabelle's blood.

He tried to calm the adrenaline that pounded through his body and he knelt to take a closer look. A small smear of blood ran along the edge of the sheet; a scratch from when she was crawling through, maybe. His breath left him in an exhale of relief.

If that was the worst of both their injuries tonight, they'd be lucky.

As carefully as he could manage, he bent the iron further, gritting his teeth at the creaking of metal. He was still for a moment as he waited to see if the noise drew any attention. When there was no sign of movement, he squeezed through the tight opening, staying low to the ground.

The warehouse was large and open-plan with metal racks surrounding the perimeter. Old boxes covered in green mould lay discarded on the shelves. The hole he'd squeezed through was behind one of the many shelving racks and, for the moment at least, he was out of sight in the dark shadows.

Without the walls to act as a buffer, the air had grown even murkier with dark magic. Ethan shook his head in an attempt to clear the fuzziness and surveyed the scene around him. He could hear the low chanting of the witches not far from where he stood, but the boxes that kept him from sight also kept them from his. The space along the wall to his left was empty save for a few packages that had fallen over. But to his right was a sight that both eased and sky-rocketed his worry in equal measures: Annabelle, crouched in the corner, hidden by shadows. Visibly trembling, but very much alive.

The relief in her eyes when she looked up and saw him made his gut twist.

We're not out of this yet, kid.

Crouching low, he made his way to her side and held her close when she threw her arms around him, burying her face in his chest. Annabelle quickly pulled herself together, wiping the back of her sleeve across her running nose, and in hushed tones she filled him in on the scene before them.

Through a break in the shelving he could see a young girl, no older than Annabelle. She was crouched on the floor in a white nightdress, tears streaming down her face as she begged and pleaded. The circle of seven witches surrounding her paid no heed as they continued their chanting.

"Okay, Annabelle, I need you to very quietly start moving back the way you came in." He placed his hands on her shoulders, urging her to look at him. "We need to get you out of here. Now."

She shook her head stubbornly. "I can't leave Izzie. They're going to kill her because of what she told me." Her voice broke on the last words.

"I'm not going to let anything happen to your friend, kid. I just need you safe first, okay?"

She hesitated long enough to make him worry he'd have to carry her out, but finally, she nodded. With one more glance towards her friend, she edged slowly towards safety.

She made it less than ten feet from him when the chanting began to pick up pace. Ethan's adrenaline surged as he felt his wolf aching to break free. The magic around them was like static shocks prickling at his nerves and he struggled to maintain control.

In the centre of the warehouse, a circle of thick, inky-black candles flared to life, casting an eerie glow on the young girl huddled at their centre. The witches surrounded her, heads thrown back, hands clasped together. Their chanting began to reach a crescendo and one of the witches stepped free of the circle, holding a large ceremonial dagger in her hand. The razor-sharp edge of silver glinted in the candlelight.

Annabelle's forward momentum halted and she turned to peer through a gap in the shelving with a look of horror on her face. Everything seemed to move in slow motion. Before Ethan could do anything, Annabelle instinctively reached out a hand towards her friend, knocking boxes to the ground in the process.

The chanting ceased abruptly and the witches turned as one in her direction.

Realising their time had run out, Ethan's movement became a blur and he pushed over the metal shelving as he hurled himself towards the witches. Their circle broke apart with shrieks of surprise, but Ethan found himself rebounding off an invisible barrier before he could reach them or their young sacrifice.

Stunned, he was only vaguely aware of Annabelle screaming his name. He turned just in time to see the head witch lunge for him. The ceremonial dagger was still in her hand, and her face was contorted in rage. Ethan flung himself to the side, the downward swipe of the blade only just missing him.

As he blocked her next lunge, he allowed his claws to extend and swiped the razor edge cleanly across her throat.

With their leader fallen, a number of the witches fled. The ones that remained took up their chanting again and their words caused the hair on his arms to stand on end.

"Annabelle, a little help here," he called, trying again in vain to reach the girl held within the circle of candles.

"Working on it," she replied, her voice strained. A second later the flames of the black candles flickered out and the chanting came to a sudden halt.

Ethan kicked the candles clear and a whoosh of air passed him as the spell lifted. The girl, however, remained sobbing on the floor.

Dammit, why can't people ever help out when they're being saved.

Just as he reached for the girl, he heard Annabelle yelp behind him. He turned in time to see her flung through the air into a pile of boxes on the floor. One of the remaining witches stalked towards her, the ceremonial dagger now clutched firmly in her hand, having obviously been confiscated from the dead witch.

With a growl rumbling deep in his throat, Ethan leapt at the witch and knocked her clear of Annabelle. Caught off-guard, the witch scrambled for the dagger, but a swift elbow to the jaw stopped her short.

He kicked the dagger well out of reach, but before he could finish her off, a low mumbled chant sounded behind him. The air became leaden as a tangible weight crushed him into the ground.

Using all of his strength, Ethan pushed to standing and

searched the warehouse for the source of magic. He found the one remaining witch standing in the shadows with her head thrown back and palms spread wide. Melodic words tumbled from her mouth.

Each step he took towards her almost brought him to his knees. His limbs crumbled under the onslaught of the invisible weight, but he forced himself to move. One limb at a time.

The closer he got to her, the faster the words came. The more each bone in his body felt like it was being crushed. His wolf raged against the attack, giving him a surge of adrenaline that pushed him the final steps. Sweat slid down his forehead as he wrapped his large clawed hand around her throat and squeezed.

With a choke, her words cut off. The weight in the room lifted so suddenly Ethan nearly fell to the floor with relief.

His wolf clawed at its mental restraints, eager to finish the witch off. But just as he prepared to end her worthless life, the air around him crackled with electricity. He turned with the witch in his grasp only to find himself blinded by a fierce blue light that momentarily scrambled his senses.

"Noooo –" Annabelle launched herself in front of him. Her scream abruptly cut off as that same blue light sent a jolt of electricity through her.

In shock, Ethan watched her fall to the ground, her body spasming as the currents ran through her. The witch he'd stunned earlier now stood fully conscious on the far side of Annabelle. Her hands and lips moved frantically as she worked to draw more electricity to her.

Ethan's vision turned red, and in an instant, all conscious thought ceased and his wolf took the reins. With a roar, the hand that held the dangling witch clenched. In one clean motion, he tore out her jugular.

Blood ran down his arm as he stared numbly at Annabelle's crumpled, unmoving form before shifting his attention back to the one remaining witch.

His teeth elongated as he stalked towards her. Rage and the full moon combined to overpower his usually iron-clad control. Ethan fought the change with what little of his human consciousness remained. Annabelle needed him.

The ball of electricity began to form again in the witch's hand as her chanting grew more frantic. But it wouldn't save her this time.

Ethan waited until she was close to the end of her chant. A brief flash of hope flared in her eyes just before he plunged his fist straight through her chest and gripped her still beating heart in his hand. He crushed it slowly, his wolf looking in fascination at the thick, black blood that ran down his forearm.

A haze filled his vision, and it took all the willpower he had to stumble back to Annabelle on two legs. He fell to his knees beside her, an invisible fist clenching his own heart.

He knew already, but still he checked her pulse.

Nothing.

He could sense no thread of life from her, no small spark to cling to. She was gone.

Her arms hung limp by her sides as he clutched her small frame to his chest, and his wolf howled in anguish. It was his job to protect her. He should have protected her.

A soft whimpering slowly broke through the haze of his grief. Looking up, he found himself staring into the glazed, green eyes of Annabelle's friend, Izzie. As she took in the sight of him covered in blood, canines still elongated, her eyes widened in terror. Scrambling away from him, she let a bloodcurdling scream and ran for the doorway.

Ethan watched her go, too tired to follow. She would have to fend for herself. He rose to his feet and gently cradled Annabelle's body as he walked out into the dark night.

CHAPTER FOURTEEN

Phoenix was just putting out the bins, ready to lock up for the night, when she heard a noise behind her.

Seriously? Again?

This time instead of freezing, she turned, ready and willing to fight. The sight in front of her stopped her short, adrenaline turning to ice in her veins.

Like before, Ethan stood in the alley with her. But unlike before, he was now holding a girl in his arms and dripping blood. His eyes had a haunted look that sent chills through her.

"Is she …" Her breath caught and she couldn't bring herself to finish the question.

Ethan nodded, looking lost as he cradled the small body close to him. "I couldn't save her. I was meant to protect her."

Phoenix stared in shock at the perfect, unblemished skin of the girl's face, ashen now that the flush of life-giving blood had been stolen. Her eyes were closed and she looked almost peaceful, at rest. But the image was wrong. She wasn't at rest. The girl was only a child, sixteen at best. What the hell could have happened to her?

Scanning the alley around them, Phoenix noted a large motorbike lying on its side in the shadows, not far from where Ethan stood. She was vaguely aware that there was something strange about the fact he was standing, something about the full moon, but she couldn't focus on anything other than the girl.

"Ethan, tell me what happened," Phoenix said softly, instinctively taking a step towards him.

"The prophecy ..." He shook his head, eyes clenched tight as if to shut out the images. "She wanted to help, and they killed her."

He turned on her then, eyes flashing yellow with anger. "She wanted to help."

His words were like a blow. The prophecy? This girl was dead because of the prophecy? Guilt flooded Phoenix in a wave that nearly choked her. All the time she'd spent burying her head in the sand and hoping it would all go away when this young girl had been trying to help.

"I'm sorry. I shouldn't have come here ... I only had the bike, I couldn't carry her well, I needed somewhere close ..." Ethan shook his head and his arms tightened protectively around the girl. "I needed you to understand."

Phoenix gave herself a shake, suddenly aware of how exposed they were, even in the darkness of the alley. There would be time enough for allocating blame later, but they needed to get inside before someone saw them. Grateful that Abi had already gone to bed, Phoenix ushered Ethan through the side door and into the kitchen at the back of the bar. A small terrified voice in the back of her mind screeched at her the whole time. What the hell was she doing getting involved? She resolutely ignored those thoughts and focused only on the child in Ethan's arms. The girl was the priority.

"The girl is ... was a Supe?" Phoenix pushed past the lump forming in her throat.

"Annabelle. Yes, she ... was a witch." A small smile pulled at the corner of Ethan's mouth as he tenderly brushed a strand of hair from Annabelle's face. "A bloody good one too."

Phoenix noted the pride in his voice but didn't pry further. "Then we need to help her pass?"

Ethan looked up at her, surprise in his eyes. He nodded. "Her soul can't rest without the Ritual."

The Ritual of Passing was one of the few Lore traditions her parents had made certain to pass on to her from a young age. Supes liked to believe they were invincible, but the truth was they could be killed just like everyone else – once you knew their weaknesses. Unlike humans though, a Supe's soul couldn't easily move on when the body was destroyed. Without the Ritual of Passing, the soul would become trapped and never be reborn. It was a thought that filled her with terror.

"I think I have everything we need." She turned on her heel, making her way towards the stairs. "Bathroom's down the hall, get yourself cleaned up."

"Phoenix."

She stopped and looked back at him.

"You don't have to do this."

The smile she gave him was sad but resolved. "Yes, I do."

Taking the stairs two at a time, she slipped quietly into her bedroom and pulled out the small oak box she kept buried at the bottom of her wardrobe. The wood was ornately carved with a sun emblem that matched her medallion; it had been one of the few things her mother had taken with her when she left Faerie.

Opening it to check everything was inside, a sudden thought stopped her in her tracks and made her stomach clench painfully. What about her parents? Would someone have cared enough to do the Ritual for them? She had to assume they were dead after all this time, but it had never occurred to her that they might be stuck and unable to pass on.

Phoenix dug her fingernails deep into the palm of her hand and forced the thought from her mind. There was nothing she could do to help her parents, but she could help Annabelle.

"Fifi, what're you doing?"

Phoenix froze at the sound of Abi's sleepy voice behind her. Heart pounding furiously in her chest, she willed a relaxed smile onto her face and turned to find her friend standing in the doorway, watching her with a look of curiosity.

"I'm just grabbing my jacket. A friend is stranded so I'm going to pick him up."

"Oh really?" Abi raised her neatly manicured eyebrows, making air quotes as she repeated, "You're going to *pick him up*?"

Crossing her arms, Phoenix glared at her friend. "Yes, Abi. I'm going to *pick him up*."

Abi held up her hands in surrender, but was laughing as she retreated to her bedroom.

Air left Phoenix's lungs in a whoosh as she released the breath she'd been unconsciously holding. She hesitated for a moment longer in case Abi came back, then grabbed the box and a blanket, and ran quietly down the stairs.

Ethan was waiting for her in the kitchen, thankfully looking less like a scene from a horror movie. Maybe no one would even notice that they were carting a dead body around.

She helped him carefully wrap Annabelle's body in the blanket and they slipped out the side door of the bar, moving quietly to her old, imported Mustang, which sat patiently in its parking spot behind the bar.

Phoenix focused on the road ahead, trying hard to give Ethan privacy while he talked to someone named Nate – not an easy thing to do with him sitting mere inches from her. As snippets of the conversation breached her consciousness, she wondered again about Ethan's frequent use of "we". The dead body in the back of her car was proof that others were involved in this prophecy conspiracy, but she had no idea how many, or what she'd signed herself up for.

From the conversation, she knew there was a sister, Lily, that was soon going to receive some of the worst news of her life. There was also reference to someone called Shade – a nickname? – and Nate, the person Ethan was speaking to directly. If there were others, they weren't mentioned and didn't seem relevant to tonight's events.

Ethan kept the details brief and to the point, asking Nate to bring the others to their meeting point so he could break the news himself. Phoenix noted the change in his demeanour with a morbid fascination as he put aside his grief and took charge of the task ahead.

As they drove further from the city, the night grew darker around them until eventually the only light was from the car headlights and the glow of the moon breaking through the clouds. The shimmering silver light reminded her once more that it was a full moon and her heartbeat ratcheted up a notch as she suddenly remembered another concern even more pressing than the upcoming Ritual.

When Ethan hung up the phone she blurted, "How are you not in wolf form?"

Her question seemed to catch him off guard, and for a moment he looked at his hands in confusion, almost as if wondering himself why they were human. But then he shook his head, regrouping.

"I don't change at the full moon. Not while I'm away from my pack."

Well, that clarified things – not.

Before she could push any further, Ethan pointed at a narrow dirt road swiftly approaching on the left. "Turn here."

Cursing, Phoenix dropped gears and turned just in time. The rear of the car skidded out behind and she had to fight to straighten it, narrowly missing the trees that caged them in on each side.

"Jeez, a bit of notice would be helpful."

Ethan gave her an apologetic smile. "Sorry, it's been a while since I was out this direction."

"Where are we going anyway?"

Phoenix knew it was best to conduct the Ritual where the gateways were weakest, but she'd been following Ethan's directions blindly ever since they left the pub and she was none the wiser as to where they were.

Ethan looked at her for a moment, then turned away as he quietly replied, "The Cathedral."

The car veered as Phoenix turned to him in surprise. "We're going to a church?"

Reaching one hand for the wheel as if to steady her erratic reactions, Ethan shook his head. "No ... well, yes. Kind of. But not in the way you're thinking. It dates back long before the church as you know it now. Back before the church's true meaning was lost."

Phoenix shook her head and added yet one more point to her list of things to be confused about. She really didn't have the energy to play twenty questions. For a while she drove along in silence, leaving Ethan to his thoughts as she concentrated on the narrow winding back roads.

But the longer she stayed quiet, the more anxious she became. Anxious about the werewolf in her car, anxious about the people they were going to meet, anxious about the dead body she was carting around. Until eventually she needed a distraction.

"Tell me about her." Phoenix inclined her head towards the young girl lying across the back seat of her car.

Ethan was quiet, and for a moment she wondered if he'd heard her.

"Annabelle was a sweet kid," he said eventually. "She looked at the world like no one else I've ever met. Just an innocent curiosity, never judging."

"That's a rare quality."

He nodded and the skin around his eyes tightened as he glanced into the back seat. "We all tried so hard to protect her, but we were wrong. We didn't see how strong she was."

"How did you meet?"

Ethan turned back to stare out into the passing night. "I met her and her sister, Lily, about a year ago in Galway. They were on the streets and running scared." He drummed his fingers on the dashboard. "Their parents had been killed, accused of using black magic and sentenced to death by their coven."

Phoenix's throat grew dry at the thought of two young girls wandering the streets alone and scared. Memories clawed their way up from the darkness and she gripped the steering wheel tightly. She'd been the same age as Annabelle. But she'd been alone. Sitting in the dark, waiting for her parents to come back, knowing they'd been gone too long.

She forced her hands to relax on the wheel. "The girls didn't believe it?"

Ethan shook his head. "No, and it wasn't long before their questions started drawing attention. I helped them out of a spot of bother and they've been with me ever since."

Mulling over the new information, Phoenix tried to reconcile the man sitting beside her with the man that attacked her only a week ago. Sure, he claimed not to have actually attacked her, but he definitely gave a girl mixed signals. That situation seemed so at odds with a man that would help a couple of strangers in trouble; never mind that the man was a werewolf, and the strangers were witches.

Phoenix opened her mouth to ask about the others they were going to meet, but they turned a sharp bend in the road and the charged air around them froze the words in her throat. The hairs on her arms stood on end, but she could see nothing past the dense blockade of trees that lined the road.

"We're here."

CHAPTER FIFTEEN

At Ethan's instruction, Phoenix pulled the car over to a narrow break in the trees and killed the engine. Silence.

The energy she felt in the air had an almost tangible quality to it, drawing her towards the trees and what lay beyond. Still, she stayed in the front seat, suddenly afraid to leave the safety of the car. A buzzing drew her attention back to Ethan, and she watched as the rough stubble on his chin was illuminated by the harsh glare from his phone.

"The others are here."

Phoenix sucked in a breath and tried to calm the sudden carnival in her stomach. She didn't know these people, hadn't even had a chance to ask about them, and now she was going to get a front seat pass to their grief. Nothing about this felt right.

As if sensing her discomfort, Ethan turned to her. "Maybe it's best if you wait in the car, at least until I speak to them."

She nodded her agreement and tried not to let her relief show.

Ethan took a deep breath and slid out of the car. He disappeared into the night before Phoenix could even blink.

Time seemed to pass in slow motion, and with each minute that flicked by on the screen of her dashboard, Phoenix became more on edge. Needing some air, she let go of the safety blanket that was her car and greeted the sharp cold of the night.

No sooner had the car door closed behind her, than a heart-rending scream of anguish cut through the night, chilling her to her core. The cry was filled with such agony that Phoenix's heart ached, and she wanted nothing more than to get back in her Mustang and leave.

But there was a dead girl lying across the back seat. A dead girl that needed help passing on. So she stayed put, focusing intently on the ground in front of her as she wrapped her arms tightly around her middle.

Phoenix wasn't sure how long she'd been waiting when she heard Ethan clear his throat. She lifted her surprised gaze only to find him standing a couple of feet in front of her. Three others stood in the shadows of the trees.

When did he come back?

"Is she in there?"

The girl, Phoenix could only assume to be Lily, looked vacantly at the car as her quiet, almost toneless voice broke the silence surrounding them.

Feeling awkward and in the way, Phoenix nodded and edged further from the car. "She's in the back seat."

Lily continued to stare blankly as if Phoenix hadn't spoken.

"I brought everything we need for the Ritual but I don't know where ..." Phoenix cleared her throat, unnerved by the watchful gaze of the two male Supes standing on either side of the girl.

As if suddenly becoming aware of the tension around him, Ethan quickly jumped in. "Phoenix, this is Nate, Shade, and Lily, Annabelle's sister."

Smiling weakly, Phoenix lifted her hand in acknowledgement.

Nate barely spared her another glance, having shifted his attention to Lily. He seemed young to her; his messy brown hair and casual clothes gave him a relaxed air that she was sure was misleading based on the concern that marred his features. The energy that came from him was similar to Ethan's, but different somehow, less primal. His features reminded her almost of a fox. A shifter, perhaps?

Shade, on the other hand, kept his icy blue eyes fixed on her. Animosity emanated from him in waves. Although the scowl looked quite at home on his pale face, Phoenix had a strange feeling this one was especially for her. Having lived around a vampire her whole life, his signature was clearer. He appeared young, eighteen or nineteen perhaps, but that was no real indication of his age, only how old he was when turned.

Lily, Phoenix noticed, looked very much like the young girl lying on the back seat. She had similar long blonde hair and the clear sun-kissed skin she imagined Annabelle would have if death had not taken the flush of life from her. But where Annabelle's features looked youthful even in death, Lily's eyes bore lines of tension that seemed out of place on someone so young.

Without another word, Ethan leaned into the car and carefully lifted out Annabelle's body.

Lily whimpered as she reached a hand toward her sister, but quickly pulled it back as if burned. Her whole body was visibly trembling, but her expression remained a fixed mask of uncomprehending shock.

In silence, they each followed Ethan through the forest until the path ahead opened into a clearing. Trees lined the space, forming a natural amphitheatre, and at the centre stood the most beautiful ruins Phoenix had ever seen.

Solid grey stone stood defiant against time and the elements while clearly outlining what had once been a magnificent building. High walls framed the north and south points, each showcasing three large arched windows that stood as proud now as when they were first built. The east and west sides were edged with a jagged perimeter of varying heights, allowing a clear view of the interior with its moss-covered walls and colourful flowers coating the floor.

The silver light of the moon highlighted their path and cast shadows from the imposing stone structure. Power filled the night, growing stronger and stronger with each step they took.

"So, this is the Cathedral?" Phoenix said breathlessly.

Ethan nodded and stepped over a low section of the wall into the ruins. He moved to the centre and gently laid Annabelle's body on a patch of soft green grass before brushing her hair back from her face.

A little piece of Phoenix's heart broke as she watched him fix the blanket around the young girl, as if worried she might get cold. Immortality had a tendency to make Supes very blasé about life; it wasn't often they were confronted with the pain of loss. The harsh reminder made her think of Abi and what she might stand to lose if her own immortality had definitely come to pass.

Retrieving the wooden box from her bag, Phoenix quietly placed it on the ground beside Ethan. She watched as he lay the sprigs of rosemary, lavender, and sage around Annabelle's resting form with care. Even the cold night air couldn't dampen the soothing fragrance that came from the herbs, and her senses eagerly soaked in the comfort they provided.

The others stood beside them, but no one spoke or made any move to take over. Feeling awkward and unsure, Phoenix busied herself grinding the remaining herbs before bringing the bowl to Ethan's side.

"Help me?" Ethan's voice was soft. His large hand rested on her smaller one as she began to move away. For a brief moment, he allowed her to see the raw pain in his brown eyes.

Phoenix took a deep breath, let go of her insecurities, and knelt beside him. She smudged the herbs between her fingers and rubbed them on Annabelle's energy points: forehead, solar plexus, and just below her naval. With the final preparations complete, she accepted Ethan's offered hand, and picking up the box, stood back to join the others.

The night fell silent around them, the usual rustle of leaves no longer evident as though even the trees held their breath. All that remained was for someone to speak the necessary words. To complete the ritual.

Aware she was the one with the least emotional attachment, Phoenix considered offering. It seemed unfair for a stranger to speak the final words for Annabelle, but if it had been her sister, she couldn't imagine having the strength. Thankfully, her internal debate proved unnecessary.

Ethan placed a large hand on Lily's shoulder and spoke quietly into her ear. Though Phoenix couldn't make out the words, whatever he said seemed to rouse Lily from her catatonic state. She straightened and squared her shoulders as she shook her head in answer to Ethan's question. This seemed to be the response he was hoping for because he smiled and squeezed her shoulder before moving to the side.

With a shuddery breath, Lily picked up a rucksack that lay by her feet. She pulled out a small stuffed unicorn and held it to her chest for a moment as she bowed her head. The unicorn was worn and a little dirty; a much-loved possession. Lily ran her hands tenderly over it once more before gently placing it into her sister's arms. She then turned to Phoenix and held out her hand.

Realising what Lily intended to do, Phoenix handed over the box with its remaining contents. The young girl raised haunted green eyes briefly to meet her gaze before turning to stand by the body of her sister. In a soft, melodic voice, Lily began to speak the words of the Ritual. Verses older than time, written in a language unknown by many, but understood by all.

Phoenix joined the others as they formed a circle around their fallen friend, heads bowed in respect and reverence for the young witch that lay before them. The words grew in strength and filled the air. And with the words, a low keening wail filled the night, making the hairs on Phoenix's arms stand on end. The sound was laced with such sorrow that it spoke to her soul.

A quick glance showed no reaction from the others, but the sound continued until it became a part of her. As the wind began to pick up, so too did the keening wail grow louder in her ears. The calming aroma of herbs overwhelmed her senses, but there was something else. Something Phoenix couldn't place.

Before her eyes, the most extraordinary thing happened: Annabelle's form began to fade. Her extremities dissolved into the currents of air that swirled around them, and Phoenix watched in awe as the body in front of her became little more than a glittering memory carried on the wind.

As suddenly as it began, the wind stopped.

The small stuffed unicorn dropped to the ground, and the night fell quiet. With one final word, Lily crumpled, sobbing as she curled tightly in on herself. Nate rushed to her side and lifted her trembling frame. He cradled her close to his chest, and without sparing the others a second glance, he carried her off into the darkness of the trees.

For a moment, Phoenix, Ethan, and Shade stood inside the Cathedral in silence. Then, with a final glare in her direction, Shade followed Nate, his vampire speed making it seem almost as if he disappeared.

Ethan crouched to pick up the unicorn and placed his hand on the ground for a brief moment before he stood, staring into the darkness after the others.

The simple truth weighed heavy on Phoenix's shoulders. "They blame me," she said.

Ethan shook his head. "They're just hurting."

"They should …"

He looked at her quizzically, the hint of yellow in his normally brown eyes telling her his wolf had also been present in the clearing with them.

"Blame me …"

"This isn't your fault, Phoenix. I was wrong to make you think that. Annabelle made her choices. We all make our choices."

His voice was firm, conviction evident, but his words from earlier that night replayed in her mind. *I needed you to understand.* He had asked for her help, but she had clung to the safety of her ignorance.

Yes, she'd made a choice. She just wasn't sure if it was the right one anymore.

"Will they trust me enough to let me help?"

The intensity of his gaze burned into her as if trying to see into her soul. "Do you want to help?"

"Yes," she said, letting him see the truth of her words as she looked him in the eyes.

"Then we'll find a way to make them trust you."

CHAPTER SIXTEEN

Leaning back in his office chair, Il Maestro forced his expression to remain neutral as the vampire in front of him finished providing his report.

The witches were dead. And not a single one of them for the purpose of the sacrifice.

His blood boiled.

He picked his glass of whiskey up from the desk and slowly stalked towards the other vampire. "So, you're telling me no one knows who killed the witches?"

The vampire shook his head and visibly stiffened as Il Maestro moved closer to him.

"Belinda?"

"Dead," the vampire responded with his eyes fixed straight ahead.

"The sacrifice?"

A hesitation. "Missing."

Considering this new turn of events, Il Maestro stared at the rich amber liquid as it swirled around the crystal glass. He walked in circles around the vampire and mused on how difficult it was to find good security nowadays.

"Il Maestro, if I might just say –"

The security guard's words were cut off with a gurgle as two sharp fangs pierced his flesh, and in one swift motion, a chunk was torn from his throat.

"No, you may not just say." Il Maestro spat the thick, viscous blood out and wiped his mouth with the silk handkerchief from his pocket.

He stepped over the still-twitching body and reached for the phone on his desk. "Raphael, get me Belinda's second-in-command.

"Oh, and get a cleaner to my office. One of your staff has made something of a mess."

CHAPTER SEVENTEEN

Ethan stared out of the car window and into the night beyond. The darkness gradually shifted from almost complete black, to an odd, orange luminescence as they got closer to the city. His mind raced with unanswered questions. Despite what he'd told Phoenix, it was highly likely that the others would blame her, at least indirectly, for Annabelle's death. He had no idea how to convince them to accept her help, but he knew he needed to.

"Did you hear it?"

Phoenix's softly spoken question broke his train of thought and he looked around in confusion, listening intently for any unusual sounds.

"Hear what?"

She kept her eyes straight ahead and adjusted her hands uncomfortably on the leather steering wheel. "The keening ... during the Ritual."

Well, that got his attention.

Twisting his body as much as he could within the confined space, he looked at her intently. "What are you talking about?"

"It was so sad. I mean, of course the Ritual was heart-breaking," she quickly clarified, throwing an apologetic glance his way, "but I've never heard a sound filled with such sorrow."

A shiver ran down his spine.

Shit. A banshee's wail?

He blew out a long breath and watched her closely for any sign of awareness. Could she really not know?

"Phoenix, one of your parents is fae, right?"

She hesitated for a moment before nodding. "My mother."

"Did she ever mention anything about the banshee?"

The look she gave him was one of such complete and utter surprise that he could guess the answer even without a response.

"No, she ... Are you saying I heard a banshee?"

"Well, I didn't hear anything so I can only guess. But it fits."

"You really didn't hear it?" she asked incredulously.

Ethan shook his head. "The banshee is only connected to particular families, and only members of that family hear her cry."

Phoenix drummed her nails impatiently on the steering wheel as she pulled to a stop at a red light. "Why did you ask about my mother?" She turned to face him.

"I've only ever heard of the banshee being linked to fae families. Powerful families."

She seemed to mull this information over, not offering any further insights to confirm or deny his observation. When the light turned green, they drove along the quays in silence until they hit another red light and she faced him again.

"Ethan? You're meant to hear the wail of the banshee whenever someone close to you dies, right?"

He nodded.

"I've never heard it before," she whispered.

An odd look of pain crossed her features that he couldn't understand. Surely it was a good thing that she hadn't heard it before?

Ethan directed Phoenix to the old converted warehouse he currently called home, and she drove in subdued silence. Nate's blacked-out Civic was already parked at the side of the building as they pulled up in front, and he could feel her tense beside him. He waited to see if she'd back out, but she got out of the car, closed the door firmly behind her, and followed him up to the top floor without a word.

She'd surprised him tonight. Any sane person would have turned him away. Would have ran a mile screaming, for that matter.

It hadn't even been a conscious decision to go to her, not really. He just remembered cradling Annabelle close to him on the bike, not wanting her to get cold from the bitter wind that slapped at him insistently. Everything had been a blur, until suddenly he was at the pub where Phoenix worked. It had been the closest place to him, but it was more than that. He needed her to understand the cost.

And now, she was at his side as they walked in to find the others waiting in his apartment.

Nate was fussing over Lily, who seemed to have returned to her previous trance, and Shade leaned against the window, staring out into the night while he played with his penknife. The mood was solemn, and Annabelle's absence was painfully obvious.

"What's she doing here?" Shade drove the tip of his penknife into the windowsill as he turned to scowl in their direction.

"I want to help." Phoenix met his gaze steadily until he looked away, directing his anger into the darkness beyond the window.

"You've helped enough," he muttered.

The weariness of the night washed over Ethan, swiftly eroding his patience and all good intentions of diplomacy. "That's enough, Shade. Phoenix is here to help, and you *will* treat her with respect."

Shade pushed away from the window, glaring at him defiantly. "I don't have to do any –"

"Enough!" Lily's voice surprised them all into silence. She was staring intently at Phoenix, green eyes more alert than they'd been all night. "We need all the help we can get. If she wants to help, let her help."

And just like that, it was settled. Phoenix took a seat beside Lily and listened quietly as they filled her in on everything they knew so far. Before long, the night sky began to lighten with the first signs of dawn, and everyone around Ethan looked to be feeling the same bone-deep fatigue he was.

They'd covered a lot of old ground, but really, they were no closer to reaching an answer. A mind-numbing headache was beginning to form behind his eyes and the list of questions were only growing. What were the witches up to? How did Phoenix fit into it all? Could Lily's source have been wrong? He didn't know what to believe anymore.

"Let's call it a night." He stood to stretch his legs and gave his neck a resounding crack.

Nate, Shade, and Lily muttered their goodnights, leaving him alone in the kitchen with Phoenix as they made their way to their respective apartments. A sharp tinge of anxiety clenched his gut as he watched the others walk out the door, and he nearly had to stop himself from calling them back. They were only down the hall.

They're safe.

He busied himself making a pot of coffee and repeated the mantra again in his head. When the coffee was steaming, he poured it into a cup and handed it to Phoenix who stood fidgeting uncomfortably behind him.

"Don't want you crashing on the way home. It's been a long night."

She took the cup from him, her small nose wrinkling in the cutest way as she looked at the black, tarry liquid. "So, you decided to kill me with this instead?"

Her vibrant green eyes sparkled as she smiled, something he hadn't seen her do very often, and he couldn't help his own responding grin.

"You'll come back tonight?" They'd discussed the idea of her going on patrol with them, but still he held his breath, waiting for her to make an excuse and walk away.

Phoenix nodded and her face turned serious as she clutched the warm cup in both hands. "I don't know how much help I'll be, but I'll be here."

"You've already been more help than you realise." His words elicited a surprisingly girly blush from her as she looked away, clearly uncomfortable.

Clearing her throat, she placed the cup down on the counter.

"Right ... I think it's probably time I make a move. Abi will be getting worried."

Moving aside to give her access to the door, he watched her leave, more curious than ever about the hybrid.

CHAPTER EIGHTEEN

"I can assure you, Il Maestro, that Belinda's mistakes won't be mine."

Deep blue eyes met his gaze with an unwavering surety that did, indeed, encourage confidence. The witch's blood red robe made her seem strangely at home in the dark chamber where they stood. Flickering torch flames cast shadows over the stone walls, and her power filled the space, falling like a sweet temptation on his tongue.

"Tell me, Esme, how is it you reached only second in command before Belinda's untimely demise?" Il Maestro tilted his head and watched her with a mild curiosity.

"It was how I preferred it to be ... Until I was sure the coven's ambitions aligned with my own." There was no arrogance in her tone, merely fact. Had she wished it, they both knew she would have been head of the coven.

"And now?" he asked, raising a neatly manicured eyebrow.

"Now, it's time for the Dublin coven to reach the greatness it was intended for." Esme's blue eyes flashed fervently even as her face remained expressionless. "Tell me what you need from us and it will be done."

He assessed the woman standing before him. She had an imposing presence and spoke such pretty words. But words were useless to him. Perhaps it was time to test the loyalty she was offering.

"I want you to find a way to speed up the prophecy."

For the briefest moment, surprise registered on her face.

"The clock began to count down when the prophecy was triggered, Il Maestro. Its course will not be easily deterred. Nor will it be easily rerouted –"

"Can it be done?" He wasn't interested in listening to excuses. He was tired of the interruptions.

After a moment, she nodded. "It would require a particular talisman. And a blood connection to the prophecy – the hybrid being preferable," she added thoughtfully, "but yes, I believe so."

"The blood will not be a problem," he said with a dismissive wave of his hand. "Can we obtain the talisman?"

"It is ... close. Though I may require assistance to acquire it."

Satisfied, Il Maestro nodded. "You'll have all the assistance you require."

In a blink, she was gone.

CHAPTER NINETEEN

"And what time did you get home last night?" Abi leaned her elbows on the bar and wiggled her eyebrows suggestively.

Phoenix kept her eyes fixed on the tap she was hooking up, resolutely avoiding her friend's probing gaze. The third degree had been going on all afternoon, and there was no sign of it letting up.

"Aw come on, at least tell me who the guy is," Abi pressed, just to prove the point.

Phoenix sighed and looked up from her crouched position under the bar. "He's just a friend, Abi. You know it *is* possible to have those."

Abi threw her a look that clearly said, "Yeah right!" before walking off to chat with the band setting up on stage.

Phoenix leaned her forehead on the edge of the bar top in front of her as an uncomfortable feeling settled in the pit of her stomach. She hated lying to Abi. Not that Ethan was more than a friend, if he was even that, but what could she tell her that wouldn't just lead to more lies?

She gave herself a mental kick up the arse and hauled herself up from the floor to set about stacking the glasses. There was enough to worry about without feeling sorry for herself on top of it all. She'd go to Ethan's once she got off work, help him find a way to stop whatever was happening, and go back to her normal life. Simple.

Except it wasn't, because she had no idea how to help. Having avoided that world her whole life, she knew sweet F.A. about the Lore. And having avoided that side of *herself* her whole life, she had little or no understanding of her own powers either. How she was supposed to be involved in the prophecy was a mystery to her. Ethan was crazy to want her on board.

Idly reorganising the bottles of alcohol, she stifled a yawn. Sleep hadn't come easily once she got back from Ethan's that morning. Every time she'd closed her eyes, Annabelle's lifeless form was there, burned into her retinas. And when it wasn't Annabelle, it was her best friend. Reaching for her. Begging for help, as all around her, the world burned. The whole thing was like a nightmare she couldn't wake from.

The shrill ring of her phone made Phoenix yelp in surprise and she fumbled awkwardly to catch the bottle of Jameson that slipped from her grasp. Already on edge, her heart leapt in her throat as she pulled the phone out of her pocket.

Shit, please not more bad news.

Darius's name flashed on the screen, filling her with relief and apprehension all at once. Did he know something? Surely he couldn't have found out about last night, could he?

The sound of laughter drifted down the bar to her, and her attention was pulled from the vibrating phone back to her current surroundings. Abi was flirting outrageously with the lead singer of the band, her head thrown back as she laughed with pure, genuine delight.

Phoenix hesitated, her finger hovering over the answer button. More sounds of laughter filtered into her consciousness from around the pub: customers chatting animatedly, friends laughing and joking as they put their worries aside for the evening. The life she'd built for herself suddenly seemed unbearably precious. And oh so very fragile.

A fierce need boiled up in her to protect it.

Biting her lip, she put the phone on silent and slipped it back into her pocket, ignoring the persistent vibration. She needed time to think before she spoke to Darius. He'd want to help. She understood that, but she needed to figure this out for herself.

It would've been nice to ease in gently, Phoenix thought wryly as she followed Ethan through Temple Bar in search of witches. Sure, she'd signed up for it, but shouldn't there be an induction or something?

The late hour, coupled with it being a Monday, meant the streets were thankfully quiet. A few straggling tourists loitered about, reluctant to give up even though the pubs were now closed. The occasional homeless person huddled in a doorway as they sought what shelter they could in their sleeping bag. Some unsavoury characters argued amongst themselves over their poison of choice for the night. All were human, and all were of little consequence to their current goal.

Traversing the cobblestones, she was aware of every person and every sound. First night jitters were only compounded by the covert meeting awaiting them. Phoenix gripped the medallion around her neck as she matched Ethan stride for stride.

Lily had been surprisingly active in acquiring an update on the witches in the few hours since her sister's death. She had pretty strong motivation, Phoenix supposed, but it was still impressive considering the grief she must be feeling. With her help, they managed to confirm that the Dublin coven had gone to ground; their second in command had taken the reins since Ethan had killed the previous leader during the attempted sacrifice.

Annabelle's young friend, Izzie, hadn't been seen or heard from since, but Lily did find another witch who was willing to speak to them – under duress. Unsurprisingly, the witch had conditions for the meeting to ensure her safety.

Creepy location in the dead of night: check.

Ridiculous codeword no one would ever guess: check.

Complete lack of backup in case of ambush: check.

Phoenix personally thought they were taking a stupid risk, given the events of the previous day. Yet here she was following Ethan like a lapdog to the agreed meeting point. Some would say she was an idiot. Some would be right.

She blew her unruly hair out of her face and noted a strange shift in the atmosphere as they passed the small square in the centre of Temple Bar. It was like all signs of life suddenly disappeared. The pubs were free of stragglers, and the doorways were empty.

Beside her, Ethan came to an abrupt halt. He looked around and sniffed the air, his body tense. It was only then that she noticed it. Blood.

She'd been so caught up in her own thoughts, and the coppery tang had been so subtle, that her vampire senses had written it off as just another part of their surroundings. But this was fresh.

She looked at Ethan and nodded when he inclined his head towards a side-street just past The Temple Bar pub. Her breath caught in her throat, but she followed him silently as he edged towards the corner.

Empty kegs stood stacked at the side of the pub and the metal shutters were pulled halfway down the windows, making the place appear almost as if it had been abandoned in a hurry. Glasses littered the footpath outside; dregs of beer and spirits were the only remaining sign of their owners. The night around them was quiet.

Ethan pressed Phoenix behind him with a gentle hand before he crouched low and risked a glance around the corner.

"Dammit," he cursed, hurrying towards something not yet visible from her position.

She cast a wary glance around and followed him, only to stop short at the sight that met her.

A woman, largely hidden by the stacked kegs, lay slumped on the ground, her neck twisted at an unnatural angle. She was in her forties, Phoenix guessed. Pretty, but in a forgettable way. A look of fear formed her death mask and a single trickle of fresh blood ran from a cut on her forehead.

Her hand was clenched tightly in a fist, and when Ethan pried it open, a small amulet clattered to the ground. He stood and punched the wall in anger before turning away to pace.

"It's the witch, isn't it?" Realisation hit Phoenix with a dull thud.

Ethan nodded but didn't speak. He just continued to pace and fought to take slow, deep breaths.

"She didn't even make it to the meeting pl –"

A woman's scream tore through the night and ripped away the veil of silence surrounding them.

With a quick glance at each other, they turned and sprinted in the direction of the sound. As they reached the small square once more, they found another woman in a heap on the cobblestones. She sobbed as her partner tried to console her and angry shouts came from the arched stone walkway that led to the quays.

Whatever had happened to this woman, she was in no immediate danger. So, Ethan and Phoenix ran through the archway and followed the shouts down the stone steps and across the road to the Ha'penny Bridge.

At the top of the bridge, Ethan skidded to a stop so suddenly that Phoenix ran straight into his back. She opened her mouth to ask what gives, but the scene in front of them stopped the words before they could leave her throat.

A middle-aged woman, fully equipped in tailored jacket and pencil skirt, stood over an old man. With her stilettos in hand, she rained merciless blows down on his frail form. A maniacal grin covered her face as the man cowered beneath his arms and tried in vain to protect his head. Each strike from the five-inch heels caused him to cry out in pain and only seemed to spur the woman on.

The image was wrong in so many ways that Phoenix couldn't even begin to list them, but more than that, the woman *felt* wrong. There was an energy to her, almost like that of a Supe, but thicker, more tangible and viscous. And her eyes ... her eyes were glowing like the flames of Hell.

"Demon," Ethan whispered, his skin visibly pale even in the darkness of the night.

The woman paused mid-strike and her head twisted in their direction. The red of her eyes pulsed and the smile on her face turned to something even more chilling than before. Abandoning her prey, she stalked slowly towards them, her tongue running seductively over bright red lips.

Phoenix shuddered and fought the sudden urge to scrub her skin raw. It didn't make sense. Demons weren't able to cross over. Were they?

"Eh ... any bright ideas?" she muttered nervously, not taking her eyes off the woman.

Ethan shook his head. His fists opened and closed convulsively at his sides. "She's just a vessel. We can't hurt her." Which left them shit out of luck since the woman – or demon – looked more than ready to hurt them.

"Hybrid," the demon hissed. Her voice was deep and unnatural coming from the woman's mouth.

Not waiting for her, or it, to get any closer, Ethan lunged shoulder first into the demon. The vessel didn't budge. Instead, it grabbed Ethan around the torso and lifted his sizable frame before flinging him halfway across the bridge, laughing.

The demon turned its attention back to Phoenix and tilted its head to assess her. Phoenix fought the urge to run as she shifted into a fighting stance. The demon was blocking her view of Ethan, but she heard the thud quite clearly when he landed, and the lack of follow-up attack didn't bode well for him at all. She was on her own.

Her knowledge of demons was limited, but she knew the woman it possessed was innocent, which severely limited her options; she wasn't willing to hurt an innocent human and had zero idea how to separate a demon from its host.

Done with its assessment, the demon abandoned its slow stalking and launched itself towards her. Human hands appeared almost as claws as they grabbed for her face, nails raking across her cheek in burning slashes.

Phoenix blocked the strikes as best she could without resorting to force, but it was useless. The human now possessed the demon's impressive speed, and its strength was overwhelming.

Unable to even restrain the demon, she finally relented and put her morals aside.

Her first punch connected, and Phoenix felt the sickening crunch of a cheekbone beneath her hand. The demon stumbled, and in a moment of utter cruelty, pulled back just enough from the woman it possessed to allow conscious terror and pain to flash behind her eyes. Nausea overwhelmed Phoenix and she had to cover her mouth with her hand to stop from throwing up.

The woman. Oh fuck, she's still aware.

With a cruel grin that looked out of place on the woman's face, the demon regained full control and began to stalk towards her once more. This time it was in no rush, knowing all too well it had effectively crippled her ability to fight back. It pressed Phoenix against the railings of the bridge and ran a chipped red fingernail down her cheek as it sniffed along her neck.

Phoenix held her breath, restraining the knee-jerk reaction to lash out. She couldn't hurt the woman again; there had to be another way. If she could just –

A loud "CAW" sounded before her view of the demon was broken in an explosion of black feathers. Wings beat furiously as a large crow latched its talons on to the demon, its razor-sharp beak striking the soft flesh of the eyes.

The demon roared and moved away from Phoenix as it fought to hold off the unexpected attack. Human limbs and feathers mixed in a confusing blur, but the crow allowed no leeway as it swarmed the demon.

Stunned, Phoenix stood frozen to the spot, unsure of what to do.

A rush of wind from her left was the only indication that Ethan was up and moving before he dived for the demon's legs. Already distracted by the crow's determined attack, the impact knocked the demon off balance and into the railings. Everything moved in slow motion and, for a split second, the demon got the upper hand on the crow as it tore the black wings away.

Furious red eyes met hers. "They're coming," it hissed, and an insane laugh wracked the woman's body.

With that parting sentence, the demon gripped the top of the railing, tore itself free of Ethan's grip, and launched the woman's body into the murky waters of the River Liffey below.

A silent scream froze in Phoenix's throat, but her outstretched hand was met with only air. She ran to Ethan's side and scanned the waters in desperation, but there was no sight of the woman. The water was eerily calm, like a mirror reflecting the night back at them.

Phoenix was shaking as she rested her head against the hard metal of the railings. She closed her eyes to block out the image of the woman's falling body, but it was no use. She'd been aware. The woman had still been alive.

Another "caw" drew her attention back to the bridge, and she turned to find the large crow watching them. From its perch on top of the railings, Phoenix could now appreciate the full size of the bird. Almost two feet in height, it was covered in silky feathers that reflected a miasma of colours back at them. What had initially appeared to be inky black, now shone with ever changing blues, greens, and purples. Eyes like rubies showcased a keen intelligence, and a strange sense of déjà vu washed over Phoenix. She'd seen those eyes before ...

With one more squawk, the crow took flight and left Phoenix and Ethan staring in confusion at the now empty railings.

Ethan let out a long breath. "I think we should call it a night."

She wanted nothing more than to agree, but Phoenix suddenly remembered the old man the demon had been attacking. She turned towards the arch of the bridge and her gaze met wide, shocked eyes. Huddled in a pool of urine, the old man clung to the railings for dear life as he stared at them. Phoenix sighed.

CHAPTER TWENTY

Ethan paced the length of his living room, unable to sit still with the adrenaline still flowing through his veins.

A fucking demon.

He blew out a breath and looked again at Phoenix to reassure himself she was in one piece. She'd fallen quiet and retreated into herself on the way back to his apartment. The cuts on her face were healing quickly thanks to a balm Lily had applied, and her own healing abilities, but he could tell she was shaken. Hell, he was too.

"And you're sure it was a demon?" Lily asked for the third time as she looked up from the large tome she was scouring.

"As sure as I can be." Ethan ran a hand through his hair, trying to remember any important detail from the night.

"I didn't think demons could cross into this world," Phoenix said, finally breaking her silence.

"They shouldn't be able to," Ethan agreed. "The Council reinforced the barrier between their world and ours in order to maintain the balance. It doesn't make sense."

"Actually ..." Nate looked up from his laptop as all eyes turned to him. "It might."

He flipped the laptop around to face the room and pointed to a block of text he'd highlighted. "I've found some references to the prophecy in Council archives –"

"The Council archives, how the hell did you –"

"Don't ask, don't tell." Nate grinned and held up a hand. "Anyway, there's a reference to a tear in the fabric, a kind of 'End of Days'. Seems a little overdramatic, but given current events ..."

Shade let out a low whistle.

Phoenix cleared her throat and squirmed in her chair as she raised a hand. "Not to ask a stupid question, but tear in what fabric? You mean the barrier between worlds?"

Nate nodded, all humour gone from his face.

"But that would mean ..." Phoenix paled.

"More demons."

Ethan felt the fight leave him in a breath. The demon they'd faced tonight was only a minor demon; if it had been any stronger, it would have taken possession of a Supe rather than a human. Or worse, it would have been able to take form on its own. It had taken so little for the demon to overpower him, and even less to stop Phoenix in her tracks. How could they fight something that was stronger and harder to kill than they were?

"Have we any idea how to separate a demon from its host?" Ethan directed his question to Lily, shivering as he remembered the woman's body disappearing into the black depths of the river.

"I've found a spell ..." Lily said.

Green eyes met his, and he knew there was a but coming.

"... but it's not enough to separate the demon. We need to be able to banish it too or it will just find another victim."

Another innocent to leech the life out of. Things had been complicated enough when they just had to protect humans from the Lore. Now this?

"You said the Council played a part in banishing them the first time around?" Phoenix looked at him for confirmation. "Who'd be strong enough to breach the Council's wards?"

Ethan didn't manage to stop the surprise from showing on his face, which earned him an annoyed glare from Phoenix. It was a bloody good question and he wondered why it hadn't occurred to them already.

"The Dublin coven?" Ethan looked at Lily, who shook her head.

"They'd never be strong enough by themselves."

"So, maybe they're not by themselves," Shade said, staring pointedly at Phoenix.

Too tired to go around in circles any longer, Ethan decided it was time to call it a night. He ushered everyone to the door and found himself once more standing alone in the apartment with Phoenix as she held back from the others.

"She was alive, Ethan. The woman. She was still in there. If we could have just restrained her ..." Haunted eyes met his as she pulled her coat tightly around herself.

"We wouldn't have known what to do anyway."

CHAPTER TWENTY-ONE

Phoenix poured every ounce of frustration and every bit of confusion into the punch, viciously punishing the hard leather for the feelings of weakness and ineptitude that had been dredged up by the previous night's patrol. The punchbag merely clunked on its chain, indifferent to her inner turmoil.

"Don't take it personally, the whole gym's been rigged to withstand our strength." Ethan's tone was teasing as he dropped a 500kg bar back on the rack and strolled over to her. "I'm sure you don't really punch like a girl."

The gym really was impressive, and she'd jumped at the chance to test it out. Comprising the whole bottom floor of the converted warehouse that housed Ethan's apartment, the walls and ceiling were reinforced with thick steel beams to support the heavier weights and frames in the lifting area. Combat weapons of all kinds lined the walls, and one half of the room was dedicated purely to martial arts training. It was Phoenix's idea of heaven.

"C'mon, how about taking some of that frustration out on me?" Ethan started walking towards the training mats without waiting for her answer.

What an arrogant sod, Phoenix thought, stubbornly refusing to follow him and his presumptuous arse. Although, she did feel an irritating need to redeem herself after their first training session. He'd walked away from that fight without a clear win. Sure, he might argue differently, but he hadn't pinned her. The competitor in her needed a clear winner, even if that meant getting her arse handed to her on a plate.

"What do I get out of it?" she echoed the question she'd once asked him, back before life had turned completely upside down.

"Tell you what ..." He turned back to look at her appraisingly. "Best of three. Winner of each round gets to ask a question of their choice. Honest answers only."

Well, that made her stop.

He was definitely stronger than her, and a more experienced fighter, but vamp trumped wolf in speed. If she could use that to her advantage ...

"Unless you're afraid of losing again?" Ethan's voice was innocent, but his eyes taunted and dared her to prove him wrong.

Screw that! She could lose with the best of them. She smiled a saccharine smile, sashayed to the mat, and threw her towel and water bottle to the side.

"No weapons. External or otherwise," she said, and pointedly looked at Ethan's hands. It had been hard enough explaining the residual scratches from the demon attack to Abi. She didn't want to explain claw marks a second time.

He gave her a boy scout salute, though she doubted he'd ever been one in his life.

They started easy. A light jab here, a snap kick there; testing each other's defences in a harmless warm-up dance. Speed and strength were kept to human levels as they flowed through locks and releases, making no real attempt to attack.

As her muscles loosened and the blood began to flow, Phoenix started testing the limits of her speed. She made Ethan work harder for his strikes and managed to stay just barely ahead of him each step of the way, waiting for an opening.

A feint to the head allowed her the moment of distraction she needed to drop low and sweep his legs from under him. She turned into his stumbling body and wrapped her legs firmly around his upper arm. With a sharp tug, she pulled his arm into a lock that forced him to face-plant the mat.

And led to her winning round one.

She waited until he acknowledged her win with a tap before she released the lock and jumped up, feeling quietly pleased with herself. Accepting her offered hand, Ethan followed her to standing and cracked his neck as he waited expectantly for her first question.

So many thoughts were running through her mind, but there was one that had plagued her ever since their first training session. "How did you get involved with the prophecy?" she asked as she thought back to the change in his demeanour when she'd asked why he cared.

Again, something clouded his eyes that she couldn't quite identify. Ethan grabbed his towel and bottle from the edge of the mat. He wiped the back of his neck and took a large gulp of water before answering.

"It wasn't intentional, believe me." He sighed. "I'd left the pack and was moving around, trying to find my feet. But it seemed like everywhere I went, weird shit followed me."

She raised her eyebrows in feigned disbelief, which caused him to laugh.

"I knew I'd been sheltered by the pack, but what I saw just didn't seem right to me. Surely the Council wouldn't tolerate the level of bloodlust I was seeing in the vamps. And the wolves ... their behaviour wasn't normal. So, I started looking into it a bit, asking a few questions."

Phoenix watched silently as he threw his towel around his neck and rubbed his hair absently with it. There were a million questions going through her mind and she was itching to interrupt, but something about his tone told her to stay quiet.

"At this point I'd been gone a while and my dad wanted me home. He sent our Omega, Sean, to talk sense into me. Only, he never got the chance. The night he caught up with me in Belfast, we stumbled on a vamp feeding." A muscle jumped at the side of his jaw. "The baby couldn't have been more than a few months old. Its mother had been discarded in a heap on the ground, still reaching for her baby even –"

Ethan shuddered, his voice becoming void of emotion. "We fought the vamp, but Sean was killed and the vamp got away. I've been trying to track it since."

"And now, if you walk away from the prophecy, he'll have died for nothing," she said quietly.

He nodded, looking in surprise at the water bottle he held in his hand – now crushed.

Phoenix took a shuddery breath, needing to break the tension. "Okay, you ready to get your arse whooped again?"

He grinned, seeming to shake off the horrors of his story. Without another word, he threw his towel aside and lunged at her, almost knocking her off balance.

Mentally chastising herself, she slipped his grasp and moved behind him before throwing in a sly kidney jab. With each strike, they grew more familiar with each other's movements. Soon, they were moving at such speed that they would have been a blur to the human eye.

Just as quickly, Ethan got the upper hand and trapped her in a chokehold from behind. Without a second thought, she dropped her weight and flipped the solid lump of muscle over her shoulder. Ethan's surprise at finding himself on his back gave her just enough time to pin him, and she threw in a little wink for good measure.

She slid off him so he could sit up, but decided to save her energy by staying seated on the ground for question two. "What were you running from?"

Ethan's head snapped up. "What?"

"Why did you leave? You said you don't change at the full moon without your pack. It sounds to me like you're punishing yourself for something."

Ethan rested his elbows on his knees and rubbed a hand over his face. "I guess I set the terms, didn't I?" He paused. "My pack is in Donegal. My father is the Alpha. And I'm the first-born."

"So ... that would make you next in line for Alpha," she said as she dug deep into the recesses of her mind for the limited knowledge she had on Lore traditions.

He grimaced. "A fact I resented for a very long time. I love my pack, and my family, but growing up, it was always about the responsibility. I guess I just needed a break from it all. So I left."

"I didn't think wolves did well without their pack?" Phoenix eyed him with growing curiosity.

"They don't, generally. Stronger the wolf, easier it is. A relief even. At least for a while."

Before she could probe any further, he jumped to his feet and extended a hand to help her up. "I think it's time for me to reclaim my dignity," he said with a grin.

She snorted and adjusted her hair back into a tight ponytail. "Good luck with that."

Round three began. It was much the same as the previous rounds, with sweat making their skin slick. However, it ended with one important difference: Phoenix found herself flat on her back, not quite sure how she got there, and wondering numbly if the two previous rounds had all been a set up.

Ignoring Ethan's offered hand, she got to her feet and wrapped her arms around herself in a vain attempt to protect from whatever difficult truth he would force her to divulge.

"How have you managed to stay off the radar for so long?"

His question startled her. It was one he'd asked before, back in the bar. Why was it even relevant enough to waste his question?

"My parents were banished by their families for their relationship." She forced her voice to remain neutral. "As you can imagine, they didn't want much to do with the Lore after that. When they found out my mother was pregnant" – she shrugged – "they didn't want to chance my safety."

"So, you've been living amongst humans your whole life?" Ethan's eyebrows raised in surprise as he looked at her.

Phoenix hesitated for a second before shaking her head, reluctant to share too much, but unable to stomach a lie.

"My parents went missing when I was fifteen. I spent some time with a vampire clan until I was old enough to fend for myself."

"Did they know what you were?"

"Only the head of the clan, and a few of his top security. I was kept separate from the others so that no one would suspect anything."

He seemed to digest the information for some time before he finally looked at her again. "It sounds very lonely."

Not able to face his pity, she simply shrugged and walked off the mat. "It was fun sparring with you," she said over her shoulder, not quite sure if it was the truth.

CHAPTER TWENTY-TWO

The biting wind carried a strong, ever present, threat of rain as Ethan strolled down Grafton Street with Phoenix at his side. The late hour had transformed their surroundings to a pale representation of its daytime persona. Shop fronts were dark and uninviting. The street was empty of music and the life it attracted. Small groups of volunteers had set up makeshift tables and were working tirelessly to dole out the last of their offerings to the homeless. The queue of people in need was an even more depressing sight on the cold winter night.

Beside him, Phoenix's terrifyingly pointy stiletto boots clacked on the cobblestones. The shadows of the night did little to blunt the fiery red of her hair, and her green eyes almost glowed as they adjusted to the dim light. He had to admit that she pulled off the badass look pretty well, though he knew now it was all a front.

Though things had been quiet the past few nights, they continued their patrols, keeping an eye out for any clues or a chance to prevent attacks from rogue Supes. If he was honest, he was also looking for an opportunity to test Phoenix. She'd held her own quite well in hand to hand combat, but he'd yet to see her use her powers aside from the night he'd first met her. It worried him, especially since there had been rumours of further demon possessions.

"Abi's starting to get suspicious about me being out all night," she said, breaking the comfortable silence as they veered down one of the dark side-streets.

Ethan smiled at the mention of the bubbly human bartender. He could well imagine her curiosity being piqued.

Phoenix rolled her eyes. "She's convinced I'm seeing someone."

"So, tell her you're seeing me," he offered, surprised when his wolf took that moment to perk up its ears.

Nudging him with her shoulder, she laughed, "Yeah right, then I'd really never hear the end of it."

He shrugged nonchalantly, wondering in the back of his mind why her response bothered him. "Just thought it might help get her off your back –"

The loud smashing of glass stopped them in their tracks and was quickly followed by a screeching alarm. Phoenix met his look of surprise with one of her own before they set off at a sprint to the end of the street. They made sure to keep close to the shadows as they peered around the corner.

Across the road, just off another dark side-street, they could see two black forms highlighted by a flickering streetlight. Whoever it was stood arguing as a number of other shadowy forms leapt through the broken window of a shopfront.

Angry words drifted to Ethan and Phoenix over the din of the alarm: "Idiot", "Kill us".

Ethan sniffed the air and found the unmistakable scent of incense and herbs. "Witches," he growled.

Phoenix grabbed his arm and pointed to a dark sign above the shop that read *Ulysses Rare Books*. "What would they be doing breaking into an old bookshop?"

"Looking for some light reading?" He edged forward, gesturing for her to follow behind him.

The two witches in front of the shop were so busy arguing that they didn't hear his approach. Ethan grabbed the largest of the two from behind and his arm snaked across the witch's throat, cutting off the man's air supply before the slightest curse could be uttered. A quick glance assured him that Phoenix had the other witch under control, and they dragged the unconscious bodies into the shadows.

Standing this close to the bookshop made his fur prickle as his wolf shifted closely beneath the surface. This was definitely more than just an old bookshop.

Conscious that the alarm would have notified the Gardaí, Ethan stepped carefully over the jagged edges of the window into the shop. The jolt of electricity only lasted a second as he crossed the threshold, but it had him shaking his head to clear the static from his ears.

One look at Phoenix told him she'd felt it too. He waited for a nod to confirm she was all right before he continued forward silently.

The dark of the night, coupled with the flickering streetlight outside, gave the shop an eerie feel. Looming bookcases cast long shadows and seemed to come alive as they stood watchfully on guard.

Aside from the large tomes strewn across the glass-littered floor, the only sign of intrusion was the murmur of voices coming from a room at the back of the shop. A strange glow seeped out from under the closed door and the closer he moved towards it, the heavier the air felt.

His wolf clawed restlessly and tried to take control. Ethan fought the urge. Something was not quite right with the feeling. Instinct told him it would be a bad idea to let his wolf loose.

Without warning, the door at the back of the shop flung open and he was blinded by a scorching white light. Beside him, he heard Phoenix curse, followed by a loud crash. As the spots began to clear from his vision, someone barrelled into him from behind. He twisted his body to avoid face-planting the floor, but his shoulder hit the ground with a bone-jarring thud.

The body that landed on top of him was female. Small and unnaturally strong. Her features were twisted and ugly, any sense of humanity long since gone. Pinned beneath her small frame and the floor, Ethan struggled to free his arm. He only just managed to turn his head and miss the dagger she plunged towards his face.

Using the witch's momentum against her, he pushed up through his lower body and threw her off. But just as he tried to rise to his feet, Ethan's legs buckled beneath him.

The loud crack of bone sounded in his ears and, against his will, his body started to shift.

His wolf howled in agony at the unnatural change being forced upon him. Tendons popped as his limbs contorted. Muscles elongated and tore. Sharp fangs pierced his gums and fur sprouted from the backs of his hands.

Through the fog of pain, he heard Phoenix scream his name. Adrenaline surged at the fear in her voice, and he fought to gain control. His eyes searched wildly until they finally found her grappling on the floor with a male witch.

Ethan tried to move towards her, but his knees buckled again and he fell forward onto his hands. His sharp claws dug into the wooden floor as his spine twisted and arched.

Phoenix met his eyes, and in an instant, her expression changed from surprise to steely resolve. With a surge of power, she flipped the witch off her, sending him careening into a wall. She made to move towards him, her hand reaching out, but he pulled back, not trusting his control under the forced change.

"Witch." He ground out the syllables painfully, his now misshapen jaw making speech almost impossible.

The flash of understanding on her face was the last thing he saw before everything went black.

Phoenix's blood ran cold as she watched Ethan collapse to the ground. Every instinct in her screamed to go to him, but she ignored the pull and forced herself to look for the witch responsible.

She found him shrouded by shadows in the corner. He stood tall with his head back and palms wide open as a continuous stream of chanting oozed from his barely moving mouth. For a moment, it seemed as if the witch was oblivious to her presence, but then his head lowered, and Phoenix was met with the whitest eyes she'd ever seen.

Her previously cold blood began to ice over as the witch fixed her with an unwavering stare. She felt her limbs grow heavy, and her body refused all commands to move.

The image of Ethan slumped helpless on the floor flashed into her mind, and anger at the violation flooded her system. Anger not just at the violation of her body, but of his, and his wolf's.

She strained against the invisible bonds that held her and channelled all of her anger. With her eyes fixated on the witch, something snapped, allowing her to move forward.

The witch's strange eyes widened in shock just before Phoenix lengthened her fangs and plunged them deep into his jugular.

A sharp gasp drew her attention back to Ethan. She dropped the now lifeless body and spat out the poisonous blood that tried to slide down the back of her throat. Rushing to his side, she slid down beside him, the fear that gripped her heart only beginning to ease when she could feel the rise and fall of his chest beneath her hand. A sheen of sweat covered his skin as his body slowly, and agonisingly, started to realign itself.

Not knowing what else to do, Phoenix held him close and gave him whatever strength she could while he worked through the pain.

Eventually Ethan lifted his head. His eyes were still strained but they were now a clear brown and showed no sign of his wolf. "The witches?" he asked hoarsely.

His question brought her sharply back to their surroundings as she realised her carelessness. She hadn't even checked if anyone was left alive.

Strangely though, the store appeared to be empty. Even of bodies.

She shook her head and mentally berated herself. "Gone."

CHAPTER TWENTY-THREE

Ethan listened vaguely to the chatter of voices that filled his apartment. His head was still pounding as he gingerly stretched out each finger and checked for any lasting damage. Phoenix's concerned gaze burned into him. He wanted to reassure her, but he couldn't. In truth, he was shaken, even more than he'd like to admit. Each aching joint reminded him of the violation he'd been helpless to defend against, and the idea made him want to punch something.

How the hell had the witches been able to control his change? Nothing other than the moon and his Alpha should've been able to do that. And he was even strong enough to fight those.

"Do we have any idea what they were after?" Lily paced the length of the living room for what seemed like the hundredth time since joining them.

Ethan looked at the young witch and noticed the stiff set of her shoulders and limp lifelessness of her long blonde hair. She'd latched on to the prophecy and the witches with a determined focus that was growing unhealthy. She hadn't taken time to grieve, and it worried him what would happen when the distraction was gone.

The comforting tempo of Nate's keyboard tapping suddenly stopped, breaking Ethan's train of thought.

"Maybe ..." Nate waved Lily over to the table where he sat.

Ethan watched impatiently as the two whispered and pointed at something on Nate's laptop.

"Are you going to share with the rest of us?" he snapped as he stood to continue the pacing where Lily had left off.

"Sorry, we were just looking at something." Lily looked up from the screen, the luminescence highlighting the concerned set of her mouth.

Phoenix and Shade both edged forward on their seats in response to the obvious tension. Ethan stopped his pacing with a sigh. Could it not just be good news for once?

Everyone gathered around the table as Nate turned the laptop to face them. The screen was full of small thumbnails, each with a single line of text underneath. The pictures were difficult to make out, but all showed an object of some type. Most were old, some looked ancient.

"I found our bookshop owner on the dark web," Nate explained. "It seems he specialises in old and extremely powerful relics."

"So, the witches were after one of these relics?" Phoenix asked.

Ethan could see her mentally connecting the dots as she moved closer to the screen with interest.

Lily nodded. "It would seem like a logical assumption."

"Do we know which one?" A bad feeling settled in the pit of Ethan's stomach, and now, even his wolf was pacing.

Nate clicked on one of the thumbnails, enlarging the image so it filled the screen.

"What the hell is that?" Shade asked, a frown etched on to his features.

Ethan felt a similar sense of confusion as he looked more closely. The image showed a small plate of what appeared to be solid gold. There was a symbol carved in the middle and it looked well worn with its edges fading. From what he could make out, the symbol showed some kind of serpent or dragon eating its own tail. It didn't look familiar to him, but something about it made his skin crawl.

"This is the relic we think the witches might have been after." Lily's voice was grave as she directed her answer to them all. "It's a very powerful talisman called an Ouroboros. It was believed to represent the endless cycle of time. Some say that whoever possesses it can gain control of this cycle and bend it to their will."

"Shit," Ethan muttered under his breath.

"Um ... that doesn't sound good." Phoenix's worried eyes met his over the laptop and he looked away, yet again unable to reassure her.

His earlier sense of foreboding increased and his wolf shuffled restlessly. What the hell were the witches up to? Blood sacrifices, dark magic, and now this? Although they were a powerful faction within the Lore, witches were never a leading force for change or upheaval. They usually preferred to align themselves with a stronger contender or stay out of the spotlight altogether. That meant they had to be working for someone. And they had to believe that someone had the upper hand.

"So, what's the plan, boss?" Shade had resumed his trademark slouch against the wall and was watching him closely.

Ethan tried to organise his thoughts as he rubbed a rough hand over his face. They needed information, and aside from the witches, there was only one person that could give it to them.

"Take Lily, and go speak to the owner of the bookshop," he said, directing his comment to Nate. "We need him to confirm what was taken. I doubt there's any point checking the police report if he's dealing on the black market."

Nate saluted, shut down the laptop, and packed away a random assortment of gadgets.

Ethan looked at Phoenix, finally able to meet her eyes. Other than the persistent concerned glances she threw his way, her features showed no lasting strain from the night's events. But every time he closed his eyes, he could hear her scream his name.

She'd been left to face the witches alone, and he'd been powerless to help her. The knowledge caused an ugly, painful knot in his gut that wouldn't unravel; it also made him angry.

Despite everything, she still hadn't used her powers. Sure, she'd torn the witch's throat out with her fangs, but physical strength and a bit of extra speed weren't going to keep her alive. Not against other Supes. Or demons.

How could he keep her safe if she wouldn't fight?

Realising the room had gone quiet around him, he looked at the expectant gazes and wondered who else he would fail before this was over.

"Tomorrow," he said, "we train."

Phoenix looked at Ethan standing on the mat across from her. His face said he meant business. His yellow eyes said his wolf did too.

As soon as Nate and Lily had confirmed their suspicions with the shop owner, Ethan had ordered them all to the gym to train at the break of dawn. Even as a half-vampire who thrived at night, the lack of sleep was starting to wear on her.

"We need to up your training." Ethan gestured impatiently for her to move towards the middle of the mat. "We don't have time to take it easy anymore."

"Hey! I saved your ass, remember?" Sure, she'd been scared as hell, but she'd held her own and that had to count for something.

"What's that, boss?" Nate turned from the target that was playing victim to his knife skills with a wide grin on his face. "You're getting your ass saved by girls now too?"

Irritation clouded Ethan's face, and Phoenix noticed with amusement the rhythmic twitch in the muscle of his jaw. Curiosity tempted her to ask for clarification, but a low growl from his direction made her rethink, and she moved to the centre of the mat with a sigh.

"You were lucky last night," Ethan cut straight to the chase. "The witches won't let you get that close next time. You need to start using your other powers."

She felt herself tense. Her body became utterly still as she fought to slow her breathing and control the involuntary reaction to his words. This wasn't the first time he'd broached the subject, but something about his tone said he wasn't going to let it drop this time.

"I told you before, I don't have any. That light thing was just a weird fluke. I can't do it again." Phoenix dug her fingernails into the palm of her hand. He was expecting too much of her. She couldn't do it. *Wouldn't* do it.

"It's okay." Ethan held his hands out in a placating gesture. "We're going to start slow. But we *are* going to start, Phoenix."

Without warning, he leapt for her, giving her no chance to prepare or gather her defences. For the first time since they'd begun training together, she sensed a difference in his intensity. His eyes glowed yellow and he moved with an animalistic grace. More than ever, his energy screamed predator.

She fought with everything she had. Her vampire speed, she used. Her vampire strength, she most definitely used. Hell, her fangs even made an involuntary appearance at one stage. Still, it wasn't enough.

Ethan pushed her relentlessly and nothing she did satisfied him. The harder she fought, the more frustrated he seemed to become. Obviously convinced that she was holding out, the expectant look in his feral eyes pleaded silently with her.

Eventually, her endurance failed, and with a final tackle, Ethan pinned her beneath him. His body was firm against hers, yellow eyes searching her own for ... something.

An uncomfortable silence filled the gym around them, and Phoenix was suddenly very aware of Ethan's hips pressed tightly against hers. Squirming under the unseen scrutiny of the others, she wriggled out from under him and tried to ignore the unintentional friction it caused.

He followed her up from the ground, eyes no longer meeting hers as he grabbed his towel from the side of the mat.

"Let's leave it there for now," he called over his shoulder on his way to the door. "I want everyone back here tonight for more training."

Phoenix scrubbed her hand over her face. *What the hell just happened?*

Needing some air, she turned to find the gym empty of all but Shade.

"It's not going to work, you know." The animosity was clear in his expression as he stalked towards her.

"I don't know what you're talking about." Phoenix sighed wearily and tried to step around him. Her body was already aching from the training session with Ethan and she was in no mood for a confrontation.

Shade moved to block her retreat, pressing himself close as he let her see the full force of hatred behind his icy blue eyes. "Ethan might not see you for what you are, but I do."

Tiredness, frustration, and confusion all caught up on her at once, eroding any patience she might have had for the situation.

"I don't give a fuck what you think of me, Shade. Just get out of my way and let me go home." She squared her shoulders and looked him dead in the eye, not willing to be intimidated by his attitude.

Tension filled the air between them, causing the hairs on her arms to raise. Could she take him on if she needed to? She'd never really seen him fight, but as a full vamp he would likely be faster than her at the very least.

Just when Phoenix thought she might have to test the theory, Shade stepped to the side and opened his arm in a wide sweep towards the door. She hesitated for a moment before walking past him.

"He'll never feel the same about you."

Her feet faltered just as she made to step through the door.

"We don't want you here, Phoenix," Shade said softly. "Why don't you go back to your cushy little life and stop pretending to be a hero? You'll never be one of us."

And with that parting blow, he pushed past her and disappeared from sight.

———

Phoenix shoved open the heavy door of the pub and took a deep breath, letting the familiar scent of home wash over her. She'd broken the speed limit the whole way back in an attempt to get as much distance as she could from Shade and his words, but still they rang in her head.

He'd made it sound like she was the one trying to push into their lives, trying to be part of their little makeshift pack. But it was the other way around. They'd forced themselves into her life! All she was trying to do was get the mess cleared up so she could go back to her "cushy life" as he'd so scathingly put it.

Grateful that it was still too early for the cleaner to be in, Phoenix slipped quietly towards the back of the bar. She was hoping to catch a few hours' sleep before she had to face people again.

Fate seemed to have other ideas, however.

As she stepped through the door at the back, she ran straight into Abi. Her friend stood wrapped in a fluffy purple dressing gown that engulfed her petite frame. Her arms were crossed as she leaned against the stairs that led to their apartment.

"I heard you go out early. I was worried."

Phoenix looked away as the guilt temporarily wiped all other thoughts from her mind. "I couldn't sleep. Thought maybe I'd go for a run."

"Bullshit."

The softly spoken word pulled her attention back to Abi in surprise. Concerned blue eyes watched her expectantly and for the first time ever, she didn't know what to say to her best friend.

"I'm worried about you, Phoenix." Abi unfolded her arms with a sigh. "You haven't been yourself ... not since this guy came on the scene."

"It's not like that, I –"

Abi held up a hand to stop her protests

"If you don't want to talk to me about it, that's fine," she said, although the hurt expression in her eyes stated otherwise. "But don't insult our friendship by lying to me."

A lump formed in Phoenix's throat that caused a dull ache and made it difficult to swallow. She wanted to deny Abi's words, but how could she when they were true? Silence stretched between them and unspoken words caused a void that Phoenix didn't know how to cross.

"I'm calling Paul in to cover the bar. Take the night off and get some rest. You look like shit." Her friend turned her back without another word and started up the stairs.

At the top, she looked back over her shoulder one last time. "I love you, Phoenix. I'm here when you're ready to talk."

152

CHAPTER TWENTY-FOUR

Il Maestro regarded the silver coin as it burned an imprint into the palm of his hand. It was funny how such small, innocuous things could cause so much pain. The searing ache of silver had not subsided over the years. He merely found he'd come to enjoy the challenge it posed and the focus the pain demanded. It was now a useful reminder of the hardship that must be endured in order to achieve greatness.

Some things did not need to be endured, however, and he'd reached the end of his patience with the constant interference in his operations. There was too much on the line; he'd waited too long for this.

"Tell me again what happened at the bookshop," he ordered his head of security. He needed to get the scene straight in his head.

In quick, concise detail, Raphael recounted the botched robbery, including a list of casualties. "Esme has confirmed the talisman is now safely in her possession, however."

Il Maestro waved the comment away, troubled by something else entirely. "What could the witches tell us about the attackers?"

"Not much. The ones that got away were either more concerned with the talisman, or were feeling somewhat forgetful thanks to their injuries." Scorn laced Raphael's tone, making it all too clear what he thought of the witches' weakness.

"They've confirmed that one of the attackers bore the signature of a wolf. The other signature was ... unclear."

It was an odd choice of words. The witches were barely a generation away from being human, but even their inferior skills should have been able to identify the signature.

"It seems strange, don't you think, that we have once again run into setbacks as a result of a mangy dog." Il Maestro spoke mostly to himself as his eyes followed the path of the coin over the back of his hand.

Raphael placed enlarged images on the desk in front of him. "We managed to pull these from CCTV footage in the area of the robbery. And this" – he placed another image on the desk, grainier but still legible – "was taken from Temple Bar on the night that the test subjects were attacked."

Even in the poor quality black and white images, the similarities were evident. "So, we're dealing with the same subject."

"We believe so."

The confirmation didn't surprise him; it was as he expected. Much of their recent testing had focused on werewolves, it was possible they'd inadvertently drawn attention to themselves as a result. Still, another thought was beginning to take shape in the back of his mind.

As he looked back at the images from the night of the robbery, it was the second subject that drew his attention. Encased in shadows, the figure was little more than a silhouette in the print, but there was one very definable feature that stood out to him.

"Subject two was a woman?" He looked to Raphael for confirmation.

"None of the cameras picked her up clearly, but based on the shape, and the witches limited information, that would seem to be the case." A somewhat disconcerting smile settled over Raphael's face. "Quite a fit one too if the silhouette is anything to go by."

Not for the first time, Il Maestro was reminded why this vampire was his right-hand man. A vision of control and efficient practicality, but beneath the surface lay a level of depravity that rivalled any other he'd encountered. Generally, he could appreciate, and encourage, such proclivities, but for now, they needed to tread carefully.

He debated his decision for a moment before giving the order. "I think it's time we fetch our hybrid."

Raphael's mouth split into a wide grin, displaying his razor-sharp fangs and transforming his face into a thing of nightmares.

CHAPTER TWENTY-FIVE

Phoenix felt an unexpected sense of comfort and relief being back in her own gym. The smells, the noises, the familiar faces, and a convenient ban on supernatural powers. It seemed like an ideal place to satisfy Ethan's desire to train but keep his incessant nagging at bay. So she'd thought at least.

"Dammit, wolf, what's your problem?"

She blew sweat-soaked hair out of her eyes. Had he decided pummelling her to death was the best way to stop the prophecy?

Ethan merely grunted and flung a towel at her as he turned for the changing rooms. "Get dressed. Abi will be expecting you."

Phoenix sighed and wiped her face with the towel. It had been so tempting not to answer her phone after the last training session. So tempting to just stay home and forget it all. She'd even cancelled her round of patrol the following night by claiming the bar was short-staffed and she needed to work. However, it didn't take long for guilt to get the better of her.

As it turned out, Ethan had fallen off the radar himself for a few days, so no one seemed too concerned about her absence; a fact that only reinforced Shade's words. Questions to his whereabouts had been met with vague responses, but he was definitely crankier since returning. If she didn't know better, she'd swear it was the full moon again already.

Once at the showers, Phoenix struggled out of her now-drenched sports top, wrestling to free herself of the clingy material. Every muscle in her body ached, and even her bones were making their protest known.

The presence of humans hadn't given her the upper hand in the slightest. If anything, he'd gone harder on her since he couldn't push the issue of her non-existent powers. She was still glad she'd made him train on her terms for once, though. The distance from the others, Shade in particular, gave her a bit of the perspective she'd been needing.

By the time the scalding water finished its pounding dance over her skin, she was even feeling somewhat understanding of the stress Ethan was under. Somewhat.

She took a couple of minutes to blow dry her hair – death by pneumonia would be very anti-climactic – before grabbing her jacket and heading outside to find Ethan under the dim glow of a streetlight.

The sight made Phoenix stop. It was odd for him to place himself in such a visible, open position; he was usually more careful than that. Her concern grew as she noted the stiff set of his stance and the strain showing around his eyes.

What the hell is up with him?

Before she could comment, he shifted his weight from the lamppost and motioned for her to start walking.

She pulled her jacket tightly around herself and followed him in silence. Her breath misted in front of her face as the chilling air hit her lungs. The cold didn't seem to bother Ethan at all, and Phoenix found herself envious of the naturally high body temperature that was typical of wolves and shifters.

The streets were deserted as they walked in the direction of the pub. The near freezing temperatures and heavy threat of rain encouraged anyone with sense to curl up in front of a warm fire for the night.

"Why did you want to train here?" Ethan asked, breaking the silence that sat heavily between them.

She hesitated, wondering how honest to be. In the end, she opted for his tactic: keep it vague. "I just needed to be close to home for a while."

"Shade said you weren't around for training while I was gone."

Phoenix tensed. What else had Shade being saying to him when she wasn't around? "I'm sure he didn't miss me too much."

Clearly noticing the edge to her tone, Ethan gave her a mildly reprimanding look. She fought the urge to stick her tongue out at him and focused instead on the path in front of her.

"I know he's not an easy person to get on with, but Shade's a good guy once you get past the exterior."

"Sure."

"His Sire abandoned him before he'd even finished turning. He was all alone, yet he managed not to give in to blood lust."

Ethan's words stopped Phoenix short, just as he knew they would. Young vampires were extremely susceptible to blood lust; it was why the Council imposed such strict rules around siring. For a newly turned vampire to wake alone and control those urges was astounding.

"His Sire just left him to turn?"

Ethan nodded. "He has no memories from before he was turned. At least that's what he says."

She chewed this information over as they lapsed back into silence. Had she been too quick to judge Shade? Sure, he had a shitty attitude, but waking up dead and alone had to leave you with some issues. Rather than making her feel more charitable, the thought just made her more irritated. Shade had been a complete dick to her since she'd met him. And for what? All she was doing was trying to help.

She blew out a long breath and forced herself to let go of the silent argument that was brewing in her head. It would do no good wasting precious energy being pissed; best to just forget it.

As they passed Whitethorn Park, Phoenix's thoughts turned to the strange makeshift pack Ethan had formed. He'd surrounded himself with a member of nearly every race of the Lore and seemed oblivious to how strange that was. What would he do when it was all over?

"Will you go back to your pack? When everything is over with the prophecy?"

He looked at her in surprise, a puzzled expression settling on his face. "I hadn't really thought about it. I guess so. There'd be no real reason for me to stick around."

"Do you not think the others would miss you?"

More confusion. "Why would they?"

Phoenix let out a short laugh of disbelief. "You're their leader. They look up to you."

At her words, his expression closed down completely, only the telltale muscle tick in his jaw telling her she'd hit a nerve.

"I'm nobody's leader," he said tightly, and turned away from her.

More than ready to call bullshit, Phoenix stopped walking and stood with her hands on her hips. "Really? Well, it doesn't stop you from bossing everyone around!"

He gave her a warning glare but didn't respond.

"Oh, come on, Ethan. Lie to yourself all you want, but you're an Alpha through and through. You can't hide from what you are."

He turned on her in an instant, his eyes flashing angrily. "Really? You're one to talk, Phoenix."

She reeled, the sting of his anger catching her completely by surprise. "Me?"

"Yes, you, Phoenix! You've spent your whole life trying to run from who you are, and now you're going to judge me?"

Phoenix stood frozen to the spot. Her gut clenched as if his words had been a solid right hook. All the anger and frustration of recent weeks began to rise like bile in her throat, burning open countless old wounds.

"I don't have a problem with who I am," she spat back, digging her nails into the palm of her hands to stop them trembling. "It's everyone else that seems to have a problem with that."

"Oh, cry me a fucking river, Phoenix. You've had a hard life? Well, guess what? Everyone has. Maybe if you started accepting who you are, everyone else would too."

"I do accept who I am," she shouted, no longer feeling understanding or conciliatory in the slightest.

"Then why do you hold your powers back?" Ethan yelled, equally as loud.

Without thinking, she took a step back and a look of triumph flashed in his eyes. Anger was quickly replaced with numbness as the walls she'd perfected her whole life were thrown up to block the pain caused by his words. Funny, she hadn't even realised they had come down to start with.

Without another word, she turned and walked away. The deafening thud of her heart the only sound that followed her.

Phoenix was shaking as she strode purposefully in the direction of the bar. Adrenaline flooded her system, making her feel sick to her stomach, and she pointedly ignored the strange burning in her throat that indicated the embarrassing potential for tears.

Who the hell does he think he is? He better not even think about following me ...

Actually, why the hell wasn't he following her? He should be rushing to apologise; he'd been completely out of line!

Where had that outburst even come from? She'd obviously hit a sore spot, but that didn't mean he had to lash out at her. She was working her arse off trying to help; it wasn't her fault if she wasn't living up to his expectations –

Her mental ramblings were swiftly cut off by a snarl as a dead weight hit her, dropping her to the cold, unforgiving concrete.

Her head hit the ground with a solid *thud*, and the flash of pain caused her vision to swim. A heavy weight pinned her and made it impossible to move. Her lungs struggled to expand beneath the restriction.

She tried to get a look at her assailant, but a large hand shoved her face unceremoniously back towards the ground. Her senses screamed vampire, but the blow to her head, coupled with reducing oxygen levels, made it hard to think straight. Whoever her attacker was, he wasn't human.

The hard grit of the ground rubbed against her cheek, and she could feel his warm breath on the back of her neck. Large hands moved from her shoulders to run suggestively down along her sides. The movement caused her heart rate to ricochet and her vision to clear abruptly.

With considerable effort, she forced herself to slow her breathing and let her body become soft and compliant. The pressure on her back eased a little, and a deep, masculine voice chuckled softly in her ear. The sound made her skin crawl; it was all she could do not to scratch her skin off.

She waited until he was preoccupied with his uninhibited groping before she snapped her head back with as much force as she could muster from her limited vantage point. Her efforts were rewarded with a satisfying crunch of bone and an angry grunt as blood splattered the ground around her.

His hold on her didn't give, however. Instead, it tightened as he hauled her to her feet like a ragdoll. She struggled against him as every cell in her body screamed to get away from his touch. A heavy heat began to build in the palms of her hands.

"Uh uh, no you don't," he growled as he slammed her against a nearby wall.

His voice. There was something strangely familiar about it. A niggling memory tugged at her consciousness, but before she could think on it further, she felt a sharp prick in her neck and all strength left her body in an instant.

Fear spiked through her as she watched the needle fall to the ground. Her thoughts became hazy, and she was dimly aware of the cold air hitting her stomach as her attacker roughly pushed a hand under her top. His calloused skin grasped her breast as he shoved her legs apart.

"Il Maestro never said anything about me having a bit of fun before I brought you in. I've wanted to do this for a very long time."

The low-spoken words were filled with such malice that, even through the haze, it chilled her to her very soul.

A voice, deep in the back of her mind, screamed for her to fight back. But she couldn't move. Her limbs were heavier than they'd ever felt before. She wanted to sob, to scream out in frustration at her ineptitude.

Slowly, her vision began to fade, filling with a white light that seemed to grow stronger and stronger. Numbly, she was aware that her body was shaking and a heat was building once again. Only this time, it was building not just in her hands, but throughout her entire body. It grew hotter and hotter as the white light grew stronger.

"Argh, you bitch!" Her attacker roared in pain and slammed her against the wall again before sinking a pair of razor-sharp fangs deep into her throat.

In an instant the light was gone, and all that was left was pain.

Blinding pain.

Phoenix screamed.

CHAPTER TWENTY-SIX

Dammit that woman drives me insane!

Ethan fumed as he stared in the now empty direction Phoenix had stalked off. She had no right lecturing him about accepting who he was when she was the one who insisted on ignoring everything that made her special.

As if being unique was a bad thing.

He blew out a breath and tried to calm the part of him that was itching to continue the argument. He'd thought going home for a few days would help clear his head. It hadn't. If anything, it just made things worse. Having to face everybody, knowing Sean's killer was still walking free ...

Guilt started to seep in, slowly and insidiously. The feeling of righteousness from only moments ago was replaced with a horrible sinking feeling in the pit of his stomach.

Had he taken it all out on her?

She was oblivious to her own potential and it frustrated the hell out of him, but would he have fared better without someone to guide him? He wasn't so sure.

With a sigh, he looked again at the empty road ahead of him. He should probably follow her and apologise. A soft growl and gentle nudge from his wolf very clearly conveyed the animal's agreement.

He tucked his hands into his pockets and walked briskly in the direction of the pub.

The night around him seemed unnaturally quiet. There were no cars passing, no rustle of leaves, just an icy silence. It was almost as if the night itself was pissed at him.

As he reached the main street, a sharp scent flowed to him from beyond the now dark shopfronts: fear.

He forced himself to remain still and listened closely, allowing his stronger senses to take over. A slight scuffling sound came from somewhere to the left. After a moment, the sound became louder and more frantic. Careful to remain silent, Ethan moved in the direction of the noise. The scent of fear grew sharper with each step he took.

An odd glow seemed to lighten the night beyond the row of shops, silhouetting the buildings against the backdrop of the heavily clouded sky. He'd barely gotten ten feet when the night was ripped apart by a violent scream.

Phoenix.

All thought of remaining silent was quickly forgotten as he sprinted to the end of the street. His claws elongated, and his canines ruptured from his gums. He knew his eyes would be yellow because his wolf was tearing at its binds to be released. But he didn't care. His only thought was reaching her.

The sight that met him in the dark shadows almost made him lose what little control he had left. Phoenix was pressed against the wall of the building. Her head was thrown back in fear and agony as a large dark-haired vampire tore into her throat with his fangs.

The coppery tang of her blood filled the air and made his wolf howl. His vision sharpened like a laser on its target and he lost all sense of humanity, lunging with every bit of power his body possessed.

In the deep recesses of his mind, he was dimly aware they needed answers, they needed the vampire alive. But his wolf didn't care. His wolf wanted blood.

Even in his heightened state, he was careful not to hurt Phoenix. He attacked the vampire, taking advantage of the momentary chaos to turn the tables and latch his own teeth into the vampire's throat.

With a roar, the vampire released Phoenix and tried to fling him off, but Ethan held fast.

The shift in position gave him his first proper view of the vampire, and he found himself staring into the empty black eyes that had haunted his dreams. It was him. It was the vampire that killed Sean.

Rage overpowered rational thought and the world around him became red. The vampire's strength was phenomenal, but he was no match for the fury that coursed through Ethan. The more the vampire fought, the more Ethan tore at him.

Claws slashed. Fangs pierced.

The blood that coated his mouth was vile and poisonous. Still, he continued. Possessed. Tearing through flesh, sinew, and bone.

It was only the weakening thud of Phoenix's erratic heartbeat that pulled him back to his senses. She lay slumped on the ground, unmoving. The slow beat of her heart was like a percussive death knell.

Fear gripped him. Had she reached her immortality? He had no idea.

In the periphery of his awareness, he noticed the vampire had stopped struggling beneath him and was shaking. It took Ethan a second to realise the vampire was laughing. A deep, shuddering laugh.

The vampire's words, when they came, struck the heart of both man and wolf. "You can't save her, you know."

In an instant his vision clouded red again and with a furious roar, he ripped the vampire's head clean off his body. Lifeless blood dropped to the concrete and slowly began to fade.

As Ethan stood panting and struggling to regain control of his wolf, he heard a whimper behind him. The simple sound made his heart clench violently.

Phoenix's eyes opened wide as she surveyed the scene in front of her, unable to stop the low moan that sent a flash of pain through her throat.

A pair of blue, lifeless eyes stared at her from their position on the ground barely three feet away. A somewhat hysterical laugh bubbled up in her chest as she realised the eyes belonged to a head that seemed, strangely, to be missing a body.

She watched as the head began to disintegrate in front of her eyes. Some vague thought pushed insistently at her consciousness, something important she couldn't quite grasp through the haze of pain. As the gruesome image gradually disappeared, it was replaced by a large black crow, its red eyes glowing as it stared at her. A soft, keening lament drifted on the night, not too dissimilar to the wailing she heard at the Ritual, but quieter, more gentle.

And then it didn't matter because Ethan's yellow-brown eyes appeared and his concerned face filled her view. Except his concerned face was covered in thick, dark blood and looked every bit as gruesome as the disembodied head.

He was speaking to her. She could see his lips moving, nearly hypnotised by the sight, but she couldn't hear a thing. And then everything went black.

Phoenix didn't know how long she was out for, but when she came to, the world around her seemed to be moving. Her stomach felt queasy and she scrunched her eyes tightly together against passing flashes of light. She felt a comforting hand smooth the hair back from her forehead as the world began to drift away again to blackness.

CHAPTER TWENTY-SEVEN

Phoenix shot up with a gasp. Blood rushed to her brain, making her head explode as spots formed in front of her eyes and the strange room began to spin violently. In an instant, Ethan was by her side making soothing noises and encouraging her to lie back down. But she couldn't lie back down because he needed to know. She needed to tell him what she remembered.

She knocked his hands away and frantically tried to get the words out, but all that came from her throat was a raw croak. She tried again, but only managed a dry rasp.

Finally, recognising her distress, Ethan disappeared and quickly returned with a glass of water. He gently helped her raise the glass to her lips and slowed her movements when she would have gladly gulped it in one go.

The water felt like a solid lump trying to painfully pass through her throat, but still she gasped for more. Eventually, the cool liquid eased the burning pain enough that she could speak.

"I knew him."

Ethan froze, and a strange expression passed over his face.

"The vampire. I knew him," she repeated insistently, grabbing the sleeve of his jumper. He needed to understand how important this was.

Ethan sat down on the bed beside her – wait, how did she end up in a bed? – and took her hands in his. His thumbs rubbed soothingly across her palms to calm her frantic fidgeting.

"It's okay, it's okay. You're safe now. Just tell me what happened."

A sob threatened to escape as the memories came flooding back to her like flashes from a horror movie. The sharp piercing of fangs. The violation. The lifeless blue eyes. She forced her breath to slow. Breathe in and out. In and out. *Stick to the facts, you can do this.*

"He attacked me from behind. I tried to fight back but" – her breath caught – "he was too strong."

Ethan's grip on her hands increased painfully, and for a moment she thought she saw his eyes flash yellow. But when she looked again, all she saw was warm brown eyes full of concern.

"Something happened when he attacked me," she continued, trying to pick through the haze of memories. "I felt a strange heat build up ... Then he bit me, and there was just pain."

Ethan stiffened slightly at her words, and Phoenix wondered vaguely whether it was the mention of the heat or the biting that got his attention.

"You said you recognised him?" he prompted.

She nodded and the sense of relief at being able to move her neck outweighed the aching stiffness that was setting in.

"His voice was familiar, but I didn't get a proper look at him. Not until I came to and saw the –" Bile rose up in her throat and she swallowed with effort. "He's the head of security for the Dublin clan. He works for my ... uncle of sorts."

Ethan's jaw dropped in unmasked astonishment. "Your uncle sent someone to kill you?"

"No, no way." Phoenix sat up so quickly that the room began to spin again.

Ethan steadied her, propping pillows behind her for support.

"None of this makes sense." She scrunched her fists into her eyes and wanted to scream her frustration. "Uncle D would never hurt me."

She tried to organise the million questions that were crowding her thoughts. "Raphael, he said something. I don't think he was meant to kill me. I think he was meant to bring me somewhere."

"Phoenix, that was the vamp that killed Sean." Ethan's voice was low and shaking with barely restrained anger. "Whatever his intentions, they weren't good."

Her breath left her in a whoosh. Raphael killed Ethan's friend? Did Darius know? Surely not.

An uneasy silence fell between them, and Phoenix's thoughts turned to her surroundings. The room around her was masculine but lacking personality. Navy and cream provided clean, efficient décor, but it was lacking personal touches. There were no photos or knick-knacks to provide clues to the owner.

Was she in Ethan's apartment? His bedroom?

She lay on a king-size bed surrounded by soft pillows and a thin blanket covered her from the chest down. A large white t-shirt was the only thing separating her skin from the covers, and she tugged the blanket up to her chin self-consciously. While she was extremely grateful not to be caked in blood anymore – particularly her own – she cringed in embarrassment, wondering at what point she'd been divested of her clothes.

As if sensing her shift in focus, Ethan stood quickly and distanced himself from the bed, busying himself with a mess only he could see.

"I called Nate to pick us up. I didn't think you'd want Abi to see you hurt. And Lily had stuff here to help with the healing." Ethan seemed to realise he was rambling and stopped talking abruptly.

So, they were in Ethan's apartment then.

The wild musky scent she'd come to associate with him was flooding her senses, which meant she was most likely wearing his t-shirt too. The thought made blood rush to her cheeks. Realising he was looking at her for reassurance, she smiled weakly and nodded her thanks.

He cleared his throat and looked uncomfortable. "The others are here to discuss what happened when you're feeling up to it. I've left some clothes at the end of the bed for you. Figured you might want to freshen up before you see them."

Again she nodded, feeling awkward from the strange intimacy of finding herself in Ethan's bed, wearing his clothes.

"The bathroom's through there." He indicated to a door to her left and turned to leave.

At the thought of being left alone, panic wiped away all concerns of where she was or who had seen her naked. She pushed it back angrily, but with it came another thought. A memory that left her cold.

That sound – a soft keening lament as she lay on the cold ground.

"Ethan?"

He stopped with his hand on the door and looked at her in question.

"How badly was I hurt?" As she voiced the words, she already knew the answer. She knew what the sound had been, and what it meant. But still she had to ask.

Ethan's expression turned guarded. "Badly." A muscle at the side of his jaw ticked. "If you hadn't already reached your immortality, you'd have been dead."

It took Phoenix a long time to drag herself out of the luxurious shower. Waterfall showerheads and scalding water did little to chase away the chill of Ethan's parting words, but the pounding beat lulled her into a gentle trance that allowed her to stop thinking. At least for a few minutes.

When she walked into the living room, everyone was assembled in their usual places. Lily and Nate were at the breakfast bar, and Nate's head was buried in his laptop. Shade slouched by the window, flipping his penknife open and closed as he stared sullenly into the darkening sky. And Ethan sat pensively on the sofa, his foot tapping as he surveyed the door she was exiting.

A deafening silence fell as soon as she appeared. She tugged self-consciously at the sleeves of the baggy jumper Ethan had left her. All eyes turned in her direction, and Ethan leapt from his seat to usher her to the sofa.

"If you're feeling up to it, I thought we could talk about what happened yesterday?" he said, handing her a steaming cup of black coffee.

Phoenix took the cup gratefully and let the rich aroma fill her senses before taking a sip. It took a moment for Ethan's words to register, but when they did, the scalding liquid caught in her throat, nearly choking her.

"Yesterday?" she wheezed out between coughs.

"You were badly hurt. You needed to heal." Ethan watched her with concern. "Lily gave you an herbal remedy to keep you asleep while your body repaired."

All things considered, losing a day of her life was really the least of her worries, but this new information only made her feel worse.

Shit, Abi!

Phoenix didn't even realise she'd jumped up until Ethan gently pressed her back down into the sofa.

"It's okay, it's okay," he said as he took the half-spilled coffee from her hands and placed it on the table. "I texted Abi. Told her you had a family emergency and you'd be gone for a day or two."

Sinking into the soft cushions, Phoenix added that text to the ever-growing list of lies she needed to keep straight. It would be a miracle if Abi was even speaking to her by the end of all this.

"Ethan said you knew the vampire that attacked you?" Lily's question drew everyone's attention back to the matter at hand.

"Figures," Shade muttered, ignoring Ethan's reprimanding look as he scowled out the window.

Phoenix sighed – good to see a near death experience didn't change anything – and nodded, but confusion made her head pound. Why would Raphael have attacked her? Growing up in the Dublin clan, she'd always avoided the large man that worked as Darius's head of security; he'd creeped her out in a way she couldn't quite put into words.

But he worked for Darius. He knew who she was, and that she was under Darius's protection. What would make him go against his Master's orders? Was he working for someone else? She tried to remember his words as he attacked her, shuddering at the memory of his hands groping her and his large body crushing hers. He had said something ... a name ...

"Il Maestro," she said, speaking her thoughts out loud. "That was the name he used. The person that had given him the orders."

Nate glanced up from his laptop, gave a quick nod of acknowledgement, and resumed his furious typing.

Phoenix picked up what was left of her coffee and took a large gulp. The bitter liquid burned a path down her throat as she debated what to tell them. With nothing left to lose, she started from the beginning.

"My parents disappeared when I was fifteen. Uncle D – Darius – took me in. My parents' families both disowned them before I was even born. Darius is the only one that stood by them. He's the only other family I've ever known."

"The vamps accepted you?" Shade waved his hand vaguely in her direction, looking at her with renewed curiosity.

"Most of them didn't know about me, only his closest advisors. He kept me hidden to protect me. I left when I was twenty-one. They'd have no reason to hurt me ..."

As her words trailed off, the memories assaulted her. The night her parents went missing, waiting, knowing in her heart that something wasn't right. Going to live with the Dublin clan. The realisation, even from such a young age, that she must hide who she was if she were to survive. And the darkness. Most of all the darkness.

"What clan did you say this was?" Nate asked from behind his screen, breaking the tense silence that had fallen.

Phoenix cleared her throat and tried to keep her tone matter of fact despite the emotion that threatened to break free of her tight grasp. "The Dublin clan."

Nate nodded, chewing on his lip in concentration.

"Did you ever find out what happened to your parents?" Lily's voice was soft and childlike as she looked at Phoenix. Her green eyes begged for a happy ending to the story.

Phoenix just shook her head and looked down at the table in front of her. She couldn't talk about this, not now.

"Got it!" Once again Nate broke the building tension with his sudden declaration. "Okay, let me see ... Uh huh ... yep ... okay ..."

"Nate, are you going to share anything useful here, or just keep making a lot of annoying noises?" Ethan spoke for the first time since she'd begun her story. He glared at Nate with his arms crossed over his chest.

Nate looked up sheepishly, a crooked grin on his face.

"Sorry," he said, and flipped his laptop screen around so everyone could see. "It looks like an investment firm has made a number of payments to the Dublin witches coven recently."

From the satisfied look on his face, Phoenix could already guess where this was leading. Empty of everything except the black coffee – which now threatened to make a reappearance – her gut clenched and she had to swallow back the feeling of nausea.

After throwing an apologetic glance her way, Nate continued, "The investment firm is called IM Investments. It appears to be owned by the Dublin vampire clan."

"Which means –"

"Which means the attack on Phoenix may not have been a coincidence," Ethan finished, eyes flashing yellow.

He turned to her. "When was the last time you spoke to your uncle?"

A loud buzzing filled Phoenix's head as she tried to make sense of what she was hearing and what it might mean. "Not for a while, I've been avoiding his calls."

She sat up straight. Was that it? Had Darius grown worried when he couldn't reach her? Maybe he'd sent Raphael to get her, not realising his head of security couldn't be trusted. As she opened her mouth to voice the thought, she looked around the room and found herself met with sympathetic stares.

Of course, they all thought he was involved, why shouldn't they? But she knew Darius. He'd never hurt her. There had to be some other explanation.

Maybe if she just spoke to him ...

CHAPTER TWENTY-EIGHT

Phoenix slipped quietly into her bedroom, grateful to have avoided Abi. Now that she was immortal, her healing abilities, helped along nicely by Lily's remedies, were impressive, but the damage to her neck had been substantial, and it would be a while before she could pass off the scarring as an over-enthusiastic hickey. No doubt her friend would have questions.

She pulled out her phone and scrolled through her contact list to Darius's name. The information Nate found weighed heavily on her mind, despite the confident brush-off she'd given Ethan and the others. Uncle D had too tight a rein on his clan and its business ventures not to know if there was something going on with the witches. Yet he claimed ignorance about the disturbances in the Lore. Disturbances which the Dublin coven were heavily involved in.

The only logical explanation she could think of was that he'd been lying to protect her. He'd sheltered her from the Lore all her life, it'd stand to reason he would try to do it now. But she wasn't a child anymore.

She took a deep breath and made the call, her phone gripped tightly in her hand.

One ring. Two rings.

"Phoenix! Where the hell have you been? I haven't been able to reach you for weeks."

A sob caught in her throat at the concern in Darius's voice. This was the man she'd grown up with, the man that looked after her as if she was his own child. The others were wrong about him. They had to be.

"Hi, Uncle D," she answered after taking a moment to get a grip on her emotions. "Sorry it's been a while. Time just kind of got away from me."

"Are you okay, Phoenix? You don't sound yourself."

She hesitated, realising she hadn't really thought the conversation through before ringing. Did she just come straight out and ask why he'd sent Raphael after her? Ask why he was funding a homicidal gaggle of witches?

"It's been a crazy few days." Fuck was that an understatement.

"How about we meet for dinner and you tell me –"

"Uncle D? Do you remember the wolf I told you about? What he said about the attacks and me being involved somehow?"

"Yes?"

"Did you ever find out any more from your contacts? Is there anything I should be worried about?"

"Phoenix, what's going on?"

He didn't answer the question.

Phoenix gripped the phone tighter and mentally willed Darius to say something to ease the ever-growing knot that settled in her stomach.

"I remembered something else he said. It's been playing on my mind. He mentioned a prophecy, said something about the witches being involved ..."

Silence.

"The wolf was lying, Phoenix," Darius said, finally. "If there was any such prophecy, the Council would know about it."

"But the witches –"

"Are under the same rule as the rest of us. If their activities have been in any way questionable, the Council will deal with it. You're worrying for nothing, Phoenix," his tone softened.

She reached up and gently ran her fingers along the bandage that covered the side of her neck. "I have to go," she whispered, and hung up before he could respond.

Ethan was surprised to receive Phoenix's call so soon after she left. It made sense that she would need time to process everything they'd learned. He was even more surprised at her words.

"Are you sure you want to do this? Break into the lair?" he asked for the third time. They were all gathered back in his living room, and Phoenix sat across from him fidgeting restlessly with the medallion around her neck.

She nodded, her expression remaining emotionless despite her obvious unease.

His breath came out in a whoosh. Were they really going to break into the lair of the most powerful vampire clan in Ireland?

Beside him, Nate was rubbing his hands together gleefully and already firing up the laptop, ready to do what he did best. Lily sat beside Phoenix with a slightly shocked look on her face as if she thought they were all nuts. Shade slouched against the breakfast bar; his single raised eyebrow telegraphed more interest than Ethan had ever seen from him.

"Okay, first things first." Ethan looked back to Phoenix. "We need the exact location of the lair."

Vampire clans were among the most secretive races of the Lore when it came to protecting their resting place, and for good reason. Although the stronger members of a clan could often withstand a degree of sunlight, there still many that were particularly vulnerable during daylight hours. Open knowledge of their lair location would be a security nightmare, and vamps were anything but stupid.

Phoenix brought up a picture on her phone and set the device on the table so they could all see. Lily's face mirrored Ethan's own surprise, nicely highlighted by Nate's low whistle, and an "I'll be damned," from Shade.

176

"The lair is in the American Ambassador's residence?" Ethan asked, staring at the image of an imposing white building with grand pillars framing the entranceway.

Phoenix gave a wry smile. "Best place to hide is in plain sight."

"Nate, can you pull up the schematics for the lair?"

A couple of taps later, "Negative." Nate shook his head, pushing unruly brown hair out of his eyes. "The plans listed only show the upper storeys." And it went without saying that the official lair was buried deep beneath the earth, away from the sun and prying eyes.

Ethan chewed this over, running through and discarding the various options that might be available to them.

"I can get you in," Phoenix cut off his thought process. Her voice was quiet but determined as her unwavering, green eyes met his.

He thought about arguing. He wanted to make it easier on her, but this was her demon to face – his desire to protect her didn't come in to it.

"I used to sneak out sometimes when the darkness got to be too much for me," she continued when no argument was forthcoming. "There are some old, abandoned service passages that made it easier to get around. They're our best bet."

Her words were clipped and he could see her working to keep her emotions in check, but she sat tall, shoulders firmly set, and Ethan found himself proud of the strength she displayed.

"Not to put a dampener on things," Shade interjected, very clearly intending to do exactly that, "but how do we get in without being noticed by a lair full of vampires?"

"*We* don't," Ethan said firmly, and cut off all arguments with a commanding look. "The more of us that go in, the more likely we'll be detected. You guys can help from a distance, but Phoenix and I will be going in alone."

The lair was large and housed hundreds of vampires; they'd have no chance of escaping alive if they were detected. He could only hope Darius really did have Phoenix's best interests at heart because they'd be staking their lives on it if they were caught.

"We need to pick a time when there'll be as few vamps as possible. Anyone have any ideas?" Ethan looked around the room and his lips quirked into a smile when Nate raised his hand with a smug grin on his face. "Yes?"

"It just so happens there's a very exclusive gala ball being held in the ambassador's residence. Only one problem." Nate hesitated. "It's tonight."

"Okay, what other options –"

"No" – Phoenix held up a hand to stop him – "it's perfect. When there's an event held, the vampires are either in attendance or ordered to make themselves scarce. Security below ground would be as low as we could hope for."

"I could probably help with that side of things." Nate grinned as he rooted around in a rucksack that was leaning against his chair. He pulled out a small flash drive and held it up for them to see. "If you can get near enough to their servers to plug this in, I *should* be able to get access to their security systems and cause a few distractions."

Ethan took the drive from him and put it in his pocket. He still wasn't sure this was a good idea. If they got too close to any of the vamps, their signatures would be picked up. Phoenix might be able to mask hers enough, but he definitely couldn't.

Lily obviously had the same thought as him. "There's a spell that might be able to help change your signatures temporarily," she said as she worried at her nails. "But I'm not sure if I'm strong enough to cast it."

"It's okay." Phoenix patted Lily's shoulder awkwardly. "The bottom levels are warded. Uncle D had it done when I came to live with him to help keep my presence a secret. The wards act as a kind of buffer for our signatures, almost like sound proofing I guess."

Ethan watched her closely, waiting to see if she'd realise the significance of her words, but she seemed to be lost in the memory of her past.

"Who set the wards?" Lily's intelligent eyes met his across the room.

"The witc …" Phoenix trailed off, all manner of emotions crossing her face as realisation dawned on her.

For that brief moment she looked lost, and Ethan found himself wanting to hurt the person that put that look in her eyes. Then she pulled herself together and a steely resolve removed all trace of emotion from her face.

"Tonight."

"Can you get everything set in time?" He looked questioningly at Nate, knowing his expertise would be vital to get past what would no doubt be an impressive security set-up.

With a grin and salute from Nate, the decision was made.

CHAPTER TWENTY-NINE

Phoenix watched the city lights flash by, vibrant colours blurring together hypnotically. The late hour allowed Ethan's Audi to keep an impressive pace as they drove along the quays, hampered only by the occasional drunk that stumbled into the road.

She'd never been comfortable in big cities. The grey buildings felt cold and soulless to her, and the hordes of people made her feel even more alone. For the first time in many years, she longed for the rolling green hills that had surrounded her childhood home.

It didn't take them long to reach the lair. Nestled in the heart of the Phoenix Park, impenetrable walls surrounded a building that was both grand and understated in equal measure. White, with large arched windows and a long winding driveway, the ambassador's residence was lit by low lighting that cast eerie shadows onto the lush, manicured lawn.

That night, the tall wrought-iron gates stood open to the honoured guests of the gala, many of whom were blissfully oblivious of the truth hidden within the depths beyond.

"Keep driving for another kilometre," she directed. "There's an old service road on the left."

The tension in the car was palpable and her pulse thrummed in her veins. She hadn't been back here since the day she left four years ago, but she'd spent a lot of time within those walls, learning the secrets they held. She could only hope that everything was as she remembered it.

It wasn't long before they reached the road she was looking for. The trees and bushes had become even more unruly in the passing years and it was a struggle to get the car through. Ethan winced every time a branch scratched the side of his Audi, and Phoenix almost laughed at the forlorn look on his face. Although, she was extremely glad they hadn't taken her Mustang.

When they could go no further, they abandoned the car, pulling into a gap in the trees so it would be hidden from view if anyone happened to follow them. A frigid breeze ruffled the branches around them, grating in the otherwise quiet night. Phoenix's nerves were on edge. Every crunch of leaves and every gust of air across the back of her neck wound her tighter and tighter.

She led the way through the soft mud and explained in a low voice, "There's an old service tunnel ahead that leads to the boiler room in the basement of the house."

As a young girl in the lair, she'd kept herself busy by finding forgotten passages that allowed her to explore her underground prison without detection. She'd pretend she was on a secret mission and her task was to outsmart the vampires.

The isolation had been for her own safety, of course. Darius had risked his reputation by sheltering her. To the Council, she was a symbol of weakness; one of their most sacred edicts broken and allowed to go unpunished. An inter-species pairing that was allowed to continue and produce offspring. All it would take was a single vampire to speak of her existence and everything would fall to pieces.

So, she was kept apart and alone. Only Darius and his most trusted vampires were aware of her presence among them. All for her own safety. But things were different now. She had a life she loved, and she needed answers so she could get back to it.

Finally, they reached the entrance to the tunnel, which was largely obscured by rocks and overgrown bramble. Ethan took out his hunting knife, the one that had terrified her when they first met, and began to hack away at the thorny branches until there was just enough room for them to squeeze through. With that done, Nate handed him a small black pouch and Ethan gave a nod to confirm they were ready.

She took a deep breath and stepped into the tunnel, her clothes snagging momentarily on the remaining thorns. Ethan followed close behind her, and his warm presence helped to calm the frantic beating of her heart.

The air was stale and the smell of packed earth was heavy around them. With each step they took, the darkness became more complete, almost like they were walking into the black, gaping mouth of the beast. She'd taken this same route many times when she was younger; her yearning to see the sun had been too strong to ignore. The same clawing fear that she felt then, the fear of being caught, caused adrenaline to thrum through her veins now.

At the end of the tunnel they waited, listening intently for any noise on the far side of the old metal door. The only sounds that reached them were the whirring of machinery and the clunking of the large boiler that serviced the house.

Phoenix was uncomfortably aware of Ethan's close proximity at her back and she had a strange urge to push him away. This little trip down memory lane was leaving her raw and exposed in ways she never imagined.

With a final glance of agreement, Ethan put his shoulder against the heavy door and pushed. The loud creaking of rusted hinges made Phoenix cringe back into the shadows. Heat from the boiler hit them like a solid wall in contrast to the cold air of the tunnel, but other than that, she registered no movement within the room.

Moving silently, they edged forward and wove between the heavy-duty machinery that filled the space. Large pipes covered the ceiling in a tangled maze above their heads, adding to the claustrophobic feeling and making Phoenix's chest feel tight.

The next door led to a long, empty corridor. Concrete floors and starkly painted walls echoed even the slightest sound. Phoenix inhaled a slow breath and paused for a second to compose herself. They were in the basement of the main residence, not yet low enough to hit the lair, but that didn't mean they were safe.

The main server sat on this floor; it linked to sub-servers above and below ground. It would be guarded, but if they were to have any hope of getting into the lair unnoticed, they would need to go there first.

At Ethan's nod, she led the way, stopping them just short of the server room.

Scuffling sounds and the occasional snort confirmed the presence of a guard beyond the final corner. Phoenix felt a sudden urge to backtrack and forget about their crazy plan. But Ethan didn't give her a chance. He handed her the small package from Nate and in the blink of an eye, he was gone, leaving her alone and exposed in the corridor.

For a whole minute it felt as if her heart had stopped beating and her lungs had forgotten how to expand. Then she heard a banging in the distance and her heart stuttered back to business.

A low curse sounded and heavy footsteps faded into the distance. Phoenix counted to ten before crouching low to peer around the corner.

Empty.

She ran towards the server room, fumbled with the package in her hand, and pulled out a small black scanner. After connecting it to the pin pad at the door just as Nate had instructed, she waited, watching while numbers flashed on the small screen in a blur of red.

It seemed to take forever, and every second that passed felt like a ticking time bomb. When the screen finally flashed green and gave a soft beep, she nearly yelped with surprise.

She yanked the door open and slid quickly inside before pulling it tight behind her. A cold breeze from the air conditioning system caused goose bumps to prickle along her skin, and she rubbed her arms briskly against the chill.

Lights, cables, black boxes. It looked like a scene from the future when computers had officially come to take over the earth.

"Nate ... Nate? Can you hear me?" She pressed the small earpiece, willing him to answer.

"I've got you." Nate's answer came back through a burst of static.

"Okay, I need you to find the main server. It'll probably be the one with the most cables in the coldest part of the room."

Phoenix looked around, quickly discounting the smaller boxes and monitors.

There!

Towards the back of the room, a large cabinet stood with floor to ceiling black boxes and flashing lights. Cables ran from it like tentacles ready to crush anyone that came near.

"Once you find the server," Nate continued in her ear, "plug the hard drive into any free USB port. I'll do the rest."

Doing as she was instructed, Phoenix plugged in the hard drive and waited nervously. Where the hell was Ethan? What if he'd been caught?

Despite the icy cold air coming from above her, sweat dripped down her spine and her hands felt clammy. Every buzz from the machines or new flashing light made her heart ricochet, and when the door to the server room opened suddenly, she nearly pissed her pants altogether.

"Phoenix?" Ethan's voice whispered from the far side of the room.

Stepping out from behind the server – with difficulty since the cable tentacles had become tangled around her legs – Phoenix called softly, "Over here."

"Where's the guard?" she asked when he came into view.

"He's otherwise occupied." Ethan grinned, looking very pleased with himself. "How are we getting on?"

"Nearly ... there ..." Nate's voice came through the earpiece to both of them at just that moment. "Okay, I'm in."

And just to prove his point, the distant sound of alarms reached their ears and emergency lights began flashing red in time with the sirens.

The trip via stairwell to the lower depths of the lair was thankfully uneventful. Whatever distraction Nate had managed to concoct seemed to be working, and his newly acquired access to the security system allowed him to keep them updated of the guards' position at the far side of the building. Their luck was holding out. Temporarily at least.

When they reached the fifth floor where the lair's security team was housed, they stopped and tentatively peered through the small glass panel in the door. A lone guard sat in front of a bank of monitors, swivelling on a black leather chair as he used a sharp hunting knife to clean dirt from under his nails.

They could take him out if they needed to, but would it be worth leaving a trail? Phoenix wasn't convinced they'd find anything of use in Raphael's quarters, and the thought of getting anywhere close to the scent of him again made her sick to her very stomach.

Ethan waited patiently, giving her space to make the decision, and following her without a word when she took a breath and continued further down the stairs.

Level six: her old living quarters. She hesitated, waiting for the barrage of memories, but none came. The truth was, this place held no real memories for her, just an overwhelming sense of sadness. That realisation allowed her to walk past the door on the sixth floor and continue down to the final level. No time, or need, for a trip down memory lane when there was no lane to walk.

The seventh and final level housed Darius's living quarters and personal office. Phoenix had visited him there many times while she lived in the lair. She could vividly remember the large, solid mahogany desk and the bookcases filled with ancient tomes she longed to touch. It was one of the few places she hadn't felt alone.

What they were doing now felt like a complete betrayal of everything Darius had done for her, but there was information here they needed. Darius kept detailed files on every vampire in his clan. If there was information to be found on Il Maestro, it would be here.

Although there were no security cameras for them to contend with on this floor, access rights were even more restricted than the other levels. Relying once more on the pocket-sized wonder of technology from Nate, they waited impatiently for the right code to get them through the stairwell door.

When the pin pad flashed green, Ethan pulled the door open and ushered her into the hallway beyond.

Mahogany panels lined the rich wine-coloured walls, mirroring the décor of Darius's office. The lighting was muted, coming only from intricate candles placed in alcoves at equal intervals along the hall.

The stairwell had barely disappeared from view when a noise dead ahead stopped them in their tracks. Voices drifted down the hall, though the words were muted by the hushed tones. Phoenix's heart tap-danced in her throat as she recognised Darius's voice.

Ethan grabbed her hand and tugged her into an unlit alcove a few feet ahead of them. As they huddled in the shadows, she tried desperately to calm her heartbeat. Surely any vampire within a twenty-mile radius could hear the blood racing through her veins.

From her new vantage point, the voices became clearer, certain words jumping out vividly: Raphael, update, ritual.

She took a slow, deep breath and eased herself to the edge of the alcove to peer carefully beyond the wall. Two large figures stood, barely visible, at a bend in the corridor, just out of reach of the flickering candlelight. Darius's shape was as familiar to her as her own, but the second figure she couldn't quite make out. It was neither figure that caught her attention, however. It was what they were standing in front of.

A door.

What the ... There shouldn't be a door there ...

Just as the thought crossed her mind, the door closed and the two figures walked briskly in the direction of their hiding spot. Ethan pulled her close to him, pressing her back against the wall as he shielded her body with his. The musky scent of him, coupled with the adrenaline flooding her veins, made her head swim. Phoenix could feel his muscles tense in preparation for a fight, but his breathing remained calm as he forced her to meet his eyes. She focused on the steadiness she saw there, using it to help her to relax.

The voices drew closer and Phoenix wracked her brain desperately for a way out of the situation. She was seriously contemplating jumping out and yelling, "Surprise!" when the footsteps suddenly

186

stopped. Ethan raised an eyebrow but didn't move, his body remaining unnaturally still.

Realisation dawned on Phoenix when she heard the chime of a lift, and she nearly dropped to the floor with relief. The voices cut off abruptly with the closing of the doors, and she finally allowed herself to release the breath she'd been holding. A wide grin split her face, but the happiness was short-lived.

"Come on. We might not have long," Ethan said, stepping out of the alcove once it had been quiet for a minute.

Phoenix followed him down the corridor, but halted abruptly when she came to the spot where the two figures had stood.

"Where's the door?" She looked at the space in confusion, not seeing any sign of the door but knowing it must be there.

Ethan placed both hands on the wall and moved them systematically across the wall until eventually he nodded. "It's well hidden, but it's here. I can feel the edges."

"So, how do we get it open?"

He didn't answer, but continued his careful exploration with a look of deep concentration. Eventually, a low click sounded and the wall swung outward, forcing them to jump back.

Her heart pounded in her chest as she stared into the gaping darkness that appeared before them. Gone were the plush floor coverings and richly panelled walls. In their place was cold, hard stone with steps leading deep into the earth.

"You know where it leads?"

Ethan's question broke through her thoughts and she shook her head. "I had no idea it even existed. It feels ... wrong."

She shivered, something about the darkness making her want to run in the opposite direction, to scrub herself raw until she finally felt clean again.

"Dark magic."

She looked up in surprise and was met with a grave expression.

"What you're feeling is dark magic."

CHAPTER THIRTY

Ethan's words repeated themselves on a loop in Phoenix's head as they slowly descended into the darkness, the only light coming from a candle Ethan had grabbed from a nearby alcove.

Why would she be feeling the weight of dark magic? It didn't make any sense.

Her confusion was only heightened by the trajectory of their steps: downwards. Never in all of her years had she heard mention of an eighth level to the lair, yet here they were, very obviously descending deeper underground.

Without even realising he'd stopped, Phoenix found herself running into the solid mass of Ethan's back. She reached out for the wall to steady herself, but quickly pulled her hand back as a bone-deep chill, unlike anything she'd ever felt before, shot through her.

Everything about this felt wrong to her, and as she craned her neck around Ethan to view the large stone chamber that had opened before them, she felt no more comforted by what she saw.

In the centre of the room stood a large stone altar surrounded by thick black candles. Even in the dim light, Phoenix could make out dark stains covering its surface, and she refused to let herself think too deeply on what may have caused them.

As she turned a slow circle to take in their surroundings, Ethan walked around the chamber with a grim expression on his face. Following his lead, she stepped further into the strange room, grimacing as the unclean feeling intensified and settled over her limbs like a palpable weight.

A single lap of the chamber was enough to leave her feeling sick to her stomach. Weapons of a sort she had never seen before adorned the walls, their metal covered in thick stains not dissimilar to the altar. Intricate symbols were carved at random intervals and pulsed with energy as she passed them.

"We should probably get out of here before someone comes back," Ethan said, his face somewhat paler, even in the dim candlelight.

Phoenix rubbed her arms, trying in vain to chase away the chill that had settled into her bones. Her instincts were screaming at her that they were missing something, but for the life of her she couldn't figure out what it was.

She turned in another slow circle from her new vantage point by the altar to take in the room one last time. As she reached the end of her rotation, something caught her eye on the far wall of the chamber – a small patch that seemed different to the area surrounding it. It was so subtle that she wasn't quite sure if her imagination was playing tricks on her.

Holding her breath, she walked towards the wall. Her eyes struggled to determine what had caught her attention. As she drew closer, the dark shadow began to take form; it was small and so dark that it almost blended into the stonework. She reached her hand forward and was surprised to feel the cold touch of metal, even though part of her expected it.

"It's a handle," she called back to Ethan, impatiently urging him to come closer with the candle.

Phoenix groped around on the rough stone until her hands found the grooves of a doorframe, set so tightly into the wall that it was almost invisible, just like the entrance to the chamber had been. A solid and imposing lock sat below the handle and Phoenix gave it a tug, not really expecting it to open.

"Can you break it?" She looked at Ethan hopefully, willing to admit he was the stronger Supe if it meant gaining access to whatever was behind the door.

He reached out a hand to examine the lock, but pulled it back as if he'd been burned. He shook his head ruefully. "There's silver built into the lock. I won't be able to break it. Our only hope is to find the key. Or ..."

"Or what?" Phoenix tapped her foot impatiently, in no mood to play psychic.

"Or you could try to melt it."

That made her pause. The memory of the heat was fresh in her mind from the attack by Raphael mere days ago. It might not have been enough to stop his attack, but it had been there. And for once, it had been useful. A fae power.

Could it really hurt to try now?

There was only one problem: she had no idea how to do it, at least not on purpose. Would she even be able to call on the power of the sun so far below ground? At night?

Grinding her teeth, she mumbled self-consciously, "I don't know how to start."

Ethan placed a hand on her shoulder and looked at her with an intensity that made her squirm. "I'll help you, just trust me."

The sincerity in his warm, brown eyes calmed her, and she realised suddenly that she did trust him. So, she nodded, expecting to fail, but willing to at least try.

"Close your eyes."

He waited until she obeyed before continuing. "Place your hands on either side of the lock. Good. Now, try to picture a warm light building between your hands. Feel the heat pulling from the centre of your chest. Feel it growing with every breath ..."

She was about to tell him to cut the mumbo jumbo and speak English, when suddenly her palms became warmer. Her eyes opened in surprise, jaw dropping when a small, white spark ignited between them.

Clinging to that small spark for all it was worth, she concentrated on the warmth radiating from it and imagined it growing stronger. It flickered, and in a panic she fumbled, desperate not to lose the light.

190

Ethan squeezed her shoulder gently and she felt grounded once more. Phoenix closed her eyes and focused on her breathing. Each exhale pulled the warmth from her centre, and slowly, she felt the heat grow between her palms as it gained life.

She wasn't sure how long she stood there before a loud clunk shocked her from her trance and pulled her awareness abruptly back to the room. A lump of metal lay on the ground at her feet, and she stared at it in shock. When she looked up, Ethan had a wide grin on his face and his eyes shone with something almost resembling pride.

Together, they turned to face the door and a strange sense of dread replaced the heat in the centre of Phoenix's chest. With the lock no longer impeding the way, it was a simple matter of pulling the heavy door open to see what secrets it hid. She watched with her breath held as Ethan inched it open. Her heart hammered louder and louder with every creak.

The first thing that struck her was the smell. It was so overwhelming it almost formed a physical barrier to the small, stone room that appeared in front of them.

No, not a room, a cell.

Human excrement left a stench so putrid it was palpable, and almost, but not quite, masked the metallic tang of blood. The air was thick with decay and cloyed at the back of Phoenix's throat as she tried not to breathe through her nose.

Ethan moved into the cell first, almost disappearing in the darkness. Every instinct in her body wanted her to turn and run. Leave this place and scrub herself clean of its memory.

Instead, she followed him.

Even her heightened senses struggled to adjust to the darkness, but when they did, her stomach heaved at the sight that met her eyes. The cell was tiny, no more than ten feet wide. Sharp metal instruments of all shapes and sizes hung from one wall, and a drain sat in the centre of the floor. Dark stains covered the instruments and coated the surrounding walls.

But what troubled her most was the shadows that filled the corner furthest from the door.

Two bodies lay huddled in the corner, covered only by rags.

Chains hung from limbs that were little more than bone, and they were surrounded by the remains of human waste.

Beside her, Ethan growled low in his throat as he too noticed the frail forms. In the darkness his eyes flashed yellow, and something about his uncontrolled anger made the hair stand up on the back of her neck.

Steeling herself against the sight before her, she inched forward with trepidation.

Just as Ethan reached out a hand to stop her, one of the bodies moved. As if in slow motion, she watched the head rise. Long hair hung limply, coated in dirt, framing a face that was little more than a skeleton.

Frozen, Phoenix watched in horror as the head turned, and she was met with the anguished gaze of vivid green eyes.

Eyes that were almost identical to her own.

And she screamed.

CHAPTER THIRTY-ONE

Phoenix's scream cut through Ethan like a knife. He had known what they would find when they stepped into the small stone cell; the familiar threads of her unique signature had filled his senses before the truth could even register with her.

Moving quickly, he clamped a hand over her mouth and urgently whispered soothing words to calm her. If they drew attention to themselves now, they'd all be dead.

Ethan couldn't pull his gaze away from the green eyes that were so like Phoenix's. They reflected an untold pain back at him, but also disbelieving wonder as they stared in awe at what could only be their daughter.

As soon as he was confident Phoenix would stay quiet, he released his hold, freeing her to run to her mother. His chest clenched as he watched her reach out with trembling hands. It was obvious she wanted so much to touch the woman, but it was hard to imagine how even the slightest touch wouldn't bring pain to the frail form.

Shifting his gaze to the other form that lay huddled in the corner, his fists clenched in anger. The naturally pale skin of who he assumed to be Phoenix's father, was now almost translucent as the man lay unmoving at the feet of her mother. Even in the man's unconscious state, what was left of his muscles appeared to be clenched tight in agony, and Ethan could guess all too well what tortures had been inflicted upon him.

As Phoenix sobbed quietly with her mother, he looked around the cramped space for a way to break the chains that held her parents. It took him only seconds to spot the keys – hanging on the wall barely more than an arm's reach from the two prisoners.

Ethan's wolf growled and he had to fight back the rage that boiled up in his chest. The level of cruelty was not surprising considering the physical torture that had obviously been inflicted, but the thought of freedom being so tantalisingly close – for ten long years – was soul-destroying.

Not wasting a second more, he grabbed the keys and unlocked the chains, careful to avoid the silver coating the vampire's manacles.

"Daddy?" Phoenix's voice cracked as his movements drew her attention to the still form of her father.

When she looked up at Ethan, her tear-stained face was filled with horror. "How are we going to get them out of here?"

Ethan could feel another, similar pair of green eyes staring at him intently, beseeching him. He knew what those eyes were asking, and it went against everything in his nature. But he couldn't refuse.

Meeting the eyes of Phoenix's mother, he gave a small nod of acknowledgement and gently moved Phoenix from where she was now huddled over her father. Before he had time to think further, he allowed his claws to extend and sliced along his forearm. His wolf squirmed uneasily, but stayed silent in agreement. He forced his arm against the vampire's mouth, angling it as best he could to ensure the blood would make contact.

At first the body remained unresponsive and Ethan feared they'd reached the vampire too late. But then suddenly, like an electric shock, the body jolted, and a pair of razor-sharp fangs latched onto his arm like a vice.

The pain he expected never came. Instead, as the blood was sucked eagerly from his vein, the rhythmic pull lulled Ethan into a calm daydream; the ebb and flow of his blood formed a hypnotic wave of motion for him to float upon as his muscles relaxed with each passing minute.

His wolf growled.

The sound was the nudge he needed, a reminder that he needed to stay conscious of their surroundings. They'd been underground too long already, and though his body would quickly replenish the lost blood, he couldn't afford to be light-headed if he was to get them all out in one piece.

With that thought in mind, Ethan moved to pry the vampire's fangs from his arm, expecting a fight for the much-needed food source. Instead, he found himself meeting a pair of warm, brown eyes. Fangs swiftly – and willingly – retracted from his arm.

For a moment, he just stared at the vampire before him, filled with an awed respect for Phoenix's father. It was glaringly obvious that he'd been starved for a very long time. The strength it would have taken for him to willingly relinquish the blood was beyond comprehension.

A split second later, Phoenix flung herself at her father, tears streaming down her face as she met Ethan's eyes over her father's shoulder. What Ethan saw in her eyes made him more uncomfortable than even the feeding, and he turned away from the gratitude he didn't deserve.

Giving them as much space as he could within the cramped room, Ethan pressed his earpiece. "Nate?"

Nothing.

"Nate? You there?"

Silence. *Shit.*

Quickly assessing their options, he turned to Phoenix's father. "Can you walk?"

In truth, even with the Supe'd up blood, the man still looked like a corpse with limbs so thin and fragile they looked liable to snap, and a face little more than a skull covered in skin. But there was an awareness to the eyes that hadn't been there before, clearly reflecting the healing power of the werewolf blood. And a determination that said the man would fight to his last breath. So Ethan wasn't surprised when he nodded.

As Phoenix helped her father gingerly to his feet, Ethan turned once again to meet the bright, green eyes that reminded him so much of Phoenix's.

"I have nothing that will give you strength, but I have more than enough strength to carry you if you'll allow me to?" Reluctant to take all choice away from a woman who had very clearly been refused her dignity for a long time, he kept his tone patient and respectful, despite the niggling feeling that time was against them.

The smile he received in return was like sunshine itself, and there was nothing but gratitude in the woman's eyes as he bent to lift her small frame.

Phoenix's head was a dizzying mix of questions and disbelieving shock as they made their way back towards the boiler room. Her father's arm rested limply across her shoulder, its meagre weight very clearly confirming he was real. Yet she couldn't quite bring herself to believe it.

They had been here all this time.

She choked on a sob, but forced herself to put one step before the other. While her and Ethan might have found an excuse for being in the lair beforehand, the presence of her parents would quickly rule out any false pretences of a surprise visit. It would be a death sentence, or worse, if they were caught.

The comms had stayed silent from the time Ethan tried to contact Nate. But more worryingly, the lair was silent too. Unnaturally so.

Phoenix knew Nate's original distraction wouldn't have lasted this long. She could tell by the tension around Ethan's eyes as he carried her mother that he'd come to the same conclusion. So, they moved quickly, praying to a god they didn't believe in that the clever shifter had somehow bought them more time.

It was with surprise that she registered the sound of the boiler in

196

the distance. They'd somehow made it back to their entry level without incident. If they could just –

"Stop!"

Ethan's soft curse told her all she needed to know before she turned around. A single vampire stood in the hallway behind them, dressed in the non-descript black of the lair's security uniform. He had no visible weapons, but being a vamp, he didn't really need any.

"Did you have a nice nap?" Ethan asked, voice friendly and stance relaxed.

The vamp growled – actually growled – and Phoenix very quickly surmised that he must have been the vamp guarding the server room.

"Phoenix," Ethan said quietly, keeping his eyes on the guard. "Why don't you take your mother and head on home? I think I have some apologising to do here."

He shifted his weight to pass her the frail form of her mother, and at the same time, her father pulled his supported weight from her shoulder with obvious effort.

Phoenix hesitated.

Ethan was a good fighter, and he was damn strong, but she couldn't leave him alone in the middle of a vampire lair. It would be a death sentence.

As if sensing her reluctance, Ethan turned serious brown eyes to meet hers. "Phoenix, you need to get your parents out of here."

Dammit! There has to be another way.

And just to prove that fate can be a cruel bitch sometimes, two more vampire guards took that moment to step around the corner and into the hallway, grinning.

Ethan didn't give her any more time to argue. Pushing her mother into her arms, he turned and launched himself at the vampires, claws extending even as he moved.

She didn't want to leave him, but the feel of her mother, so light in her arms, made her turn towards freedom. The sounds of fighting followed them with every step as they moved closer to the boiler room, and it took all of Phoenix's willpower not to turn back.

Ahead of her, her father stumbled, but kept one hand on the wall for support as he continued forward with focused determination.

A strange clunk was the only warning they had. Suddenly the hallway filled with smoke, completely obscuring their view. Flashes of blue flame were the only break in the smoke, and the flames were so bright in their intensity that they were almost blinding.

Amongst the chaos, Phoenix could make out the sound of a woman chanting. Male voices shouted over one another, and the sound of footsteps running towards her made Phoenix huddle close to the wall, turning her body to protect her mother as best she could.

"Phoenix," a muffled voice said, close to her ear, "put this on."

A large black mask was shoved in front of her face, and before she knew what was happening, her mother was taken from her arms.

Her only thought was to stop them. There was no way they were taking her parents from her again. But then a hand landed on her shoulder, and Ethan's large frame was beside her. His scent filled her senses even through the haze of smoke and the acrid smell of burning.

"It's okay. We've got her," he assured, taking the mask and quickly fixing it around her face.

The difference was instantaneous.

Phoenix hadn't even realised she was having trouble breathing until all of a sudden she wasn't struggling anymore. Her view, though still hazy, cleared significantly, and even with the black masks covering their faces, she could now make out the forms of Lily, Shade, and Nate standing not more than five feet away. Her mother was held safely in Nate's arms, and her father slumped against the wall beside them.

The chanting and flames were coming from Lily in an impressive light show that was quite effectively holding back any vampire guards attempting to join the party. However, it was obvious from her slumped shoulders that she was weakening and wouldn't be able to keep up the onslaught much longer.

When Ethan urged her towards the boiler room, Phoenix ran to help her father. Just as she bent to lift him, determined to carry him out of the lair, Shade was there beside her. Without meeting her eyes, Shade lifted her father and was gone in a blur of speed towards the tunnel. Nate wasn't far behind as he carried her mother to safety.

Phoenix followed their lead, dragging Lily with her as Ethan pulled up the rear. The thunderous sound of footsteps and snarls echoed in her ears as she ran. They weren't going to make it.

Smoke was replaced by the thick, earthy smell of the tunnel, followed seconds later by a brief glimmer of light. They'd barely cleared the exit when a loud explosion rang and Phoenix was flung through the air.

She landed unceremoniously amongst the trees, her ears practically vibrating from the ringing that sounded in them. Ethan lay on the ground beside her, shaking his head as he pulled off his mask. Phoenix followed suit and turned to look back in the direction they'd come. All that was left of the tunnel entrance was a pile of rubble. Nate stood nearby, mask removed with a huge grin on his face, holding a small black handheld computer. Her mother was by his side, being tended to by Lily.

It took her a moment to realise that the night sky around them was no longer dark. While they had been in the lair, the subtle light of daylight had begun to fill the world around them, chasing away the shelter of the night.

Fuck, where's Dad?

He was a powerful vampire, and at full strength could easily withstand the weak morning sun. But he wasn't at full strength. He wasn't at any strength at all. Even the slightest hint of sun would kill him.

Phoenix scrambled, frantically trying to get her feet under her as she looked around. The world tilted viciously and she fought back the urge to throw up. She had to confirm he was safe. Ethan was by her side in a split second, steadying her. He was mouthing something at her, but Phoenix could hear nothing other than the ringing in her ears.

Shade. That's what he was saying. Shade had taken her father to safety. Her heart both calmed and clenched tight at the reassurance. Shade, as a pure vampire, was faster than the rest of them, but did she trust him with her father's safety?

Unable to do anything more than hope, she rushed to her mother's side.

The light touch of her mother's hand against her face made

Phoenix suddenly aware of the tears streaming down her cheeks. There was so much love in the green eyes staring back at her that Phoenix had to swallow past the sob threatening to choke her. Gently, she lifted her mother into her arms and followed Ethan back to the car, clinging for dear life to the precious weight she carried.

CHAPTER THIRTY-TWO

As soon as Ethan's apartment came into view, Phoenix flung the car door wide, completely ignoring the spray of gravel as the car skidded to an abrupt halt.

Please tell me they made it okay.

The relief when she found her father's pale sleeping form in one of the blacked-out bedrooms brought her to her knees. He was so still it would have been easy to assume he was dead, but she could feel the weak threads of his signature, as familiar to her as her own even after all this time.

He would sleep until darkness fell again; his body was far too weak to fight the daylight hours, even here, hidden from the sun's touch. And while he slept, he would heal. Physically at least.

As Phoenix stared at the man she thought lost to her forever, she tried in vain to wrap her head around everything. They'd been alive this whole time. Her parents had been mere floors from her, suffering, and she'd done nothing to help them.

Her thoughts continued on along this vein, swamping her in guilt, until Ethan's scent filled her nose and pulled her out of the useless ramblings of her mind.

"Your mother would like to talk to you." His brown eyes were full of concern as he helped her up from her kneeling position.

"Aria," Phoenix responded automatically.

Ethan's look of concern turned to confusion.

She shook her head to clear her thoughts. "I never told you her name," she clarified. "My mother, her name is Aria."

"Aria." He nodded, as if the name somehow fit for him. He glanced towards the still form of her father in question.

"Marcus."

Her chest constricted as she remembered back to the lair, back to Ethan feeding her father his blood. He'd saved her father's life. Emotions choked her and she fought to find words that might begin to express how grateful she was.

"Ethan ... I can never thank –"

"Shh." He stopped her words and pulled her close for a brief hug before pushing her towards the door of the bedroom. "Go to your mother. She's on the rooftop. I'll keep watch over your father."

Phoenix found her mother sitting on a soft blanket on the flat roof of the warehouse apartment. From her position, she had a perfect view of the morning sky with the most beautiful mix of reds and oranges splashed like watercolours across a backdrop of the city.

Aria wore a look of pure bliss on her face as she angled it towards the emerging sunlight. Her hair was tied in a knot at the back of her head, but the orange and blonde strands still flared like flames as the sun's rays hit them.

With the dirt now gone, her mother's skin once again looked flawless. But the natural glow Phoenix had envied so much as a child was missing. In its place, a pale, thin frame that acted as a stark reminder of the truth behind the peaceful scene in front of her. She knew it was an illusion, and it made her heart ache.

But, illusion or not, Phoenix was reluctant to disturb it. So, she merely watched. Her keen eyes noted the slow return of colour to her mother's cheeks; the healing power of the sun swift and astounding to behold when the fae was finally returned to her natural element.

Eventually, Aria smiled, pushing a loose strand of hair over a pointed ear as she turned towards Phoenix. "You turned out more beautiful than I ever could have imagined."

Suddenly self-conscious, Phoenix attempted to smooth the clothes that were now beyond ruin after the night's adventures. She made her way to her mother's side and sat hesitantly on the blanket, wondering where to even begin.

Before Phoenix could say anything, Aria reached out a trembling hand towards her. The hand lightly touched the medallion that hung around Phoenix's neck, as tears glistened in her mother's eyes.

"You kept it." The words were barely more than a whisper.

Phoenix looked down to watch as delicate fingers traced the embossed sun emblem. She swallowed hard and nodded. At fifteen, she'd understood enough to know her parents wouldn't leave her willingly. She'd known when she left her childhood home that she wouldn't be returning, and she'd needed to take some part of them with her. She chose her mother's medallion and, hidden in the depths of her wardrobe, her father's sword.

More reluctantly than she'd have liked to admit, Phoenix moved to take the medallion from around her neck. She intended to return it to its rightful owner, but her mother stopped her with a shake of her head and a loving smile. Phoenix looked at the still youthful face in front of her. Even having lived it, it was so hard to believe ten long years had passed since she last saw that smile. Ten years lost forever.

And just like that, reality hit like a frying pan to the face.

"Have you been there this whole time?" Phoenix asked.

The thought alone almost broke her and she clenched her teeth against the burning pain in her throat. The smile wavered on Aria's face and a sad understanding filled her green eyes as she nodded. Phoenix hugged her knees tight to her chest and focused all of her attention on keeping her breathing steady.

"We all trusted him, sweetheart." Aria's words were soft, and tinged with an unspoken pain as she laid a comforting hand on Phoenix's shoulder.

Darius had been their friend for many centuries before Phoenix was even born. He'd stood by them when their families banished them. He'd encouraged their relationship. He'd been family.

Covering her mother's hand with her own, Phoenix took a deep breath. "Tell me."

Aria gazed out at the city, saying nothing for a very long time. "How much do you remember?" she asked finally.

Phoenix gave this some serious thought. The feelings were so clear to her, even ten years later: the unsettled niggling in her belly, the feeling that time had slowed to a complete halt as she waited. But the details had blurred over time. Small images had become symbols for the whole, while the bigger picture was only the hazy memory of a child.

"I remember ... you coming home. You were upset." Phoenix nodded to herself. "You and Dad were talking about something, but you wouldn't tell me what was going on. You just said you had to go out and that you'd be back soon ..."

Aria's face remained expressionless, but her grip on Phoenix's shoulder tightened for a brief moment before relaxing. "I was out shopping that day, and a woman bumped into me, accidentally, I think. Anyway, the woman was a Seer –"

Phoenix nodded her understanding of the term at her mother's questioning look. A pang of sadness hit her as she thought of all the hours spent in Darius's library, learning things from a book that she should have learned from her parents.

"The woman," Aria continued, "started speaking in tongues. She spoke of a prophecy, and a hybrid that would bring an end to humanity."

At the mention of the prophecy, Phoenix froze. Her mother gave her a knowing look.

"Needless to say, I was upset. Your father and I had been so far removed from the Lore by that stage that we had no way of knowing if she spoke the truth. And we knew of only one hybrid ..."

"So, you went to Darius."

Aria sighed, a sound filled with so much regret it made Phoenix want to weep. "So, we went to Darius. As it turns out, he was all too familiar with the prophecy. I don't know what he used, but somehow he drugged our wine, and when we woke up, we were in the cell where you found us."

Phoenix's thoughts were in turmoil as her mother grew silent. She'd seen the evidence of Darius's betrayal, had seen the truth of her mother's story, but she still couldn't wrap her head around it. How could she reconcile such evil with the man she'd loved like family?

"But then who is Il Maestro?" Phoenix asked, desperately clawing through her mind for another explanation, one that might actually make sense.

Aria looked at her, confused. "Where did you hear that name?"

"Raphael. He said Il Maestro had given him his orders."

"Il Maestro was Darius's Sire. He was notoriously psychotic. If we'd known earlier of Darius's true origins ..."

Aria shook her head. "Il Maestro can't have given Raphael his orders. He's dead. Darius killed him many centuries ago."

So that was it. There was no other mysterious bad guy waiting in the wings, laughing to himself as they all ran around blaming the wrong person. No answer that would make the truth any more palatable.

"Why?"

It was the only thing Phoenix could think of, the one word that kept repeating itself in her head.

In an instant, her mother's face hardened, her eyes almost glowing with the anger that radiated through them. She grabbed both of Phoenix's hands in hers and squeezed so tightly it hurt.

"He's evil, Phoenix. Everything you know about him is a lie, an act. You must remember that."

"What did he do to you, Mam?"

Overhead, the sun dimmed and a fierce wind began to blow. A shiver ran down Phoenix's spine.

"What he did to me is nothing." Aria's voice was as cold as the ice that settled in her green eyes. "What he did to your father ... he will die for."

CHAPTER THIRTY-THREE

"Woah, careful!"

Phoenix was so caught up in her own thoughts that she had somehow completely missed the mountain of wolf standing on the stairs in front of her. As a result, she found herself face to face with Ethan's bare chest, his hands on her shoulders to steady her.

Even distracted, it was hard not to appreciate the broad expanse of muscle only inches from her. Dark hair covered Ethan's chest, adding to the animalistic aura that came off him in waves. A light tan showed no signs of stopping as it followed the impressive v-taper of his waist into the well-worn jeans that hung low on his waist. All helpfully accented by a teasing trail of hair that led downwards.

Phoenix shook herself and looked up to meet a quirked eyebrow and teasing grin, both of which faded when Ethan took in the haggard look on her face.

"How did the talk with your mother go?"

Phoenix sighed and slumped down onto the step as she leaned her head against the wall. "As expected, I guess. She's so angry."

"It's not really surprising." Ethan sat down beside her and his body heat pushed away some of the chill that seemed to have settled permanently within her.

She shook her head. "I know, but this seems different. She's not angry about what was done to her. She's angry about my dad. Only she won't tell me what happened to him."

Beside her, Ethan went still.

"You know?" Her tone was accusing. She didn't mean it to be, but why should he know when no one would tell her?

Ethan shook his head. "No, not for sure, but I have an idea."

He held up a hand to stop her before she could interrupt. "I'm not going to tell you what I think. Suffice it to say that if it was my mate, I would kill him too."

She wanted to argue, but the look that clouded his features stopped her and his ferocity sent a shiver down her spine.

"Did Aria tell you why he took them?" he asked, quickly moving the subject along.

"The prophecy ..." That stupid word seemed to echo on repeat in her head. No matter what she did, she couldn't seem to escape it. "Darius has been encouraging it all along."

There was no surprise on Ethan's face, and she guessed it was logical given the events that led to this point. But as Phoenix recounted her mother's story, she just felt numb, as if she was talking about someone else's life entirely.

"I don't understand how I could have been so wrong about him."

Her shoulders sagged, and she put her head in her hands. It was as if the uncle she loved had died. Only, she couldn't mourn him, because in his place stood a monster that made a mockery of every memory she ever had of him.

Ethan was quiet for a moment before wrapping an arm around her, pulling her close. "We've all been wrong about people before."

"Repeat that." Darius strode into his office and closed the door firmly behind him. He kept his expression calm, but his blood was simmering at a temperature that would rival an erupting volcano.

The vampire standing in front of him tried valiantly to maintain eye contact, but a stain on the desk in front of him was too fascinating to ignore. "It appears they hacked into our security systems, Il

Maestro. The guards on duty were tending to a code one alert when
–"

A hand silenced the vampire. Darius wasn't interested in hearing any more about the incompetency of his security team. They would be dealt with later.

"Raphael?"

"Has not returned, and we haven't been able to trace his phone."

Darius said nothing, merely nodding his dismissal of the vampire as he picked up the ballpoint pen on his desk and twisted it absently around his fingers. Raphael, for all his twisted inclinations, was Darius's most trusted vampire. If his head of security hadn't returned, there could be only one explanation.

Stabbing the pen into the mahogany desk, Darius stood.

As he made his way through the winding corridors of the lair, vampires moved swiftly out of his trajectory; their natural survival instincts wisely warned them against any form of engagement.

Reaching the hidden doorway to the underground chamber, he paused. There were no obvious signs of disturbance, but every instinct told him something was amiss.

Not stopping to light any of the torches lining the wall, he strode down the stone steps, easily finding his way despite the complete darkness.

The broken lock on the floor was the first clue that his instincts were correct.

The empty cell was the second.

Chains hung impotently against the wall, mocking him with their vacant shackles. His bellow of rage shook the very foundations around him as he ripped the heavy door from its frame and flung it across the room.

As he stalked from the chamber, he mentally assessed the situation. His leverage was gone, and his head of security most likely dead. It was safe to assume Phoenix was now aware of his true role in events and wouldn't be quite so amicable going forward.

He needed to move quickly. The witches had better be ready.

CHAPTER THIRTY-FOUR

"It'd be suicide to face him ourselves. We need to let the Council deal with this." The words came out of Ethan's mouth, but they didn't sit well with him.

Night had begun to fall once more, and he'd called everyone for a meeting in his living room to agree a plan of action. Their venture into the lair hadn't gone unnoticed, and it would only be a matter of time before they had vampires breathing down their necks. They needed to be prepared before that happened.

"Ethan's right." Marcus's voice was quiet as he shuffled slowly into the living area, supported by Aria.

Phoenix jumped up from her seat on the sofa and rushed to his side. The healing sleep, combined with supernatural blood, had worked wonders in healing Marcus's wounds, but his skin remained paler than death and his movements were stilted; pain caused him to wince as he was moved to the sofa where Phoenix propped up cushions behind him.

"Darius is very old," Marcus continued, "and more cunning than you ever could imagine."

The words were spoken without inflection, and without emotion, but Ethan could tell the pain they caused. The anger on Aria's face didn't go unnoticed either; it was obvious the thought of giving up her revenge didn't sit well with her.

"Why would the Council help us? Or believe us for that matter?" she said, green eyes flashing. "Darius sits as one of their Witnesses. We are nothing more than lawbreakers in their eyes."

Ethan nodded his acknowledgement of her words and forced himself to ignore the flinch it elicited from Phoenix. It would do them no good to deny the truth. "That may be, but Darius risks exposing us all with his actions. The Council won't take that chance."

"How do we know the Council aren't in it up to their necks?" Shade pushed away from the kitchen table and made a beeline for the fridge. He pulled out two fresh bags of O negative blood and handed one to Marcus before tearing the other open with a slice of a fang.

"He has a point," Phoenix said, obviously reluctant to agree with Shade about anything.

Ethan heard the weariness in her voice, noticed how she gripped her father's hand a little bit tighter, and wished he could make it easier on her somehow. But the Council wouldn't take his word as truth; they'd need proof. They'd need to see the hybrid.

"The Council's edicts go against everything Darius is trying to do. They created the barriers that protect our world and they have no reason to see that effort undone." Ethan could see scepticism on a number of the faces staring back at him. He could even understand why they felt that way, but he needed to believe what he said was true. If the Council had turned their back on their own edicts, they didn't stand a chance.

He focused his attention on Aria and appealed to her the only way he could. "You've just gotten your family back. Is revenge worth losing them again?"

He could see her anger fight to hold firm against the truth of his words, the battle raging visibly on her delicate features. Finally, her shoulders slumped and she shook her head.

"Are we all in agreement then?" Ethan asked as he held up his mobile, a strange mix of numbers and symbols visible on the screen.

A weighted silence was the only answer, and Ethan felt no victory as he made the call.

———

Phoenix tugged nervously at the sleeve of her leather jacket, idly noting the strands of thread that had come loose as a result of the bad habit. The room around her was filled with the hum of conversation, a multitude of languages and accents blurring in an excited babble of voices.

"Remind me again why we're doing this," she said as she glanced sideways at Ethan.

"The only way we'll get to the Council is by going through the Council Liaison Office first. If we can prove to their rep that we're telling the truth, we can be assured the Council will get our message."

Ethan leaned casually against the large glass window, seeming completely unimpressed by the panoramic view of Dublin that spanned out into the night beyond.

"I get that, but why here?"

Nate had explained the role of the C.L.O. to her while Ethan was on the phone stating their case. Bowing to the demands of the Council's guard dogs irritated the snot out of Phoenix, but she accepted the necessity. What no one had explained, was why she now found herself standing on the seventh floor of the Guinness Storehouse, twiddling her thumbs while night covered the city and the vampires undoubtedly began their hunt.

"I agreed to meet their rep, so long as it was on our terms. I won't risk your safety any more than I have to." The intensity in Ethan's brown eyes was at complete odds with the relaxed slouch he'd adopted, and something about the juxtaposition made Phoenix shiver.

Needing to focus on anything other than their upcoming meeting, Phoenix stared out at the lights of the city, becoming mesmerised as they blurred together in a kaleidoscope of colour. Even in the glass enclosure of the Gravity Bar, the sickening smell of the hops filled her nostrils, over-powering the various aromas of perfume and aftershave surrounding her. Abi had never understood why Phoenix disliked the smell of the Guinness brewery so much, but it always reminded Phoenix of an odd mixture of vomit and chipper chips.

Thinking of Abi now, she wished her friend was here to complain to about such trivial concerns. It felt like an age since she'd last been back to the pub. The hourly texts from Abi filled her with guilt as she responded with assurances that everything was fine and she'd be home very soon. It killed her to lie to her friend.

"The hybrid, I presume?"

The man's voice broke clearly through her thoughts, and Phoenix turned to find herself face to face with the C.L.O. representative. A well-tailored grey suit clothed an average-height body, and clean cut brown hair framed a reasonably handsome, but largely non-descript, face. Everything about the man was forgettable. Even his signature seemed vague and intangible to her.

His question was directed towards Ethan, and the smile on his face didn't quite reach his grey eyes. The man held out his hand – again directed solely towards Ethan – in a gesture that seemed to hold a lot more weight than a mere greeting.

Ethan looked at the offered hand and then back at the rep, his face expressionless. "The hybrid's name is Phoenix," he responded coldly.

The man's smile faded marginally and he dropped the ignored hand. He turned reluctantly towards her and nodded in acknowledgement. "Indeed."

A brief grimace was quickly replaced by a politician's smile as the rep gestured to the single empty table beside them. "Shall we?"

With a sigh, Phoenix pulled up a chair next to Ethan. She'd known it would be like this. How could a representative of the Council not view her with disdain? But she thought he might at least try to hide it better.

"Maybe I should begin by introducing myself. My name is Vicktor, and I'm the head of the Council Liaison Office."

The head of the C.L.O. came himself? I thought this was just a formality?

"I act as a liaison to the Council on highly sensitive cases, such as this one," Vicktor continued, glancing pointedly in her direction.

As he droned on about how unique their situation was and how it must be handled with the utmost care, Phoenix found herself growing impatient. Every minute they wasted was one more minute Darius had to track her and her parents.

"Look," she interrupted, sitting forward in her chair, "Ethan already told you everything we know. You've seen the illusive hybrid for yourself and verified my existence. Now can you please put us in touch with the Council so we can get this matter resolved and go about our lives?"

"Ah." Vicktor leaned back and rested his chin on steepled fingers. "I'm afraid it's not quite that simple now is it?"

"What do you mean?" Phoenix asked as a sense of trepidation caused her stomach to flip.

"Well, you're correct that I have indeed verified your existence – your signature is unlike anything I have ever encountered before. However," he paused, "I have not yet verified the story regarding your parents' fate."

Ethan placed a hand on her arm, stopping her before she could respond.

"I made it clear on the phone that Aria and Marcus would not be presenting themselves before you or the Council. Not unless you can guarantee that past transgressions would be exempt from punishment."

Vicktor shifted his attention fully to Ethan, sitting forward in an obvious challenge to the heated energy flowing his way. "You're saying that Aria and Marcus have parted company?"

"What? Of course not!" Phoenix leaned forward to break up the pissing contest that was no doubt about to start between the two men. They didn't have time for this.

"So, they would not be past transgressions we are speaking of, would they?"

Vicktor sat back in his chair once more, a small, victorious smile settling on his face.

She stopped in her tracks, realising too late the trap she'd walked into. Ethan had been adamant her parents stay behind, and she'd agreed it was safer. But she hadn't understood, not really.

Phoenix stood, knowing Ethan would follow her lead without argument. "This meeting is over. Thank you for your time, Vicktor." And with that, she turned and walked towards the lift.

It wasn't until the doors of the lift closed that she released the breath she was holding. She slumped against the mirrored walls and tried to force herself not to panic. What had she just done? They needed the Council to stop Darius. What if Vicktor refused to help them now?

"We'll find another way," Ethan said, as if reading her thoughts.

Plucking at the threads on her jacket, she bit her lip. "He can't keep the information to himself, can he? Surely he'd at least have to notify the Council that there's a security concern."

Ethan nodded and rubbed her arm comfortingly. "It would be a big risk not to. And I'll speak to my father, he'll help us get a message to the Council, just in case Vicktor doesn't." The last words were almost a growl. Ethan's opinion of the C.L.O. rep was clear by the very mention of his name.

When the lift reached the ground floor, they made their way through the throngs of tourists in silence and out beyond the large, black gates to the waiting night. Heavy clouds hung overhead like ink stains in the sky, and the damp pavement served as a reminder that rain was never far away.

"It's not going to be safe for you once the Council knows," Ethan said. He stared ahead and avoided her eyes.

"Was it ever safe for me?" She laughed wryly.

He gave her a small smile in acknowledgement before shoving his hands into his jacket pockets. "No, probably not. But –"

"But you think the Council will come for me now too?"

Ethan sighed as he finally turned to her. "I honestly don't know. Technically you haven't broken any edicts, but your parents have, and the Council will want their pound of flesh."

"They avoided the Council before, they can do it again."

He watched her closely.

It took a moment to click. Having spent so long alone, Phoenix had forgotten what it was like for her life to be closely linked with anyone else's fate. The realisation hit her like a ton of bricks.

"And if they've to run ... I've to run," she said quietly, wrapping her arms around herself.

CHAPTER THIRTY-FIVE

"What can I get you?" the petite female behind the bar asked with a smile.

"I'll have your finest whiskey and the pleasure of your company for a drink," Darius said, allowing his natural persuasion to seep into the words.

Her blue eyes sparkled, but she took only a single glass from the counter.

Stretching to the highest shelf behind her, she grabbed an old bottle, causing Darius to raise a neatly manicured eyebrow. She knew her whiskey. It almost made him feel bad about his plans to torture her ... Almost.

"I haven't seen you around before." She poured the rich golden liquid into a glass and slid it towards him.

"I travel a lot for business," he replied as he noted her appreciative glance at the black Armani suit he'd chosen. "It's not often I get to appreciate the benefits the area has to offer. It appears I've been missing out."

The female snorted and gave him a look that very clearly said "cut the bull".

Swiftly changing tactic, Darius leaned back and rested his arm along the back of his chair. "You own this place?"

She nodded and he looked around, wondering what it was that Phoenix had loved so much about the small, dingy pub. Although, the whiskey *was* good, he conceded as he took a sip of his drink, savouring the rich burn as it slid effortlessly down the back of his throat.

"It's impressive," he said out loud. "Could I be so bold as to ask the name of the owner?"

She shook her head with a wry smile. "I'm Abi. Might I be so bold as to ask your name?"

"A lady as beautiful as you may be as bold as you like." He inclined his head and took another sip of his whiskey. "I'm Darius."

With introductions complete, his prey relaxed noticeably; her smile came more quickly to his carefully placed compliments, and her pupils dilated ever so slightly as he ran his tongue over his bottom lip.

He allowed the conversation to flow, imagining creative ways to make her pale skin bleed as he smiled and laughed along at the appropriate moments. Eventually though, he grew tired of the small talk and decided to cut to the chase.

"What time do you get off work?" he asked, subtly brushing against the fingers she'd been moving subconsciously closer to him.

Abi gave a quick glance around the bar, then smiled at him. "Any time I want. I'm the boss."

"Let me buy you dinner."

She hesitated.

Darius took her hand in his as he stood and met her uncertain gaze with his most seductive smile. "I'm sure your barman can manage without you for an hour. You wouldn't leave a man to eat alone, now would you?"

She looked around the bar once more. Only a handful of tables were occupied, and the few customers at the bar were happily nursing their pints.

"Feck it, why not." Abi's smile grew bigger and her eyes sparkled. "Let me tell Paul I'm going and leave a note in case my friend comes back."

The smile that watched her back as she hurried away was his first genuine one of the night.

CHAPTER THIRTY-SIX

Even with the benefit of Ethan's motorbike, the journey took forever. Ethan had wanted to go straight back to his apartment, but though Phoenix knew it was dangerous, she needed to see Abi. She needed to say goodbye.

The angry growl of the engine only highlighted the crushing weight of things unsaid, and her heart was heavy as they pulled up in front of the pub. Phoenix braced herself for what she needed to do. It wouldn't be forever. As soon as the whole mess was fixed, she'd come back.

With a deep breath, she paused at the door and turned to Ethan. "Can you wait here for me?"

"Phoenix –"

"Please, Ethan. This is hard enough."

She could see the battle rage across his face. He wanted so much to protect her, and this was the easiest place for Darius to find them. But she knew her friend; Abi would think she was being pressured into leaving and that Ethan was the bad guy.

Eventually, he sighed and nodded. "Make it quick, Phoenix. It's not safe here."

As she turned towards the door of the pub, he reached out a hand to stop her. "I called my father before we came out tonight, just in case things didn't go to plan with the Council. He's agreed to give you and your parents refuge with the pack until everything blows over."

Ethan watched her closely, as if trying to gauge her reaction. "You'll be safe there. I'll make sure of it."

A strange feeling tightened Phoenix's chest and all she could do was nod her gratitude. She pulled open the heavy door and was hit with a blast of warm air along with the familiar scent of home. Low music formed the background soundtrack to the hum of conversation and occasional laughter.

She looked around apprehensively as she made her way through the pub, but there was no sign of Abi. Grateful that Paul, their part-time barman, was preoccupied with customers, Phoenix gave a small wave and slipped behind the bar, running upstairs to find her friend.

The dark silence that met her at the top of the stairs caused her steps to falter. There was a strange feeling of abandonment to the apartment. The darkness muted all the bright colours that usually brought it to life, and shadows hinted at ominous possibilities.

"Abi?" Phoenix called, trying to ignore the niggling sense of unease that was tapping its way along her spine. As she made her way down the hallway to check Abi's room, she chastised herself for being so jumpy. It'd been a long few days and she needed sleep.

Abi's room was empty and the bed neatly made. A subtle hint of musk permeated the air. Phoenix instantly recognised the scent of Abi's 'good' perfume.

She debated whether or not to call Abi's mobile as she made her way back to the kitchen, but when she got there, she noticed a small sheet of white paper stuck to the fridge with her name on it. Abi's bubbly script was immediately recognisable and her shoulders loosened their rigid hold with a sigh of relief as she pulled it from the door. Trust Abi to resort to stone age communication on the off-chance Phoenix returned while she was gone.

A smile began to form as she read, almost able to hear her friend's enthusiastic voice describing the tall, dark, handsome man that had come into the bar and insisted she join him for dinner or his life would not be complete. She shook her head, laughing, clearly able to picture the scene in her mind. Abi loved flirting with the customers, but she also liked to make them work for it.

As she reached the end of the note, the laughter died abruptly in her throat. The words leapt off the page at her, turning her blood to ice in her veins.

You better get home soon. I need my roomie back. Wish me luck with Darius! X

Time froze around her, and the words blurred on the page. She clutched desperately for any other explanation; a random coincidence of names, a spelling mistake. Anything.

It was with an oddly calm sense of detachment that she pulled the phone out of her pocket and scrolled through her contacts. The roar of her heart beat was all she could hear as she pressed the call button and raised the phone to her ear.

"Phoenix, darling, I've been waiting for your call."

Darius's voice was rich and warm on the other end of the phone, but now she could hear something in his tone she'd never heard before – a cruel mocking; subtle but very present.

"Where is she?" Phoenix was surprised at the steadiness of her voice and amazed that her hands remained still, even as a crushing weight bore down on her chest.

Laughter rolled through the phone, sending chills through her.

"What? No time for small talk? But we have so much to catch up on."

"Don't play games with me, Darius."

Darius's voice turned cold, devoid of its feigned warmth. "I don't play games, Phoenix. You should know that."

For the first time, Phoenix realised she was hearing Darius for who he really was, and a little part of her heart – the part that still held a childish hope – broke.

"What do you want from me?" she asked softly, gripping the phone so tight it was a miracle it didn't snap in half.

"It's time we had a little heart to heart. Come to the lair. Alone. If I even sense your little werewolf friend, I will kill the human. And then I will take much pleasure in killing him too."

The thump of her pulse grew louder and louder until it was like thunder pounding through her head. She knew the question she needed to ask, but the words stuck in her throat like razor blades.

"How do I know Abi is alive?" she said finally, and braced herself with resolve.

The line was quiet for a moment before the silence was shattered by a muffled scream.

Phoenix's heart stopped short, and fear for her friend threatened to overwhelm her completely. "I swear, Darius, if you hurt her –"

"Now is not the time for idle threats, Phoenix. If I were you, I'd get here quickly. It wouldn't be a good idea to leave me alone too long with such a fragile toy."

With a click, the phone went dead and Phoenix let it slide limply from her hand. She stood frozen, her mind desperately grasping for any options available to her. But really, she had none.

He would kill her. Despite her difficulties comprehending this new reality, she was under no illusions about that point. It didn't matter though, she wouldn't leave her friend at his mercy. Whatever happened, she would get Abi out.

A satisfied smile spread over Darius's face as he let the phone fall to the ground and crushed it under the heel of his shoe. She would come. There was no way she'd leave her friend to suffer. Always such a bleeding heart.

As his thoughts returned to the human, he assessed the small frame hanging from chains fixed to the wall of the main chamber. She was a curious sight, so small and fragile, her blue eyes wide with terror. Yet, a strange defiance remained, and even with her fear, she continued to look him square in the eye.

It would be fun to try to break her while he waited for Phoenix to arrive.

He moved closer to her and ghosted his hand slowly down her jaw. Her heartbeat quickened, but still she refused to look away. Driven by her defiance, he let his finger trail down the front of her throat, moving ever lower until it hit the opening of her loose blouse and brushed against the pale mound of her breasts. Her fists clenched tightly as she tensed against his touch, eliciting a rich laugh from him.

Turning to the metal table that had been set up to the left of the shackles, he ran his hands over the various toys he'd laid out. Soft leather lay in stark contrast to hard, cold steel. Each object held tantalising possibilities.

Which to choose, which to choose …

He picked up the heavy iron scissors, enjoying the weight of the metal in his hand. With slow, deliberate movements he made his way back to the girl, twisting his hand so that the flickering candlelight glinted off the blood-stained blades.

Following the same path his finger had taken, he slid the tip of the scissors gently along her jaw and down the front of her throat. With careful precision, he allowed the razor-sharp blades to continue down before slicing through the soft material of her blouse like it was tissue paper. He paused only when he reached the soft, vulnerable skin of her stomach.

Sweat beaded on her forehead and she held her breath, as if she could make herself invisible by remaining completely still.

With a swift upward slice, he tore through the gag covering her mouth. He'd expected her to beg and plead, but was surprised when, instead of doing either, she reared back her head as far as the restraints would allow and spat in his face.

Warm saliva slid a mocking trail down his cheek and he clenched his jaw in fury. Turning once more to the table, he wiped his cheek and put down the scissors. In its place, he chose the soft leather whip that was his toy of choice for pretty ladies.

As he faced the human, Darius allowed his fangs to extend. And this time, as the candlelight glinted off the silver spikes that graced the end of the whip, the screaming started in earnest.

CHAPTER THIRTY-SEVEN

Ethan paced restlessly in front of the pub. It wasn't safe for them to be here. How had he let her talk him into coming?

The night around him was quiet and the streets were empty as midnight drew closer. There'd been no sign of the vampires, and no trouble since they'd made their getaway from the lair. That fact alone worried him.

Needing to do something productive while he waited, he pulled out his phone and called Nate.

"Is Aria with you?"

A huffy response regarding his lack of manners, and some muffled noises preceded Aria's breathless voice.

"Is Phoenix okay?"

"Yes, yes, everything's fine," he quickly assured her, realising too late the thoughts that must be going through her head. He kept one eye on his surroundings and one on the door of the pub as he quickly relayed the details of their meeting with the C.L.O. rep.

"It's not safe for us to stay here any longer is it?" Aria said after a long pause, her voice heavy with resignation.

He resisted the urge to apologise, knowing his words wouldn't change the reality she'd faced ever since meeting Marcus.

"I think it's best that we head to Donegal tonight," he replied instead, focusing on the ways that he *could* help.

"We'll be ready. Just bring my baby girl back safe, Ethan." And with that she hung up, leaving him staring once more at the door of the pub, wondering how long Phoenix had been gone.

His wolf paced restlessly, something about Aria's words setting his animal instincts on edge. Phoenix would be furious at him for interrupting a heart to heart with Abi, and he wanted to give her time to say goodbye, but they'd been lucky until now. That luck wouldn't last forever.

With a sigh, he pushed his way through the heavy door and was met with a blast of warm air. Dimmed lights and hushed conversations gave an intimate feel that seemed suitably matched to the cold winter night beyond the pub's confines. Ethan gave the room a quick scan, not really expecting to find Abi or Phoenix in the main part of the bar. He waited until the barman was busy cleaning tables before he slipped quietly to the back of the bar and through the door that led to the living quarters. He took the stairs two at a time, noting vaguely the cool draft as he stepped into the apartment.

Phoenix's scent clung to every surface of the small space, but the bright, artistic décor seemed to him the complete antithesis of her personality. Any other time he'd have smiled trying to picture her here with Abi, surrounded by so many colours and soft furnishings. But the silence of the apartment distracted him from any other thoughts of colour charts.

Phoenix's scent was fresh, confirming she'd come up to the apartment. So where was she?

He looked around each room, but saw no signs of struggle and no obvious cause for concern, yet something was setting alarm bells trembling in his head. The cold blast of air when he opened the door to the kitchen explained the draft he'd been feeling. And the open window at the far side of the room sent those alarm bells screaming at full force.

She wouldn't have ...

In his rush to the window, Ethan struck something with his foot, sending it sliding across the tiled floor with a clatter. The soft glow of moonlight filtering in from the open window glinted off the object and caused his heart to leap in his chest.

Phoenix's phone lay abandoned on the floor, cracked screen causing the shine that had drawn his attention. With a new sense of urgency, he picked it up, temporarily grateful for her negligible sense of security as he easily flicked to her call list without a pin code.

He knew what he'd find before he saw it – Darius's name at the top of the list, mocking him. What he didn't know, or understand, was why she'd call him. Was she that desperate for revenge?

He forced himself to stay calm as he continued towards the open window. Her scent was particularly strong there, and as he looked down on the alley at the back of the pub, he cursed his incompetence for letting her go in alone.

Wanting to roar in frustration, he slammed his fist down on the kitchen counter.

Another quick scan of the room showed nothing out of place, aside from a crumpled piece of paper that looked odd for no other reason than the relative cleanliness of the room. After pocketing Phoenix's phone, he unfolded the paper. Bubbly script covered the page before him, and as he quickly scanned the words everything became clear.

If there was one thing he'd learned about Phoenix, it was that she was unfailingly loyal. She may not be stupid enough to face Darius for revenge alone, but if he had Abi, she wouldn't hesitate to offer herself up as a sacrifice.

Without wasting another second, he left the apartment, pulling his own phone from his pocket as he went.

"Nate, we have a problem."

CHAPTER THIRTY-EIGHT

The trip back to the lair was the longest of Phoenix's life. Her heart had twisted in her chest as she snuck out the back and slipped away into the night in her trusty Mustang. Ethan would be crushed by her betrayal, but there was no other choice.

Ahead of her, familiar imposing walls loomed, blocking her view of the large, white mansion that lay at the end of the winding drive-way. Thick, metal security gates opened silently as she approached, and she drove solemnly into the mouth of the beast. She could feel unseen eyes watching her every move as she pulled up in front of the lair and stepped out of the car.

The night around her was completely silent, devoid of all signs of life, and shivers ran down her spine that had little to do with the chilling wind. The unnatural silence and the feeling of being watched followed her as she entered the large mansion that housed Darius's vampires.

A single vampire stepped into the hallway in front of her, and Phoenix tensed. She didn't recognise the man, but his black uniform clearly identified him as security, and his seemingly calm demeanour was no indication of his orders. The vampire merely sneered in acknowledgement of her obvious fear and held out a large hand with his palm up.

Her weapons. He'd been sent to collect her weapons.

Phoenix almost laughed out loud, realising they'd given her far more credit than they should have. Fear for Abi had overwhelmed her so much that all she'd been able to think about was sneaking out of the pub without Ethan noticing. The large carving knife stuck down the side of her boot wouldn't have been much help against a lair full of vampires anyway, so it cost her little to hand it over.

Unsatisfied with her pathetic offering, the vampire flung the knife; it lodged deep into the door behind her with a thud. It took all of her restraint not to lash out, but one quick frisk later and she was free to pass.

Phoenix wasted no time moving through the halls, more convinced now that Darius wouldn't allow his vamps to hurt her. At least not before he could. Regardless, adrenaline thrummed through her as she kept a close eye on her surroundings, all the while grasping desperately for a plan that might get Abi out alive.

In the space of what seemed like a heartbeat, she found herself once more standing in front of the entrance to the underground chamber. The door stood open, and the darkness beyond beckoned her forward for the final descent.

She faltered only for a moment, knowing that once she took the final step through the door, there would be no going back. Hell, maybe there'd never been a way back for her. Maybe she'd been screwed from the moment she found out about the prophecy.

As she crossed the threshold into the darkness, the same feeling of wrongness she'd felt previously enveloped her. It was stronger now, an almost palpable weight that made her every movement sluggish. She clenched her fists, and took slow, deep breaths through her nose, willing her heartbeat to calm. It would be no use, of course. Darius would hear the blood coursing through her veins. Like any good predator.

She came to the final bend before the steps would spill her out into the open chamber and paused. A low murmuring chant, rhythmic and almost hypnotic, came from the room beyond. A woman's voice.

Phoenix was picturing the layout of the chamber, trying to wrack her memory for any possible cover, when Darius's warm voice broke through her thoughts. "Phoenix, darling, how good of you to join us."

Chills swept across her skin and she held herself frozen on the spot. Was he bluffing? A heartbeat. And then the sound of metal scraping against stone. Followed by a low whimper.

"Don't you want to see your friend?" he asked, his voice projecting an almost amicable curiosity.

At the mention of Abi, her gut lurched. She took the last few steps that would bring her into view of the open chamber, fearing the sight that would greet her.

The flickering flame of candlelight cast ominous shadows around the already dark chamber. Phoenix's eyes were immediately drawn to the stone altar where a woman stood, head bowed, arms extended towards the earth. It was from her that the chanting came, and from around her, the heaviest aura of magic seemed to fall.

Phoenix felt a brief flash of relief when she saw the altar empty, but the relief was short lived. As she cast her gaze around the chamber, she found her friend hanging by thick metal chains from the wall furthest away. Abi's head was slumped forward. Her long hair was ragged with sweat and obscured the view of her face.

She could sense, almost better than she could see, the rise and fall of Abi's chest as her heart frantically pumped blood around her body. And though her mind tried to shut out the implications, Phoenix could make out a number of tears in her friend's clothes, flashes of pale skin shining in contrast to the dark clothing.

Darius stood next to Abi. His posture was friendly and relaxed, even as his fingers gently caressed the knives gleaming on a small folding table beside him. He smiled in welcome at her as she stepped into the room, but made no move in her direction.

The image was so disconcerting that for a moment Phoenix wanted to weep. He looked so like the man she'd known as a child that her mind struggled to comprehend the new reality she'd found herself in. So many memories from her childhood – all lies.

"Abi are you okay?"

She was proud of how steady her voice sounded. Darius would be able to sense her fear, but for her own sake, she needed to at least maintain the illusion of being calm.

"Oh, she's fine." Darius waved a hand dismissively, the reassuring sentiment somewhat lost by the fact that the hand held a long, gleaming knife.

Beside him, Abi raised her head. Slowly. As if the simple movement took all of her energy. Her face was pale and beads of sweat ran a trail down her forehead, but her eyes were a flame of blue defiance. Phoenix could feel the anger behind her friend's glare and even through the darkness, she could see the implied order: leave.

Ignoring the burning glare – and the order – she edged cautiously into the chamber, assessing her surroundings for any hidden surprises.

"So, why did you call me here, Darius?"

The smile he turned on her was worse than any of the lethal blades he had close at hand. It was so reminiscent of the man she'd known and loved that her steps faltered yet again.

"Can't a man just want to catch up with his favourite niece?"

Swallowing past the lump in her throat, she shook her head sadly. "If you'd said that a couple of days ago, I'd probably have believed you ... I've learned a lot since then, Uncle D."

He tilted his head in acknowledgement and an almost rueful expression replaced the smile on his face. "I guess so."

She pushed away the grief of acceptance and tried to focus on her surroundings. She needed a weapon, something that might give her even a fighting chance. Losing was inevitable, but she would damn sure cause some damage before she did. She was vaguely aware that Darius was still talking – something about Raphael overstepping his orders – when a glint against the wall caught her eye.

Almost hidden by the dark shadows of the chamber, she could just make out the curved blades that leaned against the stone wall barely ten feet from where Abi hung. It left her little room for error with Darius standing so close, but the options weren't really stacked in her favour anyway, and there was something about the blades that drew her attention.

Needing to keep him distracted – that's what they did in the movies, right? – she asked the question that was eating away at her. "Why did you do it, Uncle D? My parents trusted you."

"They found out about the prophecy. They would have gotten in the way." His tone was so matter of fact that the shock of it brought her to a complete stop.

"But why? Why do you want the prophecy fulfilled?"

The blade closest to her, a short sword with a curved edge made of a dark metal, was almost within reaching distance. But she didn't move. Because on some soul deep level, Darius's answer was more important than the weapon.

His expression changed to one of genuine surprise, as if the answer should've been obvious. "Have I taught you nothing, Phoenix? For power, of course."

He actually seemed disappointed as he looked at her, and for a brief moment she was a child again, wanting desperately to make him proud. A stupid notion given she was obviously talking to a psychopath, but some habits were hard to break.

"This is not how it was," he continued, staring vacantly at the altar. "Not how it should be. We were once worshipped as Gods. And now, we will be again."

With a shake of his head, Darius turned his attention back to her, seeming to regroup. "Thanks to you we will regain our rightful place. The people who rejected you will bow down at your feet. Think about it, Phoenix."

A shiver of apprehension ran down her spine. Whether from his words, or the growing fervour in his eyes, she wasn't sure. "You're insane."

Anger flashed in his eyes, and she knew she had to do something. Pushing her abilities to their limits, she moved faster than she even believed herself capable of. As she grabbed the dark, curved blade closest to her, she lunged forward to place herself between Abi and Darius. Phoenix had a bare fraction of a second to register Darius's lack of concern for her attack before the strangest thing happened. She froze.

Confusion hit her, followed swiftly by terror.

She couldn't move. At all.

Her brain was screaming at her limbs, but there was just ... nothing. Her muscles failed to contract, and her joints remained locked in position. Her hand clung desperately – and uselessly – to the blade it held. Darius's laughter washed over her like ice as she looked up to meet his black gaze.

"You always did have so much spunk." A tilt of his head and the laughter faded. "Did you really think I'd be that foolish?"

"Well, a girl can dream," she said, relieved to find herself able to speak as she pulled her reflex for sarcasm around her like a comfort blanket.

"I think it would be best if you drop the knife now, Phoenix."

Just like that, the blade fell from her grasp and hit the ground with a clatter. There'd been no change in the grip of her hand. How had the knife fallen? She gritted her teeth and tried to push through the inertia, but everything from the neck down remained still. Panic began to build to such an overwhelming degree that she almost missed it – the heavy weight of witchcraft, wrapping itself around her like a snake.

And she knew she was truly in deep shit.

CHAPTER THIRTY-NINE

I let him trick me.

As the realisation dawned on Phoenix, her panic was temporarily overshadowed by anger. Anger at Darius for not being the man she looked up to. Anger at the witch for betraying her calling. Anger at fate for dealing her such a fucked-up hand. And mostly, anger at herself.

How could she help Abi when she couldn't even help herself?

With that thought, her attention was pulled back to the wall behind her. Testing the limitations of her movement, Phoenix twisted her head as far as she could while her body was held in stasis. The muscles protested, but still she strained, needing to see her friend.

Familiar blue eyes met hers, filled with a sorrow that made her want to weep. But there was no judgement, no anger. There should have been both.

"Abi ..." she whispered, but the word died on her lips as she grasped in vain for a way to convey how sorry she was.

Steel took the place of sorrow in her friend's eyes as Abi shook her head firmly, shutting down anything more she might say.

The sound of scraping metal made Phoenix's heart jump, and she quickly shifted her gaze back to Darius. There was no time left for self-indulgent pity.

He seemed momentarily oblivious of her as he sharpened a roughly hewn blade on the edge of a jagged stone. The metal of the blade was dull and any real sense of craftmanship was missing, but it appeared well-used, and there was very little question of the damage it could cause. Darius looked up as she watched him in silence, his black gaze meeting hers briefly before flicking back to admire the sharp edge.

"Your mother was fond of this blade," he said. "She could refrain from screaming for so many of my other toys. But this one" – he turned the blade slowly from side to side – "this one she screamed for."

Phoenix clenched her jaw so tight it made her teeth ache. Anger turned her blood to molten lava, but she forced herself to remain quiet.

"It's strange really," Darius continued, unperturbed. "It's not even made of iron. In fact, I'm not really sure what it's made of, just that it's very old. It was my Master's favourite toy."

He moved towards her with slow, deliberate steps, while his fingers played along the edge of the blade. As he stopped in front of her, she looked up and found herself face to face with a complete stranger. There was no sense of recognition, no affection remaining in his eyes, just a strange luminescence that leant itself to the semblance of crazy.

Slowly, he trailed the flat edge of the blade down her cheek; the cold metal unlike anything she'd ever felt before. Like ice, it scalded her wherever it touched. Phoenix held her breath and waited for the sharp sting to follow, but Darius merely continued talking as he ran the blade almost absently down the line of her jaw, burning a path down her neck.

"Your father stopped screaming far too early for my liking. He really was no fun at all."

Phoenix felt her breath freeze in her chest.

"I really thought he'd give in." Darius's brow furrowed in confusion. "I was so sure he couldn't resist forever. Not when her sweet blood was so close."

Realisation hit like a forty-foot truck, and suddenly Phoenix knew. Knew what her mother had kept from her. Knew that if Darius had succeeded, it would've been a fate worse than death for her father.

"You starved him." The words left her mouth in a whisper of disbelief. The horror she felt was so vast that she couldn't even find words to describe it.

He looked at her in surprise. "Well, of course. Although, I guess it's really a matter of perspective since he had such a tasty food source so close at hand."

The ice that had begun to fill her veins at the touch of his blade, turned to flames, burning through her like wildfire. She struggled with everything she had against the magic that held her, but even her rage was not enough to break the invisible bonds.

"I swear to you, Darius, on my very life, that I will find a way to make you pay."

Cold laughter filled the chamber. "Oh, don't worry, Phoenix, dear, I don't require your life just yet."

And with that, he slashed the blade downwards.

For a moment confusion was the only thing Phoenix felt, then a searing pain tore up her left arm. She was dimly aware of Abi's screams as she looked down to see a thin line of blood trickle down her arm. Funny, it hurt so much more than it should for such a shallow cut.

Darius stared at the blood, mesmerised, and she could almost feel the force of the hunger coming off him. "So much power," he muttered, as he reached for a dull metal bowl on the table beside him.

He held the bowl under her wrist, watching as the blood drew a path down towards her fingers, and slowly dripped into the waiting container. A sense of dread purer than anything she'd ever felt before swept through her, and she twisted her head once more to focus on her friend.

The look of terror on Abi's face grounded her in a way that nothing else could. She committed every line of Abi's face to memory and swore to herself that her friend would not die here with her. Not like this. She closed her eyes and tried to focus deep inside herself for any thread of power she could grasp.

All of a sudden, the chamber around her was filled with silence, and it took her a moment to realise that the low murmuring chant of the witch had stopped.

When she opened her eyes, she was surprised to find that Darius was no longer standing in front of her. It took her another precious few moments to realise that the indescribable heaviness had also lifted from her. And when she tried once more to move her fingers, they miraculously responded. Aware that her window of opportunity was narrow at best, she dived for the blade Darius had discarded on the table in exchange for the bowl.

His rich laughter filled the silence around her, skittering over her skin. "Oh, Phoenix, have we not already established how futile it is for you to fight me?"

He was right of course. She wasn't strong enough to beat him, but that didn't mean she would stop trying. She clung desperately to the blade and wracked her brain for any kind of plan that would get Abi free. Suddenly, Darius's words came back to her. *I don't require your life just yet.*

He may not require it, but he wouldn't keep her alive if he didn't need to. Would he?

Turning to face Darius once more, Phoenix flipped the blade towards herself, the sharpened tip poised directly over her thumping heart as her eyes met his defiantly. His flinch was so fleeting, the mask so quickly back in place, that if she hadn't been watching for a reaction, she'd have missed it.

"You have what you want now, Darius. Let Abi go. This has nothing to do with her."

He laughed again, but something in his tone rang so much hollower this time. "Now why would I let my leverage go?"

"I'll make this very simple." She pressed the icy edge of the blade closer and felt the cold seep through to her very soul as the blade met the resistance of her chest. "Let her go or I will end this, and you'll never see your precious prophecy fulfilled."

The eyes that stared back at her blazed with a fury unlike any she'd ever seen, and for a moment Phoenix felt true fear. But instinct told her that her assumption had been right, and that knowledge brought with it a strange sense of calm.

She wasn't afraid to die. Not if it meant Abi would live.

For an eternity Darius simply watched her, as if trying to read her thoughts and decide if she was bluffing.

She wasn't.

As if coming to the same conclusion, he shrugged nonchalantly. "If you're going to make a big deal of it, the human can go. She really is of no interest to me now that she has served her purpose. Humans are far too ... breakable."

Abi struggled against her restraints, stretching towards Phoenix with muffled protests. Blue eyes blazed their anger and she shook her head, pointlessly refuting the trade that had been made.

With effort, Phoenix ignored her friend, keeping her emotions in check and her gaze firmly locked on Darius. She nodded for him to unlock the chains and held her breath as she waited for the slightest twitch that might indicate betrayal.

He reached one hand slowly towards the key hanging on the wall to the right of Abi. His other hand was slightly hidden from sight. A split-second flash of fangs was her only clue, and knowing she'd never reach Abi in time, Phoenix turned the blade from her chest and flung it towards Darius's head in blind panic.

The blade missed by millimetres, lodging in the stone wall with a thud.

Darius smiled at her, a victorious glint in his eyes. As he stalked towards her, Phoenix heard it – a loud inhuman roar, followed by a commotion that could only mean one thing. Help had arrived.

CHAPTER FORTY

The sight that met Ethan's eyes as he forced his way into the chamber made his blood run cold and his vision cloud red. Phoenix was on the opposite side of the room, about as far from him as it was possible to be. A vampire he could only assume to be Darius stood facing her, much too close for comfort.

Even across the space he could smell the blood that dripped down her arm, and the scent caused his wolf to roar as it crashed against his mental barriers, years of control eroded by the simple knowledge that she'd been hurt.

Behind him, Nate, Shade, Lily, Aria and Marcus pushed their way into the chamber, followed closely by the remaining vampire guards as their fighting spilled into the large stone room. He had to trust the others had it under control, because the only thing he could focus on was the vampire and Phoenix.

Unleashing control of the wolf, he gave himself over to instinct. The wolf's speed enabled him to close the distance in fractions of a second and his razor-sharp claws tore free of his skin as he moved.

Ethan lashed out and felt the warm gush of blood over his hand, but his vampire target seemed to simply disappear, as if he'd never been there.

The faintest of breezes caressed the back of his neck, and he spun around in time to see the glint of silver move towards his throat. Instinct drove his body back from the blade, just enough that it lightly grazed his neck, the silver leaving a burning trail in its wake. But the sudden shift threw him off balance, and it was all he could do to avoid the blade a second time as he fell.

Darius's attack was relentless, the slashes becoming little more than a blur. Even with the speed of his wolf, Ethan was no match for a vampire of Darius's age, and the lethal edge of silver came closer and closer as he fought to get up from the floor.

It was only the brief flash of red that gave away Phoenix's movement as she attacked Darius from behind, giving Ethan the precious seconds needed to lunge to his feet.

He used the temporary distraction to launch a second attack at Darius, forcing the vampire to divide his attention between both of them. Weeks of training together allowed him to fall into an easy rhythm with Phoenix as he complemented her movements with his own. But Darius was too quick. Each fist merely glanced off the intended target and each claw merely grazed.

Ethan's wolf pushed against the final restraints that bound it, but he fought back. They needed to find a weakness, and he needed to think clearly. He was slowly pulling back from the haze of animal instinct when his concentration was shattered by a high-pitched scream of terror.

Lily.

Spinning out of the way of Darius's fist, he used the momentum to pivot so he could seek out the young witch in the chaos that surrounded him. His eyes found her, little more than ten feet to his left where she was pinned to the ground with a stocky, blonde vampire looming over her. Ethan could tell by the frantic movement of her lips that she was trying to cast a spell, but the vampire was twice her size, and was easily overwhelming her.

Torn between the need to save Lily, and his wolf's instinct to protect Phoenix, he hesitated.

"Go!" Phoenix yelled as she shoved him insistently.

Lily screamed again as the blonde vampire reared back to lunge for her throat, effectively cutting off any further argument.

Ethan propelled himself to the side, sending his full weight barrelling into the vampire and knocking him away from Lily; leaving Phoenix to once more face Darius alone.

Phoenix's heart thudded in her chest. The terror she felt for Abi now extended to each and every person that had come to fight by her side. People that were willing to risk their lives for her.

Darius waited patiently for her to make a move. The smile that graced his face was one of complete arrogance, filled with the surety that he was faster and stronger.

He was. But it changed nothing.

They had come for her, and she would fight.

Drawing on every ounce of resolve and strength she had, Phoenix moved in a blur of speed, trusting her instincts to guide her strikes. For each blow Darius evaded, she followed with another from a different angle.

Another scream tore through the air, coming from Ethan and Lily's direction. The momentary fear she felt for them distracted Phoenix long enough that she failed to see the glittering blade swinging towards her in time. She threw up her arms in defence, but a blaze of fire burnt through her left shoulder as the blade struck.

Pain blackened her vision momentarily until there was only numbness. The arm fell limply to her side, useless and unmoving.

Darius's blade dripped with blood, and a look of satisfaction filled his cold stare as he stalked towards her. He slowly ran his tongue along the blade, shivering with undisguised ecstasy.

Disgust and terror washed over her in equal measures.

Backing away from his advancing form, she abruptly hit a cold, hard surface with a thud. The jagged wall dug into her sweat-soaked back, effectively cutting off one avenue of escape. The smile on Darius's face widened as he looked to her right and his shoulders appeared to relax ever so slightly.

Every instinct told her not to take her eyes off the snake in the grass, but she needed to know what could've possibly made him even more sure of himself. Tentatively, she reached her only working hand out to the side to blindly feel along the wall until it hit something. The rattle of cold iron made her stomach drop.

How many bloody chains are there in this place?

A frantic urgency clouded her thoughts, but she pushed it back forcefully. She needed to get away from the wall. If he managed to chain her, she'd be at his mercy.

Just like her parents.

The thought brought with it a desperate need to act, and Phoenix shoved forcefully away from the wall before lunging to the right. In less than a blink, Darius was there, his body an unmoving barrier as she barrelled into him, damaged shoulder first.

The impact brought a burst of pain that caused her vision to go black again, followed immediately by a flare of colour behind her eyes.

Darius's chilling laugh filled her ears as she fought to regain her orientation. His empty black eyes swam in and out of focus, mere inches from her face, and his hot breath brushed against her skin as he placed an almost tender palm against her cheek.

The burning itch in her palm was so unexpected that for a moment Phoenix thought her bruised consciousness was causing her to hallucinate. An instinctive desire to pull back from the feeling caused her gut to clench. With a surge of hope, she did something she'd never truly done before – she embraced it.

She grasped the infant thread of power and held it for all she was worth. Letting go of all doubts, she urged the burning to grow, to expand, to take on a life of its own.

Darius leaned closer, his fangs extending as his hand moved down to her neck. "Maybe one more taste …"

Her body rigid, Phoenix fought to stay controlled, to encourage and nurture the heat that continued to rise in her palm, even though all she really wanted to do was scream and fight back.

She waited until she felt the first sharp scratch of his fangs before placing her hand on his chest. And finally, she let go.

The light left her body in a blinding explosion of white. Brighter than anything she'd ever before called to her.

When she could finally see again, she found the space in front of her empty. Darius lay slumped against a wall almost twenty feet from where she stood, and spiderweb cracks began to spread through the stone behind him.

Slowly, he began to rise to his feet. He looked so much like something from a horror movie that Phoenix felt a strange urge to laugh hysterically. Charred skin covered his face and hands. Patches of glistening red showed through as blood oozed down his cheek. White fangs glowed in contrast to the blackened flesh surrounding them. And the rage in his eyes was clearly visible even at a distance.

Desperately, she began to call the light to her again, pushing her untrained abilities to their limits as her hand shook and sweat ran down the back of her neck. Her vision faltered and the pain in her head grew, but still she raised a trembling hand.

A slim, pale hand wrapped itself around hers, squeezing gently. The warm, comforting scent of the sun filled her senses, and her trembling hand steadied. Phoenix looked into her mother's green eyes, and the pride she saw there made her breath catch in her chest.

She wasn't alone.

Marcus came to stand on the other side of her, a similar look of pride in his eyes. He placed a large hand on her injured shoulder, and warmth spread through her arm, chasing away the chilling numbness.

Together, they turned to face the vampire before them. The man that had betrayed their family.

CHAPTER FORTY-ONE

Phoenix saw the surprise register on Darius's face. Rage filled his eyes at the sight of her parents standing whole and healthy by her side, and he snarled.

"Hello, old friend," Marcus said softly, moving forward to place himself in front of his wife and child.

She moved to protest, but Aria squeezed her hand once more, giving an almost imperceptible shake of her head before pointedly closing her eyes. Reluctantly, she followed her mother's lead and tried to slow her breathing by blocking out the sound of fighting.

A strange pulsing sensation began in the palm Aria held, and Phoenix's eyes flew open with a gasp. Each little pulse felt like a mild electric shock, an oddly comforting electric shock that began to gradually build in heat.

Aria threw her a wicked smile, and as if on command, Marcus launched himself at Darius, moving so quickly he became an indiscernible blur. Phoenix tried to pull her hand free of her mother's grip; fear for her father's safety demanding action. But Aria held fast, her green eyes urging Phoenix to trust her.

The recent infusion of werewolf blood seemed to give Marcus an edge the other vampire didn't possess. He matched Darius blow for blow and more wounds appeared between the charred patches of skin as Marcus's strikes landed true.

When a well-timed throw sent Darius flying in their direction, Aria squeezed her hand tightly and yelled, "Now!"

The flash of light was effortless this time. Controlled and beautiful in its simplicity, it struck its intended target, causing Darius to roar in pain.

Aria moved forward and Phoenix realised her mother had finally released her hand. She watched in shock as the gentle woman she called mother viciously kicked the fallen vampire in the gut. Blood and spit flew from Darius's mouth with the blow, but he remained on the ground.

A second kick to the head lifted his body clean in the air, causing him to land a couple of feet away on his back. His body started to shudder. It took Phoenix a moment to realise he was laughing; full-bodied, soul-deep laughter.

Aria stalked towards him, her green eyes flashing with barely contained wrath. Her pale skin began to glow with a white light that emanated into the darkness of the chamber.

Darius rolled to his side, and Phoenix had just enough time to register the blade in his hand before it was flying through the air towards her mother. A silent scream froze in Phoenix's throat and her heart stopped beating as Marcus threw himself in front of Aria, knocking her to the ground.

In an instant, she found herself standing between her parents and Darius, unsure quite how she got there. The scent of her father's blood filled her senses as she faced the other vampire.

"Mam?"

"We're okay, Phoenix."

The sound of shuffling followed the muffled response and Marcus's pained voice concurred, "Just a scratch."

Darius snarled and spit blood as he slowly rose to his feet. She noticed with surprise that he wasn't healing, at least not like a vampire normally would. The parts of skin that had been burned by their fae powers remained exposed and oozed blood.

As if he had been burned by the sun.

244

Realising this, Phoenix encouraged her still fledgling heat to grow once more. She fuelled it with all the fear and anger she felt as she walked towards Darius.

A single tear ran down her cheek as she placed her palm to his cheek.

In a vague recess of her mind, she wondered why he didn't stop her and felt an uneasy confusion at the victorious look in his eyes. But then her only thought was of the sun. The bright heat and the warmth of it on her skin.

This time the light was not as strong, but it came. Bringing with it the acrid smell of burning skin, screams of agony, and a headache unlike anything Phoenix had felt before. She pulled her hand away and stumbled backwards as she grasped her head to keep her brain from leaking out with the pain.

Then everything went completely black.

Time seemed to hold its breath. A silence so complete and a darkness so never-ending filled the entire chamber. With it came a whole new level of fear.

And then, on an exhale, it was gone.

Phoenix looked immediately towards Darius, expecting some form of attack. But there was nothing. No attack. And no Darius.

The floor was covered in a pool of blood that almost appeared black in the dim light of the chamber, but no other signs remained of the vampire.

"Where is ..."

Her own scepticism was met with similar perplexed expressions from her parents as she turned a slow circle and waited for the shadows to attack.

Guards littered the floor around her. Many lying motionless, some even missing their heads and beginning to fade. Blood soaked the walls and seemed to pulse with life as it seeped back into the earth. The remaining vampires were swiftly retreating, leaving Phoenix to stare in confusion.

A cold breeze began to fill the chamber, and the skin on her arms pebbled with goose bumps that had little to do with the chill of the wind. Electricity charged the space around her, and the air became heavy, like the weight just before a storm. Every cell in her body screamed danger. She held her breath and waited.

A shuffling sound to her left caused her heart to leap into her throat. Relief flooded through her as she saw Ethan moving towards her, holding Lily. Phoenix ran to him and added her support as she wrapped her arm around Lily's waist. The knot in her stomach eased somewhat as she looked at him.

The young witch appeared to be limping, and blood dripped from a number of cuts along Ethan's forehead and chest, but both were alive. A further look around the chamber and she found Nate and Shade, both in a similar state of disrepair. Nate's cocky grin as he flipped a long knife in his hand told her that he had sustained no serious damage. Shade's trademark scowl could have indicated he was at death's door and she'd have been none the wiser.

Finally, her eyes fell on Abi.

Her friend hung limply from her chains, no longer conscious, but breathing.

Without a word from her, Aria and Marcus rushed to unlock the chains, gently lowering her friend to the ground. Even as the wind picked up, blowing strands of red hair into her damp eyes, relief wrenched a sob from her throat. She'd been so afraid. So afraid they would die because of her. Her friends. Her family.

A sharp cackle echoed around the chamber and Phoenix whipped her head around, her adrenaline spiking once more. Everyone stood to attention with weapons drawn, waiting for the next threat to make itself known. But for a moment there was just silence, and the wind.

The cackle came once more, changing to a gurgling cough that choked off abruptly.

Phoenix followed the sound, ignoring Ethan's attempt to pull her back as she walked slowly towards the stone altar. The shadows seemed deeper somehow, more complete, but she could just about make out a woman's form lying hidden from view.

The witch.

Cursing the stupidity that allowed her to forget such a dangerous foe, Phoenix picked up a long, black blade that lay on the altar. Slowly, and deliberately, she made her way towards the woman that, not long before, had held her completely defenceless at Darius's mercy.

CHAPTER FORTY-TWO

Even in the shadows Phoenix could see the dark stain that surrounded the witch. It slowly expanded as the blood continued to flow. A quick glance showed a jagged object protruding from the witch's chest that shuddered with each wracking cough. The dagger in Phoenix's hand suddenly seemed unnecessary.

"Kill me if you want, hybrid. It won't change anything." The witch's words wheezed out and were quickly followed by a coughing fit that brought up more than just phlegm.

In a blink, Ethan was by her side, extended claws gripping the witch's throat. Phoenix wasn't ashamed to admit that a large part of her felt satisfaction at the shift in power. She could easily turn her back and let the woman die. If she was so inclined. But something about the shrewd gaze that met hers made her hesitate.

"Ethan, wait."

She held out a hand towards him, as if the gesture alone would stop him if he decided to rip out the witch's throat.

"Let her speak."

Dark eyes met hers from the floor, assessing and calculating, even as the life force behind them seeped out onto the floor.

"Your friends may have saved you, child, but it's too late."

"Speak plainly, witch," Ethan growled, and his fist tightened on the pale throat beneath his grip. "Or I will gladly end your suffering."

"Nothing you can do will change my fate now, wolf." The witch's eyes briefly flicked towards his face before their heavy weight fell once more on Phoenix. "The spell was complete. The prophecy will be fulfilled tonight."

Phoenix felt her stomach drop as the tension she'd been holding left her body in a gasp. She had known. It had been too easy. Some part of her knew there was more to come.

Around her, everyone began to speak at once, but it was only noise. Her mind was unable to focus on anything besides the witch's words, repeating themselves over and over again in her head.

"Unless ..." The witch spoke in little more than a whisper, but it brought the noise to a sudden and complete halt, all eyes falling on her.

"Unless what?" Ethan shook her impatiently.

The witch glared at him even as another choking fit took hold of her failing body. When she'd caught her breath, the weight of her gaze landed on Phoenix and it softened as something akin to pity settled in the dark depths of her eyes.

"By your bloodline this was started," the voice that came out of the witch's mouth changed, becoming deeper as the wind began to whip around them with more force. "By your bloodline it may end."

Phoenix looked around nervously as confused murmurings echoed her own thoughts. The wind was picking up speed, and strands of red hair blew across her face, blurring her vision as it grew in strength.

Pushing the hair roughly from her face, she turned back to voice the multitude of questions flying around her head, only to find a lifeless form lying on the ground in front of her, shrewd eyes now staring blankly at the ceiling.

She glanced towards Ethan and the look he gave her mirrored the feeling of dread that was beginning to rise from the empty pit of her stomach.

"What the hell ..." Nate's voice drew everyone's attention as he pointed a shaky finger at a small vortex that was forming from the wind above the altar.

The centre of the vortex was growing darker by the second, as if sucking away what little light filled the chamber.

A sharp intake of breath drew Phoenix's attention to her mother, who stood ghostly pale and stared at the blackness forming.

Phoenix rushed to Aria's side and grabbed her arm. "Mam? What is it?"

"He's done it," Aria said, haunted eyes turning to look at her daughter. "He's torn the fabric."

An icy fear washed over Phoenix, but her mind struggled to make sense of what she was seeing, and she felt a growing sense of hysteria. "I don't understand. What do you mean he's torn the fabric? He can't have torn the fabric."

Ethan came to her side and placed a gentle hand on her back, almost as if he needed to touch her. "The talisman." He looked at Aria for confirmation. "He's found a way to speed up the prophecy. And when the fabric becomes weak enough, they'll be able to get through."

"They –" Phoenix stopped suddenly, memories of a night not so long ago flashing through her mind. "Demons."

"Not just any demons," Aria said, her voice little more than a whisper. "Darius was planning on bringing through the Horsemen."

Phoenix backed away, shaking her head. Her knowledge of the supernatural may have been sorely lacking, but every Supe knew of the Horsemen. They were the things that even the strongest supernatural feared; the bringers of death and destruction to all.

The voices around them raised, panic-filled questions that blurred into one.

"How long?"

"What happens if they get through?"

"How do we stop it?"

Phoenix knew the answer because the witch had told them. Her bloodline had started this, and only her bloodline could stop it. She looked around at the people who had risked their lives to save her. People that had become her friends. Family she'd only just gotten back. The thought of something happening to them hurt her heart. The knowledge that it would be her fault almost brought her to her knees.

But she could stop it. That was what the witch had been saying. She was the key.

Phoenix walked closer to the blackness. Her movements went unnoticed amongst the panic. As she watched, it pulsated and expanded. What had started as small as the narrow gash on her arm, now stretched almost three feet in length, suspended in nothingness.

The closer she got to it, the more she could feel its inexplicable pull. Darius had only used a small bit of her blood to complete the spell, but the darkness wanted more. Somehow, she knew it would take a much larger sacrifice to undo the wheels that had been set in motion.

Tears pricked the back of her eyes as she looked around again. She wasn't ready to say goodbye. For the first time in a very long time, she had more to lose than just Abi. But even that would've been enough. She wouldn't let these people die for her.

And with that thought clear in her mind, she stepped towards the void.

CHAPTER FORTY-THREE

"Phoenix, no!"

Ethan grabbed her just in time. His heart raced like a freight train in his chest as the blackness reached eager tendrils towards its willing victim. She turned to look at him, a single tear rolling down her cheek, even as she resisted his pull.

"It's the only way, Ethan. You have to let me go."

He shook his head vehemently, unable to form the words as he pulled her forcefully away from the void and into his arms. For a moment, Phoenix resisted, but then he felt her body soften and she wrapped her arms around him, laying her head on his chest.

"It's the only way," she repeated, words muffled against the remnants of his torn shirt.

Ignoring her words, he held her closer and focused only on the heat of her body next to his. There had to be another way; there just had to. As the thought formed in his head, the wind began to pick up speed. A strange murky smoke trailed from the bottom of the gaping black hole, and as he watched, the edges pulsated and stretched. The smell of sulphur drifted up from the smoke that was settling on the ground around their feet. Ethan cast a worried glance towards Aria to find a similar look of concern filling her green eyes.

"Em ..." Nate cleared his throat awkwardly, "not to break up a touching moment and all that, but can I make a suggestion?"

Reluctantly, Ethan relaxed his hold on Phoenix as she twisted in his arms to look at Nate.

"Couldn't we just destroy the talisman?" Nate eyed the tear warily. "The Ouroboros. I'm assuming this was why they needed it?" He waved a hand towards the growing void.

A terrifying thread of hope surged through Ethan, but he cautiously held it in check. "Could it work?" he asked, directing the question to Lily, who stood looking uncomfortable by the stone altar.

She fidgeted nervously, averting her gaze from his as her shoulders dropped. "I already searched the witch. I couldn't find the talisman." Her soft-spoken words drove home like a knife, and Ethan felt the whisper of hope bleed from him.

"Do you mind if I check?" Aria looked in askance to Lily before moving to crouch by the witch's frozen form.

As she rustled about, searching every inch of the witch and the surrounding area, the smoke began to thicken. The blackness that had seemed so complete only moments before, formed shadows that brought with them terrifying possibilities.

The bottom edge of the tear pulsed. Once. Twice. Three times. Then a black ink-like substance began to pour over the rim. It flowed and morphed in such a way that no one particular form could be discerned. He heard Phoenix's gasp as she too noticed the movement and her grip on him tightened involuntarily.

"Aria," he said, urgency biting at the edges of his tone. "I don't mean to rush you, but we seem to have a situation here."

A blade flew through the air, flipping handle over tip, and abruptly sliced through the inky mass, causing it to pool motionless on the ground.

"Not anymore we don't." Shade shrugged nonchalantly and spat on the ground.

But the blackness pulsed again, and yet more shadows began to slowly seep from its depths. Sinuous tendons reached out, searching the possibilities of their new surroundings.

Aria's face was sombre as she met his questioning look with a silent shake of her head and she looked longingly towards her daughter. Everyone began to speak over each other again, and he could feel Phoenix's deep breath as she stared intently at the hole that was now almost five foot long.

She'd do it. Despite her fear, and the unknown terrors beyond that void, she would sacrifice herself if there was no other way. Ethan looked around desperately. There had to be something he could do, someone he could kill. Instead, he found Marcus staring at him intently.

It was then he noticed the subtle prodding in his mind. Almost like a politely cautious knock on the door. Something told Ethan he could choose to answer the call or not, but the sadness and regret he saw in Marcus's eyes made him lower his defences.

I'm sorry, Ethan, I would never use your gift like this if I had a choice, but we're running out of time.

Marcus's words, although only in his head, were so clear that Ethan looked around to see if anyone else acknowledged the vampire's statement.

They didn't.

He looked back to Marcus in surprise, realising immediately what gift he was referring to. His blood had created a link with the vampire, however temporary, allowing Marcus to speak to him in a manner far more intimate than was comfortable.

The witch said bloodline, Ethan. Her bloodline *is the key.*

The words registered, but it took Ethan a moment to truly understand them. He had to stop himself before he spoke aloud, suddenly conscious once more of Phoenix's warm body still held in his arms.

No, he thought fervently, *she'll never let you do it.*

Dark eyes met his, filled with a sadness that had no words. *I know. That's why I need your help.*

Moving silently through the shadows, Marcus grabbed a small knife and stepped closer to the tear. Ethan tensed, preparing to shout his objection, when a light touch on his shoulder turned his focus to Aria, who now stood by his side. The shake of her head was barely perceptible, but the look in her eyes spoke volumes.

He hesitated, torn between protecting the woman in his arms and

254

the truth that was staring them all in the face. The prophecy was coming, and if they didn't find a way to stop it, everyone would suffer. Conflicted, he watched silently as Marcus ran the blade along the palm of his hand. Blood flowed from the wound and dripped down towards the tendrils that were eagerly pulling themselves out of the black void.

The thick, viscous liquid hit the inky mass with a hiss, and the tendrils recoiled. Clumps fell to the ground, disintegrating in a cloud of sulphur. Marcus met his gaze for a brief moment, before turning to look at Aria. The look they shared was so full of love that Ethan almost felt like he was intruding on a private moment just by being in the same room.

We've had our time, Ethan. Marcus's voice came once more, steady and sure. *It's her time now.*

Phoenix chose that very moment to pull back from him. She squared her shoulders as she turned to face the others, oblivious to the panic that was constricting his chest.

She will never forgive me. He clenched his fists, wanting to reach out and pull her back to him.

The look Marcus gave him was sympathetic, but unwavering.

She will forgive you. And in time she will understand.

CHAPTER FORTY-FOUR

Phoenix's throat was achingly tight as she pulled back from the comforting warmth of Ethan's arms. The feeling of safety was just an illusion, but damn if she didn't want to cling to it. Which was why she had to move now. Before she lost her nerve.

Looking around, she was once again struck by the knowledge that these people had risked their lives to come for her. They knew who – and what – she was, yet they still came. She held that thought close to her and pointedly ignored the creeping tendrils and cloying smoke, turning first towards Nate.

The sparkling humour that seemed to show in his eyes no matter how dire the situation acted as a balm to her soul and allowed her to smile past the tightness in her chest as she hugged him. Phoenix couldn't tell if his eyes seemed just a little bit duller when she pulled back, but she quickly blocked the thought.

Lily was next to him, still slumped against the altar. She looked as dejected and broken as the night they first met. Phoenix wanted so much to wrap the young girl in her arms and tell her it would be okay.

But that would be a lie.

The best she could do was hug her tightly and pray to whatever god or goddess might be listening to watch over the young witch.

There was no hugging when it came to Shade. He simply paused his ongoing knife attack on the inky tendrils, looked her in the eye, and gave a single nod; the small gesture meaning more than words ever could.

Her heart shattered as she turned to look at Abi, still lying unconscious against the wall. She'd never get to tell her friend how sorry she was. Never get to tell her how much her friendship meant. Kneeling by her side, Phoenix gently brushed the hair back from Abi's sweat-soaked face. She let her forehead rest against Abi's cheek for a brief moment, and whispered, "I love you," before giving herself a brisk shake and rising to stand once more.

Phoenix took a deep breath and turned to face her parents, who were now standing side by side at the altar. Tears threatened to break free of the prison that had held them for ten long years. Memories of laughter and childhood innocence brought with them a yearning so strong she almost doubled over.

"At least this time we get to say goodbye," she said, attempting a weak smile.

The returning smile her mother gave her was so full of love and pride that it was almost painful to look at. She let herself fall into Aria's open arms as a sob of pure, raw grief broke free from her throat.

Her mother held her close, gently rocking her as Phoenix breathed in the warm scent that reminded her so much of happier times. Another set of arms surrounded them both. Broader. Stronger. She knew without looking that it was her father, and even with what was to come, she felt safe.

"We're so proud of you, sweetheart." Her father smoothed back her hair and his warm voice became deeper as it strained with emotion. "So proud of the woman you've become."

At his words, the tears came. She shook her head and pressed her forehead against her mother's shoulder as she fought to stay strong for a little longer.

Just a little longer.

"I failed, Dad. I couldn't stop him."

Marcus turned her firmly towards him and lifted her chin to

ensure she was looking him in the eye. "It wasn't your job to stop him, Phoenix. We should've protected you better. We should've prepared you better."

His dark brown eyes were full of such sadness that all she could do was hug him tightly.

Eventually he pulled back, took a deep breath, and smiled as he held her at arms-length. For a moment, he seemed to be taking in her every feature, then he turned her with a knowing nod and gentle push towards Ethan.

The look of raw pain that met her as she raised her eyes to meet Ethan's stole her breath away and brought the tightness back to her chest tenfold. She searched in vain for something to say, some way to let him know how much it meant that he'd come for her, but she couldn't find the right words. She didn't even know where to start.

His strong arms reached for her and pulled her against the warmth of his chest. She felt small in his embrace, and for a moment, she let herself revel in the safety of the solid muscle that seemed almost contradictory in its welcoming softness.

"I'm sorry. I'm so sorry. Please forgive me," he whispered desperately, lips pressed into her hair.

The words registered with her, but they didn't make sense. Why was he apologising? Phoenix moved to pull away. She needed to tell him it wasn't his fault, but as she tried to pull back, his arms locked tighter around her.

A mild sense of panic washed over her as she pushed against the restriction, but she fought it back, understanding his desire to protect her. However pointless it might be.

He needs to let me go. There's no other way.

She raised her head, ready to reason with him – plead with him, if necessary – so that he wouldn't make this harder than it already was, but the look in his eyes stopped the words before they even left her mouth. The earlier sadness was there, but now it was overshadowed by a resolve unlike anything she'd ever seen in those rich brown eyes.

And he wasn't looking at her.

It was then that Phoenix realised she'd missed something. Something important. Panic overwhelmed her as she began to struggle in earnest, twisting her neck to follow his gaze towards her parents. They stood together holding hands, looking at her with eyes filled with so much love she almost missed the subtle shadow of regret. As she watched, they stepped closer to the blackness, and the inky tendrils grasped for their legs.

A wordless scream clawed its way up her throat as she wrenched against Ethan's arms, her hand reaching for them. Willing them to step back towards her. Praying the look on their faces meant something other than what she feared.

Her mother smiled, her face peaceful. "I'm so grateful we got to see you one last time, sweetheart. It was more than I ever hoped for."

Marcus put one arm around his wife's shoulders and tucked her close to his side. His other hand reached out, revealing a folded piece of paper with tattered and torn edges.

The banshee wail began before they even moved. The sorrowful keening filled the chamber and ripped her aching soul to shreds.

"We love you so much. Don't ever forget that."

With that, they turned as one and stepped into the void.

Her scream was swallowed in a flash of blinding light as the folded paper fell to the ground.

CHAPTER FORTY-FIVE

Flashes of light. Snippets of conversations. It was all a blur. Phoenix had no idea how much time had passed. For all she knew, the fabric could have torn and the black void swallowed them whole.

For all she cared.

As the sounds started slowly filtering into her consciousness, she looked around in a daze. It seemed as if everything was moving in slow motion. The image was made even more surreal by the smoke that filled the chamber.

She was dimly aware that Ethan's arms still surrounded her, but she couldn't hear any of the words he spoke. They didn't matter anyway. There was no sign of the tear, no sign of any demons. And no sign of her parents.

They were gone.

A strange numbness filled her body from the knowledge, providing a detachment that was almost comforting. It was all just a sick joke. Or a bad dream. Maybe she'd never really found her parents again, and everything to this point had been the wishful imagination of a lost child.

A fluttering movement on the ground caught her eye and pulled her out of her rambling thoughts, drawing her attention to the spot she last imagined her father standing. On shaky legs, she pushed away from Ethan. This time he let her go.

The floor rushed up to meet her as she stumbled and fell to her knees. She pushed an unsteady hand out to grasp the yellowing piece of paper that lay on the ground. Some part of her consciousness told her it was important, but her thoughts were so jumbled that the dots weren't connecting.

The paper was old, edges fraying, with dark splattered stains marring the surface. In the far recesses of her mind, she recognised the shiny surface of a photograph, and she was overcome with a sudden need to see what secrets it held.

Her fingers fumbled ineptly, shaking so badly she was terrified she'd rip it. Ethan's large hand appeared before her, and she hesitated for a second before handing it over. She watched him unfold it, gently, as if it was the most fragile thing in the world.

The picture revealed itself and her breath left her completely. The smiling green eyes of an innocent child and the loving gaze of two adoring parents. The scene burned itself into her mind, searing open old wounds even as new, deeper scars were forming.

So many memories. So much happiness. All buried deep in order for that innocent child to survive.

A scream of anguish left her throat raw.

Strong arms enveloped her as the tears began to fall in earnest, blurring her vision. They tried to pull her close, but she resisted, recognising his scent. Recognising the arms that had restrained her while her parents sacrificed themselves.

With a cry of fury, she beat her fists against the solid wall of Ethan's chest. She wanted to hurt him. She wanted to make him feel even a fraction of the pain that was shredding her apart. But he didn't budge. He stood before her, making no move to stop the blows, arms ready and waiting to hold her.

Eventually the sobbing slowed and a bone-aching weariness washed over her. She slumped against him, empty and shivering. The heat that burned through his blood-soaked t-shirt did nothing to chase the chill away.

"It should have been me."

Ethan's body tensed at her whispered words, and he pulled back so suddenly Phoenix almost fell over. He grabbed her shoulders in a bruising grip as fire blazed in his brown eyes.

"Don't you dare say that."

Anger wrapped around her like a familiar blanket and she clung to it eagerly.

"It should have been me! My blood, Ethan. It should have been my blood that closed the tear. And you stopped me."

"Dammit, Phoenix. Don't you get it?" Ethan yelled, his voice cracking. "I had to do it. I couldn't lose you."

He pulled her forcefully to him. His lips crushed hers and stopped her anger in its tracks. His hands were like fire as they pressed against her back, pulling her tight against him. The fierce eagerness of his mouth created a luscious contrast to the softness of his lips and her head swam with the muskiness of his scent.

She couldn't think straight. The cold that had overtaken her body shifted to molten lava as shock was replaced by an almost primal need. She gave herself over to the sensations, and for a moment, the world became little more than lips, and teeth, and hands.

And then once again the world was empty.

Ethan stood away from her, breathing ragged with an uncertain look in his eyes. His hands clenched into fists by his sides, almost as if he needed to stop himself from reaching out for her.

The silence in the chamber was deafening.

Her heartbeat roared in her ears, and her lips burned with the memory of him. She was suddenly acutely aware of all the eyes that watched them.

"We need to get out of here." Shade's voice was cold as he pushed past her on his way to the stairs.

CHAPTER FORTY-SIX

Phoenix hovered by the bedroom door, nervously twining the platinum medallion around her fingers. For the first time since she'd come to the pub, she was unsure of her welcome.

She'd stayed away for twenty-four hours, but even with Lily's assurances, she needed to see for herself that Abi was okay. And she needed to say goodbye.

Ignoring the sickening twist of her stomach, she pushed open the door and peeked hesitantly into Abi's bedroom.

"I was wondering how long you were planning on loitering outside the door." Abi smiled up at her from the bed where she lay engulfed by soft, fluffy cushions spanning the colours of the rainbow.

Her naturally pale skin held a deathly hue that made her seem almost green. Fortunately, the shade nicely accentuated the mottled bruising which formed a patchwork over her cheek. Her arm was held tight against her body in a sling. Much of the damage had been minor or superficial, thankfully. But psychological damage was always harder to quantify.

That had been Darius's pleasure – psychological torture. It could last so much longer than mere physical pain, and hurt in so many ways the body couldn't.

"You're awake." Phoenix fidgeted nervously. "I wasn't sure you would be." The attempt at casual sounded pathetic even to her own ears, but for the first time, she didn't know quite what to say to her best friend.

Sorry I've lied to you for all these years?

Or, how about, sorry that lie almost got you killed?

"Would you come sit on the bloody bed. You're making me feel like I've got the plague." Abi's tone was light and teasing as she scooted over awkwardly, but her eyes were serious as she watched her friend.

Phoenix stepped fully into the room and steeled herself for what was to come as she shut the door behind her. She deserved whatever Abi threw at her.

She perched on the edge of the bed, itching to reach out and take her friend's hand. To apologise. To find any way that might make her understand. But she kept her hands clasped firmly in her lap.

"I should have told you –"

"Yes, you should have." Abi's blue eyes turned to steel.

Phoenix looked down at her hands, unable to face the anger that blazed behind those eyes. "I wanted to apologise. I don't expect you to ever forgive me, but I needed you to know how sorry I am before I left."

"You're leaving?" Abi sat bolt upright, only just managing to disguise the wince of pain.

"I didn't think you'd want me around after –"

"Phoenix," Abi said firmly, "Phoenix, look at me."

The hand that grabbed her arm looked so frail and pale, yet it held an unexpected strength as Abi demanded her attention. "I'm not angry that I got hurt – well okay, I am, but not at you – I'm angry that you didn't trust me."

The words registered, but they didn't make sense. Confused, Phoenix raised her gaze to meet blue eyes that had softened considerably, but still held firm with resolve.

"Phoenix, I don't care if you're a vampire, or whatever the hell you are –" Abi stopped for a second, a confused look on her face. "Actually, what are you?"

"I –"

264

"No, no," Abi shook her head, waving the thought away with her hands, "it doesn't matter. You can tell me later."

It was Phoenix's turn to shake her head as her confusion increased by the minute. "Abi, what do you mean it doesn't matter? Of course it matters."

"Why? I know who you are, Phoenix. You're my best friend. Sure, you're irritating and stubborn as hell, but how does any of that change?"

You're my best friend? Present tense?

Phoenix stared at Abi in complete and utter disbelief, the tears that burned the back of her eyes coming on so suddenly she had to swallow hard to hold them back. But Abi wasn't planning to let her off the hook that easily.

"That doesn't change the fact that you should have told me." The stern look was back, chastising her like a bold child that had just written all over the newly painted white walls. "You should have trusted me."

There was nothing Phoenix could say in her defence. How could she explain to Abi that she'd grown so used to the idea of being rejected that it never even occurred to her to try? Of course, with Abi being a human, it was slightly different, but that didn't make it right.

As Abi continued to berate her, Phoenix watched her friend silently. There were so many things she wanted to share with this wonderful human being. A huge part of her wanted to embrace the acceptance and forget everything else. But she couldn't. And Abi wasn't going to like what she had to say next.

"He's still out there," Phoenix said softly. "Darius. He's out there and he's dangerous."

Tentatively, she took Abi's hand in hers and allowed, for once, the full force of her fear to show on her face. No more hiding. "He's not going to stop until he gets what he wants. And now he knows he can get to me through you."

Abi squeezed her hand tightly. "What are you trying to say, Phoenix?"

"Ethan knows a place, a safe house you can go to. It's run by shifters. They can protect you there. He won't be able to find you."

"No." Abi pulled her hand away and sat further up in the bed. "I have a life here. A business. I'm not going to run scared."

"Dammit, Abi. You could have been killed!"

"Don't you think I know that? I was there, remember."

"This isn't your fight."

"Yes, it is."

Abi relaxed against the headboard of the bed with a look of utter surety settling over her features. "I know what he's planning, Phoenix. You can't tell me this isn't my fight. It's humans that will suffer if he succeeds. We have more right to be counted in this than anyone."

And just like that, every argument Phoenix had was taken from her. Because Abi was right. "I can't watch you die too," she whispered as the tears began to fall for what felt like the umpteenth time in the past twenty-four hours.

Abi smiled as she wiped a tear from her cheek. "Then you'll have to teach me how to kick some serious ass."

Phoenix laughed, her first genuine laugh in what felt like a very long time.

The gentle smile on her friend's face turned devilish.

"So, when are we going to talk about that kiss?"

<<<<>>>>

BONUS SCENE: A FINAL FAREWELL

Phoenix sat curled up on her bed, staring numbly at the faded photograph that lay on the blanket before her. Rain pelted against the window as she absorbed every detail of the three smiling faces: her own, much younger and naïve to the evils of the world; her mother's, so full of life that it was almost as if the sun shone from the image; and her father's, so full of love and pride that it hurt to look at.

There was an obvious sense of contentment in the picture that seemed utterly foreign to her now, and it struck her that she'd never allowed herself to look back on old photos of her parents after she'd lost them the first time.

The first time. Hell, that sounded like a bad joke, even to her. How many times was it possible to lose one's parents? It's not like it's that easy to just misplace a person, never mind two of them. And yet she'd managed it. Then to find out that they'd been there all along, imprisoned mere floors below her in Darius's lair while she lived her life, oblivious ... Even now the knowledge was enough to steal the breath from her chest.

But this time was different. This time there was no hidden chamber that could return them to her if she could just find it. This time, they were really gone.

Gone. The word repeated itself over and over in her head to the steady beat of the rain, and she just sat and stared.

A knock sounded at the bedroom door and she jerked her head up just as Abi pushed open the door and peeked inside. Her best friend had a careful smile on her face, but it did little to hide the concern that shadowed her blue eyes as she took in the unmade bed and photo resting atop it.

"Ethan will be here soon."

Phoenix glanced down at herself to check that, yes, she had in fact gotten dressed. She'd chosen the simple green top because the colour reminded her of her mother's eyes. Her mother's platinum medallion rested over it, and even in the dull grey light of the room, the sun emblem glinted back at her.

With a last look at the photo, she folded it back up and unfurled herself from the bed. "I'll be down now. I just ... I need a minute."

Abi nodded in understanding and closed the door with a quiet click.

Phoenix listened to her footsteps retreat down the hallway, photo gripped tightly in her hand. She squeezed her eyes shut.

She had no idea how she was going to do this. To finally say goodbye. She owed it to her parents to lay them to rest properly. But with no bodies, they had no way of knowing if the Ritual of Passing would even work. Still, she had to try.

Taking a deep breath, she put the photo into her pocket and picked up the wooden box that rested on her bedside locker. The rich aroma of herbs drifted up to her as she ran her hand over the sun emblem that was etched into the lid. Her mother had passed the box to her as a child and had ensured she understood the importance of the Ritual. She could never have imagined then that she'd be using it for this purpose.

Ethan had already arrived by the time she made it downstairs. The pub was shadowed in darkness, the empty tables waiting for the customers to return and bring the space to life once more. He was leaning against the bar talking quietly with Abi as she approached, and it was clear by the sudden cessation of conversation and the worry creasing his forehead that they'd most likely been talking about her.

"It's okay," she told them drily. "I'm not going to break." *At least not yet.*

"The others send their love and positive energy for the Ritual," he said.

She nodded absently. It had meant a lot that they'd wanted to be there for her today. Even Shade, who was her biggest critic at the best of times, had wanted to lend his support. But she couldn't face their sympathy and still stay strong for what she'd needed to do, so she'd asked Ethan to keep the ceremony private – just her, Abi, and Ethan.

When she gave no further response, Ethan held out an arm to her. "Ready?"

No. "Yes."

She hooked her arm through his elbow, as much to stop herself from bolting as from politeness. The icy dread numbed her to the jolt of awareness she usually got when he touched her, and they made their way outside to his waiting car in silence.

The Cathedral wasn't far from the pub she and Abi called home. A little over half an hour later and they pulled off the motorway and wound their way along the ever narrowing country roads. Trees bordered them on either side, and through their still bare branches, she caught glimpses of the red sky as the sun set on the horizon. She'd only ever been to the Cathedral once before when they'd laid Annabelle to rest. It had been the first time she'd ever witnessed a Ritual of Passing, and a naïve part of her had still believed then that it would be the last – at least for a very long time.

Energy prickled over her skin even before Ethan pulled the car off the road and came to a stop in a small space surrounded by trees. As she climbed out of the car, she caught sight of Abi's wide-eyed expression and wondered if, even being human, her friend could feel it too. Phoenix offered what she hoped was a reassuring smile, and Abi seemed to shake herself off.

Ethan was the last to climb out of the car, and after retrieving the small wooden box for her, he beckoned them forward into the forest. They followed the overgrown path to the ruins in a silence that was broken only by the thunderous beat of Phoenix's heart in her own ears. The sky had taken on a purplish hue by the time they emerged into the wide clearing where the Cathedral sat. There was an unnatural calm in the place, and as Phoenix took in the jagged stone walls and moss-covered interior, she was transported straight back to the night she'd come here with Ethan to lay Annabelle to rest. It seemed like a lifetime ago, and yet it was as real to her now as it had been then.

She knew in that moment that she'd been right to ask the others to stay away. It was true that she'd done it partly so she wouldn't have to worry about breaking down in front of them, but she'd also done it for another reason too. She hadn't known Annabelle, and though the young witch's passing still filled her with sorrow, she knew that the loss cut so much deeper for Lily and the others. To bring them back here and remind them ... it would be cruel.

The three of them paused at the Cathedral's boundary wall. Last time it had been Ethan that took the lead in preparing. This time, he waited patiently by her side, ready to take his cue from her. She took a deep breath and stepped over a low section of the wall and onto the blanket of flowers that covered the soft earth within the sacred space.

Unlike Ethan had with Annabelle's passing, she didn't have any bodies to place in the centre. That fact settled heavy in her heart as she took the folded photo from her pocket and knelt down in the grass.

For a minute, she just stared at the yellowed backing of the photo. She didn't need to see the image hidden within its folds to clearly picture her mother's or father's face. Didn't need to see the captured moment of happiness to understand she'd never again have that moment with them. It took everything she had to force her fingers to unfold the paper and smooth it out flat on the ground.

Hurriedly, she rose to her feet and stepped back away from it.

When she returned to his side, Ethan held out the small wooden box to her. She didn't meet his eyes as she reached out to take it, but when he didn't release his grip, she reluctantly looked up.

So many unspoken emotions danced behind his brown eyes: guilt, sympathy, pain. She knew he blamed himself for her loss –

he'd said as much after the night her parents stepped into that black void. But she also knew he'd make the same decision again if he had to.

Her parents had given their lives to protect her, just like she'd been willing to die to protect them and everyone else. Evening if she'd wanted to blame someone, anyone, in those dark days afterwards, she knew now that blaming Ethan was futile. The end would have been the same whether he'd held her back or not; her parents would never have allowed her to make the sacrifice if they could stand in her place.

Ethan opened his mouth to speak, but she gently tugged the box from his hands and turned back to face the centre of the ruins. "I don't really know where to place the herbs. Without their bodies ..."

"I don't think the placement matters so much as the ritual," he said quietly.

Abi moved to her side and wrapped an arm around her waist. "I can help if you like?"

Phoenix swallowed past the lump that had wedged in her throat and nodded.

Together, the three of them set about laying out the herbs. She'd chosen the photo to represent her parents in the absence of their bodies. The fact she was in the picture seemed fitting too since a part of her heart would also pass over this night.

Once everything was prepared, they stepped back into a line – Abi on her right side, Ethan on her left. Her throat was barren and, at first, she didn't think the words would come. Abi reached out and took her hand. Ethan did the same. The heat of their touch flowed through her, and when she finally opened her mouth to speak, the ancient words of passing came.

She had no idea what language the words were in, but some base part of her knew and understood them innately. They spoke to her soul, and to the souls of all who had lost. They were an ancient song of sorrow, but also of celebration. Celebration for the life that was. And the life that was still to come.

With each word, the power grew around her. The evening that had only moments ago been calm, stirred, and wind whipped through the ruins of the Cathedral, blowing loose strands of hair in front of her face. The hands holding her tightened their grip.

As the wind picked up speed and the words continued to flow, almost unconsciously, from her mouth, a keening lament drifted to her. The banshee's song was softer than the previous times she'd heard it, but somehow that only made it more sorrowful. It wrapped around her, enveloping her in its embrace.

She let them fill her, the words and the lament both. She focused on their strength rather than on the aching void that had existed in her chest ever since that night, and she let her voice rise above the wind. All the pain focused on one thought: let them be at peace.

The photo rose like a feather on a gentle breeze, calm and undisturbed by the gale that blew around them. As her words reached a crescendo, a white light glowed around it and, oh so slowly, the picture dissolved, turning to dust on the wind.

Everything fell silent.

The evening was once more calm around them, and the banshee's sorrowful lament was no more now than an echo within her bones.

"Do you think it worked?" she asked quietly.

Ethan turned to her and reached up to wipe away the tear she hadn't even felt sliding down her cheek. "It worked."

2 MINUTES TO MIDNIGHT

CHAPTER ONE

"I thought you said this one would be easy?"

Phoenix shoved her way through the sea of bodies that waited impatiently for the next Luas tram outside Jervis Street Shopping Centre. If Ethan answered, his response was lost in the drone of conversation that surrounded them as they moved deeper into the throng of people. Mindless chatter about the weather and slurred requests to "spare some change" all seemed so *normal*. She envied the blissful ignorance of the humans.

Rain pelted down relentlessly as she shoved sopping strands of bright red hair from her face while dodging the lethal corner of yet another carelessly wielded umbrella. Ahead of her, Ethan was swallowed by the black hole of rush hour madness. She craned her neck to keep sight of the werewolf's broad shoulders.

A jangling bell announced the approaching tram and the horde surged forward. She dug her heels in to stop herself from getting carried along with the tide as everyone jostled for prime position on the moving sardine tin.

"Phoenix!"

Ethan's yell forced her attention to the furthest carriage where a flash of yellow slipped through the doors of the tram.

Dammit!

She pushed through the crowd with renewed vigour, murmuring vague apologies as she went. Angry shoves and not so pleasant words were the only thanks she got for trying to save the oblivious humans from their own ignorance.

Her eyes fell on the frail old man in the bright yellow rain jacket, clutching tightly to a handrail in the furthest carriage. The tram's warning bell sounded once more. Time was up.

Glowing red eyes met her own, and a wide smile split the man's wrinkled face into a grimace of satisfaction as the doors began to close.

Ahead of her, Ethan moved in a blur, disappearing into the packed tram carriage after their target. She cursed under her breath and made a last-minute dive for the doors nearest her. She pulled herself clear just as they snapped closed.

The smell of stale sweat was the first thing that hit her, carried on a wave of recirculating heat and assaulting her heightened senses. Damn the vampire side of her genetics that left her open for such torture.

With a laboured jolt, the Luas began its sluggish shuffle forward. She shifted her position to see past the bobbing heads and found Ethan at the next set of doors. He gave her a grim nod and turned his menacing stare back to the frail old man standing a couple of feet from him.

Only it wasn't a frail old man. Or at least it wouldn't be for much longer if given a choice. Because the demon was on the hunt for a new host. A stronger host. And they couldn't let that happen.

The rattling of the Luas over the tracks became an audible sound-track to the tension as they picked up speed. Ethan stared at the demon. The demon stared at her. She stared back at the demon. Waiting.

The commuters swayed with the motion of the tram, and every split-second that they blocked her view made the adrenaline in her veins ratchet up even further. There was a veritable smorgasbord of casualties between her and the demon. Her skin crawled with the need to act.

She reached into the pocket of her leather jacket and gripped the small amulet Lily had given her earlier that evening. Her thumb rubbed over the smooth stone at its centre.

Would it work?

The young witch had been working hard on a spell that would allow them to trap a demon, but it was still all trial and far too much error for Phoenix's liking.

Once more the tram began to slow, and her body tensed in preparation.

The intercom announced the next stop. "Four Courts, Na Ceithre Cúirteanna." With a whoosh, the doors opened and a blast of cold air formed a sharp contrast to the unnatural heat encasing them.

The demon moved faster than the frail body should have allowed, diving for the open doorway. Shouts of surprise followed in its wake, quickly turning to angry yells as Ethan set off in pursuit, shoving unwitting bystanders to the side to get past.

I guess that's my cue to go. She leapt to the footpath and raced to catch up, grateful for the fresh air that filled her lungs.

The irate passengers gawked as she passed, and she gritted her teeth with the effort of restraining her speed. Only when she hit the thick shadows afforded by the stone buildings did she let go.

They needed to stop the demon before it reached the River Liffey. She was still trying to get over the nightmares from her last demon encounter there; she'd be damned if she was doing it again.

A low growl pulled her up short at a narrow side street. Ethan's familiar signature called to her from the darkness and her breath hitched. Careful to keep her back tight to the wall, she edged around the corner.

Ethan had the old man cornered at a dead end. Even from a distance, the demon's energy crawled over her skin like a wave of insects. She shuddered.

Red eyes flickered like flames and glowed in the dim light. Foam dripped from the corner of the demon's mouth. It stood tall and defiant, forcing its hunched body into a position it probably hadn't seen for many years. Arthritic hands were held in claws that looked as deadly as any blade she'd ever faced.

"Have you got it?" Ethan asked, his voice deeper than normal as he allowed his wolf to play close to the surface.

She nodded, eyes fixed on the demon as she held up the small amulet still clasped in her hand. At the sight of the smoky black stone the demon hissed; it was an unnatural sound that should never have come from a human mouth, let alone the old man before her.

"Do you think it'll work?" Lily's confidence had seemed shaky at best, and last anyone had filled her in, there was no plan B here.

Ethan gave her a wry smile. "Only one way to find out."

Without warning, he launched himself at the demon.

The sudden movement took Phoenix by surprise and she fumbled with the amulet, almost dropping it before she managed to regain her composure.

Grunts of pain and screeches of fury filled the small space, and she tried in vain to block it out. *Concentrate,* she ordered herself, forcing her breathing to slow.

Daily practice meant she could now access her fae power and call on the sun with ease, but her control was still tenuous at best. If she didn't focus, the results could be ... unpredictable.

Heat pulled from the centre of her chest and flowed down through her arms, warming the amulet that was cupped in her hands. The words that came from her mouth made no sense to her and felt completely foreign to her tongue, but she repeated them as Lily had instructed.

A glaring white light burst from her palms, blinding her before she had a chance to close her eyes. For a moment, the light was all there was. In a flash it was gone, and Phoenix found herself unceremoniously dumped on her arse on the cold, wet concrete.

The distant sound of tyres sloshing over the rain-slick roads filled her ears and she looked around in surprise. Not far from her, Ethan lay slumped against the side of the building with the old man in a heap at his feet. She realised immediately that her hand was empty and scrambled to her knees. Frantically, she searched the ground for the smoky black stone.

Only, it was no longer black.

Midway between her and the demon, what she could only

assume was the amulet rested on the pavement. No longer dormant, it now pulsed with life, glowing a fiery red that was eerily similar to the demon's eyes. She plucked it from the ground and quickly shoved it into her pocket, half expecting it to burn her.

A deep, rumbling groan came from Ethan's slumped form, and he raised his head to cast a wary eye towards the old man lying at his feet.

"Did it work?"

CHAPTER TWO

Everything ached and Phoenix was beyond weary as she shoved open the heavy wooden door to the small pub she called home. Long past closing, darkness filled the space with a calm sense of waiting; the jukebox sat quietly in the corner, and beer mats were placed on the wooden tables ready for the next cold glass. She sighed.

The pub had been her sanctuary ever since she left Darius's vampire lair four years earlier. She'd passed by just as the jukebox was playing her mother's favourite song, and something about the darkness of the place had called to her, pulling her in.

The friendship and acceptance she'd found within these walls were beyond her wildest dreams, and she wanted nothing more than to lock the door behind her and leave the world outside to fend for itself.

"You're back. I was getting worried."

With a tired smile, she turned towards the bar where Abi stood. A fluffy purple dressing gown encased her petite frame, and her long brown hair was tied in a messy bun on top of her head. Worry lines creased Abi's forehead and guilt gnawed at Phoenix.

Humans weren't meant to know about her world; it was one of the primary edicts of the Lore. Abi had taken it all in her stride, but Phoenix could see the knowledge was taking its toll. Darius might have been the one to expose Abi to the Lore, but it was Phoenix who kept her there.

"Sorry for leaving you to close up again." She waved a hand towards the bar, her chest tightening as she tried to remember the last night she'd spent behind it, laughing and joking with customers.

With a dramatic huff, Abi grabbed two bottles of water from the fridge beside her. "What can I say? It's hard to get good staff these days."

Phoenix laughed and a little bit of the tension eased from her shoulders. She jumped up on one of the wooden bar stools and gratefully accepted the bottle Abi held out to her.

"Did it work?" Her friend's blue eyes were filled with concern, but there was a spark of curiosity in their depths.

Ever since Darius had given her a crash course on all things supernatural – in the form of kidnapping and torture – Abi had demanded to be kept up to date with everything related to the prophecy. Having learned the hard way that lying to her friend was a bad idea, Phoenix had kept her promise to provide Abi with updates, even though she expected Abi to run screaming for the hills any day now.

"I think so. I hope so." She scrubbed a hand over her face. "The man was old. I'm not sure if he'll make it. We managed to trap the demon in the amulet, but the possession takes its toll."

"You're finding more and more demons lately. It's not a good sign, is it?"

She let the silence speak for itself.

It had been a little over a month since Ethan had arrived at her door and she'd learned of the prophecy that would end humanity – the one she was supposedly the cause of. In those few weeks she'd been attacked more times than she could count, found her long-lost parents, been betrayed by the man she'd thought of as family, and lost her parents all over again. You'd really think she was due for a break.

Fate seemed to disagree.

No one wanted to say it, but they all knew what was happening. More demons meant only one thing: the fabric was growing weak.

Her parents' sacrifice had been enough to stop Darius's spell and close the tear he'd created, but it was becoming very apparent that it hadn't been enough to stop the prophecy. Their sacrifice had been pointless.

The thought brought with it a throbbing ache in her chest that matched the one forming between her eyes. She took a long swig of water and hopped down from the bar stool.

"Phoenix ..." Abi bit her lip, hesitating.

She gave her friend what she hoped was a reassuring smile. "I'm going to try get some sleep. Take the night off tomorrow. I'll cover the bar to make up for being such a lousy employee."

"I might need more than one night off to make up for that."

She swatted Abi playfully and let her friend's laughter wrap around her like a comfort blanket as she headed upstairs to the apartment they shared. Not bothering to put on any lights, she made a beeline for her bedroom, closed the door, and flopped onto her bed fully clothed.

The cool, fresh sheets did little to ease the pain in her skull. The pillow over her face didn't work either. She sat up with a huff, leaned back against the headboard, and hugged the pillow to her chest.

Why wouldn't her head just shut up? Every night after patrolling it was the same. Memories and what-ifs consumed her thoughts, growing louder and more insistent the moment she closed her eyes. The ever-looming threat of the prophecy and the distinct feeling they were doing little more than fire-fighting was exhausting.

The close proximity to Ethan didn't help either. Especially not when he was making such an obvious effort to avoid any kind of physical contact with her. It wasn't that she cared or anything, but he'd kissed her, not the other way around.

And still, all of that felt irrelevant.

She reached her hand towards the small wooden box that sat on her bedside locker. Her fingers traced the rough etchings of the sun emblem that represented her mother's fae lineage, and she let the lingering scent of herbs wash over her. The ache in her chest turned into a crushing pain that made it difficult to breathe.

It had been almost a week since Ethan had helped her prepare the Ritual of Passing for them, two weeks since they'd sacrificed themselves to save her. She still couldn't bring herself to put the box away. If she did, she'd have to admit the truth.

They were gone.

Ten years. Ten long years she'd spent wondering if they were alive or dead, and never once had she felt their loss as acutely as she did now. When they stepped into that void, they took with them any possibility of denial.

All she was left with now was the crushing fear that the Ritual hadn't been enough, that their souls were trapped forever.

Ethan peeled his eyes open with effort. Sunlight streamed in through the bedroom window and he squinted, trying to untangle his thoughts from their stupor. Vague fragments of a dream clung to him: green eyes, red hair, a kiss that lit his whole body on fire.

What time is it?

He shook his head in a vain attempt to clear the fog. Late night patrols were taking a toll on his body clock, and it took a minute for the vibration of his phone to register through the grogginess. He bolted upright in the bed.

Adrenaline chased away the last of the sleep fog as he rummaged in the tangled sheets to find his phone. The name on the screen only calmed his heart rate marginally.

"Dad."

"I've been waiting on you to call." Cormac's deep voice held an edge of irritation, but Ethan was more than used to his Alpha being frustrated with him.

"I know. I was hoping she'd have changed her mind by now, but the bloody woman just won't see sense. So long as Abi is here, she refuses to leave."

He ground his teeth in frustration. It had been two weeks since they'd contacted the Council Liaison Office stupidly looking for the Council's assistance. Two whole weeks during which the Council had no doubt been notified of the existence of a hybrid and were making plans to act. Not to mention the fact that Darius was still out there somewhere. They were working on borrowed time, and every second Phoenix insisted on being stubborn just put her in more danger. But would she listen?

"It's not safe for her, Ethan. Or for the human."

"Don't you think I know that?" He tugged a hand through his unkempt hair. "I'd like to see you convince her."

Cormac's hearty laugh boomed down the phone. "She sounds like your mother."

The thought of his stubborn, strong-willed mother brought a smile to Ethan's face, and after a moment, he found himself laughing too.

"There's something else you should know." Cormac grew serious. "I contacted William. I was due to check-in with him anyway, so I thought I could feel him out a bit. The Council has called an emergency assembly tomorrow night."

Ethan's blood ran cold. William was his father's cousin and sat on the Council as head of the werewolves. If he'd been called to an emergency meeting, it could only mean one thing.

"Did you tell him about Phoenix?"

"What do you think I am, a young pup?"

"Sorry, it's just ..." He trailed off before he could put his fear into words and give it life.

The meeting couldn't mean anything good for Phoenix. It was true that she hadn't technically broken any of the Council's edicts – she could hardly be blamed for being born a product of an inter-species relationship. But with her parents now dead, the Council would need someone to make an example of, and what better person than the hybrid who was also responsible for triggering a doomsday prophecy.

"She's still welcome here." Cormac's soft-spoken words broke through his thoughts. "All of your friends are welcome here. Come home, Son."

And with that, he was gone.

284

CHAPTER THREE

Darius pulled the black cloak low over his head as he stepped out of the portal and into the large indoor amphitheatre that formed the centre of the Council headquarters in Brussels. He kept his face angled, allowing the material of his robes to shadow the burns that still covered the left side of his face. His right hand clenched the silver coin he held, and he relished the distraction of the burning pain. That pain, he could heal from.

Around him, the chamber began to fill as other Witnesses stepped through similar portals and formed a sea of identical black robes. The supernatural signatures were so potent that they mixed together to form something almost unrecognisable, but all were accounted for: vampire, werewolf, fae, witch, and shifter.

All pure blood.

He weaved between the stone pillars, keeping to the shadows as he made his way closer to the platform at the front of the room. The low hum of conversation surrounded him, but he ignored the other Witnesses. They were irrelevant.

Once the last portal closed and they were closed in by solid stone walls, a hollow gong rang out. A hush fell over the room and the lights dimmed.

All eyes turned towards the raised platform where five figures now stood. Shrouded in blood red cloaks, their faces were hidden and their forms indistinct. Power emanated from the group and the air became heavy with its oppressive weight.

The Council.

Anger flared in Darius's chest and he clenched his teeth against their not-so-subtle show of superiority. They knew nothing of power, but they would soon enough.

Like sheep, the Witnesses took their places, forming a semicircle around the platform. Another gong rang out, and a man stepped forward through a break in the crowd. His fitted grey suit immediately set him apart from those surrounding him, and Darius sneered.

Vicktor. He knew the snivelling weasel wouldn't be able to hold his nerve.

As he watched, the chief representative of the Council Liaison Office bowed his head in reverence to the five figures before him. One by one, the Council lowered their hoods.

First, the long red hair and sultry pout of Méabh, the head of the fae, became visible. Darius couldn't help but note the resemblance to Jessica Rabbit – if Jessica Rabbit had magic powers and was inclined to slit your throat.

Next, William's rugged features were revealed as he shoved the hood back from his face. The head of the werewolves had a wild, unkempt appearance that matched the feral quality of his signature. He seemed completely out of place in such an official setting, yet he held himself with an assurance that left no question as to his position.

Diana, the head of the witches, followed suit. Her long blonde hair appeared almost as a halo that was starkly contrasted by her resting bitch face. Kam, the head of the shifters, who was easily identifiable by his shorter stature, stood beside her. He, too, lowered his hood, revealing Asian features and an unreadable expression.

Vlad, the head of the vampires, was the last to remove his hood. More like a politician than the head of a powerful supernatural species, he graced the room with his smarmy smile.

Darius gripped the coin tighter in his hand as he pushed down the urge to wipe the smile away in a slow and excruciating manner. This vampire wasn't fit to stand where his Sire had. It was an insult to Il Maestro's legacy and their entire species that they were now forced to bow down to *this*.

Patience, he reminded himself as the silver seared into his palm.

In a gesture filled with all the arrogance of the man, Vlad stepped forward, taking centre stage. "You may speak," he ordered, his voice ringing clear throughout the chamber.

"Council." Vicktor cleared his throat and straightened his suit jacket. "Witnesses. It is with a grave heart that I stand before you today. The CLO was recently contacted by a member of our society. A werewolf. He expressed some concerns regarding recent activity in the Lore and wanted to speak to the Council. Of course, we don't normally entertain such requests, but this werewolf had knowledge of a certain prophecy ..."

Murmurs filled the chamber, creating an anxious hum. Darius tensed. Just how much did Vicktor intend to divulge?

"... And he claimed to be in the presence of a hybrid."

Silence.

For what felt like an eternity, no one spoke. The implication of Vicktor's statement settled around the room, acting like a weight that pinned everyone in place.

"So, Cassandra saw true," Diana whispered, her words and the resignation they held clearly audible in the deafening silence.

At the mention of the Seer's name, chaos broke out around Darius, angry exclamations and worried cries that achieved nothing. The prophecy was infamous among those privy to the Council's history; it was a closely guarded secret that many centuries ago foretold the coming of the Horsemen ... and an end to their way of life.

Fools, all of them. They clung to their way of life like it was something of worth, like they'd all forgotten the true greatness of the Lore. They settled for scraps and fought against the inevitable. Not Darius.

While they cowered in fear of the rising tide, he welcomed it. And for that, he would be rewarded. They would see the folly of their ways when he finally took his place at the right hand of the Horsemen. *They* would bow to *him*.

"How do we know it's true?" a voice called from the crowd.

Murmurs of agreement and similar questions followed, the room only falling quiet when Vlad held up a hand to silence them.

"Did this werewolf provide any proof of his claim?" William crossed his arms in front of his chest and raised an eyebrow in undisguised scepticism.

There was something oddly familiar in his expression, but Darius didn't have time to think on it as Vicktor nodded in response to the question and the room once more erupted around him.

"SILENCE." Vlad motioned for Vicktor to continue, a single warning glance enough to bring order.

"The werewolf spoke the truth. There is a hybrid," Vicktor confirmed solemnly. "I met with them both personally ... to discuss their concerns."

"It would appear our attempts to stop the prophecy have failed." Méabh sashayed forward, stopping just ahead of Vlad. She flipped her hair over her shoulder and gave him a saccharine smile. "Your edict doesn't seem to have had the effect you hoped for."

The vampire snarled.

"Enough." Kam didn't move from his position or raise his voice. If anything, the Japanese shifter appeared almost bored with the proceedings. Looks could be very deceiving however, and both Vlad and Méabh retreated back into line at his order. "The prophecy has been triggered. We must decide our next steps."

Each of the Council members pulled up the hood of their cloak, and the lights of the chamber dimmed while they deliberated among themselves.

Darius turned his gaze to Vicktor while he waited. The CLO rep stood stiff, his hands clasped in front of him as he pointedly kept his eyes forward. All it would take was one wrong word on his part and Darius's plans would be made significantly more difficult. Perhaps the weasel had outlived his usefulness.

Only a couple of minutes passed before the room brightened, and the Council turned back to face the Witnesses with their hoods lowered. There was a tension between them that indicated not all were happy about the decision they'd arrived at.

Once more it was Vlad who stepped forward. "For the sake of all the Lore, the hybrid must die."

The night air was crisp as Darius slipped unseen from the Council chambers. He'd heard all he needed to hear, and the fraught discussions and concerned murmurings were of little consequence to him.

A block away from the Council building, he found Vicktor waiting for him in a narrow alley that stank of garbage and other unfavourable aromas that burned the back of his throat. The CLO rep squirmed and tugged the collar of his tailored coat close as he made a concerted effort not to touch anything in the dingy space.

"I was hoping to speak to you." Vicktor gave an impatient huff as his body twitched with its obvious desire to escape the alley.

Darius inclined his head and stepped into the shadows, effectively blocking the other man in.

"I assume you heard the decree?"

"Yes. And I'm not pleased, Vicktor. We need the hybrid alive. I warned you not to approach the Council with this information."

The CLO rep squared his shoulders, his defiance and snooty air bringing him closer to a final death than he could have possibly imagined.

"You've been missing for two weeks, Darius. I couldn't wait any longer. Your name has been kept out of it for now, and I've convinced them to let the CLO organise the hit. That is already more than I'm comfortable doing."

Darius's hand flexed involuntarily, and he put it into his pocket to stop himself from tearing out the man's throat.

"Comfort is not something we have the luxury of if we're to restore the Lore to its former glory. You know that." Darius kept his tone amicable despite the murderous thoughts playing through his mind. "If the Council succeeds, we'll be back to square one. All of our work will have been for nothing."

Vicktor picked his briefcase up off the ground and brushed it off with a grimace. "If your hybrid is as impressive as you say, she will be able to fend for herself. If not? Well then ..."

With that, he pushed past Darius and stalked from the alley.

CHAPTER FOUR

Lily tossed and turned in the bed. Sweat-soaked sheets tangled around her legs and she kicked at them, biting back a scream of frustration. Her eyes burned with exhaustion and she longed for a single night of dreamless sleep, but every time she closed her eyes, the thoughts came.

Darkness had become a familiar companion since Annabelle's death. Night after night she lay in her sister's bed, clutching the stuffed unicorn that had been Annabelle's since she was a baby. If she tried hard enough, she could still catch a hint of her sister's scent from the soft toy and unwashed sheets. When she closed her eyes, she could still picture her sister's innocent smile. But it was all fading. She was running out of time.

That thought brought with it a panic greater than any of the other memories or what-ifs that plagued her. The thought that her sister would fade from memory before she could do anything to stop it.

She flung the covers off her legs and sat up in the bed, panting as her chest grew tighter. Her fists clenched and unclenched reflexively. It was as if all the oxygen had been sucked from the room. She forced herself to close her eyes and count to twenty.

You're not going to die, she reminded herself. *You wouldn't be that lucky.*

After a time, her breathing slowed and her lungs once more obeyed the command to expand. Resigned to yet another sleepless night, she slipped from the bed and checked the bedroom door to make sure it was locked.

Ethan and the others had turned in hours before, but she paused for a second, listening for any sign of movement in the apartment.

Only when she was satisfied did she return to the bed. She reached her hand under the mattress and pulled out a box roughly the size of a book. Wooden, and covered in paint that wasn't quite white anymore, there were scuff marks along the edges and the glass top was smudged with fingerprints. Four faces smiled back at her from the photo held within that glass, and her fingertips shook as she tenderly traced the image of her family.

Two minutes. That was all the time she would allow herself. If she looked at the picture any longer, she would break.

With a shuddering breath, she opened the metal clasp on the edge of the box and raised the lid. Even in the darkness the Ouroboros gleamed. Preparing herself for the guilt that always came with her first touch, she lifted the gold plaque out of the box and held the weight in her hands.

Memories came flooding back unbidden: standing in the dark underground chamber, the walls painted with blood and the aftereffects of death. The lingering taint of black magic. The realisation that it wasn't over.

When the fabric began to tear and they discovered exactly what Darius had achieved with his spell, she'd almost been relieved. They'd failed. They didn't have to fight anymore. Soon, it would be over and she could be with Annabelle and her parents again. The aching emptiness would be gone.

It was only when someone mentioned the Ouroboros that a new possibility occurred to her. She could fix it all. Annabelle's death, Darius's spell, all of it. She could turn back time and make it as if it never happened.

But in order for her to do that, she would need the Ouroboros. Which meant no one else could have it.

On the rare nights when sleep came, Lily found herself back in that chamber, watching Phoenix's world shatter as her parents stepped into the black void. The weight of the Ouroboros would grow heavy in her hands as she silently let Marcus and Aria sacrifice themselves. It would pull her down and she'd find herself drowning in a sea of red. Only then would she wake up, gasping for breath with tears streaming down her cheeks.

What was worse than any of that, however, was the look on Aria's face. The quick glance of compassion she'd turned towards Lily before confirming to the others that her search of the witch had shown no sign of the Ouroboros. She'd sacrificed herself knowing that Lily held the means to save her.

And she could still save her. She could make it all right.

Lily clutched that thought to her like a life buoy as she closed her eyes. Focusing on the weight of the Ouroboros, she opened her mind to its energy and prayed. *This time it would work.*

CHAPTER FIVE

The sun was setting low on the horizon as Phoenix pulled her Mustang up outside Ethan's apartment and cut the engine. The converted warehouse was surrounded on three sides by the docks, and the lights of the city reflected like a mirage on the water, ebbing and flowing with the tide.

She cast her eyes towards Abi in the passenger seat and noticed her friend absently picking at her nails. The drive there had been unusually quiet, and attempts at conversation had been met with distracted, one-word answers. The strange atmosphere was making Phoenix antsy.

It wasn't the first time Abi had come with her to Ethan's place. Ever since Abi had gotten a crash course on the Lore, they'd all made a conscious effort to ensure she was as comfortable in their world as possible, Ethan especially. And now that Phoenix thought about it, Abi had asked to come; she'd even organised cover for the bar.

So, why did this suddenly feel like a very bad idea?

"Come on. The others will be waiting." She flashed Abi a reassuring smile and climbed out into the chill of the evening. There'd be time enough to question her friend's strange mood later; first, she had a lecture to face.

Ethan had called two days ago to fill her in on the update from

Cormac. It had been clear from his tone that he had his knickers in a twist, and she'd resigned herself to yet another argument about her safety. It didn't stop her putting him off ... or winding him up a little.

The memory of his frustrated growl when she'd regrettably informed him she wouldn't be free for a group meeting until Saturday brought a smile to her face. She could even picture the small muscle at the side of his jaw that was no doubt twitching as he ground his teeth together.

As much as she wanted to though, she couldn't put him off forever.

The rich smell of coffee beckoned her through the door of the upper floor apartment and into the open-plan living room where she found the others already assembled. Nate was perched on the edge of the leather sofa. His floppy brown hair fell into his amber eyes as he leaned over something that looked suspiciously like a Rubik's cube. The tech-loving shifter gestured excitedly to the vampire beside him as he held the object up for closer inspection, completely oblivious to the new arrivals.

Not impressed by Nate's enthusiasm, Shade slouched in the corner of the sofa with a surly expression held firmly in place. As she walked further into the room, his icy blue eyes flicked to her and the temperature seemed to drop to Arctic conditions.

She gave the vampire her friendliest smile, just for the satisfaction of making his scowl deepen.

A further survey found Lily at the large oak dining table with a mug clasped in her hands and a vacant expression on her face. The sight of the young witch pulled Phoenix up short.

Lily had seemed haggard when she'd last seen her a few days ago, but now she looked like she hadn't slept in weeks. The circles under her eyes had grown darker and appeared almost black in the dim light, and her once lustrous blonde hair hung unwashed in a limp ponytail.

Phoenix bit her lip and frowned.

At only eighteen years of age, Lily had seen more death than anyone should ever have to. The passing of her sister had hit the hardest though. Phoenix could still remember Lily's anguished scream when Ethan broke the news to her. And yet somehow, Lily had shoved all of her grief aside to focus on helping them stop Darius and the witches. It was only now that the toll was beginning to show.

The thing about grief was that it couldn't be ignored forever. Eventually, it found its way to the surface.

She pulled her eyes away from the young witch to look at Ethan, who stood with his back to the panoramic window that spanned the length of the room. A rough coat of stubble covered his jaw, highlighting the tense set of muscles as he, too, watched Lily. When he finally turned his gaze towards her, his brown eyes echoed her own concern, and she couldn't help but notice that he also looked worn out.

Behind her, Abi cleared her throat. "Hi," she said with a pointed wave.

As if a spell had been broken, everyone suddenly seemed to remember why they were there and set about rearranging themselves to make space. Phoenix plonked herself between Nate and Abi on the sofa after Shade moved to one of the lone recliners with a glare in her direction. Ethan joined Lily on the smaller two-seater. Not that his choice of seat mattered to her.

"Okay, so we know the Council were due to meet last night," Ethan started, bringing the low murmur of conversation to a halt. "My dad hasn't been able to reach William, and he needs to tread carefully in case the Council find out about our involvement. So, for now we're on our own."

Phoenix pointedly ignored the piercing stare he directed at her and the uneasy flutter in her stomach.

"The Council called that meeting for a reason," he continued when she didn't react. "Vicktor will have told them about you, even if he hasn't told them about the prophecy, which I think we can assume he has. It's not safe, Phoenix, and the longer you stay in Dublin, the more dangerous it becomes."

She blew out an exasperated breath, sick to death of the broken record. "Why should I run? I haven't done anything wrong."

Shade snorted and sat forward to rest his forearms on his knees. His icy blue eyes held hers, the challenge clear. "Do you really think

296

it matters? Your very existence calls into question their authority. An inter-species relationship allowed to continue and produce offspring? If the Lore find out about you, the Council will appear weak. Do you really think they'll let that happen?"

The rebuttal stuck in her throat. Phoenix knew he was right, but still she rallied against the idea of being punished for something completely out of her control. Their edict was bullshit anyway.

Ethan stayed silent, watching her as she battled the conflicting emotions churning in her gut. She didn't want to face the Council – she really didn't – but she wasn't leaving. They had no right to make her.

"What will happen to Phoenix if the Council does come?" Abi reached out to give her hand a squeeze.

"It's hard to say," Ethan answered. "We've got no precedent for this situation, but the Council doesn't tend to look kindly on anything that threatens the order of things."

"And Phoenix does that?"

Ethan nodded.

Abi turned to her, still gripping her hand, and Phoenix felt her heart drop. Her friend's face was tight with worry; she knew immediately this was why Abi had come. Tonight had been a carefully orchestrated setup.

"Why are you still here?"

The question was rhetorical, of course. Abi was smart enough to figure out the answer for herself, but it hung in the air between them.

After they'd met Vicktor, the CLO rep, Ethan had convinced her to go stay with his pack in Donegal. She'd been so afraid she'd lose her parents all over again if they were forced to face the Council. Well, she lost them anyway. And when Darius took Abi, he'd shown her just how much more she stood to lose.

"The pack's offer of protection still stands. It wasn't solely for the benefit of your parents." Ethan's voice was gentle, his gaze sympathetic, but the determined set to his jaw remained.

"As long as Abi stays in Dublin, I'm staying." It wasn't up for debate. She wouldn't leave her friend vulnerable again.

All eyes in the room turned to Abi. Her hand tightened in Phoenix's and she squirmed under their scrutiny.

"Have we had any luck locating Darius?" Phoenix quickly diverted, taking pity on her friend. She knew how hard Abi had worked to build herself up from nothing. She'd never ask her to leave.

"Afraid not," Nate answered. His tone was a mix of frustration and admiration. "I don't know how they're doing it, but the vamps are doing a damn good job of covering his trail."

"Are you sure he's still alive? That sun trick of yours did a lot of damage." Shade tilted his head and considered her, his gaze intense as if he was really seeing her for the first time.

She yanked her hand away from Abi and clasped it with her other hand in her lap, suddenly conscious of the damage they were capable of. "He's alive."

"What about the Council?" Abi looked at Ethan. "If Vicktor tells them about Phoenix, he'll tell them about Darius too. Surely they should be the ones to deal with him?"

The room fell silent.

What she said made sense – logically, at least. But the tension that filled the room spoke volumes. The Council was powerful and also unpredictable. Phoenix didn't know about the others, but she could think of a million things she'd prefer to do than rely on that group of megalomaniacs for her safety. Like play Russian roulette. With explosive silver bullets.

She blew out a slow breath and forced the thoughts of Darius from her mind. *Good old Uncle D.* It was still hard to hear his name without feeling a lance of pain through her very core. She'd tried in vain to reconcile the monster with the man she'd once known, but it still didn't make sense to her. Hopefully the scars she'd given him were as long-lasting as the ones he'd left on her heart.

"What's our next step with the prophecy?" she asked, grasping for something practical, though no less terrifying, to deal with.

Ethan tried to focus on the conversation around him, but his gaze kept slipping back to Phoenix. She might've thought that redirecting the discussion would get her off the hook, but she was very wrong. He'd lock her in the apartment if needed. She wasn't getting out of here until she saw sense.

He'd hoped that asking Abi along would help him. Play the guilt card a bit. He even thought he was onto a winner for one whole, precious minute, but he'd underestimated how closely linked Phoenix's actions were to her friend's.

Even with Abi on his side, he wasn't confident their combined pressure would be enough to get Phoenix to leave, at least not while Abi stayed behind. Hell, if he was honest with himself, he could mostly understand why she was being stubborn. Maybe even respected her for it. Unfortunately, respect wasn't going to keep her alive.

With a huff of frustration, he cracked his neck and stood; he needed some space to clear his head. After a quick pit stop in the kitchen to top up the refreshments – minus Shade's bag of blood, didn't want to freak out the human – he headed to the bathroom at the end of the hall to take a leak.

As he washed his hands and splashed water over his face, a sound came from the hallway.

Can't a man get two minutes peace?

He opened the door and pulled up short when he found Abi in the hall, her hands nervously entwining as she stared towards the bathroom.

"Sorry, did you need to –" He moved aside and indicated for her to go ahead, but she didn't budge.

A battle waged war behind her blue eyes, and a sudden sense of unease set his Spidey senses tingling. "Abi, is everything okay?"

She opened her mouth to respond but closed it again and shook her head.

"Is there somewhere we can talk that we won't be overheard?" She looked towards the living area and bit her lip.

The sense of unease grew stronger. He moved past her to open the door on the opposite side of the hall and, with a gentle hand on her back, ushered her into his bedroom. The door closed with a soft click behind them and he sat down on the bed, waiting for her to speak.

For a time, she simply paced.

The room wasn't small by any standards, but the super-king size bed and wall of wardrobes left little space for her to manoeuvre before she had to turn around again. He watched her with a detached fascination and wondered if there would be a path worn in the plush navy carpet by the time she finished.

"I should be talking to Phoenix about this, but I'm afraid if I tell her ... I told myself there was no point saying anything. I mean, Darius was obviously crazy, right? And once he was gone, I just figured everything would go back to normal. The whole thing seemed so surreal. I didn't really think –"

She wrung her hands and turned to face him.

"Phoenix has to die."

CHAPTER SIX

Jaded by the conversation, Phoenix slumped back into the large cushions behind her. They were going around in circles, and everyone was starting to snipe at each other.

Well, actually, Nate and Shade were starting to snipe at each other. Lily stayed quiet, staring off into space, unless she was asked a direct question, and Abi still hadn't come back from the bathroom. How long did it take to pee anyway?

A niggle of concern crept down her spine and she pushed herself up from the groove she'd settled into. No one even looked her way as she slipped out of the living room and made her way down the hall.

She was just about to call out to Abi and offer to send a search party when she noticed the bathroom door was ajar. Low murmuring came from the room on the opposite side of the hall, and she stared at the closed door of Ethan's bedroom.

Now that she'd become aware of the clandestine conversation, Abi and Ethan's voices were clearly distinguishable. A pang of something she didn't want to examine too closely caused her stomach to do a little flip-flop.

What the hell was going on?

They spoke quietly, so she moved closer to the door, mentally ordering her internal narrative to shut up so she could hear what was being said. The distress in Abi's voice was clear even before the words became audible. When they did, Phoenix's heart stopped cold.

"That's what he said. The only way to prevent the prophecy is for Phoenix to die."

A buzzing sound filled her ears and the narrow hallway closed in on her. Whatever was said after that was lost as her head begin to spin and her vision blurred.

She'd known. Some part of her deep down had known. Sure, she'd even used the threat of ending her own life against Darius. But to hear the words out loud ...

The bedroom door swung open and Phoenix found herself face to face with Ethan. The small muscle in his jaw was hopping, and the earlier image she'd had didn't seem so funny anymore. Behind him, Abi sat on the bed, looking dejected as she stared at the ground.

The moment stretched forever, the silence tangible and oppressive. Eventually, Abi raised her tear-filled eyes and whispered, "I'm sorry."

A heavy silence filled the living room, and Phoenix could feel their eyes burning into her. She pulled her knees to her chest and tried to make herself smaller in the black leather recliner that mirrored Shade's.

What were they expecting her to do? Scream? Cry? A small part of her actually wanted to laugh. But the rest, well, that was just numb.

Ethan's announcement that they knew what the prophecy said had grabbed everyone's attention immediately. Even Lily in her subdued state had jerked her head up in surprise. The same question came from everyone's lips: "How?"

How indeed.

Abi cast a pained glance in her direction before repeating the explanation she'd given Ethan in the bedroom.

"When Darius ... had me, he spoke about the prophecy. Gloated might be more accurate." Abi shuddered, a haunted look darkening her red-rimmed eyes. "He liked to play head games to show he could hurt me without even touching me. He took great pleasure in informing me that the only way to stop the prophecy was for Phoenix to die."

She spoke the last words softly, but every one of them was like a blade slicing through Phoenix's skin.

"So, if Ethan had killed her to start with, this would already be over." Shade's voice was cold as he broke the silence.

The answering growl from Ethan made the hairs stand up on the back of Phoenix's arms.

But she didn't need him to defend her because Shade was right. Her death would've stopped it all. Annabelle's murder. Abi's torture. Her parents' sacrifice. All of it had been for nothing.

"Oh no you don't." Ethan pointed a warning finger at her. "You don't get to play martyr in this."

She opened her mouth to argue – she wasn't playing anything – but before she could speak, Nate stood with his hands held up in surrender.

"How about we get all the details before anyone goes making any rash decisions?" He looked pointedly at Shade and Ethan, then her before turning his attention to Abi. "Did Darius say anything else? Anything at all that might help us?"

"There was a scroll. It looked pretty old and had some kind of wax seal on it. I couldn't make out the seal properly, but it seemed familiar, like a scales or –"

"The Council," Lily whispered.

Phoenix's stomach dropped and she swallowed back the bile that forced its way up her throat.

"Shit." Shade let out a low whistle and leaned back in his seat.

Abi looked around, her brow furrowed in confusion. "What does that mean? Is Darius working with the Council?"

"Not necessarily." Nate flicked his hair out of his eyes and started pacing as he worked through his thoughts. "We found texts on the prophecy in the Council archives, so we knew they were aware of it."

"How did Darius get the scroll if he's not working with them?"

Nate shrugged. "There was no mention of a scroll in anything I found. There was reference to someone named Cassandra, the

Horsemen, and a tearing of the fabric that protects our world. That's all."

"Terror, destruction, death to man. The fires of hell o'ertake the land." Abi's voice shook as she spoke the words. Everyone froze.

"What did you say?" Ethan leaned forward, barely contained urgency visible in the tension that ran from the hunched muscles of his upper back to his clasped fists.

"That was what the scroll said. Or at least, how Darius read it." Abi stared into the distance, her nose scrunching in concentration. "So long as she alone does stand, shall the Horsemen walk the land." She shook her head, tears glistening in her eyes as her shoulders slumped. "I'm sorry. I should have said something. I just –"

A strange sense of detachment settled over Phoenix. It hurt to see the look of regret on her friend's face, and a part of her wanted nothing more than to wrap her arms around Abi and tell her it'd be all right. But she couldn't. Because Abi's words had forced her to face the truth she'd been ignoring: It wasn't over.

For the past few weeks, her parent's death had given her something to focus on other than the stupid prophecy, and she'd let herself wallow in the haze of grief. She'd become complacent. Even with the nightly patrols, and the work she'd been doing on her fae powers, she'd forgotten what was really at stake. She'd taken each demon possession as an inconvenience to be dealt with rather than a sign of what was to come.

"How long?" she asked, her tongue like sandpaper in her mouth. "Did the scroll say how long we have?"

"When the clock strikes midnight on your twenty-fifth year."

Ten months. A lot of innocent people could die in ten months.

She pushed herself up from the recliner, suddenly feeling like the room was shrinking around her. "Nate, you mind if I go patrolling with you tonight?"

Ethan was in front of her in a flash. His hands gripped her upper arms and his expression pleaded with her. "We have time to figure this out. Promise me you won't do anything stupid."

A tight nod was the only answer she gave before she yanked her body out of his grip and grabbed her leather jacket from the back of the chair. She pulled her car keys from her pocket and threw them to Abi.

"I'll be home late."

With that, she made her way to the door, not waiting to see if Nate followed.

CHAPTER SEVEN

The buzzing in Lily's head grew louder as she watched Ethan pace the living room. Without a word, she stood from her chair and squeezed past Shade. His eyes followed her as she left, but she ignored him. She needed to get out of there.

First stop was her bedroom. She locked the door quietly behind her before lifting her mattress to retrieve the Ouroboros, still tucked away safely in the wooden box. She averted her eyes so as not to see the photo on the lid, but Annabelle's smiling face drew her gaze back like a magnet she couldn't resist. Bitterness welled up inside her, making her gut roil painfully.

No one called after her as she slipped out of the apartment without bothering to grab a jacket. No one noticed.

The night was icy cold as she walked along the docks, focusing only on her breath as it fogged the air in front of her and the burn of the wind against her face. The cold was an anaesthetic and she welcomed it.

For so long, she'd let the guilt eat away at her. Night after night she'd lie in bed, thinking of the people who had sacrificed themselves so she could have the Ouroboros. But what about her? What about what she'd sacrificed?

With Abi's words, the guilt had changed. It was shifting around inside of her, morphing into something alien and terrifying.

None of it mattered. The sacrifices, the Ouroboros, the chance to fix things. All of it was pointless. Because Phoenix still lived. And as long as she lived, the rest of them would continue to suffer.

She walked for a while, trying to sort through the screaming thoughts that fought for attention in her head, and when she looked up, she was surprised to find herself at a busy junction near O'Connell Street.

How had she gotten there? She didn't recall walking so far.

A car horn blared and she leapt back to avoid being splashed as a car drove straight into a puddle at her feet. Lily muttered a curse under her breath and slipped through a break in traffic to the safety of a nearby footpath, drenched and freezing. The few pedestrians passing by gawked at her as if she was crazy and her cheeks heated.

A small cafe sat on the corner, and the soft lights beckoned her like a lighthouse. She pushed open the chipped wooden door to the sound of jingling bells, and the rich aroma of caffeine engulfed her senses.

The clock on the wall indicated that it was near closing, and the cafe was empty of customers. Still, the kindly old woman behind the counter ushered her to a table and placed a cup of steaming coffee in front of her. She shook her head when Lily tried to dig some money out of her jeans pocket and gave her a pat on the shoulder before returning to her cleaning.

Lily clutched the cup in her hands and waited for the heat to sink in. But the cold she felt wasn't physical, and it wasn't one that could be fixed with a cup of coffee.

So many people dead. Not just Annabelle, others too. Was Shade right? Could all of those people have been saved if Ethan had just killed Phoenix in the beginning? How many more would die now? Even if she managed to use the Ouroboros, it wouldn't matter; she'd be dooming her sister all over again. There was no happy ending for any of them. Not while Phoenix was alive.

She reached down to the bag that sat by her feet and drew out the wooden box. It felt heavier than normal as she placed it on the table. The photo on the lid lost focus as tears burned her eyes.

"Please, Annie, tell me what to do," she whispered, scrunching her eyes shut.

CHAPTER EIGHT

Ethan's gaze followed Phoenix around the pub as he tapped his foot absently in time to the band's music. His pint of Blue Moon sat untouched on the wooden table in front of him, and the paper beer coaster was in shreds beside it instead of absorbing the condensation that ran down the glass.

"Has she spoken to you?" Abi appeared beside him. Her line of sight followed his as she twisted a cloth in her hands.

"Just to inform me she doesn't need a babysitter, and that everything is fine."

"Ooooo."

Ethan laughed. He'd grown up around enough women to know that when a woman told you it was "fine", you were in deep shit.

It didn't help that he had no clue why Phoenix was pissed at him. But based on the ice-cold welcome he'd received, she obviously was. His arrival that evening had been met with a dagger stare, and she'd spent the entire night avoiding him. He'd watched her laughing and joking with the other customers; a general observer would be fooled into thinking she was happy and relaxed, but he could see the telltale tightness in her shoulders. Hell, he could almost see the steam coming from her ears.

"You?" he asked, noting the tightness around Abi's eyes and the frown that creased her forehead.

Abi blew a strand of hair out of her face with a sigh. "I waited up last night to talk to her, but I guess it was a late one."

She looked at him for confirmation and he muttered non-committally, avoiding her gaze. Nate had gotten home sometime around midnight, but he didn't think Abi needed to know that. It was obvious Phoenix needed space to process everything. The last thing he wanted to do was cause a rift between the two best friends in the meantime.

His phone buzzed on the table before she could ask anything further, and he gave her an apologetic smile as he noted his father's name on the screen. Leaving his full pint behind, he slipped outside into the night.

"Have you managed to get in touch with William?" he asked as soon as he answered, all form of pleasantries foregone.

"Is that any way to greet your Alpha?" Cormac growled. "Or your father?"

Ethan closed his eyes and took a breath. His father wasn't the bad guy here. All he'd done was try to help; it wasn't Cormac's fault a certain redhead put him in a bad mood.

"Sorry, it's been a long few days. We got more information on the prophecy."

"Nothing good I take it?" Cormac's voice softened, no trace of the Alpha remaining, only a father's concern.

He shook his head even though his father couldn't see him. He had no idea how to start explaining the clusterfuck they were in or the heavy weight of dread Abi's words had triggered.

"Ethan?"

"Yeah, sorry, I'm still here. It turns out Darius had a scroll." In concise, emotionless detail he brought Cormac up to speed. He forced himself to focus only on the facts; the implication spoke for itself.

For a minute, there was silence.

"We have time, son. We'll find another way."

The words struck Ethan in a place he wasn't ready to examine yet, and he swiftly changed the subject. "What about the Council? Did you speak to William?"

"He seems to have fallen off the radar since the meeting." Cormac's frustration was palpable even through the phone.

"Maybe if I try to contact him?"

"And say what? He expects me to take an interest in Council business. It's my job as Alpha. If you start asking questions, you'll only draw attention to yourself."

"So, I'll tell him the truth."

The line fell silent once more.

"Make no mistake, Ethan," Cormac said, eventually, "William's loyalty is to the Council. The fact you're family will mean nothing to him if he believes your actions pose a risk to the Lore."

Ethan's free hand clenched. They'd had this argument before and he just couldn't understand it. Family came first. Always. Besides, if Vicktor had informed the Council of his meeting, there was every chance he'd mentioned the wolf by Phoenix's side. That alone would be enough to raise questions. It would be better if William heard the truth from him.

"Think carefully, son. If the Council knows of your connection to the hybrid, you put the whole pack at risk. Are you ready to ask that of them?"

An uncomfortable knot settled in the pit of Ethan's stomach, and he cursed. "I have to go. Let me know if you hear anything from William."

He hung up and shoved the phone into his pocket, biting back a roar of frustration. His father was right. Whether he liked it or not, anything he did reflected on the pack. It didn't matter how far he ran from his responsibilities.

With that thought gnawing at him, he turned to go back into the pub, only to find himself face to face with Phoenix. Her vivid green eyes were unreadable as she watched him with her arms folded tightly across her chest.

"I don't need you to save me, Ethan."

His jaw dropped. Was that what she thought he was trying to do? Play the knight in shining armour?

"I know you're trying to help," she continued, tone cooler than he'd heard from her since they first met. "But I'm a big girl, and I can look out for myself."

His anger flared. She was so bloody stubborn. Did she not realise it was going to get her killed?

"And what about the people that get hurt while you're busy looking out for yourself?" He growled and pushed past her, stalking into the night.

As Ethan's form disappeared from sight, Phoenix bit back the urge to scream. Frustration mixed with anger, churning into a mess of emotions that crawled over her skin. He didn't get to push her around or decide what was best for her. She'd done fine before he came along; there was no need for his self-sacrificing bullshit. She wasn't asking anyone to put themselves in danger for her. She didn't *want* them to put themselves in danger for her.

The anger wrapped around her like a protective blanket and she turned to yank open the door of the pub. Even from across the room, she could feel Abi's concerned gaze boring into her. She pointedly ignored it and set about cleaning tables. She didn't need their concern ... or their pity.

The night passed in a blur and by closing time, her mood had only marginally improved. She'd avoided Abi by using customers as live body-shields and had multiple arguments with Ethan in her head – all of which she won. But as the last stragglers slipped out the door, she saw Abi approach from the corner of her eye.

"Ethan left in a bit of a rush earlier. Is everything okay?"

An uncomfortable knot of jealousy twisted in her stomach, adding more fuel to her anger.

"Everything's fine. I just made it clear I didn't need him to babysit me."

She moved to the side but Abi blocked her way, unyielding.

"He's worried about you. Why is that so bad?"

"I don't need him to be worried about me. I don't need everyone to protect me." She glared pointedly at her friend but was met with defiant blue eyes.

"Does it ever cross your bloody mind that we care about you?"

"Oh, so you kept the truth from me because you cared?"

"Yes! Just like you kept the truth from me because you cared." With that, Abi turned on her heel and disappeared through the door that led to their apartment.

Phoenix stared after her, an uncomfortable burning sensation building in the back of her throat. What was she doing? She didn't want to argue with Abi. Or anyone really. It was like she couldn't stop herself. The sane part of her brain was being held hostage, nothing more than a muffled voice trying to make itself heard through the haze that was clogging her head.

She should be upstairs with Abi right now, curled up on the sofa debating which tacky movie to watch tonight. Instead it felt like there was a huge divide – one she'd created – between them. And she didn't know how to fix it.

With a heaviness in her heart, she locked the doors and trudged upstairs to her room. The first sight that met her when she switched on the light was the wooden box on her locker. The subtle fragrance of herbs reached her nose, and an image of her parents flashed before her eyes. They'd given up so much for her. And it was all for nothing.

She crumpled to the floor and let the silent tears flow.

CHAPTER NINE

Darius sank into the plush velvet couch that had been handcrafted specially to fit the curved office. The floor-to-ceiling window offered him a panoramic view of the club below and he watched as servers wove through the crowd of writhing bodies. They were easily identifiable in their leather attire and by the desperation they reeked of. *Pathetic.*

The bank of monitors to his left sat silent, screens black. At this time of night, the private rooms they showcased would all be occupied, but he didn't think his guest would quite appreciate the show they provided.

He took a sip of his whiskey and regarded the man across from him. "You have news for me?"

Vicktor nodded and pulled a handkerchief from his pocket, grimacing as he not-so-discreetly wiped his hands. A glass of whiskey sat untouched in front of him. Amused, Darius noted the stiff set of his shoulders as he avoided looking towards the club.

"This is an interesting place you have here." The undertone of disdain was clear in Vicktor's voice. Darius smiled.

"We like to cater for all tastes ... Even those not necessarily to our liking."

A non-committal grunt was the only answer as Vicktor wiped his hands once more.

"The witches are going in tonight."

Darius stilled.

"Where?"

The other man eyed him warily. "Does it really matter? She's either strong enough to survive the hit or she's not."

Darius leaned forward, allowing himself a moment to imagine ripping Vicktor's throat out. "Humour me."

"I'll give you this information, but then I'm out, Darius. I won't betray the Council any more than I already have, even if they are misguided."

Darius took another sip of his drink, using the glass to mask his impatience.

"The hovel she calls a home. They're on their way now."

That didn't give him long to act.

With an amicable smile, Darius pushed himself to standing. "I appreciate you coming here to tell me." He brushed his hands down the front of his jacket, smoothing out the soft cashmere. "Now, I'm afraid you'll have to excuse me; I have another prior arrangement. My guards will be happy to show you out. Unless you wish to stay and partake in the entertainment?"

His smile shifted, and with pleasure he noticed the other man flinch before he turned and left the viewing room.

CHAPTER TEN

What the —

Phoenix's eyes shot open. The insistent tapping that had pervaded her dreams continued. Darkness filled the room around her, and in her groggy state it took a moment to realise the noise wasn't just a figment of her imagination.

She turned to look at the window where red eyes stared back at her through the glass. A scream bubbled up in her throat.

The crow's loud squawk broke through the terror long enough to make her pause. Even against the backdrop of night, the bird's feathers were a miasma of colours that rippled hypnotically as they ruffled in the wind.

Red eyes. Feathers like an oil-slick rainbow. She'd seen this bird before.

The crow's tapping became more frantic and its squawk more insistent. She scooched up in the bed until her back was against the headboard, but kept her eyes glued to the window. Surely it couldn't be the same bird? The one that had saved her from the first demon?

Apparently satisfied to have gotten her attention, the crow took flight and disappeared in a blur of feathers.

Well, that wasn't creepy.

Shaken, she looked around her room, half expecting the

bogeyman to jump out at her next. What she saw instead stopped her short.

A thin wisp of smoke seeped under the bedroom door and moved across the floor like fog. She sniffed the air but found no smell of burning, and the fire alarm was noticeably silent. She closed her eyes and peeked one eye open, but the smoke was still there, thicker now.

Shit! Abi.

Panic sent a spike of adrenaline through her. She leapt out of bed and ran to the door, yanking it open before her brain belatedly reminded her to check how warm it was.

The hallway beyond was a haze of smoke, a strange blue hue trailing along the ground behind it. A wisp of the smoke touched her bare legs and creeped upward in a tender caress. A light prickle of static followed its path over her skin, but aside from that odd sensation, there was nothing.

No smell. No immediate clogging of her airways. None of the things that should have come with smoke.

Abi's room was barely twenty feet from where she stood, yet in that moment it felt like miles. She sprinted down the hall and yanked the door open, not bothering to knock. The room was filled with the strange blue smoke, and she could only just make out Abi's form lying in the bed. Unmoving.

Phoenix's heart stuttered and clenched painfully. In the split second it took her to reach the bed, she did something she hadn't ever done before: she prayed.

She'd be a better person, a better friend. She'd stop being a complete pain in the arse. She'd forgive her friend for every little lie and apologise for her own, glaringly obvious double standards. She'd do anything.

The rise and fall of Abi's breathing was so subtle that, for a moment, she thought she was imagining it. Phoenix placed her hand on her friend's chest and when she felt the gentle movement, she let out a sob of relief.

"Abi." She shook the still form. "Abi."

No answer.

Panic started to overtake her once more and she shook harder.

Still no response. Then, through the haze of smoke and fear, she heard it: footsteps.

She darted to the door and crouched low. Tentatively, she peered into the empty hallway. The footsteps grew louder. A second later, a man stepped into view at the top of the staircase. Long robes draped over his lanky frame, and a trail of blue flames followed in his wake like an eager puppy lapping at his heels. His lips moved in a silent chant and his signature washed over her, bringing with it a burning heat.

The flame crawled up the walls, slowly devouring everything it touched. Everything except the witch.

She cursed and glanced towards the bed. The witch would reach her in seconds, and the only other exit from the bedroom was a small window with a two-storey drop. Could she make it without hurting her friend?

There was no time to decide, however, as the witch began to walk in her direction.

Without thinking, she lunged from her crouched position at the door and barrelled into the witch. He stumbled a couple of feet, but his mouth turned up in a satisfied smile.

Blue fire surrounded them in an instant, and she was consumed by a heat so intense it could sear the flesh from her bones. Her instincts screamed at her to run.

Instead, she drew closer to the witch until she found herself within his protective sphere and the heat reduced somewhat. Unfortunately, it also brought her within reaching distance. The witch grabbed at her but she twisted away, using her speed to her advantage. The close quarter training sessions Ethan had forced on her suddenly seemed a lot more relevant now.

Conscious of the flames growing closer and closer to Abi, she waited for an opening. The witch was strong, but a significant portion of his energy was focused on creating the magic fire and eventually she saw her opportunity.

A sharp jab to the kidney doubled him over in pain and she followed through with a knee to the jaw. The strike caught at the perfect angle and he fell to the floor unconscious.

Before she could do anything further, blue flame engulfed the narrow strip of floor between her and the witch, forming a barrier. She stumbled back, her arms raised in front of her face in a vain attempt to shield from the heat. Every instinct in her body screamed to finish him off; he'd come into her home and threatened the safety of the people she loved. He couldn't be allowed to live.

But even with the witch unconscious, the flames continued to spread. Gaping holes appeared in the plasterboard that coated the walls, exposing wooden beams that were quickly turning black. There was no time. She needed to get Abi out.

With a glance towards the witch, she ran back to Abi's room and lifted her carefully from the bed. Hoisting her over her shoulder, Phoenix shoved back the panic that rose like bile in her throat. The rise and fall of Abi's chest was shallower now, her breathing laboured. She was suddenly aware of the tightness in her own lungs. Each inhale caused an ache of protest between her ribs and burned a path down her windpipe.

Abi wasn't much smaller than her, and though her friend's weight was easily manageable, the mechanics of carrying a person proved difficult. She risked a quick glance into the hallway on the off-chance of an easier escape route, but when she saw the witch begin to stir, she turned back to the window with a grimace.

A single, full-force kick and the glass shattered. The gust of wind that blew through the opening caused the fire to explode into a violent furnace behind her. She ignored the shards of glass that stuck into her bare feet and took a running leap, clutching Abi tight to her.

The jarring thud as she hit the ground sent her tumbling and she barely managed to twist enough to protect her friend from the fall.

An abnormal blue hue filled the night around her. The sounds of nearby yelling had her on her feet and running within seconds. She didn't look back. Not once. Not even when a loud explosion shattered her hopes of ever returning home.

CHAPTER ELEVEN

Darius snapped the neck of the second witch just as an upper-storey window exploded and a flash of red leapt through the night. He watched as Phoenix rolled and stumbled to her feet with a pale human-sized form clutched in her arms.

The fucking human? He snarled. Had he taught her nothing about her weaknesses?

Three more witches still surrounded the pub; their yells confirming they, too, had spotted her. He moved in a blur, careful to keep to the shadows as he tore out their jugulars one after the other and left them in a gurgling heap on the ground. Five down, one to go.

Behind him, blue fire continued to devour the building, casting an eerie halo into the night. That meant the sixth witch was still alive. And powerful, if the magic blaze was anything to go by. Vicktor hadn't pulled his punches when he arranged the hit.

From the shadows, he watched Phoenix adjust her human baggage and make a hasty retreat, no doubt heeding the previous yells as warning of further pursuit. Well, she needn't worry; he wasn't letting her die that easily.

Just as she cleared his line of sight, a pale face appeared at the broken window. Even with the distance between them, he could see the fury etched into the witch's features.

The man's descent from the upper floor was far more graceful than Phoenix's had been on account of her bleeding-heart loyalty to her friend. A black cloak billowed behind him as he landed on the ground in a crouch, a trail of blue flame following his descent.

The man stood, his tall frame creating an imposing silhouette against the backdrop of destruction. He glanced at his fallen comrades, then clicked his fingers. A loud explosion rippled through the night.

As he stalked into the darkness after Phoenix, Darius followed. Impressive as the man's powers were, he couldn't be allowed to live.

Stones ground into Phoenix's bare feet, pushing the shards of glass further in with each step. She gritted her teeth and bent her head against the biting wind that scorched her exposed skin.

Mental note: get more practical pyjamas.

The baggy t-shirt skimming her thighs offered little protection against the freezing February temperatures. Over her shoulder, she could feel the goosebumps covering Abi's ice-cold skin through the silk nightwear she wore. Her gut twisted as she added hypothermia to the list of possible things liable to kill them both before the night was over.

Abi hadn't stirred at all. Not when Phoenix had leapt with her from the first storey window, and not now as she was being jostled about like a ragdoll. She could only hope that her friend's slumber was some strange side-effect of the magic fire and would lift once she'd gotten them far enough from the source.

Tears pricked her eyes as she forced herself to keep moving. The witch would be coming for her. Besides, there was nothing to turn back for; their home was gone.

The night was quiet and the streets empty. Anyone with an ounce of sanity had long ago succumbed to the safety of their beds, and for that, she was grateful. Still, she was conscious of being seen. A half-naked woman carrying another unconscious woman would definitely raise some questions.

She looked around, debating her options. The shop fronts afforded her some shadow, but while she stayed on the main street, she was exposed. Soon, she'd run out of shops and hit the residential areas, which would only increase the likelihood of attracting attention. Not to mention the potential for collateral damage if the witch caught her.

At the end of the street, she turned the corner, and was debating her next move when a sound from the main street made her freeze. Her heart pounded so loudly that she had to concentrate to hear past it.

The sound came again, faint and almost imperceptible. The scuff of cloth against stones maybe? The witch's cloak?

Her fight-or-flight response sent a burst of adrenaline through her system, clearly telling her she was going to bloody well fight. But even as it did, her hands grasped reflexively, pulling Abi tighter. She couldn't fight like this.

Desperate, she looked around for somewhere to place her friend that would keep her out of the crossfire, but there was nothing but an empty path as far as the eye could see.

Another sound, louder this time, followed by a grunt.

With no other choice, she lowered Abi to the ground and edged cautiously along the wall, back the way she'd come. She paused at the corner, her body tense as she waited for the witch to appear.

A full minute passed, and nothing happened. Very slowly, she crouched down and peered around the corner.

The main street was empty, as silent as it had been when she'd made her way down it only minutes before. There was no sign of the witch and no material dragging along the ground. Was her imagination playing tricks with her?

She couldn't shake the feeling that someone would jump out at her any second, but when another survey of the street showed no movement, she ran back and hefted Abi over her shoulder once more. She needed to get help for her friend.

Turning another corner, she followed a winding path back to the main road. Hopefully anyone following her would get fed up and go home ... *Yeah, because she'd be that lucky.*

She'd left the pub in such a hurry that she hadn't thought to grab her phone and she wracked her brain, trying desperately to remember Ethan's number – or if phone boxes even still existed. What other options did she have? Could she figure out a route that would get her to Ethan's apartment without attracting attention? Her chances were slim to none, and something told her Abi didn't have that much time.

She turned the final corner and barrelled straight into the broad chest of a shocked pedestrian. The man's expression was almost comical, eyes flitting between her and the body she carried as he instinctively took a step back. His mouth opened and closed multiple times before he managed to formulate any words.

"Are you okay?"

CHAPTER TWELVE

The red hue of dawn broke over the city horizon as Ethan stared out his living room window. His eyes were heavy with sleep, but his body was restless and his head wouldn't shut up. He'd gone to bed fuming after his fight with Phoenix, and the fact that he was awake at stupid o'clock only made his mood worse.

Nightmares had plagued him all night, each of them involving some kind of horrific death for Phoenix while he watched on, unable to act. The last had been the worst, and he'd woken in a pool of sweat with the image still burned into his mind: her walking into an inferno of blue flame, a serene smile on her face.

It was her fault, of course. He was only trying to help because he cared. If she wasn't so determined to push everyone away, she'd see that. Maybe he should just accept that he was fighting a losing battle?

His wolf growled at the suggestion and he dropped his head into his hands, letting out a low rumble of frustration. He was a bloody pushover.

Screw this. He grabbed his leather jacket from the back of the sofa and stood. After a quick check for the keys to his bike, he stalked out of the apartment, not bothering to lock the door behind him.

The matte black Harley sat waiting patiently for him just inside the shuttered doors of the converted warehouse. The mere sight of its sleek curves made him smile and the tightness in his chest eased a little. He slipped on his jacket and pressed the button to raise the metal doors.

The cold morning air hit him and he took a deep breath, relishing the freshness. Maybe he'd head for the Wicklow Mountains. He'd been spending too much time in the city lately. His wolf was getting edgy.

Plan set, he swung his leg over the bike. His mobile phone chose that moment to start buzzing insistently and he swore. Memories of his nightmares flashed through his mind as he struggled to free the phone from his jeans pocket and his body tensed.

The number on the screen was unfamiliar, and he hesitated with his finger over the answer button. A twist of anxiety in his gut refused to let him ignore it, however, so he brought the phone to his ear with a longing glance at the door.

"Ethan?" Phoenix's harried voice came down the line before he even had a chance to speak. "Yes, yes, I'll be quick," she said, voice muffled as she spoke to someone beside her.

In the background, he could hear a strange rhythmic beeping and the distant sound of wheels squeaking on linoleum.

"Phoenix? What's going on? Where are you?"

For a moment, she was quiet. The distant sound of shouting reached him through the phone, followed by the sudden blaring of an alarm. A deep sense of dread hit him and his mouth dried as if filled with sawdust.

"I'm in the hospital," she finally answered, a sob choking its way free. "There was a fire."

The stench of disinfectant and disease assaulted Ethan as soon as he pushed through the doors of the hospital. The smell clawed its way down the back of his throat, nearly choking him. Everything was white and sterile, from the walls, to the floors, to the people, and he shuddered at the cloud of death that hung in every fibre of the place.

Phoenix had assured him on the phone that both she and Abi

were safe, but his pounding heart refused to calm until he saw for himself.

A quick glance at the overhead signs pointed him in the direction of their ward. He ignored the protests from the hospital security guard as he took the first right turn and ran down the corridor.

Even at the early hour, the hospital was a buzz of activity; workers hurried past him in scrubs, their expressions varying between haggard, determined, or a mix of both. The occasional patient shuffled about in their dressing gown, and a young couple sat on distorted plastic chairs, clutching hands as they sobbed. They all ignored him, focused only on whatever situation had brought them there.

He knew he'd found the right room when he turned a corner and spotted two uniformed Gardaí talking quietly outside a closed door. Both seemed too young to shave, let alone guard anything, but their presence gave him pause.

Phoenix hadn't mentioned the police when she rang. Their involvement probably stood to reason given the fire, but surely they didn't need to be at the hospital?

As he approached the room, he waited for them to stop him and question his presence since visiting time wasn't for another three hours, at least. Instead, they both gave him a sympathetic look and nodded politely before moving to the side to allow him clear access to the door.

It was then he noticed the sound of arguing coming from the room, and he groaned as he realised just what the sympathy was for. Phoenix's stubborn tone was as familiar to him as his own by now, and in a strange way, it eased some of the tension that had been bubbling up inside.

He braced himself and pushed open the door to find her sitting on a stiff metal chair beside a hospital bed that looked equally as comfortable. A dirty t-shirt was the only thing covering her and blood coated her feet. Other than that, she appeared unharmed. Abi sat propped up by pillows in the bed and though her skin had a slightly grey tinge to it, her blue eyes were alert and sparkling with barely restrained laughter.

"I told you, I'm fine. I don't need to be checked out." Phoenix looked up as he stepped into the room and gestured desperately towards an old man in a white coat who stood glaring at her from the end of the bed. "Ethan, can you please tell this nice doctor that I said thank you, but I don't require his assistance. He doesn't seem to want to listen to me."

Before he could say anything, the doctor tapped his clipboard pointedly, nodding towards her feet. "It says here you had broken glass in your feet; you may need stitches."

"Nope, no stitches needed here," she insisted, crossing her arms over her chest and tucking her feet under her on the chair. Her jaw was set firm, but her eyes were pleading as she turned to him for help.

He couldn't stop the smile that caused his lip to quirk up as he watched her squirm. A small part of him was so tempted to draw it out. But she was right, of course, they couldn't let the doctor check her out. Who knew what their human tests would show, or wouldn't show, as the case may be.

With an apologetic look back to the doctor, he shrugged. "Sorry, doc. She's a stubborn one."

The doctor shook his head and shoved the clipboard towards Phoenix. "If you insist on being so stupid, you'll need to sign this release to confirm you refused medical attention."

She took the clipboard from him and quickly scrawled her name before handing it back as if it might burn her.

"What about me, doctor?" Abi chimed in.

The man turned to her and frowned. "All of your tests have come back normal, but I'd like to keep you in for observation. Smoke inhalation can be very serious."

Abi nodded in understanding, then pushed the blanket off and swung her legs over the side of the bed, wearing nothing more than a paper-thin hospital gown. She looked around the room in confusion before turning to Phoenix.

"Don't suppose I've got any clothes here?"

Ethan handed over the rucksack that Phoenix had asked him to bring and politely averted his eyes to allow Abi some degree of modesty. He'd borrowed the clothes from Lily so they should more or less fit. Either way, they couldn't really be too picky right now.

"What are you doing?" the doctor spluttered as Abi pulled on a pair of blue jeans.

"Discharging myself." She gave him an innocent smile and continued dressing. "You said all of my tests were fine."

The man's face turned a worrying shade of red, and Ethan almost felt sorry for him. He obviously recognised a lost cause when he saw one, however, as he turned on his heel, muttering something about preparing the paperwork as he stalked from the room.

When the door closed and they were once more alone, Ethan immediately shifted his attention back to Phoenix. He scanned her from head to toe, the tension he felt only fully unravelling once he was satisfied she was unharmed. Dark circles ringed her eyes, and a subtle mix of fear and sadness shadowed her features, but she seemed to be holding it together out of sheer stubbornness.

"Okay, what happened? Why are the police outside?"

In a toneless voice, she relayed the events of the night before: waking up to the blue flame, her battle with the witch, escaping with Abi.

"Needless to say, the good Samaritan was a bit concerned about the fact I was carting around an unconscious body and called the police," she finished with a wry smile.

An uneasy feeling settled low in his stomach at the mention of the blue fire, memories from his nightmare flashing to mind. He pushed them away.

"Have they questioned you?"

She nodded. "I managed to convince them that shock and adrenaline turned me into Superwoman, and that's how I was able to carry Abi to safety."

He snorted. It was amazing the things humans would believe while completely ignoring the obvious signs right in front of them. "Why are they still here? Is it because of the fire?"

Her cheeks coloured and she looked sheepish all of a sudden. Abi sniggered beside her.

"I may have had a minor argument with the doc when he tried to examine me. They said they have to wait for their boss to give them the go-ahead to leave, but I think they've been told to stick around in case I cause any trouble."

He put his head in his hand and took a deep breath. It had been a long night. The last thing they needed was to draw attention from the human authorities.

"Let's not give them reason to hang around any longer." He waved at the bag of clothes and indicated for her to follow Abi's lead and get changed.

He turned his back, mentally berating himself for the sudden urge to peek. Instead, he focused on the details of Phoenix's story. Blue flame equalled witch. A strong one. He had a hard time believing the witches themselves had organised the attack, which left Darius or the Council. Neither option was appealing.

When the rustling behind him stopped and the room fell silent, he deemed it safe to turn back around. Phoenix and Abi stood together watching him, both looking more vulnerable than he'd ever seen them before.

"Ready to go?" he asked gently.

Phoenix looked at Abi, her green eyes haunted.

"We have no place to go anymore."

CHAPTER THIRTEEN

Darius wove between the gathered Witnesses, drawing closer to the centre of the amphitheatre where Vicktor kneeled before the Council. Large candles bordered the raised platform upon which the five Council members stood, their hoods lowered. Shadows flitted across their impassive faces and he smiled in anticipation of their judgement.

Vicktor had kept the details of the attack short and sweet: pub burned down, casualties sustained, hybrid still alive. A heavy silence fell over the chamber in response to the news.

Vlad stepped forward, looking down at Vicktor with a sneer of disdain. "You say the witches are all dead?"

Vicktor hesitated a moment. "It would appear the hybrid got the upper hand on them."

Darius raised an eyebrow. *Is that so?*

"So, you failed."

A low murmur filled the chamber, and the room bristled with tension. Vicktor bowed his head in supplication before straightening up to look at each of the Council members in turn.

"It's true. I underestimated the hybrid. However, I have some information that may be of use to you, if you would allow me?"

Vlad opened his mouth to respond, but Méabh moved forward

and placed a hand on his shoulder. Red-tipped nails dug into his flesh as she smiled. Even from his position in the crowd, Darius could see the barely restrained anger darken Vlad's eyes.

"Please proceed," she ordered Vicktor, the seductive invitation carrying a very clear warning.

Vicktor stood and gave Vlad a smug smile as he brushed down his grey suit; his sense of self-preservation was obviously non-existent.

"A source has informed me that, aside from the wolf, there is also a witch keeping company with the hybrid. A young girl. I have it on good authority that the girl is a weak link you may be able to exploit."

There was a subtle shifting around the room at the news. Darius watched Diana, who had stayed silent to this point but tensed noticeably at the mention of witch involvement. He cast his mind back to the confrontation with Phoenix at his lair. Had there been a witch with her? He couldn't quite remember.

"Please elaborate," Méabh encouraged with a wave of her hand.

"It appears that the witch lost a sister. An unfortunate accident, so I'm told, but closely related to the issue of the prophecy. Loss can breed resentment, and if the hybrid is the only reason the prophecy exists ..."

"We may be able to turn this witch to our cause." Méabh tapped a viciously sharp fingernail against her lip as she regarded the CLO rep.

"You really think a young, inexperienced witch can succeed where your highly-trained witches failed?" Vlad directed the question to Vicktor but arched his eyebrow in contempt at his fae co-Council.

"That's not what I'm proposing." Vicktor shook his head. "An unfortunate side-effect to the failed attack is that the hybrid will run. It'll make it a lot harder to kill her if you can't find her. This witch can provide you information about her location. I believe you already have the means to finish the job."

The whole room stilled, except for the shadows. At Vicktor's words they began to swirl and twist, wrapping themselves around the Council before settling once more in the background.

Chills ran down Darius's spine and he shivered. Anticipation settled in his gut like a jolt of electricity. For a split second, he forgot that he, in fact, needed Phoenix alive, and he imagined the thrill of facing a true challenge again after so many centuries.

"You propose we call on the Mists." Kam cast a glance at the shadows behind him, his face expressionless.

Vicktor inclined his head.

The whole room seemed to hold its breath. In all the time Darius had acted as a Witness to the Council, he'd only seen the Mists deployed twice. The result had been a swift and sure end to the targets, despite the fact that both were Supes of immense power. The simple mention of the Council's assassins was enough to strike terror into the heart of all within the Lore, and their threat alone maintained order. Even the most powerful being couldn't fight what they couldn't touch.

The Council formed a circle, pulling up their blood red hoods as they turned their attention from the waiting crowd. Behind them, the shadows began to shift and take shape. Darius watched in fascination as, one by one, the Mists took their human form.

Two men and a woman stood in place of the shadows. Black harem pants and long flowing robes covered most of their tanned skin, and hoods were pulled low over their head, shadowing their exotic features. But even in the darkness they used for cover, their eyes were clearly distinguishable, and the most striking feature of all.

The golden eyes were a feature unique to the Mists, and one rarely seen in the world anymore. The power they signified had resulted in a long history of enslavement for the species, and for many, the Mists were now little more than a myth.

Thick bands of gold, a symbol of that very enslavement, circled the wrists of the three now standing behind the Council, and hatred blazed in their eyes. Only a spell, controlled by the Council, prevented that gold from touching their skin and draining them of their magic and very life source.

The circumstances that led to the Mists being bound were a mystery to all but the Council. Darius knew only that it had resulted from the actions of Shayan, the youngest of the three. Stupidly, the

332

male's sister, Maj, and older brother, Jannah, had sacrificed themselves to save him from death. *Idiots.*

After what seemed like an age, the Council broke apart and lowered their hoods. Kam indicated for the Mists to step forward, and they did so as if being forcefully dragged. A wave of power washed over the room, eliciting gasps from a number of Witnesses.

"By the terms of your servitude, we can only enforce your actions if all five of the Council are in agreement." Kam paused, looking at each of the Council members in turn. His gaze hesitated at Diana before finally resting on William. "That is not the case here today, so we must instead ask for your assistance."

Jannah, the oldest of the three, instantly stood taller, tension leaving his body. His answer was clear in the stubborn tilt of his chin.

Kam set out the Council's requirements and their reasoning: kill the hybrid and save the Lore.

Shayan tilted his head and assessed the Council. "You ask a lot from us. What will you give us in return?"

"We will let your sister go free." Vlad leered at the female.

Maj made to lunge for him, but he held up a finger and wagged it tauntingly. Jannah placed a hand on her shoulder and glared a warning at Shayan.

The young Mist ignored it.

"All of us. Let us all go and I'll do what you're too scared to do yourself." Shayan sneered and turned his back, arms crossed as he looked around the chamber, seemingly unimpressed with the proceedings.

"Shayan." Jannah's voice rumbled through the amphitheatre, causing every Supe in the room to shiver.

"And what if you fail?" Méabh sidled up to Shayan. She walked a circle around him, trailing a fingernail across the broad expanse of his back. Her face was a mix of calculating assessment and carnal admiration as she brushed against him.

Shayan hesitated. He glanced at his brother and sister, then squared his shoulders and fixed his golden gaze on the fae.

"If I fail, I'll be yours to command. With no restrictions."

"No!" Maj pushed herself forward and placed herself between her younger brother and Méabh, mouth set in a resigned line. "If he fails, then I shall finish the job."

Shayan put a hand on her arm, golden eyes beseeching her. "I can do this, Maj. I can fix everything. Let me do this."

Méabh tapped the blood red nail against her lips and watched them quietly for a moment. "I don't know. I think I prefer his offer." She pointed to Shayan and smiled suggestively.

Before Maj could argue further, Jannah stepped forward, his fists clenched by his side.

"If he fails, we shall both ensure the job is finished. That is the only deal you'll get from us."

Méabh pouted her luscious red lips, then shrugged and walked back to the other Council members, giving Vlad a wink as she passed him.

The vampire ignored her, turning instead towards Diana. "We have our assassins. Now we need the witch. It's time for you to make yourself useful."

CHAPTER FOURTEEN

It's all gone.

Phoenix faced the charred and crumbling building that used to be her home and bit back the tears that burned her throat. Ethan stood by her side, an unwavering pillar of strength. But nothing could comfort her at that moment.

Abi had been silent since they arrived, and when she walked ahead of them, they hung back to give her some privacy. In truth, she couldn't bear to see the look of pain on her friend's face. The pub had been everything to Abi. It was the only thing she had left after her mother died, and now it was in ruins.

The heavy wooden door was little more than a pile of ash, allowing a glimpse of the devastation inside. Windows were gaping holes of jagged glass, and the roof had collapsed in a number of places. The general shape of the building had been maintained by the brickwork, but everything that had given it its character, its soul, had been destroyed.

It had taken her two days to gather the courage to come back. She knew she had to see it for herself, but she couldn't face the truth of what she'd cost them. What she'd cost Abi. Eventually, her friend insisted she was well enough to go and Phoenix had no more excuses.

Ethan peered inside the doorway and let out a low whistle. "The witch's fire did all this damage?"

The memory of the explosion rang in her ears, and she shrugged. "The fire. The alcohol. Who knows."

It didn't really matter how the pub was destroyed. She was the reason it had happened; the how was immaterial.

To her left, Abi peered through one of the shattered windows. When she saw the wreckage inside, she let out a sharp sob and sank to the ground with her hand over her mouth. Phoenix ran to her side, ignoring the lance of pain as guilt speared her in the chest. She crouched down beside her friend and was surprised to see no tears on Abi's face. Her skin was still the sickly pale it had been since the fire, and rage blazed in her eyes, but no tears.

Abi grabbed her hand and gave it a tight squeeze, her mouth set in a determined line as she looked up at the carcass of her home and livelihood.

They sat together in silence for a few minutes, each lost in their own thoughts as they assessed the damage. Eventually, they stood and walked back to the main entrance where Ethan waited patiently.

"It's not safe for you to stay anymore. You know that."

His voice was gentle, but still the words caused her throat to tighten. She couldn't argue – not when the evidence was laid out so starkly before them – so she swallowed past the lump that choked her and nodded.

"What about Abi? She needs somewhere to go while ..." She looked at the damage before her, not even able to contemplate how it might be undone.

"I'm going with you."

Her jaw dropped and she gaped at the obviously insane human beside her. When all she got in return was steely resolve, she turned to Ethan for support. A smile tugged at the corner of his mouth and he held up his hands, backing away from both of them.

What the hell? Has everyone lost their mind?

"Abi, I really don't think that's a good idea." She waved a hand towards the incinerated building, as if the obvious needed to be high-lighted. "You could have died in that fire."

"Yep, and I could walk outside the door and get hit by a bus. I'm going with you, and you're going to train me to fight." Without waiting for a response, Abi turned and walked to Ethan's car, leaving Phoenix and Ethan staring after her in shock.

A low chuckle from Ethan was enough to redirect her irritation.

"Surely you can't think this is a good idea?" She planted her hands on her hips and glared at him.

"Of course not." He grew serious. "But it's her decision, and damned if I don't respect her for it. We'll protect her, Phoenix. She's already a target, whether you like it or not. Leaving her behind won't change that."

She sighed, wishing yet again that she could argue with him. And wasn't Abi the reason she refused to leave in the first place? One of the reasons at least?

Needing a minute to gather her thoughts, she excused herself and slipped into the wreckage of the pub. She had one more thing to do before they left.

The interior was a mess of ash and charred remains, yet there was a clear pattern to the destruction. She followed the path that ran from the entrance – or what remained of it – straight to the door that led to their apartment. There was a gaping hole where the bar had been and only small sections of the stage and seating area were intact, but the route the witch had taken was clearly marked by the lack of debris; as if the fire had burned everything clean away, even the dirt.

She only allowed herself a brief glance around before she forced her attention straight ahead and focused on her goal. There'd be time to grieve later.

The stairs leading to their apartment were barely standing. The skeleton structure remained, but sections of steps were missing and the ones that were left looked like they'd crumble under her weight. With a deep breath, she took them at a run, rebounding off the edges and crossing her fingers that she'd make it to the top before they collapsed entirely.

She did, just about.

Upstairs had fared a little better than the pub below, with the damage concentrated mainly around the hallway. The plasterboard walls on either side had burned away, and the rooms beyond were visible through gaping holes. Shafts of daylight shone down in the places where the roof was missing, and a chilling breeze filled the once cosy space.

She reached under her jacket to clasp the medallion that hung against her breastbone and hoped against hope. The floors creaked in protest as she made her way to her bedroom with her breath held.

While the rest of the apartment looked to only have sustained fire damage, her room had obviously been the focus of some serious pent-up anger. The bed, alone, remained intact, and even that was half buried under a barely recognisable pile of rubble.

She rushed towards the heap of oak slabs that had once been her wardrobe, and a mix of terror and rage welled up inside her. Panic clawed at her throat but she pushed it back with effort. She knelt and carefully began to move the pieces aside, one at a time.

When a patch of mahogany came into view, her head swam with relief. The knot of fear didn't unravel fully until she pulled the long box, miraculously intact, from the wreckage. Intricate Celtic symbols covered the wood, and her heart clenched at the familiar sight. She opened the box to reassure herself the sword was also unharmed, then quickly closed it and stood.

A niggling thought played at the back of her mind, and she cast her eyes to her bedside locker where she'd last seen the box for the Ritual of Passing. There was nothing there now besides ash, broken wood, and some stray herbs. A chilling sense of foreboding slithered down her spine as she turned and left the room.

CHAPTER FIFTEEN

The sharp wind bit at Lily's skin as she stood in front of the abandoned warehouse. She paid it little heed as she stared at the place where Annabelle had died. The industrial estate around her was silent, all the other businesses now closed for the night, but still she clutched her bag tight to her side. It wasn't the first time she'd found herself drawn to that exact spot, trying to imagine what her sister's last moments had been like.

Had she been afraid?

Had she called for her big sister?

It seemed odd that such an innocuous looking building could be the scene of something so tremendous like the shattering of her world. Yet something lingered in the air. Death wasn't a stranger to this place.

She wasn't really sure what she hoped to achieve by coming here. Inspiration, maybe?

Through the cloth of her canvas bag, the heat of the Ouroboros called to her. Judging her. She could feel its power, but still it was out of reach. Despite the cold night air, her hands grew clammy. What if she wasn't strong enough? What if it was too late?

Someone cleared their throat softly behind her and she jumped.

Lily pulled her magic to her, ready to strike as she turned to face the woman who'd appeared seemingly out of thin air.

A palpable sense of power surrounded the woman, and her signature was unmistakably that of a witch. She had a kind smile and long blonde hair similar to her own, but it was the green eyes that made Lily's heart clench; the compassion and wisdom behind them was so reminiscent of her mother that for a second, she was a child again and wanted nothing more than to be held in the safety of her mother's arms.

She shook herself and took a step back. The woman may be a witch, but that did not make her a friend. After all, it had been a witch that killed Annabelle. And their parents.

"Sorry, I didn't mean to startle you." The woman made no attempt to move closer, just watched her with those green eyes. "You're Lily, right?"

Lily tensed. *How does she know my name?*

"I'm Diana."

The name hung in the air between them and Lily's breath hitched. Diana? As in, the head of the witches?

"You're from the Council," she whispered, her heart hammering in her chest as her body's survival instinct suddenly realised how fucked she was.

Diana hesitated for a moment, then nodded. "We want to help you."

"That's very kind" – Lily cringed at the tremor in her voice – "but I'm not sure what you could help me with."

She took a small step to the left, watching closely for any reaction. A raised eyebrow directed at the canvas bag caused her to clutch it tighter as a new fear settled in the pit of her stomach.

Diana turned away from her to give the warehouse her full attention. "I knew your parents, you know. They were good witches, powerful. What happened to them was terrible, and it never should have happened." She sighed. "It must be hard for you to have lost them so young. And then your sister ... I can only imagine how painful it is, knowing you couldn't protect her."

The words sent a stabbing pain through Lily's heart. She raised

340

her hand, half expecting to find a wound there, but there was nothing. Nothing other than her own guilt and the agony of the truth spoken aloud.

"I tried, I ... Annabelle was very strong-willed."

Diana gave her a sympathetic smile. "It's a trait of some of the best witches."

Lily's throat burned as she remembered the eagerness with which Annabelle had taken to her studies; even before she was old enough, she'd watch Lily and try to copy everything she was doing. She was determined to be a great witch, and no one was going to stop her.

"She would have been ... one of the best."

"She still can be." Diana turned to face her, the warehouse looming behind her. "We can help you use the Ouroboros."

A heavy weight pressed on Lily's chest, almost suffocating her as she tried to push it back. She knew better than to give in to the hope, knew better than to trust the Council. But what if ...

"I'm not giving it to you."

"I'm not asking you to. The Council have plenty of magic at our disposal; we've no need for an old relic."

"Then what do you want from me?"

"Your help." Diana assessed her carefully. "There is only one way to stop the prophecy and save our people. The hybrid has to die."

She held up a hand to halt the protest that was on the tip of Lily's tongue. "You know I speak the truth. All we're asking from you is information. Keep us informed of the hybrid's whereabouts, and we can make sure no one else gets hurt. No one else has to die, Lily."

So many emotions rushed through Lily: fear, anger, guilt. It was Phoenix's fault this was all happening. If it hadn't been for her, the prophecy would never exist. Both Abi and Diana had now said this was the only way. But could she do it? Could she really give Phoenix up to the Council? Would she be able to look herself in the mirror again if she did? Would she be able to face her sister again?

And it was that thought that pulled her up short. The chance of seeing her sister again. She'd do anything to make that happen.

Even if it meant selling her soul.

CHAPTER SIXTEEN

The scenery all blurred into one as Phoenix rested her head against the car window. City turned to motorway, then to rolling green fields as far as the eye could see before starting the cycle all over again. Four hours they'd been driving only to end up in the Wicklow Mountains, barely an hour from where they'd first started. She hadn't argued when Ethan suggested it was worth leaving a false trail; she'd learned the hard way what it cost to take unnecessary risks.

Ethan was quiet in the driver's seat beside her. The occasional sideways glance was thrown her way between watching the road ahead and flicking to the rear-view mirror, but overall he left her to her silent musings.

After the first hour, the hum of the rental car's engine had become soothing and lulled her into a mild sense of relaxation. It hadn't kept the niggling worries from flitting at the edge of her thoughts though, and every now and then, the relaxation would turn to a suffocating panic.

"Are you sure Abi will be safe with them?" she asked for the third time.

He spared her a reassuring smile despite the frustration he was no doubt feeling.

"Nate will watch out for her. The most dangerous place she can be right now is with you. It's better this way. At least until we know the trail is clear."

What he said made sense; hell, she'd even agreed to the plan. The others would lay low in a safe house in Galway while she and Ethan ran a diversion to draw out anyone that might follow them. Nate would use the time to try to hack deeper into the Council's network and find out what they were planning next. Then, once the coast was clear, they'd all regroup and head to Donegal together. That way they'd at least be limiting the trouble they were bringing with them.

Abi's response to the plan had been less agreeable; she refused point-blank to leave Phoenix's side. It had taken a lot of convincing, and a pinkie promise to check in every hour, before her friend had conceded. Nate's offer of self-defence training helped sweeten the deal too.

It gave her a strange fuzzy feeling that Abi was so adamant to stick by her, considering everything that had happened. And that was why she knew this plan was the right one. If the Council was going to follow anyone, it would be her; she'd do everything in her power to lead that danger away from the others.

As the road sloped upward, the smooth tarmac was replaced with potholes and gravel. Trees lined the narrowing road and ditches awaited the unprepared. The 80 kph speed limit suddenly seemed a lot more questionable, even taking into account their so-called immortality.

They'd passed the last village fifteen minutes prior, and the glimpses of civilisation had become fewer and farther between: a quaint bungalow here, the occasional farm there. Instead, sheep and cows dotted the lush green fields and breaks in the treeline afforded unobstructed views of breath-taking valleys and forests.

Her chest constricted as she remembered the last time she'd been in these mountains. Ten years ago, she'd walked out of her family home. She'd never found the strength to come back. Not until now.

As if reading her thoughts, Ethan asked softly, "Do you want to go see the house?"

She bit her lip hard and shook her head.

He reached out and gave her hand a quick squeeze before returning his focus to the road, an unreadable expression on his face.

They drove for another few minutes in silence before Ethan pulled the car to a stop in front of a small pub that appeared out of nowhere. The thatched roof and white pebble-dashed walls gave the building character, even if the wooden door and window frames were weathered and in need of a lick of paint. Despite the apparent lack of civilisation nearby, cars littered the small parking area to the left and many of the wooden picnic tables were occupied with customers enjoying the rare sunshine. A B&B sign hung beside the door, swinging gently in the breeze.

She hesitated before getting out of the car. So, this was their first stop? The place seemed so normal. A whisper of anxiety bubbled up in her throat as she imagined what magic fire could do to the thatched roof.

She trailed behind Ethan as he headed into the pub. Darkness shrouded them as the light of the sun gave way to shadowy nooks and crannies filled with wood and exposed stonework. The smell of freshly poured Guinness reached her nose and her chest ached at the thought of home ... until she noticed the silence.

A glance around the room confirmed that all eyes were on them; she squirmed under their scrutiny. Two men in jeans and checked shirts sat on high stools at the bar with cold pints resting in weathered hands. A middle-aged couple sat in one corner, an unlit stone fireplace forming their backdrop. And an old man occupied the opposite corner, a newspaper in one hand, pint in the other. All were watching the newcomers with a mix of curiosity and suspicion. Phoenix suddenly understood what it felt like to be an animal in the zoo.

Ethan grabbed her hand and plastered a friendly smile on his face as he pulled her to the bar.

"Just a minute. Just a minute," came a woman's voice from a doorway behind it.

Phoenix raised her eyebrows at Ethan, but he said nothing, just leaned against the bar.

A couple of very silent, very uncomfortable minutes later, a woman came bustling from the back room, looking somewhat dishevelled as she wiped her hands on a tea towel. Her mousy brown hair was pulled back in a messy knot and her black top was covered in flour, but her smile was friendly, and she wore the lines on her face comfortably.

"Now, what can I get you folk?"

Ethan's smile grew wider. "A Malibu and coke for the lady, and a pint of your finest for me. Also, would you happen to have a room for the night?"

The woman eyed them both for a minute, her gaze flicking to Phoenix's left hand resting on the bar. Phoenix's cheeks grew hot as she realised the conclusions the woman was no doubt jumping to, and she shoved the hand self-consciously into her pocket.

Assessment done, the woman nodded and began to prepare the drinks. "Room is eighty a night, breakfast included. Pub closes at eleven, so no loud music after that. Local church is back in the village and holds a six o'clock service. Band sets up at eight to give everyone time to get back from mass." The woman placed two glasses on the bar in front of them and smiled. "Oh, and I'm Maura."

Phoenix took a welcome sip of her drink while Ethan handed over some money and received a room key in return. A low murmur of conversation had returned to the pub, but she could still feel the stares burning into the back of her head, and it was obvious the conversations were only half-hearted attempts to cover the eaves-dropping.

When he was done, Ethan nodded back towards the door and, with a smile of thanks to Maura, they took their drinks and headed for one of the empty picnic tables outside.

"Jeez," she said, once they were seated out of earshot. "That was about as comfortable as an anal probe."

Ethan snorted, choking on the first gulp of his pint. "I wouldn't know. Besides, you grew up not too far from here. You should be well used to the local welcome."

A huff was all she gave him in reply.

They sat in silence, watching as the sun sank lower on the

horizon and the air turned chilly. Ethan gave her a sideways glance. "You look tired."

She shrugged. Sleep wasn't coming too easy right now, and she'd spent the past few nights tossing and turning in Ethan's spare room. When she did finally fall asleep, her dreams went on a never-ending loop involving a gaping black hole and her dying in the most horrendous ways possible.

Last night's dream had been the worst; all she remembered were the cries for help before waking in a pool of sweat. It had taken her a long time to rid her mind of the sound and shake the feeling that there was someone she needed to save.

Ethan stood and offered her a hand. "Why don't we check out the room? You can catch a quick nap before we use you as bait."

Ethan unlocked the door to the B&B room and moved aside to let Phoenix pass. He followed her in and his attention was immediately drawn to the double bed that occupied most of the space. The floral bed covers were a complete eyesore and reminded him of something from the eighties. The room was clean though, and a matching floral armchair sat by the large picture window, affording a breath–taking view of the hills.

Phoenix came to an abrupt halt as she, too, spotted the lone bed. Ethan watched with morbid fascination as she tensed and started tugging nervously at her sleeve. A sharp pang of irritation clenched his jaw.

"Don't get your knickers in a twist." He stepped past her towards the bathroom. "I'll take the floor."

He closed the bathroom door a little harder than necessary and leaned back against it. Was the thought of sharing a room with him really that bad? It wasn't like he was going to ravage her while she slept. Hell, it was the twenty-first century; she should be the one taking the floor.

With a weary sigh, he went to the avocado-coloured sink and splashed cold water over his face. Phoenix would just have to suck it

346

up because he wasn't leaving her alone again. His wolf growled in agreement; she was theirs to protect.

What part of him had thought being alone with her would be simple? Just being near her drove him crazy. He'd basically signed himself up for a week of torture.

Ever since their kiss in Darius's lair, he'd gone out of his way to give her space. After the role he'd played in her parents' sacrifice, he had no right to push her. Some stupid part of him had actually hoped she'd come to him of her own choice if he just gave her time. Instead, her walls had gone straight back up, and the glimmer of passion she'd allowed him to see haunted his dreams.

Maybe it was time they laid it all out on the table once and for all. A straight up conversation with no bullshit. Grabbing a towel from the radiator, he dried his face, decision made. Before he could second-guess himself, he yanked open the bathroom door. And stopped.

Phoenix lay on garish bed covers, her breathing soft, in sync with the gentle rise and fall of her chest. Her eyes were closed, and for once, the tension was absent from her face.

He leaned his head against the doorframe and sighed.

CHAPTER SEVENTEEN

Darius absently swirled the golden liquid around the crystal tumbler as he stared out the viewing window of his club. Even at this height, the scent of blood reached him and his fangs ached for something with a bit more bite than the smooth whiskey. But it would have to wait; business first, pleasure later.

The door opened behind him and he pressed a button on the wall to turn the glass black. He knocked back the whiskey and turned to face the wolf that eyed him warily from the doorway.

"Sit," he ordered, indicating towards the velvet sofa.

There was a slight hesitation before the man complied. Blue eyes tracked his every movement as he picked up a file from his desk and placed it on the table between them. He opened the file and fanned out the security footage images so that each was clearly visible.

The flinch was subtle but enough to catch his attention.

"Tell me, Omega, do you recognise anyone in this image?" He pointed to a still taken from the security cameras in the Dublin lair, almost a month prior. The picture showed Phoenix leaving the lair with a number of others in tow. One of which he knew to be a wolf.

Silence was the only answer that came, and the wolf held his face in a blank mask, obscured by the tangled white hair that fell in front of his eyes. The flinch had been enough, however.

"Need I remind you that you only remain alive so long as you're useful to me?" Darius let the warning hang in the air between them before twisting the knife in fully. "What do you think will happen to the other wolves if you're gone?"

Blue eyes tightened in pain, and he knew the wolf would answer. The Omega's nature had proven key in helping Darius to control the temperament of his test wolves. That very same nature would make it impossible for the man to turn his back on the other wolves, not if it would cause them pain.

"The wolf's name is Ethan," the Omega ground out eventually, each syllable torn reluctantly from his mouth.

Darius raised an eyebrow. "How is it you happen to know his name?"

The man clenched his fists and his whole body shook as he warred with himself.

"He is the son of my pack Alpha."

Now that was interesting. He'd hoped to use the Omega to track Phoenix and maybe find out some information about her associates since they'd been such a thorn in his side. But this was an unexpected bonus.

"Your *old* pack, where was it based?"

A bead of sweat ran down the Omega's forehead and his knuckles turned white from clenching so hard, but still he answered.

"Donegal."

"Would he go there? Would his pack help him protect someone not of their species?"

"Cormac would do anything for his son."

"Even defy the Council?"

A small smile twitched at the corner of the Omega's mouth. "If it gave him a chance to defy his cousin? Most definitely."

Darius stilled. "His cousin?"

"Cormac's cousin, William, is the head of the werewolves."

CHAPTER EIGHTEEN

Confusion clouded Phoenix's mind as she climbed her way back to consciousness. The room around her was dark, and her heart pounded as she tried to place the strange-smelling sheets and the too-soft mattress. It took a moment for the fog to lift enough to remember where she was.

Flustered, she sat up. The bed covers were rumpled beneath her and a thin line of drool ran down her chin. How long had she been asleep for?

The sound of running water filtered into her consciousness and she looked around, realising she was alone in the room. An image of Ethan in the shower flashed unbidden into her head.

She pushed the thought from her mind and grabbed the backpack Ethan had left at the side of the bed for her. A quick rummage through it for her phone somehow produced a hairbrush. She looked at it in disgust, but then her gaze flicked towards the bathroom door. Shaking her head, she yanked the brush through her hair, then shoved it back into the bag. She was pathetic.

The next rummage actually produced her phone, and she pressed speed dial on Abi's number before she was overtaken by some other stupid urge, like putting make-up on.

"Fifi! Thank god. I've been so worried. Did you get there okay? Ethan's not leaving you alone, is he?"

Her mind once more flashed to the thought of Ethan naked and suddy in the shower. She had to clear her throat before answering. "Nope, he's not giving me an inch. Sorry I didn't call sooner. We got here a few hours ago, but I fell asleep. Guess I was more tired than I realised. You're at the safe house, right?"

She listened as Abi babbled excitedly about their hideout in Galway and the self-defence training Nate had dutifully started with her. He'd declared her a natural after she caught him with an unexpected knee to the balls.

"Supe or not, it works on them all," Abi proclaimed proudly.

Phoenix's laughter died in her throat as the bathroom door opened and Ethan walked into the room with his jeans slung low on his hips and bare chest still damp. The serious look on his face morphed into a cheeky grin when he caught her staring. She turned her back, cheeks burning.

"What? ... Yeah, I'm listening," she blustered, suddenly realising that Abi had continued talking. "Look, I gotta go. Promise me you'll be careful, okay?"

Even after Abi hung up, she waited until Ethan cleared his throat before turning back around. He'd taken the time to put on a t-shirt, but the twinkle was still in his eye.

"Like what you –" He was stopped from finishing his question by the ping of his phone.

A quick glance at the screen and all signs of teasing fell from his face. Something that looked worryingly like fear flitted over his features before his jaw settled in a hard line and he shoved the phone into his pocket.

"Ethan?"

He was quiet for a moment before looking at her with serious brown eyes. "We've got trouble. Let's go. I'll explain while we check out the area." He didn't wait for her to respond, just grabbed his jacket and headed out the door.

She grumbled to herself about annoying werewolves, but plucked

351

her leather jacket from the end of the bed and followed him, closing the door behind her.

They made their way through the hallway of the B&B to the bar where a band was busy setting up in the corner. The locals, fresh from evening mass, once more turned their microscopes to examine the newcomers in their midst. She kept her head down and tried to ignore the curious stares as she trailed Ethan to the front of the pub. They'd just reached the door when Maura appeared from nowhere with a tray of drinks in hand.

"All settled in?" She wiggled her eyebrows with a mischievous glint in her eyes that caused Phoenix's cheeks to burn again. "You're just in time. The band should be starting shortly."

Ethan returned her smile with a charming grin as he placed a warm hand on the small of Phoenix's back. "We were actually just going to take a stroll, have a look around the area."

The smile fell from Maura's face and her forehead creased with concern. "I'm not sure it's a good idea for you to go wandering at this time of the evening."

There was an awkward pause as the landlady hesitated. With a conspiratorial glance around her, she leaned in and lowered her voice. "The fairies have been up to no good lately. It's really not safe out there at night."

Phoenix choked in surprise and bit the inside of her cheek in an attempt at keeping a straight face. Mirth sparkled in Ethan's eyes as he patted her back.

"Oh really? What have they been up to?" he asked innocently.

"Well, there's been a lot of animals killed. And then there's them freak storms. Now I'm not saying the fair folk can control the weather or anything but ..." She gave them a knowing look.

Ethan raised an eyebrow. "What makes you so sure the fairies are responsible? Maybe there's a wild animal on the loose?"

Maura clucked her tongue and shook her head adamantly. "Ain't no wild animal doing this. Not with the way these animals are being killed. I always said that fairy ring up the hill would bring trouble. John – Lord rest his soul – said I was off my rocker, but I knew."

Before either of them could respond, a shout from across the bar grabbed Maura's attention and, with a smile, she hurried off.

Phoenix looked after her in disbelief as Ethan chuckled beside her.

"Fancy checking out a real live fairy ring?"

Night had coated the area in a blanket of darkness, broken only by the map of stars twinkling above them and a sliver of the moon. This far from any villages or towns, there was very little artificial light to guide them along the gravelly path that doubled as a highly suspect road. Phoenix shivered as she cast her eyes around at the hedges and forests that provided more hiding places than she was comfortable with.

"So, what trouble are we in now?"

She was suddenly conscious of the metaphorical target pinned to her back, and their earlier plan didn't seem quite so clever. Why the hell had she agreed to be bait? Sure, it would help draw out anyone who might be following them, but it also had the potential side-effect of death.

"They're sending the Mists."

Ethan's words broke through her rambling thoughts and she stumbled to a stop. "What?"

He turned to look at her, running a hand through his hair. "Dad texted. The Council is sending the Mists."

She opened her mouth and closed it again. Like every other Supe in existence, she'd grown up with horror stories about the Mists; tales of the bogeyman that were meant to keep young, powerful, unpredictable children in line. She'd never really thought ...

"So, they're real?"

His jaw clenched tight as he nodded. "Phoenix, I don't know if I can protect –"

He stilled.

Adrenaline shot through her veins at the sudden tension radiating from him. She strained but couldn't hear anything aside from the soft rustle of leaves and whistle of wind through the trees.

Ethan grabbed her hand, motioned for her to stay silent, and pulled her through a small gap in the hedges into the empty field beside them. He urged her to keep low and beckoned her to follow him along the thorny brambles. With the wind at their backs, it took her senses a little longer to catch up to his, but soon the stench of decay hit her and she knew instantly what had put Ethan on high alert.

It didn't take them long to reach the small farm at the peak of the hill. Sheep and cows were little more than a blob of shadows huddled together at the far end of the field. Their nervous bleating created an anxious symphony in the otherwise silent night.

The pen that should have contained them was broken in places, the fences trampled and useless in restraining its occupants. It was from there that the stench emanated. She forced herself to take shallow breaths through her mouth as they drew closer.

The sight in front of them caused her stomach to heave and tears to prick her eyes. It was impossible to count how many lambs lay mauled in the grass with blood staining their once pristine coats. Insides trailed outside, and despite Maura's earlier words, Phoenix's first thought was animal attack.

Ethan crouched down beside one of the lambs for a closer look, and when he turned back to her, his face was puzzled. "These bites are from human teeth."

"What?"

Distracted enough by his comment to block out the gore for a moment, she moved to his side for a closer look. Sure enough, she could make out marks roughly the size of a human bite circumference, and damage that was clearly done by blunt teeth rather than the fangs of an animal.

"Don't get me wrong" – she swallowed back the bile that rose in her throat – "I'm no vegetarian, but that's just gross."

He gave her a wry smile and stood, nodding towards the small farmhouse in the distance. "I think we should probably go check on the owners. It's hard to tell with so much decay nearby, but we might have a few more surprises before the night's out."

She followed him with a resigned sigh, her eyes scanning the darkness for any movement. There were no lights on in the house, but a battered SUV sat in the drive and she saw no obvious sign of intrusion from the outside. Maybe whatever got the animals was full and left?

Ethan tried the door and it opened with a creak. The stench of death hit them like a furnace of hot air. Darkness filled the hallway, and the only sound was a low buzzing noise that seemed to come from the room at the far end. Ethan drew his hunting knife from inside his jacket and motioned for her to stay behind him.

Tentatively, they inched their way down the hall, pausing at each open doorway to check the rooms beyond. The further they moved into the house, the stronger the smell became, cloying at the back of her throat and making it hard to swallow.

The door at the end led to a small kitchen. Faded flower wallpaper covered the walls and a well-used stove sat nestled between oak cabinets. A wooden table filled the centre of the room, one chair occupied and the air around it swarming with flies.

"What the –"

The words left her mouth on a whispered breath, and the look she received from Ethan mirrored her own horror. She squinted as her brain struggled to make out what she was seeing.

The form definitely appeared human, or at least something of a similar shape. But beyond that, the features were almost indiscernible. A thick layer of grey sludge coated the body. It clung in parts, forming dips and troughs that may or may not have been eye sockets and a gaping mouth. And in others, it oozed, as if it were a living organism.

A floorboard creaked overhead and she froze. Her heart tripled its rhythm. She really did not want to meet whatever was responsible for this. This was a whole new level of fucked up.

Ethan, however, didn't seem to have the same reservations, and instead of moving towards the door like a sane person would, he motioned for her to follow him as he slipped back into the hall and made his way to the stairs.

She glared at his back even as her body stupidly followed. If he got her turned into a slimy corpse, she was so going to come back and haunt him.

Soft moonlight filtered in from a window at the top of the stairs, but it did little more than add an eerie backdrop to the horror movie they were so willingly traipsing into. All except one door on the upper level stood open, and she could hear a low scratching sound coming from inside. Her skin crawled and she shuddered.

Silently, they moved to the door, side by side. She held her breath and mentally cursed him for dragging her up here. He reached for the handle, met her eyes for a second, then pushed the door open.

Nothing.

The scratching continued, but nothing came barrelling out of the room to attack them. One breath. Two breaths. She looked at Ethan. He looked at her.

Her heart hammered in her chest as she slid down to a crouch and peered around the wooden frame of the door. Her jaw dropped.

The room was an explosion of 1980s floral and impeccably tidy. None of that was what caught her attention, however.

An old lady was hunkered down on the floor. Her body was in a position Phoenix wouldn't have thought possible given the fact she looked to easily be in her eighties. Her grey hair was wild around her head, and the white nightgown she wore was covered in dirt and blood.

She watched with a disturbed sense of detachment as the woman scratched words into the floral wallpaper with her fingernail. She'd obviously been doing it for quite some time as blood ran in rivulets from her fingers. When she was done, the words "THEY'RE COMING" were smeared across the wall in jagged letters.

Slowly the woman's head turned in their direction, red eyes pulsing as she tilted her head at an unnatural angle to regard them.

"Shit," Ethan muttered under his breath.

Phoenix couldn't help but agree. The Council, Mists, and now this? Surely they shouldn't have to worry about demons on top of everything else.

For a moment everyone stood still, assessing each other. The old lady eyed them like she'd just found her next meal. Then, with a hiss that showcased rotten black teeth, the demon lunged.

Ethan met the frail body in a clash that should have caused it to crumble. Instead, the demon's essence infused it with a speed and strength that beggared belief, and the old woman easily countered his attack.

Phoenix flung herself onto the demon's back in an attempt to slow it down, but a layer of slime seeped out from the woman's pores and her hands slipped off, unable to gain purchase.

Rotten teeth snapped at her face before Ethan grabbed the demon and flung it against the wall.

"Tell me you have an amulet with you?" He grunted as the demon rebounded and threw itself at him once more.

She fumbled in her pocket for the amulet she'd tucked away, but the slime coating her hands caused it to slip from her grasp and clatter to the floor. With a curse, she lunged to grab it, the sounds of fighting a ticking time bomb to her ears. In her panic, she sent it skittering under the bed.

Before she could reach for it, a strangled noise drew her attention upward. The demon had Ethan by the throat and appeared ready to eat his face off. His face turned puce as he struggled against the vice-like grip that was crushing his windpipe.

A glint of metal caught her eye and she saw Ethan's hunting knife lying on the ground a couple of feet from her. She grabbed it and flung it at the demon.

The blade lodged in the old woman's eye, and she let an inhuman screech that caused the windows, and Phoenix's bones, to rattle. With a final shrieking roar in their direction, the demon took a running leap and crashed through the first-floor window.

Phoenix reached the broken glass at the same time as Ethan. Her resounding "Fuck!" was echoed by his own as they looked out into the empty night beyond.

CHAPTER NINETEEN

Lily gritted her teeth and tried to sidestep Nate. At the far end of the safe house training studio, she could hear Abi on the phone, but she couldn't make out what was being said because he wouldn't shut the hell up.

"I'm worried about you. I know it's been hard for you since –" Nate prattled on as she tried in vain to block him out.

Was Abi frowning? Had something happened? She craned her neck, but Nate moved with her, blocking her eye-line again. She hadn't given Diana the location yet so the Council couldn't have gotten to Phoenix already. Could Ethan have found out that they contacted her? Was Abi going to turn around any minute now and point an accusing finger in her direction?

"I just wanted you to know that I'm here if you need to talk or anything –"

What if they'd found Phoenix? What if they'd found another source and didn't need her anymore? Her heart stopped cold.

If they didn't need her, they'd have no reason to help her. At that thought, her chest tightened and she grew lightheaded, each breath she took seeming void of oxygen.

Beside her, Nate sighed in resignation. "I'll leave you alone."

She turned in a daze towards him and a distant part of her noted a deep sadness in his amber eyes; she'd never seen that look on his face before. When she didn't say anything in return, he gave her a small smile and headed for the changing room behind them.

Guilt twisted her gut, and she opened her mouth to call him back and apologise. But she closed it just as quickly. There was nothing she could say to make him understand. Nothing that wouldn't make him hate her at least.

At that moment, Abi hung up the phone and her concerns about Nate's feelings were forgotten. She made a beeline in Abi's direction, only for Shade to step out in front of her before she got across the room. She bit back a scream of frustration and met his intense blue gaze.

"What?"

His scowl deepened. "Don't push your friends away, Lily."

His words made her bristle, but she held her tongue. With a defiant glare, she shoved past him and hurried to Abi's side. "Is everything okay?"

Abi nodded and gave her a small smile that didn't quite reach her eyes. "It appears Phoenix and Ethan have run into a slight demon problem. It got away and they've been out all night trying to track it down."

Lily's knees went weak with relief. Just a demon, not the Council. They still needed her.

"What are they going to do about it?"

"She said they're going to stick around another day to try to track the demon." Abi chewed her lip and looked at the blank screen of her phone. "Is that safe? Should they not keep moving in case the Council find them? Phoenix played it down when I asked, but I could tell she was worried."

Lily rubbed the girl's arm absently, her mind busy assessing how that affected her own plan. "I'm sure Ethan knows what he's doing."

Shade let out a low grunt from behind her, making her jump. "Yeah 'cause he always thinks clearly when he's around her." With that, he turned and stalked towards the changing room.

Abi raised an eyebrow and looked at her. "I don't mean to overstep the mark or anything, but what's his deal?"

Lily stared in the direction of the changing rooms, something about the vampire's strange mood making her uneasy. "Shade doesn't exactly like Phoenix."

"He blames her for the prophecy."

She flicked her eyes back to Abi. "I guess so."

The other girl chewed that over for a few moments before excusing herself with a frown. Lily watched her go and let out a shuddering breath. Her hands were shaking from the adrenaline thrumming through her veins, and she couldn't shake that terrifying thought of "what if". The longer she waited, the more chance they'd find another way. She couldn't let that happen.

She squared her shoulders, and with renewed purpose made her way back through the winding corridors of the safe house until she came to a door that would lead her outside. The cold air hit her like a slap, and dark clouds threatened rain as she stumbled her way through the vast grounds that surrounded the property. Once she was far enough from prying eyes and ears, she pulled her phone out and pressed the call button.

"Diana, it's Lily."

CHAPTER TWENTY

Phoenix hung her head and let the water from the shower pound across her shoulder blades until it turned cold and she was forced to step away from the soothing stream or face hypothermia. Shivering, she grabbed the nearby towel and wrapped it around herself. Steam fogged the small bathroom and she breathed deeply, letting the residual heat flow through her lungs.

After almost twelve hours straight searching the area, they still hadn't managed to find the demon, and she was starting to grow antsy. They couldn't just leave the locals at the mercy of a rampant slime monster, but how long would it take for the Council to find them? And if they were really sending the Mists ... Well, that didn't even bear thinking about.

When Ethan had suggested they try get some rest before one last-ditch search, she'd agreed wearily. One more night, then they had to leave; demon or no demon.

With a sigh, she grabbed her clothes from the radiator and started dressing. She had her trousers half on when she heard Ethan's voice on the other side of the door. He was speaking quietly, but the agitation was evident in his tone. Balancing precariously with one leg in and one leg out of her trousers, she paused to listen.

"What does it matter if he knows? ... Of course I didn't contact him ... When? ... TONIGHT?"

She didn't have a chance to react to Ethan's roar before the bathroom door was flung open to reveal the werewolf with his phone pressed to his ear. He barely even blinked at her state of undress, simply ordered, "We need to go," before slamming the bathroom door closed.

Not quite sure what had happened, she gaped after him. An unreasonable voice in the back of her head mumbled that a little acknowledgement of her nakedness wouldn't go amiss as she shoved her foot through the other leg of her jeans.

When she emerged from the bathroom minutes later, she found him pacing the room, his hands clenching and unclenching as he stared at the door. Before she could even ask what was going on, he yanked open the door and waved for her to follow. She raced to catch up with him, giving Maura a quick wave as they hurried through the pub and out into the night.

"Dammit, Ethan, what the hell is up?"

"We need to find the demon and get out of here. Now."

She came to an abrupt halt, her blood running cold. "What happened?"

He stopped and shoved his unruly hair back out of his face as he turned to her. "They've sent the first Mist."

"Oh."

Well, that sure took the wind out of her sails.

Ethan, too, seemed to deflate a little before her as he nodded. "Yeah, big oh. Somehow William found out about my connection to you. He sent my dad a warning out of courtesy. He said he can't protect me if I insist on being stupid."

She blew out a breath and watched it fog in the air in front of her. "Guess we need to get hunting."

With time working against them, they started up the hill again in search of their demon. Maura had told them at lunch that there'd been even more animals killed the night before. In a hushed voice she'd informed them that the farm owners, Seamus and Betty, had

362

obviously annoyed the fair folk since the trail of dead animals led straight from their farm to the fairy ring.

Despite how ludicrous her logic was, Phoenix and Ethan both agreed it was as good a place as any to start their search. With any luck, they'd pick up a scent Ethan could follow.

"Your uncle didn't by any chance give you some idea how you might survive one of these Mists?"

Ethan grimaced. "You don't survive the Mists. You run."

Ah, just the cheery answer she was hoping for.

She opened her mouth to ask her next question – how long do you keep running for? – but he suddenly tensed and pulled up short.

Really? Again? Please let it be the bloody demon at least.

She stood completely still and watched as Ethan tilted his head, jaw clenched in concentration.

"How sure are you that the ring forts are just a superstition?" he asked, voice barely a whisper.

She raised her eyebrows and swivelled her head to survey their surroundings. They'd nearly reached the peak of the hill, and the border of trees on either side were thinning out enough that she could see an open field on the far side, bathed in moonlight.

"What kind of stupid question is that?"

She shuddered at the creeping sensation that was working its way up from the base of her spine. Humans had bizarre imaginations; what relevance could a random circle in a field have to the fae?

"Can't you feel it?"

She shook her head, but a whisper of something tingled across the back of her neck. Subtle. Easily missed.

"There's magic of some kind here." Ethan's eyes searched their surroundings warily.

"The demon?" she suggested. But she already knew the answer. This didn't feel like the demon's energy; it was lacking the taint of evil.

Instead of answering, Ethan crouched low and stepped through a break in the trees into the field on the other side. She followed his lead, keeping her eyes peeled as they moved towards the raised hill of grass that formed the ring fort.

Unease tap-danced along her spine, and the feeling was immediately justified when a shadowy form came into view.

A body lay in the middle of the ring fort, spreadeagled and unmoving. The layer of clear slime that coated it glistened under the light of the moon and made her want another shower.

"Is that –"

"The farmer's wife." Ethan took a step closer, careful to stay out of reach.

"It found another host?" She searched the darkness, fully expecting the demon to emerge from the shadows at any second.

"Not quite," came a voice as smooth as silk in response.

CHAPTER TWENTY-ONE

The air shimmered before Phoenix's eyes and she stepped into a defensive stance. Ethan shifted his position so that his back was to hers with his claws extended. Shadows entwined and coalesced, teasing a possible source for the voice, only to disappear and reappear in another location.

"Shit." Her heart hammered in her ears.

Ethan growled low in response.

"I thought you'd be grateful that I took care of your demon problem." The voice came again, brushing past her ear in a whisper.

Her body tensed instinctively at the touch. She forced her breathing to slow, and waited. The shadows swirled in front of her, turning into a black smoke as a form began to solidify. The first thing that struck her were the golden eyes. The next was the heart-stopping smile.

Should my murderer look that charming? she wondered in a daze.

The glint of a silver sabre broke whatever spell held her mesmerised and she dived to the side, pulling Ethan with her. The blade sliced so close to her face that she closed her eyes to brace for the pain. When it didn't come, she leapt to her feet and looked at Ethan in a panic.

"How do we fight him?" she repeated her earlier question.

"We don't." He grabbed her hand. "We run."

He pulled so hard she nearly fell over. She stumbled to get her footing and followed him to the forest in the distance.

How fast were the Mists? Goddammit, why hadn't she asked more bloody questions?

Somehow they reached the trees. Branches scraped her arms and face as she pushed through the dense copse. Shadows moved around her, and the night seemed alive with strange noises that filled her head and caused her sense of direction to become disorientated.

Her vision blurred, but still she kept running, forcing her instincts to focus only on Ethan's energy ahead of her.

"Run all you want," the silky voice whispered in her ear. "You're just making it harder on yourself."

The tree in front of her burst into flame and she was forced to veer sharply to the left.

Shit. Where's Ethan?

The Mist's laughter followed her, but the shadows were no longer lapping at her heels. Instead, they swirled leisurely through the trees, weaving a trail of fire that would soon box her in.

"Ethan," she yelled, frantically searching the thick block of trees around her.

"He can't help you now," came the reply at her back.

She turned just in time to see a rueful smile on the charming face of death as the Mist reached a glowing gold fist towards her.

A loud growl was the only indication she had of Ethan's whereabouts before a large brown wolf leapt between her and the Mist. The golden fist plunged through the wolf's chest, and she watched in horror as its whole body went rigid and Ethan's now yellow eyes widened in shock.

"No!" she screamed, wrapping her arms tightly around the rough fur, as if that alone could stop the fist from crushing his heart.

Heat built in her chest as fear for Ethan overwhelmed her. She clenched her eyes closed and gave herself over to the magic. They were dead either way.

With her chest pressed close to the wolf's body, she could feel when his heart began to slow. She let all of the fear, all of the anger fill her, and in a flash of blinding white light, she let it go. Once more, the night went black.

Daylight flared through Phoenix's eyelids and pain exploded in her head. She scrunched her eyes tight against the glare. The ground beneath her was hard and unyielding, and every part of her ached.

Shit. Her eyes flew open and heart leapt into her throat. Where was she?

Scorched earth filled her immediate eye-line and gnarled trees loomed over her, their barks blackened. She kept completely still even as her heart thundered in her chest.

Was he still here? The Mist. Was he waiting for her to wake so he could kill her?

When minutes passed with no sound other than her soft breathing, she glanced carefully around. She was lying in a small clearing surrounded on all sides by trees. The ground under her was little more than charred dirt, devoid of the lush vegetation that covered the rest of the forest. A large lump of brown fur lay at her feet, unmoving. She saw the wolf, but it took her brain a minute to connect the dots.

Ethan!

She scrambled to her knees, the memories flooding back: golden eyes, a glowing fist, the all-consuming heat of the sun. Her hands trembled as she ran them over the coarse fur, searching for injuries. *Please be okay. Please be okay.*

He was still alive. She knew because she could hear the sluggish beat of his heart as it laboured to pump blood around his body. But his breathing was shallow, and he showed no reaction to her touch. There were no burns that she could see. How was that? She was holding him when the sun's power had exploded from her. He should be dead. They both should be.

A light breeze blew through the trees, rustling the leaves, and her heart pounded. She looked around, suddenly aware of the ominous shadows that lurked between the trees.

What happened to the Mist when she called the sun? Did it kill him, or was he hiding in one of those shadows? A cold sweat broke out on the back of her neck. They needed to get the hell out of here.

She climbed to her feet, and with extreme effort, manoeuvred the huge wolf so that she could hoist it over her shoulder. Even with supernatural strength, the weight knocked the wind out of her.

There was no stealth to her trek back to the B&B, and she could only hope none of the locals saw her or the giant "dog" she was carrying. It was very possible Ethan sustained some bumps to the head along the way, but she figured it'd do him no harm; maybe even knock some sense into him. If he ever woke up.

The sun was cresting the horizon as she reached the pub and miraculously made it to their room. She lay Ethan on the bed and slumped down beside him, gently running her fingers through the fur at the nape of his neck.

Why hadn't he changed back? Or regained consciousness? His body should be healing any damage. She bit her lip.

On the locker beside her, red numbers flashed on the small alarm clock. A taunting reminder that they were on borrowed time. The Mist would be back. She didn't know what had happened after the world went black, but her gut was telling her he was alive. They couldn't afford to be here when he returned.

Five more minutes, she decided, staring at the blinking numbers. She'd rest for five minutes, and then they had to leave.

She set about packing their meagre belongings, wrote a brief note of thanks to Maura and looked back to the clock, resigned to her fate. Time to go.

Getting an unconscious werewolf to the car unnoticed was another feat she hadn't expected to manage, but it seemed someone up there was taking pity on her. She slid behind the wheel of their car, Ethan resting across the back seat, still in wolf form. Her gaze flicked from him to the small pub, and an icy thread of fear slid through her as she hoped like hell they weren't leaving a trail of destruction in their wake.

CHAPTER TWENTY-TWO

There was complete silence in the chamber as Shayan kneeled before the Council. Deep burns marred his handsome features, vivid red blending into blackened patches of skin. Even from where Darius stood at the edge of the crowd, he could see the defiance blazing in those golden eyes and he shook his head; the boy had a death wish.

His main focus at that moment wasn't the Mist, however, but rather the Council. More specifically, William.

The blood red cloak covering the werewolf didn't quite conceal the fists clenched at his side, and there was a tightness to his jaw that was perceptible only because Darius was looking so closely.

He'd seen that same tic the evening before when he'd innocently approached William as a concerned Witness. Of course, the reaction had been preceded by barely concealed shock when Darius mentioned rumours of a particular werewolf being involved with the hybrid.

"I can't imagine it was easy for you," he'd declared solemnly. "To send the Mist knowing it would put your own blood in danger."

The flinch had been subtle and just what Darius had hoped for. He needed Phoenix alive at all costs, which meant he needed to exploit any weak link he could find.

"I appreciate your concern, Witness," William had growled, "but the Council will do what needs to be done. The first Mist is being dispatched as we speak."

Needless to say, that wasn't the news Darius had been hoping for. He'd contacted his head of security immediately with an instruction to find Phoenix or face the final death. They'd managed to locate her, but by that stage it was dawn and the Witnesses had already been summoned for an update.

"Tell us again what happened," William ordered Shayan, his voice a low rumble filled with warning.

As the Mist once more relayed his encounter, Darius couldn't help the smirk of satisfaction that lifted the corner of his mouth. Despite all the odds, Phoenix seemed, yet again, to survive on pure blind luck. And to hear that a werewolf got injured during the fight, well, that was just unfortunate.

"I'll finish the job. Just get me the next location." Shayan stood from his kneeling position and faced the Council with his chin held high and shoulders squared.

"You failed." William's brown eyes blazed. "What makes you think we'd give you another chance?"

"You need the hybrid dead, don't you?"

Vlad moved as if to say something, but Méabh placed a hand on his arm and shook her head. She tilted her chin and observed the scene, but her expression gave no indication of her thoughts. Did she know of William's connection to the injured wolf? Darius couldn't be sure, but William's careful choice of words through the proceedings led him to believe not.

"We need discretion," William growled. "Something you've clearly demonstrated you're not capable of."

Shayan sneered. "Let's see how discreet I can be when I rip your throat out, wolf." His body started to turn translucent as shadows danced around him.

Diana stepped forward and whispered a word that was unintelligible to Darius's ears, removing the barrier that protected Shayan from his gold bonds. Immediately the Mist dropped to his knees, his body becoming solid as he arched back and screamed.

Within seconds, he seemed to wither and weaken. He slumped to the floor, his muscles taut from the agonising onslaught of the gold.

"Stop!" Maj yelled, stepping forward. "Give me the location. I'll finish this."

Darius watched the conflict rage on William's face. He was counting on the wolf to be the weak link. Would he allow another attack now that he knew about Ethan? The wolf stayed quiet, and beside him, something that looked suspiciously like satisfaction glinted in Méabh's eyes.

"All agreed?" Vlad looked at each of the Council members, then nodded to Maj. "Make sure it's done properly this time."

Diana whispered another unintelligible word and Shayan fell silent on the floor. She stepped back in line with the Council and pulled up the hood of her cloak.

CHAPTER TWENTY-THREE

Lily worried at the skin around her thumbnail as she paced the empty training room. Her hand subconsciously reached for her phone again. For the third time in as many minutes, she glanced at the blank screen. It had been forty-eight hours; surely it should be done by now. Why hadn't they contacted her?

She clutched her canvas bag to her midsection and fought the urge to scream until her throat was raw. She'd kept the Ouroboros close ever since she'd given Diana the location. Its familiar weight was a small comfort as she counted the minutes until her nightmare was over. One little phone call; that was all she needed.

"So, how did you get it?" Shade's voice came from behind, startling her out of her thoughts.

"What are you talking about?" Her brow furrowed in confusion as she tried to make sense of the question. How long had he been there? Had he been watching her?

He nodded to the bag she held. "The Ouroboros. I'm guessing it's the same one."

Her heart stopped. Icy blue eyes bore into her and she fought the sudden need to fidget.

"I don't know what you mean." Her voice was calm but her hand jerked involuntarily on the bag, clasping it tighter. She angled her body away from him in a vain attempt to block the bag from sight.

"Yes, you do. And I can even guess why you have it. But trust me, Lily, there's no good way to come back from the dead."

Anger flared white hot in her chest, overshadowing the fear and uncertainty. "You don't know what you're talking about."

His laugh held no trace of humour and his voice was bitter when he said, "Oh, don't I?"

She shook her head; she wasn't interested in his lecture. His opinion didn't matter now anyway.

"I don't know what you *think* you saw, but I don't have an Ouroboros. Do you really believe I'd be standing here wasting time with you if I could go back and make it all right?" Despite her best efforts, her voice cracked, and something akin to pity flashed across his face.

"I think you're a scared young girl who's gotten in way over her head. And if you're not careful, there'll be no way back."

Her hackles rose and defiance pulled her shoulders back and made her stand tall. "How about you stay out of my business, Shade."

She turned to stalk away, only to find Abi walking towards them, concern creasing her brow. Lily's breath caught as she scanned the girl's face for any sign of grief. Shade grew completely still beside her.

Abi's gaze flicked warily between them. "Is everything okay?"

Lily hesitated for a second before looking to Shade, only to find the vampire walking away without giving them another glance.

Abi placed a hand on her arm and frowned. "Lily, what did he say to you? You're shaking."

"He ... he was saying there's no good way to come back from the dead."

"What the hell does that mean? Was he threatening you?"

She shook her head, but then paused and glanced uncertainly at Abi. She could feel the anger and need to protect radiating off the other girl and a thought flirted at the back of her mind. What was one little lie in the grand scheme of things? One more little sin on her way to hell.

"He was talking about witches being untrustworthy. That we were too easily corrupted by dark magic or some crap like that. I just pointed out that if it hadn't been for the vampires ..." She shrugged and looked at the ground. "He got pretty mad when I mentioned Darius."

Out of the corner of her eye, she could see Abi frown. An uncomfortable knot twisted in her stomach, and she dug her nails into the palms of her hands to stop herself from backtracking. She hadn't said anything really, just a distraction; that's all.

"Shade was abandoned by his Sire when he was turned, wasn't he?" Abi chewed her lip thoughtfully. "Where was it you said he's from?"

She shrugged. "Dublin, I think."

"So, he was sired in Darius's territory."

Silence hung in the air between them and Lily dug her nails in harder.

Abi plastered a smile on her face. "I better check in with Phoenix; I haven't heard from her since last night."

CHAPTER TWENTY-FOUR

Heavy black clouds rolled across the sky, and Phoenix's hands clenched involuntarily on the leather steering wheel at a sudden bang of thunder. She wasn't sure how long she'd been driving for, but at some stage between leaving the B&B and navigating the winding country roads, the bright morning sun had shifted to an ominous and oppressing sky that mirrored her mood.

Ethan had yet to move as he lay across the back seat of the car, and fear had her heart tightly in its clutches. If it wasn't for the fact he remained in wolf form, she'd have long ago succumbed to her fear and brought him to the nearest hospital. Since bringing him to a vet was also out of the question, she took what comfort she could from the steady beat of his heart and kept driving. He'd wake up. He had to.

The question now was where was she driving to? The logical thing would be to contact the others and get their help. But what if she led the danger right to them? The Mist had almost killed both her and Ethan. She couldn't ask anyone else to put themselves at risk.

She couldn't stick to their original plan either; if the Mist found them at the last B&B, it would be stupid to assume he wouldn't find them at the next. Which only left Ethan's pack.

They'd be in the best position to help with Ethan's injuries, and

Cormac had already offered her his protection. But still she hesitated. The whole point of their little jaunt around Ireland was to limit how much trouble they were bringing to the pack's door. If she headed there now, she'd be bringing a whole lot more than trouble; she'd be bringing death.

So, she drove in the general direction of north, sticking to back roads and isolated locations, all the while urging Ethan to wake up so she didn't have to make the decision alone.

Another clash of thunder sounded overhead and moments later, thick droplets of rain pelted her windscreen. The pounding beat was so deafening, she almost missed the ringing of her phone on the passenger seat beside her.

She glanced at the screen and her breath caught when she saw "unknown number". Her old phone had been left back in Dublin as a temporary decoy for anyone who might be tracking it. Only a handful of people had this number, and all of their names should have come up on the screen.

The phone continued to vibrate insistently, and she swung the car into a gravelly lay-by that came up on her left. She fumbled to pick it up and pressed the answer button before the car had come to a complete stop. Heart pounding, she said nothing as she lifted the phone to her ear.

"I know you're there, Phoenix."

The familiar voice that came down the line sent a wave of nausea flooding through her and the world spun.

"How did you get this number?" The words came out in a whisper rather than the furious demand she'd intended.

Darius's rich laugh sent shivers down her spine and the nausea faded, only to be replaced by a confused mix of sadness and anger.

"I have my ways. Don't worry. I'm not looking to hurt you. I could've done that long before now if it had been my desire."

She sneered, his words adding fuel to her anger. "Of course not. You need me alive for the prophecy, after all."

"Exactly."

Her free hand clenched the steering wheel so tightly, the leather creaked in protest under her grip. Why was she even humouring this conversation? She already knew he was insane. But before she could force herself to hang up, Darius's tone shifted from chilling psychopath to the charming persuasion she'd always known him for.

"I'll admit I'm quite impressed you managed to survive Shayan's attack. That's no meagre feat. The Council, however, were less impressed and intend on sending the next Mist." He let the statement hang in the air for a moment. "I wish to offer you my protection."

She choked, his words causing a shocked laugh to bubble up in her throat. "Your protection?"

"You were lucky with Shayan. Maj is neither as naive or careless. And, should you by some miracle survive her, Jannah will crush you like a bug. As you quite succinctly pointed out, it is in both of our interests that you survive. Therefore, I propose a temporary truce."

"You seriously think I would ever accept help from you?"

"I think you want to live. I'll give you some time to consider my offer, but I advise you do so quickly. I'll be in touch."

With that, he hung up and Phoenix was left staring numbly at a blank screen as her hands trembled.

———

Phoenix huddled over the cup of coffee, as if its warmth might somehow chase away the chill that had settled in her centre. The watery brown liquid tasted like scorched piss and did little more than burn her tongue, but still she clung to it.

The rain had grown even heavier, teeming in sheets of water that made visibility non-existent, and when combined with her frazzled nerves, turned the treacherous country roads into a death trap. So, when she'd come across the ramshackle building that passed itself off as a petrol station, she'd done the sensible thing and pulled in.

Her automatic response after the call from Darius had been to drive, as if by doing so she could put distance between herself and the memories conjured from the mere sound of his voice. Some things you just couldn't outrun, however, and now that she'd been forced to stop, she felt lost.

Was what he said true? Was the Council sending another Mist?

The first had been bad enough, and she couldn't deny it had been anything other than pure luck that kept them alive, but a second one just added yet more unknowns she wasn't ready to deal with alone.

She blew out a breath and rested her head on the steering wheel. Hell, when had she become so reliant on other people that her biggest fear out of that whole scenario was the part where she was alone?

As if in response to her thought, her phone vibrated on the passenger seat. Her stomach did a full three-sixty and threatened to return its contents for visual inspection as she flipped the phone over to see the screen. This time, a name flashed persistently back at her and her head swam with relief.

"Abi," she answered breathlessly.

"Phoenix? Are you okay?" Abi's cheery voice immediately turned panicked, and Phoenix forced herself to take a slow, deep breath before answering.

"Yeah, sorry. I thought it was someone else calling. I ... It's just good to hear your voice."

"What's going on? And don't say nothing. I can tell you're upset."

Phoenix leaned back in the driver's seat and closed her eyes for a moment. "The Council found us. They sent one of their assassins. We barely managed to escape. And then Darius called. He said they're sending another one to finish the job. He wanted to offer me his protection; a temporary truce, he said. Is he completely insane? How could he ever think I'd trust him after everything he's done?"

The flood of words came to an abrupt halt, and she was suddenly aware of the stunned silence on the other end of the phone.

"Shit," was Abi's only response.

Phoenix started laughing. And as her friend joined her, an invisible weight lifted from her chest. The laughter turned to a hysterical fit of giggles until tears were rolling down her cheeks and she was no longer sure if they were good tears.

"I'm afraid, Abi," she whispered when she was finally spent and the energy drained from her body.

"It's okay to be afraid, just as long as you don't stop fighting. Now, first things first, where are you?"

She looked around at her grey, nondescript surroundings and suddenly felt the heavy weight of exhaustion settle over her. "I'm not sure. Up north somewhere. I just kept driving."

"Okay, let's start by getting you guys somewhere safe. Can you find a B&B nearby? Text me your location. I'll fill the others in. Nate hasn't managed to get past the Council's firewalls yet, so we can't verify what Darius said, but maybe he can find out how Darius got your number."

Abi rattled off orders, asking questions about the assassins and the Council's attack. Phoenix could tell that the calm, assured tone was an act for her benefit but at that moment, she was immensely grateful for her friend's strength.

"There's something else," she said once she had answered all of Abi's questions. "Ethan –"

A flash of lightning lit the sky and the line went dead. She gaped at the "no signal" sign on the phone and cursed. She was jinxed; she had to be. There was no other explanation for it.

A shuddering gasp from the back seat made her jump, and she spun around to see the final patches of fur fade from Ethan's now human body. His eyes fluttered open for a brief second, then closed, leaving her alone once more.

CHAPTER TWENTY FIVE

Lily methodically folded her clothes and placed everything into a neat pile, ready to go. Surely it wouldn't be long now. Diana would call to give her the green light, and she'd take the Ouroboros to the Council. They'd show her how to tap into its powers and she'd fix everything; it would be over.

The door to her room burst open, and she looked up in surprise at a frazzled Abi. "The Council found them," Abi blurted before turning on her heel and disappearing.

Lily froze in terror. *It was done?*

Heart racing, she ran out into the hallway to find Abi banging on Nate and Shade's doors. She ground to a halt as she searched the other girl's face for any sign of grief, only to fine none. *How could there be no grief? If Phoenix was dead, there should be grief.*

When there was no answer from either room, Abi swung back towards her. "How could they have known?"

"Wait, wait –" Lily held up her hands as much to pause her own racing thoughts as to calm the other girl down. "What are you talking about? What happened?"

Abi quickly relayed her conversation with Phoenix. "How could they have known?" she repeated. "We didn't tell anyone the plan. No one knew where they'd be."

Lily's pulse pounded so loud she was sure even Abi's human hearing would pick it up. Phoenix was alive. The Council failed.

"What about Darius?" she suggested, grasping for anything that might seem remotely plausible. "You said he contacted her. Maybe he's really working for the Council?"

Abi shook her head, but before she could say anything further, footsteps sounded at the far end of the hall. Nate and Shade turned the corner, deep in conversation. They pulled up short when they spotted the two girls, and the scowl on Shade's face deepened. His frosty gaze focused accusingly on Lily.

Nate hurried to their side, his lips pinched in concern. "What's going on?"

Lily's hands grew clammy as Abi filled them in. She watched the cogs turning in Nate's head; any minute now the pin would drop and they'd all realise what she'd done.

"Okay, first things first. We need to assume the Council knows our plans," he stated, jolting her out of her panicked thoughts. "Which means we need to change them. Let me make a few calls. You guys get your shit and be ready to leave as soon as I've got another safe house sorted."

"What about Ethan and Phoenix?" Shade's eyes remained fixed on her, but he didn't voice the accusation that was so clearly visible in their icy blue depths.

"Phoenix sent you their new location?" Nate looked to Abi for confirmation. "They should be safe for now, but I'm not so sure it's a good idea for them to be on their own anymore."

"They need more help," Shade agreed quietly.

A strange look passed between Nate and Shade, and Lily's stomach lurched. Had Shade said something to Nate? Did they know?

"We don't have much time. We need to move." With that, Nate hurried off to make arrangements. Shade gave her a final glare and followed after him.

Lily watched them go and tried to calm the panic that was bubbling up inside of her. "Excuse me," she muttered to Abi, mumbling a vague excuse about needing to do something before they left.

She made a beeline for the nearest exit and pushed through the door. The cold hit her with a sharp slap, and through her muddled thoughts, one fact came into sharp focus: it wasn't over. Needing answers, she pulled out her mobile and pressed the call button, only dimly aware of the ringtone as she wandered aimlessly around the property's grounds.

"Lily, I was going to call you later today," Diana answered, her voice warm and friendly.

"What's going on? Why isn't it done?" Lily could hear the frantic edge in her tone, but she couldn't seem to calm the emotions that raged through her.

There was a long pause, then Diana sighed.

"I'm afraid there was a slight miscalculation in our tactics. But it's nothing for you to worry about. It's all in hand. All I need is the next location from you and I'll get it sorted. This horrible mess will all be over."

Lily hesitated. She wanted so much to feel reassured. The Council had it all under control; she just needed to let them handle it. So why didn't she feel relieved?

"I know how hard this is for you." Diana's voice softened. "But I need you to be strong a little while longer. Annabelle needs you to be strong. You can do that, can't you? For Annabelle?"

Her throat tightened at the sound of her sister's name. Where was Annabelle now? So much time had passed. Too much. Had her soul already passed on to a new life? Would she be too late?

Before she could think any further, she spurted out the address that Phoenix had sent Abi and hung up without saying goodbye. Hot tears pricked the back of her eyes, but she refused to let them fall. Tears wouldn't help her now.

CHAPTER TWENTY-SIX

Everything went white. Then there was only darkness, never-ending darkness. Ethan could hear Phoenix's voice, whispering to him, begging him to come back to her. But no matter how hard he tried to pull himself out of the murky swamp of his thoughts, reality remained just out of his reach. The harder he tried, the more fatigue washed over him and brought with it the emptiness of oblivion.

A light touch to his cheek sent a jolt of awareness through him. His skin tingled as fingertips trailed along his forehead and smoothed the tension from his brow. The warm scent of sunshine flooded his senses, and his eyes fluttered open to meet the most striking green eyes he'd ever seen. They tightened with worry until they registered his own brown ones staring back.

A small smile lifted the corner of Phoenix's mouth and she sat back, taking her hand and her warmth with her.

"Hey."

"Hey." His response came out as little more than a croak, and she jumped up to grab him some water.

The room tilted at an odd angle as he watched her, and it took a minute for the fuzziness to clear enough for him to realise he was lying down. The magnolia walls blended into the magnolia ceiling above his head, and the musty smell that filled his nose was unfamiliar. Where were they?

Phoenix came back into his line of sight with a glass of water in hand. He made a weak attempt to shift his body to a sitting position, but she glared a warning at him. Quickly and efficiently, she propped a pillow up behind him and moved him enough that she could hold the glass to his mouth for a few sips.

"You will not so much as blink until we know what damage has been done," she ordered as she fussed about to make sure his body was fully supported.

Her words triggered a flash of memory: a hand reaching into his chest, and pain, blinding pain. He winced.

"The Mist –" He swallowed with effort past the uncomfortable dryness in his throat. "I'm guessing you didn't win him over with your charms. How are we alive?"

She arched an eyebrow at him and the tension that had tightened her features was instantly replaced with a challenging smile. "Are you sure? I'll have you know that I can be very charming."

He choked on a laugh. "I'll believe it when I see it." The memory of the fist clenched around his heart flashed into his mind again and he grew sombre. "Tell me."

Her eyes darkened and she quickly averted her gaze from his, but not before he caught a glimpse of her haunted expression.

"I don't know. I just remember grabbing you and calling the sun. There was a burst of white light and next thing I know, I woke up in the woods to find you unconscious beside me. The Mist was gone."

"Dead?"

"What are the chances we'd be that lucky?"

He sighed. She was right, and going by what she said, it was little more than a miracle they were alive. In fact … he took a mental inventory of his injuries: crippling fatigue unlike anything he'd felt before, phantom ache in his chest, raw throat. But no sign of burns. If she was holding him when she used her powers, he should have been incinerated. How was he alive?

"Where are we?" Too exhausted to think on it further, he focused on the practicalities.

Even if the Mist was by some miracle dead, there were two more at the Council's disposal; it was only a matter of time before they came.

Phoenix looked around, dazed, as if his question confused her.

"A B&B up north. I got a call and … when you changed back, I thought it was best to get you some place comfortable."

He studied her closely. Why had she hesitated?

"Do the others know what happened?"

She shook her head. "The storm knocked out my phone signal when I was filling Abi in. The weather seems to have gone a little bat shit crazy all of a sudden. I texted her our location when the signal came back, and I was just about to give her a call."

For some strange reason, her answer relieved him. It wasn't that he wanted to lie to the others, but if people knew he was out of action, they'd also know Phoenix was more vulnerable. That was the last thing they needed right now. The fact he felt like a failure was irrelevant; it was her safety he was thinking about.

"Let's keep it to ourselves for the moment. No need to worry them unnecessarily."

She raised her eyebrows in surprise but didn't push further. Instead, she chewed her lip and started pacing. Her eyes flicked nervously to the drawn curtains that hid their room from anyone passing outside the window. Then a hesitant glance in his direction.

"Ethan … Darius called."

Darius stepped through the portal and into his office in the Club of Night. He brushed his hands down his black suit and grimaced at the lingering magic that prickled across his senses. He was growing very tired of jumping every time the Council clicked their fingers. If it wasn't for the patience he'd cultivated through centuries of planning, he'd have long ago given up the charade of being a loyal puppy.

But perception was everything, and it was important that he control theirs. His Sire had learned the hard way what happened when control was lost; he wouldn't make the same mistake.

A sharp rap on the door signalled the arrival of his head of security. Raphael's replacement was a solid wall of muscle and composure. He didn't have quite the same psychotic tendencies as his predecessor, which ironically made him a better choice to oversee the security of their operations, if a less fun one.

"Erik, tell me you've found her."

The vampire gave a curt nod. "The wolf has been surprisingly efficient in tracking the hybrid and her canine companion. Are you certain the link to his pack is severed?"

Darius steepled his fingers and raised a neatly manicured eyebrow. Maybe it had been worth losing the insanity in his right-hand man for the benefit of clear, intelligent thinking.

"Our tests indicate as much, but keep a close eye on our dear Sean. The Omega's desire to protect the other wolves does not mean he's loyal to our cause."

Another sharp nod.

"What about the demon? Is everything set up for the experiment?"

"All ready to go. You just need to confirm which species you want to use as the host."

Anticipation pushed away some of his mounting frustration. Which to use? Some were more expendable, but others were more conducive to the final end game.

"Run the first trial on one of the vampires," he decided. "If they take well, we can proceed straight to the next stage."

The thought made him shiver with excitement and his fangs descended. He licked the edge of one and cast a quick glance at his Rolex. No time for a treat just yet. Maybe later, once he made sure Phoenix didn't get herself killed.

"Get me the co-ordinates for the hybrid and have some of our top men on standby. I may need some assistance if Maj arrives before I do."

"Done." Erik held the door to the office open for his boss and followed as he headed for the black Mercedes waiting in front of the club. "I take it she didn't accept your offer of sanctuary?"

Darius's smile was cold in response. "No, but she'll soon see the error of her ways. And if she doesn't, we can always use our leverage to convince her."

CHAPTER TWENTY-SEVEN

Phoenix eased the bathroom door closed as she slipped quietly back into the bedroom and tried not to disturb Ethan. He was so still on the bed that her gut clenched in a moment of panic before she could focus on the steady beat of his heart. She'd come so close to losing him ...

It was a good sign that he'd regained consciousness, but she couldn't help worry about the ashen tone to his normally tanned skin, and the light sheen of sweat that coated his forehead. Even a brief conversation that afternoon had exhausted him, and he'd been resting since.

"You don't have to wait until I'm asleep to ogle me," he mumbled. His lip quirked up in a cheeky grin even as his eyes stayed closed.

She scowled at him and turned to the dressing table to plug in the small kettle. "I just wanted to make sure you hadn't wussed out on me and kicked the bucket."

"Aw, would you miss me?" He peeked one eye open and his grin widened, softening his deathly appearance somewhat.

"Yeah, about as much as I'd miss having my fingernails pulled out."

Ignoring the satisfied look on his face, she grabbed two tea bags and threw them into the paper cups provided by the B&B, before filling both with water. Three sugars later and hers was just how she liked it. Ethan's she plopped unceremoniously on the bedside table beside him.

He looked up at her with pathetic puppy dog eyes. With a mock sigh, she turned back to the tea station to grab some of the individually wrapped biscuits. She flung two at him, then sat down in the armchair beside the bed, hugging her knees to her as she cradled the tea between her hands.

"Did you manage to reach Abi?"

"Hmm?" She looked at him in confusion for a minute. "Oh, yeah. I called her while you were asleep. They're getting ready to move to another safe house Nate has organised."

"You okay?" Ethan's forehead creased in concern as he watched her.

She gave him a wry smile. "Shouldn't I be asking you that?"

Without answering, he shifted over in the bed and shuffled his way up to a semi-reclined position. "Sit. Talk to me." He patted the empty space beside him.

She bristled at the order and opened her mouth to tell him to get stuffed, but was once again struck by just how fragile he looked. The simple process of clearing a space for her seemed to have worn him out completely as he leaned back against the headboard for support.

Softening, she scooched out of the chair and onto the bed beside him. The bed was large; two singles pushed together and covered with oversized sheets to make it appear as one – assuming you didn't roll into the dip in the middle. Even still, she was conscious of the heat of his body at her side.

They sat in silence for a few minutes, him getting his strength back from the small effort and her musing on just how fucked up her life had become while pointedly ignoring the way his musky scent made her head swim.

"It couldn't have been easy hearing his voice."

Her heart gave a pained spasm as she remembered Darius's call. She had no doubt left that he was evil, but it seemed her heart still hadn't quite come to terms with the revelation.

"You know the funny thing? He wanted to help me." Her laugh

was bitter as she leaned against the headboard. "He said the Council was sending the next Mist and he needs me alive." Her throat burned. "He offered me sanctuary."

"No!" Ethan lunged forward, his eyes flashing yellow for a split second before he collapsed back.

Her jaw dropped in surprise at his almost feral response. "Well, of course I wasn't going to take him up on it." She gave him her best "well, duh" look as she helped him fix the pillow behind his body for support.

He blew out a slow breath with a sheepish grin. "Sorry, I didn't mean it like that. It's just the thought of him coming anywhere near you ..."

His eyes darkened as they examined her face. Uncomfortable with their intensity, she averted her gaze to focus on her fidgeting hands. He wrapped a hand around hers to still their nervous twitching. His one hand was large enough to cover both of hers and so much warmer than her own naturally cool temperature. The heat seeped from his skin into hers, and the chill that had started with the mention of Darius began to ease.

Her instinct was to pull away from the comfort he offered, but the weight of his hand was oddly reassuring. Instead she leaned back against the headboard once more and rested her head next to his.

They sat like that for a while before he turned to her with a puzzled look on his face. "How did he get your number?"

She tensed and pulled her hands from beneath his. The question had been running through her mind ever since Darius called. Not to mention the still unanswered question of how the Council found them at the last B&B. Only a handful of people knew where they'd be, and those same people were the only ones with her number. The thought made her uneasy in a way she couldn't quite explain. And it didn't help that Abi had – hesitantly – raised some concerns when she spoke to her earlier that evening. But she had a strange feeling Ethan wasn't going to appreciate her thoughts on the subject.

"Only our group have this number. I made sure of it."

"Well, we know none of them would have given it to him."

She looked at him, searching for any kind of doubt on his face. There was nothing but certainty.

When she didn't immediately respond, he frowned. "Surely you don't think –"

A part of her wanted to just agree with him and shut her mouth. No matter how hard she tried, she couldn't think of a way to voice her concerns that wouldn't piss him off.

"Abi asked me something earlier that got me thinking." She bit her lip, trying to think past the little voice in her head that was begging her to just stay quiet. "If Shade was turned in Dublin, he'd be under the rule of the Dublin vampire clan, wouldn't he?"

Ethan shifted away from her ever so slightly, his expression hardening. "What are you saying?"

"I'm not saying anything. I'm just asking a question. He's never liked me. You can't deny that."

"That doesn't mean he'd ever help Darius."

"What about the Council?"

A heavy silence followed as she finally voiced the thought that had been niggling at the back of her mind. Ethan was right. It was unlikely Shade would help Darius if he truly had been the one to abandon him. But the Council was a different story. If he helped them, he not only got to ruin Darius's plans for world domination, but it also had the added bonus of getting rid of her. She could see him jumping for glee at that prospect – or at least cracking a smile.

"There's a big difference between disliking someone and wanting them dead. Shade has been nothing but loyal," Ethan eventually responded.

"To you, perhaps." She clenched her jaw and pushed off the bed. "I should've known there was no point trying to talk to you about this. I'm going out. I need some air."

She grabbed her jacket and flung open the door to the room.

"Phoenix –"

His protest was cut off with the slam of the door behind her.

Would it have really killed him to hear me out?

Phoenix shoved her hands into her jacket pocket and bent her head as the wind whipped around her with an angry howl. Trees bowed under the force and heavy, black clouds overhead promised more rain to come.

Hell, even Abi could see Shade had a bad attitude. Not Ethan though. He just thinks Shade's the golden boy because he didn't turn into a blood fiend. Well, maybe that's because someone was keeping him in check all along. Maybe the sob story about his Sire is exactly that – nothing more than a story.

Aimlessly, she followed the dirt path that wound from the back of the B&B to a small lake, her only goal to put some distance between herself and Ethan. The biting wind was sharp against her face and the muddy waters swirled restlessly.

With a low rumble, the sky opened. Fat droplets pelted her from all angles and broke the flat surface of the lake. Within seconds, her hair was plastered to her face and she bore a stark resemblance to a washed-up rat.

Damn you, Ethan.

This was all his fault. If the stubborn fool had been capable of having a mature conversation, she wouldn't be standing out here freezing her wet arse off. Alone. When lethal assassins were trying to kill her –

Shit, what am I doing?

She sighed and shoved the hair out of her face. The thought of going back really grated on her, but it would be pretty hard to make a point if she ended up dead. She'd just have to suck it up for now ... Or hide in the bathroom.

She was about to turn around when a warning prickle ran down her spine. She spun around, braced for an attack, and froze. A tall figure stood under a nearby tree, watching her. His profile was as familiar as her own, and she didn't have to see his face to recognise him.

Darius.

Her heart did that awful stutter again, and her breath stalled. He made no move towards her, but she found her feet glued to the spot as she stared at the man she'd considered family, and all thoughts of the torrential rain evaporated.

Of course, the water seemed to simply glide off his tailored suit while his black hair held perfectly in place, impervious to the blustery wind. The only thing in any way flawed about him was the subtle hint of scarring on the left side of his face. Scarring she'd caused.

"I thought it was time we spoke in person." His rich voice reached her despite the distance and the pounding of the rain.

"I've nothing to say to you."

Darius inclined his head and gave her a knowing smile. "I wouldn't be so sure of that. I came to warn you. The second Mist is on her way. I'd advise you leave quickly. She won't be as easily deterred as her brother."

Icy fear ran through her at the mention of the Mist, and she couldn't stop herself from quickly glancing around.

"I've already told you what you can do with your so-called protection." She crossed her arms defiantly, but inwardly winced at the slight tremor of her voice.

"Indeed. And I've no doubt you mean it. For now. But I'm confident that in time you'll come to me willingly. If I can find you this easily, what chance do you think you stand against the Council?"

His words cut straight to the quick, and she pulled her anger tightly to her as if it could act as a shield from the truth. "How did you find me?" she demanded.

"I have my sources. You really should be more careful who you associate with, you know."

Her breath caught in her throat and she became deathly still. The niggling suspicion that had been plaguing her sent a chorus of butterflies fluttering around her stomach. Words turned to ash on her tongue as she battled with herself on whether or not to ask the next question. She already knew she couldn't trust a word he said, but she couldn't help herself; she needed to know.

"He's one of yours, isn't he? It was you that sired him."

Darius said nothing, just gave her a knowing smile. She felt an insatiable urge to put a fist through his smug face.

A loud rumble rolled through the sky, and a flash of lightning struck the ground mere feet from where she stood. She jumped back in surprise, adrenaline shooting through her as she prepared again for an attack. None came.

Just as suddenly as it had begun, the rain stopped, and when she looked towards Darius again, she found nothing other than an empty space where he'd stood.

CHAPTER TWENTY-EIGHT

Ethan leaned his head back against the headboard and closed his eyes. He growled, not even sure who he was more frustrated with, himself or Phoenix. No, Phoenix. It was definitely Phoenix.

She was so bloody stubborn. Trying to make her see sense was like talking to a brick wall. Only the brick wall didn't talk back. Was it really so hard for her to try see the good in people? Or at least see something other than the worst?

A bone-deep weariness filled him, and his whole body felt heavy. It had been almost twenty-four hours since the Mist's attack, and the slightest movement still left him panting for breath. His body should have healed by now.

The Mist. Shit! He bolted upright, sluggish brain cells finally making the connection. Phoenix was out there alone and the next Mist was coming.

His heart hammered in his chest as he pushed the blanket off and swung his legs over the side of the bed. The room swam and the edges of his vision turned black. He closed his eyes and took slow, deep breaths until the world stopped tilting.

Luckily, he was already wearing jeans and a t-shirt because he didn't think he had the energy to get dressed. He just had to put shoes on; that should be easy enough.

As he bent to retrieve one of his shoes from under the bed, he toppled forward, only just managing to catch himself on the armchair. Not so easy after all.

A couple of minutes, and a lot of cursing later, he had shoes on his feet and had somehow managed to stumble outside. Heavy black clouds hung overhead and rain soaked him through in seconds. The chill permeated his very core, but he used the cold to focus his foggy thoughts.

One step at a time, he moved sluggishly forward. The wind felt like a wall of resistance against him, and by the time he reached the dirt track, he was forced to stop. He panted as he leaned against a tree for support. Leaves rustled above his head and a large crow landed on the ground in front of him. Strange red eyes watched him with an eerie intelligence that made him freeze. He'd seen those eyes before.

The air around the crow shimmered, and Ethan blinked against the rain that blurred his vision. Between one blink and the next, the crow disappeared. In its place stood a black wolf with the same red eyes.

His own wolf stood to attention, and when the black wolf turned and trotted down the path towards the nearby lake, he gritted his teeth and stumbled along after it. More than once, his vision turned black, but his instincts screamed at him to push on. One foot in front of the other: left, right, left, right.

Exhaustion was like a leaden blanket draped over him, and each blink he took seemed to last longer than the previous. He was dimly aware of Phoenix's voice in the distance, but he couldn't make out what she was saying. Who was she talking to?

He tried to call out, but his words were swallowed by a crash of thunder. And then the world went black.

Phoenix held her breath as her eyes scanned the clearing around her. Darius would reappear any second. Or, if not him, the Mist. She was sure of it.

A minute passed. Then two. Nothing.

The longer she waited for the hammer to fall, the more tense she became. Had she really seen him at all? Maybe her overactive imagination was playing tricks on her, or she'd just finally lost her marbles.

Another loud rumble overhead sent the rain pelting down once more. Thick raindrops mingled with hardened lumps of hail. It took only a few knocks to the head before she came to her senses; why the hell was she standing there waiting for someone to kill her when she should be getting a head start?

She pushed the sopping strands of hair out of her face and moved tentatively in the direction of the B&B. The pounding rain made it hard to hear anything other than the symphony of nature, but she strained for the slightest noise and watched for any sign of movement. Her heart pounded in her ears with each step and she fought the urge to break into a panicked run.

Just as she rounded the corner and the B&B came into view, she noticed a dark shape half-obscured by the hedges and long grass that bordered the trail. What looked like a shoe peeked out of the overgrowth, and she edged forward for a better look.

It took her a second to recognise the shoe as Ethan's, and a second more to make out his unmoving form attached to it. Her stomach flip-flopped and she closed the gap between them in an instant. A multitude of terrifying scenarios ran through her head as she crouched down beside him. Had Darius hurt him? The Mist? What the hell was he even doing out of bed?

Her hands trembled as she shook him. "Ethan. Ethan, wake up, dammit."

The plea was met with a weak murmur, but his eyes didn't open. Despite the chill of the rain, his skin was feverish beneath her touch. Instead of the strong, sure rhythm she expected, his heartbeat was rapid but thready. She needed to get him out of here, and she needed to get him help.

With a grunt, she hoisted the dead weight of his upper body off the ground and manoeuvred him until he was half draped over her shoulder. The weight was significant as she put one foot under herself and pushed to standing. But it was more his size that posed the biggest hindrance. Talk about déjà vu.

"I thought it was meant to be the man carrying the damsel in distress," she groused as she trudged back up the dirt trail and hoped like hell no one saw them.

She didn't even bother heading for the room. Instead, she made a beeline straight for their car, where she once again slung Ethan's unconscious form across the backseat. Darius knew where they were now. There was nothing in that room worth facing him for. Plus, if he was to be believed, every second they stayed increased their odds of coming face to face with the next Mist. And that wasn't a scenario she was up to dealing with right now.

It wasn't until she'd gotten them on the road and a comfortable distance from the B&B that she allowed herself to take a breath. She glanced in the rear-view mirror at Ethan's still form and her chest tightened with worry. A sheen of sweat coated his grey-tinged skin and his breathing was shallow. He shouldn't be like this; he should have healed long before now.

With a slight twinge of guilt for betraying her promise to Ethan, she pulled out her phone and called Abi on loudspeaker. As soon as her friend answered, she blurted out the rest of the information about the Mist attack – the part that had left Ethan gravely injured.

"I don't know what the Mist did or how he did it, but his body's not recovering the way it should. I was hoping he'd get better but he's not, and I don't know what to do. If the next Mist comes, we're in serious shit."

Abi was silent at the other end of the phone, and Phoenix blew out a long, shaky breath.

"Okay," Abi said finally, "I'll speak to the others and see what we can find out about the Mists. It sounds like they've got some weird mojo at their disposal, so we'll need to figure out how to counteract it. And I do mean *we*, Phoenix. You're not doing this on your own any longer."

She opened her mouth to protest, but shut it just as quickly. She didn't want to do this on her own. She was tired of trying to figure shit out by herself. Her nerves were fried. Besides, she had a vampire to confront, and what better way to do that than to show him just how much damage he'd caused.

So, she agreed a fresh plan with Abi and hung up, feeling a mixture of relief and trepidation as she pulled onto the motorway with a clear destination.

"Where are we going?"

She jumped in surprise at Ethan's mumbled question. When did he wake up?

"The others are leaving for a new safe house shortly. We're going to take a detour and meet them there in the morning." She threw a quick glance in his direction before fixing her eyes on the road.

"Do they know I've been hurt?"

She nodded, not really sure whether he was looking or not. A weary sigh and some shuffling were the only response from the back seat. When she glanced in the rear-view mirror again, Ethan's eyes were closed and he sat with his head leaning against the window.

Her grip loosened on the steering wheel a touch when she sensed no anger from him, but any relief was immediately replaced by a twist of anxiety. She might have just avoided an argument with Ethan, but there'd be a lot more to come if she was going to confront Shade face to face about his betrayal.

CHAPTER TWENTY-NINE

Lily trudged into the kitchen, idly wondering if it was possible to die from exhaustion as she made herself yet another cup of bitter coffee. The walls of the safe house were starting to close in on her and if they didn't get moving soon, she was afraid she'd start screaming and not be able to stop. Then again, what did it matter where she was? The location was all the same to her. Once she got the confirmation that Phoenix was dead, she'd be heading straight to the Council to fix everything.

Her nerves were completely frayed from the waiting. Every time someone's phone rang, her stomach dropped and a wave of nausea rolled through her. She felt like she was on a never-ending roller-coaster, blindfolded. She was trying to keep the end goal in sight, but it was getting harder and harder the more time passed.

The steaming cup was halfway to her lips when the sound of a phone ringing reached her ears from the living room next door. She froze, instantly recognising Abi's ringtone. Her heart jack-hammered in her chest as she waited for the cry of grief, or some sign that the deed was done. None came.

With a shuddering breath, she forced her feet to move one step in front of the other, out of the kitchen and into the hall. She paused at the open doorway of the living room where Abi stood completely still with her phone held to her ear. Unable to hear the other side of the conversation, Lily tried to read between the lines of the girl's furrowed brow and intense concentration.

After listening for a moment, Abi straightened up and strode purposefully from the room without even a glance in her direction. Before Lily could move, Shade appeared in front of her, his face an unreadable mask.

"If he doesn't recover from this, it'll be your fault." He didn't wait for a response, just followed in Abi's wake, calling over his shoulder. "You're going to want to hear this."

An insidious thread of fear wove its way through her confused thoughts as she stared at his receding back. What had his vampire hearing picked up that she'd missed?

With clammy hands and a very bad feeling, she ran down the hall, stopping only when she caught up to them at the office Nate had commandeered for the duration of their stay.

A metal desk sat in the centre of the room, covered in an assortment of screens and gadgets that obscured Nate from view. Only the rapid tapping of fingers on the keyboard gave away his presence. Abi stood over his right shoulder with her arms crossed and lips set in a determined line as she stared at the screen.

Shade waited inside the door and pointedly ignored her as she stepped into the room. Lily returned the favour and moved closer to the computer for a better look. "What's going on?"

Nate shifted in his chair but didn't look up from the screen. "Ethan's been hurt."

"What?" The question came out in a whisper as the bad feeling turned into a churning pit in her stomach.

"He told Phoenix to keep it quiet so we wouldn't worry, but he was hurt when the first Mist attacked. He's not healing the way he should be."

A low, buzzing noise filled Lily's ears as she tried to make sense of the words. She slumped against the wall, her legs going weak beneath her.

"But he'll be okay, won't he?"

Abi gave her a sympathetic look that did little to soften the grim expression on her face. "Nate's trying to get as much information as he can so we know what we're dealing with. We're thinking the Mist left some kind of poison in his system. Maybe you can start researching spells that might help?"

Lily nodded absently, the buzzing in her ears growing louder. Abi was still talking, outlining the plan she'd agreed with Phoenix, but the words seemed distant.

Diana promised. She promised me no one else would get hurt.

While the others crowded around the computer and brainstormed ideas for dealing with the Mists, she slipped from the room with her phone gripped tightly in her hand. She barely made it out of earshot before she had pressed the call button.

Diana answered on the third ring. The warm greeting that, until now, had helped to calm and reassure Lily, this time left her numb.

"You said it'd just be her. That no one else would get hurt."

The line was silent for a moment.

"There are always casualties in war, Lily." Diana's voice turned cold and a deep chill settled in Lily's chest.

"We're not at war."

"Aren't we?"

"Ethan is innocent," she insisted. "He's trying to stop this thing, just like you. He's not healing, Diana. He's really hurt."

"The wolf got in the way. If he hadn't, this would be over now. You'd have your sister back and my witches would be safe."

The buzzing in her head turned to a barely contained scream as all the conflicting emotions fought for attention. Of course she wanted her sister back, dammit, but this wasn't right. Every part of her being was telling her this was wrong.

"I can't do this," she said quietly. Her final thread of hope faded and took a piece of her soul with it.

"I'm afraid it's too late for second thoughts now." Diana's voice turned hard, no hint of her earlier warmth and compassion remaining. "What will your friends think when they find out you betrayed them? Do you think they'd still accept you? You'd be even more alone than you are now. No, you *will* go through with this, Lily. And when it's over, you'll be reunited with your sister. Just like you wanted."

CHAPTER THIRTY

The morning sun was splitting the sky as Phoenix navigated the winding coastal road, finally en route to their destination after a long night laying diversions. The clear blue sky formed a surreal juxtaposition to the erratic thunderstorms of recent days and she raised her face, relishing the warmth of the sun as it beamed through the car's windscreen. Rolling sandy beaches followed their path on the left, and jagged cliffs covered in lush green foliage bordered them to the right.

In the bright light of day it seemed almost idyllic. Yet there was an energy to the place that she couldn't quite explain. She'd felt it as soon as they'd reached Portrush, and it had only grown stronger as they drew near their meeting point. It made all of her senses tingle, like a feather whispering across her skin. There was something both foreign and strangely familiar that called to her and pulled her in.

She debated asking Ethan if he felt the same thing, but an awkward silence had settled between them once he'd regained consciousness. There were so many things unsaid from their disagreement the night before, and they'd only increased in significance after her run-in with Darius.

Arguments played over and over in her head, but she knew that voicing them again was a waste of time. It was okay though, because very soon she'd confront Shade herself and prove the truth to Ethan. And didn't that thought just make her gut twist painfully.

Beside her, now slumped in the passenger seat, Ethan gave a low whistle. She looked over at him, and her jaw dropped as they crested the hill and she was awarded a clear view of the ancient ruins that had caught his attention.

Dunluce Castle stood proud and imposing on the edge of the cliff. The sea was calm behind it, but an image filled her mind: waves crashing against the rocks as lightning split the sky. A shiver of anticipation ran through her.

Craning her head for a better look, she slowed the car as they neared the entrance. Coaches were parked along the grass verge and tourists milled about with cameras. They all seemed suitably impressed with the historic site, pointing and posing at random locations around the grounds. Were any of them aware of the immense power vibrating from the place? It was almost impossible to think that even the most mundane of humans could be oblivious to it.

"You feel it?" Ethan asked, his eyes glued to the castle as he sat up a little straighter.

She nodded even though he wasn't looking at her; she was too in awe to speak.

A car horn blared and she was snapped from her trance. At some point she'd slowed the car to a complete stop, and they were now blocking the narrow road with an irate driver making angry gestures behind them.

Ethan glanced at the car and gave her a somewhat dazed smile. "We better go meet the others. We can come back and explore later."

The rest of the drive was a blur. Colourful seafront houses came into view ahead and minutes later, the sat nav instructed them to turn into the drive of one of them. The mint green facade was a questionable choice of colour and the white paint surrounding the windows was cracked and flaking, but the views were stunning. Situated right on the seafront, she could easily imagine herself nestled behind one of the large bay windows and curled up with a cup of tea while she watched the waves beat tirelessly against the rocks. It wasn't quite what she'd expected from the safe house.

Before she had two feet out of the car, the front door swung open and Abi sprinted down the driveway towards her. She braced herself to avoid being knocked over by her friend's enthusiastic embrace and laughed while hugging Abi back just as tightly. For a brief moment, her heart felt lighter than it had in days.

Nate and Lily followed Abi from the house, their expressions tight with concern. Her happiness soured a little as she saw them. Shade was no doubt waiting inside to avoid the morning sun. Her stomach twisted at the thought of the confrontation to come. Would the others take his side too?

Lily hurried to Ethan's door and helped him from the car. He tried to brush her off, but his movements were slow and laboured, even the smallest exertion causing a sheen of sweat across his forehead.

Abi cast a worried glance in his direction before turning back to her with a reassuring smile plastered on her face. "Come on. Let's get you inside."

Together they followed the others into the house and upstairs to living room, which was ideally situated to make the most of the stunning views. Nate and Lily helped Ethan to the sofa, and Lily muttered something about a serum before scurrying out of the room.

Phoenix couldn't help but notice the lines of worry that now seemed permanently etched on the young girl's face as she passed by. Lily had lost weight in the short time the group had been apart, and her once tanned skin was almost as pale and sickly looking as Ethan's. The signs of grief were all too familiar to her. She wished there was something she could say to take Lily's pain away, but no words could ease the loss; she knew that better than anyone.

"Did you manage to find anything that will help him?" Phoenix turned her concern to Ethan and frowned as she noticed the fist he held clenched over his sternum. He had his eyes closed, and the rise and fall of his chest was shallow as he fought to catch his breath.

"We think there might be some kind of poison in his system that's stopping him from healing." Nate's amber eyes met hers, worry depriving them of their usual sparkle. "Lily has put together a serum we hope will work, but we'll need you to melt some gold for us."

"Gold?"

"Yeah, we've found some references that indicate the Mists react badly to it. We're hoping their magic will be the same." He shrugged. "Worst case scenario it does nothing, but it won't hurt him to try. Not any more than he already is."

"*He* is still here, you know," Ethan grumbled but didn't open his eyes.

Phoenix bit her lip and looked around for Lily. How long did it take to prepare? She pushed back the niggling fear of what would happen if the serum failed. It would work; it had to.

Abi grabbed her hand and pulled her down to sit on the second sofa. Plump cushions swallowed her as if the sofa itself was trying to force her to relax. She didn't want to. She couldn't.

A large clock hung on the wall over an open fireplace, and she watched the second hand move around at a snail's pace. She was vaguely aware that Abi was telling her all about the training she'd been doing with Nate. She nodded in the appropriate places and gave her friend a weak smile, but her eyes were glued to Ethan. His whole body seemed tense. Every now and then he'd wince as if in pain.

She'd just about had enough of waiting when Lily walked back into the room holding a glass full of greenish-blue liquid in one hand and a gold ring in the other. The girl's eyes flicked to Ethan and she flinched before looking to Phoenix.

"You ready?"

Lily closed her bedroom door with a soft click and rested her forehead against the cool wood. She scrunched her eyes tight and tried to force air into her lungs. Each breath she took pulled the invisible band tighter around her chest, and her head swam as she struggled for much-needed oxygen.

It was too much. Seeing Ethan's body spasm with the crippling pain that overtook him as the serum fought the poison in his system. It was all just too much.

She had no idea if the serum would work, and she'd been too much of a coward to stay and face the consequences of her actions. If he died, it would be her fault; she as good as murdered him herself. The knowledge twisted like a knife in her gut.

Silent tears streaked her cheeks and she slid to the floor, curling into a ball and hugging her knees to her. The pain in her chest increased, and she idly wondered if she was too young to have a heart attack. A dark place in the back of her mind welcomed the idea with relief.

The walls felt like they were closing in around her, and Diana's word echoed in her head. "It's too late for second thoughts now." This couldn't be the way she got her sister back. Annabelle would never want to be saved at the expense of someone else, least of all Ethan. And even if the Ouroboros managed to reset everything, could she live with herself, knowing the pain she'd caused?

She felt dirty, as if her insides were turning black with every lie and betrayal. She was losing a little bit more of herself each time; it felt like she was disappearing. A scream burned her throat as it tried to force itself free. She bit it back and clenched her fists in a vain attempt to hold it all in. She needed to fix this. She needed to make it right.

With a laboured breath, she pushed up from the floor and stumbled to the bed. She reached under the mattress for the white box before turning to the locker where her grimoire rested. The book lay open at the page she'd used for Ethan's serum, and the image of him contorted in pain once again flashed before her. She gritted her teeth and flicked past the page. That spell had already done its job; it would either work or it wouldn't. What she needed now was another spell, one that would help her end this.

Scrawled writing and roughly drawn images blurred past until she finally paused her search. Her breathing slowly returned to normal as she scanned the details. This was it. This was what she needed.

A strange sense of calm settled in her chest as she sat back on the bed and pulled the box onto her lap. She opened it and took a long look at the object she once thought would solve everything, then closed the lid and reached for her phone.

"I have your location," she said as soon as the call was answered.

CHAPTER THIRTY-ONE

Phoenix paced the length of the small kitchen as she waited for the kettle to boil. Adrenaline still trickled through her, setting her nerves on edge.

Ethan's response to the serum had been instantaneous and terrifying. Spasms had overtaken his whole body, and her heart had frozen in pure terror as she watched the veins bulge in his arms and neck, his back bowing. Her body had screamed at her to do something, but that was the problem, wasn't it? There wasn't always an enemy to fight. So, she'd watched helplessly as Nate held him down to stop him from hurting himself even more.

It had passed in a couple of minutes, but those minutes had been some of the longest of her life. What followed was a puke session worthy of a horror movie, but after that, Ethan's deathly pallor seemed to fade somewhat and his breathing had become less laboured. He fell into a deep sleep, which Nate assured her was a good thing. She still wasn't convinced.

Just as she was about to throw her cup at the wall, Abi popped her head through the door.

"He's awake."

She hurried after her friend and into the living room to find Ethan sitting up on the sofa, looking healthier than he had in days.

He gave her a crooked smile and her heart stuttered in overwhelming relief.

"How are you feeling?"

"Better. Still pretty tired, but my body seems to be doing its thing now that whatever stopped it from healing is gone."

She slumped onto the sofa beside him, all the energy draining from her body along with the unspoken fear she'd clung to. She closed her eyes and allowed herself that moment to just breathe.

"We'll stay here until you get your strength back. Then we can all head to Donegal together," Nate was saying in the background.

Her eyes flew open as she suddenly remembered the other reason she was so determined for them all to regroup.

"Where's Shade?"

She hadn't seen the vampire once since she'd gotten here. Her first priority had been to get Ethan help, but now that he seemed to be doing better, she didn't want to waste time playing happy families while Shade found another knife to stick in her back.

"He's gone to follow up on a possible lead that might help us with the Council," Nate answered. "He reckoned we needed more help, and I'm inclined to agree."

On the sofa at the other side of the room, Abi shifted uncomfortably, not meeting her gaze. Ethan gave her a weary look and his brown eyes pleaded with her not to start an argument. She gawked at him. How could he still believe that Shade was innocent?

Darius rats him out and suddenly he disappears to "follow up on a lead"? Come on, what a load of bullshit.

"Help us with the Council? Shade's working against us. He betrayed us to the Council, and he's the reason he" – she stabbed a finger emphatically in Ethan's direction – "almost got killed."

"Enough, Phoenix." Ethan sat forward, hanging his head in his hands as he propped his elbows on his knees. "You need to drop this ridiculous notion. Shade may not like you, but none of this is his fault."

"Darius confirmed it."

Ethan's head jerked up, his face a mask of shock. "What?"

"Darius paid me a little visit. Back at the B&B while you were having your catnap. He was only too happy to claim Shade as one of his own."

Ethan's face paled and Nate placed a hand on his shoulder, calmly encouraging him to rest back in the seat. "What exactly did Darius say?" he asked, his tone far too reasonable for her liking.

She cast her thoughts back, trying to remember Darius's exact words. It was all a bit of a blur. Her emotions had been on such a rollercoaster since seeing him and the exhaustion was starting to cloud her mind.

"It doesn't matter exactly what he said. He confirmed that Shade was betraying us."

She waited for the lightbulb to switch on and understanding to dawn on their faces. Ethan just shook his head, and Nate appeared as relaxed as ever. Only Abi frowned in concern at her words.

Nate gave her an apologetic shrug. "Sorry, Phoenix, but I don't buy it. Shade's a pain in the hole, but he's a good guy. You of all people should know what Darius's word is worth."

She gaped at him in disbelief as anger bubbled up inside her. What the hell was with these people? How could they sit there and defend him when it was obvious he'd screwed them over?

"Are you shitting me? The guy was turned in Darius's territory and has some crock story about not knowing who his Sire is. How can you not see the connection here?"

Ethan sighed heavily. "It's not that we don't see your point, but you can't deny that your source is dubious at best. Even if Darius is his Sire, Shade is our friend. You can't really expect us to condemn him without even hearing his side of things."

A strange numbness filled her chest as she looked at each of them in turn. They didn't believe her.

With a stiff nod, she stood up. "I thought you might respect me enough to trust my word, but I guess I was wrong. If you want proof, I'll get it. I just hope no one else gets hurt while you hold on to your denial."

She turned and walked out of the room, nails digging into the palms of her hand as she swallowed past the burning in her throat.

CHAPTER THIRTY-TWO

Darius stepped through the portal and followed the rest of the Witnesses to the Council chambers. His face was a mask of indifference, but inside he was seething. A last-minute summons by the Council was an irritating show of power at the best of times, but this one had come at the most inconvenient moment.

Everything had been set up for the first test to transfer the demon. If the test was a success, not only would his plans take a significant leap forward, but he would also have a very useful weapon to help protect Phoenix from the Mists.

Low murmurs and restless shifting filled the antechamber. He caught snippets of conversation suggesting Maj had fulfilled her oath, and that was the reason for the sudden meeting. If not for the team he now had tracking Phoenix's movements, he'd have feared the same thing.

He hadn't exaggerated when he'd warned her the second Mist was coming. Less than an hour after she'd vacated the B&B, Maj had arrived. He'd watched from the shadows since there was no need for him to reveal himself just yet. Not surprisingly, there was no sign of Maj when he looked around the chamber. The Mist was a lot smarter than her younger brother and he strongly suspected she'd gone to ground to await her next opportunity rather than returning to admit failure.

And it was only a matter of time before that opportunity came. If Phoenix didn't come to her senses soon, it would make his job of keeping her alive a whole lot harder.

A sudden hush fell over the room, drawing his attention to the platform at the centre. All five Council members stood in a line with their hoods pulled low enough that their faces were cloaked in shadow.

The large double doors at the back of the room opened and Vicktor entered, making his way to the centre to stand before them. His pristine grey suit was complemented by his usual pompous air and arrogant confidence, but there was a subtle tension that held his shoulders a little too still.

To what do we owe the honour of this weasel gracing our presence yet again?

As Darius watched, Vicktor bowed his head and kept his gaze fixed to the ground until all Council members had lowered the hoods of their cloaks.

Méabh stepped forward with only a brief glance of acknowledgement for the CLO rep. "I'm sure you're all wondering why you've been summoned here at such short notice. It has come to my attention that one of our own has withheld key information from us. Information that may have contributed to a swifter end to this unfortunate situation."

Darius tensed, his eyes flicking back to Vicktor. Had the little weasel informed the Council of his involvement? He'd been sure the man would value his survival far too much to betray him. Not to mention it would risk bringing to light his own duplicitous actions. Had he been mistaken in not dealing with the rep sooner?

Vlad held up his hand to halt the intrigued murmurings filling the room. His face remained stoic, but there was a curious glint to his eye as he nodded for Méabh to continue.

She gave him a saccharine smile before turning to address the room once more. "The hybrid poses a threat to us all. And as such, it has been agreed that she must be sacrificed for the sake of the Lore and all humanity. We know from Shayan's failed attempt" – she cast a cold glance towards the youngest Mist who stood in the shadows scowling – "that there are others of our kind assisting her. With the help of key sources, we have managed to identify these accomplices."

She paused dramatically before nodding to Vicktor.

Vicktor straightened and smoothed invisible creases from his tailored suit jacket. "We at the CLO have been working tirelessly to gather information that may be of assistance to the Council in bringing this unfortunate matter to a swift conclusion. From our investigations, we can now confirm that, aside from the werewolf and witch, there is also a shifter and vampire aiding the hybrid in her endeavours. The concerning point, however, relates to the wolf. It appears that the man who intervened in Shayan's attack has a familial connection to one of the Council members."

He didn't have to speak the name for every eye in the room to turn to William. The apologetic glance the CLO rep cast in the head were-wolf's direction was as genuine as Darius's supplication to Council rule. William, for his part, didn't react. He held his hands clasped loosely in front of his body with his steely gaze fixed dead ahead.

Of course, this wasn't new information to him. Darius himself had seen to that. But it was obvious from the tension radiating from the other Council members that they'd been kept in the dark about this little fact.

Diana's eyes blazed as she crossed her arms. Vlad's expression didn't change so much as his energy shifted with a subtle movement of his body and a darkening in the colour of his eyes. Darius wasn't sure what it meant, but he could clearly see the cogs turning in the vampire's mind.

Kam tilted his head and regarded his fellow Council member closely. It was he that stepped forward and called a hush to the rumble of speculation moving around the antechamber.

"William, would you care to speak in your defence?"

The wolf looked at him and a muscle jumped at the side of his jaw. Just once.

"What exactly am I expected to defend? I was as unaware of this connection as you. It changes nothing."

Diana gaped at him before snapping her mask of composure back into place. "Of course it changes things. How do we know you haven't been feeding him information?"

"I haven't."

She opened her mouth in retort, but William turned to address the other members of the Council before she could utter another word.

"As we've just heard, there is also a shifter" – he nodded towards Kam – "a vampire" – nod in Vlad's direction – "and a witch" – a pointed look to Diana – "helping the hybrid. My priority is as it's always been: the safety of our people. If a member of my family chooses to get themselves caught in the crossfire, that's their choice."

Darius raised an eyebrow as he watched the interchange. He knew the wolf was bluffing, and any other Supe in the room with a good nose should have also been able to smell the lie. Yet, William appeared completely assured, and the lack of condemnation from the crowd would suggest the Witnesses were sold on his declaration. *Interesting.*

"May I make a proposal?" Vlad held his arms wide and pasted the perfect politician smile on his face as he addressed the room. "The second Mist has already been deployed. It's only a matter of time before we receive confirmation that she has fulfilled her duty. Perhaps William might agree to remain within Council chambers until such a time we receive that confirmation ... Just a formality, of course. To put everyone's minds at ease regarding his loyalty."

William bared his teeth at the vampire, and Vlad's smile widened.

"That seems a fair proposal to me," Méabh agreed, a long red fingernail playing at the corner of her full red lips as she regarded William with a calculating gaze.

The other Council members nodded their agreement. William inclined his head in acknowledgement and stalked from the room.

CHAPTER THIRTY-THREE

Phoenix drove aimlessly, no real destination or plan of action in mind. It wasn't like you could outrun your own thoughts, was it? The numbness that had started in her chest now wrapped around her like a protective bubble and she clung to it, grateful for the temporary reprieve it afforded. She'd switched off her phone, too, but only after sending Abi a message to reassure her she was okay and promising not to leave without her.

Did she intend on leaving? She had no idea. Where would she even go? She just knew that somewhere under the protective layer of numb, she was angry. And hurt. Even with everything pointing to his guilt, they were taking Shade's side over hers. She was still the outsider, and he was their friend.

If she stayed and they stuck to the original plan, there was a high chance it'd put her in more danger. But when she thought of walking away, her stomach churned uncomfortably. Had she gotten so used to having others to rely on that she was afraid to be alone? Or was it the thought of walking away from Ethan?

As the sun dipped low on the horizon, she found herself drawn back to a familiar view: the castle.

At the edge of the jagged cliff, the setting sun framed the ruins in a glowing halo of red that seemed to pulse with the energy filling the air. She slowed the car to a crawl as she neared the entrance and watched the last coach of tourists pull away.

An old man in a green duffel coat and tweed cap pulled the barrier to the carpark closed, his movements painstakingly slow as he fitted the large padlock. When the lock clicked into place, he turned to look at her car, which was now stopped at the end of the dirt road, and inclined his head. Phoenix couldn't be sure from where she sat, but she could've sworn there was a satisfied look on the old man's face.

A glint in the distance drew her attention towards the cliff edge and she squinted, trying to see what had caused it. Nothing obvious jumped out at her, so she turned her gaze back to the gate to find the old man gone and the locked gate now open and waiting.

Curious, she put the car into gear and eased the car up the narrow dirt road. She killed the engine and got out, expecting to feel the bite of the salty sea breeze on her skin, but there was nothing. The air was unnaturally calm, and it held a weight that seemed almost pensive.

A strange vibration ran down her spine and thrummed through her solar plexus. She looked around, searching for a possible source, but she was completely alone.

Slowly, she walked towards the low stone wall that formed a barrier between the carpark and lush green lawns of the castle. As she passed the rear of the car, the vibration turned into an odd tugging sensation, almost like an invisible rope was attached to her sternum, pulling her backwards.

She eyed the boot of the car warily and stretched an intrepid hand out to open it. She held her breath, half expecting something to jump out and attack, but the boot opened with an anticlimactic click.

A tentative peek inside revealed nothing other than the few belongings she and Ethan had brought with them: two rucksacks of clothes, some emergency supplies, and the wood box covered in Celtic symbols that held her father's sword.

Her hand reached towards the box and the insistent pull grew stronger. She bit back a nervous laugh as she envisaged opening it to see the sword inside glowing. Thankfully, it wasn't. When she lifted the lid, the sword sat innocently cushioned on the bed of red satin casing. The blade was as simple as the box was ornate. It was only with a closer look that similar Celtic designs could be seen shimmering along the metal.

Without a thought, her hand closed around the smooth wooden grip, and instantly a sense of calm fell over her. A tension she hadn't even fully acknowledged unravelled itself, and she took a deep breath. The salty air tickled her nose as she filled her lungs.

The bronze hilt sat snuggly against her hand, the long blade perfectly balanced. Shafts of light radiated from the sword when the sun's rays touched it, and for a moment, she was mesmerised. An answering heat came to life in the centre of her chest.

She took a step back in surprise at the visceral reaction of her body. Suddenly uneasy, she moved to place the sword back in its casing but the vibration started again, more insistent this time. A heavy sense of foreboding replaced the heat in her chest and she swallowed, stepping away from the car with the sword still in her hand.

All of her senses were on high alert as she stepped over the low wall. The grass beneath her feet was unnaturally green and luscious. Flowers dotted the fields around the castle in a spectrum of colours she'd never seen before, or at least not since she was a child following her mother around the garden. Power ran across her skin like static electricity and increased as she moved forward with careful steps.

What is this place?

It didn't take her long to reach the large stones that formed the boundary wall of the ruins. A gust of wind ruffled her hair, and she could've sworn it brought with it the echoes of a soft lament.

An unseen force urged her forward and into the castle. With a blink, she found herself surrounded on all sides by the thick stone walls, what remained of them anyway. The sword vibrated in her hand once more and she raised it, testing the weight.

Though she'd never held this particular sword before, it felt like the most natural thing in the world to let the blade move through the pattern of movements her father had taught her many years before.

The air shimmered and she stared, hypnotised by the iridescent trail it left.

She was so entranced by the sight that everything else around her faded until a familiar voice called from behind her.

"What're you doing here?"

CHAPTER THIRTY-FOUR

Startled by the sound of Lily's voice, Phoenix snapped out of her daze and turned, only to freeze in shock. It was Lily's voice she heard, but it wasn't Lily standing before her. Instead, the person standing before her was a mirror image of herself. A living, breathing doppelganger.

"What the –" Her mouth opened and closed in confusion as she blinked to clear the illusion. It didn't disappear.

"You're not supposed to be here," the doppelganger said with Lily's voice. "She'll be coming any minute."

Phoenix clasped the sword in front of her and frowned as her brain tried to make sense of what it was seeing. The more she concentrated, the more she could catch a faint trace of Lily's signature, but the image was all wrong.

What the hell is going on?

She was just about to demand answers when the not-quite-Lily rushed towards her, her head swivelling from left to right as if searching for something.

"Lily, why do you look like me?" She took a step back but forced her voice to stay calm to avoid making the young girl more agitated.

"I was going to make it right. You have to believe me."

Desperate hands grasped at Phoenix's sword-free arm and her own wide, green eyes stared pleadingly at her. Alarm bells rang in the deep recesses of her mind, but she couldn't focus past the strange image, or Lily's frantic ramblings, to think straight.

"Lily, calm down. Just tell me what's going on."

"Please, Phoenix, you need to leave. I was wrong. I know that now. I'm sorry. She promised to help me get Annabelle back." Lily's voice broke in a strangled sob. "I just wanted to believe her so badly. But I'm going to fix it. I promise."

A sense of dread wrapped around Phoenix, freezing her to the spot. The hairs on the back of her neck stood to attention and her hands grew clammy.

Lily abruptly halted her profuse apologising, and her eyes widened into a mask of fear as she stared over Phoenix's left shoulder.

Not one to ignore a warning, Phoenix ducked just in time to miss the blade that sliced through the air where her neck had been less than a second previous. She brought her sword up the meet the follow-through strike and found herself looking into expressionless golden eyes.

The woman wasn't much taller than her, and her body was lean with muscle and a lethal air. Her energy screamed power but had an almost intangible quality that made it hard to identify; just like the first Mist.

"Shit," Phoenix whispered as the woman became a shadow dispersing into the air.

Breath held, she turned in a slow circle, waiting for the attack she knew to be inevitable.

It came from the left, but not in the form of the Mist herself. Rather, one of the large stones seemed to free itself from the jagged structure to fly at her head.

She only just managed to side-step in time and found herself moving straight into the trajectory of an oddly shaped dagger held by the Mist. The blade sliced through her upper arm and pain blazed in its wake.

Too late to avoid the damage, she continued turning until she was pressed in tight against the Mist. Close enough to make another blade strike difficult, and close enough to look death in the eyes.

She placed her hand against the Mist's chest and called the sun to her. It came more swiftly than ever before and burst from her in a flash of light, but the air beneath her hand was empty. Behind her, Lily screamed, and she turned just in time to see the young witch throw herself in front of the blade that was plunging for her back.

It was all Phoenix could do to yank her backwards, sending them both tumbling to the ground.

The coppery tang of blood filled the air, and Lily's body shimmered beneath her until she was no longer looking at a mirror image of herself but at the true version of Lily. A slight twitch from Lily was enough to assure her the witch was alive. She rolled to her back with the sword still miraculously clutched in her grasp and held it up in a vain attempt to stave off another attack.

But the Mist was gone.

The wind whipped into a frenzy and the sky overhead darkened with oppressive grey clouds. Lightning split the sky, filling the centre of the castle in an eerie white light.

Lily let out a pained groan and rolled to a sitting position beside her. A red stain coated one side of her blue jumper and she clutched her ribs, wincing with each inhale.

"Leave," she pleaded.

"Too late for that," responded a disembodied voice on the wind.

Phoenix jumped to her feet. She turned in a slow circle, sword at the ready, as she stood guard over Lily. Suddenly, sounds berated her from all angles: wordless cries, her name, a language she didn't recognise.

The wind grew in force until it became a visible barrier around her and Lily. Shadows appeared and disappeared, making it impossible to concentrate on a single point. The dizzying sight made her head spin and the world tilted at an odd angle.

A vibration through the hilt of the sword and into her hand shocked her back into focus. Somewhere in the deep recesses of her mind, she heard her father's voice whisper, "Trust your instinct." Words spoken long ago, in another lifetime.

With a deep breath, she let the tension ease from her body and closed her eyes. She fought past all the noise and distraction and tried to centre herself.

Inhale. Exhale.

She raised the sword and sliced through the swirling vortex that surrounded them. There was no resistance, but when she opened her eyes again, the wind was gone, and just as suddenly as it had changed, the sky overhead was cloudless once more.

Atop the northern wall of the castle, the Mist – Maj, Darius had called her – stood watching her. There was a curious look on her face as she eyed the sword in Phoenix's hand. Something had shifted in the woman's demeanour. It was almost as if her determined stance now held a hint of reluctance.

"Why are you doing this?" Phoenix called, not really expecting the other woman to answer.

For a moment Maj was silent, but then her weary voice carried on the wind. "I have no choice."

Her physical form dissolved to mist once more, and Phoenix braced herself.

The blows came from every angle, invisible but no less painful for their lack of substance. It was all she could do to remain standing. All attempts to block the unseen attacks proved fruitless.

Beside her, Lily stumbled to her feet, hissing in a breath as she attempted to straighten. She pushed the young girl behind her, using herself as a shield as she closed her eyes again. *Focus on the energy,* she reminded herself, and raised the sword before her.

Her next slice met with resistance and a grunt. Then something slammed into the side of her and sent her spinning. She opened her eyes and spun just in time to see the odd-shaped dagger plunging for her chest.

Lily whispered a word Phoenix didn't understand, and time fractured.

The next thing she knew, the witch was standing in front of her, and as she watched, the dagger plunged through Lily's chest. Her body arched back and a scream of agony tore free from her throat.

Phoenix clutched her in disbelief, taking the weight of her body as it crumpled. She fell to her knees and wrapped her arms tightly around the young girl.

"No, no, no," she demanded, shaking her head as she willed Lily to live with everything she had.

Rage, and pain, and fear, and grief welled up inside her until it felt like she might explode. She squeezed her eyes shut and pushed it all down, but it was too much; she couldn't contain it. The scream ripped from her as all the pain she was feeling combined into the burst of power that exploded from her chest.

Everything went white and her ears rang. It was a few moments before Lily's soft, gasping breaths brought her back to her senses. She opened her eyes, almost expecting to see a large crater surrounding them, but the castle grounds were just as they had been. Minus the Mist.

Lily's body started to shake in her arms and when she looked down, her stomach dropped. The other girl's face was deathly white, and clammy sweat glistened on her forehead. Her body felt so cold. A soft lament drifted on the wind, and panic seized Phoenix.

"It's okay. It's okay. We'll get you help," she said, even as her eyes were drawn to the growing pool of blood surrounding the dagger in Lily's chest.

"I ... I'm sorry ... I was ... I was going to make it right." Lily clutched her hand with surprising strength and gave her a sad smile. "I can be with her now."

The soft lament turned to a keening wail and grew stronger, filling every cell of Phoenix's body. Her grief merged with it, until it was all encompassing, and as Lily's eyes closed for the final time, a single tear broke free.

CHAPTER THIRTY-FIVE

Ethan tapped his foot and mentally willed Nate to drive faster. The flash of light in the distance only meant one thing, and every second it took them to reach Phoenix's side was a second too long.

He'd stubbornly refused to follow her when she stalked out of the house in a huff. She was being completely unreasonable, and truth be told, his whole body felt battered and exhausted as it fought the remnants of poison in his system. He couldn't face yet another fight with her.

Once the anger had worn off, reality filtered back in and he'd started to get antsy at the thought of her out there alone. By that stage, he'd had no way of knowing where she'd gone, and he couldn't find Lily to do a locator spell. Abi had stubbornly refused to help him too, at least until he made her realise the danger Phoenix could be in.

Now, as he saw the castle looming in the horizon, his instincts screamed at him, calling him an idiot of the highest proportions. Adrenaline pushed back the fatigue that still weighed heavy on his body and mind, and he gripped the car's door handle, ready to leap from the moving vehicle as soon as they were close enough.

Seconds later, the car screeched to a halt and he was running, vaguely aware of slamming doors behind him.

He passed the car Phoenix had taken and leapt the low wall.

There were no sounds of fighting. There was only an eerie silence broken by the crunch of soft green grass under his feet as he ran.

Please don't let me be too late.

The jagged edge of the castle wall blocked his view, and it was only when he reached the boundary that he saw them. Phoenix knelt in the grass with a body draped across her lap and sword on the ground by her side. He slowed to a halt as his brain tried to make sense of the scene before him. Was it the Mist? A tourist?

His senses stayed on high alert, fuelled further by the potent energy that enveloped him. Tentatively, he stepped through what had once been a doorway. A soft wind blew in from the coast and it was then he noticed the blonde hair, ruffled by the breeze even as the body lay still. His heart froze.

Phoenix raised her head and turned dull, shocked eyes towards him. A single tear glistened in the fading light of the sun.

His mind struggled to fit the puzzle together, trying valiantly to protect him by offering alternative interpretations. But he knew.

He fell to his knees in the clearing and howled.

Time became inconsequential and Phoenix had no idea how long had passed before the others arrived. She was dimly aware of Ethan's howl of anguish, shortly followed by Abi's gentle sobs and Nate's repeated denials, but she couldn't take her eyes off Lily.

The young girl's face seemed so peaceful now that the lines of tension were finally gone. The flush of colour had left her lips, but there was a softness to them that made it almost seem as if she was smiling, something Phoenix had never seen her do in the short time she'd known her.

But the peaceful image was all wrong. Death shouldn't have been a release for Lily. At eighteen years of age, she should have been full of life and willing to fight with every ounce of her being, not giving it up so readily.

A heavy weariness filled Phoenix and when Nate's haunted eyes appeared in front of her, she let him take Lily. Strong arms wrapped around her and lifted her from ground. Voices spoke incoherent words, and moments later she was placed gently in the passenger seat of a car. Whose, she had no idea. It didn't matter.

The world blurred past and she let the numbness protect her. But at the back of her mind, a niggling memory was trying to push through to her consciousness.

The box.

She bolted forward only to be jerked back by the seatbelt. The car swerved as beside her in the driver's seat, Abi jumped at her sudden movement. It was only then that Phoenix looked around the small confines of the car and realised she was alone with her friend.

"Where's Ethan? I need to tell him about the box."

Abi's eyebrows scrunched in confusion and she indicated backwards with her head as she righted the car. "He's behind us with Nate and ..."

Phoenix deflated in the seat as her gut twisted with the remembered sense of foreboding. The dream. The cries for help. Had it been Lily? She should have done more to save her. Somehow they needed to make sure Lily passed. She needed to be with her sister. The thought caused a fierce burn in the back of Phoenix's throat and she closed her eyes. So much pain. So much death.

Eventually, they reached the house, followed moments later by the others. Nate carried Lily inside, her body cradled close to his chest as if he wanted to keep her warm. Before she could speak to him, Ethan disappeared into the house behind them, his face haggard and drawn. Abi placed a hand on her shoulder and she jumped.

"Come on. I'll make you tea. It'll help."

Phoenix followed obediently, not sure anything could help at that moment. She sat in silence as Abi fussed about the kitchen with determined focus, and accepted the steaming cup liberally laced with sugar.

It didn't ease the crushing pain in her chest, but by the time she was finished, she at least felt capable of forming a coherent sentence again. She gave Abi a grateful smile. The smile she got in return didn't reach her friend's blue eyes, and she noted the black circles and bloodshot lines that replaced their usual sparkle. Phoenix added yet another tick to her guilt list before pushing the thought aside; it would help no one.

With a resigned sigh, she stood. "I should go find Ethan and tell him about the box for the Ritual."

Abi gave her a strange look. "He needs you, Phoenix. No matter what he says, don't let him push you away."

Her steps faltered, the words striking a chord in some deep hidden part of herself. After a moment, she nodded, then turned and headed downstairs to find him.

The door to one of the bedrooms was cracked open, and through the narrow gap she could see him sitting on the bed with his head bowed. She knocked tentatively, unsure of her welcome, but when no response came, she slipped into the room anyway.

Ethan didn't look up or acknowledge her, though he had to be aware of her presence. He just stared at his hands, looking utterly lost. The need to comfort him overwhelmed her.

"I was wrong about Shade. I'm so sorry," she admitted softly.

He nodded but didn't raise his eyes.

She hesitated, Abi's words replaying in her head. When, after a minute, he didn't order her to leave, she moved further into the room and sat down on the bed beside him. She could still smell the salty sea air lingering on his skin and an aching sense of loss filled her.

When Ethan finally raised his brown eyes to hers, they were full of anguish, mirroring that ache. "It's my fault."

She grabbed his hand and shook her head vehemently. "You didn't cause this."

"I didn't stop it either."

"We will."

"What if we don't?"

She shrugged. "Then I guess we'll all end up dead and it won't matter."

His jaw dropped and he gawked at her in disbelief. Then suddenly, they both burst out laughing. The kind of hysterical laughter that came when your only other option was to cry. When the laughter finally subsided, she leaned her head on his shoulder. He put an arm around her and pulled her close with a squeeze. His body was warm against hers, solid, and for that moment, the fear faded.

"I think your pep talk needs work."

He pulled away to lift something from the bed behind them. His eyes darkened as he turned back with a white box in his hands. "I think you should see this."

She frowned in confusion, looking from him to the box. The first thing she noticed was the photograph, and her heart spasmed as she recognised Lily's smiling face. Before she could say anything, Ethan lifted the lid and revealed the box's contents.

"I found this in Lily's room."

A solid gold plaque gleamed up at Phoenix, the serpent mocking her from its wooden resting place. Bile rose in her throat and she blinked, her head trying to make sense of what she was seeing.

"Is that –"

"The Ouroboros."

"She had it all along," she whispered in disbelief.

Tentative fingers reached out to trace the symbol that could have saved her parents. Her skin tingled where she touched the gold, the relic's magic tangible even to her. She pulled her hand back as if burned and clasped it in her lap.

"We don't know that it would have made a difference," Ethan said softly.

The image of her parents stepping into the void flashed into her mind, stealing her breath. Even now she could remember the gut-wrenching pain in that moment of realisation; time hadn't dulled its sharp edge, and she doubted it would ever heal. It was that under-standing that brought clarity.

She looked up at Ethan and saw the conflicting emotions warring behind his brown eyes: anger, hurt, betrayal, pain, grief. They'd all experienced so much loss in such a short time, and none of them were really equipped to deal with it. Could she blame Lily for wanting the relic? It was obvious why she'd taken it. If Phoenix had a chance to bring back her loved ones, she'd grab it with both hands.

None of it mattered now. What was done was done.

"It needs to be destroyed," she said finally. "No one else can be allowed to use it."

He nodded and closed the box with a firm click, reminding her of the reason she'd come to find him.

She gave him a sad smile. "I don't have the box for the Ritual. It was burned in the fire."

His eyes searched her face, as if trying to understand what she was feeling. "We'll sort it out, don't worry. We'll make sure she finds Annabelle," he said eventually.

Tears burned at the back of her throat, but she swallowed them. If she let go now, she wasn't sure she'd ever stop. She needed to be strong if she was going to do what had to be done.

"If we can't find an alternative soon, I'm ending this, Ethan. I can't let anyone else die for something I could stop."

He jerked around to face her, his hands grasping her shoulders in a bruising grip. "No!" The one word was filled with command, but his eyes were desperate and pleading as he dropped his guard and let her see the fear and need hidden under the surface.

And that was her undoing.

His lips found hers, and she hesitated for only a second before she gave in to the firm pressure. The fire was instantaneous as it consumed her. She pressed herself closer, needing the heat of his body against hers. All the while terrified he'd pull away. More terrified he wouldn't.

Her body came alive with sensation, and for once, she let go of the doubt. When he pulled her back with him onto the bed, she didn't resist. She met his need with a hunger of her own, consequences be damned.

CHAPTER THIRTY-SIX

Darius stalked through the corridor of the Council headquarters, a mask of indifference hiding his deadly intent. Following the Council's decree to confine William, it was decided prudent to keep all Witnesses on site to save on the need for constant portalling. That didn't mesh with his plans, however, and he was damned if he was going to be grounded like a school child while Phoenix ruined centuries of hard work by getting herself killed.

Unfortunately, as much as the Council was full of idiots, they were still powerful idiots, and Diana's barrier spell wasn't one he'd be able to easily break through unnoticed. Which left only one option: he had to kill her.

A sense of anticipation increased his pace and helped to dull the rage he'd felt at their order. This was just another test on the path to claiming his rightful station. And truth be told, the witch had it coming to her. Hers was merely a token position on the Council, and the loss would have no great impact; her species was barely a step above humans anyway.

He headed further into the depths of the building, noting a slight downward slope to his trajectory as he moved silently over the marble floor. Each of the Council members had private high security chambers below ground level that were off limits to Witnesses, with only rare exceptions. For the duration of Il Maestro's reign on the Council, Darius had been one of those exceptions, and so he proceeded through the private quarters with a confidence that allowed him to blend into his surroundings.

He slowed when the sound of low voices from a nearby room reached him. The two voices he recognised immediately, but it was only when the conversation grew more heated that they spoke loud enough for the words to become clear.

"Tell us where they'll go," Vlad demanded. "If your loyalty truly lies with the Council, tell us where he'll take the hybrid."

The hybrid? The Council had Phoenix's location; did that mean Maj had failed?

There was a long silence before William responded. "He'll take her to Donegal, to the pack. It's the only thing that makes sense."

"Indeed."

"The pack will stand with him; that's why he'd go there. They won't let you kill her."

"Then they will be destroyed as well."

Vlad's response held no emotion, but Darius could almost feel the satisfaction oozing from him on the far side of the door. The rumbling growl from William said the werewolf could clearly feel it, too.

Both men stalked out of the room, only to come to an abrupt halt when they saw him. Vlad barely acknowledged his presence. Instead, he straightened his suit jacket and bid William farewell with a friendly smile that didn't quite reach his eyes, before continuing down the corridor. William, on the other hand, narrowed his gaze.

"It seems odd that mere days after we last spoke, the CLO have brought my relationship to the attention of the Council, don't you think?"

Darius inclined his head but met the man's gaze without flinching. "I appreciate how it must seem, but I assure you that information was held in good faith and passed my lips to none other than you. Unfortunately, it seems Vicktor is a little greyer on the matter of loyalty. With his considerable resources, it's actually surprising it took him this long to discover the connection."

William regarded him closely, his nose twitching subtly as he searched for a lie in the words. "The second Mist failed," he offered eventually.

Darius raised an eyebrow but said nothing.

"Needless to say, the Council is less than happy." His careful tone clearly implied he wasn't including himself in that statement. "Jannah will be sent, the others alongside him. She won't stand a chance. My cousin's pack won't be enough to protect her and my hands are tied."

The words hung heavy in the air, their implication clear. With that, William turned and disappeared down the corridor.

Well, that was a curious turn of events. Phoenix had managed to evade yet another Mist? She was proving more resourceful than he'd given her credit for.

It wouldn't matter though. Jannah was one of the most powerful Supes Darius had ever encountered; only the bonds of the Council, and his own misguided sense of morality, held him in check and prevented the Mist from being a terrifying force to reckon with. What a waste.

With a renewed urgency, he pulled out his mobile and stepped into the recently vacated office beside him. The phone rang once before being cut off by a robotic answering machine.

"Phoenix," he chastised. "There's really no need to avoid my calls when I'm trying to help you. It seems the Council have reached the limit of their patience. They are sending all three Mists, and they will destroy anyone that chooses to stand with you. My offer of protection still stands. The pack aren't strong enough to survive what you bring to their door, but I am. You have less than twenty-four hours; I suggest you make your decision quickly."

He hung up and immediately called the next number on his list: the Omega.

"Sean, I think it's time you take a little trip home. Just make sure you're not seen. I wouldn't want to have to kill your old pack."

With that task done, he strode out of the office and continued down the corridor. His fangs descended as he walked. He needed a stiff drink.

CHAPTER THIRTY-SEVEN

Phoenix kept her gaze firmly on the car ahead of her. Ethan and Nate were leading the way to the pack lands in Donegal and if she lost sight of them, there was every chance she and Abi would end up back in Dublin; her sense of direction was questionable at the best of times. It also helped to focus on something so mundane as the car bumper. The fact that car currently contained the dead body of a young girl was something she was trying hard to forget.

For a short time, she'd been able to block it all out – the warmth of Ethan's body chasing all thought away – but then she'd gotten Darius's voicemail, and reality had come rushing back so fast it had nearly given her a concussion. Warmth and comfort had been replaced by a chilling sense of fear, and awkward conversations with Ethan had been replaced with strategic group discussions.

The general consensus was that they needed to get to the safety of the pack as soon as possible. She couldn't argue with the logic, but a sickening sense of dread had set up camp in her stomach and she couldn't shake the certainty that she was bringing death to Ethan's home.

"Are you nervous?" Abi asked, after a long stretch of silence.

She clutched the steering wheel with sweaty palms. "I don't want anyone to get hurt for me."

"That's not what I meant."

Phoenix sighed. She knew exactly what her friend was asking; she just didn't want to think about it. Anyway, meeting Ethan's parents wasn't a big deal. What happened the night before had been a one-off. There was no need to make this into something bigger than it was.

"What if they blame me?" she blurted out, her mouth obviously not on the same wavelength as her head.

"For what?"

She waved vaguely. "For everything. Ethan being hurt, Lily and Annabelle getting killed. Oh, you know, the upcoming apocalypse."

Abi let out a snort of laughter. "Then they'd be idiots. I know there's a big bad prophecy trying to lay all this shit at your feet, but none of this is your fault. Besides, we both know that's not what you're really worried about."

Shrewd blue eyes met hers, and she squirmed. *Not a big deal,* she reminded herself again. *So what if they don't like me?*

Only, it was a big deal. She was going to the pack because of Cormac's offer of protection. Would he rescind that offer when he realised she'd tainted his son? Would she have to look his parents in the eye and face their disgust?

Brake lights glowed from the car ahead. Ethan took a sudden left turn and disappeared between a row of trees. She followed his lead, holding her breath as she swung into an opening barely wide enough for the car. The suspension shuddered and groaned as they bounced over rough terrain and trees engulfed them. With no other option, she continued up the winding trail.

After a couple of teeth-chattering minutes, they emerged from the forest to find themselves surrounded by lush green fields and rolling hills. An occasional dot of colour marked the landscape, hinting at civilisation buried within the untamed wilderness.

"Wow," Abi said on an exhale.

Phoenix stared open-mouthed, her attention split between following Ethan and gawking at the stunning scenery.

They rounded a bend and a small hill came into view. A glorious house composed equally of brick and glass sat at its peak, looking like something from those designer shows that she'd binge-watched with Abi last summer. Ahead of her, Ethan indicated and turned into a gravelled area at the bottom of the hill before killing the engine. She followed suit and climbed out of the car, still staring in awe at the house.

Ethan grinned and walked over to her. "You like?"

She just nodded, dumbfounded, and his grin widened. He grabbed her hand and tugged her up the path. "Come on. I've a few people I want you to meet."

Suddenly panicked, she turned back to look for Abi. When she spotted her friend lending support to Nate as he gently lifted Lily's body from the car, she sighed and straightened her shoulders, resigned to her fate. If Ethan noticed her reluctance, he didn't comment on it, even though the hand he held was clammy by the time they reached the house.

The front door flung open and a blur of wild brown hair was all Phoenix registered before a woman threw herself, mid-run, at Ethan, breaking the grip he had on her hand. She could hear him laughing as he picked the woman up – not an easy feat considering she was almost as tall as him – and swung her around.

A strange twinge of jealousy stabbed her in the gut, and she crossed her arms around her midsection. It was only when Ethan finally set the woman down and Phoenix got a proper look at her that relief loosened her arms. The face was more feminine, and had significantly less stubble, but the eyes were a mirror image of Ethan's as they assessed her shrewdly.

"Phoenix, this is my twin sister Sasha. Sash, this is Phoenix."

The other woman tilted her head and looked her up and down. Sasha's expression gave away nothing of her thoughts, so Phoenix did the only thing she could: she met her gaze head on, attempted a friendly smile, and offered her hand, not too sure whether it would be accepted or bitten off.

After a moment, a wide grin broke out on Sasha's face, making her look even more like Ethan, and she shook the offered hand. "Thanks for bringing my big bro home." She pulled him to her side for another hug.

Ethan rolled his eyes but gave her a tight squeeze. "I'm only four minutes older, Sash."

"Four of the most painful minutes of my life," came a voice behind them.

Phoenix turned to see a man and woman walking in their direction. Energy thrummed from them in waves. There was no doubt in her mind that she was about to meet Ethan's parents. She sucked in a breath and subtly wiped her hands on her trousers.

"Mo Faolán." The woman opened her arms and pulled Ethan into a loving embrace.

His mother's hair was long and wild like Sasha's, with only a smattering of grey visible through the rich auburn. At a glance, she could easily have been mistaken for Ethan's sister, if not for the light lines around her brown eyes as she smiled and a calm confidence earned only from life experience.

Ethan returned the embrace for a long moment before breaking away. "Mam, this is Phoenix. Phoenix, my mother, Fia."

Phoenix suddenly found herself enveloped in a hug. Not quite sure how to respond, she patted Fia awkwardly on the back. A small bubble of warmth settled in her chest at the unexpected gesture and she pulled away with a shy smile.

When she looked at Ethan once more, he was standing straighter and the gentle fondness he'd shown for his mother was now replaced with uncertainty as he faced his father. She held her breath, suddenly feeling uneasy.

"Dad –"

He was stopped in his tracks as his father closed the distance between them and grasped him in a firm embrace. They stayed like that for a moment, and then some manly clearing of throats ensued as the two separated with a slap on the shoulder.

The large open space seemed so much smaller to Phoenix as she took in the combined energy of both men. Ethan's father was a solid wall of muscle. His strong jaw and sombre grey eyes gave him a serious, unyielding air. Like Fia, threads of grey crept from the edges of his hairline and his skin was nicely weathered, but he wore his years well. She could easily imagine him leading the pack. Hell, she almost felt like bowing her head in supplication herself.

"Phoenix." Ethan turned to her. "This is Cormac, my father and Alpha of the Donegal pack."

She gave him what she hoped was a confident smile and held out her hand. He didn't accept it, just looked at her appraisingly. She bristled and squared her shoulders, never flinching from his gaze.

Eventually, he nodded. "You'll do."

He gave her a wink and cheeky smile before wrapping an arm around Fia's shoulders and turning back towards the house.

"Come on, you two. We have things to discuss."

Ethan followed his parents into the cosy sitting room that had been his favourite part of the house growing up. Phoenix trailed in after him, her head swivelling from side to side as she took in his family home. Her gasp made his chest expand with pride.

Floor to ceiling windows formed one corner of the room and revealed the most breath-taking views of the surrounding land. A stone fireplace covered another wall, and oversized grey sofas begging to be sprawled on filled the space. He managed to restrain himself as they all politely took a seat and faced each other.

"You have a beautiful home." Phoenix earned herself a glowing smile from Fia as she fidgeted beside him.

"Maybe one day you can explore it in less stressful circumstances," Cormac offered, before his steely gaze turned serious once more. "Now, tell me everything."

Ethan had already given him the headlines, but he went through it all again: what they knew of the prophecy, the assassination attempts by the Council, Darius's warning. He could feel the tension radiate from Phoenix with each detail.

"I'm sorry. I should never have come here," she blurted, jumping to her feet.

He grabbed her hand in an attempt to stop her from bolting, but it was his father who responded.

"It's my choice who I offer protection to, lass, and I do so freely." Cormac turned a weighted gaze to Ethan. "The pack, however, must also be free to choose. They'll stand with you, but it must be you that asks it of them. I won't do it for you."

He'd expected his father to say as much, but his stomach still tightened with the implication of the words. The thought of facing the pack after everything that had happened ... It would be so much easier to just leave and face the Mists alone, but that would be the coward's way out. He looked at Phoenix, the warmth of her hand seeping through his skin. He nodded.

No more running.

It didn't take long for the arrangements to be made, and within half an hour, the entire pack was gathered outside the house. He stood before them, at his father's side for the first time since he'd left – for the first time since Sean's death – and he felt the weight of every eye on him.

From the moment he was born, he'd been taught the responsibility of an Alpha, but only now did he truly understand it. Only now did he acknowledge the fear that responsibility brought, and the real reason he'd run away. He could feel the nervous energy thrumming from Phoenix as she stood behind him with Nate and Abi, and it was that alone that gave him the strength to stand tall and step forward.

"I've missed you all." He looked at the faces that had surrounded him since childhood, and his wolf sighed contently as the pack's energy wrapped itself around and through him. "My wolf has yearned to run with you again, but I denied it out of fear. I failed this pack by running away, and I failed Sean, our Omega, when he tried to help me. The thought of failing more of you terrifies me."

He let the admission hang in the air, waiting for them to turn from him or look away in disgust. They didn't.

"I've come to ask something very dangerous of you, and I know I don't deserve to. But there's something coming that's bigger than all of us, and if we don't find a way to face our fears now, many people will suffer. The Council is coming for this woman" – he pointed to Phoenix – "because of a prophecy she has no part in. One she's actively trying to stop. They want to keep this secret from the Lore and they're sending the Mists.

"It's likely they will kill anyone that tries to protect her, Supe or human alike. They've already tried, and failed, three times. I intend to see to it that they fail for a final time. And I'm asking you to stand with me. My family has pledged their protection, and you are free to make your own choice. But our strength comes from the pack. So I'm asking you, will you lend us your strength now?"

A heavy silence hung in the air and Ethan held completely still, his breath frozen in his chest.

"The Alpha said you killed the vamp that murdered Sean. Is that true?" A woman stepped forward through a break in the crowd and he immediately recognised the gentle features of Sean's mother.

He inclined his head. "I'm sorry I couldn't do it for you sooner, Sarah."

She nodded her acknowledgement and squared her shoulders, standing tall and sure of herself. "I will stand with you against the Council and in all future battles to come."

Low murmurs filled the crowd, and her words were echoed by male and female voices alike. One by one, the wolves of the Donegal pack bent to one knee around him, offering their pledge.

CHAPTER THIRTY-EIGHT

Phoenix bit her lip as she stared at the map that was rolled out over the marble kitchen table. The pack lands were substantial, with many of the wolves residing within the dotted boundary Cormac had marked. A large community building sat at the centre surrounded by woodlands, and they'd all agreed this was the best place to make their stand.

"And you're sure the Mists can't just appear wherever they like?" she asked, her stomach twisting into an uncomfortable knot.

Cormac gave her a grim smile. "As sure as I can be, lass. The entire boundary was warded by the local coven to prevent access to anyone we don't want in. But once they break the ward – and they will – there won't be any restriction on their magic."

Her palms turned sweaty, and she glanced at Ethan before letting her gaze rest on Abi, who stood against the wall listening intently to their every word.

"How do we keep everyone safe?"

"By doing the best we can." Fia gave her a compassionate smile from the far side of the table, but her eyes were hard, determined. "There are wolves monitoring the perimeter, and the rest of us will meet at the community centre to prepare. But first, I think there's something we need to do?"

Phoenix looked towards Nate. He'd been unusually quiet throughout the discussion and though he appeared to be listening, his lack of contribution worried her. He was the strategy guy; he should be in his element now, but he just seemed pensive and distant. Maybe once they conducted the Ritual, it would help him focus. They could all fall apart later – if they survived.

She nodded in response to Fia's question. "Do you have what we need?"

Ethan held up a small box wrapped with white rope. "Everything's set up and ready to go. I didn't know how much time we'd have and I wanted to make sure ..."

She reached out and squeezed his hand, swallowing past the lump in her throat as she prepared herself for yet another goodbye.

One by one, they filed out of the house and headed for the woods. Only Nate remained behind. They didn't have to walk far before they came to a small clearing illuminated by the sliver of moon that hung low in the sky. Lush grass dotted with beautiful white flowers covered the area. Energy filled the space, not quite as strong as the Cathedral, but similar.

"The clearing is blessed so that we can help pack members pass," Ethan said quietly, his shoulder brushing against hers as he came to a stop by her side.

Before she could answer, a rustle drew her attention back to the trees and Nate stepped into view with Lily cradled in his arms. He kept his head bowed, his messy hair obscuring his eyes as he moved to the centre and laid her down.

In her hands, he placed a faded photograph Phoenix had never seen before. Two smiling girls stared up at her from the picture, so full of life and potential that would never be realised. She balled her own hands into fists and focused on the sting of her nails digging into her palms.

Silently, Nate prepared the herbs, shaking his head when Ethan moved to help him. When he was done, he closed his eyes for a moment, then stepped back to join the rest of them in forming a circle around Lily. Wolves of all colours and sizes appeared in the shadows of the trees, and even without a connection to the pack,

Phoenix could feel their offer of strength as they stood together in solidarity.

The air grew heavy as Nate spoke the words that were now all too familiar to her. A soft lament, different than the keening she'd heard at the castle, or at any of the other Rituals, floated on the wind. The sound was gentle and filled with sorrow, but also hope. Warmth flooded her chest and energy danced over her skin like static electricity.

The words grew in power and the wind picked up in force, whipping her hair across her face. As Lily's body turned to dust on the wind, the wolves raised their heads to the sky and howled. Their song mingled with the lament only she could hear.

It was then that the large black wolf caught her eye. Its strange red eyes stared knowingly at her from across the clearing. There was something so familiar about those eyes, but the knowledge floated just out of her mind's reach.

She blinked, only to find a pale woman with long black hair and an unreadable expression where the wolf had been. They stared at each for what seemed like an eternity before the woman nodded and disappeared, replaced by a large black crow with those same familiar red eyes.

The lament ended and the wind calmed. The centre of the clearing was now empty of everything except the photograph. Phoenix stared at it in confusion, then looked back towards the crow, but that, too, was gone. A sense of calm settled over her, and somehow she knew that Lily was finally at peace.

"You okay?" Ethan asked quietly.

She sighed, her eyes doing one final sweep of their surroundings for any sign of the crow. "We've had to do far too many of these Rituals."

He smiled sadly. "Let's hope it's the last. Guess we should start getting everyone –"

All around her, the wolves froze.

She looked at Ethan and her breath caught. Even before Cormac said the words, she knew.

"They're here."

CHAPTER THIRTY-NINE

Ethan stared at Phoenix, memorising every line on her face. Her panicked eyes met his and he swore to himself then and there that she'd survive this, even if it meant giving his own life. With effort, he tore his gaze away and turned to his father.

"We need to get everyone to the community centre before they break the wards."

Cormac gave a short nod and set about issuing orders for the wolves to prepare. The telepathic link he held to the pack allowed him to give the rest of the wolves fair warning of what was to come.

Phoenix grabbed him by the arm. "Where's Nate? He's meant to protect Abi?"

Sure enough, when Ethan looked around, there was no sign of the shifter. The photograph that Nate had placed with Lily's body had also disappeared. He cursed under his breath.

"I can fight." Abi stood tall behind Phoenix, her head held high even as her voice trembled slightly. "Nate has been teaching me, and I have some protection charms Lily made me before ..."

He gave her a reassuring smile and squeezed Phoenix's shoulder. "I don't doubt that you'd give half the people here a run for their money, but let's get you back to the community centre first."

As if reading his mind, Sasha appeared at his side. "I can go with Abi. She can keep me safe."

She winked at the other girl, and he smiled gratefully at his sister for helping to ease the tension. In the back of his mind he could hear the buzz from the pack, and it was only with effort that he managed to block it out enough to focus. He could tell from the tightness in his father's posture that they didn't have much time left.

There were no explosions or flashes of light as the Mists worked against the wards. In fact, the night was eerily silent. But when Cormac went deathly still, he knew.

Moments later, a howl filled the night, only to be abruptly cut off.

"They're through," Fia whispered.

"Go!" Ethan ordered, shoving Sasha and Abi towards the trees.

All around him, wolves leapt into action, turning the clearing into a chaos of activity as everyone hurried to safety. Within seconds, only Cormac, Fia, and Phoenix remained with him.

"We need to buy them time." He looked at Phoenix and bit his tongue to hold back the order for her to leave; it was obvious from the stubborn set of her shoulders that she was staying whether he liked it or not.

"If we spread out along the perimeter, we can hold them off in the woods," Cormac said, his gaze distant as he mentally monitored the movements of the pack.

"Okay, dad and I will take the eastern side. You and Phoenix take the western side." He directed his instruction to Fia, allowing the plea to show in his eyes: keep her safe for me.

His mother grabbed him in a fierce hug, then pulled Phoenix into the trees with her, not giving him a chance to say anything further. A steely-eyed nod from his dad was the only acknowledgement before he, too, disappeared into the darkness.

Ethan stood alone in the clearing. He allowed himself only a second to focus his mind, then he was off, running through the woods to face death head on.

The screeches started moments later, shocking him to a halt. Birds, humans, animals, their cries echoed and faded like ghosts on the wind. The utter terror caused his every nerve ending to thrum.

They need help.

He swivelled his head, frantically trying to pinpoint the direction, but their pain and torment was everywhere.

Then his name, a cry for help. His own terror mirrored that of the screaming voices.

Phoenix.

He set off at a run again, crashing through the trees in a blind panic. But it didn't matter which way he turned; her calls always came from behind him, always out of reach.

Flashes of lightning hit the four corners of the compass and filled his vision with blotches of white light. He stumbled on blindly, his hands clawing at branches as they tangled around him

Ethan!

Cormac's voice broke through the fog in his mind, and instantly his wolf calmed. He slid to a stop with his hand on a large oak tree and forced his breathing to slow. He closed his eyes and let his wolf's instincts take over.

The cries for help stopped and the night fell silent except for the rustle of leaves in the gentle breeze. The illusion faded away, and he felt the tug in the centre of his chest as the pack link pulled him back to reality and grounded him.

"Impressive." Shayan's familiar voice drifted on the wind.

The hairs on the back of Ethan's neck stood to attention and a throbbing pain filled his chest. He turned in a slow circle, extending his claws as he did. He was going to make this hurt.

Shadows wove between the trees, teasing their way towards him only to retreat again. He stayed completely still and waited.

"I thought you'd be dead by now," the disembodied voice mused.

Memories bombarded Ethan: a fist plunging into his chest. Excruciating pain. Never-ending darkness. "I thought the Council would have killed you for your failure," he ground out.

A burst of lightning struck the tree next to him and he grinned. *Guess that hit a nerve.*

"We won't fail this time."

With that, the screeching came again, even louder than before. Ethan fell to his knees, hands over his ears as the piercing noise battered his ear drums. It was no use; the sound infiltrated his mind, growing so loud he was sure his head would explode.

He grabbed for the place deep in the core of his being that tethered him to the pack and bared his teeth. But it was the image of Phoenix that forced him back to his feet, one painstaking step at a time.

The shadows coalesced, swirling together to take the form of a man. Shayan stood before him, tanned skin now marred with healing burn patches. His golden eyes were expressionless despite the cocky smile on his face. He held his palms open and began to speak softly, the energy building around him.

Suddenly, he stopped. His head tilted as if listening to something in the distance.

Ethan's instincts roared to life and he fought to hear past the shrieking that filled his head. When Shayan turned a satisfied smile in his direction, he knew: Phoenix was near.

With a wink, the Mist disappeared and heavy fog descended over the forest.

He ran. The only clear thought in his mind to save her.

The fog was so thick he could barely see two feet in front of his face. With it came an unnatural silence that was almost louder than the previous screeching. He let his wolf guide him through the trees, trusting the instincts of the beast more than those of the man.

He tried desperately to reach his mother through the pack link, to warn her Shayan was coming, but it was as if the fog had coated him in a blanket and blocked him off from the outside world.

After what seemed like an eternity, he broke the treeline, only to find himself back in the clearing where they'd started. Shayan stood in the centre with Fia snarling at him on one side and Phoenix looking equally as feral on the other. Both were poised to attack, but the Mist appeared unconcerned.

Not breaking his stride, Ethan barrelled into Shayan from behind.

The Mist stumbled but quickly regained his footing. With a single word, Ethan was flung sideways against a tree.

Fia and Phoenix took that moment to attack, their movements lethal and beautiful to behold.

It gave him the split second he needed to climb to his feet, but before he could do anything to help, spidery tendrils of shadow slipped from the trees and combined to form a woman.

She wore similar robes to Shayan and her tanned skin was also mapped with raw, red burn marks, hers significantly fresher. Her golden eyes assessed him with cold calculation before she once more disappeared.

The first slash of the dagger came from his left, the gleaming blade aimed for his throat. He stumbled away and sliced upward with his claws, only to meet air.

Her next attack was lower and from the right, intent on gutting him. His quick side-step limited the damage to a superficial slice, but again she disappeared before he could retaliate. He growled in frustration.

Luck and instinct afforded him a minor win when she rematerialized in front of him just in time to meet the slash of his claws.

It didn't stop the dagger in her hand from plunging into his side, however. Or the solid roundhouse she sent to his knee, causing his leg to buckle with a sickening crunch.

Maj stood over him, seemingly oblivious to the blood soaking her chest, and raised her hands to the sky. Lightning brightened the night and coalesced into a ball of blue light surrounding her hands. She looked back at him, her golden eyes glowing, and he knew he was well and truly fucked.

The air crackled with building power and somewhere in the distance, he could hear Phoenix scream his name. He braced himself.

A loud growl came from the forest and before Maj could focus her energy, a huge white wolf rammed into her side. Teeth and claws attacked her unrelentingly, driving her back.

She flung the blue ball of light at the wolf, scorching its side and filling the air with the smell of burnt flesh. The wolf simply bared its teeth and leapt for her, its powerful jaws locking around her forearm in a vice grip.

Pain tightened Maj's features, but she didn't cry out. With what seemed like effort, she faded to shadow and dispersed on the heavy fog.

The wolf stood panting for a moment, then turned to look at him, blue eyes filled with an intelligence and familiarity that stopped his heart.

He'd only ever known one wolf to look like the one before him. That wolf was dead.

Ethan gritted his teeth and pushed up to standing, all of his weight on the right leg. Tentatively, he stretched out a hand, convinced what he was seeing had to be an illusion. But before he could reach the snow-white fur, the wolf turned and bolted into the forest.

The sounds of fighting filled his ears and everything pulled back into sharp focus. He turned back towards his mother and Phoenix just in time to see Cormac break through the trees on the far side of the clearing.

Shayan evaded a strike from Fia and pivoted to take in the scene. Three wolves and one pissed off hybrid stood before him. Obviously not favouring the odds, he disappeared in a blink, leaving them all staring at each other warily.

CHAPTER FORTY

Phoenix was panting hard by the time they reached the edge of the forest. The heavy fog that pervaded the air made it difficult to breathe, and her lungs burned with each inhale. As soon as they stepped from the trees, however, the fog disappeared, leaving only a calm night sky and a pensive silence.

Miraculously, their path back to the community centre had been unimpeded, and she couldn't help the healthy dose of scepticism that kept adrenaline roaring through her veins. The four of them alone shouldn't have been sufficient to deter a follow-up attack from the Mists, especially not if all three were present.

The community centre lay before them in the middle of a field the size of a football pitch. That open space was all that stood between them and backup, and it was enough to make her want to piss her pants.

Ethan hobbled up beside her, and she got her first clear look at him without the fog blurring her vision. Blood coated his side, and he was purposely keeping his weight off his left leg. A vague expression of shock lingered on his unnaturally pale face even as his eyes scoured their surroundings for any sense of threat.

She let Fia and Cormac move ahead of them and offered him a

shoulder to lean on. Her concern only increased further when he took it without complaint.

"You okay?"

"I saw something in the forest ... I ..." He shook his head. "It doesn't matter. Let's just get through this."

They moved quickly. As soon as they were in sight of the community centre, the doors flung wide. Sasha and Abi urged them forward before slamming the doors closed. Locks clicked into place, and Phoenix blinked from the glare of the fluorescent lights.

She was dimly aware of Ethan's weight leaving her shoulders as Sasha slipped her arm around him and hurried away. Fia and Cormac conferred quietly between themselves before disappearing down the stark corridor towards the auditorium. Abi linked her arm and tugged her in the same direction, their footsteps echoing around them.

"What's the plan?"

Phoenix stopped at the entry to the auditorium, a heavy weariness settling in her heart. She grabbed Abi's hands in her own and looked her friend in the eye.

"The plan is I need you to hide." She shook her head to stop the protest that was forming on Abi's lips. "Please, I need you to do this for me. The Mists are coming, and when they get here, I won't be able to protect you."

"It's not your job to protect me."

"I'm the reason you're mixed up in this shit. So yes, it bloody well is." She choked back the fear that threatened to drown her and pleaded, "People are going to die tonight, Abi. Innocent people. I need you not to be one of them."

Worry, fear, and sadness clouded her friend's features as she bit her lip and nodded. The tears that settled along the rim of her blue eyes were stubbornly held back, and when Sasha returned indicating it was time to go, Abi didn't protest. She also didn't say goodbye.

With a shaky breath, Phoenix walked into the auditorium to join the rest of the wolves. Most were in full wolf form, their strongest and most resilient form, with only the higher-ranking werewolves staying human. Cormac and Fia were busy organising everyone, but she paid little attention; she already knew the plan. Instead, she looked around the large open space and memorised every person and wolf that stood in the room with her.

How many of them would die tonight? They were risking their lives to protect her. Without question. If she somehow managed to survive this night, they'd have her undying loyalty.

She felt the comforting warmth of Ethan's presence behind her even before his hand touched her lower back.

"You ready?"

She closed her eyes and took a deep breath, inhaling his familiar scent. The copper tang of blood mingled with the earthiness of the forest that lingered on his skin. His knee was now strapped for support and the worst of the blood had been cleaned from his side, but his face was still drawn and she knew in her heart he wasn't at full strength. An ache of sadness settled in her chest and she pushed it back resolutely. She reached out for his hand and nodded.

Suddenly, a loud explosion filled the night.

The ground shook beneath Phoenix's feet, and she grabbed Ethan's arm to steady herself. Plasterboard cracked from the ceiling and dust rained down on them, sending her into a coughing fit.

"Looks like they heard us," Ethan said with a wry grin.

Snarling wolves raced passed them, ready for the fight that awaited. With one last look at Ethan, she turned and followed.

The ground crumbled beneath her feet as she ran, and she only just managed to avoid a huge crevice that appeared out of nowhere, leaping over it to grasp the doorway for balance.

She expected to hear the sound of fighting from the night beyond, but the only thing that reached her was the angry growls of the wolves. Carefully, she slipped through the door to assess the scene.

The three Mists stood in the middle of the field, unmoving. Two of the three were painfully familiar to her; the third was a man she'd never seen before. He stood ahead of the other two, and an aura of immense power surrounded him as his black robes flowed around

451

his body. His palms were held out to the side and, even in the weighty dark of the night, she could see the glow from his golden eyes. She shivered.

All across the front of the building, the wolves formed a terrifying wall of teeth and claws. They snarled and strained, but seemed unable to move forward. She glanced in confusion at Ethan as he slipped through the door behind her. A raised eyebrow was his only response.

Crouching down, she moved forward only to hit an invisible barrier. A low growl from Ethan confirmed the same on his side: The Mists had them trapped.

Lightning struck the ground mere feet to her left. A yelp of pain was accompanied by the sickening stench of burnt flesh, and Ethan roared in fury.

"Fucking cowards. Face us with honour." He rammed his shoulder against the barrier, but it didn't budge. And neither did the Mists.

"How do we fight them if we can't reach them?" She looked around in panic, expecting another bolt of lightning at any second.

The ground beneath their feet rumbled and she widened her stance in an attempt to keep her balance. The air was heavy, charged with the promise of death; they were sitting ducks.

Ethan grabbed her shoulder and turned her to him. "You can reach them."

The look on his face was so full of unquestioning confidence. She didn't share his faith in her ability, but when his hand grasped hers, she took a deep breath and closed her eyes. She had to try.

Ethan began issuing orders to the wolves to get ready. She blocked it all out and focused only on the heat simmering in the centre of her chest, waiting to be called. Magic filled the air and she knew they were out of time. She held the image of the Mists in her mind and let go.

The burst of light was so bright that it seared itself into her eyelids, causing colours to dance like a bad trip in front of her eyes. For a moment, everything seemed to move in slow motion, almost like the aftermath of a bomb blast. Then the heat wave exploded outward.

The invisible barrier shattered, and the wolves surged forward.

Everything turned into a blur of movement. Wolves leapt through the air only to have their targets disappear on contact. The Mists blinked out of existence and reappeared a hundred strong. Their illusion was so powerful, it was impossible to tell apparitions from reality.

She searched for an opening that would allow her to make further use of her powers without hurting her allies, but it was complete chaos.

The night filled with the same screeching they'd heard in the forest. A number of the wolves fell to the ground, howling in pain, while even more turned on each other, unable to recognise friend from foe in their disorientated state.

The air shimmered to her right and Shayan materialised, his once cocky grin now a grimace of burn-tightened skin. Before he could move in her direction, Fia stepped between them, teeth bared and eyes blazing.

"You hurt my son."

She dived at him in a ferocious blur of slashing claws that made Phoenix's jaw drop. Ethan moved to help, but the air solidified in front of him to reveal Maj, holding the very same dagger that had killed Lily. He growled and lunged for her.

Once more, Phoenix tried to call on her power, but before she could, the third Mist stepped in front of her. She stood frozen to the spot as Jannah's golden eyes pulled her into their molten depths. Dimly, she knew she should be afraid; he was here to kill her.

"Don't worry. I'll make it a quick death for them," he promised solemnly.

A voice inside her head screamed for her to fight, but a heavy lethargy fell over her. Her limbs were leaden and her eyelids blinked closed. She forced them back open with effort.

"They don't deserve to die. *We* don't deserve to die."

He gave her a sad smile and raised his hand. A golden light flared in his palm. It called to her, beckoning her forward.

In a distant part of her mind, she heard Cormac shout her name. Then, suddenly, he was there. He shoved her sideways, breaking the hold Jannah had on her mind. The golden ball of energy that had been meant for her skimmed the side of his body, and he tumbled to the ground.

His roar of pain pulled her back to the scene around her, and she stared in horror. Wolves littered the field, bloody and wounded. Those still standing appeared to be battling a vast array of monsters that flitted in and out of existence; illusions, but no less deadly for being so.

So much blood. So much sacrifice.

Her heart wept and every cell in her body screamed for her to protect them. Time fractured in that moment, and when, out of the corner of her eye, she saw Ethan fall to his knees in front of Maj, something inside her shattered.

Rage flooded through her and her body started to shake as a fierce pressure built in her solar plexus. She dropped to her knees and placed her hands on the cold hard earth beneath her. She called to the sun, and it came.

Grass burst into flames and a ring of white-hot fire surrounded her. Jannah stood watching her on the far side, his eyes mirroring the flames back to her in an almost hypnotic way.

She focused as hard as she could, willing the fire to spread until it formed a barrier around the wolves closest to her. Many were caged in with the illusions they faced, but no further attack would reach them.

Still she pushed further, ignoring the skull-splitting headache that flared to life as she did. There were so many. She needed to protect them.

Through the flame, Jannah looked at her with something akin to respect. "I want you to know I take no pleasure in this."

Phoenix gritted her teeth as her vision turned black.

CHAPTER FORTY-ONE

The darkness surrounded Phoenix and threatened to drown her. She was dimly aware of Ethan yelling her name, and she clung to the sound of his voice like a lifeline. But she couldn't hold the power she'd created. Her energy faded and the flames winked out of existence, leaving only scorched earth.

Through her hazy vision, she saw Jannah raise his hands to the sky. His lips moved, forming the unintelligible words that she knew would seal her fate. With gritted teeth, she forced herself to her feet; if she was going to die, she'd bloody well do it standing, not cowering on the ground. She swayed unsteadily.

A blur of movement from the forest caught her attention, and a hysterical laugh bubbled up in her chest as she imagined she saw faces flitting among the shadows. Was this it? Had her mind finally cracked now that she faced the end?

The energy coming from Jannah was so powerful that it was getting difficult to breathe. It pressed against her sternum with a crushing force and she knew that when he let it go, nothing would remain. She closed her eyes and a single tear burned a path down her cheek. That one tear for everything that would never be.

She welcomed the pressure that enveloped her, let it merge with her essence, and she focused on one simple thought: I have to save them.

The realisation brought with it an instant calm. She let the heat build inside her until it felt like she might burn from the inside out. Jannah's power pushed back against it, trying to crush her. Her flames lapped hungrily at the edges of his power, ready to break free, ready to burn.

She would die tonight. But so would he.

Her eyes snapped open and she looked at the Mist. The image that reflected back at her from his golden pupils was full of fury and fire. The nod he gave her was one of acceptance.

She could hear shouts of confusion from all around her, but she had only one goal in mind now.

The power continued to grow inside her until sweat ran in rivulets down her spine. She took a step towards him, her head feeling like it might explode as his energy enveloped her. Then another step. He reached out a hand to her and she took it, surprised at the softness of his skin.

A blur of movement and a glint of gold were the only things that registered in her mind before Shade magically materialised beside Jannah with another man at his side. They flung a large chain-link sheet of gold over the Mist, and instantly the energy holding her weakened.

Strong arms wrapped around her waist and pulled her backwards. She landed in a heap on the ground. Ethan's "humph" in her ear snapped her out of the trance she'd been in.

The field was full of men and women she didn't recognise. She could tell by their signatures that they were vampires, but her mind struggled to make sense of much more than that.

Two large groups surrounded Shayan and Maj, Fia standing guard with one, and an injured Cormac with the other. Both Mists had similar sheets of gold chain covering them, and though their magic lingered in the air, she could see no sign of their illusions, and neither of them were struggling.

"I don't know how long the gold will hold them." The blonde vampire with Shade offered his hand to help her up from the ground.

The English accent took her by surprise and she eyed him warily. The vamp appeared to be in his forties, and his grey eyes were kind but serious. She'd never seen his face before, but for some reason she was certain he wasn't one of Darius's vamps. A quick glance around her found no familiar faces from her time living in the Dublin vampire lair. Who were these people?

Before taking the offered hand, she looked in askance to Shade. At his nod, she accepted the help and got, not so gracefully, to her feet. As she did, she reached back to pull Ethan up behind her.

He hissed, yanking his hand away and she glanced at him in surprise. It was only when she saw him gripping a raw red hand that she realised she'd burned him with her touch; the power of the sun still vibrating through her body.

A quick look to the blonde vampire revealed a similar burn on the hand he'd offered, yet his face showed no sign of anger or pain.

"Who are you?"

"My name is Lucas ... I'm your father's Sire."

She sucked in a breath, expecting any answer but that. What did she say to the man who had turned his back on her dad?

"And these ..." She gestured to the field where the other vampires were helping the injured wolves.

"Are your father's clan."

"Were!" She glared at him, daring him to contradict her. Her father hadn't spoken of his past much, but she knew the scars his banishment had left; they were a shadow forever lurking behind his loving gaze.

Lucas gave her a sad smile and nodded in acknowledgement of her words.

Shade cleared his throat. "Not to break up the family reunion, but we still have a situation to deal with."

As one, they turned to Jannah, who was watching them with a blank expression.

Phoenix took a shaky breath and wrapped her arms around her midsection. Ethan moved to her side and she flinched, afraid of burning him again. He nudged her with a playful grin and when his

457

skin didn't start to sizzle, he draped an arm over her shoulder, leaning on her for support.

"If we release them, they'll never stop hunting you," Lucas said softly.

The words chilled her, and she pressed closer to Ethan's side. "I'm not a killer."

"Neither are we when we have a choice." There was no pleading in Jannah's tone, simply truth.

She assessed the Mist for a moment, then moved towards him, ignoring Ethan's attempt to hold her back. "But you won't stop."

His golden eyes darkened with unspoken pain and he shook his head. "We're bound by our debt to the Council. So long as they control us, we have no choice."

Her eyes fell on the thick golden bands encasing his wrists and the clenched fists beneath. The thin golden chain-link sheet glinted in the moonlight; it had been enough to nullify the Mists' magic. What were those thick bands capable of?

Lucas stepped up beside her, his eyes flicking to the bands as well. "What if you had a choice?"

CHAPTER FORTY-TWO

The plan was simple, Lucas explained. Release the Mists from the threat of their golden bonds by using lead – gold's magical opposite – to weaken the structural integrity enough to break them. Phoenix listened, but the logic was lost on her.

If it was really that simple, why hadn't the Mists broken free long before now? She asked as much, directing her question to Jannah, who'd remained silent as Lucas spoke.

"The vampire is right. If the bonds can be broken, we'd be free of the Council control," the Mist answered, his expression grave. "The problem isn't the bonds, however; it's the spell protecting us from them. It is only our obedience that stops the spell from releasing, and once it does, the gold comes into contact with our skin."

His tone implied dire consequences, and Phoenix looked closely at him, suddenly aware that he'd barely moved at all since the chain-link had been thrown over him. If anything, his posture seemed to have withered, almost imperceptibly. A quick look at the other two Mists showed an even more obvious weakening. If that was the reaction to such a thin sheet of gold, what would the thick bands around their wrists do?

"How bad?" she asked, turning her attention back to him.

"A minute, maybe less before the gold drains our life force completely."

She sucked in a breath.

"It can be done. We just need to be quick." Lucas gave her a confident smile that made her stomach drop.

"How exactly are you going to combine the gold and lead?" She didn't want to know the answer, she really didn't.

"I'm not. You are."

She shook her head and backed away with her hands held up. "Oh no. No way. I'd burn them to a crisp."

He shrugged. "That's the chance they'll take." With a wave of his hand, two vampires appeared beside them with Cormac, Fia, and the other two Mists in tow. "The only question is whether or not you're willing to try."

Her jaw dropped; he was actually serious. This was insane. The three people standing in front of her had each tried to kill her. One had almost killed Ethan, and another had succeeded in killing Lily.

As if reading her thoughts, Maj met her gaze square on. "You would be within your rights to take this opportunity for vengeance. In your position, I'm not sure I would do anything else."

Phoenix looked into the eyes of the woman that had killed a young girl and saw a shadow of regret. She also saw something else: steel. The Mist would accept her fate with honour.

"You hesitated. Back at the castle. Why?"

A small smile lifted the corner of Maj's mouth, but it didn't reach her eyes. "I didn't relish the death of potential."

The cryptic words just caused her head to ache even more. She sighed wearily.

"I'm not a murderer, despite what the Council may have you believe. I won't kill you while you're unable to defend yourself."

A look of surprise flashed momentarily across the Mists' face, and she nodded in acknowledgement of the uneasy truce.

Beside her, Phoenix could feel the tension emanating from Ethan. His jaw clenched tight and his eyes blazed as he stared at the woman that had killed Lily. He put his hand on her lower back and spoke close to her ear. "You don't have to do this."

A large part of her wanted to grasp the offered out with both hands, but that was the cowardly part of her. That part of her wanted the Mists gone, and for this to be all over, but it wasn't that simple.

She stepped forward, fists clenched to stop her hands from trembling. "If I do this, I want your blood vow that you will never harm anyone here again."

Something dark and terrifying swirled in the depths of Jannah's golden eyes. "If you can free us from the Council's control, you will have more than that," he promised. "You will have our vow to stand at your side when the time comes."

She shivered and a strange fluttering filled her stomach.

And so it was agreed. Lucas placed two small pieces of lead in her hand, then produced a dagger and extracted the blood oath from Jannah.

The moment he uttered the oath, the spell protecting him from his bonds released and he fell to his knees with a pained cry.

Phoenix was so surprised by the reaction that she fumbled with the lead and dropped it on the ground. She scrambled to pick it up and turned to kneel before him. Sweat coated his paling skin and his face contracted in agony. The effort it took him to lift his wrists left her in no doubt that she was working on limited time.

With shaking hands, she raised the two pieces of lead until they were under his wrists. "Ready?"

She took his grunt as confirmation and closed her eyes. It didn't take much to heat the lead in her hands, and strangely, it didn't hurt. The scary part came when she had to control her energy enough not to barbecue the Mist on contact.

Slowly, she inched her hands upwards, her heart in her mouth as she closed the gap between the lead and the gold. There was no resistance, and the stench of crispy-fried flesh never came. She opened her eyes in surprise.

Jannah's wrists rested in her palms, and the bonds surrounding them were now a strange swirling mix of lead and gold. He raised his head and stared at them in awe. His golden eyes glowed and the air grew heavy with the weight of his magic.

The words he whispered were weak, but they danced across her

461

skin as if they had physical substance. His form shimmered in a soft golden glow, and his bonds cracked in half and fell to the ground with a loud thud.

There was no rejoicing, or even a show of emotion at his newfound freedom. He simply closed his eyes for a moment before turning to Maj and Shayan. "I'll help you block it as best I can."

So, two more blood oaths were taken, and two more Mists were free of their bonds. By the end, Jannah was significantly weakened from his attempts to shield his siblings from the gold while she worked. Shayan and Maj acted as support on either side of him, the fact he allowed such a show of weakness speaking volumes of the gold's potential for harm.

Shayan gave her an assessing look, no cockiness evident in his gaze now. "The Council won't stop. You know that, don't you?"

Nate's unexpected voice answered from behind her. "That's where I come in."

Ethan led Phoenix, Shade, and Nate back to his parent's house while the others stayed behind to tend to the wounded pack members. Still, adrenaline roared through his veins, unspent and in need of release. They had come so close to losing everything.

"Where the hell have you been?" he yelled at Nate as soon as the front door closed behind them.

The shifter held his laptop up defensively in front of him. "Let me show you before you eat me."

Ethan bared his teeth as Nate pushed past, but followed him to the kitchen nonetheless. Maps from their earlier planning were strewn across the large table, and half empty cups of tea sat waiting for their owner's return.

Nate placed the laptop on top of the maps, and his fingers danced over the keyboard. The screen went black for a second before green writing started scrolling along the bottom like a breaking news bulletin.

A few of the words in particular jumped out at Ethan: hybrid, Lore, prophecy, Council, murder.

"What am I looking at?"

Phoenix leaned past him for a closer look, and his frustration was forgotten as he watched her face scrunch in concentration. How close had he come to losing her tonight? His chest constricted at the thought.

"It took me longer than I hoped to hack into the Council's security network, which is why Shade went to get us more help." Nate held up a hand to stall any questions. "I only managed to get in just before the Ritual, and by then it was too late to tell you our plan. The feed you're looking at is currently the only thing running on their operating systems and can be broadcast worldwide on all forms of human media with the push of a button."

Beside Ethan, Phoenix gasped, mirroring his own surprise. "You're going to expose the Lore?"

Nate gave them his trademark cheeky grin – the first Ethan had seen in a while.

"Of course not. That would be suicide. We just need them to think we are."

The cogs were turning slowly in Ethan's head. His body still hadn't reached full strength after purging the poison, and the night's battle had left him physically and mentally exhausted. Nate's words just didn't make sense, no matter how much he concentrated.

"I'm lost," he admitted with a weary sigh.

"It was Lucas's idea." Shade's icy blue eyes watched him carefully. "The Council have been desperate to keep the rest of the Lore in the dark about the prophecy and Phoenix's existence. They'd shit kittens at the thought of humans finding out."

The mention of the mysterious blonde vampire caused Phoenix to stiffen, and Ethan bit back the multitude of questions running through his head. It wasn't that he was complaining about the intervention, but Shade and Nate sure as hell had some explaining to do later.

Nate produced a small black mobile that looked suspiciously like an old flip phone. "We just need you to call your dad's cousin and specify our terms."

The phone was shoved into his hand, a number already on the screen ready for him to dial. He looked up at Nate.

"Which are?"

In quick concise detail, it was all laid out. He chewed on the inside of his cheek as he listened and debated their options. Realistically, it wouldn't change anything in the long term; the prophecy still hung over their heads. But it would be nice not to have everyone trying to kill them while they figured it out. And they would figure it out. The alternative wasn't an option.

Unsurprisingly, William picked up on the first ring.

"What are you doing, Ethan?" The werewolf's familiar voice was tight with tension and the underlying warning; he wasn't alone.

"What we need to stay alive."

"You know the Council can't let you do this. The Mists will –"

"The Mists are no longer answering to the Council."

A long pause.

"If you expose her to the Lore, you'll just put her in more danger," William warned. "You know the Council won't be the only ones to believe her death is the answer."

Ethan barked out a laugh. "True. But we don't intend to just expose her to the Lore. We will be exposing the Lore to the humans. Then we'll all know what it's like to be in the firing line right alongside her."

He let the words, and their implications, sink in before continuing. "Our proposal is simple. The Council backs off and gives us time to stop the prophecy. I'm sure by now you've seen our I.T. capabilities. It will only take a push of a button for us to broadcast this internationally. And we *will* do it."

A low chuckle rumbled down the phone. "They're not going to like being given an ultimatum."

Ethan smiled. "Tough."

CHAPTER FORTY-THREE

A bone-deep weariness settled over Phoenix, and she let the conversation drone on around her as she slouched over the kitchen island. The Council had kindly agreed to a temporary stay of execution, for which she was oh so honoured. They'd also received word from Cormac that all injuries were being tended to, himself included.

Two dead and a dozen severely injured. It was better than they could have hoped for, but it still felt like too high a price.

As it turned out, the vampires had been the only reason she and the others had made it to the community centre in the first place. The sudden disappearance of the Mists in the forest had not been down to their impressive show of power, but rather an unexpected attack from Lucas and his clan. It had done little more than delay the final showdown, but it had been enough to allow events to play out as they had.

She couldn't think too much about that though; her feelings for the blonde vampire that sired her father were something she just didn't have the energy to examine at that moment.

When the front door opened an hour later, she jerked her head off the cool marble that had become her pillow. Her breath caught as Fia came into the kitchen, followed by Cormac, Sasha, and finally, Abi. A dizzying sense of relief overwhelmed her, and she leapt to her feet to pull her friend into a crushing embrace. Ethan had assured her that Abi was fine, but she couldn't help the sob that escaped her at seeing the evidence for herself. A part of her had truly believed she'd never see her friend again.

Teary laughter and slaps on the back all around proved she wasn't the only one feeling a little overwhelmed by their victory. Soon, they all retired to the cosy living room where a blazing fire provided hypnotic viewing, if not fully chasing away the pervasive chill. Fia busied herself making tea and laying out plates of meat and biscuits as everyone was brought up to speed.

"Eat up. You need to get your strength back." The order was directed at the entire room, but Fia's eyes fell on Phoenix and she gave a knowing smile.

As if by magic, Fia's words reminded her just how drained she was. Her limbs were leaden, and the warm spark that normally occupied the centre of her chest seemed weak and far away. The thought of sleeping for a week was more than appealing and she snuggled back into the large cushions behind her on the sofa.

"You okay?" Ethan dropped down beside her, his brown eyes filled with concern.

"Long night, I guess." Hell, he didn't look so hot himself.

An odd feeling, almost like bubbles popping, drew her hand to her stomach and she frowned.

"Let me get you something to eat," he offered.

She reached out a hand to stop him as he started to stand. "No, it's fine, I can –"

The room spun and her vision grew hazy. It lasted only a second and when everything came back into focus, she was aware of Ethan gripping her arm, a look of alarm on his face. Heat crept up her cheeks and she cringed. Maybe food wasn't such a bad idea; her blood sugar was obviously low.

Yet again showcasing a talent for mind reading, Fia appeared in front of her with a plate of food and a kind smile. "Here, this will help. It can take a lot out of you in the early stages."

Phoenix scrunched her brow in confusion, dimly wondering if

her brain had short-circuited at some point during the night. "The early stages of what?"

Fia simply nodded her head towards the hand she had resting protectively on her stomach. Beside her, Ethan's jaw dropped, while she tried in vain to unravel what had to be the world's most confusing math equation.

"She's pregnant?" The question was barely a whisper from Ethan's mouth.

His mother nodded. "Only just, but the spark of life is strong."

Awe and anger and fear passed over his face all in the blink of an eye. "Why didn't you say anything?"

Fia's smile turned sad. "It only mattered if we survived. I couldn't take the chance that it would cloud your judgement in the fight."

Gripping terror clenched Phoenix's gut, and she wrapped her arms around her stomach. A child? How?

Of course, she knew how it physically happened; she could even now remember the feel of Ethan's body against hers as he held her close. But it didn't make sense. How could she have a baby? She'd barely survived the night, let alone the last couple of months. How could she be responsible for another living thing, never mind a defenceless baby?

Her legs were shaky under her as she stood up in a daze and muttered an excuse about needing to go to the bathroom – that was what pregnant women did, wasn't it?

She was vaguely aware of Ethan reaching out a hand towards her, and Fia quietly telling him to let her go. A sliver of guilt joined the fear twisting her gut, but she pushed it back and stumbled out of the room in need of air and a minute alone to think. She wandered aimlessly down the hall until she came to the staircase, then slumped down onto the bottom step.

"Phoenix?"

Abi's hesitant voice drew her attention from her knees to find worried blue eyes watching her. She opened her mouth to tell her friend everything was fine, then closed it again. When Abi motioned for her to scooch over on the stairs, she did, and they sat together in silence.

467

Eventually, she managed in a small voice, "I'm pregnant."

Abi's jaw dropped and her eyes widened in shock. Then her face morphed into a wide grin and she crouched down in front of Phoenix, taking both hands in hers.

"A baby?"

Phoenix nodded numbly. She'd been trying to make sense of the word ever since Fia's revelation. What did it even mean anyway? A baby. She had no context for it, no real life experience to equate it to, or no clue how she should be feeling.

"And you're not happy?" Abi asked, no judgement in her tone.

Tears pricked the back of her eyes and her stomach clenched. "How can I protect a baby, Abi? The Council won't let this go, no matter what they say. And then there's still the prophecy to deal with –"

"The prophecy." Abi jumped up suddenly, wringing her hands in excitement. "Oh my god, that's it! Don't you remember? It said, 'so long as she alone does stand.'"

Phoenix gawked at her friend, fully convinced she'd lost her mind.

Abi pulled her to her feet with a shake. "Don't you see? If you're having a baby, you won't be alone. You won't be the only hybrid."

CHAPTER FORTY-FOUR

When Phoenix finally got her head down, she slept for sixteen hours straight. She awoke feeling aches and pains in places she didn't even know she could hurt, with a nervous fluttering in her stomach that had nothing to do with the new life growing there.

After her talk with Abi, she'd pulled on her big girl pants and talked to Ethan. He'd agreed that Abi's theory had merit, and that thought alone had been the start of the tentative hope blossoming somewhere deep inside of her. But she kept that hope in check – they both did – with the unspoken understanding that they still had a long way to go if they were to have a chance of bringing their baby into this world.

Their baby. The words still didn't really make sense to her, not in any tangible form. She didn't dare let herself imagine either. And there would be no awkward "what are we to each other" conversations. Not yet. Not while the thread of hope was still so fragile.

It was with extreme effort that she pulled herself out of bed and into the shower. After, she went in search of Lucas.

She'd slept long enough that night was once again shrouding them in darkness, and she had no problem finding him sitting at the island in the kitchen, nursing a warm cup of tea and some of Fia's homemade biscuits. She pulled out a stool beside him and sat down.

"I never thanked you. If it wasn't for you and your vampires, we may not have survived to be sitting here now."

The look he gave her was sombre. "It was the least I could do."

A heavy silence hung between them as they both acknowledged the history that caused them to be strangers to each other.

"Why did you come?"

Lucas sighed and looked at the mug of tea cupped in his hands. "Your father was like a brother to me. When he broke Council edict ... I couldn't risk bringing their wrath down on my clan. I was bound to protect them, but I couldn't kill him either. No matter what our laws say."

"So, you banished him."

"So, I banished him. Every instinct in me told me it was wrong, but it was too late. I had no idea where Marcus had gone. It was only when Shade contacted me that –"

"Shade?" She jerked her head up in surprise.

"He came to me requesting my help. Demanding it, actually. I didn't know about you, that Marcus and Aria had had a child. I didn't even think such a thing was possible. Shade told me about the prophecy and the Council's vendetta. He asked me if I was finally willing to do the right thing." Lucas looked at her, his grey eyes haunted. "I failed your father. I won't fail you."

She bit her lip and nodded before hopping down from the stool. His apology had come too late for the person it was intended for, and it reminded her that she had her own apology to make. She left him lost in his memories and went to find Shade.

A quick check with Nate sent her to the large garage adjoining the house. She found him there, viciously punishing a weathered punch-bag. He stilled at her approach but didn't turn to look at her.

"I owe you an apology." She pulled at the sleeve of her top, a childish voice in the back of her mind sulkily pointing out that he'd been a dick to her, so it wasn't surprising she'd suspected him.

He shrugged.

"Lucas said you sought him out. Why?"

The question finally caused him to turn. His expression was unreadable as he met her gaze with his icy, blue eyes. "He loves you."

470

"Lucas?" She furrowed her brow in confusion.

His unreadable expression morphed into the irritated glare that was so much more familiar to her.

"Ethan. I don't want him to get hurt, so you need to stay alive." It was an order, not open to discussion or subject to emotion. He turned back to the punchbag, connecting with a solid left, right combo.

She stared at his back for a moment, confounded by the sullen vampire, but turned with a sigh to leave. His words stopped her in her tracks.

"The real fight is still to come, Phoenix. You'll need as many people on your side as possible if this world is to have a chance of surviving."

CHAPTER FORTY-FIVE

The vampire strained against his silver bonds. Foam dripped from his mouth as razor sharp fangs snapped at nothing. Crazed eyes turned fiery red and cast the metal walls of the sterile chamber in an eerie glow. A body lay slumped on the ground just out of reach; its lifeless eyes stared at the ceiling with a now permanent look of terror.

Darius walked a slow circle around their newest test subject, and a satisfied smile settled on his face as he stepped over the body without a glance. Everything was finally falling into place. Phoenix was alive, despite her continued stupidity, and for now, the Council posed no threat to his plans. It was time to take fate out of the equation.

His head of security stood quietly in front of the vampire, waiting for Darius to rejoin him before speaking.

"You were right," Erik confirmed. "We just needed to find the right kind of demon for the hosting to take. This one seems to be a good match for the vampire."

As Darius watched, shadows swirled behind the red fire of the vampire's eyes and the snarling quieted. The straining stopped and the crazed look turned into something altogether more terrifying. The vampire tilted its head and regarded them with curiosity. Darius's smile widened.

"Let's test the other species to confirm their matches. Once we know the right combinations, we can move to the next phase."

The door to the chamber opened and Darius turned to the white-haired wolf who stood reluctantly in the doorway.

"Ah, Sean. How was your trip home? You weren't seen, I hope."

The Omega's jaw tightened, but he didn't answer. Instead, he averted his gaze to take in the chained vampire and lifeless body. His hand clenched around the door handle, and it snapped off with a crack.

Darius raised an eyebrow.

"I need you to bring me one of the wolves. I'll leave the choice up to you, though I suggest you choose one that's easy to control. They can become very unpredictable when the demon takes hold."

BONUS SCENE: ETHAN AND THE PUPS

A gentle breeze ruffled Phoenix's red hair, the fresh aroma of Spring twining with the citrus hints of her shampoo. Abi walked in comfortable silence at her side as they wound their way through the forests that bordered the pack lands.

It hadn't taken much to twist her arm when Abi had suggested they take a walk. Though Phoenix was grateful to Ethan's parents for giving them all shelter here with the pack in Donegal, the cramped confines of the house had been grating on her more than usual that morning.

She knew she was being a cranky bitch, and she was grateful to her friend for tactfully offering a way to get away from everyone for a while. In truth, it was likely the pregnancy hormones getting to her, but she'd damn well rip out the throat of anyone who dared suggest that to her face.

Abi threw her a sideways glance and asked, "How are things between you and Ethan? I can't imagine things have been easy for you both."

Phoenix snorted. That was an understatement.

She sighed. "I honestly don't know. He's going out of his way to make sure I'm okay, and we said we weren't going to put any pressure on things. It's just a bit of a weird situation. And with everyone staying in the house, we haven't really had any time to ourselves to figure it out.

"Living with his parents is probably a bit of a buzz kill for any potential romance, all right."

Phoenix laughed and shook her head. "Don't get me wrong, Cormac and Fia are amazing, but yeah, they are still his parents. It's a bit awkward."

"And like it or not, the baby puts a lot of pressure on things too. Like, you shag once to check out the merchandise, and bam, suddenly you're tied together for life."

Her stomach did a little flip flop. Trust Abi to lay it out in black and white!

Life could be a very long sentence when you were immortal. Sure, there was an attraction between her and Ethan, and she definitely cared about him, but what if things didn't work out between them?

And to make it worse, they had now officially broken Council edict. They had stepped right into her parents' footsteps and broken the Lore's most solemn law: no inter-species relations.

Phoenix remembered all too well how much it had hurt her parents to be banished by their respective families and turned into pariah's simply for loving each other. Her father's vampire Sire might have seen sense eventually, but not before it had caused her parents a lifetime of pain. Her mother's family ... well, who knew?

Ethan's pack meant the world to him. So far, no one had voiced an opinion on what her pregnancy might mean for the pack, or his place in it, but she knew it would break something in him if they were forced to banish him. Or worse.

"It's definitely complicated," she muttered, as much to herself as in acknowledgement of Abi's comment.

As they approached the edge of the forest, laughter drifted towards them from the distance. They stepped from the shadowy umbrella of the trees and emerged in the large open field that bordered Ethan's family home.

A childish giggle was followed by a mock roar, and Phoenix spotted Ethan and his twin sister, Sasha, chasing two smaller figures across the lush green grass. She smiled, recognising Lucy and Jake, the pack's youngest members.

At only six years of age, the twin werewolf pups were full of energy. And based on the stories she'd been told, they had a healthy appetite for mischief.

Though they were now in human form, their animal nature was clear in their movements as Lucy pivoted, and pounced on Ethan. He fell to the ground with her, rolling over and pretending to play dead. That sent the girl into another burst of giggles.

Not to be left out, Sasha and Jake halted their own chase and looked at each other. Sasha nodded towards Ethan's prone body and Jake gave her a wicked grin. They both dived on him.

Abi laughed as she observed the four wolves and something warm and fuzzy nudged its way into Phoenix's chest. Her hand unconsciously found its way to her belly.

"He's always been good with the pups. They both have."

Abi yelped at the sudden sound of Fia's voice from behind them.

Phoenix bit back her smile; she'd sensed the Fia's supernatural signature as she'd approached, but even she'd been impressed at how quietly the werewolf moved.

"Goddamn ninja Supes." Abi crossed her arms and glared at them both.

Fia's brown eyes sparkled with barely restrained laughter, but she put placating hand on Abi's shoulder. "Sorry, I promise to make more noise next time."

Abi shook her head, her lips twitching into a smile; it was hard for anyone to stay mad at Ethan's mother. "I'm going to help the pups torture Ethan. I'll catch you both later."

Phoenix watched as her friend ran to join in the playful hunt, feeling suddenly self-conscious as Fia moved to her side.

"Looking at the pups always reminds me of when my two were small." Fia's tone was wistful as she watched the scene with a gentle smile. "It's hard to believe how quickly the time has passed."

"I didn't grow up around kids," Phoenix admitted. "I can't really imagine what it'll be like ... I'm not sure I'll know what to do." She glanced down at her still flat stomach and tried to imagine the life growing inside her.

"No one's ever really ready. You figure it out because you have no choice." Fia wrapped an arm around her shoulders and tugged her in close. "And you won't be alone."

A burning sensation tightened Phoenix's throat. She turned her face to look at Fia, but all she found in the other woman's expression was a gentle surety. No disgust or worry. Just acceptance.

Could it really be that easy? Could she and Ethan have what her parents never did – a life of love surrounded by their friends and family? She didn't know, she just knew she wanted it with every part of her being.

<<<<>>>>

MIDNIGHT MOON

ETHAN'S PREQUEL

CHAPTER ONE

"I'm sure you'll agree that the apartment boasts a rather impressive view of the city. You'd be hard—pressed to find –"

"I'll take it." Ethan stopped the pretty brunette estate agent in her tracks. He didn't need the sales pitch. He'd already made up his mind.

The converted warehouse was just what he was looking for. Nestled in the heart of the Dublin docklands, the location provided easy access to the city while still affording him some solitude. A panoramic window ran the length of the building, accounting for the estate agent's key selling point. Somehow it managed to frame the concrete skyline in a way that made it appear beautiful rather than cold and harsh. The lower level was a blank slate and came complete with heavy duty metal beam supports; he already had the reinforced gym planned in his head. Best of all, the apartment came fully furnished to save him the need to decorate.

"Brilliant, I'll get the paperwork ..." Lisa, the estate agent continued on. Her enthusiasm hadn't waned in the slightest, even now that she'd gotten the sale.

Ethan stared out the window. So, this was it. His very own bachelor pad. He should have felt excited to be finally doing something for himself, but his wolf remained silent.

"So, I take it you'll be sticking around Dublin?" She held out a stack of forms for him to sign, a glint of curiosity in her brown eyes.

He shook himself out of his melancholy and accepted the pile with a grin. "I guess so."

"It's a big change from Donegal?" His eyebrows raised in surprise and she blushed. "I'm good with accents."

The reminder of home drew his eye once more to the city skyline. It was a far cry from the lush green mountains that surrounded the pack lands. But that was the point, wasn't it? Somewhere new. Somewhere he could find his own path.

An awkward silence filled the space between them, and he suddenly realised that Lisa was still waiting for an answer to her original question. "I just fancied something different."

"I get that." She smiled and her face lit up.

For the first time, Ethan took a proper look at her. The layers of make-up she'd caked onto her face aged her at least five years and masked her natural beauty, but her energy was infectious and her easy-going air was appealing.

"Myself and a few friends hit the clubs in town most Fridays after work," she continued. "Why don't you join us? It's important to start a new adventure on the right foot, and I wouldn't be doing my job if I didn't help you get acquainted with the nightlife."

His eyes widened. That was some after-sales service.

The buzzing of his phone saved him from answering immediately. With an apologetic smile, he moved out of earshot, pulling the phone from his pocket. His father's name flashed up at him from the screen and he hesitated, finger hovering over the answer button.

It didn't take psychic powers to know what his father was calling for. In fact, at this stage he could probably relay the entire conversation even before a word was spoken:

"When are you coming home?"

"Not for a while, Dad."

"The pack needs you here."

From the moment he'd left home, it had been nothing but barely restrained arguments any time they talked. His Alpha just didn't understand. Sure, for most wolves the loss of connection to their pack would drive them crazy. But one benefit to being next in line for Alpha meant Ethan was strong enough to handle it with his sanity intact. In many ways, it was even a relief.

His father's repeated reminders of how much the pack needed him only made him more determined to stay away. He sure as hell wasn't going to admit to his father that he was lonely, or that his wolf missed home.

After a minute of persistent buzzing, the phone fell silent, saving him the decision on whether or not to answer. A mild sense of guilt niggled at him, but he pushed it back and shoved the phone into his pocket with a sigh. When he turned back, Lisa was waiting for him by the door. He gave a final glance around him and followed her out of the apartment.

She left him to his thoughts as they took the elevator back down to street level and she locked up behind them. "I should have the rest of the paperwork by the end of the week and the office will contact you to collect the keys." She held out a crisp white business card with a number scrawled on the back. "My mobile number is on this if you decide to take me up on my offer."

Ethan took the card from her outstretched hand and glanced at the number. When he looked back up to thank her for her help with the apartment, she was already sashaying towards her car without waiting for a response.

CHAPTER TWO

Ethan scanned the packed club and grimaced. The music was thumping so loudly he was amazed his ears weren't bleeding, and while not opposed to the volume itself, the DJ's taste in music made the noise closer to torture than entertainment. He debated leaving; he had a nice big apartment waiting just for him. But he'd been staring at the same four walls all day, so he gritted his teeth and made a beeline for the bar instead.

It wasn't really a bad spot, he supposed. The decor was modern and his feet only stuck to the floor in the occasional spot as he walked. The clientele seemed to range from mid-twenties to early thirties, so at least he wasn't surrounded by teeny-boppers. That was about as far as his enthusiasm for the place extended though.

The crowd around the bar was three deep, and it took him a few minutes to nudge his way to the front. "A pint of Blue Moon," he shouted to the barman, not sure if the man was lip reading or could actually hear his request over the din.

A condescendingly raised eyebrow and a wave of hand towards the very unimaginative selection of beer was the only response.

He sighed. "Fine, I'll have a bottle of Miller please." He took the cool bottle offered by the barman, handed over a tenner and pushed away from the bar without waiting for his change.

The occasional supernatural signature caused his senses to tingle as he moved through the club. A glamoured fae here, a witch there. The bouncer on the door had been a shifter too - favouring a bear, or similar large animal if he had to guess - so he'd known he wasn't the only Supe in attendance. None of them seemed to give him a second glance, however, and he didn't expect any trouble with this many humans around; only a Supe with a death wish would be that stupid.

A lap of the club found him an empty stool at the edge of the dance floor. He looked out over the sea of gyrating bodies and a familiar face caught his eye. In the middle of the floor, head thrown back in laughter, Lisa, the estate agent, swayed in time to the music. Two other girls danced with her, and a guy that was spending more time gawking at her with lovesick puppy dog eyes than actually dancing.

He hadn't seen her in a couple of weeks, not since they'd finalised the paperwork and he collected his keys. She'd reminded him again of her offer, and he'd actually debated calling her once or twice to accept. But deep down he knew there was no point. Humans and werewolves just weren't a good match; she'd never want to play fetch with him during the full moon. How he'd managed to walk into the same club as her out of all the clubs in town he did not know.

Taking a large gulp from his beer, he stood up, resigned to calling it a night. This had been a bad idea anyway.

He wove through the growing sea of bodies and made his way towards the exit. A somewhat dishevelled blonde woman stumbled into him before he reached it. She gripped his arms and swayed as she gave him what was probably meant to be a sexy smile.

"You can't leave," she slurred. "You have to dance with me."

The sickeningly sweet smell of Red Bull hit him as she spoke, and Ethan cringed. He gently tried to pry her off, but he was no match for her determination, and his protests fell on deaf ears. Before he knew it, he found himself on the dance floor, his escape cut off by the blonde who had either proceeded to dance or have a seizure, he wasn't sure which.

"I'm sorry, I need to –"

"Ethan!" Lisa's enthusiastic cry was only just audible over the

485

music, and he spun around to find her standing behind him, a grin on her face.

"Lisa, hey. It's great to see you. I was just ..." He waved his hands vaguely, having absolutely no clue what he was "just".

Her brown eyes sparkled with amusement as she glanced at the blonde who was now wriggling up and down his back in a disturbing impression of a snake. "Need saving?"

His nod might have been a little over-eager, but he couldn't help the relieved sigh when she grabbed his hand and pulled him off the dance floor and safely behind the railing that separated it from the seating area.

"I'm pretty sure you owe me a drink for that," she said with a cheeky wink.

He laughed and shook his head. "It's the least I can do."

Two beers and some light conversation later and Ethan was surprised to realise he was actually enjoying himself. Lisa's easy-going chatter nicely made up for the fact that they had little in common, and he'd somehow managed to block out the DJ's musical torture.

Finishing the last of her drink, she gave him a reluctant smile. "I better get going. I made a mistake of booking a personal training session at stupid o'clock in the morning, and my trainer tells me that if I stay out too late, I'll turn into a pumpkin."

"Why don't I walk you to the taxi rank?" he offered, grabbing his jacket.

The crisp night air was a welcome change after the sweaty heat of the club, and it was a relief to his ears when the door of the club swung closed behind them. Temple Bar was in full swing with groups of men and women spilling out of the bars and onto the street. A group of cackling women passed them by, clinging to each other as they precariously navigated the cobblestones in high heels. He offered Lisa his arm as he watched the group, fearing that at least one of them would end up with a broken ankle before the night was out and he'd rather she not suffer the same fate.

As they neared the end of the road, a strange tugging sensation made Ethan falter. He rubbed the heel of his hand against the centre of his chest, but the feeling was deeper, less tangible. It pulled at that illusive spot that tied him to the pack, the spot that had been silent ever since he left Donegal.

"So, what made you change your mind about coming?" Lisa asked.

"Hmm?" He looked at her in confusion, belatedly realising she'd been speaking while he was distracted.

"The club. I figured when I didn't hear from you, you weren't interested in checking out the nightlife."

"Oh, I thought it'd be good to get out and see what Dublin has to offer," he murmured. More like he thought it would be easier to ignore the persistent phone calls from his father if he went out and left the phone at home.

She said something else, but the words didn't register with him because at that moment an icy breeze blew, carrying with it a scent he was all too familiar with: blood.

He inhaled deeply, trying to pinpoint the direction. The odour came to him again, stronger now that he was searching for it, and intertwined with the coppery tang was the acrid aroma of fear. His gaze fell on a darkened side street on the far side of the road.

"Earth to Ethan." Lisa pulled her arm from his and raised a quizzical eyebrow.

He looked at her, then back to the side street, torn. "Are you okay walking the rest of the way by yourself? I just remembered I left something back at the club."

Her face hardened for a split second before she nodded with a smile. "I'm a big girl, I can look out for myself." She didn't give him a chance to say anything further, just turned and continued on her way, her steps sure despite the obstacle course of cobblestones ahead of her.

A low growl of frustration bubbled up in his throat, but he swallowed it back. He watched for a second to make sure she didn't look back, then sprinted across the road, hoping he wasn't too late.

Before he even reached the shadowy side street, the signatures hit him. At least one werewolf and one vampire were present aside from him, but he didn't think the blood belonged to either. Care-

487

fully he edged his way along the wall of the building, crouching low.

A large industrial skip lay ahead of him, piled high with planks of wood and broken chairs. Muffled sounds came from beyond it, and from his crouched position he could see a pale arm lying on the ground at the far side of the skip.

He inched upwards, muscles tensed as he raised his head to see over the skip. Just as he cleared the edge, a body came tumbling through the air towards him and landed with a pained groan in the debris.

Ethan stared at the familiar white hair and angular jaw in shock. The blue eyes that blinked up at him were filled with amusement. "Oh, hey, Ethan. I was hoping I'd run into you."

The smell of Guinness hit Ethan as soon as he pushed open the door of the small side street pub. A band was set up in the far corner, still in full swing despite the late hour, and the patrons sung along to the familiar Irish rebel song with vigour. Rickety wooden stools and dated dark wood decor gave the place character, and he instantly felt more at home than he had in the club.

He waited until the barman handed over two perfectly poured pints of Guinness and he'd commandeered two free stools before turning to the wolf beside him. Sean's white hair had grown long since Ethan had last seen him. For some reason, that more than anything else, drove home just how much time had passed since they'd last spoken.

The Omega of the Donegal pack, and his childhood friend, took a long sip of his pint and waited patiently.

"What are you doing here?"

Sean raised an eyebrow, unphased by the abrupt question. "Can't I just want to catch up with a friend?"

Ethan stared the other wolf down, waiting. As usual, the Alpha influence that was his by birthright seemed to have little effect on the

Omega wolf, and Sean simply tapped his foot in time to the music. Ethan gritted his teeth.

"Did my father send you? How did you even know where I was?"

"Technically, I didn't. I happened to be in Dublin for a few days and I was hoping I might get lucky and bump into you, seeing as you're not answering your phone ..." Sean shrugged nonchalantly.

Ethan didn't buy it for a second. Sean's role in the pack was far too important for him to just go wandering off to Dublin on a whim. The Alpha may have been the force that led the pack, but it was the Omega's strength and innate calm that kept the pack civilised and in control of their animal instincts. Sean took that responsibility very seriously.

"How did you get mixed up with the vamp?" Opting for a change of subject, Ethan thought back to the altercation he'd inadvertently stumbled on. The vampire had made a swift exit once he realised the numbers had shifted out of his favour. His victim was thankfully okay; she'd sustained a concussion from a knock to the head when she fainted and had minor blood loss, but all things considered, she'd been lucky.

Even with the threat of repercussion from the Council, it wasn't unusual for the occasional vamp to break the law and find a less than willing donor. But something felt odd about this one, and Ethan couldn't quite put his finger on it.

A frown creased Sean's forehead. "I smelled the blood when I was walking past. It was strange." A shadow passed over his features as he echoed Ethan's thoughts. "The vamp's eyes, they were red. But he wasn't crazed. He was in control."

A bloodlust vamp that was in control of his actions? Ethan had never heard of such a thing. Once a vampire succumbed to bloodlust, they were little more than a monster driven by the all-consuming need for blood. There was no rational thinking, therefore no control.

They both fell silent, mulling the information over. Something pricked at the edge of Ethan's consciousness, an instinct, a subtle feeling that he should be worried. But at that moment he hadn't got the energy to really give it the consideration it deserved because he was still waiting for the other shoe to drop, and Sean to get to the real point of why he was here. A heavy weariness settled over him. He didn't want to have an argument, not tonight, and not with his friend.

Draining the end of his pint, he stood. "I'm going to call it a night. You got a place to stay?"

Sean's blue eyes saw straight through him, but the other wolf followed his lead and stood. "I'm at a hotel nearby."

They ventured back out to the chilly night and made their way to Sean's hotel in silence. When they reached the arched entryway that led to the hotel's reception, Sean turned to him.

"Will you meet me tomorrow for a midnight run? I hear there's a nice park not far from the city. It's been a long time since we ran together."

Ethan hesitated, but his wolf growled and pushed at its barriers. Against his better judgement, he nodded.

CHAPTER THREE

The moon was high overhead by the time Ethan reached the Phoenix Park the following night. Its power tingled across his skin like static electricity, making his wolf restless. Sean was already waiting for him at the main gate for the park, and he silently fell into step with Ethan as they turned away from the neon glow of the city.

Trees and open space replaced the concrete jungle, and the earthy smell of nature smothered the noxious exhaust fumes. It should have been peaceful, but it wasn't long before the silence started to grate on Ethan. So much hung unsaid in the air that even Sean's calming Omega energy was setting him on edge.

Finally, he bit the bullet and asked, "How are things back home?"

Sean glanced at him, but there was no change in his expression, no sign of the accusation that Ethan was expecting.

"Good. The pups are getting really grown up now. It's almost a full-time job keeping them out of trouble."

There was no need to clarify which pups he was talking about; the breeding rate among werewolves was so poor that, despite the size of the Donegal pack, there were only a handful of kids between them. The pups were cherished by all in the pack, and everyone played a role in helping to raise them. Keeping the young werewolves out of trouble wasn't an easy feat, and it would only get harder once they hit adolescence.

"Your mam is cooking a huge Christmas dinner for the pack," Sean continued. "I'm sure she'd love to see you."

The words caused a pang in Ethan's chest. He missed his mother's roast potatoes almost as much as he missed her. Anger swiftly followed the pang and he clenched his jaw. It wasn't a big deal if he was away for a single Christmas. Why should he have to feel guilty for it?

The subtle shock of the moon's energy grew sharper on his skin as his agitation weakened his control on his wolf.

"How long has it been?" Sean asked, not looking at him.

"How long has what been?"

The Omega simply stopped, raised an eyebrow and waited. They both knew he could feel the tension radiating from Ethan, and from his wolf.

"About a year."

Well, that got a reaction. Sean's jaw dropped and for a moment he did little more than gape his disbelief. "You haven't changed since you left the pack?"

The blue gaze was so intense that Ethan looked away and shoved his hands into his pockets. He kicked a stone in front of him on the path and sent it skittering across the ground. "It didn't feel right."

Though werewolves could change form at will, very few could resist the pull of the full moon. All except the strongest of wolves fell prey to their inner beast when that time of month came. The pain had been excruciating the first time Ethan fought his instincts, but as he moved further away from the Donegal, his link to the pack had grown weaker. The thought of feeling that lost connection in wolf form had been enough motivation for him to fight through the pain.

Sean resumed walking, saying nothing for a while as he chewed over the revelation. When he turned back to Ethan, there was a cheeky glint in his eye. "Fancy breaking your celibacy?"

Ethan's stride faltered. Sure, he'd agreed to a run, but the thought of changing suddenly seemed daunting.

"Now?"

"Why not?" Sean gestured to their surroundings. "There's plenty of tree coverage. Unless you're afraid …"

The familiar taunt from their childhood elicited a mock growl from Ethan. He shook his head. "You're crazy."

Sean backed towards the nearest tree line, a challenging smile on his face. "You know you want to."

And he was right. Ethan's wolf pressed against his mental restraints, pleading to be let free. The empty space in his chest had lessened with Sean's presence, and the close proximity to pack had strengthened his wolf's will. He wanted to run. He wanted to feel the air brush through his fur as his feet pounded over the earth. He wanted to feel free for just one night.

A glance around showed no one else nearby. Ethan leapt at Sean, playfully shoving the Omega aside as he raced towards the tree line. He'd barely cleared the first tree when coarse brown fur burst from his skin, muscle and bone contorting as his wolf was finally freed.

———

Ethan fell to the ground breathless, the cold light of the moon filtering through the canopy of leaves overhead. His muscles burned and his limbs were like jelly, but still the energy thrummed through him, making him feel exhilarated and alive.

A large white wolf flopped against a tree beside him, and Sean shifted back to human form, laughing. "Now that was fun."

They'd run for hours. Once Ethan let his wolf free, the need over-took him and he couldn't stop. Sean had happily kept pace as they raced through the shadowy cover of the trees, startling sleeping deer and sending birds squawking into the sky. Only when his beast was satiated did they slow.

Ethan's body burned like a furnace after the change, and the chill night air was blissful as it cooled his skin. He lay his head on a soft bed of moss and listened to the sounds of the night around him. The hum of traffic was still audible in the distance, but if he tried hard enough to block it out, he could almost pretend he was back home on the pack lands.

"I have to go back." Sean's quiet words broke through his blissful reverie, all traces of laughter gone from the Omega's voice. "The Alpha wants me home. I was hoping to stay longer, but he needs me with the pack."

Ethan shouldn't have been surprised. Sean's calming influence was pivotal to helping Cormac keep order in the pack, particularly this close to the full moon. The fact the Omega had left Donegal at all was unusual. Yet the words took the air from his chest, replacing it with a leaden weight.

"When?" He sat up and brushed the dirt from his arms, staring ahead at the trees.

"In the morning."

Less than twelve hours before the emptiness returned. The thought made Ethan feel sick. With Sean's appearance his connection to the pack had found strength again; he didn't know if he was strong enough to let it go a second time.

"You could come with me you know."

"I've just bought a place here."

Sean raised an eyebrow. "Rent it out. I hear all the cool kids have investment properties these days."

Ethan shook his head with a weary smile and stood. His friend made it sound so simple. But it wasn't. Not for him.

He held a hand out to help the other wolf to his feet and started walking back towards the tree line without a word. They continued that way as they left the Phoenix Park and made their way back into town: him lost in his own thoughts, Sean giving him the space he needed.

The city was quiet as they neared the Ha'penny Bridge, the streets empty of pedestrians and only the occasional car passing by. It was so quiet that when Ethan heard the sound of a baby's cry, he actually thought he was imagining things. At least until the coppery scent of blood reached his nose a second later. He froze as the helpless cry came again.

Beside him, Sean let a low growl, his eyes glowing blue. Adrenaline flooded Ethan's veins and he set off at a sprint, knowing the other wolf would follow.

Left down a darkened side street. A sharp turn right past graffitied shop fronts. The copper tang grew stronger and mingled with the acrid scent of urine and fear. He skidded around a final corner and ground to a halt as he came face to face with a scene from a nightmare.

A woman lay on the pavement, her throat torn and ragged. Blood trickled slowly from the wound, and a small pool stained the ground beneath her. But there wasn't nearly enough blood. Her lifeless eyes stared unblinking even as her hands reached forward, frozen in their final plea.

The plea fell on the deaf ears of the man holding her baby.

CHAPTER FOUR

Ethan's breath left him in a gasp. Sean skidded to a stop beside him with a low whine and they both held completely still, afraid to move. The man turned to them with a chilling smile. Fully extended fangs and a blood-smeared mouth completed the nightmare image, but it was the calm brown eyes that were the most terrifying of all.

"I'm afraid there's not quite enough to share." The vampire ran a fingernail down the baby's red, tear-stained cheek, and it struggled valiantly to escape his grasp. "You're welcome to my leftovers, however."

A menacing growl wrenched itself from Ethan's chest. Razor-sharp claws extended from both his hands without a second thought, and his muscles spasmed as he fought to hold himself in check. Sean placed a hand on his arm, lending some calming energy so that Ethan could reign in his control.

"Ah, ah." The vampire wagged a finger at them both, then grasped the baby's hand in his steel grip. He raised the tiny fingers to his mouth and grazed them with his fangs.

Deep, heartfelt cries rent the night, and Ethan's control almost shattered. The hand on his arm trembled and white fur burst through the skin.

Get the baby, he mentally ordered the Omega before pulling away.

Slowly he edged towards the vampire's right side, his movements careful but obvious enough to draw attention. The vampire cast only the briefest of glances in his direction before looking back to Sean with a curious glint in his eyes.

The vampire sniffed the air in a manner not dissimilar to a wolf. "Oh, now that's interesting," he murmured.

A spike of unease stabbed through Ethan but he pushed it back; this wasn't the time to decipher crazy. Without warning, he leapt, closing the gap between him and the other man in a single breath. Self-preservation won out over food, just like Ethan hoped, and the vampire released the baby.

Sean moved in a blur, catching the infant a bare millimetre before it hit the ground.

Ethan was fast, but a vamp always had a speed advantage over a werewolf. The vampire slipped past his first strike and retaliated with a solid uppercut that knocked the wind out of him.

The blows came so quickly that he struggled to block them all, let alone land any of his own. He gritted his teeth as another fist struck home; he just had to distract the vamp long enough for Sean to get the baby to safety.

Air brushed past his cheek as the next punch missed him by a hair's breadth and struck the wall of the building behind him. Spider web cracks rippled through the brickwork, and Ethan sucked in a breath, grateful his face hadn't been an inch further to the right.

He dived to the side in time to evade the next blow and drove his foot into the side of the other man's knee. The crunch was sickening, but still the vamp's maniacal grin didn't falter. Ethan had the distinct feeling he was being played with.

A glint of silver appeared in the vampire's hand a split second before he plunged a large serrated knife into Ethan's gut. Fire exploded through Ethan's body and his eyes lost focus.

The vampire's breath was cold against his skin. "Don't worry, I'll take care of your friend."

Fury overwhelmed the pain and somehow Ethan shoved the vampire away once more. The knife, however, remained firmly lodged, the silver poison seeping into his system. He clenched his teeth against the pain. There was no way he was letting this vile creature walk away. He grabbed the leather-wrapped handle of the knife and yanked it free with a roar of agony.

His legs buckled and his vision swam once more.

The vampire watched him in fascination and reached inside his jacket to produce another knife, this one as long as his forearm. He held the blade up, twisting it so that the moonlight glinted off the edge.

Ethan's muscles spasmed as his body tried to fight the silver poisoning, but still he urged himself forward, one painstaking step at a time. The vampire's grin widened and he held his arms open in welcome.

Suddenly, a huge white wolf leaped passed Ethan and collided with the vamp, sending him stumbling against the wall. Wolf and vampire tangled in a blur of limbs that made it impossible to tell who had the upper hand.

Sean's canine fangs locked onto the vamp's left arm, and at last, Ethan saw an opening.

Delving deep to gather his remaining strength, he lunged for the vampire's back. His arms locked around the thick throat in a chokehold and he clung on for all he was worth. If he could just break the neck, it would disable the vamp long enough for them to finish him.

Too late he remembered the long knife.

The vamp snapped his head back and his free hand swung in a downward arc, driving the blade into Ethan's leg. Ethan roared. His leg buckled and his hold on the vampire loosened. The silver of the blade combined with the fragments already in his system and his entire body turned to fire.

This time, the vamp did him the honour of removing the blade. He tore it free, and brought it up in a diagonal arc passed his body, ramming the bloody knife into the white wolf's chest.

The wolf released its grip on the vampire's arm with an agonised howl and fell to the ground. The air shimmered as fur receded and limbs contorted. In seconds, the wolf was gone, and Sean lay on the ground shivering. A circle of blood was growing gradually larger around the knife still lodged in the left side of his chest.

Ethan reached out a hand to Sean in disbelief. He urged his body forward with everything he had, but the silver poisoning had already taken hold. His muscles spasmed so violently they tore, and he fell to the ground, losing all control of his limbs.

Through fading vision, he watched the vampire lift Sean's limp body up. With a gloating smile in Ethan's direction, the vampire sank razor sharp fangs into the Omega's neck. Ethan's world went black.

CHAPTER FIVE

2 Months Later

Ethan slammed the scrawny frame of the drug dealer against the wall. He gritted his teeth in an effort to restrain himself. It would take so little to snap the head off the worthless piece of shit.

"Word on the street is you've been supplying fresh blood to some unsavoury characters. Fresh as in still breathing. You're going to tell me who your customer is."

Bloodshot eyes full of defiance and stupidity met his. "Fuck you, man."

Ethan growled close to his ear and pulled a large serrated hunting knife from the sheath inside his jacket. He was careful not to touch the blade himself; the memory of the silver was still fresh in his head, even two months after the wound in his abdomen had healed. He placed the knife flat against the man's jaw, allowing the razor edge to dig ever so slightly into the skin.

"Let's try this again. You can tell me who your customer is, and I let you live. Or, I kill you. Your choice."

The drug dealer squirmed to get away from the blade, but kept his mouth shut. Ethan sighed.

He really wouldn't lose sleep if he had to kill the dealer – the world would be a better place without him – but he was getting bloody tired of all the dead ends. Someone had to know the vamp that killed Sean. Someone had to know where his friend's body was.

His hand twitched, aching to take his frustration out on something tangible. It was only with extreme effort that he released his grip on the scrawny neck and stepped back. The dealer's eyes flicked to the right and the hair on Ethan's neck stood on end as a vamp signature hit him. He turned around to find not one but three vampires blocking the entrance to the alley.

All three looked like they stepped off a production line for Gangsters R'Us, with their muscled frames clothed in black, shaved heads, and menacing snarls to complete the look. Their eyes glowed the deep red of bloodlust in the dim light, and their fangs were clearly visible.

The drug dealer took that as his cue to leave and scurried past Ethan. With only one way out of the alley, he obviously expected to receive free passage from the vamps.

As he neared, they moved to the side, opening a path for him. But just as he passed them, the vampire closest grabbed him, and in a single breath, tore out his jugular. Blood coated his mouth and he let it drip down his chin as he dropped the limp body to the ground.

Okay, that's new. Never before had Ethan seen a bloodlust vampire willingly relinquish a fresh body – or a rotten one for that matter. He'd also never seen one work as a team. Crazy didn't tend to play well with others.

Three against one weren't great odds, but no matter; he had some frustration he needed to work out, and these guys would do just fine. He waited for the vampires to move further into the alley, adrenaline roaring through his veins. *That's it, just a little closer.*

The vamp with the blood-stained mouth gave him a rabid grin and cracked his neck. Ethan grinned back just as feral and adjusted his grip on the hunting knife in his hand.

As soon as the trio got within ten feet of him, he moved. Claws extended on his free hand and he struck in a fury of slashing blows. The silver blade of his knife struck home, eliciting inhuman screeches from the vampires. The claws tore through flesh like tissue paper.

In seconds, blood coated the walls of the alley; some of it his. Still the vamps kept coming.

He was no match for their speed, but they were no match for his rage. For two months it had been building inside him, twisting and swelling, demanding a release. Well, he was going to give it its release. And he was going to get some answers.

A single slash of the silver blade left a smiling gash across the neck of one vampire. *Two more to go.*

His next strike came from low down, ramming the knife under the ribcage of vamp number two. The blade met resistance for only a fraction of a second before it pierced the heart.

The remaining vampire snarled and lunged for him. He twisted his body to the side and flung the vampire against the wall. He grabbed him on the rebound and smashed him back into the wall again and again.

Cracks formed in the brickwork, and blood poured from the vampire's skull, but still Ethan didn't stop. Couldn't stop. He was dimly aware of a voice yelling. His own voice. "Where is he?" he demanded. "Tell me his name."

The vamp just laughed, a maniacal gurgling sound that only infuriated Ethan more.

His vision turned hazy and the wolf inside him roared, demanding retribution. But this wasn't the vamp that had killed Sean, there would be no victory in his demise. Blood coated his shaking hands when he finally let go and stepped back.

"Tell your boss I'm coming for him."

He turned and walked from the alley, only dimly conscious of the worrying glances he received from passers-by as he returned to the neon glow of civilisation. His phone buzzed in his pocket but he ignored it; he wasn't ready to face his father. Not yet.

<<<<>>>>

1 MINUTE TO MIDNIGHT

CHAPTER ONE

Images flashed before Cassandra's eyes. They were the same images that had haunted her for the past millennium: red hair like flames, unnaturally green eyes, death. This time it was different, however. This time there was more.

A heartbeat. The rhythmic sound of hope.

An impatient clearing of the throat broke through the fog that clouded her mind, and the visions blurred, mixing with reality. The leather chair was rough beneath her. The lights in the room, while dim, caused her to wince. Her body felt raw, as if it had been scraped repeatedly with a razor blade, and the light chiffon of her dress grazed against skin which was now oversensitive and painful even to the gentlest touch. Her mind struggled to remember where she was. When she was.

Five pairs of eyes regarded her warily from across a large oak boardroom table. No, wait ... That wasn't right. There were only four pairs of eyes now. The witch was no longer among them. It was only her essence that Cassandra saw, the memory of her.

Diana's death hadn't been a surprise. She'd foreseen the witch's fate long before Diana had succumbed to her final breath, but Cassandra had borne the vision in silence. Even as the brutality of what she'd seen destroyed a little piece of her own soul, she'd known that it must come to pass. That was her curse: to see and to know.

Fate was often a cruel thing. Not by design, but out of necessity. One suffered so that others may live, and one lived so that many may suffer. Millions of threads weaving together. She'd learned long ago the cost of intervening in even the smallest of those threads. She'd learned to endure the visions in silence until, after more than two thousand years, she hardly knew what was real any longer.

Yet here she was, sitting in front of the Council once more. Because this was bigger than her, bigger than them all. The very existence of her people was at their mercy, and she could only pray that they'd make the right decisions.

"What have you seen?" Méabh sat back in her chair, shrewd gaze watching her closely. The cunning that lay behind those green eyes could easily have been overlooked in the shadow of the fae's sultry pout and luscious curves, but Cassandra saw it. She saw everything.

"Two hearts beat as one." The words left her mouth in a whisper, the rhythm of the heartbeat still thrumming through her. "From their love a new possibility is born."

William slammed his palms on the table and stood. "What the hell does that even mean?"

The werewolf's Scottish accent was thickened by his frustration, and tension rippled across his shoulders as he turned to pace the length of the boardroom. Cassandra knew that he, out of all the Council members, was the least likely to ever cause her harm, but still she shrank back, eyeing him like one might a wild animal.

"Cassandra." Kam's tone was soothing as he drew her attention to where he sat on the opposite side of the table. "Can you tell us exactly what you saw?"

She tilted her head and looked at the shifter with the kind eyes. His Asian features had always fascinated her. They brought to mind faraway lands and magical adventures. She never let herself dwell on such thoughts for long, however; they were not her adventures to have. And she never let herself be fooled by his kind eyes.

When her response wasn't immediately forthcoming, there was another impatient clearing of the throat from Vlad at the furthest end of the table. The vampire's face was fixed in a scowl, and though he was the picture of composure, she was almost certain his ridiculously shiny black shoe was tapping the floor impatiently beneath the table. Overcome by a sudden urge to stick her tongue out at him, Cassandra bit back the childish giggle that tried to slip past her lips. His scowl deepened.

"The girl has triggered the prophecy," she said, after taking a moment to compose herself. "But she also holds the means to stop it."

The images played before her eyes once more, and they, not the room she was in, became her reality. "A new life grows from their love. A chance to end the prophecy. The child must live. Or we all will die."

The images shattered, and she came back to the present with a gasp.

Méabh leaned forward, her red-tipped nails clutching the table like claws. "The child? You're saying the hybrid is pregnant?"

Cassandra stayed silent. She'd said too much already. Anything she said had the power to influence the future, and the balance was already precarious. She couldn't risk saying more; not now. So, she fixed her gaze firmly on the frosted glass that covered one entire wall of the room and pinched her lips together.

William's pacing ceased abruptly, and he glared at Vlad. "I guess it's a bloody good thing we didn't kill her then, isn't it!"

"The child is no guarantee. The Seer said it herself." Vlad waved a hand dismissively. "The hybrid's death ensures our safety."

"We gave our word to give them time."

"We also gave our word to protect our people. Or have you forgotten that?"

William growled low in his throat and leaned over the table towards Vlad. "Don't try to pretend it's 'our people' that you're worried about."

Vlad pushed back his chair and stood.

"Enough," Kam ordered quietly. Both wolf and vampire paused but didn't take their eyes from each other. "This hybrid child, will it prevent the Horsemen from returning to our plane of existence?"

Cassandra looked at him once more, debating how much she

could safely say. "If it survives, they will not be able to return in their true form."

"Well then, we need to ensure it does."

Kam turned to the figure sitting in the corner behind Cassandra, the one who had been observing their discussion in silence. She'd been aware of the man's presence but had purposely avoided looking in his direction. Every instinct told her that the man was important, that his presence here would change everything. She hadn't looked at him yet because there were some things even she didn't want to see.

"Vicktor," Kam addressed the man, "perhaps the Council Liaison Office may be able to act as a contact between the hybrid and the Council? It's important that we assist her in whatever manner we can, but I fear, given recent events, that she may be less than amenable to dealing with us directly."

The conversation faded into the background as Cassandra finally gave in to the compulsion that had been tugging at the deepest part of her mind. Slowly, she turned to look as the man in the neat grey suit stood and nodded.

An icy chill shot through her as the vision came. Flashes of red. Screams of agony. Fires hotter than the depths of hell. He would bring death to them all.

CHAPTER TWO

The nausea kicked in at the worst possible moment. Phoenix scrunched her eyes tight and tried to slowly breathe through it. The small ball of light she held in her hands flickered and winked out.

"Dammit." She bit back a scream of frustration. It had taken her half an hour to get that far. The makeshift target she'd been aiming for mocked her from where it stood, untouched, fifty feet away.

Her stomach lurched, and the image of a small boat on roiling seas came to mind. She hunkered down on the ground and let her head hang between her knees. Was this what it felt like to be hungover? Dammit, it would be easier if she just got sick already. But no, her body insisted on torturing her with relentless, unproductive nausea instead.

All around her the familiar sounds of fighting continued. The field that the Donegal pack used as their main training ground was huge. Thick, lush forests bordered it on all sides, and rich green grass covered the open space. Groups of werewolves dotted the field around her, some in their wolf shape, some in their human one. Cormac, their Alpha, yelled training drills at them, and they obeyed with lethal grace and efficiency.

To her left she could hear Sasha's hearty laugh as Abi unexpectedly flipped her. While Nate had started Abi's self-defence training,

Ethan's sister had taken it upon herself to help Phoenix's very human, very breakable best friend up her game. She was adamant that given guidance, Abi could be every bit as skilled as the Supes she was surrounded by, and Abi had taken to the training with an enthusiasm that made Phoenix proud.

On the other side of her, by the forest treeline, Lucas and Shade were deep in discussion. Shade had been spending quite a bit of time with her father's Sire ever since Lucas had arrived to save them all from almost certain death at the hands of the Council's assassins. Of course, the Mists didn't answer to the Council anymore, thanks to her. She wasn't quite sure who they answered to now. They'd disappeared after striking a tenuous truce with her, but not before making the ominous promise to return when they were needed.

With the sun high in the midday sky, Lucas and Shade kept close to the shadows provided by the trees. Lucas was old enough to withstand the sun, but Shade was still severely weakened by it. Every few minutes, she would hear a sharp hiss from their direction as Shade stepped into its bright rays and gritted his teeth while Lucas counted, providing intermittent instructions and encouragement as Shade worked to build his resistance.

It was the sounds of training that she focused on now, the familiar routine that had become her life in the three weeks since the Mist attack. At first it had been strange not having someone try to kill her anymore. The Council had agreed to a stay of execution – temporarily at least. And Darius, well, he needed her alive in order for his stupid prophecy to be fulfilled. The gold-gilded note he'd sent to her with a single red rose had reminded her as much.

After the last few months, it all seemed almost anticlimactic, but she took the reprieve while she could because she knew it wouldn't last.

A few slow breaths later, and the nausea subsided enough for her to rise to her feet. Ethan's mother, Fia, had assured her this was normal in the early stages of pregnancy, even more so with the accelerated growth of Supes. If that was the case, Phoenix couldn't help but wonder why women willingly signed themselves up for it.

A niggle of guilt immediately followed the thought, and she

placed her hand on her still-flat stomach. "Sorry, munchkin, I don't mean it, really."

She sighed and straightened her shoulders, focusing her attention on the wooden target. *Small ball of light, pinpoint control,* she reminded herself yet again.

The heat resting in the centre of her chest was strengthened by the sun on her bare arms. It was warm for March, and the cloudless sky was a welcome reprieve from the recent crazy weather that had varied from sudden snowstorms to sun showers in a single day. Given that she was half vampire and the pregnancy had brought with it an inconvenient aversion to blood or any food heavy in iron, the elemental fae half of her genetics was having to do a lot of heavy lifting to make up for the shortfall in sustenance. The sunny day was a much needed chance to replenish her energy.

Focusing her thoughts, she directed the heat into her arms and down to her open palms, cupped together in front of her. The spark of light was hesitant at first, her power confused by the willing barrier she placed on it. Sure, she could blast the target with a huge ball of light in the blink of an eye, but that would only get her so far. She needed to start learning real control of her fae powers instead of just blowing shit up and blinding everyone around her.

Gently, Phoenix urged the spark of light to grow, mesmerised by the tiny ball of light that radiated the sun's heat back up at her. It was getting easier to draw on the power of the sun, the connection as natural to her as breathing once she'd finally embraced it. She smiled. She could do this; she could be a force to be reckoned with, even if she had to stop to retch every once in a while.

She coaxed the light to grow until it was almost the size of a tennis ball. It began to emit a tremendous amount of heat as she focused the energy into the small space. She raised her eyes and zeroed in on her target.

Head? No, that was too adventurous to start with. A larger body part, maybe. The chest? That was doable, wasn't it? She just ... needed ... to ... concentrate ...

The image of the ball striking the wooden figure dead centre held in her mind, she released the power. An ear-splitting *BOOM* sounded, and she was flung backwards, landing with a heavy thud on the ground.

The field around her grew completely silent. Phoenix shook her head in confusion and looked at the target. Only it wasn't there. In its place was a muddy crater in the ground where the target had once been.

The front door flung open as Ethan stepped out of the kitchen and into the hallway, steaming cup of tea in hand. Phoenix stomped into his parents' house, her vibrant red hair in disarray, dirt on her clothes, and her shoulders tense. He froze, gaping at her. "What –"

She cut off his question with a warning glare and stormed up the stairs without a word. A couple of leaves fell from her top as she went, and Ethan looked from the stairs to the front door and back again. What the hell had happened at training?

He moved to follow her but hesitated with his foot on the first step as he remembered the look on her face. Her mood had been rather unpredictable after training sessions recently. The battle with the Mists had taken a lot out of her, and for a time she'd worried that she had burned out her fae powers entirely. He'd tried pointing out that her body was under a lot of pressure, what with the pregnancy and all that, but his suggestion that she maybe take it easy for a while had been met with a snarl that would rival any wolf in his pack.

She hadn't seemed injured. Maybe she wanted to be alone?

Before he could make a decision on whether or not to check on her, Nate appeared in the hallway, eyes glued to the tablet in his hand. "You got a minute?"

Ethan gave a final glance at the empty staircase and sighed, following Nate into the living room. A low fire simmered in the stone fireplace even with the sun streaming through the large picture windows that covered one wall of the room. He placed his cup of tea on one of the small oak side tables and settled into the oversized sofa facing the window and the view of the rolling hills that made up the pack lands.

Nate sat down beside him, still distracted by whatever was on the screen. Ethan couldn't help but notice the dark circles under the young shifter's amber eyes, and the unkempt appearance of his clothes. Ever since Lily's death a few weeks prior, Nate's usual cheeky sparkle had been missing. It was understandable given Nate's feelings for Lily, yet Ethan couldn't help but worry that he wasn't coping well with the loss.

"What did you want to talk to me about?"

Nate flipped the tablet around to give him a clear view of the screen. Ethan frowned.

"What the hell is that?" He squinted at what looked like a rough sketch of a vaguely human shape composed almost entirely of writhing insects.

"Greed. At least the only visual depiction I've been able to find of him. Unlikely to be his true form, of course." Nate flicked to another image that looked disturbingly like a person devouring his own flesh. "My research suggests he's the lowest ranking of the Horsemen, but still one scary motherfucker. Anyone he touches is consumed by an insatiable hunger that ultimately leads to –" He waved a hand at the screen with a grimace. "Well, you can see for yourself."

Ethan shuddered, unable to look away from the images. "What about the other three Horsemen?"

"All I've managed to find on Envy are the articles collating the aftermath: an unprecedented increase in child abductions, people murdering their next-door neighbours for their possessions, whole communities wiping each other out to gain access to their resources. It doesn't make for good bedtime reading. I'm drawing a pretty big blank with Fear and Hatred."

Ethan blew out a slow breath and tried to ignore the growing knot of unease twisting around his gut. "Makes sense. It's been millennia since the Horsemen were free to wreak their destruction here. If the stories are to be believed, survivors were a rarity wherever they went so there wouldn't have been anyone to pass on the information about them."

"The very first Council were charged with banishing them and creating the barrier. Surely they must have more information than this. Can't your dad contact William? I've gotten as much as I can from the online archives, but maybe the Council have physical records or something. At the very least we're going to need details of the banishment spell."

A heavy weight settled in Ethan's chest at the mention of the Council and his father's cousin. Not too long ago he'd have gone straight to William himself without hesitation. But after everything that had happened in recent weeks, maybe Cormac had been right when he said William would put the Council before blood. Could they really take the risk of turning to him for help now?

"That'll have to be a last resort. Now that Phoenix has broken their edicts and is pregnant ... We can't take the chance that they'll come for her, even with the truce."

Something darkened in Nate's amber eyes and he nodded. Once more Ethan was struck by the strain that was visible on the young shifter's face. Not too long ago he'd seen a similar strain on Lily's face as she attempted to bury the grief of her sister's death. That hadn't ended well.

"Nate, do me a favour?" Ethan stood, an inexplicable sense of exhaustion settling over him. "Take a break from this. Clear your head and do something to blow off steam. We have time to figure this out." At least he hoped they did.

CHAPTER THREE

The werewolf snarled, white foam dripping from one side of his mouth. He wrenched against the silver bonds that held him in the centre of the sterile white room. Muscles corded along his naked body, and veins protruded as his face turned a dangerous shade of red.

Darius glanced sideways at Sean. The Omega's face was pinched and beaded with sweat as he watched the suffering of the bound wolf. Sean's very nature allowed him to calm and ease the pain of other wolves – a discovery that had been invaluable in the early stages of testing – but Darius had no patience for this bleeding-heart reaction.

"You might want to get a better hold on your wolf, Omega, or this is not going to be pleasant."

Sean's jaw and fists clenched in response to Darius's order. His body trembled as he fought to calm the shackled werewolf. "He can't take any more," he ground out. "You need to stop."

As if to prove the point, the other man suddenly went rigid. His head flung back, and his spine bowed at such an unnatural angle that Darius expected to hear it snap. To their left, the witch's low chanting grew faster, more urgent. The air became charged, and the growing power raised the hairs on Darius's arms.

"Why would I want to stop? If this transfer fails, you'll just have to select another wolf until we find a match." A low whine came from the Omega wolf at his side, and Darius resisted the urge to strike him. It wouldn't do to break Sean's concentration while he was assisting with the transfer – albeit under duress.

It had been unfortunate that the last test had been a failure, but that was the difficulty in trying to find the correct combination of Supe and demon. So far they'd only successfully managed the transfer with vampire subjects. The barrier between worlds wasn't yet weak enough for the higher-level demons to come through, even with the magical assistance of the witches. Success balanced on a knife edge of timing, power, and compatibility. It was a frustrating but necessary process.

Patience, he reminded himself. Soon he would have his army and stand at the side of the Horsemen. Soon he would return the Lore to its true glory.

Electricity crackled over Darius's skin as the energy built to bursting point within the square chamber. Sean dropped to his knees with an agonised groan, and an inhuman scream ripped from the wolf he was trying to control.

Darius could feel the exact point when the fabric tore around them. The power waiting within the void was breathtaking. It was alive and straining to break free from its confines. Not long now.

There was a hollow *POP* and the energy disappeared. The barrier knitted back together, and the power became little more than an echoing memory. But it was there, waiting until the moment that the veil came crashing down entirely.

A clang of chains drew Darius's attention back to the centre of the room. Low growls rumbled from the bound wolf's throat, and his fangs elongated to vicious points. The sinewy muscle covering his body tensed as if poised to attack. Wild yellow eyes darted around the room without seeming to focus on anything.

A minute passed. Then two. There was no noticeable change in the wolf that Darius could see.

No sooner had he finished his observation than the werewolf started to thrash about. The yellow eyes went wide with fear as the skin on the left side of its body darkened, growing almost black in

516

places. Darius watched with morbid fascination as small patches of skin appeared to rot and decay. Pus oozed from the wounds and a rancid odour filled the room.

Another failure, he noted with a clinical disappointment, and prepared to turn for the door.

The wolf's eyes flashed red. As quickly as it had started, the thrashing stopped. The pattern of decay slowly faded. When the skin was once again smooth, the wolf grew deathly still. He raised red eyes to meet Darius's, and a vicious grin split his mouth.

———

Darius took the secure elevator to the upper level of the Club of Night, musing on the progress of the testing. Another demon-Supe match confirmed. It was a step in the right direction, but it still wasn't enough. He had less than nine months before the prophecy would reach its conclusion. Less than nine months to build an army fit for the right hand of the Horsemen. The fabric was failing too slowly; he needed more power if he was to pull through higher-level demons.

His head of security awaited him when he entered his office. Darius joined him at the panoramic window that provided a one-way viewing platform to the heaving dancefloor below. The stocky vampire stood with his hands clasped behind his back as he observed the crowd in detached assessment.

"It's busy tonight," Erik commented.

Darius didn't respond. He'd known long before setting up this little enterprise that there would be a rabid market for the services he offered. On the face of it, the club was simply an underground hotspot that allowed Supes to blow off some steam without the need to hide; any human within its walls knew well what they were walking into. But the true heart of the club's thriving balance sheet was funded by the darker services available to select patrons.

Sordid and depraved individuals, all of them. Of course, the humans were no better. They came here serving themselves up on a silver platter, blinded by some ridiculous fantasy that had been implanted in their head by Hollywood. They made his job far too easy.

He turned from the viewing window and went to the mahogany bar built into the wall behind his desk. He poured a dram of whiskey from the crystal decanter and settled on the plush velvet sofa that faced the bank of monitors covering the opposite wall of the room. Each screen showed one of the private rooms available to the club's elite members. Barely past midnight and already the rooms were fully occupied.

The images before him showcased a variety of depravities, ranging from temptingly sensual to unspeakably brutal. All of the participants had entered under their own free will. But not all would leave.

He took a sip of his drink, relishing the burn as the liquid slid down his throat. "Have you found him yet?"

"According to our sources at the Council Liaison Office, Vicktor has been away at a private meeting in Brussels. He's due back this evening. I have men stationed to apprehend him as soon as he returns."

So, he'd been with the Council. Darius mused on this, debating just how much risk the weasel posed to him. Yes, it was very possible that Vicktor could have informed the Council about Darius's plans to nudge the prophecy along, but that would mean admitting to his own culpability, given he'd previously assisted Darius's endeavours.

The CLO rep was too much of a coward to take a stand against him. That didn't change the fact that he'd become a dangerous loose end, however. In the wake of Diana's untimely demise, the Council would be looking closely at everything that was happening around them. He could no longer rely on Vicktor's sense of self-preservation to ensure his loyalty.

"Good. See to it that he's brought here immediately." Darius stood and surveyed the horde of writhing bodies below. "I'm going to find someone to eat."

CHAPTER FOUR

Phoenix eyed the steaks in the middle of the large oak table with a strange mix of longing and revulsion. Her mouth watered even as her stomach somersaulted. The dining room was buzzing with conversation as everyone settled down for dinner. It had been their daily ritual ever since they'd arrived at Ethan's family home – no matter what else happened during the day, they all made an effort to eat dinner together. Of course, for Phoenix eating had become a rather loose term of late.

She looked up as Ethan pulled out the chair beside her and sat down.

"How are you feeling?"

She eyed the amazing spread of food and gave a martyred sigh. "Like I got the short end of the stick with this pregnancy business."

His brown eyes glinted, and he attempted to look suitably apologetic but failed miserably. "It could be worse. You could be the one listening to you complain."

She glared at him and raised her fork threateningly, but she couldn't help the smile that tugged at her lips when he started laughing.

"Dig in, folks," Cormac ordered, placing two more steaming

dishes in the centre of the already packed table before taking his seat beside Fia.

Phoenix assessed her options as one might the coloured wires on a live bomb. She couldn't even bring herself to look at the rare slabs of meat that had once been her preference. The vegetables were all homegrown and provided a rainbow of colours that were full of the nutrients the baby needed, so naturally her body rejected that option with a surge of nausea. Which just left the potatoes.

She leaned over to reach for the bowl of mashed potatoes only for it to rise into the air and float towards her. Her eyes widened in surprise before she belatedly noticed the pale hand holding it and looked up into Lucas's grey eyes. She gave him a sheepish grin and accepted the offered bowl.

Her father's Sire had been the main reason they'd all survived when the Council had sent their deadliest assassins, the Mists, to kill Phoenix and anyone that helped her. Lucas had sent his vampires back to England once the dust had settled but had decided to stay behind himself in case he could be of further use. She'd had mixed feelings about that at first, given the role he'd played in her parents' banishment, but in a strange way it had been nice to have some connection to her family.

"I have to say, Phoenix, pregnancy suits you." Lucas relinquished his hold on the bowl with a kind smile.

Beside him, Shade snorted, not even bothering to look at her with his icy blue eyes. "He's full of shit. You look like hell. Get some blood into you before you turn any paler."

Before she had a chance to retort, a hand snaked around behind Shade and gave him a clatter in the back of the head. "Never tell a pregnant woman she looks like shit," Fia warned, pointing a finger at him before turning towards Phoenix. "How are you feeling? Have you had any luck keeping any blood down?"

Heat burned Phoenix's cheeks as all eyes turned to her. Did they really need to be discussing her blood drinking habits over dinner?

Seated on her left-hand side, Abi glanced at her, clearly realising her discomfort. Her friend plastered a huge smile on her face and

520

interjected. "Oh my god, did I tell you all about the deadly new move Sasha taught me today?"

The attention shifted to Ethan's twin sister, Sasha, as she animatedly began describing Abi's new-found prowess with throwing knives. Grateful, Phoenix reached out to squeeze Abi's hand under the table and gave her a small smile. It still amazed her how well her friend had fit into their insane world. By all accounts Abi was putting her past experience in dealing with drunk pub customers to good use and was embracing some of the more violent forms of expression that were necessary in the Lore. Looking at her now, Phoenix could almost believe that Abi didn't miss her old pub at all, but that was just wishful thinking and a vain attempt to ease her own guilt over its destruction.

Phoenix contemplated the remaining mashed potato on her plate as the dishes around her were scraped clean of every last morsel of food. It was only when she noticed the sudden absence of laughter that she looked up and noticed the mood had turned sombre.

"Did the witches get the ward finished?" Ethan asked his father.

Cormac had been working with the local witch coven to restore and reinforce security around the pack lands ever since the Mists had shattered the original wards. Wolves had been stationed to guard the perimeter in the interim, but they couldn't take any risks; it was only a matter of time before Darius or the Council decided to target them again.

"They finished the last binding this morning," Cormac answered, leaning back in his chair and placing his hands on his stomach with a satisfied sigh. "Going forward, only pack members, or people invited by the pack, can cross onto our land."

"Let's hope they did a better job of it this time," Ethan muttered under his breath.

Phoenix jabbed him in the ribs with her elbow and frowned. He shrugged, looking suitably chastised. They both knew he didn't really blame the witches for what had happened; none of them had expected to face opponents as strong as the Mists. The thought sobered her.

It was possible they hadn't even faced their strongest opponents yet. If the prophecy was fulfilled ...

A shiver ran through Phoenix and she placed a protective hand on her belly. She couldn't contemplate that possibility right now.

"Phoenix? I was hoping we might speak."

Phoenix looked up in surprise to find Lucas standing in the doorway of the living room. She'd been so mesmerised by the flames blazing in the stone fireplace that she hadn't realised he was standing there. Would it be rude to say no? She so rarely got a moment alone now that so many of them were staying with Ethan's parents that she was sorely tempted to make an excuse.

Instead, she bit back a resigned sigh and gave him what she hoped was a friendly smile as she motioned for him to join her. "To what do I owe the pleasure?"

He closed the door behind him and settled beside her on the sofa. His posture remained poised despite the soft cushions behind him, but he managed to make himself look powerfully composed rather than stiff and unapproachable.

"How are you feeling?" he asked. "While I stand by my earlier assessment that pregnancy suits you, I see you're still suffering with some rather unpleasant side effects."

Phoenix snorted. He was ever so polite, her father's Sire. "Fia assures me it's normal and should pass once I'm over the earliest stage of the pregnancy. Whenever that might be."

And that was the million-dollar question, wasn't it? How long exactly would her pregnancy be? And would it be soon enough to save them? Even for pure werewolves, the length of each pregnancy varied. The mix of wolf and human genetics meant full term could be anything from a wolf's sixty-odd days to a human's forty weeks. The average often fell somewhere in between the two, which would give her plenty of time to have her bun cooked before the prophecy reached its endpoint at midnight on thirty-first December.

But that was the simplified timeline, if they only took into account

Ethan's contribution to the gene pool. Her own contribution was a little more complicated since they hadn't yet been able to establish the gestation period for fae. And vampires supposedly couldn't have babies – a fact her own existence highly called into question.

"That was actually part of what I wanted to speak to you about."

"Huh?" She looked at him in confusion.

"It's true we haven't known each other for a very long time, and I've been hesitant to overstep any boundaries, but I wondered if you've considered reaching out to your mother's family?"

Phoenix couldn't help the wall that slammed down at his words. She sat back farther into the cushions, trying hard to keep her expression composed. "And have them report me to the Council for breaching the same edict that my parents were banished for?"

A shadow darkened Lucas's grey eyes, but he accepted her words without flinching. "It's possible that they now regret their decision as I do."

"With all due respect, Lucas, you may have turned my father into a vampire, and you may have been friends with him for a very long time, but you weren't blood. My mother's *parents* banished her. They turned their back on their own daughter because of an outdated, prejudiced law that makes absolutely no sense." Phoenix swallowed, surprised at the sudden burning in her throat as the anger swelled inside of her.

The vampire looked down at his hands, lines tightening the corners of his eyes. "I could argue that I loved Marcus as if he were my own blood, but that only makes my actions even more unforgivable. I can only say that I tried to do what was best for my clan. Perhaps Aria's parents also carried the same burden for their people."

"What do you mean 'their people'?" The phrasing was odd enough that it momentarily distracted her from her anger.

He looked up at her, grey eyes seeming to assess her, but for what she wasn't sure. "How much did your mother tell you of your fae heritage?"

Sweet fuck all because it hurt her too much to ever speak of it. Phoenix bit back the retort. "Not much."

"Your mother's family descend from a great lineage. I guess you could say they are considered royalty among the fae."

Her jaw dropped. "Royalty?"

Lucas nodded. "Not exactly in the human sense, but yes, royalty of sorts. They are descended from the Tuatha Dé Danann, the original rulers of the fae. The political structure has changed significantly over the millennia, but your family still hold a great level of power and responsibility over the courts. As such, they would be expected to uphold a certain level of ... ideals."

"Why are you telling me this?" Phoenix wrapped her arms around herself, not quite sure what to make of the information or why it should change how she felt.

"I guess I'm trying to explain why your mother's family might now, as people, be regretting the choice they made then as leaders."

She bit her lower lip. A detached part of her could understand his reasoning, but the part that had witnessed her parents' pain at their banishment wasn't so willing to listen to logic. Whatever regret her mother's family had was their burden to bear. She wouldn't risk the safety of her child on the assumption that they'd had a change of heart, not even for more information on fae reproduction.

"There have to be other ways to get the answers we need."

"In truth, information around your pregnancy is only one of the reasons I feel it may be worthwhile reaching out to your family."

She raised an eyebrow but stayed quiet.

"I wasn't alive when the Horsemen last roamed this plane, but I am old enough to have heard rumours about their banishment. It was said that the magic of the Tuatha Dé Danann was used to forge the fabric that keeps them at bay. Fae magic is unlike the magic of any other species in the Lore. It's an ancient magic that existed long before much of humanity. Back when demons ruled our world."

Back when demons did what now? Phoenix shook her head, trying to clear her reeling thoughts. Even if what he was saying was true and her family had some connection to the magic that bound the Horsemen, why would ...

She froze. Her stomach clenched with something other than her usual pregnancy nausea as the realisation hit her. "You think we'll need that magic to banish them again."

It wasn't a question, and his suggestion shouldn't have been a surprise. Lucas was only voicing what they all secretly feared. She grew cold despite the fire that blazed in the hearth.

"I think we'll need to be prepared for that possibility. Your baby is a miracle, Phoenix. A beautiful miracle. But it is innocent, and it should be us protecting the baby from the world, not the baby protecting us."

CHAPTER FIVE

Darius stared at the screen in the centre of the bank of monitors. The image showcased an empty, square space, containing only a metal table and a lone figure seated before it. Even from the visual on the screen, Darius could detect the man's pompous air. His posture was rigid despite the chains that held him in place, and his nose was turned up in distaste as he stared directly ahead.

"Did you have much trouble acquiring him?" Darius asked Erik.

"No, though he was adamant that we would pay for our insubordination."

A sliver of satisfaction ran through Darius. He would show the little weasel what insubordination really looked like. "I'll be sure to give him my deepest apologies."

He stood and removed his suit jacket, rolling up the sleeves of his crisp white shirt. "Cancel my next meeting," he ordered, before striding from the viewing room.

The music was a dull thudding bass as he made his way through the darkened hallways that ran along the rear of the club. Blue lights bordered either side of the black carpet, casting an eerie glow as he passed the windowless doors of the private rooms. At the end of the hall, he stopped in front of one such door.

Vicktor's glare was the first thing he noticed as he entered the room, and he smiled wide in greeting. "Vicktor. It's been a while."

"What the hell do you think you're playing at, Darius?" The CLO rep shifted on the metal chair, setting his chains clinking. His eyes darted to the questionable stains on the table and he licked his lips.

"Playing? Oh, I don't believe this is a game."

"The Council know it was you who killed Diana. They have witnesses who saw you heading to her quarters. If something happens to me, they'll –"

"They'll what? Come avenge your death?" Darius sneered. "Don't fool yourself. Even if they cared to expend the energy – which I highly doubt – it won't change the fact you're dead, will it?"

Vicktor swallowed and a vein pulsed at his temple.

"But I don't want to kill you, Vicktor." Darius walked a slow circle around the table, coming to a stop behind the chair. He placed his hands on the other man's shoulders and smiled when Vicktor tensed. "I just want to know what your meeting with the Council was about."

"Why should I tell you anything?"

Darius shrugged and continued his circle until he was once more standing in front of the table. "You shouldn't. Though I'd hate to have to reconsider my decision to keep you alive."

Vicktor licked his lips again. His grey eyes flitted from side to side, searching for an escape that didn't exist. The restraints in all of the private rooms were of the highest quality and could be easily tailored to suit any species of Supe. The doors were magically reinforced, and a building full of highly trained vampires stood between Vicktor's chair and freedom. There was no escaping.

Clearly coming to the same conclusion, Vicktor swallowed audibly. "If I tell you, I want your word that you'll let me live."

Darius brushed the demand off with a wave of his hand. "You have my word."

"The Seer has had another vision. It seems there's a possible solution to the prophecy."

Darius became deathly still. The only *solution* was for the prophecy to be fulfilled. Any other alternative was unacceptable.

"The hybrid is pregnant," Vicktor continued. "If she births the child before the prophecy endpoint, the balance will be restored."

"What do you mean she's pregnant?"

Vicktor grimaced. "Another abomination to the Lore."

Darius paced the small confines of the room as he considered this development. Every day the fabric was growing weaker; he could already see signs of it as they managed to pull stronger demons through with each transfer they conducted. But the Horsemen were a different story; they were more than mere demons. The fabric would need to fail entirely for them to pass over.

"Did the Seer happen to offer the odds on this outcome?" It wasn't unusual for a scenario to have many possible paths. Perhaps this was just the Council clinging desperately to the sinking ship.

"It was unclear. It seems the future balances precariously on a series of key events."

"Indeed."

"The Council will protect the hybrid now that they know. It doesn't matter that she's broken their edict; they'll do everything in their power to ensure the baby is born."

"I fear you overestimate your dear Council. As you so rightly pointed out, one of their own has already met an untimely demise. Without the Mists to do their bidding, they are little more than an inconvenience." Darius stopped once more in front of the table and leaned forward until his face was mere inches from Vicktor's. "The prophecy will come to pass. I promise you that much. It's just a shame you won't be here to see it."

Vicktor jerked back, his pinched features paling. "You gave your word that you wouldn't kill me."

"Oh, I'm not going to kill you. I'm going to do something much worse." Turning away, Darius pulled his mobile phone from his trouser pocket and pressed the first number on his speed dial. "Erik, I believe we've found ourselves our next test subject."

Darius headed for the stainless-steel lift at the end of the corridor,

Vicktor's protests and fruitless threats still ringing in his ears. He had debated with himself over recent months whether or not to keep the CLO rep alive. Vicktor had long ago outlived his usefulness when it came to getting information about key Council actions, but Darius hadn't wanted to take the risk in drawing attention to himself too soon, should the weasel have a failsafe in place. Now it seemed patience would bring its own reward.

In all their testing to date, they hadn't yet managed to find a suitable demon match for shifters. While not the rarest of the Supe species, myths about their skin being able to transfer the shifting magic to the wearer of same had led to the species being hunted. As a result, they were notoriously private and less inclined than their wolfen counterparts to live in groups. It had meant fewer opportunities to test them than he'd have liked.

Vicktor would make an ideal candidate. If the transfer was successful, it would move their testing along even further. And if it didn't? Well then, the weasel would be out of his hair once and for all. And since it would technically be the demon that killed him, Darius would have even kept his word.

He paused in front of the retina scanner and the lift doors opened with a hiss. There was only one button and it deposited him five floors underground, in the complex that been built below the club.

Significantly smaller than the space they'd previously used at the Dublin clan's lair, he'd felt it prudent to move the most vital of their operations after Phoenix and her little band of do-gooders had breached the lair's security a couple of months previous. The space at the club allowed for a well-equipped laboratory, a testing chamber, and a number of holding cells for the subjects. The remainder of their operations had been moved to the pharmaceutical complex that had been the starting point for the testing, and now also accommodated his ever-growing army of demon-Supe hybrids.

Stepping from the lift, Darius strode past tables laden with tubes, computers, and strange gadgets that meant little to him. A technician in a white lab coat bustled about, preparing for Vicktor's transfer, while a witch readied himself for the ritual on the opposite side of the room.

Darius vaguely recognised the sharp, pale features of the man who stood with his head bowed, chanting in a low voice over a bowl that was coated in a tar-like substance. A streak of white ran through the witch's mousy brown hair and that, more than any personal knowledge of the man, was what triggered Darius's memory.

Though he wasn't always present for the transfers, it was unusual for Darius to see any of the witches more than once. The spell to weaken the barrier, even temporarily, drained a significant amount of energy and burned many of the weaker witches out entirely. Of course, that was the benefit of having the Dublin coven at his disposal; he always had another witch on hand when needed. The coven's greed had long ago left them beholden to him, and now that they floundered without a strong leader, it was even easier to bend them to his will.

Satisfied that all was in hand for the transfer, he made his way to the heavy steel door at the far end of the room. Two feet thick, the door offered much needed soundproofing from the cells that lay beyond it. He stepped up to a second retina scanner, and there was a moment's pause before the door crept open. Immediately, his senses were assaulted by the howls of pain and the stench of days-old filth. He grimaced in distaste before stepping through to the waiting darkness.

Metal bars ran the length of the room on either side of him, and perpendicular sets of bars sectioned each side into smaller cells. The segregation had become necessary when some of the first test subjects had torn each other to shreds in a rather undignified manner.

He passed the first few cells with only a cursory glance at their occupants. A werewolf coated in his own dried blood. A shifter curled in the foetal position, mumbling incoherently as he clawed obsessively at his skin. A vampire so starved he could almost see her skeleton. A witch that did little more than stare at him with eyes that flickered repeatedly between red and a wide-eyed green. Dejected figures, each in a varying state of disrepair.

New candidates for the trials were held in the pharmaceutical complex until their genetic manipulation and psychological conditioning were complete. Only then could they be considered for progression to the next stage – demon transfer. Occasionally candidates didn't take well to the treatment. Or they progressed to the second stage, but the demon transfer still failed due to an incompatible match. Rejects were housed here until it could be decided what to do with them. Sometimes he released them into the general population for his amusement, others were destroyed depending on his mood. It was an unfortunate waste given the time spent on bending each subject to his will, but only the strongest would suffice for his army.

A guttural growl came from the last cell on the left, followed immediately by a sharp yelp and hushed words. Even in the dim light, Darius could see Sean crouching by the silver-coated bars. He was speaking in a low, soothing tone, but the wolf occupying the cage was far past the point of listening.

There was a clang as the wolf hurled himself against the bars. It roared in pain as it came into contact with the silver. *Stupid mutt.*

Sean tensed at Darius's approach, not taking his eyes from the wolf. "He just needs time," he said, his voice strained.

"I'm not concerned with your rabid pup." Darius eyed the werewolf in the cage as he approached. Crazed red eyes stared back, a mix of fear and desperation haunting their depths.

According to Erik's report, the transfer hadn't gone well with this subject. Whether it was due to weakness on the witch's part or a natural rejection of the demon, they didn't know. It was clear from looking at the wolf that they would be adding another number to their tally of failures, something that did not put him in a good mood.

They needed to refine the process. And the witch involved would have to pay for their ineptitude, of course.

But that wasn't why he'd come. "I have a job for you," he informed Sean. "I need you to go back to Donegal and retrieve the hybrid."

Sean's blue eyes flashed in the darkness before he managed to rein in his emotions. He swallowed before answering. "They'll never let me waltz in there and take her."

"On the contrary. You're part of the pack. If anyone here can do just that, it's you."

"The hybrid is of no threat to you. Why not just leave her be?"

Darius levelled his gaze on the Omega. Fear for the other wolves had been more than enough to keep the man in line before now, but ever since Sean had returned from his last visit to Donegal there'd been a change in him. Perhaps it was time to remind him just who his Alpha was now.

"You will go to Donegal. And you will bring me back the hybrid, alive and unharmed. Take one of the other wolves with you." He turned to walk back towards the metal door, casting a final disparaging glance over his shoulder. "Oh, and Sean? Kill the mutt before you leave."

CHAPTER SIX

A strange thudding noise broke through Phoenix's consciousness and she peeled one eyelid open gingerly. Her body was leaden, and it exhausted her to do even that much. Sunlight filled the bedroom she was sharing with Abi and she squinted against the glare. It took a moment before the knocking registered in her muddled brain.

Before she could call out – or pull the duvet over her head and hide – the door opened a crack and Ethan peeked his head in. "Hey."

"Hey," she mumbled, ducking her head under the covers when she suddenly noticed the thin line of drool running from the corner of her mouth to the pillow. "What time is it?"

"Nearly noon," he said, stepping into the room and closing the door behind him. "We all thought you could use a lie-in."

Noon? Wow, she'd slept twelve hours straight. She'd never done that – not even after a heavy night working behind the bar. The munchkin growing inside her was really wearing her out.

With what felt like monumental effort, she sat up and patted the bed beside her. Ethan's brown eyes sparkled with a cheeky glint, his mouth opening to say something that would no doubt get him into trouble. She glared a warning at him even as her cheeks heated and a smile tugged at her lips.

Obediently, he came to sprawl next to her on the double bed and with a flourish of his hand, he produced a chocolate bar – her favourite dark Belgian kind.

She grabbed it and eagerly tore at the wrapper. "You're the –"

Before she could even raise the luscious chocolate slab to her mouth, the heady aroma of cocoa reached her nose and her stomach lurched. Her eyes widened and she glared at the bar accusingly. "No!" She shook her head in denial.

Her body chose that moment to revolt with another wave of nausea. She shoved the bar back at Ethan before burying her face in her pillow with a wail. "This sucks!"

The mattress beneath her shifted as Ethan jumped up. A soft thud signalled his swift eviction of the chocolate bar from the room, then his weight returned again, causing her to roll into the dip he created in the mattress.

"Sorry. I thought the sugar hit might help your energy levels. My mam's downstairs brewing some strange concoction that she says will help calm your stomach. It's some ancient family recipe apparently. I thought the chocolate seemed like a better idea."

Phoenix peeked an eye out from her behind her pillow. Fia was making a family recipe for her?

A strange feeling that she couldn't quite clarify caused her chest to tighten. She'd grown very fond of Ethan's mother in the short time she'd known her. Fia only ever treated her with respect. Never once had she made Phoenix feel like an abomination because of her hybrid nature. And even when the unexpected pregnancy quite clearly confirmed that Phoenix had led her one and only son astray – an act punishable by death under their laws – she was downstairs preparing a family recipe rather than condemning her.

She looked up to see concern shadowing Ethan's gaze as he watched her. He'd been careful not to put pressure on her or smother her over the past few weeks, but he'd always been there if she needed help. What was it like for him? Did it feel real to him that they were having a baby together? Because it still didn't to her, and she was the one growing it.

"We haven't really had much chance to spend time alone since we've gotten here," he said, breaking the silence. She arched an eyebrow at him and he laughed, shaking his head. "I don't mean like that. All of this has been pretty sudden, what with the pregnancy and everything. I just realised we've never even had a first date."

A sound of surprise slipped past her lips. A date? That was definitely not what she'd expected him to say. "Are you asking me out?"

He grinned. "Well, I feel it's only the gentlemanly thing to do. What d'ye say? Mam will make her magic herbs, and I'll get a picnic ready in case you feel up to eating something?"

A nervous flutter tickled her belly as she forced her expression to stay carefully neutral. She pretended to contemplate his offer for a full minute before putting him out of his misery. "I suppose I can grace you with my presence."

Ethan stood and gave her a mock bow. "I'm honoured … I'm sure." With a wink, he turned to leave, calling back over his shoulder. "Meet me in the forest clearing in half an hour."

She watched the broad expanse of his back as he retreated. Their first date. She gave herself and surreptitious sniff. Maybe she could squeeze in a quick shower before she went to find Fia.

Phoenix gritted her teeth as she yanked the brush through her unruly hair. With a frustrated sigh, she flung the brush on the bed and turned away from the mirror. This was stupid. Ethan had seen her at her absolute worst more than once; if he was put off by her uncooperative hair, then this was all pointless anyway.

Refusing to allow herself a final glance at her reflection, she left the bedroom and went in search of Fia. The strong aroma of herbs hit her the second she stepped out into the hallway. The fresh scent of ginger was particularly familiar given she'd all but taken to chewing on the stuff to help her nausea. Beneath that was a lighter, flowery scent. Chamomile maybe? She shrugged and followed her nose to the kitchen. If it helped, she'd try anything.

Fia turned from the pot she was stirring at the stove and gave her a warm smile. "An old family recipe. It looks awful, but I promise you it doesn't taste that bad. It was a godsend when I was pregnant. I was waiting for the last herbs to grow, otherwise I'd have made it for you sooner."

With a final stir, she poured the contents of the pot into a plain white mug and held it out in offering. Phoenix wrinkled her nose as she assessed the highly questionable brown liquid but took the mug with what she hoped was a grateful smile.

Best to do it quickly, she decided, and closed her eyes, knocking back the mystery concoction before she could second guess herself. The flavours came in waves: the light taste of chamomile was followed by an uncomfortable burn, then eased to a cool aftertaste of mint.

Satisfied, Fia took the empty mug from her, and nudged her towards the door. "Go. Have fun," she ordered.

The afternoon was unseasonably sunny for March, and Phoenix paused outside the house to soak in the warmth of the sun. Her cells tingled at its touch, and a spark of power flared to life in her solar plexus. The freshness of the calm air brought with it spring's promise of new life, a promise of possibilities. The distant sound of laughter reached her from the back of the house where she knew Cormac was tending the garden with some of the pack's younger pups. With a smile and a nervous flutter of anticipation, she headed for the forest at the far side of the garden.

The bright light of day faded and was replaced by leafy shadows. The moss was springy beneath her feet, and the privacy afforded by the trees was blissful. Even the birds were leaving her to her moment of peace, their birdsong silent, undoubtedly due to the number of large predators nearby. She filled her lungs with the earthy scent of the forest as she wove her way through the oak trees to the small clearing.

There was no sign of Ethan when she got there and she had to push back the involuntary pang of disappointment. She was early, that's all. Sunlight filtered in through the trees and the lush green grass looked as tempting as any picnic blanket. So with nothing to do but wait, she picked a spot and settled down to do just that.

She let her eyes drift closed and noticed that, for the first time in weeks, the permanent threat of nausea didn't seem to be lurking under the surface, waiting to pounce at the most inopportune moment. Damn, maybe Fia's family recipe really did work. She'd happily drink all the brown sludge in the world if that was the case.

A soft rustle sounded behind her and she stilled, suddenly aware that she wasn't alone. Her senses picked up the signature of a wolf, but she knew instantly that it wasn't Ethan. She frowned, turning to look behind her. Surely he wouldn't have sent one of the other wolves if he planned to cancel on her?

The wolf who stood at the edge of the clearing was taller than Ethan, his frame leaner. His long white hair partially obscured his eyes, which were a stunning shade of blue, and there was a roughness to his features that made him seem almost feral. But despite the wild edge to his appearance, his energy felt calming. Which was odd, given that wolves were predators and naturally triggered an innate survival instinct buried deep within a person's genome. Even a human who was oblivious to the existence of werewolves would feel an inexplicable sense of unease in the presence of one.

"Did Ethan send you?" She cringed inwardly at the edge of accusation in her tone. If Ethan *had* decided to stand her up, it wasn't this wolf's fault that he'd been sent to deal with the dirty work of telling her.

The man was quiet for a moment, his gaze piercing. "He asked me to get you. There's been a change of plans." His voice was hoarse, as if he was unused to speaking, and he glanced around uneasily.

Phoenix narrowed her eyes and took a closer look at him. Had she seen him around before? They hadn't been here that long, but she was pretty sure she'd met most of the pack and this wolf wasn't familiar to her.

"I'm sorry, I didn't catch your name?"

The wolf hesitated. "It's Sean."

CHAPTER SEVEN

Feeling very pleased with himself, Ethan loaded up a cooler box with succulent cuts of meat, fresh fruit, and freshly baked scones. He could already imagine the look on Phoenix's face when she discovered his hidden talent for baking. Hopefully his mother's herbal remedy had done the trick and she'd even be able to enjoy some of the food.

With a final check to make sure he had everything, he threw a blanket over his shoulder and left the kitchen. He had the front door opened when Nate called his name. Ethan groaned inwardly but tried to keep impatience from showing on his face as he turned.

"You got a minute?" Nate didn't wait for an answer before shoving an iPad in his direction. "Look." He jabbed his finger at the newspaper article on the screen.

Ethan scanned the words while at the same time wondering just how pissed Phoenix was going to be at him for being late. A bold headline cited, "An unexplained surge in crime," and he noted plenty of buzzwords to highlight the point: *aggravated assault, petty larceny, arson, vicious murder.*

"What am I supposed to take from this?" he asked with a resigned sigh.

Nate jabbed the screen emphatically. "It's getting worse. There are headlines like this popping up all over the place, and the dark web is full of talk about demon sightings. Their influence is beginning to affect anyone they come into contact with."

A now all-too-familiar sense of apprehension settled over Ethan, dulling his good mood. Frustration welled up inside him, and he handed the iPad back to Nate.

He wasn't going to do this. For a just a few bloody hours, he was going to focus on something positive. "We already know there are demons breaking through. The fabric is weak, but we'll find a way to repair it."

"I want to go to Belfast. The most recent headlines are all centred around there. If I can capture one of the demons, I might –"

"What?" Ethan cut him off more forcefully than he'd intended. "Are you insane?"

Nate shoved his messy brown hair back off his face and Ethan noticed again the dark shadows around the shifter's eyes. "It's still only minor demons coming through. If I can catch one, I can study it. Maybe I can figure out a way for us to fight them."

Ethan let out a sharp laugh, remembering all too clearly what it was like to fight a minor demon. Hell, he and Phoenix had barely escaped with their lives. "How exactly do you plan on capturing one? We are out of the amulets, and now that Lily's gone, we have no one to make more."

He regretted the words immediately. The brief flash of pain that passed across Nate's face sent a pang through his own heart.

"I might know someone who can help us," Nate said quietly, averting his gaze.

Ethan sighed and put a hand on the shifter's shoulder. "Let's talk about this later when everyone's together. Maybe my dad can spare a few wolves to go with you, just to check it out. Now's not the time for taking unnecessary risks, Nate."

Nate gave only a brief nod before turning away. Ethan watched, torn. Then, with a sigh, he walked through the doorway and pulled the front door closed behind him. Nate may have missed his chance with Lily, and Ethan was sorry that he was hurting, but he wasn't going to make the same mistake with Phoenix.

Phoenix stared at the white-haired wolf, transfixed. She'd only ever heard the name Sean mentioned in one context in relation to the pack. And it wasn't a context that resulted in a living, breathing wolf standing before her. She should be afraid, the sane part of her knew that. Instead, she got to her feet and gave him what she hoped was an amiable smile. "So, what's this change of plans?"

He assessed her somewhat warily as she moved towards him but didn't respond. His nostrils flared and his blue eyes widened with surprise. He took a step back, shaking his head. "You're – He didn't tell me – I can't –"

She wrinkled her brow in confusion, but before she could ask what he meant, a large black crow burst through the trees, startling them both. Phoenix recognised the oil-slick feathers and red eyes as soon as the bird landed beside her, and when the it issued a warning "*Caw!*" her pulse ricocheted. She shot a nervous glance back towards Sean and her mouth went dry.

Another man had somehow appeared at Sean's side without making a sound. He was a solid wall of muscle and had a square jaw that looked like it could easily take more than one punch. But it was his eyes that struck her the most. They were so dark they appeared almost black in the shadows of the trees. However, when he shifted into the light of the sun, she could see blood-red swirling in their depths.

Heat left her body in a rush, and an icy fear slithered through her. His signature felt like a wolf's, but it was murkier, almost slimy. And those eyes ...

The crow let out another "*Caw!*" but this time the warning was unnecessary.

"It would be best if you come with us," the other wolf growled, placing his hand on Sean's shoulder.

A pained look flashed across Sean's face and his fists clenched at his sides. "Let's just leave it," he pleaded in a quiet voice.

The hand resting on his shoulder tightened. As Phoenix watched, the skin on the back of the hand turned a dark, brownish-grey and began to split. Cracks formed along the surface, and a wriggling maggot slid from between one of the gaps. Followed by another. And another.

The stench of decay hit her, and her stomach lurched.

"Need I remind you of the consequences should you fail, Omega?" The wolf spoke to Sean, but his grin was all for her – a gruesome smile which showcased rotten teeth and a mouth crawling with maggots.

Phoenix swallowed back a scream. Then she blinked, and somehow the image disappeared. The hand on Sean's shoulder was blemish-free, and no maggots crawled from his menacing grin. She shook her head in confusion.

Sean's blue eyes screamed at her to run, even as he stood silent and pale beneath the other man's bruising grip. Heat flared in her chest and her fingers twitched. The power was there to be called, but doubt mingled with her fear.

She took a step back. Then another. The two wolves just watched her, one with a pained look, the other with a confident grin.

Without warning, the large crow took flight. There was a blur of feathers, followed by a yell of surprise. Phoenix didn't pause to see what happened; she turned and bolted.

Her blood pounded so loudly in her ears that she couldn't tell if anyone was following her or not. She stumbled through the trees, almost tripping over the tangle of roots that had broken through the soil in her haste to get away. She swerved left and then curved right. Within moments she'd lost her sense of orientation but was too terrified to stop.

The large werewolf lunged from her left and barrelled into her. The force of impact sent her colliding into a tree, and her breath left her in a gasp. Rough hands grabbed her in a bruising grip.

"Let's not make this harder than it has to be." Red eyes flashed a warning at her, and her skin crawled as she stared into their swirling depths.

She opened her mouth to scream, but the sound was smothered by a large hand. The wolf smashed her head against the tree, and the world around her swam.

"Don't worry," the wolf assured her. "He won't kill you. Just your baby."

Terror flooded her at the mention of her unborn child, and heat burst from her chest in an involuntary flare of power. The flash of light sent the wolf flying to the ground in a roar of pain. Not waiting to see if he got up, she pushed from the tree and ran.

Where was the other one? Where was Sean?

The thought had barely entered her mind when the Omega stepped out in front of her, and she slammed into his chest. He grabbed her shoulders to steady her, but before she could strike out at him, he let go of her and urged her on.

"Go. I'll hold him off as long as I can."

There was a rustle of movement behind her, and Phoenix turned to see the other man prowling towards them. The left side of his face was a scorched mess and his blood-red eyes blazed with fury.

"Go!" Sean roared and shifted into a huge white wolf.

The last thing Phoenix saw before she turned and ran was the huge white figure leaping through the air.

CHAPTER EIGHT

Ethan hurried towards the forest, wondering just how late he was. Dammit, knowing his luck Phoenix would've decided he'd stood her up and left. What a great bloody start to their first date. He broke into a light jog as he hit the trees and followed the short trail to the clearing.

He drew up short when he came upon the empty space. A patch of flattened grass was confirmation that someone had been here, but there was no sign of Phoenix. His heart plummeted. Surely he wasn't that late? He lowered the cooler box and blanket to the ground and looked around.

Okay, let's not blow this out of proportion just yet. He sniffed the air, intending to follow her trail, and froze.

Phoenix's scent was strong enough to confirm that she had indeed been there very recently, but that wasn't what gave him pause. Mingled with her scent was another, long-forgotten one.

Sean.

Ethan frowned. That couldn't be right – Sean was dead. But then a memory came to him, unbidden, of a white wolf that had saved him from Maj during the faithful battle against the Mists. He'd long since convinced himself that it had been his imagination playing tricks on him, that the illusions cast by the Mists had confused his memories.

There was no way those blue eyes had belonged to his dead friend. But scents didn't lie.

Heart hammering in his chest, he followed his nose deeper into the forest. Both Sean and Phoenix's trail moved in the same direction until suddenly Sean's veered left. He eyed that path, torn, but continued straight on.

A third, unfamiliar scent intersected Phoenix's not long after Sean's disappeared. He'd sensed this one back at the clearing too, but had been too distracted to pay attention to it. Now he took a moment to examine it and frowned. His first thought was that it was from another werewolf, but there was something off about the scent; it left him with a strange, rotten taste in his mouth.

A twig snapped just ahead of him and a voice he recognised all too well yelled in pain. Adrenaline shot through him and he bolted through the trees, unusual scent forgotten. A flash of red caught his eye, and he made a beeline for it. The sounds of a struggle preceded yet another scream, and his wolf roared, forcing him onwards with mindless urgency.

He leapt over a fallen tree in his path and skidded to a stop when he came to a small break in the trees. His breath caught in his throat, and his body froze in fear as he saw Phoenix lying on the ground with a stocky man looming over her.

Her eyes were wide with terror as they met his, and Ethan took in the man's vicious grin as he pinned her to the ground with one knee pressing into her abdomen. Ice-cold rage washed over him. The man was going to die.

He leaped for the man, knocking him clear of Phoenix and sending them both tumbling across the ground. The man was on his feet before Ethan had a chance to rise. Ethan lunged upwards, slamming his shoulder into the man's gut. There was a jarring *thud* as the man's back slammed against a tree.

Ethan had a moment to notice something odd about the eyes that were gleaming back at him before the man grabbed him by the shoulders and flung him aside as if he weighed nothing. A sharp *crack* signalled Ethan's own collision with a tree and he slid to the ground, winded.

Phoenix crawled towards him, one arm clutching her abdomen. The man simply watched her, the relaxed look on his face making it clear he was in no hurry to end the fun.

"Get out of here," Ethan ordered, even as he knew by the stubborn set of her jaw that she wouldn't leave him.

"Sean. I think he's –"

"Later," he ground out, even as his gut clenched at the mention of his friend. Painfully, he rose to his feet and angled himself between Phoenix and the red-eyed wolf.

"I can take you to Sean," the man offered amicably. "You can get reacquainted while I get to know your girlfriend better."

A low snarl forced itself from Ethan's throat, courtesy of the wolf within him. He allowed his claws to extend but kept a tight hold on his inner beast as he held still and waited.

"No?" The man shrugged. The air around him changed and his body began to shift.

At that moment, a huge crow burst through the trees and slammed into him. There was a blur of feathers and furious roar before the werewolf caught hold of the bird and flung it away from him.

The crow landed to the right of Phoenix and the air shimmered around it. From one blink to the next, it changed from a bird into a huge black wolf, and with mesmerising grace, it launched itself at the man.

Ethan had no idea what the hell was going on, but it didn't matter – he was going to kill the man for hurting Phoenix. He moved to help the black wolf.

An apparition stepped between him and the fight, pulling him up short. White hair and blazing blue eyes were scarcely visible on a face that was covered in so much blood it was barely recognisable. But Ethan did recognise it. It was the face that had haunted all his nightmares ever since his friend's death.

For a moment their eyes met. The pack bond flared like a rope tethering them together. Then Sean tore his gaze away, and just as quickly the connection was gone.

"Get her out of here." The Omega didn't spare him a second glance as he shifted into his wolf form and dived into the fray.

Ethan's shock was shattered by a groan of pain behind him and he turned to find Phoenix on her knees, bent double and clutching her stomach. The memory of the man's knee on her abdomen flashed into Ethan's mind, and fear for her well-being pushed away all other emotions.

The fight raged mere feet from him, and instinct roared at him to help the friend he thought he'd lost. But an even stronger instinct demanded that he protect his mate and his child. Unable to do anything else, he sent an urgent call for help through the pack bond, praying that someone would be close by. Then he scooped Phoenix up into his arms and ran, leaving his friend to his fate once again.

Phoenix could focus on little else other than the fear for her baby as Ethan raced through the forest, holding her in his arms. At any other time, she'd have protested the show of chivalry, but the sharp pain shooting through her abdomen blocked out everything else.

Fia and Cormac met them at the edge of the forest, and without a word, ushered them back to the house and into the living room where the pack doctor was already setting up. She dimly wondered how they'd known to get the doctor as Ethan placed her gently on the sofa and brushed the hair away from her face with an unreadable expression. She watched as he turned to speak to his father in a low voice.

A sharp twinge in her belly elicited an involuntary gasp from her lips, and when she tried to sit up, Fia rushed to her side.

"Don't move," Ethan's mother urged, gently pressing her back against the soft cushions. "Not until the doctor checks you over."

"How did you know?"

Fia smiled, though it didn't reach her eyes. "Ethan sent out a distress call through the pack bond."

The mention of the pack brought the image of the white-haired

546

wolf to Phoenix's mind, and she grabbed Fia's hand, panicked. "Sean –"

"I know," Fia assured her, pain shadowing her features. "We'll find him."

Before she could ask anything more, Ethan and Cormac finished their hushed conversation and Ethan crouched down beside her. "The doctor's ready to check you over, if that's okay?"

Phoenix swallowed. The worry she'd been trying in vain to ignore caused bile to rise in the back of her throat. She knew the pains in her abdomen couldn't be good. She knew exactly where the wolf's knee had pressed.

"He's sworn an oath of secrecy," Cormac assured her, taking her pause to be from reluctance. "Nothing he learns here will leave this room. You have my word."

Not trusting herself to speak, she bit her lip and nodded.

With her consent given, the doctor ushered Fia and Cormac from the room, only allowing Ethan to remain at her say-so. The doctor fired questions at her as he finished setting up an assortment of gadgets in a frighteningly efficient manner.

"Can I please clarify your species?"

She cleared her throat, hands suddenly clammy. "Half vampire, half fae."

No obvious reaction.

"Which is from your mother?"

"Fae."

A nod. "Species of the baby's father?"

Phoenix's cheeks heated with a shame she didn't want to feel. Ethan took her hand and gripped it with a reassuring squeeze before answering for her. "Werewolf."

"How far is the pregnancy?"

"Em, three weeks, maybe four?" Time had lost all meaning to her in the chaos of the recent weeks.

The doctor pulled on a pair of latex gloves, then looked at her with kind eyes. "Do I have your permission to examine you and the baby?"

She nodded, even as a knot of panic settled in her chest. Ethan released his grip on her hand and moved to the end of the sofa to give the doctor room to work, but stayed within eye line.

As the doctor raised her top to expose her stomach, a sharp hiss from Ethan made her look down. Mottled purple bruising marked her abdomen where the wolf had used his knee to pin her. The violent discolouration marked the exact spot where she often found herself unconsciously resting her hand, and tears pricked the back of her eyes. A sob threatened to tear itself from her throat and she bit down on her lip hard enough to draw blood in an attempt to hold it back.

She watched in numb fascination as the doctor smeared a clear substance on a wand-like contraption that was connected to a small machine. He placed the wand on her lower abdomen and there was an initial shock of cold as the jelly touched her skin. She winced as he applied gentle pressure, but stayed quiet.

A deafening silence filled the room, seeming to go on for an eternity. Then she heard it. A heartbeat.

It was like a freight train, strong and sure. And it was the most amazing thing she'd ever heard.

She looked at Ethan, and the awe on his face caused her own heart to skip a beat. She followed his line of sight, turning her gaze to the monitor beside her. The screen was small, but she could just about make out a small shape moving. "Is that ..."

"Your baby." The doctor gave her a smile. "It's more developed than a human child would be at this stage, but that's not unusual for Supe pregnancies. Typically, we see more progress in the early stages, and then development can slow depending on the species. It's one of the reasons the pregnancy takes so much out of you in the beginning."

Phoenix squinted at the screen, trying to make out the shape. Was that the head? It looked like it could be a head ... maybe. Shouldn't she be able to figure out what part of her baby was what? What kind of mother didn't know what her baby's head looked like? Her chest tightened in panic.

Ethan cast her a worried glance before addressing the doctor. "Is the baby okay?"

548

The doctor was quiet for one terrifying moment as he focused on the screen and adjusted the position of the wand. "I can't see any damage to the placenta. Blood flow to the cord appears to be good, and there's plenty of amniotic fluid around the baby. I'd like to monitor you a little while longer, but it looks like you have a strong one here."

His words brought with them an overwhelming sense of relief, but still there was another worry, a deeper sense of anxiety that gnawed at Phoenix. "Can you tell what the due date might be?" she asked quietly.

"I'm afraid not. With a mix like this it could be a few months, or even as long as a year."

She looked at Ethan, and the shadow that passed over his face mirrored her own thoughts. They didn't have a year.

CHAPTER NINE

The doctor was only just out the door when Abi rushed into the living room with Sasha hot on her heels. Both hurried to Phoenix's side, and it was all she could do to concentrate on their questions. The sound of her baby's heartbeat still rang in her ears, and although the cramping had subsided, fear still held her firmly in its grip.

Fia and Cormac followed close behind Sasha and Abi, and Ethan hurried to his father's side. "Did they find him?"

Cormac shook his head, frown lines creasing his forehead as he turned his attention to her. "I'm sorry, lass. I promised that you'd be safe here, and we failed you. I don't know how they managed to break the wards."

"They didn't." Nate appeared in the doorway, laptop in hand, face grim. "The wards recognised Sean as pack, so he was free to enter. As was anyone he invited."

A shiver ran down her spine at the thought of the red-eyed wolf. Sean's taste in company seemed to have gone downhill since he "died".

Sasha's face scrunched in pained confusion. "I don't understand. Why wouldn't he have come to us before now if he was alive? And what does he want now?"

Phoenix's heart broke as she saw the same look of pain mirrored on all the wolves' faces. "He was sent for me."

Ethan's eyes flashed yellow for the briefest moment as they met hers. "Darius sent him."

Sasha's frown deepened. "He's working for Darius?"

Phoenix thought back to the torn look on Sean's face. Whatever else he'd done, he'd helped to save her. "I'm not sure he has a choice."

"There's always a choice," Ethan snarled. He blew out a breath, grabbing his hair in a fist. "We need to find him."

Fia moved to his side and placed a hand on his shoulder. "We'll do what we can, Mo Faolán, but our priority right now is for the safety of Phoenix and the baby."

The room fell silent. No one said what they were all thinking: it wasn't safe here for her anymore.

Phoenix pushed her way up to sitting, ignoring Ethan's protests. She'd be damned if she was going to lie there all helpless while they discussed her safety. "The wolf with Sean, there was something odd about him. He didn't ... feel right."

Ethan nodded. "His eyes were strange too. A deep blood red."

"Like a demon's."

Phoenix looked up in surprise and saw Lucas in the doorway of the living room, Shade standing behind him. Damn vampires could sneak up on anybody.

"What do you mean?" Nate asked, blowing a mop of hair out of his face.

Even before Lucas explained his thought process, Phoenix knew he was right. She remembered back to her previous demon encounters, and that same feeling of wrongness had been present. It had been muted this time, less obvious, but that could have been from the strength of the wolf signature or just the blinding fear.

"So Darius is somehow combining Supes and demons?" Nate said thoughtfully. "But how? None of the demons we've encountered so far have been strong enough to possess a Supe."

No one answered. Everyone in the room bore a similar look of apprehension, and Shade summed it up best when he whispered, "Well, fuck me to high hell."

A bone-deep weariness settled over Phoenix. She'd gotten complacent over the past few weeks. She'd almost forgotten what it was like to be in constant fear for her life. "What do we do now?"

Lucas moved to come to her side, but froze, becoming deathly still.

Beside her, Ethan's whole body tensed, and the hairs on the back of her neck stood up. Shifting awkwardly on the sofa to follow his gaze, she turned to look out the window behind her.

In the distance, she could see the forest, and from the trees, a huge black wolf emerged. The very same black wolf that had saved them from the demon-Supe hybrid. It moved towards the house with an otherworldly grace that made all the other werewolves she knew seem clumsy in comparison.

Phoenix watched, mesmerised. The tension in the room cloyed at the back of her throat, and she knew from the reaction of the others that this wolf wasn't one of their own. Yet, none of the wolves that Cormac had ordered to stand guard in front of the house moved to attack as the black wolf drew closer.

The air around the wolf blurred, and without missing a step it transformed into a woman. Her pale skin seemed to glow in the light of the sun, and long black hair flowed behind her. Even from a distance Phoenix could see the miasma of colours that shimmered through the ebony strands. Purples, blues, and greens all reflected back at Phoenix, bringing with them a forgotten memory: Lily's Ritual of Passing, the wolf. She'd seen this woman before.

Without realising she'd moved, Phoenix found herself standing, staring out the window as the woman came to a stop in front of the house.

"Morrigan," Lucas whispered, drawing all eyes to him.

Phoenix gasped and looked from her father's Sire back to the woman who waited patiently at the bottom of the steps leading to the house. She walked out of the living room and made her way to the front door, ignoring the protests behind her.

An odd sense of calm settled over her as she pulled the door open and made her way down the steps to meet the woman she'd only ever known by name. Morrigan. Her mother's guardian.

She stopped a few feet away from the figure, conscious of the others stationed behind her, ready to react to the slightest twitch. "Your eyes aren't red anymore." The words left her mouth before she could think, and she cringed.

Morrigan laughed, a rich, musical sound that wrapped around Phoenix and made her skin tingle. "No child, they're not. It's a side-effect of the magic I use to shift." She paused, and a sad smile settled on her ethereal face. "You've grown into such a beautiful woman. I wish we might have met under different circumstances."

Phoenix said nothing, unsure of how to respond. Her mother had told her many stories about Morrigan when she was a child. The goddess who'd helped lead the fae to greatness in the midst of their darkest hours. The high being who heralded victory and doom alike. The woman who had watched over their family for many centuries. They were little more than fairy tales to her, and yet her mother had spoken of Morrigan as if she were a friend.

"You know who I am?" Morrigan asked.

"I do." Phoenix thought back to the various times in her life when an intervention from the large black crow had meant the difference between life and death. "You've been watching over me. Keeping me safe."

"When I can. Like all, I'm limited in the actions I can take without disrupting the natural order."

"Thank you."

Morrigan inclined her head, her dark eyes glistening. "Your mother meant a great deal to me, Phoenix. As do you. I wish I could do more to spare you the pain of what you are to face, but that is not my place. I've come here to offer you what little help I can."

A tremor of fear ran down Phoenix's spine as the words brought forth a premonition as yet unformed.

"You're not safe here, child. I'm sure that has already become apparent to you. The forces at work behind this prophecy will stop at nothing to ensure it is fulfilled. They will come for you again, and next time I fear they may succeed. You need to go somewhere that they cannot reach you."

"Where?"

"Faerie."

Phoenix barked out a harsh laugh. "Faerie? What makes you think I'd be any safer there?"

"Your mother was banished because she broke a Council edict that normally carries the punishment of death. Banishment was the minimum punishment that would have been deemed acceptable by the Courts. But propriety is very important to the fae, and it would be improper in their eyes for the fae, or your family, to apply that same judgement to you."

"Assuming they don't realise that history has repeated itself." Phoenix hated herself for the bitterness that laced her tone, but she couldn't help it; the fear for her baby was still so raw that she didn't give a shit about the Council or their edicts, or fae propriety.

There was no surprise in Morrigan's expression, only a hint of sorrow as she inclined her head in acknowledgement of the truth. "Your baby is vital to the survival of this world, but some prejudices are deeply ingrained. I will not lie and tell you Faerie is a safe place. It will be filled with much treachery, and I fear I will not be able to assist you while you're there. But it is the only place that Darius cannot follow you, and for that reason alone it is the safest place for you right now."

"No!" Ethan stepped up to Phoenix's side, clearly done with staying quiet in the background. "We can protect her. There's no way she's going to Faerie."

Morrigan met his challenging glare with dark eyes filled with an ageless understanding. "You have done a valiant job in keeping her safe, wolf. And you will be the difference between life and death for her before this is over. But you can't protect her from what is coming. She must leave here if she is to live."

He opened his mouth to protest further, but Phoenix put a hand on his arm. Trepidation filled her and she wanted more than anything to argue alongside him, to stay here, safe with the people she loved. But some part of her knew that what Morrigan said was true. Darius wouldn't give up. And so long as she was here, she was putting them all in danger.

"How long would I have to go for?"

Ethan spun her to face him, eyes blazing. "Are you mad? You can't go to Faerie. What if they find out you're pregnant? You'll be all alone and –"

"She won't be alone," Morrigan interjected softly. "Tomorrow is the Equinox. The veil will be weak enough that, with my help, she'll be able to pull you across with her. But you must make the decision now, or it'll be too late."

Phoenix didn't take her eyes off Ethan as fear, doubt, and determination all warred behind his dark eyes. She knew that he would do everything in his power to protect their child, but he was right – they had no idea what might await them in Faerie. Was it fair to ask this of him? She didn't know; she just knew she couldn't stay.

"Will you come with me?" she asked, her heart halting its rhythm in her chest as she waited for the answer.

He opened his mouth and closed it again. Looked at his family, then back at her. For an agonizing moment she thought he might refuse. Then he blew out a long breath and ran a hand through his hair, shaking his head.

"It was getting a bit boring here anyway," he answered finally, his lip quirking up in the ghost of a grin.

"There's one more thing."

They groaned in unison and turned to look at Morrigan. She gave them an apologetic smile but continued anyway.

"Four ancient fae weapons were used in the original banishment of the Horsemen. Afterwards, the weapons were scattered so that no one could ever use them to undo what had been done. The time has come to unite them once more."

Phoenix frowned in confusion. "What's that got to do with us going to Faerie?"

"I need you to help gather the weapons." Morrigan held up her hand to halt the protest that was on Phoenix's lips. "One of the weapons is here in the human realm. Lia Fáil, the Stone of Destiny, sits on the Hill of Tara, and is easily accessible when the time comes to act. The second, Claíomh Solais, the Sword of Light, is already in your possession."

A collective gasp sounded as Phoenix's jaw dropped. *The Sword of Light?*

Realisation dawned. "My father's sword."

"Yes. Your mother gifted it to him as a sign of her devotion. The sword is a fae weapon and should have only answered to a fae, but her love allowed for a new bond to be formed. It created the possibility of a new future."

Phoenix let the information sink in as she thought back to the first time she'd ever wielded the sword. The pull she'd felt, and the power that had vibrated through the blade, was still fresh in her memory. After that one and only time, she'd put the blade away, afraid of the strange feeling it had triggered. But now she understood. It had called to her, recognised her as a fae.

She shook her head, trying to organise her thoughts. "You said there are four weapons?"

"The third weapon, the Spear of Lugh, remains in Faerie. I need you to find it. The weapons call to each other. If you bring Claíomh Solais with you, it will lead you to the spear."

"What about the fourth weapon?" Ethan asked.

"Dagda's Cauldron. It is safe. It was taken many millennia ago so that it wouldn't fall into the wrong hands. When the time comes, I will call on its guardians and they will bring it to us."

CHAPTER TEN

Darius stared at Sean in silence as fury scorched a path through his veins. It was bad enough that the Omega had disobeyed his order to retrieve Phoenix, but now the mutt dared to stand before him with his shoulders squared defiantly, no trace of fear on his face. Well, that would soon change.

"And why, pray tell, did you see fit to return empty-handed when I gave you a direct order?"

"She's pregnant," Sean ground out from between clenched teeth. As if those two words should explain everything.

"And?"

"I won't have the death of an innocent on my conscience. I don't care what you do to me, I won't help you with this."

Darius gave a humourless laugh. "My dear Sean, you and I both know you already have the deaths of many innocents on your conscience. And you're about to have even more." He pulled out his mobile phone and redialled the most recent number. "Erik, can you please gather any remaining wolves that haven't yet completed the transition? Our Omega has decided that they're not fit to continue the process and he'd like to oversee their termination himself."

Sean blanched, and the defiance that had moments ago dared to darken his blue eyes shifted to an agonised look of disbelief. He shook his head, but it was a futile denial. He would comply just like he always did because for every wolf that Darius hurt or killed to control him, there were always more that needed the Omega to save them.

Darius held Sean's gaze with a cruel smile and continued speaking to Erik. "When he's finished, see that he's made comfortable in one of the chambers. I shall inform the witches that there's another transfer to be done."

Thick, rich blood slid down the back of Darius's throat as he drained the last drops of precious life from the nameless woman. Her body lay limp in his arms, the weight an inconvenience now that he'd taken what he needed from her. With swift efficiency, he retracted his fangs and tossed her to the floor beside his mahogany desk like a discarded tissue.

The warm blood coursing through his veins did little to abate his fury. Sean's failure had put everything in jeopardy. Even now Phoenix was likely on the move, the failed abduction attempt giving her more than sufficient warning that she wasn't safe within the confines of the pack.

Licking an errant drop of blood from the corner of his mouth, he slipped his hand into his pocket and wrapped it around the silver coin resting there. His flesh burned where the precious metal made contact, and he forced his hand to grip it tighter. The pain was searing, but he focused on it, letting it clear his mind of all distractions.

The witches were already busy at work trying to track Phoenix. They'd had little trouble following her whereabouts in the past, and this time would be no different. It was inconvenient, but still only a minor setback. He'd have the hybrid under his control within twenty-four hours, and he'd deal with the abomination growing inside her.

He stood, stepping over the woman who lay in a heap on the floor beside him, and made his way from the office down to the lowest level of the club.

The laboratory was abuzz with activity as Darius stepped from the elevator. Preparations were being made for Sean's demon transfer, and it gave him no small sense of satisfaction to imagine the Omega's horror at the knowledge that pure evil would soon live inside him. It had been a nice little touch to the punishment, if Darius did say so himself.

He glanced around for a witch, intending to enquire on the progress of the tracking spell, and was surprised to once again recognise the sharp features of the witch with the white streak of hair. As when Darius had last seen him, the man was in the middle of preparing for the transfer. Despite his scrawny frame and pale features, the man seemed in no way weakened from having conducted the same spell only the previous day. Darius watched him with curiosity, a thought forming in the back of his mind.

"You," he said, when the witch's preparations seemed to be complete. "What's your name?"

The man straightened and met Darius's eyes without flinching. "Richard."

"What's your affinity?" Witches drew their power from the world around them, and while they could work various common spells, their individual strengths tended to have a more specialised focus. Darius had found that some affinities proved more useful than others when he required someone to do his bidding.

"I can control animals."

Oh, now that is interesting.

"Tell me, Richard." Darius placed a hand on the man's bony shoulder. "What are your ambitions in life?"

"What does any self-respecting man want?" Richard's beady eyes flashed. "I want to be the most powerful witch that history has ever known."

Darius smiled. This one would do.

"What if I told you I could help you with that? You do something for me, and I will give you power unlike anything you've ever known."

Richard regarded him closely, making a poor attempt to mask his interest. "What would I need to do?"

With a comforting pat on the shoulder, Darius led him towards the empty chamber that was being prepared for Sean's transfer. He gave a subtle nod to the scientist who was eyeing the interaction with curiosity and guided Richard into the sterile white room. The door closed tightly behind them.

CHAPTER ELEVEN

Phoenix stared at the rolling hills that zoomed past the car's window. It was easier to focus on the blur of green than the apprehension twisting itself into a complex knot in her stomach. She hadn't been back to Dunluce Castle since Lily's death, and the thought of returning to the place where she'd held the young witch's dying body filled her with a sickening dread.

It had been no real surprise when Morrigan told them the old castle was one of the main gateways to Faerie; Phoenix still remembered the power the place held, and how it had called to her. In truth, she wasn't quite sure how much of her trepidation about returning was because of Lily's death, and how much was fear of facing that power again.

But even on the Equinox they needed a place of great energy to enable her to pull Ethan through to Faerie with her. So, they'd left Donegal as soon as the sun had crested the horizon that morning, and Ethan had treated every speed sign as if it were a gentle suggestion rather than a legal limit in his haste to get them to the gateway where they'd meet Morrigan.

It was hard to believe that she'd finally get to see the place where her mother had been born. She'd never once had the urge to visit Faerie – had never even been sure if she could, given her hybrid nature – but now that she was going, she couldn't help but wonder what it'd be like. Of course, they weren't exactly going on a summer holiday. Morrigan had warned them more than once to be on their guard, and with time moving differently in Faerie than it did here, they'd have to make haste in their search for the Spear of Lugh.

For the umpteenth time, Phoenix glanced behind her to the back seat of the car and the long mahogany box that rested there. Intricate Celtic designs covered the wood protecting her father's sword, and she pictured the blade that lay cushioned inside. Claíomh Solais. Had her parents known? Did they know they'd someday need the sword to protect the world because of her?

She pushed the thought from her mind and asked Ethan, "Did you get a chance to speak to Nate?"

Ethan glanced sideways at her. "He pinkie-promised not to let Abi out of his sight. He's enlisted her to help with his research. I'm not sure that's a good thing for her, but he seems happy to have someone who's actually willing to listen to his tech waffle."

A tinge of sadness laced Phoenix's laughter. "She loves learning about our world and feeling useful. I just wish she'd gotten the chance under better circumstances."

"She will," he assured her, reaching over to give her hand a quick squeeze.

The warmth of his touch chased away some of the chill lingering deep inside her, and when he took his hand away, she felt its loss so acutely that she shivered. She wrapped her arms around herself, her abdomen still tender to the touch. The pack doctor hadn't been too happy to discover he wouldn't be able to monitor her further, but he'd grudgingly agreed that the baby seemed largely unharmed. Phoenix, for her part, took comfort in the memory of the strong heartbeat, and the soft flutters that let her know the munchkin was still with her.

"Are you nervous about meeting your family?" Ethan asked, when she lapsed into silence for a time.

"I've been trying not to think about it. They may be the least of our problems once we hit Faerie."

Morrigan believed that Phoenix's half-fae blood should be

enough for them to avoid a direct attack once they crossed over, but all they really had to go on at this stage was supposition. They'd need to make their way to her family as quickly as possible if they were going to utilise the protection of her family name.

"Did your mother tell you much about them?"

"She didn't like to talk about them; it hurt her too much." Even now Phoenix could remember the look of pain on her mother's face when, as a child, she'd innocently asked about her family. She shook her head with a wry grin. "Hell, I didn't even know I came from royalty. I could have demanded that you address me as Princess all this time."

Ethan burst out laughing, a hearty chuckle that she couldn't help but join in with. "Keep dreaming!"

"How do you think we'll find ..." She trailed off, squinting at the horizon. A heavy fog rolled towards them, the thick grey mass a striking contrast to the bright cloudless sky directly above.

"What the –" Ethan leaned forward over the steering wheel as he too noticed the strange sight.

The fog engulfed the landscape before them, muting the vivid greens of nature as if an unnatural grey veil had been dropped over everything. Ethan eased his foot off the accelerator, putting on the hazard lights as he slowed the car and pulled it to a stop at the side of the road.

"That's a pretty sudden change in weather," Phoenix noted, a nervous tingle running down her spine. She looked behind them and her unease was only increased at the sight of the sun shining high in the sky.

Ethan was quiet for a minute as he too watched the grey wall of fog move closer with each passing second. "There's no turnoff on this road for another mile."

That would take them straight into the fog.

Phoenix worried at the sleeve of her jacket. "We could turn back?"

"We're not far from the castle now. Besides," he added with what she assumed was false confidence, "it's not unusual for Ireland to have four seasons in one day."

She said nothing as he slowly pulled the car back onto the road, but a tightness settled in her chest. The air grew heavier as they moved forward. Her fingers twitched and she looked back at the mahogany box that held her father's sword.

In less than a minute the grey mist blanketed them, bringing with it a weighty silence that made it almost seem as if they were underwater. Visibility reduced to little more than a couple of feet in front of them, and even the car's fog lights struggled to pierce the veil.

They inched forward, tension building as they both acknowledged the creeping sensation that warned them this fog wasn't natural. The car jerked, and Phoenix's seat belt halted her forward momentum with bruising force. Ethan cursed loudly, slapping the steering wheel as they shuddered to a sudden stop.

"Wait here," he ordered, and jumped out of the car before she could respond.

Like hell was she staying there alone. She fumbled to unbuckle her seat belt and reached over to retrieve her father's sword from its box in the back seat. By the time she climbed out after him, Ethan was standing staring at the wheels on the driver's side with a grim frown.

Both tyres on her side hung limply around the alloy wheels, and a quick walk to where Ethan stood showed her the same. Deep gashes ran across each tyre, shredding them beyond repair. Phoenix looked in dismay from the tyres to Ethan.

"How –"

A loud "*Caw!*" broke through the muted silence of the fog, cutting her off. Morrigan's crow form swooped down towards them.

"What's she doing here? I thought we were meeting at the castle?" Phoenix had barely finished her question when chilling howls sounded in the distance. Her breath caught and she looked at Ethan with wide eyes.

In a single movement, the crow landed beside them and shifted into a woman. Morrigan grabbed Phoenix by the elbow, her eyes tight with tension. "Go. He's coming."

A primal fear ran through Ethan at the distant howls. He met Morrigan's dark eyes and recognised the unspoken order in their depths: *protect her.* He had no idea who was coming for them, or what could possibly have the goddess so on edge, but he wasn't about the ignore the warning.

As the air shimmered and the large crow propelled itself once more into the air, he grabbed Phoenix's hand, mentally calculating the distance to the castle. It had been less than twenty-four hours since she'd been hurt and the last thing he wanted to do was put her body under more stress, but injuries would be a moot point unless they survived.

"Can you run?"

She clutched her father's sword tighter and gave him a determined nod despite the fear that glistened in her green eyes.

They broke into a sprint, letting instinct rather than sight guide them as they moved deeper and deeper into the fog. It didn't matter how quickly they ran, however; the snarls and howls continued to grow closer. Not breaking his stride, Ethan risked a glance behind him. His stomach lurched.

Through the thick blanket of fog, he could see a blur of black on the horizon. As it grew closer, he could just about make out the shapes of huge black dogs. They moved faster than the wind, and the pounding of their paws was like thunder in the unnatural denseness of the fog.

Phoenix gasped as she too spotted their pursuers. Her steps faltered. He grabbed for her as she stumbled. "Just a little bit further," he urged, hoping like hell he was right.

Vicious snarls punctuated his words. But this time the sound didn't come from behind them. It came from in front of them.

Ethan skidded to a halt, pushing Phoenix behind him with a low curse. The blanket of fog parted and a tall, wiry man with sharp features stepped into their path. A streak of white ran through the man's mousey brown hair, and his eyes flickered from black to red as he smiled at them. Two huge Irish wolfhounds stood on either side of him, reaching almost to his shoulder. Acrid black smoke rolled off their dark grey coats, and they too had red eyes.

A sickening aura permeated the man and his dogs, the tainted sensation of black magic mixing with something otherworldly. Ethan's skin crawled, and even the beast within him shrank back to try to escape the magic's vile touch.

"Here, doggy," the man hissed and clicked his fingers.

A blinding pain ripped through Ethan. Ligaments tore away from bone as his body started to shift and change against his will. Claws ruptured from his fingertips, and fangs burst through his gums, filling his mouth with blood. His wolf howled.

He was dimly aware of Phoenix screaming his name as his knees buckled. The memory of another such violation of his will caused every cell in his body to roar in protest, but try as he might, he couldn't resist the shift any more now than he had the last time. Then something changed.

Phoenix's hand gripped his shoulder, and the warmth of her touch sent a jolt through him. A white light surrounded them, and he could feel the heat of the sun as his wolf latched onto her scent. He clung to it for all he was worth, drawing on her power to help fight back against the unnatural magic that tried to crush him to its will.

Sweat soaked his body as he visualised silver bars slamming down around his wolf, caging it within him. Inch by agonising inch, he forced his body to straighten, his limbs to realign.

"You dare defy me!" the witch roared, red eyes blazing. The wolfhounds at his side snarled and foaming saliva dripped from mouths filled with impossibly sharp teeth. They jerked forward, but the man stopped them with a snap of his fingers.

His face relaxed to a chilling calm. "I would've liked to add a wolf to my collection of pets. Never mind. I'll deliver your bitch to Darius and I'm sure he'll gladly provide me with one. Maybe even your white-haired friend."

Low growls began to emanate from all sides. Ethan's blood ran cold.

"Shit," Phoenix whispered, moving closer to him as he risked a glance away from the witch.

The swarm of black hounds that they'd seen on the horizon had finally reached them. Slowly and deliberately, the dogs formed a circle and caged them in. Pairs of red eyes shone like torches of fire through the heavy fog, and their blade-like teeth gleamed.

Ethan noticed the witch making minute gestures with his hands, and the hounds began to move with an eerie synchronicity. Beside him, Phoenix tensed, raising Claíomh Solais before her. The noose tightened around them and Ethan tensed for the attack.

A blur of black swooped down from the sky, and a cawing shriek shattered the tense bubble of silence. Morrigan swept past Ethan with a rush of air, her feathers skimming his cheek right before she collided with the witch.

The man stumbled backwards, hands flapping in a desperate attempt to keep her striking beak away from the soft flesh of his face. His momentary distraction broke the hold he had on the hounds and the red disappeared from their eyes in an instant. The dogs shuffled about in confusion, and a couple whined pitifully as they cowered down on the ground.

The two wolfhounds at the witch's side were a different story, however. Without their master to hold them back, they fixed their feral stares on Phoenix and Ethan and stalked forward. Acrid black smoke swirled around them, and fear choked Ethan as he looked into the emotionless depths of their eyes.

As one, the wolfhounds tensed and leapt. Phoenix slashed out with her sword and caught the one on the left with a glancing blow. A swipe of Ethan's still extended claws tore through the side of the one on the right, but the sheer weight of it leaping at him threw him backwards.

"Morrigan!" Phoenix yelled as they struggled to hold their ground against the wolfhounds.

A piercing shriek sounded from the witch, only to be abruptly cut off. The black crow shot through the air towards them, shifting mid-flight. When Morrigan struck the ground, she no longer bore the oil-slick feathers of the bird but instead took the form of a huge black horse.

The horse reared up on its hind legs before the wolfhounds, using its sheer size to drive the dogs back. It gave a sharp whinny as the front hooves struck the ground, and Ethan grabbed Phoenix. He got her up on the horse's back a fraction of a second before the wolfhounds regrouped.

He lashed out with his claws as the one on his right snapped vicious teeth towards him. He drew blood, but not nearly enough. The wolfhound on the left followed the attack, its teeth latching on to his shoulder. Fire blazed through him as the dog's canines locked onto bone and refused to let go.

A flash of metal came from above and Phoenix plunged the blade of her sword down into the wolfhound, who released its grip on Ethan's shoulder.

With his one remaining good arm, Ethan swung himself up behind her on the horse. "Go!" he roared.

CHAPTER TWELVE

Phoenix's heart thundered so hard she thought it would shatter her ribcage at any moment. She gripped the horse's oil slick mane with one hand and her father's sword with the other as the wind whipped at her face. The heavy fog didn't thin as they shot towards Dunluce Castle, and there were eerie cries in the distance, but Morrigan moved faster than the horrors that followed and nothing caught them before they reached the castle's boundaries.

A wave of power washed over Phoenix as the castle's jagged structure came into view, stealing her breath away. It called to the very core of her, and this time she recognised it for what it was: like calling to like. The power wasn't the only thing that came, however. Memories came too. She gritted her teeth and pushed them away. Thinking about Lily's death wouldn't help her now.

The black horse pounded up the dirt track and leapt over the metal barrier that blocked entry to the empty car park. Through the unnatural grey veil, the castle ruins loomed up from the edge of the cliff, the broken walls and crumbling stone somehow making it seem more imposing rather than less.

Only when they reached the entry wall to the castle did Morrigan come to a stop. Ethan dismounted in a single graceful movement behind her. Phoenix handed him the sword, relieved to see the wound on his shoulder already appeared to be healing despite the blood that soaked one side of his jumper. She swung her legs over to the right side and slid rather ungracefully to the ground.

The air shimmered and the horse disappeared, leaving the goddess with flowing black hair in its place. "We don't have much time," Morrigan said, eyeing the horizon as if she expected danger to appear at any second. "The witch isn't dead, or the fog would have lifted. He'll be coming for you." She urged them through the jagged arch that had once been a doorway and into the centre of the ruins.

The castle was just how Phoenix remembered. Colourful flowers dotted the lush green grass, their vibrancy in no way muted by the unnatural grey shroud surrounding them. Her gaze was drawn to the stone wall where Maj had once stood with that strange look of regret on her face. Some part of Phoenix still wondered at that look, and whether she'd made the right decision in freeing the Mists. The other part of her was just glad they'd decided not to stick around after the uneasy truce was struck.

She blew out a long breath and turned to face Morrigan and Ethan. "What now?"

"Now I'll show you how to cross the barrier to Faerie. As your guardian it is my job to watch over you and protect you in any way I can, but once you reach Faerie, I fear my hands will be tied. The rules that govern my power also serve to hold back others more powerful than me. If I overstep my boundaries while you're there, they will be allowed to overstep theirs. So, I urge you again to take care. I did not lie when I said Faerie is the safest place for you right now, but it is by no means a safe place."

Phoenix swallowed at the ominous warning and nodded her understanding.

"Keep the secret of your union close to you." Morrigan looked from her to Ethan with a sad smile. "It is a precious gift you carry, though others may not yet see that."

She held out her hands in invitation. Phoenix took the sword back from Ethan and gripped it tightly in her hand as she reached forward to place her other hand in Morrigan's. Ethan stepped forward next and placed his hand in the goddess's without hesitation.

"Time moves differently in Faerie. What seems like days there may be weeks, or even months, here. Waste no time in seeking the spear." With Morrigan's final words, the world around them disappeared.

Blinding white filled Phoenix's vision, and she groped desperately for Ethan. Her heart pounded and her head spun. She was both weightless and heavy at the same time, floating with nothing beneath her feet but infinity. A wave rippled through her body and she lurched forward. She gasped when a hand grabbed her, and only when her panic calmed enough to feel the familiar heat radiating from the touch did the tightness in her chest ease. Slowly the light faded from her vision, leaving specks of colour dancing before her eyes.

The boundaries of Dunluce Castle were gone, now just a memory etched into her eyelids from the light. Instead, trees surrounded them in all directions. Gnarled trunks twisted, their thick branches coated with an unusual mix of colours – greens so vibrant they were almost illuminous, azure blues which brought to mind the ocean, yellows that varied from the palest lemon to rich golden tones. Mushrooms and toadstools dotted the ground, making the tableau seem like an illustration from a children's book.

"Is it just me, or does all this feel a little cliché?" Ethan muttered, taking it all in with a look of disbelief.

Phoenix giggled, imagining little gnomes popping up from the grass to greet them. "It's kind of quaint."

"I guess we should try find a way out of here. It would have been helpful if Morrigan had supplied a map or something." He looked at her and stopped in his tracks, mouth gaping. "Where did you get that?"

"Huh?" She looked down, patting her torso in confusion. Her hands found a thick leather strap running diagonally across her body that hadn't been there before. She followed it up over her shoulder where she found the hilt of her father's sword within easy reach.

Ducking carefully, she pulled the strap over her head and stared at the simple black scabbard covering the sword's blade. She hadn't even realised the sword wasn't in her hand anymore. Where the hell had this come from?

She was about to voice the question aloud when a piercing shriek shook the trees, jerking her head up to meet Ethan's wide eyes. "Any chance that was my imagination?"

He shook his head, body instantly alert as he eyed the area around them. "We should get moving."

She drew Claíomh Solais from the scabbard and slung the leather strap across her back. The weight of the sword was comforting in her hand, but it didn't chase away the icy fear as they cut a careful path through the cheery landscape.

Something about that sound had tapped straight into her primal senses, and as they moved, Phoenix realised that her first impression of their surroundings had been subtly deceptive. The closer she looked, the more she realised that the forest around them was alive, and she had the creeping sense that it was watching them. Waiting.

As soon as the thought came to her mind, the lush green grass disappeared. In its place, twisting ropes of ivy covered the forest floor, writhing like snakes.

One of the vines edged towards her, slithering around her foot and up her leg. She jumped back with a yelp and kicked out at the space around her with a shudder. Yet more vines snaked their way down from a nearby tree to tenderly caress Ethan's cheek before moving to his neck.

For a split second he seemed almost entranced by the touch, but then he snapped his hand out and grabbed the vine, yanking it away from him before it could fully encircle his throat.

More and more vines edged in their direction. The quicker Phoenix moved, the faster they closed in. Slowly, her heart pounding with the effort, she edged closer to Ethan, never once taking her eyes off the green mass. "What do you think will happen if we make a run for it?" she asked under her breath.

Ethan's response was cut off as another shriek filled the air, closer this time. In a flash the ropes of ivy retracted, leaving only barren earth in their wake.

They looked at each other and back to the now empty space around them. When the creepy things fled, it was really time to go.

"Run!" Ethan grabbed her hand and pulled her behind him as he started to run.

They sprinted blindly through the ever-changing colours of the forest. Phoenix swung her head left and right, frantically seeking a break in the trees, or anything that might indicate they were near the edge of the forest. But the trees seemed to only close in tighter around them.

A third shrill cry sent chills skittering along her skin. She had no idea what could possibly be making the noise; she just knew that every instinct in her body commanded her to run. So when Ethan came to a jarring stop in front of her, she slammed straight into the broad expanse of his back.

"What the –" A sharp *click* froze the words in her throat.

Tension radiated from Ethan, and her mouth was dry as she moved her head an inch to the side to glimpse past him. What she saw was the gleaming tip of three arrows pointed straight at them.

The arrows were loaded into sleek, curved black crossbows, and at first glance Phoenix almost thought they were floating in the air. Then the three men holding them moved into a V formation, the movement breaking their camouflage from the surrounding foliage.

Each of the men had pale skin tinged with green. Long, green-blue hair was pulled back into braids entwined with twigs and leaves, showcasing the pointed tips of their ears. Steady yellow eyes fixed on her every movement, reminding her of the watchful gaze of a cat. A vine of ivy slid across the forest floor and wound itself around the foot of the lead fae. It crawled up his body and faded to form a faint shimmering pattern on his skin.

Ethan shifted his body to block their view of her and held up his hands, palms forward. "We're not looking for trouble."

One of the men let a humourless laugh. "What else could a wolf be looking for by coming to Faerie?"

Phoenix slid her body past Ethan, ignoring his frustrated glare. It wasn't that she didn't appreciate the show of chivalry, but he could get stuffed if he expected her to hide behind him like a scared little girl.

She squared her shoulders and with as much authority as she could muster, declared, "We've been sent by Morrigan. We wish to be brought to Lord Aodhán and Lady Clíodhna."

The ivy-covered fae in front sneered, his companions remaining stony-faced as they held the crossbows pointed unwaveringly at her heart. "You claim the great Goddess sent you here? And who might you be to demand an audience with our Lord and Lady?"

"I'm their granddaughter."

CHAPTER THIRTEEN

Home – 1 day gone

Abi chewed on the jagged edge of her thumbnail as she stared out the window to the sprawling expanse of the pack lands. The weather had taken a turn from clear blue skies and sunshine to an ominous blanket of grey clouds that perfectly matched her mood and the atmosphere in the house.

Six hours and thirteen minutes had passed since Phoenix and Ethan set off for Dunluce Castle. There'd been no news, and as time continued to tick on, her nerves were becoming even more frayed. Most likely they'd crossed over to Faerie by now, but would it really have killed them to send a quick text before they jumped ship to a magical land?

It wasn't getting to just her either; the whole house was on edge. As if the prophecy and Darius weren't enough, the pack had to deal with the shock of Sean's reappearance now too. The strain was painfully visible on Cormac's and Fia's normally composed features as they talked quietly to Nate on the far side of the living room. The shifter's fingers danced over the keys of his laptop as he concentrated on the screen, giving the occasional nod or grim shake of his head.

Sasha sat quietly beside Abi on the sofa, her playful humour noticeably missing as she stared at the ashes in the unlit fire. More than once Abi had opened her mouth intending to say something reassuring, anything to take the look of pain from those brown eyes, but every time she'd closed it again before ever speaking a word. What could she say? She was only human; she knew nothing.

The rhythmic tapping of Nate's fingers on his keyboard ceased as he blew out a frustrated breath and leaned back into the sofa, scrubbing his hands over his face. "Unless we've missed something on the CCTV cameras around the Dublin clan's lair, Darius hasn't been back there in months. It stands to reason he's hiding out somewhere connected to the clan, but they've more than twenty businesses to their name. And they have an indirect or minority interest in dozens more."

Cormac let a low growl. "We need more information. If we go in gung-ho and start attacking the clan's businesses, it'll just make Darius go deeper underground and we'll never find him."

"So, what, we just sit around and do nothing?" Sasha's composure finally broke and she jumped up from the sofa and started pacing, fists clenched at her side.

Fia moved to put a hand on her daughter's shoulder, but Sasha shrugged her off and sat back down, seeming to deflate. Abi's heart ached for the wolf and she reached out to give Sasha's hand a gentle squeeze.

"That's not what I'm saying." Cormac's eyes were fierce, determined. "We need to be smart about it if we're going to get Sean back. And we *are* going to get him back."

"He'll be okay," Abi quietly reassured Sasha as the wolf gripped her hand. "Sean's survived this long; he can hang on a little bit longer."

Even as she said the words, she wondered if they were true. She could still remember every second of her time as Darius's guest, and it terrified her to even imagine what Sean must be going through. She'd only just managed to survive a few hours with him. How did someone endure years of that torture and still remain sane?

The door to the living room opened, and they all turned as Lucas and Shade strode into the room. At Cormac's questioning look, Lucas shook his head. "I'll keep asking around."

Of all of them, Lucas was the best connected within the vampire networks of the Lore. His clan was well respected, and from what she'd heard, Darius had even been a member of it once upon a time. He'd gone to Lucas seeking a new clan after his own Sire had died and subsequently ended up meeting Marcus, Phoenix's father. It had been a long shot to hope Lucas might be able to track Darius through his connections, but it seemed their avenues were few and far between at the moment and it had been worth a try.

A heavy silence fell over the room, only to be broken by a shrill ringtone.

They all reached for their pockets instinctively, but it was Cormac who pulled out his mobile and sighed. "It's William again."

The wolf head of the Council had been calling incessantly for days. Cormac had been avoiding his cousin, but he'd only be able to do that for so long before the Council lost their patience and decided to stop playing nice.

Once again Cormac moved to decline the call, but Fia put a hand on his arm to stop him. "Maybe you should talk to him? Darius was one of their Witnesses. If they can help us find Sean ..."

He hesitated, a muscle twitching in his jaw as he glared at the phone. He gritted his teeth and nodded, slowly bringing it to his ear as he hit the button to answer the call.

Abi didn't need supernatural hearing to catch William's furious tirade on the other end of the phone.

"Where the hell have you been? I've been trying to reach you for days. You know it's an offence to ignore contact from the Council."

Cormac waited until his cousin had paused for breath before asking, "Did you want something?"

Abi watched his expression closely as the conversation settled into a more civilised tone – if Cormac's grunted responses could be considered civilised, or even conversation. His expression remained stony and unchanging, but at some point since getting involved in this crazy world she'd become attuned to the more subtle signs that gave away a person's mood. The darkening of his eyes worried her the most.

"We'll be there," Cormac said after a long silence, and hung up the phone without a goodbye. He looked around the room at the impatient expressions. "We're going to meet the Council."

White-hot rage filled Darius as Erik brought him up to date on the morning's events. He leaned back in his office chair, knuckles whitening when his grip tightened on the crystal tumbler in his hand.

"We've been unable to trace the hybrid," his head of security summed up, expression carefully neutral. "Last known location was Dunluce Castle, then the tracking spell we had on her just stopped working. Our sources confirm there is a gateway to Faerie on the castle grounds. Given our inability to track her, it would seem likely she's crossed over."

Darius took a slow, deliberate sip of his whiskey. He stood, and with a roar flung the tumbler at the window overlooking the heaving dance floor below. The tumbler shattered and golden liquid ran down the glass in rivulets to soak into the plush carpet. Erik waited silently.

"What about the witch who was sent after the hybrid?"

"He's been dealt with."

"Gather the remainder of the coven. It's time they understand the price of their failures." Too often now he'd overlooked the coven's mistakes. Mistakes that could cost him everything he'd worked for. Well, no more.

Erik gave a sharp nod and left to see to the arrangements. Darius waited until the door clicked closed, then made his way to the mahogany desk and pulled open the top drawer. Faded red velvet lined its interior and a scroll rested inside. Carefully, he lifted it out.

The scroll was ancient, made of vellum that had long ago been preserved by magic. The flowing words were as clear now as the day they were written, and he soaked them in as he unrolled the scroll.

Terror, destruction, death to man.
The fires of hell o'ertake the land.
So long as she alone shall stand,
Shall the Horsemen walk the land.

These words were his destiny. These words had shown him the way to restore the Lore to its former glory. He would do what his Sire had not been able to; he wouldn't succumb to weakness and death.

An icy calm settled over him as he rolled the scroll back up and returned it to its resting place. A thin haze of red clouded his vision as he strode from the office and made his way down to the lowest level.

Seven witches remained in the Dublin coven, and Erik had them all lined up and waiting by the time Darius reached the laboratory. Vampires stood on either side of them, and a heavy silence filled the room. The tension tasted bitter on his tongue and he noted more than one finger or eye twitch from the instinctive need to draw magic. It wouldn't matter though – their magic wouldn't save them now.

He assessed the witches one at a time. A mere three of the seven were brave enough to look him in the eye, and only one of those managed to maintain a stony composure while doing so.

"One of your witches has put me in a very difficult position." He kept his tone conversational as he addressed them. "Because of him, a key element of our plan is now out of my reach, putting everything we've worked for at risk. I'm sure you'll agree, that is simply not acceptable. Now ..." He paused to steeple his fingers as he paced. "I will give you each a chance to rectify this unfortunate situation. The one who provides me with a solution gets to live. The rest of you die." His smile was cold as he looked at them expectantly.

"But – but – You need us," a tall man in the middle stammered. His face was a mask of shock and beads of sweat dotted his forehead.

Darius regarded him for a moment, then, in a blur of movement tore his throat out with his razor-sharp fangs. He pulled a handkerchief from his pocket and dabbed delicately at the blood running down his chin before turning to address the remaining witches.

"Make no mistake in believing you're indispensable. Your coven has grown weak. I've kept you here out of convenience to me, but I grow tired of your incompetence. There is another coven is already lined up to take your place, and if you wish to be alive to join them, I suggest you get creative."

The next to open their mouth was a female witch. She lost her life when his fist ripped her heart from her chest cavity. The stammering terror of another two witches pissed him off enough that he didn't even give them a chance to speak before he tore them to shreds. One of the three remaining witches was foolish enough to draw on his magic and was buried under a pile of vampire guards in a feeding frenzy.

Two remained: a cocky-looking man that reminded him of a lawyer, and the stony-faced witch, a woman barely five feet tall.

The man opened his mouth to speak but broke off in a choked gurgle. The woman at his side quirked a lip and raised an eyebrow at Darius. Her magic skittered over his skin even as the man at her side turned a worrying shade of purple and fell to his knees.

The guards moved to subdue the female witch, but Darius held up his hand, halting their movement. "Someone with initiative. I like that."

"I don't plan on dying for other people's incompetence."

"Well then, let's hope you have an acceptable solution for me."

The witch considered him, no trace of fear in her steely gaze. "I can't give you the hybrid. If the rumours are true and she has passed over to Faerie, no witch can; that magic is beyond our reach and any who tell you otherwise are lying to you. But I can offer you a possible alternative to the prophecy."

Darius waited for her to continue, his curiosity peaked.

"The Horsemen need the fabric to fall completely in order to cross into our world in corporeal form, but their essence does not. If the prophecy was to fail – say, for example, due to a particular child being born – there will be a pivotal moment during which our world and theirs collide. If we can time this precisely, I can use the point of collision to draw their essence into this world. All I need is a vessel."

"A vessel? Someone to hold the Horsemen within them?"

The witch nodded. "The vessel would not hold indefinitely; the

580

Horsemen's power is too immense and would destroy the body before long. But it would buy us time."

"Time for what?"

"Time to reverse the original spell and free them back into this world. With or without the prophecy."

Darius pivoted on his heel and paced the length of the laboratory, stepping over the fallen body of one of the witches. A solution that didn't require reliance on the prophecy was awfully tempting, but when something seemed too good to be true it usually was.

"I see one very large flaw in your suggestion." The witch raised an eyebrow and waited. "The timing of the child's birth is impossible to predict."

The witch gave him a satisfied smile. "Not if we decide the timing ourselves. With the right ingredients, I can create an elixir that will speed the progress of the hybrid's pregnancy and induce labour."

"And how do you propose that we get her to take such an elixir, given she's currently out of our reach?"

"A powerful man such as yourself must have some connections who are open to a more ... enlightened way of thinking. It would be a simple matter of getting some assistance."

He considered this. The fae were notoriously difficult to deal with, and his influence with them was a lot more limited than some of the other species – like the witches. However, he now conveniently had the head of the CLO at his disposal, and Vicktor had become infinitely more agreeable following his demonic upgrade. It stood to reason that the CLO rep would have some connections that could be of use to them. Darius knew enough about the power structure of Faerie to know that many of the high-ranking fae were not above temptation.

"If it's as simple as convincing someone in Faerie to assist us in giving Phoenix an elixir, why then would we not just give her one to end the pregnancy?"

The witch shrugged. "It could be done if you wished, though I would have thought you were more forward thinking than that."

Darius grew deathly still. The vampires in the room shifted

nervously, but the witch continued, unphased by the obvious threat of death that was but a hair's breadth from her.

"If you force a termination of the pregnancy, it will indeed remove the current obstacle to the prophecy. But what of the next obstacle, and the one after that? There is still a significant amount of time to pass before the prophecy reaches its conclusion. Why wait, when you can control the outcome once and for all?"

CHAPTER FOURTEEN

Faerie — day 1

Phoenix followed the fae guards in silence, Ethan sticking close to her side. Her father's sword was a comforting weight across her back, though the fact they'd allowed her to keep a weapon was concerning.

There were no more terrifying shrieks as they walked, and the forest was suspiciously quiet. She scanned her surroundings warily, not fooled by the sudden calm. The path out of the trees was so straightforward that she was convinced the landscape had to be shifting to accommodate them. A ridiculous thought, really, but given Faerie was an unknown entity to them, it was entirely possible.

They emerged from the trees to stop in front of a towering stone wall. It ran as far as her eye could see in both directions, and guards patrolled the battlements at the top. Many sported a more traditional bow and arrow than the crossbows carried by the three fae surrounding her, and others carried what appeared to be long, coiled whips. Each looked more than capable of dealing with a potential intruder, though she had to imagine that the wall itself acted as sufficient deterrent to most.

Just as she was wondering how far they'd need to trek to find an opening in said wall, the lead guard stepped forward and placed his hand against the stone. He bowed his head and spoke so quietly that even with her enhanced hearing, she couldn't make out his words. A section of the wall dissolved, and an archway formed. A cobblestone path led into the distance, bordered on either side by rolling lawns of green and gold.

"Don't stray from the path," the guard with the ivy skin warned, giving them an accusing glare before leading them through the arch.

Phoenix exchanged an uneasy look with Ethan but followed without a word.

A large building loomed in the distance, its opulence so apparent even from afar that it could only be considered a castle. Beautifully ornate turrets framed huge panes of glass that glistened like crystal in the sun. Oak trees larger than any she'd ever seen before bookended the building on either side and seemed to meld into the walls. Thick branches snaked out from the trees and reached towards each other, making it look as if the castle had sprouted up from the centre of one giant tree.

Despite the knot of apprehension that was twisting in her gut, Phoenix couldn't help but stare in awe. *So, this is Faerie?*

Of course, it was easier to focus on the unusual scenery than the fact they really were in another world now. Alone and away from their family and friends. She took a shaky breath and forced the thought away as they drew closer to the castle.

Stone steps led up to two large oak doors that opened, seemingly of their own accord, at the group's approach. A long hallway led from the entrance, boasting a plush cream carpet that was so spotless Phoenix could only assume the fae were capable of hovering. Vines of ivy wound along the walls and across the ceiling, giving the effect of a long green tunnel.

She hesitated at the top of the steps for a moment before following the others across the threshold. The doors slammed shut behind her and she jumped, heart ricocheting in her chest. Ethan put a hand on her back, his brown eyes searching her face for confirmation that she was okay. She gave him a small smile which might have been more of a grimace, then followed the fae guards, grateful for the comfort of his touch.

A gentle breeze blew through the interior, and Phoenix could have sworn she heard the chirping of birds. She eyed the vines of ivy, expecting them to close around her at any moment, as the ones in the forest had. When another pair of wooden doors came into view at the end of the hall, she hurried her steps with relief.

These doors didn't open in welcome as the first ones had. Instead, two sentinels dressed entirely in black stood on either side of the doors, hands clasped behind their backs, steely gazes focused ahead. The ivy guard broke from their group and stepped forward to speak with the one on the right.

The sentinel's silver eyes locked on Phoenix as he listened, his face blank. She wondered if he was going to simply stare at her, but after some consideration, he turned and slipped between the doors.

"Now what?" She clasped her hands together in an attempt to stop from fidgeting.

"Now you wait," the ivy fae answered coolly.

Minutes passed, each one feeling like an hour. Finally, the sentinel returned, his expression no friendlier. He held open one of the doors and indicated for them to enter. "Lord Aodhán and Lady Clíodhna will speak with you."

Phoenix's palms were sweaty as she stepped into a cavernous room with Ethan close by her side. Butterfly arches drew her gaze upwards to a ceiling that sparkled as if encrusted with diamonds. The cream carpet from the hallway continued down a long aisle, bordered on either side with rows of empty chairs. It came to a stop at a raised platform that boasted two large thrones carved into the ashen bark of a tree that rose upwards and disappeared from sight. Both thrones were occupied.

On the right, a slender woman with strawberry-blonde hair sat with her hands folded primly in the lap of her flowing green dress. Her expression was one of cold calculation, but there were enough similarities to her mother that Phoenix instantly recognised her grandmother, Clíodhna.

The other throne was occupied by a man with shoulder-length

grey hair and a face that seemed experienced rather than old. His gaze was piercing, and from his assured posture and broad shoulders alone she could see he had an imposing presence. So, this was her grandfather.

A strange numbness wrapped itself around her as she stepped forward to address them both. "My name is Phoenix. My mother was Aria McGrath."

Silence.

"Was?" Aodhán asked eventually, his expression giving no indication of his thoughts.

Phoenix froze as a chilling realisation hit her: they didn't know her mother was dead.

"She ... I mean ..." Her throat constricted and the words refused to leave her lips.

Ethan stepped forward. He lowered his head respectfully but didn't take his eyes from Aodhán. "We regret to inform you that your daughter, Aria, has met her final death. She died nobly and saved many lives, including her daughter's and my own."

Phoenix cast her eyes down, but not before she caught her grandfather's flinch. She didn't want to see her grandparents' reaction; whether she was afraid of witnessing their pain or a lack of grief, she wasn't quite sure. But the very fact she had to question it made her angry in a way that she had no words for. Aria had been their child, and she didn't even know if they cared.

"And who might you be?" Clíodhna demanded, her voice betraying no reaction to the news of their daughter as she addressed Ethan.

"I am Ethan Ryan, son of the Donegal Alpha, and friend to your grandchild."

"Our grandchild." Clíodhna sounded the word out slowly as if it was difficult to say. "This is what you claim to be," she said, turning her cool gaze on Phoenix. "But how do we know you speak true?"

Phoenix forced herself to look up, taking in the paleness of her grandmother's skin, and pinched lips. "Why would we risk our safety to come here and lie to you? My mother was fae. She was your flesh and blood. My father was the vampire you banished her for loving."

"You know nothing of the choices we made." Clíodhna's eyes flashed with anger – her first real show of emotion.

Aodhán, who had been quiet since the news of his daughter's passing, placed a hand on her arm for a moment and stood. His tone was reserved when he spoke, but the tension in his body was clear. "We fae are bound to speak only the truth, but that is not the case for others, so you must forgive our scepticism. Though it's true your signature is different than any I've ever encountered, never in the history of the Lore has there been a vampire offspring, let alone a mixed species as you claim to be. Do you have any proof of what you speak?"

She'd expected this, of course, but still Phoenix had to swallow back the bitterness that burned her throat like bile. Reaching under the collar of her top, she pulled out her mother's pendant, ever close to her heart. "My mother's medallion, engraved with our family emblem."

Clíodhna arched a single, unimpressed eyebrow.

Not waiting for the dismissal of evidence she knew would come, Phoenix reached over her shoulder and grasped the hilt of her father's sword. Slowly, so as to appear as non-threatening as possible, she slid the blade from its scabbard and held it flat across her open palms.

"And I believe you may recognise Claíomh Solais."

Clíodhna gasped, leaning forward in her throne even as her hands gripped the armrests. Aodhán became deathly still, gaze riveted on the blade in her hands. Phoenix held her breath and made a conscious effort not to move.

Disbelief and shock passed over her grandfather's face as he stepped down from the raised platform and walked towards her. He stopped just out of reach of the sword, but he was close enough for her to see the pain darkening his violet eyes.

"I gave this to Aria when she reached her immortality," he said quietly. "She ... Your mother gave it to you?"

"She gave it to my father as a symbol of her love and commitment. It was his prized possession."

"You lie," Clíodhna declared, her icy tone cutting. "That is a fae weapon, passed down from the Tuatha Dé Danann themselves. It would never have allowed itself to be possessed by another species."

Anger twisted once more inside Phoenix. "Perhaps the sword doesn't hold the same prejudices you do."

"Enough." Aodhán's didn't raise his voice but the command in his tone was clear. "My lady does not mean any offence. She is speaking the truth as we understand it. If your father owned this sword as you say, then my daughter's love for him must truly have been something of magic." He paused, seeming to deflate. "You have her eyes."

Phoenix swallowed and clung tightly to the anger; it was preferable to the confused mix of emotions cloying for her attention. A heavy silence hung in the air for a moment. Then Aodhán cleared his throat and straightened, composing himself.

"What brings you to Faerie, my child?"

Phoenix hesitated. Morrigan had warned them about revealing her pregnancy, but what about the prophecy? Would her family also decide that killing her was the best way to prevent it? Her blood ran cold with fear, and when she glanced at Ethan, she could see the same concern shadowing his face.

"My parents were betrayed by someone they believed to be their friend," she said eventually. "Because of him, they were forced to sacrifice themselves to save us. This man now wants me, and will stop at nothing until he gets what he wants. Morrigan promised me I'd be safe here." She'd promised no such thing of course, only that it was the lesser of the evils. "Will you, my family, refuse us sanctuary in our time of need?"

Her grandfather gave a subtle jerk at the accusation in her tone, and Ethan sucked in a breath beside her. Too far? Well, tough shit. These people may be related to her by blood, but they had yet to give her any reason to forgive them for what they had done to her mother.

"You will have your sanctuary," Clíodhna's cool voice came from where she remained seated in her throne. "We would not turn away a child of our blood for the sins of the mother."

Ethan's hand grasped Phoenix's arm and squeezed gently in warning. She bit down on her tongue and focused on the stinging pain as she inclined her head in acknowledgement of her grandmother's words.

Her grandfather watched her closely, his shrewd gaze seeming to peer straight through to her soul. It was clear from his guarded expression that he believed she was holding something back, but he too nodded. "I would like to learn more about my grandchild." His eyes darkened, turning a stormy black. "And I would like to know more about the man responsible for my daughter's death."

A shiver ran through Phoenix at the calm tone that held more threat than any degree of anger would have. A part of her relished the thought of sending this powerful fae leader to deal with Darius, but some small voice in the back of her head warned that, as powerful as he may be, he wouldn't survive.

She was saved from responding when the door behind them opened and a woman with vibrant orange hair strode into the room, her face obscured by the clipboard she carried. "Mother, the convoy from Darkhaven have sent another message requesting an audience –"

The woman came to an abrupt halt as she looked up and realised there were others present in the room. "I'm sorry, I didn't mean to interrupt."

Phoenix took in the woman's face and her knees buckled. She crumpled to the floor, hands cupped around her mouth to hold in a breathless cry as she stared at a face that haunted her dreams. The face of her mother.

CHAPTER FIFTEEN

Faerie – day 1

Phoenix couldn't take her eyes from her mother's twin as she and Ethan followed Aoife out of the room, leaving her grandparents behind. She'd known Aria had a sister, of course, but the stark resemblance still came as a shock. A deep ache filled her chest and settled in the gaping hole that had been left in her heart with her parents' death.

There were differences between the sisters once you looked closer than a cursory glance. Aoife's eyes were green like her mother's had been, but less vibrant somehow, as if the mischievous sparkle was missing. And though her face was the same shape as Aria's, there was a sharpness to Aoife's features that made her seem older. She also showcased her pointed ears proudly, something Phoenix had rarely seen her mother do, even in the privacy of their own home.

"You'll have to forgive my mother for such an abrupt dismissal." Aoife looked back over her shoulder with a smile. "The court demands a lot of her attention. At times it can make her seem unapproachable."

"I can't really say she gave me the warm and fuzzies," Phoenix muttered, eliciting a laugh from her aunt.

"No, she's certainly not known for that."

"What role does your family play in the fae courts?" Ethan asked as they came to a large foyer with marble floors and a sweeping staircase.

He'd been quiet through much of Phoenix's conversation with her grandparents, careful not to encroach on her authority within the situation. But she'd been grateful to have him at her side – even more so after the shock of meeting Aoife.

"Many believe the Faerie courts can be viewed simply as Seelie and Unseelie, light and dark. But that's far from the case. Seven courts make up our political structure, and each play a role in maintaining the tenuous balance of rule. Our family ..." She paused and looked at Phoenix somewhat wistfully. "We are direct descendants of the Tuatha Dé Danann. We preside over a significant portion of the fae, and as such, my parents have the pleasure of babysitting the other rulers who would happily tear each other's throats out. It's a rather thankless job."

Unimpressed by the strains of her grandparents' positions, Phoenix followed Aoife up the stairs and down several winding corridors. Stained-glass windows lined one wall, turning the path into a kaleidoscope of colours. At random intervals Aoife pointed out rooms and areas of note: the kitchen and family dining area, a large library filled with ancient tomes, and her grandparents' private quarters, should she ever wish to speak with them.

At the end of one long corridor, Aoife came to a stop in front of a mahogany door. "I hope you'll find the room comfortable," she said, opening the door to reveal a spacious bedroom filled with a four-poster bed covered in the plushest cushions Phoenix had ever seen. "My mother has arranged a dinner for us all this evening, if you would both honour us with your presence."

Phoenix nodded, hoping her face didn't show just how unappealing the invitation sounded. She moved to go into the room, but Aoife placed a hand gently on her arm, stopping her.

"Did she have a happy life?"

Phoenix looked at her aunt, momentarily puzzled by the question.

Aoife pulled her hand back and cast her eyes to the floor. "Aria and I weren't close the way you'd imagine twins to be. In truth, I spent a lot of our childhood jealous of her. She had a special bond with our father; his golden girl who never seemed to do any wrong. While I on the other hand ..." She gave a small smile. "Well, let's just say it came as a surprise to us all when she was the one standing before them for punishment. I always wondered what became of her after ... I hoped she was happy."

"My father made sure she was." Phoenix swallowed, unable to say anything more than that. The resemblance to her mother made it impossible for her to cause her aunt pain, but it just wasn't in her at that moment to soothe her family's guilt. Even if Aoife hadn't been the one to banish Aria from their family, she'd stood by and allowed it to happen.

"You will join us for dinner?" Aoife asked softly as Phoenix slipped past her into the room.

Phoenix swallowed again and nodded, a throbbing headache starting to form behind her eyes.

Ethan made to follow her into the room but her aunt looked at him with a smile, seeming to compose herself once more. "Your room is down the next hallway. Come, I'll show you the way."

Ethan took a large gulp from his crystal goblet as he cast another surreptitious glance towards the entranceway to the dining room. Where the hell was Phoenix? A guard had summoned him from his room when it was time for dinner, as he assumed one had for her. But when he'd arrived at the family dining hall, he found only Aodhán, Clíodhna, and Aoife waiting. He'd been making polite small talk for nearly fifteen minutes and was running out of safe topics to discuss.

Much of the room was filled by a magnificent oak table surrounded with six high-back chairs covered in soft, green velvet. The table looked as if it had been carved straight from the heart of a tree and highlighted the intricate patterns of the wood grain beautifully. A masterpiece of a flower arrangement had been placed at the centre of the table. The flower petals sparkled like diamonds under the lights and the blooms moved in a way that made them seem alive. He had to give it the fae – they really knew how to make their décor magical.

"So, what brings a wolf to my grandchild's side, and to Faerie?" Aodhán's shrewd gaze assessed him as he took a drink from his own goblet.

Ethan met his gaze, letting the man see the truth of his words. "Phoenix has been a loyal friend and ally. Her safety is important to me."

"In what matters have you required her allegiance?" Clíodhna's cool tone made no attempt to disguise the suspicion that had tinged her every question since he'd sat down.

"She –"

"Sorry I'm late." Phoenix stumbled into the dining room, out of breath and a little flustered. "I got lost."

The filthy clothes she'd been wearing previously had been replaced by a flowing emerald-green dress which accented her eyes, and she looked as uncomfortable in it as Ethan felt in the tunic that had been brought to his room. He stood and pulled a chair out for her, noticing the slightly green tinge to her pallor, and the dark shadows under her eyes. She gave a grateful smile but avoided his concerned look as she sat down.

"I hope I haven't missed anything important?"

"I was just getting to know your acquaintance," her grandfather responded, with a pointed look at Ethan. "It seems you've managed to make some powerful friends."

"Now, father," Aoife interjected with a frown. "I'm sure the last thing Phoenix and Ethan need is the third degree from you after the day they've had. Let us enjoy our meal and celebrate the discovery of new family and friends." She raised her goblet in salute.

Ethan followed her lead and took a sip of his own drink, the heady spices and rich aroma titillating his senses. He generally preferred beer, but this wine was unlike any he had ever tasted before.

Beside him Phoenix raised her goblet as well, but placed it back down on the table without taking a drink. Her left hand rested on her lap and he noticed the twitch of her fingers as they seemed to be drawn to touch her stomach. He couldn't even imagine how unnatural it must feel for her to have to conceal something as huge as the child growing inside her.

Two fae males and two females bustled into the dining room laden with trays bearing every food imaginable. They were all silent as the lushest fruits and most succulent meats were laid out before them. The mouth-watering aroma of freshly baked bread filled the room even before the loaves came into sight. Ethan's stomach growled and he suddenly realised he hadn't eaten since they left Donegal.

Aoife gave him a bright smile. "Help yourself," she said before proceeding to fill her own plate.

He reached over to pick up a silver platter filled with juicy chicken legs and was about to offer it to Phoenix when he saw her complexion turn a worrying shade of green. Swiftly changing course, he grabbed a basket of bread rolls instead and placed one on her plate. She gave him a smile that was close to being a grimace and accepted some plump strawberries from him too before a subtle shake of her head warned she was at her limit.

His own plate full, he turned to Clíodhna with his most charming smile. "This all looks amazing. You honour us with your hospitality."

She arched an eyebrow. "Did you think we'd do otherwise?" Her eagle-eyed gaze zeroed in on Phoenix, who was picking forlornly at her bread roll but not eating. "You need not fear, child. We aren't trying to trap you here by feeding you the fruits of Faerie."

Phoenix's cheeks flushed. "Oh, no, I –"

"Or is blood more to your liking?"

"My Lord." Ethan turned to Aodhán before Phoenix could respond. "I'm curious about something you mentioned today. You said it was your understanding that a fae weapon could only be wielded by a fae. Forgive my ignorance, but as a child I heard of many great battles fought and won using fae weapons, often in the hands of other species. Are those stories little more than myths?"

The question had bothered him all day. Not because it shattered any childhood illusions he might have had, but if what Aodhán had said was true, what did it mean for their search for the spear?

Phoenix already possessed the sword, so it was possible her part-fae blood would be sufficient to wield the spear. But the sword had also belonged to Marcus, so maybe it held to different rules? He'd like to believe Morrigan wouldn't have set them a task they had no hope of completing, but then what did he actually know about the goddess?

"Some are myths, though many were borne from true events," Aodhán answered. "I assume you're familiar with the story of the Horsemen's banishment from the human realm?"

Ethan fought to keep the surprise from his face as he nodded.

"The four treasures of the Tuatha Dé Danann were used as part of the banishment ritual. In fact," Aodhán looked at Phoenix, "the sword you now carry is the very same blade that was used all those millennia ago. That is the last time, to our knowledge, that a fae weapon has allowed itself to be possessed and wielded by another species. And I think you'll find that's when the stories ended too."

"So, what happened?" Phoenix asked, perking up in her curiosity.

Aodhán's violet eyes darkened. "One of the treasures was stolen from us. After the ritual was complete, it was discovered that the cauldron of Dagda was missing. All were questioned – some even tortured – but it was never found. Maab was the Council head of the fae at the time and was not known for her benevolence. She saw the situation as a betrayal and crafted a curse that would prevent fae weapons from ever again coming to the aid of a non-fae."

Phoenix frowned, her brow furrowing. "Obviously something must have changed if my mother was able to pass the sword on to my father?"

"Perhaps, though I know not what. The cauldron has never been recovered, and though Maab is no longer the head of the fae, the magic she used to fuel the curse is ancient and formidable."

Maybe the magic knows something we don't. Ethan mulled over this new information as he took a sip of his wine. Morrigan had told them the cauldron was safe and that it would be returned when the time came. Had she always known where it was? If so, that would mean she kept it from the fae intentionally, and he wondered at her reasons.

The table lapsed into silence as each of them indulged in their fill of food – Phoenix's fill being little more than a cursory nibble or two so as not to draw further attention to herself. When they finished, Aoife gave them a kind smile. "I expect you'll want to get an early night so that you're well rested for the gala tomorrow."

Ethan glanced at Phoenix in question, but she just gave a confused shrug in answer. So he asked Aoife, "What gala?"

It was Clíodhna that responded in her clipped tone. "The gala to present Phoenix to the fae gentry, of course."

Phoenix froze, doing a remarkable impression of a deer caught in headlights.

He cleared his throat, attempting to keep his tone polite and reasonable. "We've had to pack rather lightly for our journey to Faerie. I'm afraid we wouldn't have anything suitable to wear to such an event."

Clíodhna pinned him with a steely gaze. "Our tailors have already been provided with your sizes." She indicated pointedly to the fresh clothes he and Phoenix wore. "It's all been arranged."

CHAPTER SIXTEEN

Home – 2 days gone

"Tell me again why we're entertaining this shit show," Shade muttered as his eyes skirted the cliff edge where he waited with Lucas and Cormac. The Atlantic Ocean crashed against the rock face below them, vicious and unrelenting. At this height the air was cutting, and the longer they had to stand around waiting, the more pissed off he got.

It had taken less than half an hour to drive the winding roads from the pack lands to the top of the cliff where they now stood in the middle of a wide stone circle. The area was one of many dotted around the country that was considered neutral territory by the Lore. The circle had long ago been warded with powerful magics to ensure no blood could be spilled within its boundaries. But magic or no magic, he felt as if they had glaring targets on their backs. And hey, words could hurt too.

"We can't face Darius alone." Lucas scanned the darkness with equal wariness. "We need the Council's help if we're to have any chance of getting Sean back."

"And we're meant to just believe their sudden change of heart?"

When Cormac had agreed to meet with the Council, they'd all felt that keeping close to the pack's territory was the best option – it wouldn't look good for the Council to attack them here when the local pack Alpha was meeting in good faith. But considering the Council had tried to wipe out the pack once before, Shade had trouble reining in his usual scepticism.

Before Lucas could answer, the air in front of them shimmered and two figures materialised. The power that emanated from them was almost suffocating, and Shade sneered as he took in the red robes of the Council. William and Kam stepped forward into the moonlight, hoods down so that their faces were clearly visible. There was a tense silence as the wolf and shifter heads of the Council stepped across the boundary of the circle.

"Cousin." William greeted Cormac before nodding to Shade and Lucas in acknowledgement. "We had hoped the hybrid might join us for tonight's meeting."

Of course you did. Shade bit back the words but kept his scowl firmly in place as he watched the two men closely.

"I'm afraid *Phoenix* isn't available right now." The pointed emphasis Cormac placed on "the hybrid's" name didn't go unnoticed, and William bristled at the correction.

Kam placed a hand on William's arm in warning. "I believe William has explained to you that our position regarding Phoenix has been reviewed. We mean her no harm. In fact, we are here to offer her our protection."

"Bit fucking late for that." This time Shade couldn't keep the words to himself, and when Lucas gave him a censoring look, he glared right back.

Cormac, who had been quiet since their arrival at the meeting point, didn't look too impressed with the declaration either. He raised an eyebrow and crossed his arms over his chest, causing his biceps to bulge. "So kind of you to quell your bloodlust. Might we enquire as to what led to this change of heart?"

"We know about the baby." William's words caused them all to freeze, and the air became charged as they all regarded each other evenly.

"We sent a messenger to explain the situation and extend our offer of protection," Kam explained, his soft voice cutting through the tense silence. "When we realised he didn't make it to you, we began trying to contact you ourselves. We would have done so in person, but we were concerned it would mistakenly be seen as an act of aggression, given recent events."

Shade's disbelief expressed itself as a derisive snort. "So, you're done trying to kill us and now you want to be best buddies?"

"Hardly." William gave him a patronising look and Shade barely resisted the urge to give him the middle finger.

Lucas spread his arms wide in a placating gesture. "I think it's understandable why we wouldn't be willing to reveal Phoenix's location to you." His tone, though polite, held an edge of steel that brokered no room for negotiation on the matter. "We do, however, have a common enemy, and it would be in all our interests to work together."

"What enemy is it you speak of?" Kam assessed the vampire with a thoughtful look.

"One of your Witnesses has been working hard to ensure this prophecy comes to pass."

"He's taken someone of mine," Cormac interjected. "I want him back."

William and Kam glanced at each other, their blank expressions giving nothing away. But Kam's voice was low and deadly when he asked, "What Witness?"

"His name is Darius," Lucas answered. "Long ago he was a member of my clan and is now the head of the Dublin vampire clan. He was sired by one of your predecessors on the Council – Il Maestro."

A low growl rumbled from William's throat and Cormac met his cousin's eyes, jaw set in a tense line. "He has my Omega, William."

The wolf head of the Council froze, and pain flashed behind his eyes. Shade had never quite understood the structure of a werewolf pack – the thought of being so tightly bound to others made his skin crawl – but he'd seen how much Cormac cared for the wolves under his charge. And if the role of Omega was as important as he'd been led to believe, only a heartless wolf could feel indifferent to Cormac's predicament.

There was another tense silence as William digested the news. Something ancient and terrifying swirled in Kam's dark eyes despite his otherwise outward calm, and it was he who finally spoke.

"Darius has come to our attention recently for a reason more personal to the Council. We too would like to speak with him, but ... Well, we've been unable to locate him. Our enquiries with the Dublin vampire clan indicate that he's no longer in charge there, and they claim to have no knowledge of his whereabouts."

"Bullshit!" All eyes swung to Shade and he shrugged. "Well, it is. There's no way he'd just walk away from the clan and give up all that power."

Kam inclined his head. "Eloquently put. Yes, we believe this is unlikely also. But the Council is bound to act within the confines of our laws, and without proof that Darius is still involved in the clan, we've been limited in the steps we can take against them. If what you say is true about Darius's role in the prophecy, we may have grounds to take emergency measures that enable us to conduct a more in-depth investigation into the clan's affairs."

"What about Sean?" Cormac interrupted. "Darius has been holding him against his will. We need to get him out. Now."

"It would seem that the best way to help your Omega might be to determine Darius's location. As I said, we've had no luck doing that to date. We are, however, willing to work together to resolve this situation as quickly as possible."

Shade could tell from the subtle drop of Cormac's shoulders that the Alpha had been hoping for something more concrete than a game of Where's Wally. It didn't bode well that the Council hadn't been able to track Darius, but then again, they'd been oblivious to everything he'd been doing thus far. Maybe they just needed stronger motivation.

"There's something else you should know," Lucas said, voice sombre. "We believe Darius is actively arranging the demonic possession of Supes."

And there it was.

Kam's eyes darkened. A wave of power rolled off him that seemed to suck the oxygen from the circle. The wards flared a bright white for a split second before fading. His voice was carefully even when he asked, "What makes you think this?"

"They sent one for Phoenix. A wolf with red eyes and a strangely tainted signature. He was stronger than a normal Supe. If it wasn't for some outside assistance, things might have gone very badly."

William's nostrils flared at the mention of the wolf and his frown etched deep lines into his face. Kam appeared troubled, though Shade couldn't have said exactly what it was that made him think that since the shifter's expression never changed.

"That is concerning indeed," Kam said finally. "Reports of demon activity have been increasing on a weekly basis, but it is early days yet in the prophecy timeline. The barrier should still be strong enough that only minor demons are crossing over. We didn't expect to be dealing with possession of our own for a number of months yet."

Shade thought back to Darius's previous attempts at manipulating the timeline. It was unlikely the vampire had become any more patient with his recent failures. "How bad can this thing get?" he asked.

There was a weariness that defied age in Kam's eyes when the shifter met his gaze. "When the Horsemen last walked this world, it took all of our strongest people working together to stop them. Not all of them survived, and some might have been better if they hadn't. Our Seer believes that the child can prevent this, but if it doesn't …"

"Then we're back to you trying to kill Phoenix."

"It would be the only way."

"What if we recreate the ritual that banished the Horsemen? Reinstate the barrier?" Lucas asked.

"Until the Horsemen cross over into this plane of existence, the ritual would simply buy us time by reinforcing the barrier. It would not stop the prophecy. Besides, I'm afraid we no longer have the means to recreate the ritual. Four key artefacts are required for the spell, one of which was long ago stolen. Your hybrid freed the only man who may have been able to tell us where it is."

Shade frowned, thinking back to what Morrigan had said about the artefacts. According to her, Phoenix had the sword, the stone was somewhere here in Ireland, and Phoenix and Ethan were to bring the spear back from Faerie. That only left the cauldron, and Morrigan had said she had that under control. So, who was Kam talking about?

He looked at the shifter, light dawning. "The Mists."

Kam nodded solemnly. "The ritual requires power from all the species. The Mists assisted us in banishing the Horsemen, but afterwards, Shayan, the youngest of the three, betrayed us by taking Dagda's Cauldron. We've never been able to ascertain why, nor has the threat of ultimate death persuaded him to divulge its location."

"You forced his family into centuries of slavery because he wouldn't tell you." It wasn't a question, and Cormac shook his head in disgust, turning away from the two Council members before either could answer or justify.

Kam didn't flinch or show any signs of remorse at the accusation, but William shifted slightly, looking away uneasily.

Diplomatic to the end, Lucas forced the attention back to the problem at hand. "Let's assume we can get the cauldron, and the assistance of the Mists. Will you aid us in completing the ritual if it's needed?"

"You don't believe the child will be born in time?" Kam asked.

"I don't believe in relying on chance. Will you stand with us or not?"

CHAPTER SEVENTEEN

Home – 5 days gone

Darius stared through magically reinforced glass into the small white chamber. A single occupant crouched in the centre of the room, bonds of silver chain glistening where they were bolted to the floor. Blood coated wiry muscle and dirt matted shaggy white hair. The Omega was deathly still.

"Has there been any change?" Darius turned to Erik, who stood beside him, hands clasped behind his back.

"None. He still has moments of lucidity despite the strength of the demon possessing him. Last night he managed to partially shift and almost clawed his own face off before we could tranq him."

When Darius looked through the viewing glass again, red eyes stared at him through the hair that obscured Sean's face. There was no emotion in them, only the chilling calculation of the demon. But he'd seen the footage for himself; some part of the Omega remained inside the shell and fought back against the possession. It was unprecedented in all their trials to date.

"How did he manage to shift with the silver shackling him?"

"We don't know. He shouldn't have been able to. Tests confirm that silver is still as detrimental to him as it was before the posses-sion. It's possible the regeneration ability of his demon element is mitigating the damage in some way."

"Interesting." Darius gave one final glance into the white room before turning to walk down the sterile white corridor, Erik keeping step with him. "Keep him under control however you need to. He may still be of use to us yet, and I don't want him finding a way to kill himself before I've decided what to do with him."

They made their way through the pharmaceutical complex to the front lobby, an odd mix of disinfectant, bleach, and herbs drifting to them from the various laboratories. Men and women in white lab coats nodded at them as they passed, barely looking up from their clipboards. The humans who worked in the complex were well aware of the supernatural presence that surrounded them. He had to admire their arrogance; the only time they batted an eyelid to the situation was when a test subject ended up underneath their microscope.

He'd purchased the floundering pharmaceutical company under an alias twenty-five years earlier when it had become clear that the time had come to make preparations. With a bit of financial backing and some ... motivation, the company had quickly become one of the top players in the field of genetic engineering. Some of the less savoury trials he'd kept off site until recently, but the facility offered the perfect space he needed to house his growing army.

"We have another problem." Erik handed him a letter with a familiar emblem in the top corner. "The Council have frozen the clan's assets. It seems that they have grounds for an investigation into the clan's affairs, whether or not we currently claim association with you. Our lawyers are dealing with it, but it's making business difficult to say the least."

Darius clenched his teeth. He wasn't afraid of the Council, or their so-called influence, but he had too much to do right now to humour such interference. He considered his options as he watched a sleek black Mercedes pull up in front of the glass doors of the building.

"Perhaps the Council need something better to do with their time than bothering hard-working members of the Lore," he mused. "We still have the more unruly transfer subjects contained, correct?" At last count Darius was aware of close to fifty subjects who had survived the demon transfer but proved too difficult to be controlled to add to the ranks of their army. The worst of these had been detained in a secure part of the facility until he was ready to make a decision on their fate.

Erik nodded.

"Release them. I want them sent to Brussels. I've heard the neighbourhoods around the Council headquarters are some of the safest areas to live in the world. Let's see if we can rectify that, shall we?"

Erik's lips twitched, but his expression remained serious. "If you do this, you know it'll show your hand? They will double their efforts to find you; it will only be a matter of time before they come."

"And when they do, we'll be ready for them."

With that, Darius strode outside to the cool night and waiting car. He opened the rear door and slid into the leather seat beside Vicktor.

"Well?"

Vicktor's smile was as smarmy as it had always been, but there was a cunning calculation in his red eyes that belied the new intelligence behind them. "I believe we've found a member of the fae gentry sympathetic to our cause. They are aware of the hybrid's presence in Faerie and have agreed to monitor her on our behalf while the witch makes the necessary preparations."

"Very good." Things were finally starting to go right. Darius leaned back in the seat with a satisfied smile. "Take us to the club," he ordered the driver.

CHAPTER EIGHTEEN

Faerie – day 2

Phoenix stared at her reflection in the floor-length mirror. But no matter how long she stared, she hardly recognised the image looking back at her. The silver gown that had been brought to her room earlier that morning fit as well as her own skin did. The material was light and delicate despite the sparkling crystals covering every inch of it; she'd never seen anything like it before. A male and female had come to her room an hour previous to attend to her hair and make-up, and the results convinced her that they must have used some kind of fae magic on her.

She turned sideways and ran her hand over the soft swell of her abdomen. The flowing material of her dress managed to make the bump unnoticeable, but still she could have sworn that it had grown overnight. If time moved differently here in Faerie, how would it affect her pregnancy? It was all well and good keeping her secret so long as her body didn't give her away.

A soft flutter tickled her belly just beneath her hand and she smiled sadly. "Hey, munchkin. I'm sorry I have to keep you hidden.

I'm sorry that I'll be bringing you into a world that's so full of hatred for things people don't understand."

A knock sounded and she jerked her head up, yanking her hand away from her stomach. The closed door mocked her paranoia and she shook her head, mentally berating herself for being an idiot. She took a deep breath, smoothed down her dress, and went to answer it.

Ethan stood in the hallway looking awkwardly handsome in a traditional fae tunic, embroidered with gold thread that brought out the hint of his wolf's yellow eyes hidden beneath the surface. His normally unruly hair was slicked back, and though rough stubble covered his jawline, the contrast only accentuated the raw masculine energy that oozed from him. His eyes widened in surprise as he took her in.

"I see they got to you too," she said with a wry smile, fighting the urge to fidget self-consciously.

He laughed and moved to run a hand through his hair before stopping himself with a grimace. "I guess they're hoping it might help me blend in a bit. You look stunning." He offered her his arm with a wide grin.

Blend in? Fat chance of that. She closed the door behind her and slipped her arm through his, allowing him to lead her down the hallway.

Two guards waited for them in the large foyer, tasked with escorting the so-called guests of honour to the gala. Phoenix raised her eyebrows, but neither she or Ethan commented as they were led to a balcony that overlooked the open courtyard at the centre of the castle.

She'd caught a brief glimpse of the courtyard through the window when Aoife had shown them to their rooms the previous day. It was even more beautiful now. Flaming torches lined the walls, complementing the dimming light from the dusky pink sky. At the centre of the courtyard, azure-blue water cascaded over a marble fountain that had been carved into the naked form of a couple entwined in a loving embrace. Four trees that looked like weeping willows marked the compass points, and small fluttering balls of light moved in an intricate dance between the hanging branches. It was breathtaking.

Fae mingled in the courtyard with drinks in hand, few bothering with the glamours Phoenix was used to seeing back home. They proudly showcased the subtle points of their ears, and many made a conscious effort in their outfit or make-up to highlight the trademark features that marked their respective heritages: pale green skin faintly patterned with leaves identified the earth elementals, while Phoenix spotted more than one fae with the orange and red flame-like hair that marked sun elementals like her. The water nymphs were nearly impossible to miss thanks to their oozing sensuality, and the accompanying harem of males and females hanging on their every word.

The guard beside her cleared his throat impatiently and ushered them forward to the top of a stone staircase. Curious gazes swept in their direction, and she was struck with a vivid image of falling on her face as she descended the steps. She clung tighter to Ethan's arm.

"Should we go find my grandparents?" She cringed at the low murmuring of the crowd as hundreds of eyes observed their descent. No one had explained the etiquette for the gala so she had no idea if she was supposed to present herself or slip quietly into the shadows, which was her preference.

"Let's get a drink first."

As if summoned by Ethan's words, a waitress appeared at his side with a tray in hand and a seductive smile on her face as she gave him a blatant once-over. He accepted two champagne flutes with a polite smile and handed one to Phoenix.

"You don't have to drink it," he assured her when she eyed the purple liquid suspiciously. "It's like armour. Holding a glass is a requirement for surviving awkward social engagements."

"He's not wrong, you know." Aoife appeared beside Ethan, a champagne flute in her own hand, and gave Phoenix a conspiratorial smile. The turquoise dress she wore made her green eyes sparkle, and she looked even more like Aria in that moment. "Mother and Father have been waylaid; they send their apologies. Let me introduce you around."

Driving hot pokers through her eyes sounded more appealing to Phoenix, but she dutifully followed Aoife and Ethan, smiling when expected to, and keeping to polite, mundane conversation where possible. Of course, polite seemed to be a relative term given that the fae's sense of personal boundaries varied wildly from any she'd ever encountered before.

"You don't *feel* right. What are you?"

"Are you sure you're fae? Your ears are awfully round."

"Oh, you live in the human realm? How very quaint."

The comments were delivered with such open curiosity and bluntness that in most cases she sensed no real malice behind them. Just ignorance.

Ethan stuck close to her side the whole time, and she felt him tense at more than one inappropriate comment about her tainted genetics. Aoife, for her part, moved the conversation on with the ease and relaxed air of someone well versed in managing the political minefield of Faerie.

Oddly, the fae seemed less disturbed at having a werewolf with absolutely no fae blood among them than they did by her half-fae status. In fact, many of the fae – males and females alike – flirted shamelessly with Ethan. He engaged in playful banter in return, his cheeky smile and suggestive comments enough to make even the water nymphs blush. Phoenix knew he wasn't seriously considering their advances, but a small part of her sulked as she watched them preen and flutter their eyelashes at him.

"Aoife, where have you been hiding this beauty?" A tall man with silver hair stepped into Phoenix's view. His grey eyes sparkled as he took her hand and raised it to his lips. "Please, let me introduce myself. I'm Eoghan, high lord of Eldridge."

Startled, Phoenix looked to Aoife, noting that her aunt's smile didn't quite reach her eyes.

"Eoghan, this is my niece, Phoenix. You might want to return her hand now."

"Oh, but it is such a lovely hand." He gave a cheeky wink, but did as asked.

Heat flared in Phoenix's cheeks and she fought the urge to fan herself with a girly giggle.

What the hell? Is he using a glamour on me? She straightened up and frowned at him. The smile he gave her in return didn't look the least bit apologetic.

"Forgive me. I couldn't resist."

The urge to giggle disappeared in an instant and she glared at him, "Don't do that again, or you'll find no amount of glamour will make up for the damage I do to your manhood." She gave a pointed look at the bulk that was nicely highlighted by the tight fit of his trousers – and no doubt also accented by magical means.

The fae lord bowed his head, attempting to look suitably chastised, but amusement and something else she couldn't put her finger on danced behind his grey eyes. "Will you be staying long with us here in Faerie?"

"Just a few days," Aoife answered coolly before Phoenix could respond.

She looked at her aunt in surprise. Though Aoife appeared relaxed, and even friendly, her green eyes had a hard edge that piqued her interest. If Eoghan noticed the chilly response, however, he didn't show it.

"I do hope you'll give me a chance to show you some of the delights Faerie has to offer," he said, his attention and smile still firmly fixed on her.

A collective gasp rose from the crowd, smothering her polite decline. She turned, looking around in confusion to see what had caught everyone's attention. And froze.

Her grandparents stood at the top of the stone staircase. Clothed in fine silks of purple and silver, they were every inch the regal image as they looked down upon the rapt audience. A woman with vibrant red hair cascading in loose waves over one shoulder stood between them. Her sultry red lips were held in a delicate pout and the pale skin of her thighs flashed teasingly from between the slits of a shimmering gold dress that clung like water to her body. It was this woman whom all eyes were fixed on, a sense of reverential awe oozing from the crowd.

"Who's that?" Phoenix whispered. A shiver of trepidation ran through her.

Eoghan's eyes were riveted on the stairs as he answered. "That's Méabh. Leader of the fae."

CHAPTER NINETEEN

Faerie – day 2

Phoenix's head spun as Eoghan's words sank in. Leader of the fae? That meant Council. Her eyes met Ethan's as she tried to keep the fear from showing on her face. The tight set to his jaw did little to reassure her, and she could see the same thoughts racing through his mind – the Council had agreed to leave them alone, to give them time to find a solution. What had changed?

She could almost see Ethan's muscles twitching as he fought against his instincts to get her the hell out of there. But they both knew leaving wasn't an option, and the slightest movement from either of them would likely draw the attention of everyone present.

As if the whole courtyard was suddenly released from a trance, Méabh began a steady descent down the stairs and low murmurs of wonder filled the air. Clíodhna and Aodhán followed in her wake, Phoenix's grandfather holding himself proud as he looked over the crowd, while her grandmother's stoic expression told little of her thoughts.

Everything moved in painfully slow motion as Méabh glided along a clear path towards Phoenix. The fae she passed watched her with a mix of reverence and awe. A few wore poorly disguised looks of envy that suggested a well-placed dagger in the back wouldn't have been unexpected. Méabh for her part seemed unconcerned by the attention, her shrewd green eyes focused solely on her target.

When the procession finally came to a stop before Phoenix, Aodhán stepped forward, meeting her gaze for a second before turning to formally address Méabh. "If I may, I'd like to introduce you to our granddaughter, Phoenix."

The weight of all eyes in the courtyard fell on them. Phoenix cringed, sinking into herself in a futile attempt to escape their scrutiny. Her throat was barren, and she gripped the champagne flute tightly in her hand as if it really was the shield Ethan had promised.

"Leave us," Méabh ordered with a flick of a hand tipped with lethal red-enamelled nails. "I wish to speak with Phoenix and the wolf alone."

Looks of surprise were quickly masked by bows of obedience, and suddenly Phoenix found herself standing alone with Méabh and Ethan at the centre of the courtyard. Around them, music and conversations resumed, but everything seemed muted, far away, as if they'd been encased in some sort of bubble.

As soon as the area cleared, Ethan growled. "The Council agreed to leave Phoenix alone."

Méabh's green eyes traced a slow path down his body, and she ran her tongue over her bottom lip. "Down, boy. I have no intention of breaching any agreements here tonight. I simply wished to verify some interesting new information for myself."

"What new information?"

All traces of flirtation were forgotten and Méabh's expression turned thoughtful as she shifted her attention to Phoenix. "You're not what I expected."

Phoenix bit back the urge to tell her to go fuck herself, and instead said, "Sorry to disappoint."

The smile she got in return held no trace of humour. Méabh looked down at Phoenix's stomach. "Cassandra may be right, but it appears there's a long way to go before any saviour might be born of your union. Time passes very differently back home than it does here

613

in Faerie. It remains to be seen what, if anything, is left to save even if the vision proves true."

Ice ran through Phoenix's veins and all thoughts fled her mind except one: *she knows.*

The terror must have shown on her face because the leader of the fae laughed, cold and harsh. "Oh, do calm down. I'm not here to harm you or the child. I simply wished to see for myself."

"You've seen, and now you should leave," Ethan said, the muscle at the side of his jaw jumping, even as a deadly stillness held him in place.

Méabh purred low in her throat and placed a hand on his chest. "You have so much pent-up aggression. Is she not helping you to work it off?"

She pulled her hand away with a wink, all business once more. "When Cassandra informed us of her vision, the Council voted to offer you assistance. A messenger was sent, but it seems they never reached you. Perhaps that's for the best. I, for one, am not yet convinced you're worthy of that assistance. I guess time will tell."

A loud buzzing rang through Phoenix's head. The Council knew. Who was Cassandra? What did Méabh mean that there might not be anything worth saving? A strange numbness settled over her as she asked, "Will you tell them? My grandparents?"

The fae woman waved a hand, looking suddenly bored. "I have more pressing matters that require my attention right now. I have no interest in being dragged into any family drama. I will keep your secret. For now."

Clearly deciding the matter was settled, Méabh plucked the full champagne glass from Ethan's hand and swallowed the purple liquid. She ran a nail across her lip to clear some imaginary droplets and handed the glass back with a seductive smile.

Phoenix's tongue felt strange and swollen in her mouth, but still she managed to form one last question. "The vision ... Will we have enough time? Will the baby ..."

Stormy shadows passed behind Méabh's eyes. "Let us hope so."

The drinks continued to flow and there was no break in the hypnotic music that had revellers dancing with abandon around the courtyard. Ethan leaned against the wall of the castle, sipping his drink as he watched Phoenix dance with Eoghan. He made a conscious effort to keep the scowl from his face. The fae male hadn't been shy in expressing his interest in Phoenix since Aoife had introduced them earlier that evening. Phoenix, for her part, had kept the conversation polite and humoured him with the occasional dance when pushed. Ethan knew the attraction wasn't reciprocated, but it took more restraint than he cared to admit to stop himself from marking his territory.

As the music shifted tempo, she pulled away from Eoghan's grasp and excused herself. She slipped from the crowd and headed for a quiet corner of the courtyard, moving out of sight. Noting the subtle slump of her shoulders now that she thought no one was looking, he followed her. She stopped under what looked like a cherry blossom tree except for the fact the small blooms continuously shifted colour, and sat on the stone bench beneath it. Even in the dim light he could see the shadows under her eyes and the sharpened edges of her cheek bones. When had he last seen her eat properly?

She gave him a tired smile as he approached and shifted over to make space for him. "Hey."

He sat down next to her and gave her a gentle nudge with his elbow. "How you holding up?"

"I just needed a break. It's been a long night."

It had been a long few days, never mind a long night. The fact she'd had to flee to Faerie before she'd even had a chance to recover from Darius's attack – because he couldn't quite bring himself to think of it as Sean's doing – still bothered him. The stress couldn't be good for her, never mind the baby. He'd kept the thought to himself so as not to worry her further, but he couldn't stop watching her for even the slightest sign that something may not be right.

"At least Méabh didn't stick around for long," she said with a sigh.

"Do you think she'll say anything to your grandparents?"

She shook her head. "The fae can twist words, but they can't lie.

The 'for now' part will only cover us so long as it suits her, but I don't think we need to worry about it right now. It's the other part that bothers me."

"That we might not have enough time?"

Phoenix stared at her hands in her lap, eyes tight with tension. She didn't answer, instead chewing on her bottom lip.

"We can't think like that," he told her firmly, pushing back his own sense of unease. "All we can do is focus on the things we can control. Méabh said the same thing Morrigan did, that time passes differently here. We need to find the spear, and sooner rather than later. How the hell we're meant to do it, though, I've no idea."

Phoenix's brow furrowed. "It has to be here, or somewhere close by at least. Otherwise, what was the point in Morrigan telling us to find it while we were here? If the four treasures call to each other like she said, then I guess we bring the sword on a treasure hunt and hope it lights up like a Vegas casino with big flashing arrows."

She sat back against the bench and closed her eyes. "I'm exhausted. You think anyone will notice if I slip off to bed?"

He looked back at the courtyard and the party that was still in full swing. "I think you've served your time in the zoo." He stood and offered her his arm. "I'll walk you up."

She rose and linked her arm through his without a word. Nobody intercepted them as they made their way back into the castle, keeping to the shadows. Inside, they followed the winding corridors until eventually the music of the gala was little more than an echo on the wind.

"So, other than tired, how are you feeling?" he asked when he was sure they were alone. "You haven't been eating much."

She grimaced. "Apparently even lands filled with ancient magics can't defeat morning sickness. I could really do with your mam's special tea right now." They came to a stop outside her bedroom and she turned to look up at him. "It's hard. Having to hide ..."

His chest ached at the sorrow that darkened her eyes. Hesitantly, he reached out to touch her cheek. He'd had to fight the urge to touch her so many times since they'd arrived in Faerie that he took a moment to relish the softness of her skin beneath his fingers. A smile tugged at one corner of her mouth as she covered his hand with her own and rested against his palm.

He moved closer to her.

His eyes fixated on her mouth as he ran his thumb over the soft swell of her bottom lip. Her scent wrapped around him, warm and inviting, drawing him further in.

"Oh, there you are."

Phoenix jerked away from him as if she'd gotten an electric shock. He dropped his hand, heart pounding as he turned towards Aoife's approaching form.

"You caught us," he said with what he hoped was a relaxed grin. "We were both a bit worn out from all the excitement, so we slipped away when no one was looking."

Aoife's friendly smile never faltered, but something unreadable passed behind her eyes for the briefest of moments.

Before she could say anything more, he stepped away from Phoenix's door. "If you'll excuse me, I shall bid you fair ladies a good night." He swept a low, theatrical bow and turned on his heel, careful to keep his pace relaxed as he headed for his room.

CHAPTER TWENTY

Faerie – day 3

Phoenix groaned as she rolled over somewhat clumsily in the bed and struggled up to sitting. Sleep clung with determination to her eyes and she blinked at the sunlight streaming in through the window. Surely it couldn't be morning? She'd only just fallen asleep.

She'd been exhausted when they'd left the gala, but as soon as her head had hit the pillow, the internal monologue had begun. Thoughts of exactly what Méabh's words might mean for them and the prophecy alternated with memories of Ethan's gentle touch. All of it, combined with her body's inability to get comfortable, had plotted against her quest for sleep. It would be a miracle if she could keep her eyes open for the day, but they had a spear to find so she'd just have to pull on her big girl pants.

Indulging herself with a martyred sigh, she set about making herself look somewhat presentable. She eyed the swell of her abdomen critically in the mirror and grabbed a loose-fitting tunic from the wardrobe before strapping Claíomh Solais across her back. It was becoming clearer to her that they should have pressed Morrigan for details on just how long they were likely to be here.

She left the room and made her way to the place she knew she was most likely to find Ethan: the dining room. Sure enough, she found him at the large oak table, the remnants of what looked to be a hearty breakfast on the silver platter in front of him.

He gave her a sheepish grin. "I can see where the myths about accepting fae food came from. I'm not sure I want to leave now that I've tasted it either."

Laughter came from behind her, and Phoenix turned to see Aoife approach, her eyes sparkling.

"Oh, don't be fooled. Not all of the stories are myths, and there are plenty of foods here in Faerie that have undesirable effects for the unaware. But fear not," she said, gliding into the room and plucking a luscious red apple from a bowl on the table, "we simply like showing off the fruits of our land. So, what have you two got planned for the day?"

"We were hoping to explore the grounds a bit more." Ethan pushed back from the table with a contented sigh and stood. "We haven't really had a proper chance to look around since we got here."

Aoife smiled widely. "Why don't I come with you? I can show you the rest of the castle and introduce you to some of the fae who tend the lands."

Phoenix opened her mouth to politely decline, but Ethan caught her eye and gave a subtle shake of his head. Taking his hint, she pasted a smile onto her own face. "If you're sure we wouldn't be taking you away from your duties?"

Aoife laughed. "I'd be more than happy for the excuse, believe me."

"Did many of the gentry remain in the castle after the gala?" Ethan asked, sweeping his arm out in an invitation for her to lead the way.

"A few."

A troubled look passed over her aunt's face, gone so quickly that Phoenix wasn't sure if she imagined it. She followed Aoife out of the dining room, casting a questioning glance at Ethan to see if he too had noticed it. His face remained impassive, but his eyes were watchful and alert.

They skipped the parts of the castle Aoife had shown them when they first arrived in Faerie, and instead made their way through the farthest reaches that extended away from the family's living quarters. As they walked, Aoife supplied intriguing explanations and facts about the castle's history. On the uppermost levels, the glass walls allowed for stunning views of the land surrounding them, and the high wall that bordered it. Thick branches snaked across the exterior of the glass from the trees on either side of the building, turning the image into a patchwork of artistry.

"What's beyond the wall?" Phoenix thought back to the creepy forest that had been their first introduction to Faerie and shuddered.

Her aunt's face darkened. "Death," Aoife answered softly, before beckoning them on with smile.

Phoenix gaped after her, and Ethan's eyes widened in surprise. They hurried to catch up with her, neither really sure how to respond.

With each floor they explored, Phoenix was painfully aware of the sword hanging silently across her back. She didn't know what exactly it was meant to do if it came close to the spear, but as it was their only guiding point, even the slightest shift of it against her spine made her breath catch. It got to the point that, at times, she even imagined it was vibrating.

"How are the trees so interwoven with the building?" Ethan asked when they passed yet another hallway of glass windows displaying a spider web of branches on the exterior.

Aoife placed her hand against the glass and the branches writhed, seeming to respond to her touch. "Everything in Faerie is derived from nature in some form. The environment is malleable and changes as requirements demand it. This castle wasn't always here, and may not always be. Nature responded to the need of our people."

"Do many people live here?" Phoenix watched as small forms moved about the land in the distance. Aside from the gala, she hadn't yet encountered too many fae during her time in the castle.

"More than you may realise. Some live here in other quarters. Some have their own dwellings on the land. There's no obligation for them to stay within our boundaries, but much of Faerie is wild and unforgiving for the less-powerful fae, and they choose to stay where it's safest."

Phoenix chewed her lip, wondering what it had been like for her mother growing up here. Had she been sheltered from whatever horrors lay beyond the wall? Knowing her mother's fierce spirit, Phoenix doubted it.

Back on the ground level of the castle, they came to a long, dark corridor which led towards the west wing. Aoife paid it little heed, turning to head back to the main foyer, but an odd tugging sensation stopped Phoenix in her tracks. The shadows seemed to almost beckon her forward.

"What's down there?" she asked, her voice little more than a whisper.

Her aunt looked at the corridor in surprise, as if only just remembering it was there. "Oh, there? Nothing as far as I know. It used to lead to old escape tunnels that ran under the castle, but it's a dead end now. I guess the building decided the tunnels weren't necessary anymore." She shrugged as if the suggestion was perfectly natural, then turned back towards the main part of the castle. "Let me show you the grounds outside. We have the most magnificent stables."

Ethan gave her a quizzical look, and Phoenix discreetly placed a hand on the leather strap that crossed her body. She wasn't sure if it was the sword drawing her towards that corridor or something else; she just knew she'd be coming back later.

As with every day since they'd arrived in Faerie, the sky was a cloudless blue when they made their way outside. If Phoenix hadn't already known that magic filled this place, the constant sun would have proved it to her; no place could have weather this perfect all the time.

The estate was larger than it had appeared from the castle, housing hundreds of residences that blended seamlessly into the landscape. Aoife stopped at regular intervals to introduce them to the fae who were tending the grounds. They all greeted her with warm welcome, and Phoenix was pleasantly surprised by her aunt's friendly ease with those whom some might have considered beneath her.

As they drew close to the stables, Aoife deep in conversation with

Ethan about the unique herbs they grew in the medicinal gardens, a male came riding over the horizon on a magnificent white steed. Phoenix recognised the silver hair immediately, and the scowl that settled on Ethan's face told her that he too had spotted the rider. Eoghan waved and headed in their direction.

It was only as he neared that Phoenix realised he was riding bareback. Even she had to admit that he looked terribly regal sitting astride the beautiful beast, his hair glistening in the light of the sun. His dismount from the steed was equally impressive, and she rolled her eyes with a smile as he bent to kiss her hand in greeting.

"Well now," he said. "I believe my morning has just brightened considerably."

Ethan's scowl deepened.

"To what do we owe the honour, Eoghan?" Aoife asked, something slightly off with her polite expression. "I thought you were returning to Eldridge this morning?"

"I decided to stay a little longer. The views are much more interesting here." He gave Aoife a wink while still somehow managing to keep his attention firmly on Phoenix.

Squirming uncomfortably at the intense focus being aimed her way, Phoenix grasped for a way to redirect it. "That's a beautiful horse. Is it yours?"

"Yes, his name's Jack. Would you like to meet him?"

She choked in surprise. "Jack?"

"Well, I couldn't make his name too impressive. He's already far too spectacular. If I gave him an impressive name, the ladies would surely think I'm trying to compensate for something."

She laughed despite herself and shook her head.

Aoife turned towards the horizon, where another rider was heading towards them on a steed the colour of rich chestnut. "I didn't realise you were riding with my father."

"We had some business matters to discuss. It seemed a shame not to make the most of this wondrous morning as we concluded them."

Aoife's eyes narrowed on the fae lord, but before she could say anything further, Aodhán brought his horse to a stop next to them.

Phoenix noticed with interest that he avoided his daughter's questioning gaze as he greeted them.

"What a pleasant surprise." He dismounted with an ease even more impressive than Eoghan's and patted the horse's back. "Are you going riding?"

"Actually," Eoghan jumped in, "I was just about to ask your granddaughter's assistance in getting Jack here settled after our ride."

Phoenix moved to protest, but her grandfather nodded approvingly and turned to Ethan. "Perhaps I could interest you in some sparring then? It's been a long time since I've had a chance to test my reflexes against an opponent of another species."

Ethan didn't even glance her way to acknowledge the plea in her eyes before he inclined his head and said, "I'd be honoured."

That settled, her grandfather passed his horse over to the stable hand who had rushed to assist him. Phoenix tried once again to politely suggest alternative plans, but somehow she found herself standing alone with Eoghan as Ethan followed her grandfather to the training fields, and Aoife distractedly muttered an excuse about needing to speak with her mother.

———

Ethan eyed the impressively stacked weapons rack and wondered exactly what kind of sparring Aodhán had in mind. For some reason, he didn't think Phoenix would appreciate him slicing her grandfather to shreds with the wickedly sharp blades of the twin daggers or bludgeoning him to death with a mace. Though their search for the fae weapon would never be that easy, he scanned his eyes over the rack for any sign of a spear. Oddly enough, it was one of the only weapons not represented in the vast selection.

"Many of these weapons were passed down to me by my father," Aodhán said, coming to stand beside him. "Claíomh Solais I kept in my own personal collection, of course. At least until I passed it down to Aria. She was impressive with the blade, even at a young age."

Ethan thought back to the battle in Darius's underground chamber, the images still etched in his mind. "I fought at her side once. She was a magnificent fighter. Phoenix is too, despite her lack of training."

Aodhán frowned. "Her parents never taught her to fight?"

Ethan hesitated. Phoenix's story wasn't his to tell, and yet some part of him wanted it to be known, wanted the man before him to understand just what she had lost, and how strong she was.

"They trained her as much as they could, but they disappeared when she was quite young. The man who hunts her held them prisoner for ten years until we found them. She was left alone, without any family to train her or help her understand her powers. She feared who and what she is because that's all our world ever taught her to do." He stopped, clamping down on the anger that welled inside him on her behalf.

Her grandfather stood deathly still beside him, his expression unchanged except for the storm swirling in his dark eyes. For a minute he was quiet.

"When you live a long time, you make many decisions that haunt you," he said eventually. "It's clear that you care for my grand-daughter a great deal. I would hate for you to have to understand firsthand what it's like to make a decision like that."

Ethan met his gaze silently. There was a warning in those words, he knew that much. But he also knew it changed nothing. He straightened and gestured to the training area. "Shall we spar?"

CHAPTER TWENTY-ONE

Home – 10 days gone

Abi watched over Nate's shoulder as rows and rows of code filled the black computer screen. Not so long ago the words and numbers would have meant less than nothing to her, but Nate had been a patient teacher. In the week and a half since Phoenix had left, Abi had found the art of hacking to be an exciting distraction from her racing thoughts. Of course, it probably didn't count as hacking since the Council had voluntarily handed over their data this time.

From all accounts, the meeting with the Council had yielded an uneasy acknowledgement that they needed to work together to stop Darius. True to their word, the Council had set about making life very difficult for the Dublin vampire clan by freezing their assets pending investigation. Coincidentally – or not, as the case might be – they began seeing a surge in suspicious and violent attacks in the communities surrounding them shortly after that, with all information suggesting crazed demon-Supe hybrids were to blame.

Despite the incentive to find him, the Council's best trackers had failed to pinpoint Darius's location, and so William had shocked them all by willingly providing Nate with access to the Council databases. She felt it was gracious of Cormac not to point out just how easily the shifter had gained access to their security systems in the past, and was only a little disappointed that she didn't get to properly test her new-found hacking skills.

"What exactly is it we're looking for?" She scanned the data, waiting for something to magically jump out at her.

They'd already run checks on all businesses even remotely connected to the Dublin vampire clan. She'd reviewed their financials for any odd changes in recent months, and Nate had trawled through countless hours of security footage in and around the businesses. Everyone was acutely aware of how much time was passing and what it might mean for Sean.

Nate leaned closer to the screen, squinting in concentration. "I was up all night trying to figure out how we might approach things from a different angle. We've already covered Darius and any of his known aliases, but I remembered that when we first discovered his link with the prophecy, he was going by his Sire's name, not his own."

"Il Maestro." Abi shuddered as she thought back to the fevered light that had burned in Darius's eyes when he'd talked about his Sire. "He told me that Il Maestro was the one who gave him the scroll."

"That would make sense. Il Maestro served on the Council when Cassandra proclaimed the prophecy. No doubt it was written down to preserve the wording; he'd have been in a prime position to take it or make his own copy ..."

He trailed off as an icon flashed in the bottom corner of the screen, notifying him of a new email. He moved to click on it but suddenly the lines of code halted their scrolling, and there was a sharp beep as one of the lines flashed green.

"Bingo!" Nate slapped a hand on the table and pushed back from the computer with a triumphant smile, email notification forgotten.

Abi leaned closer and scrunched her brow in confusion. "Who's Alessandro Rossi?"

"*That* is the birth name of Darius's Sire. And it's our answer to finding Darius." Nate slid his chair back towards the desk and tapped the keyboard in a blur of movement. "Look." He pointed to a list of three names with dates beside them. "These are all the companies that Alessandro Rossi acquired in the past twenty-five years. Quite a feat for a man who's been dead for centuries."

She scanned the list, the letters thankfully forming words that made sense to her now. "A law firm, a pharmaceutical company, and a night club. A bit of a strange combination. So, how do we find out which one he's hiding in?"

Nate was quiet for a few moments as he flicked between various screens and websites. He chewed on his lip, eyes darkening as he digested the information quicker than she could follow.

"It's the club. It has to be. I can't find any record of it in normal channels, and from the limited information I can find on the Dark Web, it seems to cater to the" – he grimaced – "less savoury of our kind. A psychopath like Darius would be in his element in a place like that."

Butterflies skittered around in Abi's stomach. Was this it? Had they finally found him? "What do we do now?"

Nate gave her the most genuine grin she'd seen from him in months. "Now we call in reinforcements."

He tapped a few more buttons to transfer information over to his mobile phone, then pushed away from the table and beckoned her to follow him. They made a beeline for the kitchen where they found Cormac sitting at the table, deep in discussion with Lucas. Shade leaned against the counter with a mug of blood in hand. All three looked up at their approach, and Abi felt a pang of sympathy at the wary hopefulness on Cormac's face.

Nate placed his phone face-up in the centre of the table and grinned at the Alpha. "Call the Council and tell them we're going to need backup at this address, and distractions at these two."

"You found him."

"I think so." Nate turned to Abi, his grin widening. "How do you feel about going back to Dublin?"

627

CHAPTER TWENTY-TWO

Faerie — day 3

Phoenix had never been the type of person who became drained by interacting with others. Though she loved having time to herself to recharge, she was well used to making polite small talk with customers in the pub and generally managed to keep up her side of a conversation without too much effort. But conversation with Eoghan? That was a different story altogether.

The fae lord's definition of talking with another person involved him spewing a never-ending monologue about his formidable achievements, with not-so-subtle hints as to how that might translate to his prowess in the bedroom. At first she'd listened with some interest, figuring it might be an opportunity to learn more about Faerie. However, it didn't take long to deduce that she'd be better off finding an alternative source of information. She wasn't even lying when she pleaded the start of a headache and excused herself.

She checked Ethan's room first to see if he had returned from sparring with her grandfather, but when she found no sign of him there, she made her way to the family dining room. That too was empty except for a kindly fae female who worked in the kitchen.

The female offered to make her some honey tea and Phoenix accepted with an embarrassing rumble of her stomach and a gracious smile. She was surprised to find hunger gnawing at her as she sipped the warming liquid and was warily contemplating trying actual food when Ethan strolled in.

He gave her a teasing grin as he shoved his damp hair out of his face. "Where's his Lordship Smarmy Pants?"

She glared at him, crossing her arms. "I can't believe you just abandoned me like that. Do you know how much he likes to talk about himself?"

He snorted and grabbed a bread roll from a basket of fresh-baked bread on the table. "I can imagine. Anyway, I wasn't really given a choice. It seems your grandfather had a few things he wanted to get off his chest so he decided to do it while kicking my arse. He's pretty spry for an old guy."

"Get what things off his chest?" she asked, the subtle tension underlying his tone making her forget her irritation.

"Nothing important." He dismissed the issue with a wave of his hand and bit a chunk out of the bread roll. "He did mention having an important meeting this afternoon. I got the impression your grandmother and Aoife would be involved too, so it might be a good opportunity to go back and check out that corridor."

He didn't have to ask her twice. She hopped to her feet and grabbed Claíomh Solais from where it rested against her chair. "Let's go."

Phoenix tried to look casual as they made their way through the castle back to the corridor they'd passed earlier that day with Aoife. Her palms were sweating and she was convinced that she had guilty written all over her face. What if she'd only imagined the strange pull? She'd been so focused on finding any clue to the spear's where-abouts that she wouldn't be surprised at all if it turned out to be little more than wishful thinking. But as they drew closer to the dim corri-dor, the tugging sensation came again. The inexplicable pull beck-oned her forward as if the darkness itself were calling her. She kept walking, only dimly aware of the logical voice in the back of her mind that warned her to be careful.

Tension radiated from Ethan as he kept close to her side, but he stayed quiet and let her lead the way. The light was almost non-existent as they moved deeper into the corridor. So much so that even with her enhanced sight she had to strain her eyes. She didn't need to see, however; not when the sword, and her gut, were telling her exactly where she needed to go.

Eventually they reached the end of the corridor and came face-to-face with a blank wall. Just as Aoife had said, it appeared to be a dead end. Ethan let out a low curse that mirrored her own sentiments. The pull had turned into a vibration, and it was thrumming though her now, insisting that she go forward. But there was no forward.

Frowning, she reached out and placed her hands on the wall and ran them methodically over the smooth surface. A hidden doorway seemed awfully cliché, but it wouldn't be the first time they'd found one.

Ethan followed her lead, concentrating as he searched with her. After a minute, he shook his head.

"Maybe there's a password or something?" She stepped back with a huff of frustration to assess the wall. As she did, her heel got caught on an uneven stone, and before she could regain her balance, she landed unceremoniously on the ground with a thud.

Ethan was at her side in an instant, checking for injuries. "Are you okay?"

"I'm fine. I'm fine." She brushed him off and twisted around to see what she'd stumbled over. Nothing obvious caught her eye so she rolled onto her knees and ran her hands over the floor. A ridge ran across the cool stone, barely noticeable. "Look."

Ethan bent down to examine the spot where she indicated. His eyes flashed yellow for a second before huge claws extended from both his hands. He gripped the ridge and pried the floor upwards. A cloud of dust preceded the musty smell of earth as he revealed a decrepit wooden staircase. Thick mud and spindly roots surrounded the opening, and Phoenix could only see a few steps down before complete darkness consumed everything. Were these the escape tunnels Aoife had mentioned?

Ethan pulled a small torch from his pocket. "I'm game if you are?"

When she nodded, he lowered himself into the narrow space. The stairs creaked with each step he took, but held firm. Carefully she manoeuvred herself into the hole after him and he reached back to steady her. The air was heavy and stale and she had to fight the urge to hold her breath.

At the bottom, a tunnel led deeper into the earth. It was narrow enough that they had to walk single file, so Phoenix let Ethan lead the way with the torch while she kept one hand on his shoulder and the other firmly gripped to her scabbard's leather strap. The light of the torch threw shadows around them and lent an eerie feel to the darkness.

After a few minutes, the tunnel widened and she was able to move to Ethan's side. The earth beneath their feet was smoother now, and she noticed that the dirt walls also seemed smoother, more intentionally carved. Thick roots ran through the walls like veins, and she guessed they must be moving towards the tree that braced the west side of the castle.

The vibration that thrummed from the sword rattled through her with every step forward she took. When the passage suddenly branched into three separate directions, she took the far left one, without hesitation. Muck turned into a stone walkway, and a light breeze caressed her skin. The fragrance drifting through the air was so unexpected that she stopped and looked at Ethan in surprise.

"Is that ..."

"Roses," he confirmed, looking every bit as puzzled as she felt.

Though the air seemed fresher in this tunnel, there had been no let-up to the darkness, suggesting there was no opening to the outside world nearby. So where was the smell coming from?

Her question was quickly answered as the passage veered around a bend and they found themselves in front of the most magnificent sight. The walls were no longer coated in mud, but instead thick green stems covered every inch of the walls and ceiling. Deep-purple roses bloomed from the ends of the stems, their perfume subtle yet pleasing. Finger-length thorns protruded from the shadows and Phoenix shivered as she took in their vicious tips.

A single wooden door stood at the end of the passage, as if

waiting just for them. There was no sign of a lock or even a handle, but her head buzzed with the surety that what they sought was behind it. She took a step forward, but Ethan grabbed her, halting her motion.

"Let me go first."

She opened her mouth to argue and stopped. The stubborn set of his jaw was far too familiar by now, so she just sighed and waved a hand for him to proceed. He'd gone less than two feet before she followed.

About halfway to the door, the plants around them came to life.

The thick stems covering the walls writhed and the blanket of green seemed to undulate. A couple of particularly large stems lazily slithered down the wall and along the floor, making their way towards her and Ethan. The light of the torch glistened off the blade-like edge of the thorns. She swallowed and looked back the way they'd come, debating whether retreat was necessary. But instead of the open entrance that they'd stepped through, there was now just a tangled web of thorns and roses.

"Ethan," she whispered, tugged on his arm with barely restrained urgency.

A vine darted out from the wall and before she could even yelp her surprise, it latched on to her right wrist. She froze, afraid to even breathe.

Ethan turned, paling when he took in her newly acquired restraint and the blocked exit. His eyes glowed an eerie yellow in the torchlight. "Don't move. I'll cut it with my claws."

She shook her head, eyes riveted on another vine creeping closer on her left, this one sporting a terrifying thorn. "I think that will just piss it off."

"Shit." He growled.

"I have an idea." She tried to keep the tremble from her voice but failed. Tentatively, she reached out towards the approaching vine with her free hand. She scrunched her eyes closed as she inched closer to the thorn.

"What are you –"

A burn of pain caused her to hiss, cutting off Ethan's protest. She opened her eyes and watched as a single bead of blood ran along her palm and dripped onto the plant. The blood absorbed into the fibrous skin of the plant's stem, and an instant later the grip on her right wrist released, the vine sliding back to its spot on the wall.

She blew out a shaky breath. "Come on," she said, her attention once again focused on the wooden door as she started forward.

A strangled cry halted her mid-stride.

CHAPTER TWENTY-THREE

Faerie – day 3

Horror clutched Phoenix in its claws as she turned and saw the thick vine wrapped around Ethan's throat. The muscles in his forearms bulged in his attempts to pry it away, but he might as well have been tickling the plant for all the good it was doing. She cursed as panic threatened to choke her. Whatever spell protected this place either didn't like his werewolf blood, or was keyed to her family line only.

"Okay, don't struggle," she said in a calm, soothing voice, as if that might stop the vine from squeezing the life out of him.

She inched towards him, hands held out as if to assure the roses she was coming in peace. But even as she moved, more vines snaked their way towards Ethan. Their blooms looked full, and dare she say it, hungry.

He gave her a pained look, but did as she asked and calmed his attempts to remove the fibrous rope that was a mere contraction away from strangling him. His hands remained firmly in place, however, in case the vine took the opportunity to tighten further.

It felt like an eternity before she reached his side. Slowly, so as not

634

to spook the plant, she placed her still-bloodied palm on the vine and held her breath. Nothing happened.

"Looks like there's no option for a plus one," Ethan said wryly.

The vibration of the sword on her back was so strong now that between it and her fear, she couldn't think straight. She looked from the vine around his throat to the wooden door and back again. They were so close, she could feel it. Maybe she could grab the spear and then find a way to free him? The vine hadn't tightened enough to cut off his oxygen; maybe it just wanted to restrain him.

Even as the thought crossed her mind, another thick rope of green latched on to Ethan's right foot. This one was barbed with an entire row of small thorns and he hissed as they pierced his skin.

"Go. I'll be fine."

Another wince of pain belied his words, and she hesitated.

"Go!"

She sucked in a breath and with a final look at the noose around his neck, she turned and sprinted down the short passage. A muffled grunt behind her sent her heart ricocheting in her chest, but she kept her focus firmly on the door. *It's not like the thorns are made of silver,* she reminded herself. *He'll be okay.*

She skidded to a stop and immediately began searching the door for a handle or catch of some sort. The wood was rough beneath her hands, but she could find no mechanism to open it. She cursed and kicked the door in frustration. It didn't even shudder in response.

"Phoenix," Ethan called, his voice sounding strained. "Any chance you can hurry it along?"

She turned to look back and a sharp cry escaped her lips as she took in the vines that had latched themselves on to his arms and legs. Blood seeped from a multitude of cuts made by the thorny edges, and thick purple blooms caressed him almost lovingly.

Forgetting all about the door she ran back to him, drawing Claíomh Solais from the scabbard on her back as she did. New vines reached out from the wall and tried to pull the blade from her hands, but she cleaved clean through them and kept moving.

Once she was within reaching distance, she swung the sword at the ropes binding Ethan. They fell to the ground, but others replaced them before he barely had a chance to move. She bit back a scream of frustration.

Gritting her teeth, she hacked at the plant over and over again, hoping that if she just kept cutting it would slow its ability to regenerate. A black, tar-like substance oozed from the severed limbs, and by the time she managed to get Ethan's arms and legs free long enough for him to move, she was covered in it.

He extended his claws and sliced clean through the remaining vine around his neck. Still more came for him. He snatched her free hand and pulled her towards the mouth of the passage, writhing vines and razor-like thorns clutching at them from all sides. Neither his claws nor her sword ceased slashing for a moment.

Attempts to hack through the wall of roses that blocked their exit made little impression, and sweat mixed with the black tar covering Phoenix's skin as she tried in vain to create an opening.

A shudder ran through the ground and she stumbled. She reached out to steady herself and let out a cry of pain as a thorn pierced her palm. The wound burned with an intensity that caused her vision to swim.

"Phoenix." Ethan grabbed her elbow as another tremor rippled beneath them. He hissed as he looked at the damage to her hand and back to the barrier that kept them trapped. "Can you call the sun?"

This far underground? And with her power as glitchy as it had been recently? Doubt niggled at her, but she forced herself to take a slow breath and focus on the exit. "Get behind me," she ordered, hoping like hell she would be able to control the power enough not to incinerate him.

With her bloody hand she gripped her mother's medallion hanging warm against her chest. *Please let this work, please let this work.* The heat came slower than normal, but it came. It stuttered, and her chest tightened in panic for a split second before she regained her focus. Inhale. Exhale.

As the warmth built, she let it flow from her chest down her arm and into the sword gripped tightly in her hand. She raised the sword towards the exit and unleashed her power.

A blinding flash of light seared her retinas and in the moment of silence that followed, her heart stopped. Only when she heard Ethan groan behind her and felt his hand grip her arm did it start beating again.

Where once an impenetrable wall of roses stood before them, a large, charred hole now opened into the dark passage beyond. Her legs went weak, but the relief lasted no time at all. The ground began to shake under their feet and dirt rained down from the ceiling above them. She looked at Ethan with wide eyes.

"Move," he commanded, pushing her through the opening.

Her feet caught on vines and she fell to her knees on the far side of the tunnel. Ethan's hand disappeared from her back and she heard a strangled cry behind her. She turned in time to see him yanked backwards by a thorn-filled vine that had locked itself around his throat.

"Ethan!"

An ear-splitting roar filled the air and the ceiling collapsed around her.

CHAPTER TWENTY-FOUR

Home – 2 weeks gone

A slow smile spread over Darius's face as he observed the writhing bodies on the dance floor below his office. The vampires not rostered to work that night had been warned to make themselves scarce, but that still left plenty of bodies to act as an obstacle for the coming fun.

"How many?" he asked, turning to Erik.

"Twenty-five from the south, another thirty or so from the north. The wolves and their companions seem to be heading for a point between the two. Presumably a rendezvous point."

The Council had sent little more than fifty of their security team? *Hmm.* They either highly underestimated him, or the present he'd sent them the week prior was still keeping their resources tied up back in Brussels. It didn't matter; they could have sent double the number and it wouldn't make a difference to the outcome of tonight's events. The Donegal pack might think they had strong allies on their side, but he would show them just how wrong they were.

"And everything's in place?"

"The wolf was transferred earlier today," Erik confirmed, a wicked gleam in his eye.

"Good. Leave guards on the main doors of the club and clear out the rest of our people. Get the car started out back, I'll be down in a moment."

Erik left without a word. Darius sat down at his mahogany desk and pulled out a cream sheet of paper and a gold pen. He composed a brief note and folded the page, leaving it resting in plain sight. Pity he wouldn't be able to greet its recipients in person, but he had work to do.

Shade shoved his way through a sea of sweaty bodies and flailing limbs. The Club of Night was in chaos. Humans ran in panicked circles like headless chickens as they scrambled towards anything that even remotely resembled a door, while the Supe patrons had chosen to vent their anger at a ruined night by turning the dancefloor into a scene from *Battle Royale*.

Strobe lights flashed to a now-silent beat, allowing him glimpses of the Council security team that was busy securing the exits. He'd been surprised that the Council had come through on their promise of backup, but sure enough, they'd found the best part of fifty Supes waiting for them at the agreed rendezvous point, each carrying enough weapons that they looked like they were ready to go to war.

Cormac had taken five of his wolves and made a beeline for the upper floor of the club, where the offices were likely to be. Another ten wolves were busy rounding up the staff while the Council team corralled the less-helpful patrons. For his part, Shade had his sights set on an auspicious set of double doors at the back of the club, and anyone who got in his way was going to get hurt.

A beefy shifter with beer stains down his torn shirt clearly hadn't gotten the memo, however, and lumbered into his path with a sneer. Shade didn't even slow as he lashed out with a well-placed strike to the windpipe that left the man gasping in a heap on the floor. Two more vamps tried their hand at him before he made it to his target on the far side of the dancefloor. One ended up with a penknife in the eye for good measure, while the other would likely need to drink his blood through a straw for the foreseeable future.

Lucas reached the double doors at the same time as he did. The wary look on the vamp's face told Shade he wasn't the only one suspicious about the obvious lack of security; nothing was ever that easy. They each moved to either side of the doors. Lucas mouthed a silent countdown to him, and they yanked them open.

Shade held his breath waiting for a flood of vampires or an explosion, or hell, anything. But no nasty surprises greeted them.

They slipped through the doors and made their way soundlessly through the darkened corridors that wound along the back of the club. At each turn he expected to be faced with some form of attack, and at each turn they were met with silence. Rather than allowing him to relax, it only made him warier.

On the second floor below ground level they reached a corridor with a row of nondescript black doors lining both sides of the hallway. A shiver ran through him as he eyed the doors; something told him he didn't want to know what was behind them.

Lucas moved ahead, indicating for Shade to take the doors on the left while he took the ones on the right. Shade grimaced but nodded in acknowledgement before moving to the first door.

He shoved it open and was hit with a stench of decay so strong it sent his head spinning. Whatever had been in that room was no longer alive enough to be a problem, so he made a swift retreat before he was tempted to empty his stomach contents in a very undignified manner on the floor.

The second room was oddly sterile, a complete dichotomy to the previous one. A single metal table sat in the middle of the room and a tray was laid out on a rolling stand beside it. No amount of bleach could hide the metallic tang of blood, and no stretch of imagination could convince him that the instruments spread out on the tray had been used in enjoyable endeavours. The space was thankfully empty.

The third room was not.

The girl who hung limply from chains in the centre of this room looked to be barely eighteen – an impression only heightened by the schoolgirl outfit and pigtails. Her head lolled to one side, eyes glassy and unfocused as a vampire knelt before her, trousers around his ankles while he ravaged her femoral artery.

Red haze filled Shade's vision.

Before the vamp could turn from his helpless prey, Shade pulled his penknife out and rammed it into the side of the vamp's throat.

The vampire roared and stumbled backwards, tripping over the trousers tangled around his feet. The sight was so pathetic that Shade couldn't even bring himself to make the man's suffering last; he snapped the vamp's neck in one swift movement and retrieved his penknife in disgust.

He turned to walk from the room but stopped before he could reach the door. Unable to stop himself, he looked back at the girl's limp body. There was no helping her, he knew that. Either she'd come here voluntarily, in which case she'd do it again, or she'd been stupid enough to be tricked into coming. If so, it wouldn't be long before some other predator would scent her out for the easy prey that she was. Whichever way he looked at it, it was only a matter of time before she was dead. And yet, he couldn't bring himself to leave her in her current state.

"Fucking idiot," he muttered to himself.

He unhooked her from the chains as quickly as he could and lowered her to the ground. There was no hint of awareness from her as he did, and he didn't make any attempt to get a response either. He simply tore the end of his T-shirt off and tightened it around the wound on her upper thigh. Whether it would be enough to keep her alive, he had no idea. He left the room, his head pounding in rage and the scent of the girl's blood clinging to his nostrils.

The remaining rooms were each different variations of depraved. Lucas's features were as strained as his own when they had finally cleared them all. Grateful to be away from the black doors, they continued down the corridor until they reached a dead end and an elevator. Metal doors stood open, beckoning them into the empty interior. A retina scanner to the left of the lift glowed green.

Shade looked at Lucas.

The older vamp pressed a small earpiece in his left ear that allowed them to communicate with the others outside the club. "Nate, did you hack the elevator security on this level?"

Shade couldn't hear Nate's response in his own earpiece, but Lucas frowned and shook his head. "This wasn't Nate. Which means someone is expecting us."

Footsteps could be heard in the distance, and they both tensed until Cormac's signature reached them. The wolves came into view seconds later, their expressions grim.

"Darius is gone." Cormac's eyes blazed in the dim light and blood spatter dotted his cheeks. "We found this in the main office." He held out a piece of white paper, crumpled and smeared with blood.

Lucas took it from him, and Shade read the words over his shoulder: "He's my pet now." He sucked in a breath and risked a glance at Cormac. The tightening of the wolf's jaw was subtle, but there was a calmness to the Alpha that was more terrifying than any show of anger could be.

Lucas indicated to the waiting lift. "It appears he may have been expecting us."

Cormac's answering smile was terrifying. "We wouldn't want to be rude then, would we?"

CHAPTER TWENTY-FIVE

Home – 2 weeks gone

It was a tight fit, but the two vampires and six wolves squeezed into the small tin container. *Now would be a perfect time for someone to cut the cables,* Shade thought as Cormac pressed the single button and the lift doors closed.

The descent took seconds, and they all spaced out around the sides in preparation for the attack that was surely waiting. The doors opened to silence.

Warily, they edged out of the lift one at a time. The room appeared to be a laboratory of sorts. Complicated-looking gadgets lined metal tables running along one side of the room, while the faded remnants of a chalk circle could be seen on the other. A large window allowed visibility into an empty white chamber on the left.

The fragrance of herbs mingled with the burnt aftertaste of chemicals and the odour was so potent it choked him. Yet none of it hid the coppery tang of blood, or the rot of days-old faeces. He shuddered as his mind offered him possibilities for what the lab and chambers had been used for.

A man in a stiff grey suit stepped through a shadowed doorway at the back of the room. "Oh, there you are. I was wondering when you might join us."

The man's posture was relaxed and open, and his smile made Shade want to punch him in the face. Even from a distance the swirling red of his eyes was apparent, and his signature, although familiar enough to be recognised as a shifter, felt tainted in a way that made Shade want to scrub his skin raw. Low growls rumbled from the wolves, but they all held still, awaiting Cormac's orders.

The newcomer moved further into the room, completely unphased by their reaction. "Please, let me introduce myself. I'm Vicktor, head of the Council Liaison Office. Darius asked me to make sure his guests were properly welcomed. Can I get anyone a drink?" Vicktor's smile widened and he folded his hands in front of him.

Cormac stepped forward, his eyes flashing yellow in warning. "Where's Sean?"

"Oh, do forgive me." Vicktor clicked his fingers and called, "Can someone please bring out the mutt?"

A man and woman appeared from the shadows behind the CLO rep, dragging a limp form between them. Blood and dirt caked the body, and shredded rags hung loosely from emaciated limbs. The man and woman took no care as they dumped their package on the ground and stepped back, flashing grotesque grins which failed to hide the chilling calculation in their red eyes.

A deathly silence fell over the room. Shade could just about make out the faint beat of the Omega's heart so he knew Sean was alive, but there was no hiding the fact that he had been tortured to within an inch of his life.

Vicktor shrugged. "I guess some people just can't handle the pressure."

Without warning, Cormac lunged for him. Vicktor sidestepped the attack even as the other wolves followed their Alpha's lead and swarmed towards him. That left the other two demon-Supe hybrids to Shade and Lucas.

Shade faced off with the male – a vampire with a signature muddied enough to make him question whether there was truly any Supe left in the man – while Lucas turned his focus to the female.

644

Shade allowed himself a moment to remember the young girl hanging from the chains while her vitality was slowly sucked dry from her. He let all the rage he'd felt in that moment to take him over now; he was going to make this hurt.

The room turned to chaos as bodies crashed into metal tables, smashing glass bottles and knocking equipment to the floor. Darius's abominations were outnumbered almost three to one and they shouldn't have stood a chance. But Shade was dimly aware of Vicktor's maniacal laughter in the background as each of his strikes missed by a fraction of a second; his opponent was just too fucking fast.

A fist connected with Shade's jaw, spinning him a full three-sixty and causing his vision to blur for a second. He groaned.

The vampire opened his mouth in what was probably supposed to be a cocky grin, and the stench of rotten flesh smacked Shade in the face. He fought against the urge to gag as he took in the blackened maw crawling with maggots. Yellow fangs lunged for him.

A loud rumble sounded and a tremor ran through the floor. The vamp was thrown off balance mid-lunge, and Shade used the reprieve to slip behind him and slice a clean line across his throat with his penknife.

Another shudder ran through the ground, and he had to reach for the wall to maintain his footing.

"Shade!" Lucas yelled from the far side of the room.

Shade turned to see the older vampire driven back by a blur of flashing claws that were attached to one scary-ass female. Despite Lucas's fighting skill, he seemed unable to get through the strikes to launch his own attack, or even disable the woman.

"Dammit." Shade launched himself over one of the metal tables that had been shoved into the middle of the room. He was dimly aware that the wolves had managed to surround Sean in a protective circle as he moved to help Lucas. Cormac was holding his own against Vicktor, but the CLO rep showed no signs of real damage.

An explosion sounded from the back of the room and suddenly the lab swarmed with a hoard of red-eyed Supes. Everything went to hell.

Shade lost sight of Lucas and found himself face-to-face with something from his nightmares. He could hear Cormac's roars as he tried to protect Sean and howls of pain from the wolves as they were attacked.

Another rumble tore through the earth and the ground beneath his feet split apart. A groan of metal was the last thing he heard before the ceiling caved in on top of them.

The world shook around Abi as she stumbled her way down the fire escape of the abandoned building across the road from the Club of Night. Only Sasha's grip on her arm stopped her from falling down the metal steps when the next tremor hit. Her head was pounding and a thin stream of blood ran from her forehead, obscuring her vision.

"Get to the street," Fia ordered from behind them as she helped Nate haul what little of their comms equipment remained intact.

The first tremor had taken them all by surprise. Earthquakes were unheard of in Ireland, so Abi's first thought had been a bomb explosion. When the next shockwave hit and the road between their building and the club had split in two, she realised what was happening just in time to get brained by a falling plank of wood that had moments before served as a rooftop billboard.

On the far side of the road, bodies streamed out of the club. The Council security team had obviously unblocked the exits when the building had begun to crumble around them. As she raced down the final flight of steps, Abi scanned the crowd for any sign of a familiar face. Where were the others? They couldn't stay in there; the building was going to collapse.

Behind her, Nate muttered curses under his breath as he tried without luck to get the comms to connect. "I'm just getting static. Either the signal's down or ..."

"Okay," Fia said with a calm she couldn't possibly feel as they reached the chaos of the street. "We need to go in after them. Sasha, come with me. Nate, get Abi clear in case the building falls."

Abi opened her mouth to protest – she was pretty sure a collapsing building was just as dangerous for a Supe as it was for her – but the two wolves took off at a run before she could speak. They leapt over a huge crevice that bisected the road and disappeared into the wreckage of Darius's club.

"Dammit, now would have been a good time for that backup to arrive," Nate muttered.

She gave him a questioning glance, but he ignored it and beckoned her to follow. "Come on. We need to secure the back of the building."

Her legs were shaky, but she managed to keep pace with him without breaking an ankle on any of the spiderweb cracks that had created an obstacle of concrete ahead of them. Sirens echoed in the distance, and the sound seemed to spur the club's patrons to clear the vicinity at record speed. Only a few of the more badly wounded men and women stumbled about in a daze and if Abi had to guess, she'd say they were the human customers.

Miraculously, the worst of the damage appeared to be at the front of the club. The tight knot of dread eased just a little in her chest as she took in the remaining people fleeing through the emergency exits. Most were covered in dust and appeared a little worse for wear, but if they were alive she had no reason to believe their friends weren't too.

Nate pulled her back into the shadows, his eyes darting between the doors and the cracked screen of his phone. His phone did little more than flicker on and off as he pressed the power button repeatedly, and she could sense his irritation growing with each futile attempt. It had to be killing him to be stuck out here babysitting her while his friends were trapped inside. Guilt gnawed at her and she stared at the doors, willing a familiar face to appear.

Minutes ticked by.

Finally, a woman Abi vaguely recognised as being part of the Council's security team emerged from the club. She moved with a limp, carrying a lifeless body over each shoulder. The woman didn't stop for a breath as she dumped the bodies on the ground and disappeared back inside.

Not waiting for Nate's permission, Abi hurried across the street to the lifeless forms. She couldn't help the uneasy sense of relief that struck her when she realised neither face was familiar, and she didn't even have the capacity to feel bad about it.

More of the Council's team emerged from the club hauling injured men and women. Nate grabbed one of them. "Have you seen –"

The door slammed open, and Cormac's bloodied form appeared carrying an equally bloody body over his shoulder. He stumbled out into the street and his knees buckled beneath him. Nate grabbed his shoulders and eased him to the ground.

"No." Cormac gritted his teeth and pushed back to standing. "We have to move. They're coming."

The door swung open once more, bringing with it the sound of fighting and a loud crash. Fia pushed Sasha through the exit and, without stopping, wrapped her arm around Cormac's waist, urging him to move. "Shade and Lucas are trying to hold them back. We don't have long."

Abi had no chance to ask who it was they were running from before Nate lifted her off her feet and took off at a speed that sent her already-pounding head spinning. He didn't slow down until they reached a quiet street a few blocks over, at which point her stomach retched in protest and deposited its contents on the ground.

The others reached their side a moment later. Breathing hard, Cormac lay the body he was carrying down on the ground. He pushed the blood-caked hair back from an almost skeletal face. "Sean? Sean, can you hear me? Come on, Omega, your Alpha is talking to you, give me something, dammit."

Fia knelt opposite him and quickly ran her hands over the unconscious wolf, assessing his injuries. Her features tightened as she uncovered vicious slashes that exposed muscle and sent Abi's stomach reeling again. Charred bands surrounded the wolf's ankles and wrists, and now that he was lying down, Abi noticed that more than one limb was bent at an unnatural angle.

She bit back tears and bile rose up in her throat. What had they done to him?

A light breeze skimmed her face and she almost jumped out of her skin as Shade and Lucas appeared beside her. Cormac looked up from his position on the ground in question.

"They don't seem to be following us," Lucas told him, grey eyes darkening as he took in Sean's injured form. "We held them back until the emergency vehicles and human authorities arrived. After that, none of them seemed inclined to follow us out of the club."

Fia frowned, looking off in the distance to where the sounds of sirens could still be heard. "Darius clearly isn't ready to show off his new toys to everyone just yet."

Shade grimaced. "We're fucked when he is. The bastards were strong. Fast too. If that roof hadn't collapsed and trapped half of them ..."

They all fell silent, no one wanting to consider just how tenuous their victory tonight had been. Abi wrapped her arms around herself as a chill that had nothing to do with the cool night air settled into her bones.

"How is he doing?" Lucas asked, crouching down beside Cormac.

"Alive, but –"

Everyone froze. As one, the Supes all whipped their heads around to face the end of the street, tension radiating from each of them.

Abi's breath caught in her throat and she swallowed hard to hold back the whimper that tried to escape. She stared into the dark, waiting. As silent as the night, Sasha moved to her side, vicious claws elongating from her hands.

Seven shadowy figures came into view from around a corner. They walked in sync with each other, staying side by side so that they spanned the width of the street.

"Witches," Sasha whispered, her eyes flashing yellow.

The seven figures stopped about fifty feet from their group and a slender girl with long, fair hair stepped forward. If Abi had to guess she'd say they girl was little more than sixteen, but the witch showed no sign of fear as she faced them with her shoulders squared.

"We're going to need you to give us the Omega." Her voice rang clear in the silence, no hint of threat in her tone, but also no room for doubt.

Cormac and Fia stood, placing themselves as a barrier in front of Sean. Sasha moved to their side. Low growls rumbled from the wolves as three pairs of yellow eyes glowed in the darkness.

"We don't have time for this," the girl said firmly.

The wolves all tensed to attack, but Nate pushed past them, his hands held forward in a gesture of peace. "Izzie?"

Abi felt as much as saw the others around her flinch with the same confusion she felt. Nate knew this girl?

"It is Izzie, isn't it? I got your email. I'm the one who sent the message from Annabelle's account. We're on the same side."

Abi struggled to follow exactly what was happening. Who the hell was Izzie, and why was Nate messaging a witch from a dead girl's account? Was this the backup he'd mentioned earlier?

"You need to step away from the wolf," the girl repeated, eyes firmly fixed on the wolves.

Abi glanced down at Sean and gasped when she saw his body twitch. Instinctively, she moved to crouch at his side.

"No!" Izzie yelled.

She stretched out her hand and a blast of blue light shot from her palm. It wrapped around Sean just as his body jerked up from the ground, eyes wide and crazed. He froze mid-movement.

The wolves roared and moved to attack her, but Lucas shot in front of them, arms wide to halt their momentum. "Wait. Look." He pointed back at Sean, who seemed to be held in some kind of stasis by the blue light that shone like a bubble around him.

Abi's heart pounded in her throat as she too looked at the Omega. Sean's wolf fangs were fully extended, saliva dripping from them, and his eyes ... his eyes were flooded crimson red. "Is he ..."

The witch walked to their side, expression sombre. "Possessed."

CHAPTER TWENTY-SIX

Faerie – day 3

"What exactly did you think you were doing in the tunnels? Access was blocked off a long time ago, and for a very good reason."

Ethan could feel the weight of Aoife's hardened stare boring into him, but he couldn't take his eyes off Phoenix's still form. The crisp white sheets of her bed only accentuated the deathly pale of her skin, and her hand was cold as it rested in his. Every second that ticked by was torture. Every minute that she remained unconscious only increased the roaring in his head until he was convinced that he'd go crazy.

He ignored Aoife's question, just like he had every other time she'd asked, instead repeating, "We need to get her to a doctor."

Aoife huffed out a frustrated breath. "The healer has already checked her. Her vitals are strong, her body just needs time to heal."

"You don't understand." He clenched the bed sheets with his free hand to stop the scream of frustration from freeing itself from his throat. It had been hours. She should have woken up by now.

Every time he closed his eyes he could see the avalanche of earth swallow her whole. He'd watched, trapped and helpless as the

651

tunnels collapsed on top of her. He'd fought with every last breath in his body to free himself of the vines so he could go to her. His only thought as the world turned black had been of Phoenix and their baby.

When he'd come to in the glaring light of day, he thought for a moment that he'd passed to the other side. The stories always tell of that magical white place where good people go when they die. He had been a good person, hadn't he?

But then the pain had kicked in and he knew he was still alive.

Aoife had come to him soon after he'd awoken. How she'd known where to find them he still wasn't sure, but either the cave-in, or whatever ward controlled the roses, had alerted her to their presence in the tunnels. Initially, her only concern had been getting them both to safety and ensuring they were unharmed. But when he'd refused to stay in bed – ignoring her frustrated protests to stumble weakly to Phoenix's side – anger had overtaken her concern, and she'd deemed him fit for an ear lashing.

"So, tell me," she snapped. "What is it I don't understand?"

When he didn't immediately answer, she threw her hands up in the air and resumed pacing. Her hair was in disarray and her clothes were still covered in dirt from when she had dug Phoenix free of the earth that had buried her. He knew she'd kept a vigilant watch at her niece's side for the brief time that he'd been unconscious himself, and something vaguely like guilt settled in the pit of his stomach.

"I know you and Phoenix have been keeping secrets, and I won't force you to confide in me. But I don't understand what it is I've done to earn your mistrust."

He let out a growl of frustration, looking once more at Phoenix's still form. The swell of her abdomen was more noticeable than it had been when they'd left home. How much longer before it would become difficult to hide? If they had to stay here, it was only a matter of time before their secret was revealed, and he needed to know that the baby was safe.

"She's pregnant."

Aoife's pacing abruptly ceased. A tense silence fell over the room and Ethan held his breath.

"Is it yours?"

He nodded.

Aoife exhaled, long and slow. "Thank you for being honest with me. You have nothing to worry about. The baby is fine."

He looked up in surprise. "You knew?"

She gave him a sad smile. "The healer discovered it when she was examining Phoenix. She is sworn to secrecy, but I needed to know whether or not you would tell me the truth."

The soft murmur of voices reached through the fog to Phoenix as a warm heat radiated through her. Her eyes were so heavy, the simple effort of peeling them open was enough to exhaust her and make her want to sink back into blissful oblivion. A kind face peered down at her before giving a satisfied nod and disappearing. Harsh, unforgiving daylight assaulted her eyes and she scrunched them closed with a wince.

"Phoenix. Phoenix, can you hear me?"

There was a barely contained urgency in Ethan's voice as his calloused hand gripped hers. His musky scent filled her senses, and that along with his touch became her focal point to centre herself.

Where was she? She blinked her eyes gingerly.

It was Ethan's worried face which filled her vision this time as he leaned over and smoothed her brow with his thumb.

"Hey." The word came out more of a croak than she'd intended it to.

A slender hand held a small shell of water to her lips so that she could drink. Phoenix flicked her eyes up as she took a grateful sip and was surprised to find that the hand belonged to her aunt.

The familiar surroundings of her bedroom came into focus, and she struggled to think through the murkiness that clouded her head. She was cocooned by the soft cushions on her bed, and Ethan and her aunt were both here with her in the room. But how had she gotten here? And why were they looking so worried?

A thunderous roar filled her head. An overwhelming sense of

suffocation washed over her, replacing the warm feeling she'd had only moments before. The smell of earth assaulted her. The heavy weight crushed her.

She bolted upright in the bed.

Ethan grabbed her shoulder, stopping her before she could move any further. "Shh. It's okay. Everything's okay now." He eased her back to the pillow, all the while murmuring quiet reassurances and telling her again and again that it was okay.

But how could it be? The memory of the cave in hit her in full Technicolor. It had happened so fast she hadn't had a chance to be afraid, but even in that fraction of a second, she'd known it was going to be anything but okay.

"The healer said you might have a bit of a concussion, but your body is doing what it needs to in order to repair itself," Ethan said gently, propping pillows up behind her so that she could sit up a little. "You just need to rest and let your body do its thing."

She looked at him with wide eyes, trying desperately to convey without words the panic that was racing through her.

"The baby's fine," he confirmed.

She jerked, her eyes darting towards Aoife.

He gave her a wry smile. "She knows. The healer discovered it when she was examining you."

Phoenix's breath caught for a whole different reason this time as she looked from Ethan to her aunt. Neither of their expressions gave any indication of how the news had been received and nausea twisted in her gut.

"How ... how long have I been out? What happened?"

"A few hours. From what we can tell, there seems to have been an earthquake of some kind that rippled through Faerie. It caused the cave-in."

An earthquake? A few hours? How badly had she been hurt? She reached for her abdomen, seeking comfort from the small flutter of life beneath her hand.

"I haven't shared your secret with my parents," Aoife said finally. "But I'm going to need you both to start being honest with me. What were you doing in the tunnels?"

Ethan gave a slight shake of his head to indicate he hadn't told her aunt anything else. Phoenix gave sighed and met her aunt's shrewd gaze, resigned.

"When Morrigan sent us here, she also wanted us to find something. A spear."

Aoife's manicured eyebrows shot up. "The Spear of Lugh?"

Phoenix bit her lip and nodded.

"Why would Morrigan send you to retrieve the spear?"

It was Ethan who answered when Phoenix struggled for the right thing to say. "She believes it may be needed again – to banish the Horsemen."

Aoife's already pale skin turned ashen. "The Horsemen were banished a millennia ago. They can't return."

And that was the problem. How could they explain it all without revealing the prophecy? How could Phoenix admit it was her fault that there was now even a possibility of the Horsemen's return without it being seen as proof her parents' love really was wrong?

"The fabric is growing weak," Ethan said in answer. "Demons are managing to cross over again, and human possessions are happening at an increasing frequency. They've only been minor demons so far, but it's clear from the pattern that the problem is progressing and it's only a matter of time before the barrier fails."

Aoife digested his words, her brow creasing with worry as she did. She was quiet for a moment before nodding, seeming to come to some internal decision.

"As I'm sure you've guessed by now, the spear is here in the castle. The tunnels, while once used as a secure escape route, also lead to some underground chambers that have been used over the centuries to protect important fae artefacts held by our family."

"The roses ..." Ethan shivered.

"One of many wards set to protect the chambers. The artefacts used in the original banishment were created by the Tuatha De Danann themselves, and as such were passed down through our family. The sword was Aria's birthright and was passed to her when she came of age and reached her immortality. The spear is mine."

Phoenix's heart stuttered. The spear belonged to her aunt? She could help them. If they could just make her understand.

She sat up, ignoring Ethan's protests, and reached out a beseeching hand to the woman who looked so much like her mother and yet was not. "I know you have no reason to trust us –"

"It is not I who has the issue with trust."

She bowed her head, unable to refute the accusation in her aunt's words. Quietly she said, "We came here because we have been betrayed, more than once, by people we trusted. The man I looked up to as an uncle my entire life was the very same monster responsible for my parents' death." Her breath hitched, but she swallowed and forced herself to continue. "You know our secret. Surely you must understand why we would be afraid to confide in you?"

A deep sadness softened Aoife's hard expression and she inclined her head. "Be that as it may, if you had come to me with the truth from the beginning, we would be having this conversation from a place of greater understanding now. You seek the spear, and you now know the only way to acquire it is with my help, or through my death. I'm not quite sure what to do with this information."

A numb sense of disbelief settled over Phoenix. Did her aunt honestly believe they would challenge her for the spear if she chose not to help them? How had they gotten to a place where it was even fathomable for family to turn on each other like that?

Aoife sighed and straightened. "As with all children of the Lore, I grew up hearing stories of the Horsemen and the horrors that followed in their wake, so I'm well aware of what it would mean for both our lands if what you say is true. However, we have heard no mention here in Faerie of the fabric failing, nor can I see of any reason why it would after all these millennia. Unless there is more that you can tell me, I don't know if I can help you."

"It's my fault," Phoenix blurted out. "It's my fault that the fabric is failing." She looked at her hands and let the words hang heavy in the air.

When the barrage of disgust and condemnation wasn't immediately forthcoming, Phoenix risked a quick peek up from under her lashes. Aoife simply waited, looking at her in patient expectation. So she took a deep, shuddery breath and explained it all. She told her aunt about Darius, and her parents' abduction, about the prophecy she'd unknowingly triggered, the people who were trying to stop it. And about the baby, who was their greatest hope.

When she finished, her aunt smiled. The haunted look remained in those green eyes, but for that moment, there was something different in Aoife's expression that reminded Phoenix of her mother.

Aoife stood from her chair by the bed. "You need to get some rest, and I need to think on what you've told me. I will keep your secret for now, and I advise you to do the same. But I fear there will come a time when we'll all have to face our own personal demons. The Horsemen were not banished by weapons alone. It took all species of the Lore working together to defeat them. I'm not quite sure if that capacity exists within us anymore."

CHAPTER TWENTY-SEVEN

Home – 2.5 weeks gone

Abi curled her legs closer to her body as she sat on the sofa and sought warmth from the mug of tea clasped in her hands. The sun had begun its descent beyond the city skyline as she stared out the panoramic window that ran the length of Ethan's apartment, and the sky had gone from a clear blue to streaks of red and orange. Almost a week after their arrival, and it was still strange to be back in Dublin. To be so close to her beloved pub knowing that it still sat in ruins after the witch fire.

They'd all agreed that it wasn't a good idea to move Sean far; the witches' stasis spell was limited by distance, and until they could find a way to help him, they couldn't risk releasing him from it. She'd agreed to stay behind with Nate and Sasha to watch over him, though how much her bedside vigil really helped she had no idea.

It had devastated Cormac and Fia to leave their Omega. The group had barely made it back to Ethan's apartment after the earth-quake when word came from Donegal that wildfires were spreading across the pack lands and destroying homes. The whole country, in fact, seemed to have been hit with a series of freak natural disasters, and instinct warned Abi that it was not a good omen.

God, she still couldn't believe that Darius had turned Sean into one of his demon hybrids. For him to survive so long only for it to come to this ... She clutched the mug tighter to her as if it alone might push away the chill that settled in her heart.

The sharp buzz of the apartment bell sounded, and low voices drifted towards her from the hallway. She unfurled herself from the soft cushions and stood as Nate came into the open plan living area with Izzie close behind him.

Izzie shook her head when Nate offered her a drink and settled herself on a stool at the island in the centre of the kitchen. Her expression was grim, and Abi was struck once more by just how young the girl looked.

Nate had told her that Izzie had been a friend of Annabelle's – Lily's younger sister who had died before Abi had had a chance to meet her. When they'd learned that the Council head of the witches was dead, Nate had tried to reach out to Izzie through Annabelle's email account. They'd need a witch to aid them with the banishment spell if it came to it, and with the Dublin coven at Darius's beck and call, it was hard to know who they could trust. What better option than a witch whom that very coven had tried to sacrifice?

Abi pulled up a stool beside Izzie, and unable to stop herself, she reached out and placed a hand on the girl's forearm. "Are you okay?"

Izzie gave her a weak smile. "An eighty-year-old lady tried to claw my eyes out earlier, and I'm not even sure she was possessed. Things are getting a bit weird out there." She blew out a breath and seemed to pull herself together. "Anyway, that's not why I'm here."

"Did you get what you need?" Nate asked.

Izzie regarded him with a serious expression. "We did. But I'm advising you again not to go through with this."

Abi's heart sped up its pace. The witches hadn't been very confident about their chances of freeing Sean from the demon. The level of demon Darius was pulling across was far beyond anything Phoenix had managed to trap in Lily's amulets, but they'd promised to try. They had to try.

"We can't leave him like that." Abi cringed at the desperation in her voice as she beseeched the young witch to understand. He had held on so long; they couldn't let him down now.

This time it was Izzie who reached over to give her hand a comforting squeeze. "Ethan saved my life. So if you ask me to do this, I will. But you need to understand this is bigger than anything I or any of the other witches have faced. We don't have the power of a coven behind us. We might not be strong enough."

Abi's brow furrowed in confusion. "I don't understand. You all work together. Does that not make you a coven?"

She didn't know much about the group of witches who'd turned up just in time to save them as Sean regained consciousness. Nate had told her they were fugitives from their various covens – witches who had rejected the use of dark magic. From what she understood, that made them weaker than witches who chose the dark magic path, but surely it didn't make them completely powerless?

"No," Izzie said, a hint of bitterness tinging her tone. "We are all still bound to our old covens, even if we don't agree to their practices. That kind of bond is unique, meant only to be forged once. It's impossible to create another with it in place."

"So find a way to sever it," Nate said simply. "Your coven tried to kill you; surely that's an acceptable loophole? You said it yourself, Ethan saved your life. You owe him this."

"Can ... Would you do it?" Abi asked, searching the girl's face.

Izzie contemplated his words as painful memories warred behind her eyes. Eventually, she nodded slowly. "If the others agree, there may be a way we can sever the bonds so that we're free to form a new one. It will take a few days."

"We'll wait," Nate said, even as something in Abi rebelled at the thought of leaving Sean in his frozen hell for a moment longer.

"There's one more thing you should know. If we do manage to separate Sean from the demon, I can't promise you he'll still be whole. We don't know what damage has been done to him, but it's possible he may never recover from this. You need to decide if that's a chance you're willing to take."

Abi met Nate's amber eyes, unease twisting in her stomach. Is this what Sean would want? She didn't know the Omega, had no way of knowing what he might want for himself.

Footsteps sounded and Sasha came into the kitchen, her eyes appearing tired but her expression determined. She put the book she'd been reading to Sean down on the marble top of the island. "We'll take the chance."

"My dad's ready to blow a gasket," Sasha said as she dropped into the leather recliner across from Abi with a sigh.

Nate had gone to his room to do some more research on the history of demon possessions once Izzie had left, and Abi had found it impossible to sleep as worries for Phoenix and Sean both competed for attention in her head. She'd given up trying a little after midnight and decided to make some warm milk like her mother used to do for her when she was small. It didn't surprise her that her friend was still awake and looking wired. She'd heard the murmur of Sasha's voice down the hall as she'd spoken on the phone with Cormac. Even without being able to hear the words, it had been clear to Abi that things weren't going well.

"Did the fires do much damage?"

Sasha waved a hand, looking distracted. "Some, but the pack will rebuild any of the homes that need it."

"So what has him so wound up?"

"The Council. William called and thanked him for his assistance at the club, but now that we have Sean back, our part in things is done." Sasha looked up, her brown eyes hard. "Apparently, the situation is too dangerous for 'civilians' to be involved, and they will 'deal' with it from here."

Abi grimaced, imagining all too well the reaction that call had gotten from Cormac. Hell, even she thought it was insulting, given the Council probably still wouldn't have a clue what Darius was up to if not for their help.

"What's your dad going to do?"

Another sigh, this one telling her just how much the recent weeks

661

had taken their toll on the wolf despite her joking and sarcasm. "Damned if I know. It's his job to protect us, to protect the pack. Every part of him will be screaming for revenge for what Darius did to Sean, but with everything going on at the moment, and worrying about Ethan ..."

"You think it's better letting the Council deal with it?"

"Hell no! The Council can't get their own shit together, never mind deal with Darius, but I worry that if he gets into another situation like the one at the club and his head's not fully in it ... Well, you saw for yourself. It was only luck that got them out of there last time." Sasha fell quiet as she remembered whatever horrors she'd seen in the club that night.

Abi took in her friend's creased brow and the subtle tightness around her jaw. She wished there was something she could do to ease the worry they were all feeling, to make a real difference to the situation rather than hanging around the sidelines and trying not to be a liability. If Phoenix was here she could talk to her best friend about it, admit just how inadequate she felt. Phoenix might be a Supe, but she understood – she'd spent most of her life believing she wasn't good enough to be part of the Lore.

But Phoenix wasn't here, and there wasn't anything Abi could say. So she stayed quiet, and they sat together, each lost in their own worries of what was to come.

CHAPTER TWENTY-EIGHT

Home – almost 3 weeks gone

Darius leaned on the metal rail of the platform and assessed the mass of bodies below. Men and women stood with lethal readiness, their crisp black uniforms a stark contrast to the sterile white walls of the pharmaceutical complex's centre chamber. All species were accounted for except two: the Mists and the fae.

A shiver of anticipation ran through him as he finally beheld the fruits of his labour. Years of testing and failed experiments had to be endured before they'd perfected the process that allowed him to first break the subjects to his will. Hundreds of wasted test subjects. But now, here they were. His army.

Ideally, he'd have liked to manage a full house, a demon match for every species. But recent centuries had seen the Mists become so rare that many forgot they were even a species of the Lore, and something about the ancient nature of fae magic meant the few transfers he'd attempted on them had failed drastically. It wouldn't matter though, because the time had come to move forward.

Erik appeared at his side, his head of security's movements even more silent and deadly since his own transfer had been completed days before.

"They're quite impressive," Erik noted, following Darius's gaze to the army that awaited their orders.

"The final behavioural issues seem to have been resolved."

He'd waited as long as possible before placing his head of security into the transfer chamber. A strong army needed a strong commander to keep them in line, and he needed the barrier as weak as possible to have a chance of pulling through an acolyte of the Horsemen. The recent spate of natural disasters was enough to assure him that the balance was finally shifting in their favour, and it seemed his faith had been rewarded.

Erik's wide smile showcased razor-sharp fangs and caused his red eyes to gleam. "They just needed a firm hand. It was nice of the Council to give us a chance to test them in the field. Though I'm a bit disappointed that their security teams didn't provide a better challenge."

Indeed, it had been depressingly predictable when the Council followed up their raid on the Club of Night with further raids on his other businesses, the pharmaceutical complex included. Their security teams didn't get far, though he'd made sure his army left some alive to send a message back to the Council.

"How many of the rejects are left?" he asked, turning his thoughts to the subjects who had completed the transformation, but whose level of control hadn't made the cut. They could still be useful to him. He turned from the platform, Erik moving with him as he made his way down the long corridor that led back to the private laboratories.

"Thirteen are left after the last group were sent to entertain the Council. Ready to be released when you say."

"Have them prepared, we may need them as a distraction. You managed to get hold of Vicktor?"

"He's waiting in your office."

"Good. It's time he makes up for his failure at the club."

Darius stopped in front of a metal door with a retina scanner and dismissed Erik with a wave. The scanner moved across his eyes and the door opened with a hiss to reveal a small white room that was as sterile and nondescript as the rest of the building. The heady aroma of herbs drifted to him from a glass vial of green liquid resting above an unlit Bunsen burner.

The witch didn't bother to look up as he approached, her attention focused on a half-torn piece of parchment lying on the metal table to the left of the burner. Her lips moved soundlessly as she scanned the faded words, a scowl firmly fixed on her face.

"Have you found anything?"

She made no attempt to mask her irritation as she raised her head, one eyebrow arched. "Your Sire kept some interesting records, but I've found nothing to suggest that he knew the cauldron's location."

Darius had expected that answer. He'd gone through Il Maestro's records many times over the centuries; if there had been anything to find, he was confident he would have already.

"We will proceed regardless."

The surprise that widened her eyes disappeared as quickly as it came. "Without the artefacts, the vessel –"

"Yes, yes, I know." He waved a hand dismissively. "We have the ingredients we need to proceed, do we not?"

"Yes," she answered warily.

"Then it is decided. We move forward with the transfer. Once I hold the power of the Horsemen within me, it will be a simple matter to find the artefacts; no one will dare stand in my way." He turned and strode back to the door. "Come. We need to send word to Faerie. It's time for the hybrid to return."

The witch's expression screamed her disapproval, but she wisely kept her mouth shut. She walked to the Bunsen burner and removed the glass vial resting above it, plugging the top with a small cork. Without a word, she followed him from the lab and down to his office on the ground floor.

Vicktor was already seated when they arrived, his red eyes fixed firmly ahead. There was no sign remaining of the damage he'd sustained when the earthquake had hit the Club of Night, or of the punishment he'd received afterwards for his failure. It seemed the shifter's natural healing ability was significantly accelerated by the presence of the demon within him, a fortunate coincidence or he might not be alive now to make up for his shortcomings.

"Vicktor, it's time you made yourself useful." Darius leaned against the mahogany desk as the witch stood by the door watching the two men closely. "We are ready to proceed to the next stage of our plan."

"What do you need me to do?"

"Send word to our friend in Faerie." He waved for the witch to hand over the vial. "They need to ensure the hybrid drinks this just before she returns to our world."

Vicktor took the glass vial and slipped it into a pocket on the inside of his suit jacket. He was about to speak when a sharp rap sounded, and Erik stepped into the office.

"Sire, we have guests."

Darius raised an eyebrow at the glint in the vampire's eye.

"The Council are here. They are in the lobby and are demanding to speak with you."

Vicktor straightened in his chair. "As head of the Council Liaison Office, please let me kindly escort them from the premises for you?"

He moved to stand, but Darius stopped him with a hand on the shoulder. "You have a more important job to see to." He turned to Erik and the witch, both standing alert by the door, and smiled. "I think we will go greet the Council personally."

CHAPTER TWENTY-NINE

Home – almost 3 weeks gone

Abi still found the sound of her voice strange in the quiet of the bedroom. She'd first started reading to Sean while he'd been unconscious, held in a magical stasis by the witches. His being in a magic-induced coma hadn't stopped her from feeling self-conscious, but she'd kept going in the hope that some part of him could hear her and would appreciate the sound of a friendly voice. Now that the stasis had been lifted, the gentle flow of his breathing accompanied her words, and occasionally his eyelids would twitch as if he might be dreaming.

She sometimes wondered whether his dreams were pleasant. Did he have a safe haven he could retreat to in his sleeping hours that allowed him to escape the horror of his waking reality? Or did those horrors follow him even to the depths of his unconsciousness?

Izzie had warned them the spell to separate Sean from the demon would take a lot out of him and that it might be a while before he woke, even with the stasis now lifted. There had been a grey tinge to the witch's skin as she said this, and it had taken an obvious effort for her to remain standing, the spell having taken everything she and her newly formed coven could give. And even after all that, they still had no guarantees. The waiting was torture.

Cormac and the others had returned from Donegal to be there when their Omega woke. While they had more right to be by his side than she could ever claim, Abi found herself reluctant to leave him. So, she stayed and read to him, just like she had in the days before the separation. The others didn't question her presence as they took turns to check on him, and she took that as an excuse not to delve too deeply into her own motivations.

She flipped to the next page of the book and told the sleeping wolf with a smile, "This is my favourite part. Rachel goes to –"

A bang of a door and shouting somewhere in the apartment froze the words in her mouth. The book fell to the floor as she scrambled to her feet. Heart pounding, she crept to the door of the bedroom and peered out.

Cormac stood at the open front door, a look of shock on his face as a large bloody man stumbled through, nearly collapsing before Cormac caught him. A smaller Asian man followed, helping a red-haired woman through with him. Both were as battered as the first man, with vicious cuts visible even from Abi's vantage point down the hall.

She could hear Fia issuing orders to get first aid supplies as she slipped out of the bedroom, book forgotten, and hurried to join the others in the living area.

"What happened?" she asked Sasha as she grabbed the first aid box from the cupboard in the kitchen and handed it to the wolf. So much blood, god there was so much blood.

"Council" was the only response she got before Sasha hurried off to help Fia, who looked like she was about to tackle the red-haired woman to the ground if she didn't shut up and agree to have her wounds checked.

An almost hysterical giggle caught in Abi's throat as she noticed the woman's eerie likeness to Jessica Rabbit. With all the blood covering her, it looked like she belonged in a horror movie, but the resemblance was there, nonetheless.

On the far side of the room, Cormac was arguing with the large

668

man he'd hauled into the apartment, barely able to stand. Only the Asian man seemed willing to cooperate as he quietly allowed Lucas to clean up the worst of his injuries. Abi stood in the middle of it all, unsure exactly what to do.

"Dammit, William," Cormac growled, throwing the first aid box at the bloodied man. He stalked to the drinks cabinet, poured a large glass of whiskey, and slammed it down on the table in front of him. "What the hell were you thinking going after Darius without backup?"

William just glared back, his eyes blazing. But there was something else other than anger behind those eyes; there was fear too.

It was the Asian man who answered softly. "We had no choice other than to step in. In the days since the raid on the Club of Night, we have sent three teams to the locations linked with Darius's alias to retrieve him so that he might be punished for his actions. All but one of those teams failed to return, and the one that did ... Well, his message was very clear. The Council had to confront him."

"He was expecting us," William said through gritted teeth. "It shouldn't have mattered – no one person is stronger than the Council combined. But those things he's created, they're stronger and faster than all of us."

"Wait," Shade cut in, pushing away from the window where he'd been observing the chaos with a scowl on his face. "If all the remaining Council confronted Darius, where is the head of the vampires?"

The red-haired woman's expression went blank, but the look in her eyes chilled Abi to her very core. "Vlad chose to make himself scarce when it was clear things weren't going how we expected."

"He ran away?" Lucas's eyebrows shot skywards.

The three Council members stayed quiet, but their silence was answer enough.

"So why come to us now?" Cormac pushed, no sign of the anger on his face letting up. "After the club, you made it clear our help wasn't required anymore. You could have gone anywhere to sort these injuries. Why are you here?"

A tense silence fell over the room as Cormac and William stared at each other, neither blinking or looking away.

The anger drained from William's face to be replaced by pure exhaustion. "We underestimated him. Whatever Darius is planning, we need to stop it now before he gets any stronger than he already is."

"What do you propose?" Nate asked, a curious glint in his amber eyes.

Abi jumped; she hadn't noticed that the shifter had moved to her side.

"We need to cut off his access to the demons," the Asian man said quietly. "We can't stop the prophecy without killing the hybrid –"

"Still an option," the red-haired woman interjected brightly. Everyone in the room glared at her, but she simply shrugged.

"As I was saying," the Asian man continued with a pointed stare at her. "We can't stop it without the hybrid's death or the birth of her child, but it might be time we consider trying to repair the barrier to buy us time."

"I don't understand." The words came out without thinking, and Abi blushed as all eyes turned to her. "I mean, I get that demons are tough to fight, but I thought the barrier needed to be almost entirely gone before the really bad guys could get through?" She looked at Nate and he nodded in confirmation. "So how is Darius getting hold of demons strong enough to possess Supes, not to mention defeat the Council?"

An uneasy silence fell in the room. Eventually William shook his head. "We don't know."

"I do."

Everyone turned in surprise to the softspoken voice. Sean leaned against the entryway to the kitchen, his face gaunt and body looking like it was struggling to keep him upright. His shaggy white hair hung in stringy clumps around his face, partially obscuring his sunken blue eyes.

"Sean." Cormac was on his feet and at the Omega's side in an instant. He wrapped his arm around the other wolf and half-supported, half-carried him to the sofa opposite William.

Abi couldn't take her eyes off them. Though Sean appeared

remarkably lucid, the haunted look shadowing his eyes was unmistakable. That same look had stared back at her from the mirror on more than one occasion, and her heart constricted in pained recognition.

The wolf lifted his head and met her gaze. A ghost of a smile tugged at the corner of his mouth, and then it was gone as the room turned into a buzz of eager questions.

Sean answered as best he could, explaining exactly how it was that Darius was pulling through major-level demons. His voice faltered more than once, and Abi felt an unexplainable urge to yell at them all. Could they not see how hard this was for him? He needed to rest. But she knew they didn't have that luxury. As hard as it was watching him relive what was done to him and the other Supes, they needed any information that Sean could give them.

It wasn't just Abi who was on edge by the time the questioning finished. The tension simmered at near-boiling point in the room, and she had the uncomfortable sense that it would take only the barest spark for it to explode.

Cormac's head rested in his hands, his knuckles white as he took a moment to deal with whatever emotions he felt at hearing his Omega's story. When he finally looked up, his face was an unreadable mask, and his eyes were calm and calculating. "What's involved in strengthening the barrier?"

"The ritual that was used to banish the Horsemen should work with a few tweaks, but it takes a significant amount of power." William picked up the untouched glass of whiskey and knocked it back in one. "If we do this and shit keeps going south, we'll have severely weakened our ability to fight."

"But if we don't, Darius keeps getting access to more and more power. He'll be unstoppable."

"*If* we do it," the Asian man said, "we must get it right the first time. There will be no second chances."

"Which means we have to make sure we can stop the prophecy. Otherwise the fabric will just begin unravelling again." The red-haired woman examined her red-tipped nails, seeming unconcerned with the possibility.

Abi snorted in disbelief. "Phoenix can't exactly click her fingers and speed up the pregnancy so that it coincides with the ritual."

The room fell quiet and everyone averted their eyes from her except the woman, who gave her a pitying look that made it clear she thought Abi to be stupid.

Nate placed an awkward hand on Abi's shoulder. "Morrigan said time moves differently in Faerie than it does here. Maybe enough time has passed ..."

This time it was the red-haired woman that snorted.

Realisation punched Abi in the gut, knocking the wind out of her. "You don't think the baby will be enough." She looked around the room, beseeching them all to deny it.

Lucas's grey eyes were sympathetic when he finally met her challenging gaze. "We want to, Abi, but the Horsemen aren't our only problem now. Even if the baby comes in time to stop the prophecy, the longer we have to wait, the more time Darius has to amass his power. He may not need the Horsemen to destroy us all."

She shrugged off Nate's hand still resting uselessly on her shoulder and shook her head vehemently. "You're not killing Phoenix." She would fight them all with every breath in her body if that was what it took.

Lucas held up his hands. "No one is suggesting that."

She looked at William, who had remained silent throughout her outburst, and at the quiet Asian man who met her anger with calm understanding. The red-haired woman simply raised an eyebrow in amusement. "You are though, aren't you?" she challenged them. "The Council will kill her if there's no other way."

Silence was as good an answer as any.

Sean stood from the sofa, brushing off Cormac's protest. His legs were unsteady as he made his way to her and took her hand in his. "I will help you protect her. I give you my word."

There were exclamations of agreement from everyone in the room except the Council, but it was the steady assurance in those blue eyes that calmed her and allowed the tightness to ease marginally in her chest.

"What do we need to enact the ritual?" Fia asked, her voice

sombre as she watched the interaction between Abi and Sean with a glint of curiosity.

"First off, we need the artefacts," William said.

"We can get them."

"Then we'll need a member of each species. The Council are short a witch at the moment, so we need to determine which of the covens can provide a trustworthy candidate."

"I'll speak to Izzie," Nate said. "She wants to end this as much as we do."

"And then there's the slight problem of the Mists."

Cormac nodded. "The Mists have sworn an oath to Phoenix; they will honour their vow." He turned to William. "I want your word that the Council will do them no harm. If they help us with this, it clears any debt they owe."

"Agreed."

Cormac's expression darkened and Abi shivered as she caught a glimpse of the predator lurking under the surface. "And let me be clear, if the Council do anything to hurt the mother of my grandchild, I will hold you all personally responsible."

"Let's hope it doesn't come to that."

The two wolves held each other's gazes for a long moment before seeming to come to a silent understanding. Cormac turned to Nate. "Get word to Morrigan. It's time to bring them home."

CHAPTER THIRTY

Faerie – day 4

Phoenix gritted her teeth as she yanked the brush through the knots and clumps of dirt that were still embedded in her hair. She'd made it out of bed and managed to get dressed without her body protesting too much. Now she just had to make it look like she hadn't been buried alive, and she'd be good to go.

A soft knock sounded on the bedroom door, and she sensed Ethan's signature even before he peeked his head inside. An argument about her being out of bed was inevitable and she tried her best not to laugh as she watched his expression turn from concern to exasperation almost in slow motion.

"What are you doing up?" His tone was careful as he stepped into the room and closed the door behind him, eyeing her like she might actually have gone crazy.

The temptation to wind him up was more than she could resist so she shrugged nonchalantly. "I was going to go for a run, but I'm not sure I'm dressed appropriately." She waved a hand over the loose tunic and trousers she'd chosen for convenience, the leather strap of her scabbard slung across her chest.

His face turned a worrying shade of red and muscles bulged in his arms as he folded them across his chest. "You can't be serious. You're meant to be in bed resting. What about –"

She burst out laughing, unable to hold it anymore. He glared at her.

"Oh, relax. I'm just going for a very tame stroll. I've been stuck in this room for the best part of twenty-four hours, I need fresh air." She smiled, feeling a little bad for winding him up when he was just worried about her and the baby.

She walked over and reached up to kiss him on the cheek. "The baby's fine," she assured him, taking his hand and placing it on her stomach.

He stared at his hand where it rested over the soft swell of her abdomen. A mix of emotions showed on his face all at once: fear and the all-consuming need to protect. He looked so lost and vulnerable that her heart ached. Her wolf.

"Will you walk with me?"

He gave a martyred sigh but offered his arm in defeat. "Your escort awaits, my lady."

It took longer than normal for them to make their way outside, with Ethan insisting that she move at a snail's pace. And though she resented being treated as an invalid, she had to admit that her body wasn't up to its full capabilities.

She breathed deeply as the light breeze tickled her skin and the warmth of the sun soaked into her cells, rejuvenating her body in a way nothing else other than blood could. There was something oddly peaceful about being here in Faerie, she realised. Yes, they had to hide some of the most fundamental facts of their lives from her grandparents, but it was a relief to not be constantly looking over her shoulder, waiting for someone to try kill her, or for Darius to appear.

Now that she'd come clean to Aoife, it felt like a weight had been lifted. She'd confessed her sins to a member of her family, and she hadn't been rejected. It gave her a glimmer of hope that maybe, just maybe, history wouldn't have to repeat itself.

Thinking of her aunt turned her thoughts back to less cheery topics, however. "Has Aoife said any more about the earthquake that caused the cave-in?" she asked, shuddering as the smell of earth came to her as fresh as when she lay helpless beneath it.

Ethan gave her a sideways glance and hesitated, no doubt wondering if she was too fragile to have this discussion. "There's been word of similar earthquakes back home. She believes it might have something to do with the prophecy shifting the natural balance, and it's being mirrored here in Faerie." His expression tightened with the concerns he wouldn't voice.

Her mouth grew dry as she too thought of their friends back home and wondered where they'd been when the earthquake had hit.

"I'm sure they're all fine," she said as much for her own benefit as for his. "Morrigan would have sent for us if they were in trouble."

"Phoenix." Clíodhna's sharp voice stopped them in their tracks. "There you are."

Phoenix's breath caught in her throat. Aoife had promised not to say anything to her grandparents, but still her heart raced as she plastered a smile on her face and turned to see her grandmother striding towards them. Eoghan followed in Clíodhna's wake, and though his expression was carefully controlled, Phoenix got a strange sense that he was feeling particularly smug with himself. Beside her, Ethan bristled as he too spotted the fae lord.

Eoghan stopped before her and took her hand to place a soft kiss on the back of it. "Might I say, you are looking quite radiant this morning."

She squirmed uncomfortably under the intensity of his gaze and gave him a small smile.

"Indeed." Clíodhna's shrewd gaze assessed her. "Aoife mentioned that you were feeling unwell. Naturally we were concerned, given how few ailments afflict our kind. But perhaps it's just another quirk of your more ... unusual nature."

Phoenix fought to keep the smile in place. "I'm feeling much better, thank you, Grandmother." She extricated her hand from Eoghan's grip. "Eoghan, how lovely to see you again. I thought you'd be heading back to Eldridge by now?"

"Lord Eldridge has decided to remain in our court for a while longer," Clíodhna answered before he could speak. "He has declared his intentions to pursue you, and I have given him my blessing." She smiled, but there was no warmth in her expression, only determination.

"He – you what?" Phoenix's ability to speak coherently failed her and she gaped at her grandmother, wondering if she'd missed the joke.

"With all due respect, my lady, surely Phoenix should be the one making that decision." To anyone that didn't know him, Ethan's words would have sounded polite, but Phoenix could see the danger that lurked in the lightening of his eyes and the tense set of his jaw.

Clíodhna's eyes flashed. "With all due respect to you, I do not expect a *werewolf* to understand our ways."

A low growl rumbled from Ethan's throat and Phoenix looked from him to her grandmother in panic. "Might I have a word with you in private, Grandmother?" she asked, moving her body ever so slightly as to place herself between them.

Of course, privacy was little more than an illusion in supernatural company, but nonetheless, Clíodhna humoured her by stepping aside, leaving the two men glaring at each other.

"While I appreciate the sentiment – and I am truly honoured – I didn't come here to find a mate," Phoenix said. "It would be unfair of me to lead Eoghan on."

If she hoped to find compassion beneath the steel of her grandmother's façade, she was sorely disappointed. Clíodhna shook her head, a mild look of disgust on her face. "Lord Eldridge is a very eligible match. You *should* be honoured. I will not have you disgracing this family further by denying him."

The look in her grandmother's eyes said everything her words did not. Phoenix might not be her mother, and Clíodhna might not realise just how much she'd followed in Aria's footsteps, but all she was to her grandmother was a reminder. She couldn't be punished for the sins of her mother, but she sure as hell wouldn't be allowed to forget them either.

Clíodhna turned from her and returned to the men, clearly deciding the matter was settled. Phoenix followed, a cold numbness settling through her as Eoghan offered her his hand.

Phoenix was physically and mentally exhausted by the time Eoghan finally took a breath from his incessant prattling and stopped walking. She looked up in surprise to find the huge wall that bordered her family's land in front of her. A shiver ran through her as she remembered Aoife's ominous comment about the lands beyond. She'd been so lost in her own thoughts that she hadn't even realised what direction they were walking in. Now, a creeping sense of unease made its way up her spine and she looked around, hoping to see someone who might question their presence. They were alone.

"What are we doing here?" she asked, hoping her voice sounded more curious than nervous.

The silver-haired fae lord gave her a conspiratorial wink. "I thought you might be up for a little adventure. It can't be much fun being stuck here in the castle all the time."

"We haven't exactly been prisoners."

"Ah, but have you had any adventures?"

If you only knew, she thought to herself.

She should have resisted more when Eoghan had led her away from Ethan and her grandmother. She'd been so afraid that Ethan's reaction to the lord would make Clíodhna suspicious that she'd hurriedly agreed to the walk and hadn't thought to insist they stay close to the castle.

Some naive part of her had even thought that maybe she could use the time to make him realise why a relationship between them would never work; but that had assumed she'd be able to get a word in edgeways to the very one-sided conversation.

Eoghan strode up to the wall, made an intricate gesture with his arms and said, "Open sesame." He gave her a cheeky grin. A wooden door appeared in the solid rock of the wall, and he opened it with a flourish.

"I don't think –"

"Nonsense." He waved away her protest. "We wouldn't want to waste this beautiful day. Let me show you some of Faerie's secrets. If nothing else, it will give us a break from your grandmother's interfering, well intentioned though it may be." He said this as though he hadn't been the very reason for Clíodhna's meddling, and Phoenix had to grit her teeth to stop herself from pointing it out.

She glanced behind her, hesitating, then stepped through the doorway after him. A solid line of trees faced her and she shivered again as she remembered the terrifying screeches that had sent her and Ethan running through the forest when they'd first arrived in Faerie.

She turned to step back through the door, suddenly convinced this was a really bad idea. But the door had disappeared, and she found herself looking at a solid wall of brick. Unconsciously, her hand reached for the leather strap that crossed her body. The weight of her father's sword was comforting and she focused on it, taking a shaky breath. It was fine; she was freaking herself out for nothing.

Eoghan beckoned her forward, clearly unphased by the shadowy recesses of the forest. He offered her his elbow. "Don't worry, I know this place like the back of my hand."

Not in the least bit reassured, she allowed him to lead her between the trees. The eerie silence of the forest seemed every bit as unnatural as the screeching had been. The scenery was still as weird and wonderful as she remembered, but it didn't hold the same appeal now that she understood just how quickly that beauty could turn ugly.

When they'd walked far enough that she was worried about finding her way back, the thick expanse of trees opened to a clearing. Perfect golden grass formed a blanket in the centre and a ring of daisies surrounded it. A decadent display was laid out before her: juicy berries of all colours, succulent legs of lamb, and glasses filled with a clear bubbly liquid that glinted like crystal.

Eoghan swept his arm out in a grand gesture. "I thought you might care for a picnic."

Her stomach rumbled – the traitor – and though she was starting to think that she should have listened to Ethan and stayed in bed, she gave him what she hoped was a grateful smile and settled herself down on the ground before the feast.

Eoghan fussed about for a moment before finally folding himself elegantly beside her. He offered her a glass with a delicate crystal stem. Her attempt to politely refuse fell on deaf ears, and she finally accepted the glass with a resigned sigh.

He picked up a second glass and raised it. "A toast. To strong women. And to strong kingdoms."

She clinked her glass against his and took a small sip of the fizzy liquid, as much to hide her grimace at the pretentious words as to mollify him. The drink tasted like summer exploding in her mouth, and she couldn't stop herself from taking another small sip before placing the glass back down.

The picnic he'd laid out was beautiful, and she should have been grateful for the effort he'd gone to, but her mood turned sombre as she realised that it wasn't so long ago she'd gone to meet Ethan for a similar picnic. It was going to be their very first date. Instead, here she was with a male she had no interest in while Ethan was back at the castle having to conceal his feelings at the fact.

"How have you enjoyed your time in Faerie?" Eoghan asked, watching her intently.

"It's a beautiful place. Though I do look forward to returning home soon." *And a long-distance relationship would be naturally doomed to fail.*

His face dropped in cartoon-like shock and disappointment. "Surely you can't wish to leave?"

"I have a life back home. I'm eager to return to it." *Get the hint!*

"A life among humans?" His face twisted into a grimace of distaste before he smoothed out his expression to one of interest, the change so quick that she almost missed it. "I'd imagine it must be quite quaint."

Before she could reply, he offered her one of the plates laden with colourful berries. She plucked a few from the bunch with a half-arsed attempt at a smile.

"What of your father's people?" He popped a plump berry into his mouth, not waiting until he finished before asking, "Do you have much dealings with them?"

Wariness mingled with a vague sense of disgust at his eating manners. Where was he going with this? "I'd rather not speak about my family, if you don't mind."

"Ah, but the vampires are hardly your family, are they? It's not like their blood runs in your veins. Lucas is no more your grandfather than he was Marcus's father."

She froze. "How did you –"

"And Darius isn't really your uncle either, is he?"

Her blood turned to ice in her veins. The amicable look on the fae lord's face hadn't changed, but now she took a closer look, forced herself to really see him. There was steel behind his grey eyes. The playful sparkle that she'd been quick to dismiss as flirtation had been little more than a screen to distract from the cool calculation.

Pasting an apologetic smile onto her face, she rose unsteadily to her feet. "I'm very sorry, Lord Eldridge, I'm feeling a little unwell. Perhaps it would be better if we return to the castle."

A terrifying stillness came over the fae lord, and Phoenix's fingers twitched with the urge to reach for her sword. After a moment, he smiled widely and got to his feet as well.

"Of course. I know a shortcut back." He brushed some imaginary dirt from his clothes and offered her his arm again.

Her skin crawled as she rested her hand lightly on the crook of his elbow. Maybe there had been nothing behind the comment? Maybe his ego was just bruised because she'd been making it clear she wasn't interested in pursuing anything with him and he was looking for a reaction? But why use Darius's name? And how did he even know about Darius?

The questions raced through her head with a pounding beat that made her close her eyes in pain. When she opened them again, her surroundings were blurry and unfocused. Her feet suddenly felt leaden and each step she took was a monumental effort. Her tongue felt strange and fuzzy in her mouth as she tried to speak.

Her legs buckled beneath her and she sank to the ground, still clutching Eoghan's arm. He looked down at her with a chilling smile as the world swam to black.

CHAPTER THIRTY-ONE

Faerie – day 4

Ethan paced the length of the castle's family dining room. He had the completely irrational need to punch something – preferably Eoghan's face – and it was taking all his willpower to keep a leash on his wolf.

It wasn't that he thought Phoenix would ever be interested in the smug prick, but the idea of her having to humour her grandmother's blatant scheming when she should be in bed recovering was more than he could take. He was meant to be keeping her and their baby safe; that was the whole point of him being here. He'd done a damn shit job of it so far.

He stopped his pacing and gripped the back of one of the wooden chairs surrounding the table as he tried to get his frustration under control. There was a low groan and the wood splintered beneath his hands. He looked down at the chair in surprise.

"What's wrong? Did we run out of teabags?"

He turned to find Aoife standing in the doorway decked out in tight, black training gear with her hair pulled back from her face. She had one eyebrow quirked and was watching him with something approaching mild amusement. At least until she took in his expression.

"Is Phoenix okay?" All hint of teasing instantly disappeared and she stilled.

With effort, he unclenched his jaw and cracked his neck. "She's fine. Your mother just coerced her into going on a date with that insufferable twat."

"Insufferable –" Aoife froze, light dawning in her eyes. "Eoghan."

Ethan nodded. "She's still weak. She should be in bed resting, not having to entertain pretty-boy fae lords."

"Ethan. How long ago did they leave?"

There was an edge to Aoife's tone that made his wolf stand to attention. Her face was a mask of control, but her green eyes turned stormy. His pulse sped up. "What is it?"

"How long?" she repeated.

"An hour. Two, maybe. Aoife, what's going on?"

"It may be nothing, but I think we should go speak to my parents."

He hurried after her towards the large greeting room where he'd first met Phoenix's grandparents. He didn't even bother trying to rein in the tension that prickled along his skin and it took all his willpower to keep quiet, conscious of the curious glances they received from the fae they passed.

Two sentries stood before the closed doors of the greeting room, just like they had on that first day. Aoife paid them no heed, shoving her way through, her head high and eyes flashing in defiance. The guards recovered swiftly from their surprise and moved as if to block Ethan's passage, but he let the yellow of his wolf flash in his eyes and they stepped back, clearly deciding it was pointless to try and stop him.

Aodhán and Clíodhna's hushed conversation cut off abruptly as they looked up from where they sat in their thrones on the raised dais. They made no attempt to hide the annoyance at the sudden interruption, but Aoife stalked up to the dais, unperturbed, and stopped in front of her mother.

"What did he promise you?"

Clíodhna arched an eyebrow. "Is that any way to greet your mother?" She frowned slightly, looking in Ethan's direction.

"Eoghan. What did he say to you? What did he promise you to get you to agree to this?"

There was a pause before her mother answered, her tone conveying nonchalance even as her eyes hardened. "He simply expressed his interest in our darling granddaughter, and I gave him my blessing to pursue her."

Aodhán straightened, confusion evident in the frown lines that creased his forehead. "What did you do, Clíodhna?"

She shot him a withering glare. "I merely arranged for them to spend some time together. I really don't see why everyone is making such a fuss."

Aoife's mouth dropped open and she shook her head in disbelief. "You fool! You know he's been scheming and plotting against this court for years. What were you thinking?"

"How dare you speak to me like that?" Clíodhna stood from her throne, eyes blazing.

"How dare I? How dare you, Mother? It is because of *his* court that you were forced to banish your own daughter. And now you offer Phoenix up to him on a silver platter. How could you do this?"

Both Ethan and his wolf stilled at Aoife's words. Blood pounded in his ears, blocking out the argument that continued before him. A red haze filled his vision and his claws began to push through his skin. Eoghan's family was the reason for Aria's banishment? He would tear the fae lord into confetti and enjoy every moment of it.

No. He stopped himself, clamping down on the animalistic rage that bubbled inside him. Whatever role Eoghan or his family had in matters, they weren't the ones who ultimately made the decision to banish their daughter. The only thing that mattered now was ensuring Phoenix's safety; the rest could wait.

"Lord Eldridge can't be held accountable for his predecessor's actions," Clíodhna said, as if reading his thoughts. "It is a suitable match – one that will ensure history does not repeat itself." She lifted her chin with the stubborn determination of one who would never be swayed from her deep-seated prejudice.

"Don't be so damn naive." Aoife's voice shook with barely restrained anger. "Eoghan is a hundred times worse than his father ever was. And you sent my niece out there with him."

She gave her mother a disgusted look and turned to Ethan. "Wait here," she said and stalked from the room.

The door slammed behind her and a charged silence settled between the three Supes who remained. Clíodhna glared at Ethan with hate-filled eyes that almost dared him to attack her. He simply stared back, refusing to look away from her challenge. Aodhán ignored both of them, pain creasing the corners of his eyes as he looked into the distance, lost in his own thoughts.

Ethan knew he'd be wasting his breath trying to reason with Clíodhna, so he turned his attention to the fae lord. "Phoenix is pregnant."

He let the revelation hang in the air before turned back to Clíodhna, steel in his voice. "Because of your actions, your decisions, your daughter died without you even knowing. She had a whole life that you weren't part of. A child that you didn't get to see grow. I hope the guilt tears you up because you deserve every bit of it. My mate is out there alone with my unborn child, both of them likely in danger, all because you can't see past your stupid prejudice. So, I swear to you here and now, if anything happens to either of them, I will destroy you. You won't need to worry about the purity of your line, because there will be nothing left of it when I'm finished."

Clíodhna turned bone white. Flames flickered in her eyes, and she moved as if to lunge for him. Aodhán grabbed her arm, his expression a storm of emotion.

She reeled on him, pure venom in her voice as she hissed, "What do you think you're doing?"

"Enough! Ethan is right. I told myself all those centuries ago that the only way our people could be safe was if our court presented a united front. I told myself that even as I allowed my own child to be banished by my silence. But I won't stay silent anymore. Not while it puts our granddaughter at risk. Or our great-grandchild."

The double doors slammed open, and before Clíodhna could respond, Aoife strode back into the room and came to a stop beside

Ethan. She carried a long, narrow object wrapped in black velvet and the look she gave her parents was of pure defiance before she turned to him.

"My mother is right. We need to ensure the mistakes of the past are not repeated."

Ethan jerked backwards as if slapped, but she continued. "I, too, watched my family bow to pressures from the other fae courts. They banished my sister for breaking an antiquated law created by bigots, and I stood by and said nothing while they turned their back on my kin. I won't do it again."

She raised the long package in her hand and unwrapped the velvet cloth to reveal a spearhead made of a metal so bright it almost appeared white. The shaft of the spear was weathered wood, its natural markings forming an intricate pattern which reminded Ethan of the Celtic symbols he'd seen on Claíomh Solais. Energy thrummed from it.

Clíodhna gasped. "How could you?"

Aoife didn't spare her mother a second glance; her attention remained fixed solely on him. "If Eoghan wishes Phoenix harm, he'll take her beyond our walls. Can you track her?"

Ethan nodded, his eyes riveted on the spear he could only assume to be the Spear of Lugh.

"Then let us go save my niece."

He didn't waste a moment arguing, just turned with her towards the large doors. Aodhán's quiet plea was the last thing he heard before the doors closed behind them.

"Find my granddaughter. Please."

CHAPTER THIRTY-TWO

Faerie – day 4

Two fae guards fell in beside Ethan and Aoife as they made their way from the castle. When Aoife didn't protest their presence, Ethan ignored them, his only thought and focus on finding Phoenix before something happened to her.

It didn't take him long to latch onto her trail once they crossed beyond the barrier of the wall. Even with the unfamiliar surroundings battering at his senses, her scent called to him. He stalked into the trees, unconcerned by the dangers that might be hidden within their depths. If anything was stupid enough to stand between him and his mate, it would find out what terrifying really was.

The group was silent as they cut a swift path through the forest. The guards and Aoife swept the terrain with watchful gazes. Somehow, he knew they weren't looking for Phoenix but whatever hidden threat had his instincts also on high alert.

After a couple of minutes, the trees parted to reveal a clearing. He inhaled deeply and Phoenix's scent caused his wolf to perk up. She'd been here recently.

His eyes scoured the abandoned picnic of berries and meats, deli-

688

cate glasses toppled on their sides and left lying like fallen soldiers. There were flattened patches on the golden grass where people had clearly sat or trod, but other than that the clearing was empty.

It was ridiculous, but he couldn't help the sharp pang of jealousy at the sight of the picnic, or the thought of Phoenix here with Eoghan. He clenched his fists and forced himself to block out the feeling; emotion wasn't going to keep her safe.

As he stared at the wasted remains of the picnic, one of the guards checked the perimeter. The other guard moved forward to pick up the discarded glasses. He raised one to his nose and then the other, closing his eyes as he inhaled deeply. His mouth tightened and his eyes were dark when he opened them. Dropping one glass to the ground, he ran his finger around the rim of the other glass and held it up to examine it.

His expression was grim when he met Ethan's and Aoife's questioning gazes. "This one has been tainted."

A vicious growl ripped from Ethan's throat before he could stop it. His wolf shifted inside him, agitated, as he digested the words and what they might mean. "Do you know with what?"

The guard glanced at him with something that almost looked like sympathy and shook his head. "Something to incapacitate, if I had to guess. Whatever it was, it was strong. Most fae tinctures are nigh untraceable, but the stronger the formula, the more residue remains."

"He probably didn't want to take any chances on how a hybrid would metabolise it." Aoife spoke quietly, but her eyes blazed as she surveyed the scene.

Ethan didn't need to hear any more. He walked around the edge of the clearing until he found where the scents were strongest and beckoned the others forward.

They'd barely gone ten feet when a chilling cry rent the air. Ethan froze, power crackling like electricity around him, pricking at his skin. Another shriek followed the first, and a sense of déjà vu sent a burst of adrenaline shooting through his veins.

The guard closest to him pulled an arrow out of the quiver that hung across his back. He stared into the dense shadows of the trees and said quietly, "If you want to see your lady again, you better run."

689

Aoife grabbed his hand and they didn't look back.

Phoenix struggled to focus on her surroundings. The world tilted and shifted at odd angles, and colours flashed before her eyes only to disappear again. Her limbs were leaden, the ability to move them so far beyond her capacity that they didn't even feel like they belonged to her anymore. Yet somehow, she was moving. She could tell that much by the way the world blurred past; she just couldn't figure out how, or why.

There was a sudden jolt and she landed on the ground with a painful thud. She was grateful when the world stilled, even though her head continued to spin. The bright blues and greens that had filled her vision were replaced by a blurry face. She squinted.

There was something strangely familiar about the face, but the more she tried to concentrate, the more her head felt like it might explode. The image warped and twisted into a terrifying grin and a scream bubbled up in her throat, but no sound came out.

"It will be harder for you if you fight. Just accept your fate and I'll make the pain go away."

A gentle hand smoothed damp hair from her face and the need to scream was replaced with the inexplicable desire to giggle hysterically. The voice, it was so familiar. Why couldn't she place it?

Then the face was changing. The hard grey eyes staring down at her morphed into kind brown ones; the smooth jaw became bristled with stubble that matched the hair that had moments ago been silver and was now brown. *Ethan*. Her mind reached for him eagerly.

He placed a rough hand on her cheek and gave her a cheeky grin. She leaned into his touch and froze. Something wasn't right.

Through the murky fog that filled her head, her brain screamed a warning at her. She tried desperately to grasp at the meaning, but her thoughts were so jumbled that she couldn't make sense of it.

Ethan was here; he'd make it better. But he didn't *feel* right, and though she wanted to believe her eyes more than anything else in the world, some part of her knew. The realisation solidified in her mind and she jerked back from the touch. Her head struck something hard behind her, sending a lance of pain through her skull.

The smile disappeared from Ethan's face, and his expression twisted into a snarl that looked unnatural on the face of her wolf. She cringed, shrinking away from him.

The hand that had moments ago touched her cheek with tenderness shot out and closed around her throat in a bruising grip. "You filthy half-breed. You think you're too good for me? You're an abomination!"

The man wearing Ethan's face yanked her up by her throat so that his breath burned against her cheek. "I could have made this easier for you. We could have had a little fun before I handed you over to Darius." He flung her to the ground and stood.

Darius. Alarm bells shattered the fog holding her mind. *He can't be here, he can't be.* Panic threatened to drown her as she willed her body to move. A finger. A toe. Anything.

As she watched, the man's image morphed once more until familiar grey eyes stared down at her, full of disdain. Eoghan – she remembered his name now, could think clearly enough to remember – reached a hand into his tunic and pulled out a small vial of green liquid. He used his teeth to pull the cork out and bent down to her. An eerie calm settled over his features as he grabbed her jaw in a steel grip, forced the vial to her lips, and held her mouth closed until she had no choice other than to swallow. Hot tears ran down her cheeks as pure, undiluted fear gripped her.

"Not long now," Eoghan promised in a chilling voice. "Once I have the gateway open, you'll be his problem. Don't worry though, I'll make sure all the courts know who's responsible for destroying the natural balance of our world. All of these disasters that are damaging even our protected lands." He shook his head. "I'll make sure your family are suitably punished and –"

He paused, cocking his head, and smiled. "I do believe we have company."

CHAPTER THIRTY-THREE

Faerie – day 4

Ethan sensed more than heard the string of a bow being pulled taut. He dived for the trees to his left, knocking Aoife into the brush with him. An arrow whistled through the air, grazing his shoulder in a blaze of fire. He let the momentum of his fall continue into a roll and came up to a crouch, only to meet the smug smile of Lord Eldridge pointing a bow and arrow directly at him.

He growled; he was going to enjoy wiping that smile from the fae lord's face.

He launched from the ground just as another arrow struck the dirt where he'd been mere fractions of a second before. Aoife was hot on his heels as he closed the distance between himself and Eoghan, intent on shredding the male to pieces.

Eoghan stood watching them with that cocky fucking smile, right up to the moment when Ethan barrelled into him with claws extended. Then he disappeared.

Instead of hitting solid flesh like he'd expected, Ethan found himself tumbling through the air. His breath left him in a huff of pain as a tree halted his momentum. Eoghan's laughter floated on the wind, seeming to come from all corners of the forest at once. He snarled, looking around but unable to see the fae lord.

Aoife appeared on his right and offered him her hand. "Do not trust your sight alone. Eoghan is a master of illusion."

He nodded and closed his eyes. There was one thing he knew wouldn't lie to him no matter what tricks the fae lord had up his sleeve: Phoenix's scent. Warily he beckoned Aoife forward, every muscle in his body tensed in preparation for the attack that was sure to come. They made it ten feet before his instincts roared to life.

Aoife pushed him aside as a small blade spun through the air and lodged in the tree behind where he'd been standing. Two more blades followed in quick succession, forcing Ethan and Aoife to separate further apart from each other.

A blur of movement in the trees caught Ethan's attention and he lunged towards it. A pained groan froze him mid-motion.

Phoenix.

"Help her," Aoife ordered before reaching out with her free hand and flinging a ball of bright white light into the trees. She sprinted after it, disappearing out of sight.

He was torn. His wolf wanted blood – the fae lord's, to be precise – but another moan sounded from the opposite direction and set his heart skittering. Bearing in mind what Aoife had said about Eoghan's skill with illusions, he closed his eyes again. Phoenix's signature came to him instantly, but it was weak, almost like it had been muted somehow. Still, he grasped that connection for all it was worth and followed it.

The flash of bright red hair was the first thing he saw when he opened his eyes and spotted her slumped against a tree. Her skin was pale and clammy, and her body was limp. All thoughts of going after Eoghan fled in an instant and he rushed to her side.

Claíomh Solais's scabbard was tangled around her, but the blade remained in its sheath, showing no sign that she'd attempted to use it in self-defence. The start of a bluish bruise was visible on her cheekbone, and it took all his effort to quell his fury long enough to check her for injuries.

When he was sure there was no obvious physical damage that

needed attention, he cradled her face in his hands. "Phoenix. Phoenix, can you hear me?"

A low whimper escaped her lips, and though she didn't open her eyes, she flinched away from him. A single tear slid from her eye and burned a path down her cheek.

His chest ached with the need to help her, but he had no idea what to do, and in that moment he felt completely lost. Gently he lifted her body up from the hard ground and cradled her in his arms. He rested his forehead against hers, willing her to open her eyes as he whispered to her over and over. "Come back to me. Please. You're safe. I promise, I've got you."

He could feel her heart beating in her chest, could tell by her breathing that she was alive, but still the fear wouldn't loose its grip on him. Despite the lack of visible injury, every instinct he possessed told him that something was wrong, that she needed his help.

An agonised groan ripped from her throat, and her whole body clenched. His heart clenched too.

A rustle of leaves came from above and he tensed for an attack as he cursed himself for letting his guard down. A large black crow burst through the trees, and before it landed, the air shimmered and Morrigan appeared beside him. Her ethereal beauty was marred by worry as she looked down at Phoenix. She ran her fingertips over Phoenix's pale cheeks and when she looked up to meet Ethan's gaze, his stomach lurched at the troubled look in the goddess's eyes.

"I couldn't interfere," she said softly, pain evident in the tone of her voice. "I wanted to, but some things ..." She shook her head. "You need to help her. We don't have much time left."

His throat constricted. "What can I do?"

"We need to slow down the effects from the potions Eoghan gave her. We need to dilute them in her blood so that her body might have a chance of clearing them out, or at the very least buy us time."

"How –" He cut off as realisation dawned.

She nodded in confirmation at the thought that was written across his face. He didn't hesitate. He extended a claw and slashed a thin line down the inside of his left arm. "Go, help Aoife. I've got this."

Red swelled from the wound and he pressed it against Phoenix's too cold lips. "Come on, Phoenix, drink for me. Please, baby."

Phoenix could hear Ethan's voice through the haze of pain clouding her mind, but she knew better than to believe the illusion this time. Something warm and wet pressed against her lips and she cringed away, shaking her head in helpless desperation. No more. She couldn't take any more.

A drop of blood hit her tongue and a jolt of electricity shot through her. Before she could stop them, her fangs elongated and latched onto the throbbing pulse of life. She sucked eagerly, and with each pull the fog lifted. The vile poison that tainted her blood lost its hold and somewhere between one swallow and the next, her awareness sharpened.

Don't leave me, Ethan's voice whispered in her mind, more real to her in that moment than she was even to herself.

Her eyes fluttered open, and she met a gaze so full of fear and love that she knew instantly no illusion could ever have replicated the pure honesty of it. The real Ethan smiled down at her and the chill that had permeated the very depths of her began to fade away.

His blood coursed through her, forming a connection at the most primal level as it rejuvenated her cells and repaired parts of her that until a moment ago had felt utterly broken. Even when her fangs retracted and he eased his wrist away, the connection remained. She clung to it like one might a life buoy when stranded in a never-ending ocean.

As everything came back into focus, fragmented memories tried to piece themselves together in her mind. Every muscle and ligament in her body ached as if they had been stretched to the point of tearing, and her head pounded to a beat that only she could hear.

Razorblades scoured her throat as she asked hoarsely, "Eoghan?"

Ethan's eyes flashed yellow, fury and violence burning like golden embers within them as he looked towards the trees. "Aoife –"

His words were cut off by the snap of a twig. His arms tensed around her as her breath froze in her chest. She snapped her head around towards the direction of the sound, but it wasn't Eoghan who stepped through the trees a moment later.

Her aunt was barely recognisable as Phoenix took in the fierce fire hardening Aoife's features beneath the bright red blood smeared across her cheek. She was favouring her right leg, a vicious gash visible on her thigh. The ancient spear she used to support her weight seemed oddly clean of blood, its almost-white tip glinting in the stray rays of sunlight that filtered through the trees.

Morrigan stood beside Aoife, looking as beautiful as the first time Phoenix had seen her. There was a hint of sorrow in the goddess's smile and a shiver of apprehension went through Phoenix. She placed a hand on her abdomen, seeking comfort in the movement of new life there.

"Eoghan?" Ethan asked, saving her the trouble of repeating her question.

Aoife's mouth tightened into a hard line, but there was no regret in her voice when she said, "The spear's aim was true."

The spear? Phoenix looked again at the weapon gripped in her aunt's hand. Surely it couldn't be the Spear of Lugh, could it? She jerked forward, suddenly reminded of her own artefact. Panic robbed her of breath as she scrambled on the ground, looking for her father's – her – sword.

Ethan grabbed her shoulder to halt her frantic movements and held a black scabbard out to her. "It's here, it's okay."

She pulled the scabbard in close to her, not caring if any of them thought her foolish for hugging a sword. Its power was like a gentle caress as it wrapped around her and soothed the terror that still balanced on a finely honed knife edge inside her.

"I wish I could give you more of a chance to recover," Morrigan said, "but I'm afraid time is against us."

Phoenix looked up at her guardian's grave expression, unease once more settling in her centre. "Is it time to go back?"

"We need to get you and the artefacts home, and we need to do it quickly," Morrigan said, her expression turning guarded. "Eoghan had prepared a gateway to return you. We'll have to take our chances with it."

"But why would Eoghan want to send Phoenix back?" Ethan's brow creased in confusion as he looked from Morrigan to her.

"Darius." Phoenix's answer was little more than a whisper, and even saying the name out loud sent a bolt of adrenaline through her. Much of the time since she'd agreed to the walk with Eoghan was now a foggy blur, but the one thing that stuck clearly in her mind was that name. Eoghan had known Darius's name.

The expected growl never came from Ethan and she was surprised enough to look up at him. His expression was one of deadly calm and surety, and it terrified her more than any anger could have. She knew without a doubt that he'd make Darius pay for hurting her. Even if it meant getting himself killed in the process.

"Yes, Eoghan was working for Darius," Morrigan confirmed.

"Which means using his gateway will lead us straight into danger." Ethan shook his head. "No. No way."

The goddess ignored his outburst, instead letting Phoenix see the solemn plea in her eyes. "Here in Faerie, my hands are tied. But back in the human world, they're not. I need you to trust me, Phoenix. Please."

Phoenix stared into those fathomless eyes, searching for an answer or something to tell her the right thing to do. Eventually, she nodded. At this point she was too tired and numb to feel fear at the thought of stepping into yet another of Darius's traps. And as a strange twisting sensation shot a bolt of pain through her lower abdomen, she couldn't help but think that Morrigan was right. Time was running out.

With difficulty, she secured Claíomh Solais across her back and indicated for Ethan to help her to standing. She hid a wince of pain as she got to her feet and turned to her aunt, who was watching them with obvious concern.

"I know you haven't had long to think on things," she said to Aoife, "but if Morrigan believes we need the artefacts back home, I'm inclined to believe her. Will you come with us?"

Aoife assessed her niece for a long moment. The thoughtful

expression was so reminiscent of her mother that Phoenix's heart ached at the similarity that was both a reminder of her loss and a gift that allowed her to remember.

"No," Aoife said finally. "I can't go with you. I have a duty to my court to warn them about the prophecy and what might face us if it comes to pass."

Something inside Phoenix broke at her aunt's words, but she forced herself to nod in acceptance. They hadn't given her enough time. Blood or not, how could she expect the woman to trust her when she'd given her absolutely no reason to do so?

As if understanding the thoughts going through Phoenix's head, Aoife reached out and brushed a hand over her cheek with a regretful smile. Her aunt turned to Ethan, shifting her weight to her good leg before holding out the hand that held the spear.

"Ethan Ryan, before the Goddess Morrigan and all of those who stand here in witness, I willingly bequeath you the Spear of Lugh. So long as your quest remains honourable, so too will your aim."

Ethan's jaw dropped and he stared at her outstretched hand in disbelief. When he didn't move to take it, Aoife limped forward, lifted his hand and wrapped his fingers around the wooden shaft.

"I know now that you are the one who is meant to protect my niece. Show them you are worthy." Before Ethan could react, Aoife turned back to Phoenix, eyes glistening. "I'm so glad I got to meet you. You remind me so much of her."

She reached inside the neck of her tunic and pulled out a small, milky-pink crystal on a black silk cord. She placed the crystal in Phoenix's hand and closed her fingers over it. "I hope that the next time I see you, it'll be in happier circumstances. But if the worst should come to pass, use this crystal to call for me. The fae will come to you, I will make sure of it."

Tears stung Phoenix's eyes. There was so much she wanted to say to her aunt, so much she wished had been different. Before she could say any of that, however, a cramping pain unlike anything she'd ever felt twisted her insides. She was dimly aware of Ethan grabbing her, asking what was wrong, then Morrigan was at her side. There were whispered words she didn't understand, and the world fell away.

CHAPTER THIRTY-FOUR

Home – 3 weeks gone

The corridor was quiet as Darius made his way along the lower levels of the Dublin vampire's lair. It was the first time he'd returned to the clan's main base of operations since that night all those months ago when he'd enacted the spell to expedite the prophecy. He may have failed on that occasion, but things were going to be very different this time.

Only a skeleton security crew remained dotted throughout the building now – enough to maintain the façade of an ambassador's residence that had kept the humans from prying for many decades. He'd relocated most of the clan to the pharmaceutical complex when the Council began their incessant meddling. Of course, the Council had since been deterred from their prying too, but the lair no longer suited his needs save for one last task.

Erik was waiting patiently for him when he reached his old quarters, seven floors below ground level. He'd briefed his head of security the day before, but still he asked, "Is everything in place?" as he stepped into the room he'd once used as an office.

Distracted, he realigned one of the priceless paintings on the wall and eyed the files and papers strewn across the floor. He had no doubt that the Council had been thorough in their search of the office and the lair, but they wouldn't have found anything. It was almost insulting that they believed him to be so amateur as to leave any evidence of his plans lying around for them to find.

"The gateway should open at the Cathedral soon. Vicktor has taken five soldiers with him to await the hybrid's return, and he'll notify us as soon as she crosses back to this world."

Darius absently gathered the papers covering the mahogany desk and arranged them into a neat pile – chaos and order didn't have to be mutually exclusive. "Vicktor knows she's not to be harmed under any circumstances?"

"He's been given strict instructions. The hybrid will be allowed to birth her offspring, then they will retrieve any artefacts in her possession. Everything will be in place by the time the transfer is complete."

A shiver of anticipation ran through Darius. *Soon.*

Assuming Phoenix returned with both the sword and the spear as they expected her to, they would only need to worry about finding the cauldron. It bothered him that this final piece continued to elude him, but he refused to allow the witch's warning to sway his decision; he was done waiting. Once he carried the essence of the Horsemen inside him, he would simply destroy anyone who got between him and the last artefact.

"And what of the witch?" Erik asked, calculating red eyes watching him closely.

Darius paused, considering the question. The ritual would place him completely at the witch's mercy should she wish to betray him. He had seen the ambition in her steely eyes and had no reason to doubt anything she'd done or said to date, but he hadn't gotten this far by being careless.

"If she so much as breathes wrong during the ritual, kill her."

CHAPTER THIRTY-FIVE

Ethan was simultaneously light and heavy. Nothing felt real to him anymore except the spear clutched in his right hand and the warmth of Phoenix's hand in his left. The world around him ceased to exist and somewhere in the depths of his mind, Morrigan's voice whispered a warning: *be prepared.*

Everything came back into focus with a violent jolt. He had only a second to register the crumbling ruins of the Cathedral in the dim light of the moon before Phoenix's hand was jerked from his. Something struck him, sending him sideways. He scrambled to regain his footing, allowing the momentum to pivot him around to face his attacker.

The next blow came from overhead, and instinctively he brought the spear up to block it. He found himself staring into a snarling face that was hardly recognisable as human.

A woman stood before him, patches of grey fur covering her cheeks and forehead as if she'd gotten stuck midway through a shift. Her rabid fangs dripped yellow slime as they snapped at him, and the red of her eyes had bled from their pupils so that no white remained in their terrifying depths.

Ethan thrust out with his foot in an attempt to push away the weight bearing down on the shaft of the spear. She barely budged. With a feral grin, she stalked towards him, driving him back.

In his peripheral vision he caught a flash of blue light, followed by inhuman screeches of pain that told him this *thing* wasn't the only member of the welcoming party. Instinct roared at him to find Phoenix, to make sure she was safe, but he didn't dare take his eyes from his assailant for even a second.

The abomination before him reached out, dark shadows wrapping around her arms and seeming to slither from her clawed hands.

"Don't let her touch you," Morrigan yelled in a strained voice, her warning punctuated by another guttural screech and flash of light.

Too late he swung the spear up to knock away the hands that reached for him. The thing batted it away as if it were a mere nuisance, and the shadows wrapped around his wrists.

Screams filled his head. They were not the sounds of fighting that had moments ago surrounded him, but visceral sounds that froze his body in primal terror. All thought and logic left him in an instant. All he knew was fear.

Black filled his vision. Then as soon as it came, it was gone. The screaming, the fear ... All of it just gone. The creature still stood before him, her predatory gaze watching his every breath with what he could only describe as hunger, but she had stepped back, her posture one of relaxed preparedness.

He risked a quick, confused glance to his left. Morrigan stood facing another three monstrosities like the one before him. She watched them warily, but though she was outnumbered, none made a move to advance on her.

When he could see no sign of Phoenix, panic gripped him. Before he could check his right-hand side, a man in an expensive grey suit stepped into the dim light cast by the moon, another of the creatures beside him.

Ethan did a double take.

It had been months since he and Phoenix had met the head of the Council Liaison Office, but the sanctimonious prick had made such an impression with his snide dismissal of Phoenix that Ethan would have recognised him anywhere. It looked like the CLO rep had undergone a few changes since they last met him – and Ethan highly doubted that they'd improved his personality.

"Please." Vicktor's voice rang clear in the sudden stillness, his eyes an eerie glow of red. "Let me be the first to welcome you home. I hope my friends here have made you feel comfortable."

"What the fu –" Ethan was cut off by a low moan from behind him. His blood ran cold and all other threats forgotten, he whipped his head around in search of Phoenix.

He spotted her on her knees, body bent double in the centre of the ancient ruins. The moonlight glinted off the sweat that beaded her pale forehead and her eyes were scrunched up in pain. He rushed to her, thoughts of the fae poison in her body filling him with a new source of terror.

It was only as he drew closer to her that his brain registered the rest of the picture. He slowed to a stop, and all coherent thought left him as he looked at her belly. No longer the gentle swell that had filled him with such pride in Faerie, it was now distended and straining against her tunic as if a full term had passed in minutes.

She looked up at him, eyes wide in shock. Then a contraction seized her and she cried out in pain.

That was all he needed to break through his own confusion, and he hurried the last few feet to her, dimly aware of Morrigan also backing towards them. He dropped down on his knees beside her. "Phoenix? What happened?"

A hoarse sob was the only response.

He cast his eyes around the ancient ruins of the Cathedral, counting six demon-Supe hybrids, Vicktor included. The odds were most definitely not in their favour. "We need to get you out of here. Can you stand?"

She shook her head, face twisting in agony. "There's no time," she gasped. "I think the baby's coming."

"Oh goodie." Vicktor clapped his hands. "It's time to get the party started."

Ethan watched in disbelief as the CLO rep pulled a phone from his pocket. He clicked his fingers and the five others with him spread out to form a rough circle around the ruins. Their red eyes glinted in watchful anticipation. Vicktor raised the phone to his ear and stepped back into the shadows.

Phoenix's body clenched once more as another contraction took hold. Ethan looked up at Morrigan in desperation. "Do something. Open a gateway, anything."

The goddess gazed down at them with a mix of sorrow and acceptance, and he didn't know which terrified him more. She turned from him and her expression grew distant as she murmured a low chant.

There was a flash of light and a silver dome appeared around them before fading into the night. Morrigan's shoulders slumped as if drained by whatever spell she'd woven, but her eyes were alert as she stared out into the darkness.

"The ward will hold them back should they choose to attack again."

He looked at Phoenix and back to Morrigan, helpless. "How long?"

Worry tightened her mouth as she too looked down at Phoenix. "Long enough."

Darius ran his hands over the stone altar. Blood still stained its surface and there were dark patches visible on the stone walls too. He'd missed this chamber buried deep beneath the lair. For many years it had been the place he'd come to indulge his frustrations, biding his time while he waited for Phoenix to trigger the prophecy on her twenty-fifth birthday. It was fitting that his new beginning start here.

Footsteps echoed on the stone steps and he turned to face the witch. "It's time," she said.

"Do you have everything?"

She gave him a scathing look. "Worry less about what I'm doing and focus on surviving the ritual."

He raised an eyebrow, unphased by her warning. The witch would ensure his survival since it was the only way to guarantee her own.

Walking in a slow circle around the chamber, he took in the cell that had held Marcus and Aria for almost a decade, the chains that had held many a plaything, the spiderweb cracks in the wall from when Phoenix had used her power against him for the first time. He raised a hand to touch the rough scars that still covered the left side of his face. Everything he'd done had led up to this moment. Even his Sire's death had been necessary. He knew that now.

The witch waited until he returned to the altar before speaking again. "The power I'm going to transfer into you is unlike anything that exists in this world. You may be powerful, and old as hell" – she gave him a toothy grin – "but your flesh won't survive for long. You better be ready to finish this."

Silently, Darius unbuttoned his black shirt. He held the witch's gaze as he removed it and stepped up onto the stone slab. Carefully he picked up the skull that rested there and climbed up onto the altar. As he lay back, he looked into the skull's empty eye sockets and thanked his Sire for his sacrifice.

One by one, the witch lay out the offerings to the Horsemen. She took the skull he held out and placed it in the fourth and final position. A shock of electricity shot through Darius. His back arched and his muscles spasmed involuntarily. It passed within a second, but the dark excitement in the witch's eyes told him that worse was yet to come. Much worse.

The witch started chanting, and as she did, her voice changed. The words came faster and ghostly voices joined hers, echoing the chant until there was nothing else. Energy filled the chamber, sucking all the oxygen from the space until the pressure grew so great that it felt like it might crush him.

Darius clenched his teeth as every cell in his body was twisted and transformed. One minute particle at a time, he was changed. Fire burned through his veins, scorching him from the inside. He could feel all of them pulsing inside of him, their thoughts, their power, their thirst for destruction.

His vision turned black, and he screamed.

CHAPTER THIRTY-SIX

Pain lanced through Cassandra's abdomen and she gasped for breath. The contractions came quickly, shocking and sudden, the strength of the vision so forceful that the frosted glass walls of the Council office faded away and she could no longer distinguish reality from thought.

"The baby is coming," she gasped, curling in on herself against the pain that wasn't her own, but felt as real as if it were.

There was a distant sense of commotion around her as the Council members reacted to her cry. A figure crouched down beside her, and when she managed to blink the tears away, she saw William's kind eyes, full of concern. He reached out to touch her but stopped himself, realising the contact would only cause her more pain. The helpless look on his face warmed some part deep inside her, and she used his presence to ground herself back in reality.

When the world righted itself enough that the images faded to the background of her sight, she pushed herself up to her elbows. William quickly moved to right the chair that had toppled over with her, but before Cassandra could reseat herself, Méabh was shoving the wolf aside, her beautiful face tightened with tension.

"What did you see? Tell us."

Cassandra took a shuddery breath, conscious of the pensive stares fixed on her. Salty tears ran down her cheeks but she ignored them.

In truth, she wasn't even sure what the tears were for – the pain or the child, as yet unborn.

"Phoenix has returned. The child will –" White-hot agony flared through her again, choking off her words. No images came, just pain. All-consuming pain. It set every cell in her body on fire, unmaking her and remaking her in its flame of eternal torture. She flung back her head and screamed.

Shouts of surprise. Hands grasping her. She was aware of it all, and yet of nothing. Her body was lowered to the ground, no longer her own. Uncontrollable tremors took hold of her and she could do nothing, see nothing. Nothing except for the devastation to come.

Her back arched and everything went black.

An eternity passed before Kam's soft voice reached her, calling her name, willing her to come back. It hurt to open her eyes, and she cringed back from the light that burned her. Instructions were snapped for the lights to be dimmed. Tentatively she eased her eyelids open once more.

For a moment, she could remember nothing. Then it flooded back in an instant. She opened her mouth to speak, but all that came out was a desperate sob. She curled her knees up to her chest as racking sobs took hold of her body. All the fear. All the pain. She'd felt it all. Everything that was to come.

When she'd finally been scraped raw of all emotion, she blinked the water – Were they tears? She wasn't sure – from her lashes and sat up. She looked around at the Council members who remained, seeing them, truly seeing them.

William, bless him, had gone from looking concerned to looking downright panicked. Méabh's expression was a haughty one of impatience at what she clearly classified as dramatics, but it did little to conceal her true worry. Even Kam's unflappable façade was ruffled.

Vlad was the only one not looking at her. His eyes darted nervously to the door of the office, and she was reminded of a scared rabbit caught between the urge to freeze or flee. She knew which he'd choose, and she knew the price they'd all pay for it.

There was no emotion in her voice when she turned to the others. "The Horsemen are here."

CHAPTER THIRTY-SEVEN

"You can do it, Phoenix. That's it. Just keep pushing."

Ethan's words barely registered through the haze of pain that consumed Phoenix. On all fours, her body tightened reflexively and she bore down with everything she had. Sweat drenched her skin and her arms were ready to collapse as she dug her fingers deep into the earth. A scream, part desperation and part determination, ripped itself from her throat. Just when she had nothing left to give, she heard it: the cry a new life announcing itself to the world.

Her arms buckled, and she rested her forehead onto the soft ground. Tears of relief slid down her cheeks, and all she could hear was Ethan's repeated murmur of disbelief. "You did it. You did it."

Exhausted, exhilarated, numb, and still completely terrified, she raised herself up with Morrigan's help and turned for the first time to look at her baby.

The small red squished-up bundle was cradled in Ethan's arms and he was looking at it like it was both the most precious and most terrifying thing in the world. He smiled at her, his brown eyes wide with awe. "We have a little girl."

Oh so carefully, he placed the baby in her arms. Phoenix stared down at the little button nose, and the tiny hands. Her chest constricted with an aching joy. How had she gone from those small flutters of hope to this tiny little human?

As if seeking comfort from the harsh reality of the world it had been thrust into, the baby nuzzled in closer to her. She wrapped what she could of her tunic around her daughter, but her clothes were as sweat soaked as she was and gave little protection from the chill night air.

Morrigan bent and ripped the bottom of her flowing black dress. Gently she helped wrap the baby in the dry cloth. The goddess smiled and placed a hand over Phoenix's heart. "All she needs is your warmth."

Realising what Morrigan meant, Phoenix reached tentatively inside her. She was surprised to find the spark of her power burning so brightly when she felt so completely spent, but she was grateful as she carefully called the sun to her and wrapped its heat around them. When Ethan crouched beside them and held them both in his arms, she allowed herself that one moment of pure happiness. That one moment to just be.

It couldn't last though, because in the shadows, death waited.

She looked from the helpless human in her arms to the shifting darkness. "How long do we have before your ward fails?" she asked Morrigan quietly.

There was a long pause. "I can hold it a while longer. But the longer I hold it, the weaker I'll be when the time comes."

When the time comes to fight.

Ethan's arms tightened around her, a low growl rumbling through his body.

She looked down at the miracle she held against her chest, and the need to protect it overwhelmed her. A rage beyond words filled her at the thought of harm coming to her daughter, at the knowledge that Darius had sent these men and women, these things, to take her child. She would die before she let that happen.

"What day is it?" Ethan asked suddenly.

Confused, she looked from him to Morrigan. She had no idea. She hadn't even had time to register that they were home before the change overtook her body and pain made thought impossible.

"It's April. You've been gone three weeks," Morrigan said, her tone carefully neutral.

"So we did it?" Ethan sat up straighter. "We stopped the prophecy."

A shadow passed over the goddess's face, and a sense of dread filled Phoenix. "I fear it may not be that simple."

"What do you mean?" Phoenix forced herself to push back the panic clawing at her chest. "We did it, she's here. She was born before the deadline; it has to have worked."

Morrigan's smile was sad as she bent to run her fingers gently over the baby's cheek. "She is indeed a miracle, but her birth was not a natural one. I fear there are forces at play here that we haven't yet discovered." Her gaze flicked to the shadows, now moving more impatiently just beyond her ward. "Let us worry about first getting out of here before we concern ourselves with what is to come."

A soft gurgle drew Phoenix's gaze down to the baby that was looking up at her with wide, innocent eyes.

Ethan took one of the small hands in his, the tiny fist wrapping around his finger. "We need to give her a name."

An unexplainable sorrow filled Phoenix's chest. She'd never understood just how much it was possible to love a person. She realised now that this must have been how her parents felt when they'd first held her. They'd never seen a hybrid, or an abomination; they'd only seen their daughter. They'd seen the miracle that had been created by their love.

There was nothing she wanted more in that moment than to see this little girl grow up. To show her just how beautiful she was, and that her unique blood was something to be proud of. She wanted to help her daughter become a strong woman who would stand defiant in the face of all the hatred and prejudice she'd no doubt face and know she was not alone. She wanted her to live.

"Saoirse." Phoenix looked up at Ethan and saw all her emotions reflected back in the raw vulnerability of his expression. "I want to call her Saoirse."

He smiled, though his eyes remained sad. "Freedom. I like that."

Phoenix bent her head and placed the gentlest kiss on her daughter's brow. Tears blurred her vision as she said to Morrigan, "Promise me you'll keep her safe."

The goddess was solemn as she took Saoirse from her arms. "I promise."

With a wince of pain as her battered and spent body protested, Phoenix picked Claíomh Solais up from the ground beside her and rose to her feet with Ethan's help. She stared into the darkness that stood between her daughter and the life she deserved. "I'm ready."

The hardest part about facing death was not the thought that she might die, but what would happen to her daughter if she did. They all knew the goddess had the best chance of keeping Saoirse safe, yet as Phoenix stood at Ethan's side waiting for Morrigan to drop the ward, she wanted nothing more than to run back and pull her baby into her arms.

Ethan glanced at her, the Spear of Lugh gripped firmly in his hand, his eyes yellow. "Thank you," he said quietly.

She didn't ask what he was thanking her for; she didn't need to. Instead she just gave him a sad smile in return. "Let's make this count."

There would be moment, a split second between Morrigan dropping the ward that surrounded them all and erecting a new one around her and Saoirse, that their child would be in danger. As exhausted and spent as she was, Phoenix was going to do everything in her power to buy the goddess that moment.

She cleared her mind and focused on the heat that burned inside her. She let it build, fuelled by a soul-deep ache at the knowledge of what she now stood to lose. Slowing her breathing, she held up a hand and gave Morrigan the signal.

The air shimmered, the ward becoming visible for a second before dissolving. Colours danced in her retinas and she blinked them away. She waited, the sense of being watched a palpable thing. The shadows were restless, but the creatures didn't move closer.

"Let's not make this harder than it has to be." Vicktor's pompous voice rang clear in the quiet of the night. "We don't want your child. Its purpose has been served. Give yourself up with the artefacts, and the baby will be spared."

Her throat went dry, her heart stuttering as the words caused it to miss a beat. It was a trap, she knew that. But still ...

"Don't even think about it," Ethan growled low.

She didn't look at him as she nodded. Claíomh Solais's power thrummed through her arm like a magnet drawn to the power building in her solar plexus. It took all she had to keep her voice steady as she called out, "Okay, I'll do it. Just don't attack."

"Phoenix, what are you –" Ethan reached out to grab her with his free hand, but she slipped from his grasp, stepping forward to carefully angle her body in front of his.

"Drop the sword and throw it towards me," Victor ordered. "The spear too."

She moved as if to do what he asked, but at the last minute she swung the tip of the blade up and let loose the power inside her. White-hot light blasted through the sword's blade, illuminating the darkness in a blinding glare.

Inhuman shrieks of pain filled the night, but still she had less than a breath before a blackened figure leapt at her with fangs glistening from a gaping maw.

She slashed out with the sword, only just managing to deflect the vicious claws that swiped at her. Chaos erupted all around her, and though power thrummed in her veins, her assailant's attacks were relentless, and she couldn't get a reprieve to focus it.

Two more of the figures emerged from the darkness and stalked towards her. Their newly charred flesh, combined with their already hideous features, turned them into a thing of nightmares. Her fight or flight alarm blared a warning to run.

She edged backwards as the demon-Supe hybrids surrounded her. Their strikes came one at a time, attacks that would hurt but not be fatal. It was as if they were playing with her, when suddenly there was a blur of movement and a hand locked onto her throat from behind.

Vicktor's breath was rotten as he hissed in her ear. "You should have taken the easy option." His black tongue ran a slimy path up her cheek, and he gave a contented sigh. "I can taste your fear."

A gust of wind grazed her cheek and hot, black blood splattered the side of her face. Vicktor's body stilled, his grip on her throat loosening.

Shock held her frozen to the spot as Ethan carved an unrelenting path through the three creatures that had herded her into the CLO rep's path. Everywhere his claws struck, blood was drawn, and by the time he reached her side he was coated in the thick black substance.

It was only when he reached over to yank the spear from Vicktor's eye socket, the shaft of which she'd numbly noted in her peripheral vision, that her brain finally connected the gruesome dots. She shuddered as Vicktor's lifeless form slumped to the ground, the last of his limp grip sliding from her.

Ethan gave her a feral grin and spun the spear around, driving it back into a fourth creature that she hadn't even seen creep up on them.

A spark of hope kindled within her as she took in the bodies surrounding them. There had been five of the demon-Supes with Vicktor. Four now joined him on the ground and a little further away from them, near the edge of the ruins, she could just make out a fifth. Was that all of them? Had they done it?

"Shit."

She jerked her head around to look at Ethan and found him staring at the bodies that littered the ruins of the Cathedral, a look of horror on his face. Icy fear ran through her as she followed his gaze and saw what had elicited the snarled curse: the bodies were twitching. They weren't dead.

A chilling laugh carried on the wind and she turned in horror-movie-slow-motion to see Vicktor rise to his feet behind her. There was a great gaping hole in his eye socket where the spear had impaled him, but clearly his brain was small enough to have been missed and he grinned at her, very much alive.

Her tiny spark of hope was snuffed out in an instant. If they couldn't kill these things, they didn't stand a chance.

She was about to yell at Morrigan to get Saoirse the hell out of there when a strange, shimmering mist appeared in the space between her and Vicktor. The mist solidified and she had only a moment to register golden eyes before the world disappeared from beneath her.

CHAPTER THIRTY-EIGHT

Darius looked around with a curiosity that was not his own. The stone of the altar was solid beneath him, and the witch was slumped on the floor of the chamber, unconscious but breathing. He raised his hand to his face, turning it from side to side as he examined the lines covering the back of it.

This form was new to them. The Horsemen. The confines of flesh both a fascination and irritation.

Their thoughts vibrated through him. Not so much words as feelings. Their power filled his veins, crackling like electricity. It begged him to call it forth, a temptation unlike any he'd ever felt before. Desires that were alien to him battled for dominance until they all blurred into one loud demand.

To be set free. To consume. To destroy.

Slowly he slid from the altar, testing the responses of this new body. Their body. A smile stretched his lips – their lips – and he stepped over the witch's limp form. He walked a slow circle around the chamber, skimming his hand over the cool stone of the wall. Shadows trailed in his wake and as he passed the torches that lined the walls, their flames flared.

He instinctively knew that this world was different than they remembered. Much had changed in the millennia since they'd been

715

banished. But here, deep in the earth, surrounded by the harshness of the stone and the smell of blood, this was familiar.

When he'd finally come full circle, he made his way up the stone steps that led from the chamber. A man stood guarding the door at the top. Erik, his mind informed him. Head of security. Vampire. Acolyte.

Erik stiffened as he noted Darius's presence. Recognition dawned in the red of his demon eyes and they widened in awe. He bowed his head in subservience. "My Lords."

Darius didn't acknowledge the gesture – it was no more than their due – he just continued down the long hallway, indicating for the man to follow. The surroundings had an odd sense of newness to him, even though he knew these eyes had beheld them for many years. He observed it all in silence, yet the voices still filled him, greedy, impatient. Attempting to focus, he turned to his head of security who followed just behind him. "Give me an update," he ordered.

There was a hesitation, and the voices inside him grew quiet. They were displeased.

"We have confirmation that the child was born, and indeed the ritual appears to have been a success." Erik gave a small bow of his head in acknowledgement of their presence. "Vicktor was there to intercept the hybrid and the artefacts, but it appears she had unexpected help."

"And?"

Another hesitation. "They got away."

It wasn't rage that filled Darius's veins in that moment. Rage was a human emotion – weak and insufficient. Fire burned through him as his vision turned red. Shadows swirled around the flame, seeking a target, someone to make suffer. The shadows shot out and wrapped around Erik's throat. His eyes bulged, but it was only when bones began to crunch that he uttered a choked protest.

The sound managed to break through the fog that had clouded Darius's mind. He blinked and the shadows dissolved.

Erik coughed out a breath and grimaced as he gave his neck a resounding crack. His face had paled, but he straightened to attention and met Darius's eyes. The Horsemen approved.

"There's someone here to see you," Erik said, returning straight to business, if somewhat hoarsely.

Darius raised an eyebrow and indicated for him to lead the way.

They made their way up to the ground floor of the building and into a small reception room. Two wing-backed chairs faced a blazing fire, and a tall man with greying hair and a stiff posture occupied one. At Darius's entrance he stood, smoothing his tailored black suit and pasting a politician's smile on his face.

He held out a hand. "Darius, good to see you again."

Darius looked at the hand and back up at the man, who flinched ever so slightly. The Horsemen watched with interest. *Vlad*, he informed them silently, *vampire head of the Council*.

Vlad cleared his throat and straightened his suit again. "Yes, well, I wanted to see you because I have information that may be of use to you."

Darius tilted his head, considering the other man coldly even as the voices inside his mind provided subtle suggestions of what he could do to the vampire with his new power.

When no response was forthcoming, Vlad continued. "If I understand correctly, you're looking for the four fae artefacts. I thought you might be interested to know that the Mists have returned to Ireland, and they have the missing cauldron in their possession."

The Horsemen stilled.

"And why would you tell me this?"

Some of the tension in Vlad's shoulders relaxed. "My colleagues in their esteemed wisdom have chosen to ally with the hybrid. They intend on uniting the artefacts and reinforcing the barrier to stem the influx of demons. I, however, can see the tide of change for what it is, and I bow to it willingly. I'm offering this information as a gesture of good faith, and I simply ask that you remember my support ... when the time comes."

Darius was quiet for a moment. A smile crept across his face, and taking it a sign of gratitude, Vlad's shoulders relaxed even further.

Without turning around, Darius called to Erik, who had stationed himself at the door of the room. "See that our friend here is made comfortable."

There was a soft burst of static as Erik spoke into his walkie-talkie.

"I'm glad we've had this talk," Vlad said, the politician's smile returning to his face. "I really feel that you and I could do great things together."

Darius's smile never faltered as two vampire guards came to escort the Council head away. When the vampire was gone, he turned to his head of security, "You say the hybrid had help?"

Erik nodded. "We believe it was the Mists."

Interesting. That would support some of Vlad's information, at least. As for the rest ...

"Send a healer to the witch," he ordered. "And prepare our army. We move at sundown tomorrow."

CHAPTER THIRTY-NINE

The world solidified around Phoenix. Two hands gripped her shoulders to steady her, and when her knees buckled, those hands stopped her from sinking to the ground. She looked up and found herself staring into the golden eyes that still haunted her dreams.

Maj watched her warily, as if expecting her to attack or bolt at any second.

Phoenix jerked back out of her grip, too panicked to process the conflicting emotions that came every time she saw or thought of the Mist. She swung her head around, desperately searching the unfamiliar wooded area for any sight of Saoirse or Ethan.

"My baby, where's my baby?"

The air to the left of her shimmered and Shayan, the youngest of the three Mists, appeared, holding Ethan's arm in a bruising grip. Ethan, for his part, looked ready to drive his spear through his handsome rescuer, and her heart skipped a beat at the sight of him. But her relief was short-lived as she turned frantically in a circle waiting for Morrigan to appear with Saoirse.

It was barely a second before a third disturbance appeared in the air to the right of her, but it might as well have been an eternity. When Jannah materialised with his arms around Morrigan and

Saoirse, Phoenix's legs did finally buckle, and this time Maj let her slide to the ground.

Ethan rushed to them and pulled Saoirse into his arms before moving to Phoenix's side. He snarled a warning at the others not to come any closer.

Jannah's serious gold eyes met Phoenix's. "We gave our word that we would come to you. We are here to fulfil that oath."

Maj and Shayan moved to his side, their black robes shifting like shadows in the chill night breeze. They bowed their heads in acknowledgement of their older brother's words.

Phoenix's eyes flicked to their wrists, where thick gold bands had once rested before she'd freed them of their servitude to the Council. "How did you know where to find us?"

Morrigan stepped forward, her dark eyes glinting in the moonlight. "I contacted them before I came to retrieve you from Faerie; I needed them to return with the cauldron. Their oath allowed them to sense the danger you were in and find you tonight."

The idea that the Mists could track her did not sit comfortably, even though she was grateful that they had. So, she focused on the rest of Morrigan's comment instead. "The cauldron? You mean Dagda's Cauldron? My grandfather said it had been taken after the original banishment."

"It was," Shayan answered quietly, an odd tension settling between him and his siblings.

Her next question was cut off by a soft gurgle from Saoirse. She shook her head; the questions weren't important. They needed to focus on getting out of here before those things found them again.

For the first time since the world had rematerialized, she looked around and actually took in their surroundings. Tall trees circled them, blocking all but the view of the moon, near full overhead. She scanned the shadows for any sign of danger.

"Where are we? Can those things find us here?" Because they hadn't been dead, and she had absolutely no idea what that meant for their group if Darius decided to send even more in their wake.

"We brought you as far as we could from the Cathedral," Jannah answered, his calm golden eyes doing a sweep of the darkness also.

"It takes a lot of power to transport others with us, so we couldn't move you far. It will take them a while to track you, but we shouldn't delay here."

Ethan looked up suddenly from where he'd been soothing the baby cradled in his arms. "How *did* they track us?"

A heavy silence fell around the group.

"We used Eoghan's gateway," Phoenix said softly as realisation struck her. She looked at Morrigan, and the goddess met her gaze with an unwavering one of her own. "You knew. You knew that the baby was coming." Her throat tightened even as her voice rose. "Why did you bring us home? We could have stayed in Faerie. You brought us back here knowing they'd be waiting for us at the time I'd be completely defenceless."

"Some things need to happen. The details are not always revealed to me, nor the reasons why, but you needed to be here for the final pieces of the puzzle to come together. What picture we make from those pieces still remains to be seen."

Frustration and anger flared in Phoenix at the goddess's cryptic response. She was so sick of being a pawn in some stupid game the fates were playing. And if it wasn't bad enough that her life got fucked around for their amusement, her child had been forced into this world surrounded by monsters and death.

Burning tears pricked the back of her eyes. "I trusted you," she said hoarsely.

She turned and held her arms out in a silent request for Ethan to give her the baby. He placed Saoirse in her arms without a word. Phoenix cuddled the small bundle to her and let the tears roll down her cheeks as she ran her fingers along the soft skin that was still so pure and untouched by the world.

It should have been different. She should have been able to experience her child growing within her, should never have had to be ashamed of such a miracle. Instead, she'd had that time ripped away from her and her little girl had been violently thrust into this world. Well, she was done with it. She was done playing by everyone else's rules.

She rested her forehead gently against Saoirse's cheek and made the silent promise that she wouldn't let this be their life. And when she lifted her eyes to Ethan's, she could see the same solemn promise mirrored back at her.

"We need to get moving," Jannah said finally.

Ethan moved towards her but froze at the sudden sound of a car engine in the distance. He tensed, hand instinctively gripping the spear that rested on the ground beside him. She reached for the sword on her back even as her other arm hugged Saoirse tighter to her.

Jannah held up a hand, urging them to wait. His solid form turned to a wisp of shadow and he disappeared. Barely a minute passed before he returned, but to Phoenix it was one of the longest of her life.

"It's okay," he said, his posture showing no sign of the tense readiness the rest of them held. "It's your family."

Phoenix looked at Ethan in confusion, a mild sense of panic darting through her before she realised it was unlikely Jannah had meant her family. But still, how would any of their friends have known to find them here?

A car door slammed, closer now. She moved to Ethan's side, careful not to disturb Saoirse, who seemed to be blissfully unaware of her mother's frayed nerves as her tiny, red-tinged eyelids drifted closed with a sleepy yawn. He wrapped an arm around her waist, his other still holding the Spear of Lugh ready despite Jannah's reassurance of safety.

There was no stealth in the crunching of feet approaching them, no attempt to catch anyone unaware in the low mumble of voices. The signatures of Ethan's parents hit her a moment before they crashed through the trees. Ethan let out a gasp of disbelief.

She didn't blame him when he let go of her waist and ran to them, but she'd have been lying if she said she wasn't a little envious. Cormac and Fia enveloped their son in a great big bear hug, their laughter and relief ringing clear for all to hear.

"Phoenix!" A third figure stumbled through the trees, and Phoenix let out a shocked sob at the sound of her best friend's voice.

Abi dashed towards her, arms open wide for a hug, but she

722

skidded to a sudden stop, her eyes going wide at the sight of the small bundle cradled in Phoenix's arms. She looked from the bundle down to Phoenix's belly and back again. "Is that ..."

Phoenix choked out a laugh that was half sniffly sob, half joy, and nodded. A shocked silence fell as the others were distracted from their reunion long enough to notice what Abi had.

Ethan tugged his parents over to join her and Abi. His eyes glistened with pride as he said, "Everyone, we'd like you to meet Saoirse."

CHAPTER FORTY

The car rumbled down the motorway, taking him away from creatures that would haunt his nightmares for a long time to come, but all Ethan could focus on was the little girl nestled in Phoenix's arms beside him – their little girl. It was only now that the danger had passed, however temporarily, and they were surrounded by family and friends, that the reality was truly hitting him.

He had no words for the feeling that stirred in his chest as he looked at her, no measure for the love, or the fear. Because this tiny human was their responsibility now, and didn't that just highlight to him exactly how much trouble they were in.

When the tearful reunions were finished and he'd introduced his parents to their new grandchild, Cormac updated them briefly on the situation. His parents had sent Morrigan to retrieve him and Phoenix from Faerie, but the goddess had only just left when a panicked call came through from William warning them of Cassandra's newest vision; Darius had somehow found a way to pull the Horsemen through to their world.

His parents had wasted no time in calling on Izzie to perform a tracker spell so that they could pinpoint the exact place and moment when he and Phoenix crossed back over. The witch it seemed had grown significantly from that young, frightened little girl he'd saved from being sacrificed all those months ago.

Realisation had dawned on Morrigan's face as his father had spoken, as if she then understood why Saoirse's birth hadn't resulted in the shift they'd all expected. Ethan had been too exhausted by that stage to make sense of what it all might mean, but when the goddess had gathered the Mists and left to make preparations for the ritual, he knew any reprieve they'd gotten would be short-lived.

Leaning back against the headrest, he forced his eyes to stay open even as his eyelids grew heavier by the minute. In front of him, Cormac focused on the road with the determined caution that only came from driving with a newborn baby in the car. His mother cast surreptitious glances back at Saoirse from where she sat in the front passenger seat, and a smile tugged at his lips as he imagined what they'd be like as grandparents. On the far side of Phoenix, Abi too kept looking at the baby with a wide-eyed awe, and it struck him just how loved this tiny little person was already.

For a while there was nothing other than the lulling roll of tyres over asphalt, then suddenly Phoenix jerked beside him. "Oh no. We haven't bought any baby stuff. Where the hell are we going to find anything at this hour of the night?"

He looked at the clock on the car's dashboard and grimaced. It wasn't yet midnight, but it was late enough that shops would be closed, even if it happened to be a late-night shopping day. But wait … What bloody day was it anyway?

Abi cleared her throat, the colouring of her cheeks noticeable even in the dim light of the car. "Actually, I may have bought a few bits. Just some basics …" She held up her hands in defence. "I know you're not meant to buy things too early, but I needed to keep busy and some of the stuff was just too cute."

Phoenix burst out laughing, and Abi's relief was obvious as she too joined in. "You're going to love the crib I got. The only thing I don't have is baby formula. I figured it was too early, and I didn't know if you were planning on feeding her yourself."

The laughter disappeared from Phoenix's face, and she looked down at Saoirse, sorrow shadowing her eyes. "I don't know if I can feed. My body didn't exactly go through the natural developments. And if something happens to me ..."

His heart broke as he looked at her, and he wanted more than anything to swear he'd never let anything happen to her. But how many times now had her life been put at risk and he'd been powerless to help?

Fia turned to look back at them, her brown eyes sympathetic. "We can stop at an all-night chemist and get some formula so that the option is there if you need it. She's sleeping soundly enough for now; you don't have to make the decision until she wakes."

Ethan stared out at the lights of the city as the car idled on the side of the road. Apparently, it took three people to decide on the most appropriate baby formula, and he and Cormac had been left in the car with the sleeping Saoirse while the women went into the all-night pharmacy to stock up on milk and "other supplies," as they cryptically stated.

Cormac glanced in the rear-view mirror at him and his Alpha smiled. "You look good with a baby."

Ethan snorted. "Are you mad? I'm afraid to breathe too hard in case I break her."

"She's stronger than she looks, trust me."

Hell, he really hoped so because when he looked down at his little girl, the thought of her growing up in their world terrified the life out of him.

He was quiet for a few minutes as he thought about that. What must it have been like for his parents? They hadn't just had him and Sasha to worry about; they had the whole pack. Their every decision decided the fate of the wolves under their care, and sometimes even the best leaders got things wrong.

"How's Sean doing?" he asked quietly. Cormac had filled him in on the basics of the Omega's rescue, but he'd been so focused on getting Saoirse somewhere warm and safe that he hadn't had the mental capacity to really think about it before now.

Cormac stared out the window, lines of worry showing at the side of his face. "The witches did better than we could have hoped with the separation spell, but even with the demon gone, it'll be a long road. You don't go through what he has and come out the other side unchanged."

A weighty silence fell, broken only by the steady hum of the car's engine. Ethan was just about to admit how nervous he was at seeing his friend again, when his mother, Phoenix, and Abi emerged from the pharmacy laden with bags. Cormac jumped out to help them put everything in the boot, and then they were on the road again, his confession left unspoken.

The lights that were a constant in the city even at this late hour added an eerie glow to the silhouette of the Dublin City skyline. The traffic was light and it wasn't long before they pulled to a stop in front of the converted warehouse he'd come to call home while in Dublin. It seemed like a lifetime since he'd been back, and the feeling was only heightened by the fact he now held a brand new person in his arms.

They'd barely climbed from the car when a familiar figure came running towards them from the doorway. His sister grabbed Phoenix in a tight hug before turning to him, smile wide and brown eyes glistening. Though he knew his mother had sent word ahead about Saoirse's surprise arrival, Sasha's expression was still one of awe as she took in her little niece.

"She's actually cute!" she said, genuine surprise in her voice. "Like, I know everyone says to the parents that their baby is cute when they're just being polite because the kid looks like a squished up old man, but I really mean it." Her smile turned mischievous. "She must take after her mother."

Ethan chuckled, giving her a gentle nudge with his foot. "Don't forget we're twins, so you've got the same gene pool as me."

She tilted her head back and laughed, the sound acting like a balm to his soul. When she demanded to hold her cute new squishy niece, he handed Saoirse over obediently, even if something inside him rebelled at the thought of letting her go.

He helped his dad grab everything from the car and followed the others inside. As he made his way upstairs to the apartment, his steps slowed. He hadn't thought to ask who would be here, and though he was grateful beyond words to be able to come home to his family and friends, a tinge of apprehension tightened his chest.

On the top floor, the door to the apartment swung open to reveal a glowering Shade. Ethan grinned at the vampire, and the glower broke into a lip twitch that was the closest semblance of a smile he'd ever seen from his friend.

Before he could utter a hello, Nate shoved past the vampire and threw himself at Ethan, wrapping arms and legs around him in an enthusiastic embrace that almost sent them both stumbling to the ground. "Good to have you back. I'm sick of being the mature, sensible one around here."

Cormac cleared his throat behind them, and Nate unwrapped himself from Ethan with a cheeky grin. "Sorry, Alpha."

Lucas, at least, allowed them to enter the apartment before greeting them, something akin to pride in his grey eyes as he looked at the sleeping baby now back in Phoenix's arms.

For a few minutes, everything was in chaos as they rushed about setting up the basics they'd need for Saoirse. Ethan had no idea what half of the stuff was for, but he couldn't keep the smile from his face as he watched his friends and family work with an efficiency that would make any tactical squad proud.

They'd just finished organising the crib when the room suddenly fell silent.

The signature that reached him was achingly familiar. He turned slowly towards the hallway.

Sean's white hair was cleaner than the last time he'd seen it, though still long and unruly. The solid jaw that, in the past, had always been clean-shaven was now covered in a light stubble. But it was the eyes that were the biggest shock of all.

The blue eyes he remembered were now tinged with the red remnants of the demon that had tried to claim Sean's body. Tried and failed. That wasn't the cause of his shock, however. It was the haunted look behind those eyes.

"I wanted to leave before you got back, but ..."

"We wouldn't let him," Abi said in a firm voice, moving to stand at the Omega's side.

Ethan couldn't look away. His father had tried to warn him that it would take a long time for Sean to heal, but staring at his childhood friend now, Ethan wondered if healing was truly possible after everything he'd been through.

Words caught in his throat. All the things he'd wanted to say for so many years, yet nothing would come. "Are you ..."

Sean gave a bitter smile that looked wrong on his kind face. "Okay? Evil? Angry at you? No." His shoulders slumped, and he suddenly looked world-weary.

Ethan swallowed past the emotion choking him. "It's good to see you."

CHAPTER FORTY-ONE

It was like a surreal dream. Not just to be back in Ethan's apartment again, but to be surrounded by her friends and family. It was more than Phoenix had truly hoped for. When she'd stood in the ruins of the Cathedral facing off with Vicktor and the rest of the demon-Supes, she'd been fully prepared to die.

Of course, some of the reunions had been more difficult than others. She couldn't quite look at Sean without having the unnerving sensation that Darius was somehow watching their every movement through him. She kept her feelings to herself for Ethan's sake, but she made herself scarce while he and Sean had their awkward reconciliation.

A hot shower and a change of clothes seemed like a luxury she couldn't afford given they still had a ticking time bomb hanging over them – if Cassandra's vision was to be believed. So she got Saoirse fed and settled with Abi's help, and rejoined the others in the living area. Izzie had arrived at some point while she'd been in the bedroom, and Phoenix was struck by the strange mix of youthful features and experience-aged eyes. She'd never met Annabelle's friend before, but as she looked at her now, she was reminded of the night Ethan had landed on her doorstep with Annabelle's limp body. The night that had changed it all for her.

When everyone was gathered, Cormac finished the private phone conversation he'd been having with William and placed his mobile on the table in the centre of the group, pressing the button to switch over to loudspeaker. "Everyone's here," he told William.

There was a moment of static, then William's voice rang clear in the room. "The Council – or what remains of us – has been considering what Cassandra's vision might mean for our plans. We've agreed to go ahead with the ritual, but without the adjustments we'd planned. If Darius has managed to pull across some element of the Horsemen, we need to recreate the original banishment, preferably before we have to face him or any more of his abominations again."

"How do we know it will work if we can't even confirm exactly what he's pulled across the barrier?" Shade asked, his usual scowl unchanged by their predicament.

"The ritual is tied to their magic," William said. "Four artefacts for the Four Horsemen. It shouldn't matter what form they're in here – so long as their magic is here, the artefacts will find them."

"But if their magic is here, doesn't that mean Darius has access to it?" Abi visibly paled as she asked the question. Phoenix reached out and squeezed her hand, but no one offered any comments of comfort.

"Like I said, we need to complete the ritual before we're forced to engage him again."

Phoenix looked around the room, feeling a bit lost. She'd been dimly aware of Cormac and Fia giving an update on the plans they'd agreed upon with the Council during the drive back to the apartment, but in truth she'd been focused only on Saoirse's sleeping face. She didn't remember any magical solution as to how they were going to avoid Darius, however.

She cleared her throat. "How exactly are we going to do that? I mean, he's always been a step ahead of us. How can you be sure he won't just attack us while we're conducting the ritual?"

"The witches will hold a barrier with the Mists," Izzie said quietly. "Only one witch is required for the actual spell itself, and the rest of the coven will buy us whatever time they can."

Phoenix's breath caught in her throat and she felt Ethan tense at her side, but they both stayed silent. The young witch might have been little more than a child to them, but she'd more than proven her worth already and she had as much right to be there as any of them.

Lucas pushed away from the window he was leaning against and looked around the room. "We all know what's required of us for the ritual. The Mists will bring the final artefact with them to the Hill of Tara tomorrow, so that just leaves the question of defence. If we are attacked and the witches' barrier falls – which we should assume it will – we're going to need people who are able to fight and hold back whatever Darius sends our way. My clan will be here before night's end to help in whatever way they can."

"The Donegal pack is in transit too," Cormac confirmed. "And the Dublin werewolf pack have also pledged their aid."

"I'll contact my aunt. She promised the fae would come." Phoenix reached into the pocket of her blood splattered clothes and wrapped her hand around the smooth crystal resting there.

"Well shucks," Nate chimed in. "I'm afraid I don't have any shifter friends to offer up, but I did manage to acquire a few of these babies." He reached behind him and pulled out a small black ball that was completely nondescript except for a single button on its surface.

When no one fell at his feet in congratulations, he huffed out a martyred sigh. "How are we friends when none of you have a clue what this is?"

"Because you just can't resist our charming wit?" Shade suggested, rolling his eyes when Nate looked even more forlorn. "Please do enlighten us."

"*This* is a top of the range incendiary device, filled with pure silver. Shove it down one of those demon thing's throats, and I'm sure even they are going to be a little too preoccupied to bug us."

The vampires and wolves in the room winced, subtly shifting away from the small silver bomb. Even Phoenix grimaced, despite the fact that her hybrid nature meant silver wasn't as lethal to her.

"The Council are securing whatever forces we can without triggering all-out panic across the Lore," William said. "But there's still one more species needed for the ritual."

They all looked around the room in confusion. It was only when

Phoenix's eyes fell on Abi that she froze, her lungs forgetting to expand for a minute. "Human," she whispered.

William's silence was all the confirmation she needed. It made sense, she supposed. This prophecy, the Horsemen – it was about their world being destroyed, not just the Lore. How self-absorbed had they been to forget they weren't the only ones who would suffer if things went wrong? Hell, Abi had reminded her of it more than once when she argued for her place at their side. But still ...

Phoenix shook her head. "It can't be Abi. She needs to stay and protect Saoirse. We'll find someone else. We'll –"

Abi turned to her, blue eyes looking sad but determined. "Let me do this. Please. Morrigan can protect Saoirse. If this all goes to hell, she'll be able to keep her safe better than I ever could."

Phoenix just continued to shake her head, the thought of her best friend standing in the middle of such danger impossible for her to accept. "You can't, Abi. You'll die! William, tell her. What happened to the human who stood in the original banishment?"

"He died." There was a long pause. "As did many of the Supes that stood at his side."

A heavy silence fell over the room as they considered what they knew to be the truth: not all of them would make it back tomorrow night.

Phoenix hung her head. The hopelessness of the situation burned her throat. She clenched her fists, wanting to scream or punch something. Anything, just to release the frustration. But it wouldn't change facts.

In the quiet of the room, Izzie spoke softly. "I may have another way to keep Saoirse safe."

Ethan watched Phoenix's eyelids droop as she struggled to stay awake. It was past two in the morning, and after everything she'd been through, he had no idea how she was still functioning. With the plans for the ritual agreed upon, everyone in the room had fallen deep into their own thoughts. They all knew what was on the line, and they all knew how uncertain the outcome was.

A small cry from his bedroom shocked his body to attention at the same moment that Phoenix jerked her head up. Their eyes met across the room and the ghost of a smile tugged at her lips. "I think someone wants to be fed."

He pushed himself away from the kitchen island that had been propping him up and offered her his hand. "Come on, let's get her settled and get some rest."

There were mumbles of "Goodnight" from around the room, but his only focus was on the woman at his side. The woman who, against all odds, had given him the most precious gift. He kept hold of her hand as they walked the short distance to his room, relishing the feel of that simple touch.

His heart both lightened and clenched in agony when he saw the little red screwed-up face wailing for food and comfort. He picked Saoirse up from the crib and realised he had no idea how he would leave her tomorrow. If Izzie could do what she said she could, he could think of no better protection for his daughter. But to leave her knowing he might not return ... the thought hurt in a way he couldn't put into words.

When Phoenix offered to take Saoirse from him, he shook his head wordlessly and took the bottle from her, ushering her into the ensuite bathroom for the shower she more than deserved. Carefully he settled down on the king-size bed, leaning back against the headboard. He held his little girl as she fed and memorised every inch of her. She was perfect.

He'd just finished winding Saoirse when Phoenix emerged from the bathroom looking clean, if not exactly refreshed. With a tired yawn, she settled down on the bed next to him. She reached out to touch Saoirse's tiny little feet, staring at them with the same wonder that he no doubt had on his face.

"She should have ended this," she said softly, her green eyes darkening with pain. "She should be enough."

Once more his heart clenched. He wanted more than anything for that to have been true, for it all to be over so they could just enjoy this miracle together as a family.

"She is enough. She should never have had that responsibility fall on her. Just like you should never have had the blame fall on you. No child, no one person, can be responsible for the lives of every person in this world."

When Phoenix spoke again, something changed in her voice. Gone was the uncertainty that he'd always sensed under the surface of her confidence. In its place was one thing: strength.

"I know that now. I know they were wrong."

Shifting Saoirse into his right arm, Ethan wrapped his left around Phoenix and pulled her close. He kissed the top of her head and closed his eyes. "I love you," he whispered.

CHAPTER FORTY TWO

Darius stared at his hand, watching as the flesh and bone melted before his eyes. The slow-motion decomposition was mesmerising, if not a little disgusting; it would make a neat party trick. Pity he couldn't keep the power. He concentrated until the process reversed, the cells reforming and skin knitting back together. A small patch of skin on the back of his hand refused to cooperate, the flesh remaining blackened and charred even as he willed it to repair.

He snarled and threw his whiskey glass at the stone wall of the chamber. It shattered into pieces, and the golden liquid glistened in the dim light. Flames erupted on his hand, flickering with insatiable hunger. He closed his eyes, and when he opened them the fire was gone.

The voices were louder in his head now. *Use the power,* they ordered. *Let it fill you. Let it become you. Devour. Consume. More.*

Slowly he stalked over to the body that hung from chains, back against the chamber wall. No blood or wounds marred Vlad's naked chest, but sweat drenched his clothes, and the moan of agony as he sensed Darius draw near was a drug unlike any other.

"Maybe we'll try this one again." Darius placed his hands on either side of the vampire's face. He closed his eyes and let the power fill him. Fill him and unmake him.

His body turned to shadows, and in the shadows came fear. In an instant he knew every nightmare Vlad had ever had, his worst fears. He took that knowledge and turned it into something tangible and real, then he let it flow through his hands.

The vampire screamed in pure terror.

Darius inhaled, they inhaled, breathing in his fear. The Horsemen's power fed on it, growing and growing until the world swam around him. Only when it felt like he might not be able to piece himself back together again did Darius let go of the shadows.

Every cell of his body was electric, alive. The voices inside him purred in pleasure. He extended his fangs and with the sweet scent of fear filling his nostrils, he struck. The vampire's normally poisonous blood tasted like honey to them, and they savoured its power. When the body was finally drained dry, he opened the manacles holding the limp meat sack aloft and let the body flop to the floor. More. He needed more blood to feed the power.

This time when he held his hand out and called the fire, he smiled and watched it burn. Everything was in place. His army was finally ready. Soon it would all be his for the taking.

CHAPTER FORTY THREE

The night passed far too quickly. One minute Phoenix was lying in Ethan's arms listening to Saoirse's soft breathing, the next she was standing in a circle of candles, preparing to raise the dead.

"Do you think she can do it?" she asked Ethan quietly.

He looked up from the centre of the circle where he was busy fussing over Saoirse's crib and glanced at Izzie as she carefully placed the last candle. "I've only ever heard of necromantic magic in legends. I want to believe she can, because I don't know if I can do this without knowing Saoirse is safe." His eyes were pained as he looked down at his daughter once more and gently caressed her cheek.

Phoenix's heart clenched. Of all the things she'd encountered in her life, watching him with his child was the most magical thing she'd ever seen. She let that magic ignite a small spark of hope in her, and she held it close, tucked away in a private little part of her heart.

"We're ready," Izzie said, composing herself as she picked up a black candle that seemed to absorb the light around it. She looked so much older than her sixteen years, her face sombre and focused.

Ethan hesitated. Every muscle in his body telegraphed his reluctance to step away from his child.

Izzie gave him an understanding smile. "You saved my life, Ethan. Let me do what I can to repay the favour."

He closed his eyes for a minute, then nodded. With a final look at Saoirse's sleeping form, he stepped away from the crib and placed himself on the opposite side of the circle facing Phoenix.

Izzie began chanting, softly at first, her words growing stronger as she continued. The hairs on Phoenix's arms stood on end, and a shiver ran down her spine. The saying that someone had walked across her grave was completely inadequate for the creeping sensation she now felt. It was more like a stampede.

In the dim light of the bedroom, Ethan's yellow eyes glowed. As Izzie's power expanded, filling the room, her own power responded. A ball of light flared to life in her chest and the sun's energy flowed through her.

The whispers were the first thing she heard. The ghosts of memories. She heard her mother laughing, her father calling her name. There were other voices too. Some she didn't recognise, but they called to something familiar inside her. They were her past, her present, her future. They were part of her.

Across the room Ethan's eyes widened in surprise and she could only assume that he was experiencing something similar.

Izzie's voice changed as her words took on a power of their own. The chant filled the room, mirrored back by the ghostly echoes. Phoenix closed her eyes and focused on the voices of her parents, on the fact that she got to hear them again one more time.

When someone touched her hand, she didn't jump. She opened her eyes slowly, her breath held. The warmth of the sun embraced her, the glow of light blinding for a minute before it faded to reveal the smiling face of her mother. Tears glistened in Aria's luminous green eyes, and her smile was one of pride.

Slowly, as Phoenix watched, Marcus appeared next to her. He reached out a hand and brushed a tear from her cheek, his face full of love.

So many emotions roiled inside Phoenix that they threatened to choke her. She knew from the transparency of the forms that her parents weren't really there. But in that moment, they felt so alive to

739

her. She could feel their touch, she could breathe in their scent, she could see them.

Other shadowy figures filled the room, but Phoenix refused to take her eyes away from her parents for fear that they might disappear. "I miss you," she whispered, not sure if they could even hear her.

"We're so proud of you," her father answered. "We're always with you,"

As one, Aria and Marcus turned towards the crib in the centre of the circle. Their faces seemed to glow with love and happiness as they moved to Saoirse's side. They looked down on their granddaughter, and in that moment Phoenix knew that no matter what happened, her child would be safe.

Hot tears burned tracks down Phoenix's cheeks and she tore her gaze away to look at Ethan. Similar emotion blazed in his eyes as he lifted his head from the two young girls who stood with him to look at her.

When the oldest girl turned to smile at her, Phoenix let out a soft gasp. Lily looked younger than she remembered. The heavy weight of her grief had finally lifted, taking away the pain that had been her constant burden in the final part of her life. Her blonde hair glittered in the light of the candles, and there was a life to her green eyes that seemed almost contradictory to her current state.

Lily whispered something to the girl beside her, who also turned in her direction. Phoenix wasn't surprised to see Annabelle's smiling face, and her heart filled with happiness to know the sisters had found each other again.

Annabelle gave her a shy wave and mouthed "thank you". Two other figures moved to stand at their side, their forms not quite as defined as the girls', but visible and very much present. They pulled the girls into a tight embrace, and there was the faint echo of laughter and joy as the family reunited.

Phoenix blinked away the tears that clung to her eyelashes and looked around her. So many people filled the room. Most were little more than whispers of a thought, their features indistinguishable, but somehow she knew they were all there for the same reason.

As if reading her mind, Aria looked back at her from where she stood by Saoirse's crib, her eyes sad. "All of these people have been hurt by him. Because of his greed. We can't stand with you, no matter how much we want to, but we can do this for you. Let us protect her while you protect the innocents of this world who cannot defend themselves. Be their voice when they have none and bring them light in this darkest of times. Go. Show him what hell really looks like."

CHAPTER FORTY FOUR

Phoenix squinted at the sun as she waited at the bottom of the Hill of Tara. It seemed wrong somehow for the sun to be shining so brightly given what lay ahead of them. Her body wasn't complaining, however, as it soaked in the healing energy and tried valiantly to recover from the trauma of the past twenty-four hours. In truth, she'd have happily found herself a hole in the ground to curl up into if she'd had the choice. But she didn't have the choice, so here she was.

Ethan stood by her side, keeping a watchful eye on their surroundings. The tension in his body was as evident as her own, and no amount of slow breathing or restless pacing seemed to help either of them.

The Hill of Tara was eerily quiet. There was no sign of the dog walkers or cyclists that often frequented the spot, and the tourists wouldn't be quick to venture this way thanks to a subtle spell the witches had placed at dawn that morning. They wouldn't know quite what deterred them from the place, but it would be enough to keep innocent people from becoming cannon fodder if things went badly.

A shiver ran through her at the thought, and she looked over her shoulder to reassure herself that Claíomh Solais was still strapped to her back where it should be. Though where exactly she thought the sword might disappear to, she had no idea.

Beside her, Ethan had a firm grip on the Spear of Lugh and she could tell by the whites of his knuckles that he too was taking what comfort he could from the tangible weight of the artefact. Now all they needed was the cauldron.

Where the hell are they?

She scanned the broad expanse of green that surrounded the small hill where Lia Fáil sat. The Stone of Destiny. Would it decide their destiny here today?

The witches had already formed a wide perimeter around the hill. Once the Mists arrived with the cauldron, Maj and Shayan would join them and erect a ward, effectively sealing off the hill from any possible attack. It wasn't foolproof of course, so groups of Supes were gathered behind the witches, ready to form a second line of defence should the ward fail. She didn't want to think about what might happen if they were needed.

"What if they don't show?" She bit her lip and shuffled restlessly from one foot to the other.

"They will."

As if summoned by his words, there was a soft flutter overhead. They both looked up just as a large crow swooped down from the sky and Morrigan shifted to her human form to land beside them. Her black training gear shimmered with the same oil-slick effect that Phoenix had grown used to seeing on her feathers, and the clothes clung to her almost as they were a second skin.

Morrigan turned three-sixty, her watchful eyes checking their surroundings. Then she raised her fingers to her lips and let out a low whistle that vibrated through Phoenix's bones.

At her call, a light mist fell around them. It coalesced, solidifying to form three bodies. The Mists' golden eyes glowed, and their bronzed skin shimmered in the sunlight. Shayan stood in the centre between his older brother and sister, a small cauldron in his hands.

The sword on Phoenix's back sent vibrations rattling down her spine. Even without holding Claíomh Solais, she could feel the power thrum through the blade as like called to like. From the shocked expression on Ethan's face, she assumed he was feeling something similar from the spear gripped in his hand.

Dagda's Cauldron was remarkably nondescript. It bore a striking resemblance to an old-school cast iron pot, though she assumed it wasn't actually made of iron, given it was a fae artefact. She eyed it with curiosity. Had it been worth it? The price the Mists had paid for keeping it safe?

"We need to get into position," Morrigan said. "The sun will set shortly and there's much to do."

Without another word, they made their way to the perimeter where the witches were making the final preparations to raise the ward. Jannah stopped a little behind them, pulling Maj and Shayan to the side to speak quietly to them.

Phoenix watched the exchange closely, paying particular attention to Shayan's tense expression. It was he who had taken the cauldron, but they'd all agreed that it was best for Jannah to stand as the Mist representative in the ritual. In order for that to happen, the youngest Mist would have to be willing to hand over his ownership of the cauldron, like Aoife had the spear. For a moment she wondered if he'd refuse to do it. Her hand twitched on the leather strap holding her scabbard as he seemed to hesitate, but then he gave a solemn nod, said the words needed, and handed the artefact to Jannah. She released a breath.

Maj looked over at her, an unreadable expression in her golden eyes. "We'll hold it as long as we can." With that, she and her younger brother stepped back to join the witches and close the circle.

An ominous chill ran through Phoenix, but she pushed it away. She'd promised herself that no matter what happened, she'd find some way to get back to Saoirse. She intended on keeping that promise. Still, she had to fight the urge to turn around and flee as the near-translucent ward flared to life like a dome around them. Together, she, Ethan, Morrigan, and Jannah continued their way up the hill.

Immediately behind the ward circle, the Council's troops dotted the field. They were easily identifiable by their matching fighting gear and professional-looking badassery, but she paid them little heed.

The werewolves were stationed next in the line of defence. Some of the faces she recognised from the Donegal pack, others she assumed were the Dublin wolves who'd pledged their aid. She scanned the field but couldn't see Ethan's family among them. They must be helping to prepare for the ritual, she realised with an anxious twist of her gut.

In the limited tree cover that dotted the field, she spotted Lucas's vampires. Though many of the vampires were strong enough to withstand even the glaring sun that beat down on her now, it would weaken them unnecessarily. The shade allowed them to conserve their energy until the sun began to set, or someone tried to kill them all, whichever came first.

She continued to search the horizon, hoping.

She told herself it was stupid to feel let down, but still the pang of disappointment settled in her chest like an ache.

Just as they reached the bottom of the hill where Lia Fáil awaited them, Cormac and Fia intercepted them. "Everyone's in place," Cormac informed them.

A quick glance around showed Nate off to their left, his attention firmly fixed on the silver-laden explosives he was checking. Sean stood close to him, staring into the distance with grim determination while Sasha bounced restlessly on her heels beside him. Shade was nowhere to be seen, and she assumed he was taking shelter with the other vampires.

"The Council came," she noted as she spotted William prowling along the base of the hill. He looked every inch the wolf, even in his human skin.

Cormac grimaced. "They're all here except Vlad. Apparently, he never resurfaced after the botched attack on Darius."

She'd never met the vampire head of the Council, but no one around her seemed too surprised by the revelation, and since they weren't short on vampires, she guessed it didn't really matter too much.

"Did my aunt ..."

Cormac shook his head, but Fia gave her shoulder a reassuring squeeze. "They'll be here."

She took a shuddery breath and squared her shoulders. If they had to, they'd make do without the fae's support.

They all looked towards the rock that sat atop the hill and the others who waited there to start the ritual. Ethan opened his mouth to say something, but before he could speak, Cormac pulled him into a firm embrace, turning to Phoenix and bringing her in close as well. Fia kissed them both on the forehead, then took her mate's hand and stepped back with a nod of encouragement.

"I guess it's time to get this show on the road." Ethan placed a hand on Phoenix's back. She gave him a nervous smile and together they followed Morrigan and Jannah up the last stretch of hill.

Lia Fáil was nothing like Phoenix had expected. Sure, the fae artefacts all seemed to have been designed in an understated way, but this was just ridiculous. She tilted her head as she assessed the rock that was said to have heralded the rightful king of Ireland. All she saw was a random stone pillar sticking out of the ground. It reminded her of those strange phallic-like artefacts ancient civilisations used to encourage fertility.

But the power. Holy shit, the power!

The tug she'd felt from her sword when she was close to the spear or cauldron was nothing compared to what she felt now. One look at the surprise on Ethan's face told her he felt it too.

As she, Ethan, and Jannah stepped closer, a bright light flared to life, seeming to come from within the stone itself. Familiar Celtic symbols appeared on its surface, and her hand reached out involuntarily to touch them. A slender hand with red tipped nails grasped her wrist in a vice-like grip, and Phoenix looked up to be greeted by Méabh's sardonic smile.

"I wouldn't advise that."

Phoenix snatched her hand back, and with an extreme effort of will, forced herself to step away from the stone and turn to face the others gathered on the hill.

Izzie watched them with interest and gave a small nod of acknowledgement as their gazes met. Abi stood quietly at the witch's side, as they'd agreed. Phoenix had made her swear on every god and goddess in existence before leaving the apartment that morning that she'd stay with Izzie and allow the young witch to keep her safe, no matter what happened. She was simultaneously terrified for, and fiercely proud of, her best friend as she took in the fierce determination that shone in Abi's blue eyes. She may have been scared shitless, but she was sure as hell going to stand here with her head held high.

Lucas was waiting with the group despite the bright sun that was only then beginning to drift towards the horizon. His expression was carefully schooled, but she could feel the weight of his concern as he watched her. She knew he felt a responsibility to her father to keep her safe, and they both knew it was something that wouldn't be possible.

Remembering the love that filled her on getting to see her parents again, she stepped up to her father's Sire and took his hand. She stood on her toes so that she could speak quietly in his ear. "He forgives you."

She squeezed his hand and stepped away, but not before she caught the emotion glistening in his eyes.

On the far side of the stone, an Asian man stood next to Méabh. Though he was clearly a Supe, his appearance somehow made him seem the least threatening of all – Abi included. But the energy that oozed from him almost took her breath away. When his eyes met hers, something ancient stared back. Kam, Phoenix guessed. She swallowed hard.

A sudden darkness fell around them as heavy grey clouds rolled in to block out the sun. Morrigan raised her face to the sky and her eyes turned stormy. "It's time."

CHAPTER FORTY-FIVE

Ethan scanned the horizon as the sun set beyond the hills. Adrenaline buzzed through his veins, fuelled further by the power that emanated from the spear, down his arm and into his very core. Some distant part of him knew he should be afraid, that in reality, none of them were guaranteed to survive the next couple of hours. But he wasn't.

Only two things mattered to him in that moment: Phoenix and Saoirse. If he had to give up his life this night so that they could live, he would without a thought. He'd find a way, for them.

With Dagda's Cauldron in hand, Jannah went around to them one at a time requesting a blood sacrifice. His own blood to represent the Mists, Méabh's to represent the fae, Kam's for the shifters, Izzie's for the witches, Lucas's blood for the vampires, Ethan's for the wolves, Abi's for the human, and finally, Phoenix's as the only hybrid.

An oddly sweet odour mingled with the metallic tang as the combined blood settled at the bottom of the cauldron. The metal changed colour wherever the blood made contact, and faint Celtic symbols glowed around the outside.

Once it was done, the others formed a circle around Lia Fáil, and Ethan and Phoenix moved to opposite sides of the stone. Morrigan gave the order and he turned the Spear of Lugh upside down and

748

stabbed it into the ground. Opposite him, Phoenix did the same with Claíomh Solais.

A shock of power shot through him and for a moment he couldn't breathe. It receded as quickly as it came, but the low hum of energy remained, and something told him that he'd need to brace himself when the fourth and final artefact was added.

He looked up and met Phoenix's wide eyes. The connection that had been formed between them when he gave her his blood in Faerie was still faintly present. Enough so that he could have spoken to her without saying a word. He could have told her how much he loved her, how amazingly strong she was, and how proud he was to call her the mother of his child. Instead, he gave her a cheeky wink and got a wry smile in return.

Morrigan stepped back out of the circle and gave them a solemn look. "So long as you all hold together, the power will distribute evenly through you. If you break the circle ..."

"Don't break the circle," Kam ordered, his voice heavy with warning.

Ethan rolled his shoulders and gave his neck a resounding crack. Hold the spear, don't move. How hard could it be? Unease settled in the pit of his stomach as he looked out over the hilly landscape once more. It was quiet. Too quiet.

Izzie's words were low and indecipherable as she began to chant over the cauldron. Ethan held his breath for the sudden whammy of magic that would likely hit when the witch completed the blood circle. A heavy silence fell. And nothing happened.

He turned in confusion to see what was going on. Izzie was kneeling by the cauldron, her eyes wide with panic as she stared at it.

"It's not working." She looked up, frantically seeking out Kam. "Why isn't it working?"

"What do you mean it's not working?" Méabh snapped, an edge of fear tingeing her impatience.

"I did it exactly how he told me," Izzie said, indicating to Kam as her voice grew higher pitched. "There's something wrong. I can't feel any power." She took a deep shuddery breath in an obvious attempt to calm herself and closed her eyes. With her hands splayed above the cauldron, she repeated her chant and waited.

When nothing happened for a second time, she opened her eyes and shook her head. "Tell me the steps again," she demanded. "We must have missed something."

Kam frowned, and his ancient eyes took on a distant stare. "The blood of each species was mixed in the cauldron. An incantation declared the intention and infused the blood with power, then a circle –"

"Wait," Lucas interjected. "Have we got everyone's blood?"

They all looked around in askance, but no one stepped forward to claim they'd been missed. They'd covered the same basics as the original ritual: witch, vampire, fae, shifter, werewolf, Mist, human. The only difference this time was that Phoenix's hybrid blood had been added.

Abi raised a hand, blushing a little as all eyes turned to her. "Are we sure Phoenix's blood should be included? I mean, if there's never been a hybrid before, it can't have been included in the original banishment."

There were low murmurs as everyone debated the logic. On the one hand, her birth had technically created a new species and therefore was required as a representative of their world. And on the other, her blood was simply a mix of two species already represented – fae and vampire – so it shouldn't do any harm even if it wasn't required.

It was this last idea that caught Ethan's attention. A cold sense of dread crept through him as a terrifying thought formed. Any hybrid created from existing species did, in fact, carry the blood of their parentage and should therefore be covered within the group gathered on the hill. But there was one exception to that logic; there was another hybrid, less natural, but no less present this side of the barrier.

"Shit," he whispered, causing everyone to fall silent around him. "I think I know what species we're missing."

Phoenix listened to Ethan's theory with a sense of foreboding. She didn't want what he was saying to make sense, but it did. Her blood was just a combination of two species that had already offered up their blood willingly. But Darius's new creations, they were something different.

Demons weren't of this world, and as such, their blood hadn't been necessary to fulfil the original requirements. Now that the blood was mixed with a species natural to this world, however, it was a different story.

She was just about to ask what the hell they could do when movement in the periphery of her vision distracted her. The light was growing low in the evening sky and eerie shadows danced around them, but as she squinted into the distance, she saw it again: movement beyond their perimeter.

The ward flared blue, and surprised yells came from down the hill.

"What the fuck was that?" Ethan asked.

"They're here," Morrigan answered, her tone resigned.

The ward flared again, and the field turned into chaos around her. None of it registered though, because the familiar sense of wrongness hit Phoenix. It stole her breath away and left her gasping even as her vision swam black. She gritted her teeth and forced herself to focus.

Suddenly, it was like a veil was lifted. The movement she'd seen only moments before hadn't been her imagination. She turned in a slow circle and beheld the swarm of black that surrounded them on all sides, held at bay only by the ward. There must have been hundreds, maybe thousands.

"How long will it hold?" she asked in a whisper.

Jannah's expression was grim as he stared out at the sea of writhing bodies. "Not long enough."

Even as he said it, a blast of fire lit up one side of the protective circle. The witches cried out, but the ward held firm.

Phoenix's heart hammered in her chest. If what Ethan believed was true – and she was convinced it was – what they needed was beyond that protective barrier. But if they dropped it now, there would be no going back. They were outnumbered, and if their previous experiences were anything to go by, outmatched. They'd all die.

"I hate to rush you guys," William roared from the base of the hill, "but I think we've got a situation here. Any chance you can hurry up and do the damn ritual?"

Lucas turned to Jannah, his voice tight with urgency. "Can you materialise beyond the ward?"

The Mist shook his head. "We had to make it airtight. We didn't know what Darius might have at his disposal."

And just to punctuate his words, fire struck the wards again, spreading to cover the entire surface of it. The ward glowed red hot and cracks formed across its surface.

The cries of pain were more than Phoenix could bear. She spun to Morrigan and pleaded. "Is there any way to complete the ritual without the circle?"

Morrigan's expression was sorrowful as she stared at the field below as if already mourning the losses to come. "The artefacts and the intention are what is important. The circle is to bind you all so that the power can be dispersed through you. It can be done without the circle, but not without the blood." Morrigan turned to her. "Phoenix, if there is no circle, then the power will be channelled solely through the holders of the artefacts."

The look in her guardian's eyes told Phoenix everything she needed to know: the fewer the people to absorb the power, the lower their chances of surviving its force.

Phoenix looked to Jannah, who met her gaze unwavering. He would keep his oath to her, even if it meant his death. It was harder to look at Ethan, but she did, and when her eyes met his, she found comfort and surety.

With a deep breath, she yanked Claíomh Solais from the ground. "Let's start by getting the missing blood."

CHAPTER FORTY-SIX

The Horsemen observed from deep in the recesses of Darius's mind as their army launched a relentless assault on the ward that formed a wide circumference around the Hill of Tara. Shrieks of pain followed each strike against the ward, and a vicious smile split his face. It wouldn't be long now.

At his side, the witch watched silently. Her power crackled around her, ready and waiting to be used when the time came.

They'd wanted him to turn her, the Horsemen. To combine her with one of their most powerful acolytes. But there was something about her humanity – or natural lack of it – that appealed to the person he had been. They'd been displeased with him for his decision, and they'd made sure he knew it.

Unconsciously his hand pressed against his side where rotten flesh covered his ribcage. Oh yes, they had an interesting way of conveying their displeasure. But right now they were pleased with him, and he bathed in the warmth of that feeling, in the satisfaction that soon he would prove to them just how worthy he was of their praise.

A flash of fire lit the sky, flaring out over the dome of protection covering Phoenix and her foolish friends. The flame called to the power that welled inside him, caressing and tempting him, demanding to be set free. The will to hold it back was growing weaker by the hour. The Horsemen wanted chaos. They wanted fear. They wanted everything to burn.

But it wasn't time yet.

His eyes scanned the mass of bodies that rushed about the field, preparing for the moment when the ward would fall and they'd meet their inevitable death. So many willing to sacrifice themselves for a cause they believed to be worthy. They had no idea they were doing all the work for him.

Then he saw it: the flash of red. Anticipation rippled through him and he licked his lips. "There you are."

His smile widened.

CHAPTER FORTY-SEVEN

Phoenix sensed the others falling in behind her as she raced down the hill, Claíomh Solais gripped tightly in her hand. Ethan kept pace with her every step of the way, his expression grim but determined. Her own heart thundered in time with the pounding of her feet and terror threatened to crush her, but she pushed the feeling as far down as she could.

Cormac intercepted them as they reached the second line of defence. "What the hell is going on?"

"We need blood from one of the demon hybrids." Ethan pointed to the swarming mass of black. "We can't complete the ritual without it."

A blur of movement came from the right and Shade skidded to a halt beside them. "The ward can't hold much longer. They've surrounded us on all sides. I don't know how long we'll be able to hold them back once it falls."

"How many?" Phoenix could see Cormac doing the mental calculation as he assessed their best strategy.

"Hundreds."

Ethan let out a low whistle. "Might as well tell the witches to conserve their energy. We need to let them through."

If Shade had been pale before, he turned positively see-through at Ethan's words. "What? Are you fucking crazy? They'll –"

A look from Ethan halted his rant and he shook his head in disbelief. He muttered under his breath, "I should have found me a less crazy family," and disappeared in another blur of movement.

Despite herself, Phoenix smiled and some of the tension eased from her. Shade was right, this was a fucking crazy idea, and yet a part of her was just grateful to be standing here with these people at her side.

There was a ghost of a smile on Ethan's face too when he turned to her and held out his free hand. "Let's go make some new friends."

They left Cormac to organise the wolves as all around the field, the other teams were preparing. Phoenix made a point of not looking at the creatures surrounding the ward, but that same sense of wrongness choked her as they grew closer to the outer circle.

Even from a distance, she could see the beads of sweat running down the back of the witches' necks and the tremble of their muscles as they fought to hold on against the onslaught. "We need to do this quickly," she said.

Ethan grimaced. "Jannah has gone ahead to warn the other Mists. When we give the signal, they'll drop the ward."

Morrigan swooped through the sky above them, once more in her crow form. The sight called to something primal deep within Phoenix, and she squared her shoulders and gathered her resolve. All around the field their friends and allies stood ready to fight, despite the possibility that their idea was, in fact, crazy.

She allowed herself to look back, just once, towards the top of the hill. Her eyes sought out Abi, and she spotted her best friend standing sandwiched between Sasha and Izzie. All three looked fiercely defiant as they stared down at the hoards below them. In front of them stood a lone wolf: Sean.

He met her gaze across the distance and gave her a barely perceptible nod. Only then did she let herself turn and truly face what was to come.

Phoenix looked beyond the witches and hissed in a sharp breath. She'd known it was bad, but she could never have prepared herself for the nightmare that was before them. Snarling faces and crazed red eyes belied the methodical way the creatures moved. There was restraint and logic in the way they relentlessly attacked the ward, and that terrified her more than anything else. At their centre, a broad man stood barking orders. They all obeyed without question.

She scanned the sea of faces. There was no sign of Darius on this side of the field, but she could feel his eyes watching her. He was there somewhere, she knew it.

"We find the easiest target and get out," Ethan said, his tone brisk. "We need to complete the ritual, or all this will have been for nothing."

She swallowed hard and nodded, not so sure there would be an easy target.

He moved to give the order, but she grabbed his arm and pointed to the man at the centre of the crowd who had caught her attention moments before. "Tell the others they need to take him out. He's in charge."

He followed her line of sight and nodded. He was quiet for a moment as he conveyed her message to the pack via bat – wolf – signal. That done, he raised his hand in the air.

Morrigan let a loud "*Caw!*" and the wards came down.

<hr />

For all of her bravado and insistence that humans be considered equal in determining what happened to their world, Abi was about ready to piss herself as she watched the sea of bodies swarm onto the field. So many. How had Darius gotten so many Supes?

At her side, a feral growl rumbled from Sasha. The wolf held herself tensely, muscles twitching with the desire to help her pack-mates, but still the other woman didn't move from the hilltop. On her opposite side, Izzie had closed her eyes and was murmuring unintelligible words. Abi didn't know what it was the witch was doing exactly, but the air was charged around them and the hairs on her arms stood on end.

Sean stood in front of them. He hadn't looked at her before

moving into that position, but she'd seen the nod he'd given to Phoenix, and she knew from the stubborn set of his jaw that he'd die before he let anyone past him.

Screams of pain filled her ears as bodies collided below. There were flashes of light and bursts of flame, all punctuated by the clash of metal on metal. And blood. There was already so much blood.

It was clear from her vantage point just how outnumbered they were, and as she reached for one of the throwing knives strapped to her waist, she felt utterly helpless. She'd wanted to be treated equally, had demanded that humans were every bit as capable even if they didn't have the same natural advantages. Now look at her, cowering at the top of the hill while everyone else risked their lives.

A deep rumble came from overhead and a streak of white lightning forked through the sky. The two women at her side jerked their heads up, worry clouding their features. Then, suddenly, they were both on their knees, screaming as they clasped their heads in their hands.

"Sasha? Izzie!" she cried. There was no response other than their screaming, and she frantically looked around for Sean.

But there was no sign of the Omega. In fact, there was no sign of the field surrounding her, or the battle she knew was raging even now. All around her was a wall of black shadows.

Ice-cold fear bathed her, freezing a scream in her throat. Tendrils of darkness crept towards her, sinuous and seductive in their movement. Every instinct in her body screamed not to let them touch her, but she could see no way of escape as the shadows closed in from all sides.

One of the snake-like ropes lapped at her foot and she jerked back, only for another to caress the back of her neck. Every muscle in her body tensed, locked in place by fear. She was dimly aware that Sasha and Izzie were still kneeling on the ground, their screams now hoarse.

It was this sound more than any true sense of bravery that finally got her moving; she had to help them.

She spun on her heel and found a spot in the wall of shadows that looked – if even just to her imagination – less dense than the rest. She held her breath and ran straight for it. The darkness wrapped around her, welcoming her. But suddenly it was gone, and she could see everything around her with startling clarity.

She saw wolves she recognised from the Donegal pack being viciously struck down by the demon-Supe creatures. She saw friends fleeing with no true chance of escaping. She saw Fia on her knees in the middle of it all. The wolf's kind eyes met hers a moment before her head was separated from her body. Abi watched it all, impotent.

"Abi! Abi, help me."

Phoenix's desperate cry shocked her out of her frozen state of horror. She swung around and found her friend standing at the bottom of the hill, a small bundle cradled in her arms. Fire blazed around her, and the terrified wail of a baby joined the screams that filled the field.

"No. No. No." Abi shook her head in disbelief. Saoirse shouldn't be here; she was meant to be safe.

Wait, something inside her said. *That can't be Saoirse. She* is *safe. The spirits are protecting her.* With that thought, everything around her faded, leaving only darkness. She stumbled backwards out of the shadows, gasping.

A low chuckle came from behind her, and when she spun around, she was met by the face that haunted her nightmares.

"Hello, Abi." Darius smiled widely. The gesture caused the rotten skin and scars on his left cheek to contort, showcasing the gleaming white of his teeth between the decrepit flesh.

Fear clawed at her throat, choking her. Memories of that dark chamber swamped her mind.

Darius tilted his head, assessing her with intrigue. "Fear is an interesting thing, is it not? It can incapacitate us more wholly than any other means I've come across in my long life. Of course, I've never had quite the level of control over it as I do now, but I did okay. I think you'll agree?"

He stalked towards her, and though Abi tried to order her body to move, her muscles were paralysed, frozen in a strange limbo between flight or fight. He walked a slow circle around her, the shadows following in his wake.

"It seems appropriate that you will yet again be the reason Phoenix gives herself up to me."

The words sent a jolt through Abi, and in an instant his hold on her mind was gone. She was weaker than him in every way possible; there was no denying that. But she was damned if she was going to let herself be his victim again. Slowly she moved the fingers of her right hand, inching them towards one of the three remaining throwing knives at her waist. Her fingers closed around the cool metal and she held her breath.

Darius came full circle to gloat face-to-face, and that was when she struck. With a scream filled with all the anger and frustration and helplessness she'd felt for the last few months, she plunged the blade into his eye. Darius roared and stumbled away from her, grasping for the knife.

It took only a moment for him to yank it free; then he wheeled on her, his rage terrifying to behold. She knew in that moment he was going to kill her, but that suited her just fine. If he killed her, he wouldn't be able to use her against her friends. She squared her shoulders and looked him in his one remaining eye.

The shadows coalesced around him, swirling into a maelstrom of fury as blood streamed down his face. She was distantly aware of someone yelling her name as she said a silent goodbye to her friends. Darius held up a hand and closed his fist.

Her throat constricted as if all the oxygen had been pulled from the space around her. She gasped for breath, her hands scratching at her throat. The burning in her lungs intensified. Her vision blurred and started to turn black when suddenly a flash of white shot past and barrelled into Darius.

Abi had only a second to register Sean's blue eyes before oxygen flooded her lungs and the world spun.

CHAPTER FORTY-EIGHT

Fire lanced through Phoenix's arm as razor-sharp claws tore through her flesh. She whirled, lashing out with Claíomh Solais. The blade cleaved through her attacker's neck, as it had cleaved through every other attacker before this one.

A swarm of maggots burst forth from the stump where the creature's head had been only seconds ago. She shrieked and jumped back, stamping her feet in a panicked attempt to squash any that came near her.

It had seemed like such a straightforward plan – get the blood and get the hell out. But the sheer numbers and strength of Darius's army had overwhelmed their defences in seconds. Her hands were slippery with the black blood she'd spilled, and not all of the bodies dotting the field around her were their enemies.

A sudden explosion came from her left and despite it all, she had to grin at Nate's exhilarated "Whoop!" Ethan was buried in a flurry of bodies to her right, but no matter how much she tried to carve a path to him, she kept running up against another obstacle.

They couldn't keep this up forever; they needed to get the blood back to the cauldron.

Even as the thought passed through her mind, another attack came from both sides. She dived just in time to avoid the flame that shot over her head. She rose to her feet and as she did, something caught her eye on the horizon.

A sea of bodies crested the hill from the west, heading straight for them. Rather than the black undulating hoard of Darius's army, this group rode magnificent horses and were led by two riders bearing a banner displaying a symbol of the sun – the symbol of her mother's people.

She ducked to avoid another strike, but something inside her began to lighten. They'd come. Aoife had kept her promise.

With renewed focus, she dispatched the two demon-Supes attempting to turn her into a shish kebab. She slashed and ducked, dodged and stabbed, every move getting her closer to Ethan.

She'd almost made it to him, when Morrigan's warning *"Caw!"* came from above. Phoenix swung around and her gaze fell on the hilltop where Abi and Sean now stood alone, facing an all-too-familiar figure.

Terror gripped her. All thoughts of getting to Ethan forgotten, she moved as if her life – her best friend's life – depended on it.

Oddly, none of the creatures moved to attack her as she sprinted for the top of the hill. A distant part of her knew that could only mean she was running straight into a trap, but she didn't care.

Despite the fact that they stood little chance against Darius, Abi and Sean had settled into an effective pattern of attack. Though she doubted they were causing true harm, their alternating strikes were enough to distract and irritate their foe.

It seemed, however, that he'd finally had enough of humouring them. Black shadows swirled around him as he held out a hand and let loose a blast of power that sent both Abi and Sean flying through the air. The ground rumbled with the force of the power.

He turned and smiled at her.

A sickening scream bubbled up in Phoenix's throat as she took in the rotten flesh covering one side of his face, and the gaping hole where an eye had once been. The man who she'd once called uncle opened his arms wide in welcome, and she ran straight for him.

Ethan drove the Spear of Lugh home time after time. Its aim never once failed him, but try as he might, he couldn't stave off the attacks long enough to get one of the bodies – or even body parts – back up to the cauldron.

He spun, plunging the tip of his spear through the chest of yet another demon-Supe and caught a flash of red in the corner of his eye. He cursed, then cursed more ferociously when he turned for a proper look.

Phoenix was almost to the top of the hill, and Darius stood there waiting for her with open arms. What the fuck was she doing? She couldn't face him alone.

"Shade!" he yelled to the vampire to his right. "Get the blood." He didn't wait for an acknowledgement before turning back to the hill, more than prepared to kill anyone stupid enough to get in his way.

A huge vampire with glowing red eyes stepped into his path. Ethan recognised him immediately as the one Phoenix had pegged as the leader, and he swore; he really didn't have time for this.

To increase his frustration further, the solid wall of muscle that was the vampire's chest obscured Phoenix from Ethan's view, and he knew he had only seconds before she reached Darius. He gritted his teeth. "Can we at least make this quick?"

The vampire gave him a slow, terrifying smile that promised a world of pain.

Ethan glanced to his left, trying to calculate his chances of getting past the demon-Supe without a fight, and quickly surmised the odds were not in his favour. He darted right.

A shadowy tendril shot out from the vamp and grabbed hold of him. Ethan lashed out with the spear and shattered the ethereal restraint, but not before the sickening sense of wrongness had seeped deep into his soul from its touch and given him a taste of what awaited them should they fail.

With renewed determination, he spun the spear around and drove the tip through the vampire's chest. True to its nature, the fae weapon found its mark.

He yanked the spear out, his mind focused again on getting to

Phoenix, but then he froze in disbelief. The gaping hole in the vamp's sternum swirled with shadows and before his eyes, the tissues knitted back together and he was fully healed.

"You've got to be shitting me!"

Life flared in the vampire's red eyes and his grin widened. He looked down at his chest, then back up at Ethan. His hand shot out, and before Ethan could recover from his shock, it clamped around his throat in a crushing grip.

Ethan's brain screamed for oxygen. He slashed at the hand with elongated claws, knowing it was pointless trying to pry the fingers away; any damage he caused simply repaired itself in a swirl of shadows. His head swam, and his vision grew black around the edges.

His vision had almost faded entirely when a blinding white light seared his retinas. There was an inhuman screech of pain and the pressure released from his throat. His knees buckled beneath him.

"Ethan, are you okay?"

He recognised Aoife's voice as someone grabbed his arm to keep him upright. He blinked repeatedly, as if that might return his vision quicker.

"Phoenix," his said urgently, as the light cleared enough for him to make out Aoife's features.

"Go. We'll cover you." She pushed him towards the hill, her order punctuated with the clang of metal on metal.

He didn't look back to see what had happened to the vampire. He just ran.

Everything else around him was inconsequential as he zeroed in on Phoenix. She stood alone on the top of the hill, facing off with Darius. Claíomh Solais glowed brightly in her hand as if she was channelling the power of the sun through it. Shadows oozed from Darius and lashed out at the sword. Anywhere they touched the blade, they seemed to swallow the light it cast. Phoenix hacked and sliced at the shadows, but they kept coming.

Darius laughed, a crazed look on his half-rotten face as he held his arms out wide, taunting her. "You fool. You think you can kill me? No one can kill me. I am eternal."

Fire flared in his hands and engulfed his arms in blue flame. A

764

maniacal scream filled the air and a ring of fire burst to life around Darius and Phoenix.

"No!" Ethan roared, skidding to a stop just out of reach of the flames.

The heat was too much. It burned his skin without touching him, and the smoke clogged his airways with each searing breath he took. His body screamed at him to stop, but still he pushed forward.

Through the flickering flames, he saw Phoenix tear through Darius's abdomen with her sword. Hope surged inside him. But then he saw Darius smile – and time fractured.

Phoenix drew her sword back to drive the blade into Darius once more, but she hadn't noticed the shadows moving behind her. They shot out, wrapping around her arm and throat. The sword fell from her hand as she clawed at her neck with her free hand, her face a mask of shock.

No! This couldn't happen. He wouldn't let it.

There was no way Ethan could reach her in time, even if he could get through the ring of fire. So, he did the only thing he could do.

He drew his arm back and prayed to every god that had ever existed, whether in truth or only in the hearts of those who believed. He prayed to all those who had gone before him, to the loved ones who were even now fighting to the death at his side, to all those who were going about their lives in blissful ignorance of the fight that was raging to decide their fate. And he let his spear fly.

CHAPTER FORTY-NINE

The witch stood watching from a distance. She felt no sympathy as the spear found its mark in Darius's heart. She had tried to warn him. Had told him time and again that the power was too much for anyone on this earth to hold for long.

And now, his once-powerful body was rotting from the inside out. The strength that had taken him millennia to develop was being consumed by the insatiable hunger that was Greed.

The spear wouldn't be enough to kill him, of course. Not with the Horsemen's essence still inside him. But his body was weak and broken now. He was no use to her.

Slowly, she dragged the blade of a curved dagger down the inside of her forearm. As the blood welled, she closed her eyes and started chanting. It was time to find a more suitable vessel.

CHAPTER FIFTY

Phoenix saw the exact moment that the spear lodged in Darius's heart. She saw the fury in his black eyes as the shadows swirled and coalesced to close the wound. Then she saw his expression change.

The flames that had been blazing at her back disappeared, leaving only icy cold where there had seconds ago been a wall of heat. The shadows binding her arm and throat loosened their grip, and she gasped in a lungful of air.

An odd silence fell around them, the sounds of battle seeming muted. Surprise flickered in Darius's eyes and he looked around, confused.

For an instant he looked almost human. Something akin to vulnerability broke through the crazed look that had twisted his features until they were almost unrecognisable, and in that moment she was reminded of a time when this man had been more than a monster to her.

Something inside her died a little, but she didn't hesitate; she lunged for Claíomh Solais where it had fallen on the ground between them. With a single, clean strike, Phoenix brought the blade up and severed his head from his body.

Darius's head hit the ground with an echoing thud. She watched it with a numb detachment, as if seeing it through someone else's eyes.

"Phoenix? Are you okay?" Ethan was at her side in an instant, his eyes wide with panic as he frantically checked her for injuries.

"Is it over?" she whispered, unable to look away from Darius's fallen body.

Ethan reached down and yanked his spear free from the now-headless chest and looked back towards the field, his expression grim. "I don't think so."

The roar of battle seeped back into Phoenix's consciousness with a sudden clarity. And with that roar came a low, keening wail drifting on the wind. She looked around at the bodies that littered the field, her breath catching as she spotted William slumped at the bottom of the hill, covered in blood.

It hadn't been enough. She'd cut the head from the snake, but still the swarm of creatures surged forward, bringing death and destruction.

"We need to complete the ritual." She grabbed Ethan's hand, intending to drag him back to Lia Fáil, but pulled up short as Sean stepped into their path.

Abi! She couldn't believe she'd forgotten what had drawn her up the hill to start with – the sight of Abi and Sean facing off against Darius. Frantically she looked around for her friend.

Phoenix's knees buckled as she caught sight of Abi's prone figure on the ground behind Sean. She didn't seem to be fully conscious, but was clearly stirring. Phoenix moved to run past him and help her friend but stumbled.

The air around the Omega felt wrong. It felt empty, like a black hole that had absorbed every bit of light and happiness that existed in the world. Simply being close to it sucked away every shred of hope she held until she too was empty. An empty, useless husk.

"Are you ..." Ethan's words trailed off. "Sean?"

Dread filled the place where hope had once been, and she turned to look properly at the Omega. Ancient, inhuman eyes stared back at her. She hadn't noticed in her panic to get to Abi, didn't know Sean well enough to notice the difference in his demeanour. But now she saw it. Now she saw them.

"Did you really think it would be that easy? We are eternal."

The voice that came from Sean's mouth was not his own. It came from all around her, filled her. She stumbled backwards, shaking her head, and he smiled.

A low rumble filled her ears and the ground beneath her shuddered. She fought to hold her balance, but a crack split the earth between her feet. She leapt to the side barely a moment before the crack ruptured, forming a large fissure.

Even as she landed, more spiderweb cracks were spreading out around the hill. A thick acrid smoke oozed up from the gaps in the earth and reached up towards the sky. She choked as the smoke burned the lining of her throat, and from one breath to the next her visibility all but disappeared.

Ethan called out to her and she tried to reach out for him, but the ground undulated and rolled again, knocking her sideways and further away from his voice. Tears stung her eyes and try as she might, she couldn't blink them away. In the heavy grey of smoke, the shadows came for her.

Desperate, she grasped for the spark of power inside her and called the sun. The light came slower than it ever had before, but it came nonetheless. For a moment, the flare of white drove back the smoke and the shadows lurking within it, but then they started pushing back against her power.

Sweat ran in rivulets down her neck and chest as she tried to hold that small spark of light. Suddenly, the light surged outwards.

A new, almost familiar power joined with hers, and her own light flared with renewed force. Through the glare of white, the shadows, and the smoke, she saw a huge white horse galloping towards her. Aoife sat atop the animal, her face strained as she focused all the power she had to drive back the shadows.

Her grandfather appeared at Aoife's side on his own chestnut steed. His violet eyes glowed and when he held out his hand, a gale-force wind rose up around them, pushing back the smoke.

"Go!" Aoife yelled at her.

Before Phoenix could speak or even think, Ethan was at her side. He grabbed her hand and pulled her towards the top of the hill. She had only a second to glance back to where Sean faced off against Aoife and her grandfather in the centre of a raging whirlwind.

"No! We have to help them," she yelled, terror gripping her.

"We have to complete the ritual. It's the only way to stop this."

He tugged on her hand again and, with difficulty, she turned and left her family to their fate. Together, she and Ethan cleared the remaining distance to where Lia Fáil sat inert at the top of the hill.

As Phoenix stood at the highest point and looked down on the hill, a crushing sense of dread filled her. The blackness surged towards them from all sides, growing closer by the second. There was no time left.

A blur of movement came from their right and Shade appeared beside them, covered from head to toe in blood, and a grim smile on his face. He held up a severed head with lifeless red eyes. "Someone request some blood?"

She gasped as she recognised the face of the large vampire hybrid that she'd pointed out to Ethan before the wards had dropped.

Ethan gave a low whistle, taking the offered head. "I don't know how the hell you pulled that one off, but this'll definitely do the trick."

Shade attempted a nonchalant shrug, but his legs buckled and he only just managed to remain standing. "Was a piece of cake."

"We need Izzie and the cauldron." The words had only left Phoenix's mouth when she spotted Izzie stumbling up the hill towards them. The witch had her arm around a limping but conscious Abi, and Nate was supporting her on the other side. All three were coated in blood and had visible wounds, but still the tightness in her chest eased just a touch at the sight of them.

"Has anyone seen –" She didn't get a chance to finish her sentence before a shimmering mist coalesced to leave a grim-faced Jannah standing before her with the cauldron in his hands.

"Do you have what we need?" he asked, his voice rushed.

Ethan held up the head, thick black blood dripping from the jagged stump that used to be a neck.

"Good." Jannah thrust Dagda's Cauldron into Shade's hands. "I do solemnly pass ownership of this artefact to you, to act as a guardian to its power, as witnessed by those who stand here now."

The vampire gaped at him as if the Mist had lost his marbles, but Jannah just turned to Phoenix. "Our defences are failing. We can't last much longer. I will do what I can to hold them off, but if you don't finish this now, it will be too late." Without waiting for a response, he turned to mist and disappeared.

Izzie, Abi, and Nate reached them a moment later, and Phoenix flung herself at them, grasping her friend in a tight hug. "Are you okay?"

Abi gave her a crooked grin. "I cut the bastard's eye out."

Phoenix choked out a laugh that was partly a sob of relief. "You sure did. You did amazing."

"Where's everyone else?" Nate asked, looking around at the significantly smaller group. A long gash ran down one side of his face and he was holding his left arm oddly, but his amber eyes were alert.

"I think we're on our own," Ethan answered.

Phoenix looked at the cauldron now resting in Shade's hands and at the people who stood with her at the top of the hill. Everyone with her now had been with her from the beginning. Even Izzie, in a strange sort of way, had set her on this path. They'd become a weird, fucked-up kind of family to her, and some selfish part of her was glad they were with her now.

"It'll have to be enough," she said, squaring her shoulders and stepping into her position at the east side of Lia Fáil. She flipped her sword over and drove the blade into the ground.

Ethan helped Izzie add the final ingredient to the cauldron before taking his place opposite Phoenix and driving his spear into the earth. Their eyes met, and a world of emotion passed between them.

Izzie's chant started, and Phoenix looked at Abi. "Stand clear of the circle. You've done your part; now I need you to be safe."

Stubborn blue eyes glared at her, filled with anger and frustration and sorrow. Abi bit her lip but stepped back to watch.

Izzie's words grew louder and as they did, the power rose with them. Claíomh Solais thrummed in Phoenix's hands and she had to clench her jaw to stop her teeth from rattling. The air around them became electric.

The witch nodded in confirmation: it was working. Nate and Shade stepped into position at the North and South points of the circle. Four points of the compass, four of them to absorb the power. Would it be enough?

As the final word was spoken, the cauldron flared to life.

CHAPTER FIFTY-ONE

"It worked," Izzie whispered in disbelief.

Fear and resolve all warred within Phoenix as she looked at the cauldron, now glowing with intricate symbols. Izzie took a shuddery breath and gave Shade a nod. She stepped back on shaky legs and joined them in the circle.

Shade sucked in a breath as he held the glowing cauldron in both hands. "Ready?"

When they all nodded, he carefully tilted it until the blood dripped over the edge. The first drop landed on the ground, sizzled, and left a scorched mark. With slow, deliberate steps, he completed the blood circle around them. He placed the cauldron on the ground and returned to his position.

Nothing happened.

Phoenix focused all of her will on their intention – the banishment of the Horsemen and all demons from this world. But she felt nothing other than the power that had already been thrumming through her sword from the artefacts being reunited.

Then it hit.

The power crashed over her like a tidal wave, and the whole world turned white. In that instant, she could feel it all: the death, the destruction, the possibility.

Her body was torn asunder, made and unmade. No longer flesh and bone, now just energy floating on the air. She looked down on the battlefield that was little more than dull images moving within a haze of white, and she was filled with such unspeakable emotion that she felt it crush her.

So much death. So, so much death. What kind of people were they if they could do this to each other? She saw it all, every life lost, every life irrevocably changed, and she hated it. She hated that it wasn't the demons who had caused this, not really. And what was more, she hated that there were people out there this very moment who were blissfully unaware that any of this was happening. They were cocooned in their safe, comfortable lives, oblivious to the fact that others were sacrificing themselves so that they could keep that oblivion.

In that moment, she knew.

Yes, they could banish the demons again. The power was theirs to harness that way, should they wish it. But it wouldn't stop the pain. It wouldn't stop the death. Because they were death. Not the demons, and not the Horsemen. Them.

The power lashed at her, bringing with it glimpses of what the future might look like. The future where the demons remained, and the one where they were once again banished. In one of those visions, fires burned and destroyed everything she'd ever loved. But in the other, people destroyed everything she'd ever loved.

So much pain. So much hatred. It could all end now. They could let the Horsemen end it quickly and save themselves the heartache. They could be at peace and leave the rest of the world to fend for itself, no more running, no more fighting.

And then a single name came to her through the haze. Saoirse.

Every molecule in her body screamed for the horrors to stop, but within the devastation, there was something else too. There was love.

She focused on the name like it was a beacon. With all her will, she pushed back the fear and the thoughts of succumbing. Giving up was not an option; so long as they lived there was hope. So, she repeated the intention over and over again. *Banish them. Banish them. Banish them.*

Still she floundered within the power, drowning in it. Even as she tried to channel it into her intention, it consumed her. She was made and unmade in an endless cycle until she didn't believe she could ever be whole again.

A voice called to her from a distance. "I'm here, Phoenix. Just listen to my voice, okay? Hold on."

The voice was familiar, someone dear to her. But it was only when Abi's hand touched her shoulder that Phoenix managed to claw her way up through the power enough to recognise it.

Abi kept talking, and though the words seemed to fade in and out, she listened. She let her friend's voice guide her as Abi told her all the reasons why this world was worth saving. Why she would stand with her to the end, magic or no damn magic.

Piece by painful piece, Phoenix's body reformed. The magic filled every cell within her, flowing through her to find her own magic settled at the centre of her solar plexus.

With extreme effort, she opened her eyes.

Izzie was on the ground beside her, blood running from her nose as she gritted her teeth and struggled to keep her head up. Shade was kneeling next to her, one hand stretched out as if he wanted to help the witch, but his head was thrown back and his face frozen into a mask of agony.

To her right, Nate's body was stretched taut. His arms and legs were pulled wide as if some force was tearing him in two, and his whole body shook with the strain. Veins bulged at his temple, and sweat ran in rivulets down his face, which was now a worrying shade of red.

And across from her, Ethan stood. Barely. He slumped against the spear, his body clearly failing, but his eyes were open and he had them fixed on her. The life and sparkle they normally contained was missing. Instead, they were glassy with pain, and sweat covered his pale skin. His muscles trembled with the effort of holding himself upright.

Phoenix let out a sob as his knees buckled and his eyes fluttered closed. She wanted to call to him, to give him her strength, but it was taking all of her energy to hold onto the power. Soon she'd have to let it go, and she didn't know what would happen once she did.

Finally, she twisted her head to look at Abi. Rather than standing a safe distance away as she'd been instructed, Abi now stood behind her, a hand on her shoulder. How she'd crossed the circle, Phoenix had no idea. All she knew was that her human best friend now stood caught in the torrent of magic that was near to breaking point.

Abi's long hair blew around her, and her expression was fierce as she met Phoenix's eyes. "Do it," she demanded, no fear in her voice.

Phoenix's heart screamed in defiance, but she nodded, tears streaming down her cheeks. She closed her eyes one final time and reached deep down within herself, further than she'd ever reached before. She called the sun, let it fill her, surround her, become her. And then she let it go.

CHAPTER FIFTY-TWO

Blinding white seared into Ethan's eyelids. He could hear nothing, see nothing. Was this it? Was he dead?

It was strange, really; he'd never considered what death might be like. Even knowing when he stepped onto that hill that he might not walk down it again, he hadn't stopped to imagine what waited for him. He'd been prepared to give up his life so long as they might live. What happened after was irrelevant.

He tried to open his eyes, but a searing pain shot through his head so he scrunched them closed again. Voices drifted into his consciousness. Familiar voices. His mother. His father. They called to him, and a deep sorrow filled him at the realisation that they must be dead too.

Something shook him, and his whole body roared in agony at the movement. Dammit, surely death wasn't meant to hurt so much?

"Ethan. Ethan. Open your eyes, Mo Faolán."

He recognised his mother's voice, closer now, beseeching him. He couldn't deny her, even in death, so he forced his eyelids to open despite the pain in his head. The white persisted for a moment, but the glare began to slowly fade until he could start to pick out shadows.

Bit by painful bit, things came back into focus: the grass that tickled his cheek, the cold air brushing his skin, the hands that touched his shoulder. His mother's face appeared before him, and something about the overwhelming relief in her expression, told him that he'd been wrong – he wasn't dead.

He sucked in a breath. He was alive?

He tried to push himself up from the ground, but his arms were like jelly and merely collapsed under him. Strong hands grasped his shoulders and helped raise him to sitting. Ethan looked up to see tears glistening in his father's eyes before Cormac cleared his throat and looked away, fussing to make sure Ethan wouldn't fall over before he let go.

Disbelief prevented him from speaking, so he just stared at his parents' bloodstained faces and let it all sink in. He was alive. They were alive.

The realisation pierced the fog of pain that clouded his mind, and he jerked his head around, overcome with a sudden panic. "Phoenix?" The word came out as little more than a rasp.

On the far side of Lia Fáil, he spotted her bright red hair fanned out across the ground. A renewed sense of terror gripped him and he struggled to rise, growling with frustration when his legs refused to obey.

Cormac was at his side in an instant. His father wrapped an arm around him and hefted him to his feet. Ethan didn't dare breathe as they crossed the distance to where Phoenix lay on the ground, unmoving. Abi crouched by her side, her face pale and expressionless. She didn't look up as he approached, and an icy chill settled deep in his heart.

He collapsed at Phoenix's side and with a shaking hand, he reached out to touch her cheek. It was so cold.

It struck him just how peaceful her face looked. For so long he'd watched her try to hide her fear and worry from everyone. He'd seen the tightness that tugged at the corner of her smile, the furrow of her brow when she thought no one was looking. Now, all the tension was gone. Washed away on the tide of magic that he'd felt surge from her just before the world had disappeared.

He looked around now and realised with surprise that the first rays of dawn were cresting the horizon. Soft light bathed the field around them in an eerie red that seemed suited somehow to the blanket of bodies covering the grass. Those who had survived wandered about aimlessly, some checking for loved ones in the carnage, others just looking lost.

It was quiet now that the sounds of fighting had gone. The ritual had worked. It had torn the demons from this world and put them back beyond a fabric that now seemed far too insubstantial to stave off the nightmares he knew would come.

A strange numbness settled over him as he looked down at Phoenix once more. Ever so gently, he lifted her head into his lap and wrapped his arms around her. "We did it," he whispered and bent his head to kiss her forehead. "We did it."

Her body gave a sudden twitch, and her eyelashes brushed against his cheek. He jerked his head up in shock and almost let her head roll from his lap before he caught her.

So slowly it was like torture, her eyes opened. She blinked up at him, winced, and closed her eyes again. She swallowed and ran her tongue over her chapped lips. "Really?" she wheezed. "That's how you kiss me after we save the world?"

One minute Phoenix was standing at the centre of the sun, heat and light blazing around and within her, the next there was just him. The thread of life, so tenuous now, connected her to him, and she knew that she could follow it back if she chose. But she also knew that in doing so, she'd leave behind the comforting numbness that cocooned her. Slowly, she blinked open her eyes.

The look of shock on Ethan's face would have made her laugh if not for the crippling pain that came with her return to consciousness. Every inch of her body felt like it had been scorched from the inside out and her nerves screamed in agony. She closed her eyes, half-wishing for oblivion to take her again, but he held her to him, refusing to let her go.

She had no idea how much time passed as she lay there. She was dimly aware of people talking around her. Their voices were familiar, but their words meant nothing. Mingled with the voices, there was a low, keening lament. It drifted on the wind, its sound both beautiful and sorrowful. She wondered distantly who the song was for.

Someone came and spoke low to Ethan. There was a moment of jostling as he seemed to adjust the position of her body in his arms, and then she felt a gentle pressure on her sternum. Heat sparked in her solar plexus in response to the touch and trickled through her body. The pain didn't disappear exactly, but the warmth dulled it enough that she could once more breathe without wanting to die. Her eyes flickered open, and she found herself looking into the smiling face of her mother.

No. It wasn't her mother. It was Aoife.

Her aunt placed a gentle hand on her cheek, her eyes glistening with tears as she crouched before her. "You did it, Phoenix."

For a moment Phoenix wasn't sure exactly what Aoife meant, then she heard it: the silence. She looked around and realised for the first time that she was no longer surrounded by the sounds of battle. Instead, there was just the quiet aftermath of death. So many bodies littered the ground that it was almost impossible to see the green of the grass, and not all were dressed in the black of Darius's army.

"Is it ..."

Ethan's arms tightened around her. "It's over," he reassured her in a whisper.

She looked again at the fallen who coated the field. How many? How many of their allies? In the distance, near the original ward line, she spotted Maj and Shayan standing together. They seemed to be staring back at her, and she cast her eyes around, wondering why Jannah wasn't with them. The two Mists stood there for a moment longer, then dissipated into the wind.

At the bottom of the hill, she spotted Kam and Méabh lifting a body between them. She wondered if it was William as a vague recollection flitted at the edges of her consciousness, but was afraid to voice the question. All around them people tended to the wounded, and high up in the sky, the black crow soared, drifting on the sorrowful notes of death's lament.

Finally, she turned back to her aunt, unable to look at such immense loss anymore. "You came."

A sadness tinged Aoife's smile. "I promised you we would. You're our family, and no matter what, you will always have a place with us. No matter how my mother may feel."

Clíodhna. Had she been here? Had she put aside her bitter prejudice enough to fight at their side? Phoenix couldn't remember seeing her, and something told her she didn't want to know the answer. So instead, she asked, "Where's grandfather?"

Aoife dropped her eyes, but not before Phoenix saw the crushing pain shadowing them. Even before her aunt spoke, a part of her knew.

"He's gone." Aoife raised her head, composing herself. "He gave his last breath to help us survive. I need to leave now to bring his body back to Faerie. I must ... I need to make sure he passes." She took a shuddery breath and stood. "I'm sorry to have to leave you again so soon, but I meant what I said. You'll always have a place with us." She turned her gaze to Ethan and gave him a fond smile. "As will you, wolf."

Ethan gave her a nod of gratitude, and Phoenix watched quietly as her aunt turned and made her way to a small group of fae soldiers who were standing guard around one of the fallen. Her grandfather, she realised now.

Phoenix was too exhausted and numb to feel sorrow for the man she'd barely known. But later, when she had the strength, she'd remember his face and mourn what could have been. For now, it was enough to acknowledge his sacrifice.

Bone-deep weariness settled over her, but also something else: hope. Yes, she had seen what the future might hold for them if they didn't find a way to all live in harmony together, but for now it was enough that they lived. She didn't want to be surrounded by death anymore; she wanted to get back to her little girl and start their lives properly.

She turned to Ethan. "Take me home. Please."

EPILOGUE

3 months later

Phoenix's jaw dropped as Ethan pulled the car over to the side of the road and killed the engine. She couldn't believe it – the pub looked exactly as it had before the fire had destroyed it. The front door was a replica of the one she'd first walked through almost five years before, and an odd sense of nostalgia caused her throat to tighten.

"They've done a great job," Ethan said with no small hint of pride in his voice.

She just nodded, unable to speak.

Once the dust had settled after the banishment, and everyone had had a chance to say goodbye to their dead – of which there were far too many – Cormac and Ethan had arranged for a group of wolves from the Donegal pack to come back to Dublin to help with the rebuild of Abi's pub.

Phoenix had been unspeakably grateful, especially considering it was her fault that her best friend's livelihood had been destroyed in the first place. She'd insisted that she pay for the work, but Cormac had refused, saying that Abi had more than earned the help with her bravery during the ritual.

She wasn't sure if he realised just how right he was. Phoenix hadn't told anyone how close she'd come to giving in that night when she'd been caught in the maelstrom of the artefacts' power. If it hadn't been for Abi stepping across that circle and lending her strength when she did, she might have made a very different choice.

The door to the pub swung open and before Phoenix could even get her seatbelt unbuckled, Abi was pulling open her car door. "You're here! Oh my god, I'm so happy to see you!"

Her friend was positively glowing with joy as she caught her in a crushing hug. Phoenix laughed. "Wow. Have you been working out?"

Abi gave her a playful shove and moved aside so that she could get out. Ethan climbed out on his side and took the car seat and sleeping baby from the back of the car.

Abi's squeal dropped to a whisper but contained no less excitement as she peered down at Saoirse. "Oh, would you look at her! She's getting so big already." She beckoned them towards the pub. "Come on, Sasha's inside. She's going to want to see her niece."

Ethan followed obediently and was ushered up to the living area where Sasha was busy unpacking her things. Phoenix trailed behind them, taking in the newly refurbished pub. It was exactly as she remembered it.

Slowly she walked around the interior of the pub, trailing her fingers over the smooth wood of the new tables and breathing in the familiar aroma of Guinness hops. She came to a stop behind the bar and looked out on the room.

Abi came to stand at her side, leaning her elbows on the bar. "I honestly never thought I'd get to stand behind this bar again."

Phoenix's throat tightened once more. "Abi, I'm –"

Abi held up a hand, cutting her off. "Don't you dare apologise again. None of this was your fault, and I wouldn't be standing here now if it wasn't for you. Even if I had a chance to go back and do it differently, I wouldn't."

Phoenix nodded. "I'll miss working here with you."

"I'm excited that Sasha decided to come help run the pub, but it won't be the same without you." Abi nudged her shoulder and smiled.

At the mention of Ethan's sister, a shadow fell over Phoenix. "Has she said if they've managed to track down Sean yet?"

The Omega had been last seen walking away from the Hill of Tara after the ritual had been completed. They knew he'd survived the banishment of the Horsemen, though what toll it had taken on him was anyone's guess. The pack had been searching for him ever since, but as yet they'd had no luck tracing him. Ethan put on a brave face anytime she asked him about it, but she knew it was eating him up inside.

Abi frowned, worry dulling the sparkle in her blue eyes. "All of their leads so far have turned out to be dead ends. I have a feeling he'll only be found when he wants to be."

They were silent for a few minutes, each lost in their own thoughts. Then Abi shook herself and smiled broadly. "One last drink for old times?"

Phoenix stared out the passenger window as the green peaks of the Wicklow mountains rolled past and the roads shifted from motorway to narrow backroads. Ethan followed her directions with ease, taking the sharp twists and turns with extra care now that they carried precious cargo in the car.

They'd driven this route together once before. It had been little more than six months since they'd first gone on the run from the Mists, but it felt like a lifetime ago. So much had changed since then. She had changed.

Twisting her head to look at the back seat, she smiled as her daughter blinked back at her with wide, curious eyes.

Ethan slowed the car and came to a stop with the engine idling when they reached a half-hidden lane that led to a small white house. Unlike last time, she didn't tell him to keep driving. She stared at the house where she'd grown up and this time, instead of being bombarded by painful memories, a familiar warmth wrapped around her.

She'd never truly be able to forget the days she spent alone in that house, hoping beyond hope for her parents to walk back through the door. But she realised now that holding onto those memories did a disservice to her parents. This had been their home, and for however brief a time, they'd been happy.

Ethan gave her a questioning look, and she nodded. He swung the car up the tree-lined lane and came to a stop in front of the house, killing the engine.

"Are you sure you want to do this?" he asked gently.

She took in the rainbow-coloured roses that edged the house's white façade, and tears pricked the back of her eyes. Her mother's flowers. How had they survived?

Ethan's expression turned worried and she forced herself to swallow past the lump in her throat to answer his question. "I want this to be our home. I want Saoirse to grow up here and know the love that I did."

He reached over and squeezed her hand, then climbed out of the car and set about freeing Saoirse from the confines of her car seat.

Phoenix climbed out of the passenger side. She looked towards the lush forest that bordered the property and saw a large crow perched in a tree, watching them. She smiled and met Morrigan's gaze for a moment, then turned and followed Ethan into the house and the start of their new life together.

<<<<>>>>

ABOUT THE AUTHOR

Thank you for joining me on this new adventure through Ireland's hidden supernatural world. If you enjoyed this book, I would be very grateful if you could leave a brief review (it can be as short as you like) on the site where you purchased your copy.

As an author, reviews are the most powerful tools in my arsenal when it comes to getting attention for my books. Honest feedback goes a long way in increasing visibility and helping me to reach other readers like you, so thank you in advance!

*To get exclusive bonus material and be the first to hear about new releases, promotions, and giveaways **Sign up for my Newsletter**!*

You can also follow me on:

- facebook.com/lmhatchell
- instagram.com/lmhatchell
- amazon.com/author/lmhatchell
- bookbub.com/profile/l-m-hatchell

Lightning Source UK Ltd.
Milton Keynes UK
UKHW042200310123
416277UK00002B/15

9 781916 365155